Praise for Zane Grey

⭐

"A story that flows as swiftly and irresistibly
as the Colorado River. His West is the rainbow
land we visit in spirit when the job palls.
The wild, lonely, fearfully beautiful Arizona
desert has never been better done."

—*The New York Times* on
The Call of the Canyon

"It is the railroad that is the center of interest,
that is both hero and heroine.
Grey's pictures of the slow, determined,
thwarted, triumphant progress of the line are
vivid and thrilling, unforgettable."

—*The New York Times* on
The U.P. Trail

FORGE BOOKS BY ZANE GREY

Betty Zane

The Desert of Wheat

The Last of the Plainsmen

The Last Trail

The Lone Star Ranger

The Mysterious Rider

The Rainbow Trail

Riders of the Purple Sage

The Spirit of the Border

To the Last Man

Wildfire

COLLECTIONS

Betty Zane and To the Last Man

Desert Gold and The Light of Western Stars (forthcoming)

The Last of the Plainsmen and The Last of the Great Scouts
(Zane Grey and Helen Cody Wetmore)

The Lone Star Ranger and The Mysterious Rider

Riders of the Purple Sage and The Rainbow Trail

The Spirit of the Border and The Last Trail

The U.P. Trail and The Call of the Canyon

Western Colors

Western Legends

Zane Grey Frontier

★ ZANE GREY ★

THE U.P. TRAIL

and

THE CALL OF THE CANYON

FORGE®

A TOM DOHERTY ASSOCIATES BOOK | NEW YORK

This is a work of fiction. All of the characters, organizations, and events portrayed in these novels are either products of the author's imagination or are used fictitiously.

THE U.P. TRAIL AND THE CALL OF THE CANYON

A Forge Book
Published by Tom Doherty Associates
175 Fifth Avenue
New York, NY 10010

www.tor-forge.com

Forge® is a registered trademark of Macmillan Publishing Group, LLC.

ISBN 978-0-7653-9843-7

Our books may be purchased in bulk for promotional, educational, or business use. Please contact your local bookseller or the Macmillan Corporate and Premium Sales Department at 1-800-221-7945, extension 5442, or by email at MacmillanSpecialMarkets@macmillan.com.

First Edition: June 2018

Printed in the United States of America

0 9 8 7 6 5 4 3

CONTENTS

THE U.P.
TRAIL

THE U.P.
TRAIL

Dedication to
RIPLEY HITCHCOCK

My dear Critic and Friend:

In the light of my quotation from Stevenson it may be presumptuous for me to aspire to tell the story of the building of the Union Pacific Railroad.

But many a night by the camp-fire on the starlit desert have I listened to my old guide, Al Doyle, while he recounted his experiences as teamster, grader, spiker, and fighter during the construction of that great work. It is as though I had lived through the blood and lust and death, the "epical turmoil," the labor of giants, the heroism and sacrifice of this wildest time in the opening of the West.

Your love of the West and your early travels there and your study of historical frontier days, from which I have profited have been strong factors in my undertaking this book; and they, like Stevenson's noble words, have made me see the wonder, the dignity, the importance of the subject.

For the romance, for the inspiration, I have my own love of wild desert, plain, and mountain; I have Doyle's stories of sudden death and terrible lust and alluring gold—unforgetable stories; and it seems as though all the labor and violence and havoc of those years have become embodied in my imagination.

So here I give you my book—for which I have written all the others—and I do it with hope and dread and fear and yet with joy.

Faithfully,

ZANE GREY.

Lackawaxen, Pa.

... When I think how the railroad has been pushed
through this unwatered wilderness and haunt of savage
tribes; how at each stage of the construction roaring,
impromptu cities, full of gold and lust and death, sprang
up and then died away again, and are now but wayside
stations in the desert; how in these uncouth places Chinese
pirates worked side by side with border ruffians and broken men from Europe, gambling, drinking, quarreling, and
murdering like wolves; and then when I go on to remember
that all this epical turmoil was conducted by gentlemen in
frock-coats, with a view to nothing more extraordinary
than a fortune and a subsequent visit to Paris—it seems to
me as if this railway were the one typical achievement of
the age in which we live, as if it brought together into one
plot all the ends of the world and all the degrees of social
rank, and offered to some great writer the busiest, the
most extended, and the most varied subject for an enduring literary work. If it be romance, if it be contrast, if it be
heroism that we require, what was Troy to this?

—ROBERT LOUIS STEVENSON,
in *Across the Plains.*

CHAPTER I

In the early sixties a trail led from the broad Missouri, swirling yellow and turgid between its green-groved borders, for miles and miles out upon the grassy Nebraska plains, turning westward over the undulating prairie, with its swales and billows and long, winding lines of cotton-woods, to a slow, vast heave of rising ground—Wyoming—where the herds of buffalo grazed and the wolf was lord and the camp-fire of the trapper sent up its curling blue smoke from beside some lonely stream; on and on over the barren lands of eternal monotony, all so gray and wide and solemn and silent under the endless sky; on, ever on, up to the bleak, black hills and into the waterless gullies and through the rocky gorges where the deer browsed and the savage lurked; then slowly rising to the pass between the great bold peaks, and across the windy uplands into Utah, with its verdant valleys, green as emeralds, and its haze-filled cañons and wonderful wind-worn cliffs and walls, and its pale salt lakes, veiled in the shadows of stark and lofty rocks, dim, lilac-colored, austere, and isolated; ever onward across Nevada, and ever westward, up from desert to mountain, up into California, where the white streams rushed and roared and the stately pines towered, and seen from craggy heights, deep down, the little blue lakes gleamed like gems; finally sloping to the great descent, where the mountain world ceased and where, out beyond the golden land, asleep and peaceful, stretched the illimitable Pacific, vague and grand beneath the setting sun.

CHAPTER II

Deep in the Wyoming hills lay a valley watered by a stream that ran down from Cheyenne Pass; a band of Sioux Indians had an encampment there. Viewed from the summit of a grassy ridge, the scene was colorful and idle and quiet, in keeping with the lonely, beautiful valley. Cottonwoods and willows showed a bright green; the course of the stream was marked in dark where the water ran, and light where the sand had bleached; brown and black dots scattered over the valley were in reality grazing horses; lodge-pole tents gleamed white in the sun, and tiny bits of red stood out against the white; lazy wreaths of blue smoke rose upward.

The Wyoming hills were split by many such valleys and many such bare, grassy ridges sloped up toward the mountains. Upon the side of one ridge, the highest, there stood a solitary mustang, haltered with a lasso. He was a ragged, shaggy, wild beast, and there was no saddle or bridle on him, nothing but the halter. He was not grazing, although the bleached white grass grew long and thick under his hoofs. He looked up the slope, in a direction indicated by his pointing ears, and watched a wavering movement of the long grass.

It was wild up on that ridge, bare of everything except grass, and the strange wavering had a nameless wildness in its motion. No stealthy animal accounted for that trembling—that forward undulating quiver. It wavered on to the summit of the ridge.

What a wide and wonderful prospect opened up to view from this lofty point! Ridge after ridge sloped up to the Wyoming hills, and these in turn raised their bleak, dark heads toward the mountains, looming pale and gray, with caps of snow, in the distance. Out beyond the ridges, indistinct in the glare, stretched an illimitable expanse, gray and dull—that was the prairie-land. An eagle, lord of all he surveyed, sailed round and round in the sky.

Below this grassy summit yawned a valley, narrow and long, losing itself by turns to distant east and west; and through it ran a faint, white, winding line which was the old St. Vrain and Laramie Trail.

There came a moment when the wavering in the grass ceased on the extreme edge of the slope. Then it parted to disclose the hideous visage of a Sioux Indian in war-paint. His dark, piercing, malignant glance was fixed upon the St. Vrain and Laramie Trail. His half-naked body rested at ease; a rifle lay under his hand.

There he watched while the hours passed. The sun moved on in its course until it tipped the peaks with rose. Far down the valley black and white objects appeared, crawling round the bend. The Indian gave an almost imperceptible start, but there was no change in his expression. He watched as before.

These moving objects grew to be oxen and prairie-schooners—a small caravan traveling east. It wound down the trail and halted in a circle on the bank of a stream.

The Indian scout slid backward, and the parted grass,

slowly closing, hid from his dark gaze the camp scene below. He wormed his way back well out of sight; then rising, he ran over the summit of the ridge to leap upon his mustang and ride wildly down the slope.

CHAPTER III

ill Horn, leader of that caravan, had a large amount of gold which he was taking back East. No one in his party, except a girl, knew that he had the fortune.

Horn had gone West at the beginning of the gold strikes, but it was not until '53 that any success attended his labors. Later he struck it rich, and in 1865, as soon as the snow melted on the mountain passes, he got together a party of men and several women and left Sacramento. He was a burly miner, bearded and uncouth, of rough speech and taciturn nature, and absolutely fearless.

At Ogden, Utah, he had been advised not to attempt to cross the Wyoming hills with so small a party, for the Sioux Indians had gone on the war-path.

Horn was leading his own caravan and finding for himself the trail that wound slowly eastward. He did not have a scout or hunter with him. Eastward-traveling caravans were wont to be small and poorly outfitted, for only the homesick, the failures, the wanderers, and the lawless turned their faces from the Golden State. At the start Horn had eleven men, three women, and the girl. On the way he had killed one of the men; and another, together with his wife, had yielded to persuasion of friends at Ogden and had left the party. So when Horn halted for camp one afternoon in a beautiful valley in the Wyoming hills there were only nine men with him.

On a long journey through wild country strangers grow close together or far apart. Bill Horn did not think much of the men who had accepted the chance he offered them, and daily he grew more aloof. They were not a responsible crowd, and the best he could get out of them was the driving of oxen and camp chores indifferently done. He had to kill the meat and find the water and keep the watch. Upon entering the Wyoming hills region Horn showed a restlessness and hurry and anxiety. This in no wise affected the others. They continued to be aimless and careless as men who had little to look forward to.

This beautiful valley offered everything desirable for a camp site except natural cover or protection in case of attack. But Horn had to take the risk. The oxen were tired, the wagons had to be greased, and it was needful to kill meat. Here was an abundance of grass, a clear brook, wood for camp-fires, and sign of game on all sides.

"Haul round—make a circle!" Horn ordered the drivers of the oxen.

This was the first time he had given this particular order, and the men guffawed or grinned as they hauled the great, clumsy prairie-schooners into a circle. The oxen were unhitched; the camp duffle piled out; the ring of axes broke the stillness; fires were started.

Horn took his rifle and strode away up the brook to disappear in the green brush of a ravine.

It was early in the evening, with the sun not yet out of sight behind a lofty ridge that topped the valley slope. High grass, bleached white, shone brightly on the summit. Soon several columns of blue smoke curled lazily aloft until, catching the wind high up, they were swept away.

Meanwhile the men talked at their tasks.

"Say, pard, did you come along this here Laramie Trail goin' West?" asked one.

"Nope. I hit the Santa Fé Trail," was the reply.

"How about you, Jones?"

"Same fer me."

"Wal," said another, "I went round to California by ship, an' I'd hev been lucky to drown."

"An' now we're all goin' back poorer than when we started," remarked a third.

"Pard, you've said somethin'."

"Wal, I seen a heap of gold, if I didn't find any."

"Jones, has this here Bill Horn any gold with him?"

"He acts like it," answered Jones. "An' I heerd he struck it rich out thar."

The men appeared divided in their opinions of Bill Horn. From him they drifted to talk of possible Indian raids and scouted the idea; then they wondered if the famous Pony Express had been over this Laramie Trail; finally they got on the subject of a rumored railroad to be built from East to West.

"No railroad can't be built over this trail," said Jones, bluntly.

"Sure not. But couldn't more level ground be dug?" asked another.

"Dug? Across them Utah deserts an' up them mountains? Hell! Men sure hev more sense than thet," exclaimed the third.

And so they talked and argued at their tasks.

The women, however, had little to say. One, the wife of the loquacious Jones, lived among past associations of happy years that would not come again—a sober-faced, middle-aged woman. The other woman was younger, and her sad face showed traces of a former comeliness. They called her Mrs. Durade. The girl was her daughter Allie. She appeared about fifteen years old, and was slight of form. Her face did not seem to tan. It was pale. She looked tired, and was shy and silent, almost ashamed. She had long, rich, chestnut-colored hair which she wore in a braid. Her eyes were singularly large and dark, and violet in color.

"It's a long, long way we are from home yet," sighed Mrs. Jones.

"You call East home!" replied Mrs. Durade, bitterly.

"For land's sake! Yes, I do," exclaimed the other. "If there was a home in that California, I never saw it. Tents and log cabins and mud-holes! Such places for a woman to live. Oh, I hated that California! A lot of wild men, all crazy for gold. Gold that only a few could find and none could keep! . . . . I pray every night to live to get back home."

Mrs. Durade had no reply; she gazed away over the ridges toward the east with a haunting shadow in her eyes.

Just then a rifle-shot sounded from up in the ravine. The men paused in their tasks and looked at one another. Then reassured by this exchange of glances, they fell to work again. But the women cast apprehensive eyes around. There was no life in sight except the grazing oxen. Presently Horn appeared carrying a deer slung over his shoulders.

Allie ran to meet him. She and Horn were great friends. To her alone was he gentle and kind. She saw him pause at the brook, then drop the deer carcass and bend over the ground, as if to search for something. When Allie reached his side he was on his knees examining a moccasin print in the sand.

"An Indian track!" exclaimed Allie.

"Allie, it sure ain't anythin' else," he replied. "Thet is what I've been lookin' fer. . . . A day old—mebbe more."

"Uncle Bill, is there any danger?" she asked, fearfully gazing up the slope.

"Lass, we're in the Wyoming hills, an' I wish to the Lord we was out," he answered.

Then he picked up the deer carcass, a heavy burden, and slung it, hoofs in front, over his shoulders.

"Let me carry your gun," said Allie.

They started toward camp.

"Lass, listen," began Horn, earnestly. "Mebbe there's no need to fear. But I don't like Injun tracks. Not these days. Now I'm goin' to scare this lazy outfit. Mebbe thet'll make them rustle. But don't you be scared."

In camp the advent of fresh venison was hailed with satisfaction.

"Wal, I'll gamble the shot thet killed this meat was heerd by Injuns," blurted out Horn, as he deposited his burden on the grass and whipped out his hunting-knife. Then he glared at the outfit of men he had come to despise.

"Horn, I reckon you 'pear more set up about Injuns than usual," remarked Jones.

"Fresh Sioux track right out thar along the brook."

"No!"

"Sioux!" exclaimed another.

"Go an' look fer yourself."

Not a man of them moved a step. Horn snorted his disdain and without more talk began to dress the deer.

Meanwhile the sun set behind the ridge and the day seemed far spent. The evening meal of the travelers was interrupted when Horn suddenly leaped up and reached for his rifle.

"Thet's no Injun, but I don't like the looks of how he's comin'."

All gazed in the direction in which Horn pointed. A horse and rider were swiftly approaching down the trail from the west. Before any of the startled campers recovered from their surprise the horse reached the camp. The rider hauled up short, but did not dismount.

"Hello!" he called. The man was not young. He had piercing gray eyes and long hair. He wore fringed gray buckskin, and carried a long, heavy, muzzle-loading rifle.

"I'm Slingerland—trapper in these hyar parts," he went on, with glance swiftly taking in the group. "Who's boss of this caravan?"

"I am—Bill Horn," replied the leader, stepping out.

"Thar's a band of Sioux redskins on your trail."

Horn lifted his arms high. The other men uttered exclamations of amaze and dread. The women were silent.

"Did you see them?" asked Horn.

"Yes, from a ridge back hyar ten miles. I saw them sneakin' along the trail an' I knowed they meant mischief. I rode along the ridges or I'd been hyar sooner."

"How many Injuns?"

"I counted fifteen. They were goin' along slow. Like as not they've sent word fer more. There's a big Sioux camp over hyar in another valley."

"Are these Sioux on the war-path?"

"I saw dead an' scalped white men a few days back," replied Slingerland.

Horn grew as black as a thundercloud, and he cursed the group of pale-faced men who had elected to journey eastward with him.

"You'll hev to fight," he ended, brutally, "an' thet'll be some satisfaction to me."

"Horn, there's soldiers over hyar in camp," went on Slingerland. "Do you want me to ride after them?"

"Soldiers!" ejaculated Horn.

"Yes. They're with a party of engineers surveyin' a line fer a railroad. Reckon I could git them all hyar in time to save you—*if* them Sioux keep comin' slow. . . . I'll go or stay hyar with you."

"Friend, you go—an' ride thet hoss!"

"All right. You hitch up an' break camp. Keep goin'

hard down the trail, an' I'll fetch the troops an' head off the redskins."

"Any use to take to the hills?" queried Horn, sharply.

"I reckon not. You've no hosses. You'd be tracked down. Hurry along. Thet's best. . . . An' say, I see you've a young girl hyar. I can take her up behind me."

"Allie, climb up behind him," said Horn, motioning to the girl.

"I'll stay with mother," she replied.

"Go child—go!" entreated Mrs. Durade.

Others urged her, but she shook her head. Horn's big hand trembled as he held it out, and for once there was no trace of hardness about his face.

"Allie, I never had no lass of my own. . . . I wish you'd go with him. You'd be safe—an' you could take my—"

"No!" interrupted the girl.

Slingerland gave her a strange, admiring glance, then turned his quick gray eyes upon Horn. "Anythin' I can take?"

Horn hesitated. "No. It was jest somethin' I wanted the girl to hev."

Slingerland touched his shaggy horse and called over his shoulder: "Rustle out of hyar!" Then he galloped down the trail, leaving the travelers standing aghast.

"Break camp!" thundered Horn.

A scene of confusion followed. In a very short while the prairie-schooners were lumbering down the valley. Twilight came just as the flight got under way. The tired oxen were beaten to make them run. But they were awkward and the loads were heavy. Night fell, and the road was difficult to follow. The wagons rolled and bumped and swayed from side to side; camp utensils and blankets dropped from them. One wagon broke down. The occupants, frantically gathering together their possessions, ran ahead to pile into the one in front.

Horn drove on and on at a gait cruel to both men and beasts. The women were roughly shaken. Hours passed and miles were gained. That valley led into another with an upgrade, rocky and treacherous. Horn led on foot and ordered the men to do likewise. The night grew darker. By and by further progress became impossible, for the oxen failed and a wild barrier of trees and rocks stopped the way.

Then the fugitives sat and shivered and waited for dawn. No one slept. All listened intently to the sounds of the lonely night, magnified now by their fears. Horn strode to and fro with his rifle—a grim, dark, silent form. Whenever a wolf mourned, or a cat squalled, or a night bird voiced the solitude, or a stone rattled off the cliff, the fugitives started up quiveringly alert, expecting every second to hear the screeching yell of the Sioux. They whispered to keep up a flickering courage. And the burly Horn strode to and fro, thoughtful, as though he were planning something, and always listening.

Allie sat in one of the wagons close to her mother. She was wide awake and not so badly scared. All through this dreadful journey her mother had not seemed natural to Allie, and the farther they traveled eastward the stranger she grew. During the ride that night she had moaned and shuddered, and had clasped Allie close; but when the flight had come to a forced end she grew silent.

Allie was young and hopeful. She kept whispering to her mother that the soldiers would come in time.

"That brave fellow in buckskin—he'll save us," said Allie.

"Child, I feel I'll never see home again," finally whispered Mrs. Durade.

"Mother!"

"Allie, I must tell you—I must!" cried Mrs. Durade, very low and fiercely. She clung to her daughter.

"Tell me what?" whispered Allie.

"The truth—the truth! Oh, I've deceived you all your life!"

"Deceived me! Oh, mother! Then tell me—now."

"Child—you'll forgive me—and never—hate me?" cried the mother, brokenly.

"Mother, how can you talk so! I love you." And Allie clasped the shaking form closer. Then followed a silence during which Mrs. Durade recovered her composure.

"Allie, I ran off with Durade before you were born," began the mother, swiftly, as if she must hurry out her secret. "Durade is not your father. . . . Your name is Lee. Your father is Allison Lee. I've heard he's a rich man now. . . . Oh, I want to get back—to give you to him—to beg his forgiveness. . . . We were married in New Orleans in 1847. My father made me marry him. I never loved Allison Lee. He was not a kind man—not the sort I admired. . . . I met Durade. He was a Spaniard—a blue-blooded adventurer. I ran off with him. We joined the gold-seekers traveling to California. You were born out there in 1850. . . . It has been a hard life. But I taught you—I did all I could for you. I kept my secret from you—and his! . . . Lately I could endure it no longer. I've run off from Durade."

"Oh, mother, I knew we were running off from him!" cried Allie, breathlessly. "And I know he will follow us."

"Indeed, I fear he will," replied the mother. "But Lord spare me his revenge!"

"Mother! Oh, it is terrible! . . . He is not my father. I never loved him. I couldn't. . . . But, mother, *you* must have loved him!"

"Child, I was Durade's slave," she replied, sadly.

"Then why did you run away? He was kind—good to us."

"Allie, listen. Durade was a gambler—a man crazy to

stake all on the fall of a card. He did not love gold. But he loved games of chance. It was a terrible passion with him. Once he meant to gamble my honor away. But that other gambler was too much of a man. There are gamblers who are men! . . . I think I began to hate Durade from that time. . . . He was a dishonest gambler. He made me share in his guilt. My face lured miners to his dens. . . . My face—for I was beautiful once! . . . Oh, I sunk so low! But he forced me. . . . Thank God I left him—before it was too late—too late for you."

"Mother, he will follow us!" cried Allie.

"But he shall never have you. I'll kill him before I let him get you," replied the mother.

"He'd never harm me, mother, whatever he is," murmured Allie.

"Child, he would use you exactly as he used me. He wanted me to let him have you—already. He wanted to train you—he said you'd be beautiful some day."

"Mother!" gasped Allie, "is *that* what he meant?"

"Forget him, child. And forget your mother's guilt! . . . I've suffered. I've repented. . . . All I ask of God is to take you safely home to Allison Lee—the father whom you have never known."

The night hour before dawn grew colder and blacker. A great silence seemed wedged down between the ebony hills. The stars were wan. No cry of wolf or moan of wind disturbed the stillness. And the stars grew warmer. The black east changed and paled. Dawn was at hand. An opaque and obscure grayness filled the world; all had changed, except that strange, oppressive, and vast silence of the wild.

That silence was broken by the screeching, blood-curdling yell of the Sioux.

* * *

At times these bloody savages attacked without warning and in the silence of the grave; again they sent out their war-cries, chilling the hearts of the bravest. Perhaps that warning yell was given only when doom was certain.

Horn realized the dread omen and accepted it. He called the fugitives to him and, choosing the best-protected spot among the rocks and wagons, put the women in the center.

"Now, men—if it's the last for us—let it be fight! Mebbe we can hold out till the troops come."

Then in the gray gloom of dawn he took a shovel; prying up a piece of sod, he laid it aside and began to dig. And while he dug he listened for another war-screech and gazed often and intently into the gloom. But there was no sound and nothing to see. When he had dug a hole several feet deep he carried an armful of heavy leather bags and deposited them in it. Then he went back to the wagon for another armful. The men, gray-faced as the gloom, watched him fill up the hole, carefully replace the sod, and stamp it down.

He stood for an instant gazing down, as if he had buried the best of his life. Then he laughed grim and hard.

"There's my gold! If any man wins through this he can have it!"

Bill Horn divined that he would never live to touch his treasure again. He who had slaved for gold and had risked all for it cared no more what might become of it. Gripping his rifle, he turned to await the inevitable.

Moments of awful suspense passed. Nothing but the fitful beating of hearts came to the ears of the fugitives—ears that strained to the stealthy approach of the red foe—ears that throbbed prayerfully for the tramp of the troopers' horses. But only silence ensued, a horrible silence, more nerve-racking than the clash of swift, sure death.

Then out of the gray gloom burst jets of red flame; rifles cracked, and the air suddenly filled with hideous clamor. The men began to shoot at gliding shadows, grayer than the gloom. And every shot brought a volley in return. Smoke mingled with the gloom. In the slight intervals between rifle-shots there were swift, rustling sounds and sharp thud from arrows. Then the shrill strife of sound became continuous; it came from all around and closed in upon the doomed caravan. It swelled and rolled away and again there was silence.

CHAPTER IV

I n 1865, just after the war, a party of engineers were at work in the Wyoming hills on a survey as hazardous as it was problematical. They had charge of the laying out of the Union Pacific Railroad.

This party, escorted by a company of United States troops under Colonel Dillon, had encountered difficulties almost insurmountable. And now, having penetrated the wild hills to the eastern slope of the Rockies, they were halted by a seemingly impassable barrier—a gorge too deep to fill, too wide to bridge.

General Lodge, chief engineer of the corps, gave an order to one of his assistants. "Put young Neale on the job. If we ever survey a line through this awful place we'll owe it to him."

The assistant, Baxter, told an Irishman standing by and smoking a short, black pipe to find Neale and give him the chief's orders. The Irishman, Casey by name, was raw-boned, red-faced, and hard-featured, a man inured to exposure and rough life. His expression was one of extreme and fixed good humor, as if his face had been set, mask-like, during a grin. He removed the pipe from his lips.

"Gineral, the flag I've been holdin' fer thot dom' young surveyor is the wrong color. I want a green flag."

Baxter waved the Irishman to his errand, but General Lodge looked up from the maps and plans before him with a faint smile. He had a dark, stern face and the bearing of a soldier.

"Casey, you can have any color you like," he said. "Maybe green would change our luck."

"Gineral, we'll niver git no railroad built, an' if we do it'll be the Irish thot builds it," responded Casey, and went his way.

Truly only one hope remained—that the agile and daring Neale, with his eye of a mountaineer and his genius for estimating distance and grade, might run a line around the gorge.

While waiting for Neale the engineers went over the maps and drawings again and again, with the earnestness of men who could not be beaten.

Lodge had been a major-general in the Civil War just ended, and before that he had traveled through this part of the West many times, and always with the mighty project of a railroad looming in his mind. It had taken years to evolve the plan of a continental railroad, and it came to fruition at last through many men and devious ways, through plots and counterplots. The wonderful idea of uniting East and West by a railroad originated in one man's brain; he lived for it, and finally he died for it. But the seeds he had sown were fruitful. One by one other men divined and believed, despite doubt and fear, until the day arrived when Congress put the Government of the United States, the army, a group of frock-coated directors, and unlimited gold back of General Lodge, and bade him build the road.

In all the length and breadth of the land no men but the

chief engineer and his assistants knew the difficulty, the peril of that undertaking. The outside world was interested, the nation waited, mostly in doubt. But Lodge and his engineers had been seized by the spirit of some great thing to be, in the making of which were adventure, fortune, fame, and that strange call of life which foreordained a heritage for future generations. They were grim; they were indomitable.

Warren Neale came hurrying up. He was a New-Englander of poor family, self-educated, wild for adventure, keen for achievement, eager, ardent, bronze-faced, and keen-eyed, under six feet in height, built like a wedge, but not heavy—a young man of twenty-three with strong latent possibilities of character.

General Lodge himself explained the difficulties of the situation and what the young surveyor was expected to do. Neale flushed with pride; his eyes flashed; his jaw set. But he said little while the engineers led him out to the scene of the latest barrier. It was a rugged gorge, old and yellow and crumbled, cedar-fringed at the top, bare and white at the bottom. The approach to it was through a break in the walls, so that the gorge really extended both above and below this vantage-point.

"This is the only pass through these foot-hills," said Engineer Henney, the eldest of Lodge's corps.

The passage ended where the break in the walls fronted abruptly upon the gorge. It was a wild scene. Only inspired and dauntless men could have entertained any hope of building a railroad through such a place. The mouth of the break was narrow; a rugged slope led up to the left; to the right a huge buttress of stone wall bulged over the gorge; across stood out the seamed and cracked cliffs, and below yawned the abyss. The nearer side of the gorge could only be guessed at.

Neale crawled to the extreme edge of the precipice, and,

lying flat, he tried to discover what lay beneath. Evidently he did not see much, for upon getting up he shook his head. Then he gazed at the bulging wall.

"The side of that can be blown off," he muttered.

"But what's around the corner? If it's straight stone wall for miles and miles we are done," said Boone, another of the engineers.

"The opposite wall is just that," added Henney. "A straight stone wall."

General Lodge gazed at the baffling gorge. His face became grimmer, harder. "It seems impossible to go on, but we *must* go on!" he said.

A short silence ensued. The engineers faced one another like men confronted by a last and crowning hindrance. Then Neale laughed. He appeared cool and confident.

"It only looks bad," he said. "We'll climb to the top and I'll go down over the wall on a rope."

Neale had been let down over many precipices in those stony hills. He had been the luckiest, the most daring and successful of all the men picked out and put to perilous tasks. No one spoke of the accidents that had happened, or even the fatal fall of a lineman who a few weeks before had ventured once too often. Every rod of road surveyed made the engineers sterner at their task, just as it made them keener to attain final success.

The climb to the top of the bluff was long and arduous. The whole corps went, and also some of the troopers.

"I'll need a long rope," Neale had said to King, his lineman.

It was this order that made King take so much time in ascending the bluff. Besides, he was a cowboy, used to riding, and could not climb well.

"Wal—I—shore—rustled—all the line—aboot heah," he drawled, pantingly, as he threw lassoes and coils of rope at Neale's feet.

Neale picked up some of the worn pieces. He looked dubious. "Is this all you could get?" he asked.

"Shore is. An' thet includes what Casey rustled from the soldiers."

"Help me knot these," went on Neale.

"Wal, I reckon this heah time I'll go down before you," drawled King.

Neale laughed and looked curiously at his lineman. Back somewhere in Nebraska this cowboy from Texas had attached himself to Neale. They worked together; they had become friends. Larry Red King made no bones of the fact that Texas had grown too hot for him. He had been born with an itch to shoot. To Neale it seemed that King made too much of a service Neale had rendered—the mere matter of a helping hand. Still, there had been danger.

"Go down before me!" exclaimed Neale.

"I reckon," replied King.

"You will not," rejoined the other, bluntly. "I may not need you at all. What's the sense of useless risk?"

"Wal, I'm goin'—else I throw up my job."

"Oh, hell!" burst out Neale as he strained hard on a knot. Again he looked at his lineman, this time with something warmer than curiosity in his glance.

Larry Red King was tall, slim, hard as iron, and yet undeniably graceful in outline—a singularly handsome and picturesque cowboy with flaming hair and smooth, red face and eyes of flashing blue. From his belt swung a sheath holding a heavy gun.

"Wal, go ahaid," added Neale, mimicking his comrade. "An' I shore hope thet this heah time you-all get aboot enough of your job."

One by one the engineers returned from different points along the wall, and they joined the group around Neale and King.

"Test that rope," ordered General Lodge.

The long rope appeared to be amply strong. When King fastened one end round his body under his arms the question arose among the engineers, just as it had arisen for Neale, whether or not it was needful to let the lineman down before the surveyor. Henney, who superintended this sort of work, decided it was not necessary.

"I reckon I'll go ahaid," said King. Like all Texans of his type, Larry King was slow, easy, cool, careless. Moreover, he gave a singular impression of latent nerve, wildness, violence.

There seemed every assurance of a deadlock when General Lodge stepped forward and addressed his inquiry to Neale.

"Larry thinks the rope will break. So he wants to go first," replied Neale.

There were broad smiles forthcoming, yet no one laughed. This was one of the thousands of strange human incidents that must be enacted in the building of the railroad. It might have been humorous, but it was big. It fixed the spirit and it foreshadowed events.

General Lodge's stern face relaxed, but he spoke firmly. "Obey orders," he admonished Larry King.

The loop was taken from Larry's waist and transferred to Neale's. Then all was made ready to let the daring surveyor with his instrument down over the wall.

Neale took one more look at the rugged front of the cliff. When he straightened up the ruddy bronze had left his face.

"There's a bulge of rock. I can't see what's below it," he said. "No use for signals. I'll go down the length of the rope and trust to find a footing. I can't be hauled up."

They all conceded this silently.

Then Neale sat down, let his legs dangle over the wall, firmly grasped his instrument, and said to the troopers who held the rope, "All right!"

They lowered him foot by foot.

It was windy and the dust blew up from under the wall. Black cañon swifts, like swallows, darted out with rustling wings, uttering frightened twitterings. The engineers leaned over, watching Neale's progress. Larry King did not look over the precipice. He watched the slowly slipping rope as knot by knot it passed over. It fascinated him.

"He's reached the bulge of rock," called Baxter, craning his neck.

"There, he's down—out of sight!" exclaimed Henney.

Casey, the flagman, leaned farther out than any other. "Phwat a dom' sthrange way to build a railroad, I sez," he remarked.

The gorge lay asleep in the westering sun, silent, full of blue haze. Seen from this height, far above the break where the engineers had first halted, it had the dignity and dimensions of a cañon. Its walls had begun to change color in the sunset light.

Foot by foot the soldiers let the rope slip, until probably two hundred had been let out, and there were scarcely a hundred feet left. By this time all that part of the cable which had been made of lassoes had passed over; the remainder consisted of pieces of worn and knotted and frayed rope, at which the engineers began to gaze fearfully.

"I don't like this," said Henney, nervously. "Neale surely ought to have found a ledge or bench or slope by now."

Instinctively the soldiers held back, reluctantly yielding inches where before they had slacked away feet. But intent as was their gaze, it could not rival that of the cowboy.

"Hold!" he yelled, suddenly pointing to where the strained rope curved over the edge of the wall.

The troopers held hard. The rope ceased to pay out. The strain seemed to increase. Larry King pointed with a lean hand.

"It's a-goin' to break!"

His voice, hoarse and swift, checked the forward movement of the engineers. He plunged to his knees before the rope and reached clutchingly, as if he wanted to grasp it, yet dared not.

"Ropes was my job! Old an' rotten! It's breakin'!"

Even as he spoke the rope snapped. The troopers, thrown off their balance, fell backward. Baxter groaned; Boone and Henney cried out in horror; General Lodge stood aghast, dazed. Then they all froze rigid in the position of intense listening.

A dull sound puffed up from the gorge, a low crash, then a slow-rising roar and rattle of sliding earth and rock. It diminished and ceased with the hollow cracking of stone against stone.

Casey broke the silence among the listening men with a curse. Larry Red King rose from his knees, holding the end of the snapped rope, which he threw from him with passionate violence. Then with action just as violent he unbuckled his belt and pulled it tighter and buckled it again. His eyes were blazing with blue lightning; they seemed to accuse the agitated engineers of deliberate murder. But he turned away without speaking and hurried along the edge of the gorge, evidently searching for a place to go down.

General Lodge ordered the troopers to follow King and if possible recover Neale's body.

"That lad had a future," said old Henney, sadly. "We'll miss him."

Boone's face expressed sickness and horror.

Baxter choked. "Too bad!" he murmured, "but what's to be done?"

The chief engineer looked away down the shadowy gorge where the sun was burning the ramparts red. To have command of men was hard, bitter. Death stalked with his orders. He foresaw that the building of this railroad was to resemble the war in which he had sent so many lads and men to bloody graves.

The engineers descended the long slope and returned to camp, a mile down the narrow valley. Fires were blazing; columns of smoke were curling aloft; the merry song and reckless laugh of soldiers were ringing out, so clear in the still air; horses were neighing and stamping.

Colonel Dillon reported to General Lodge that one of the scouts had sighted a large band of Sioux Indians encamped in a valley not far distant. This tribe had gone on the war-path and had begun to harass the engineers. Neale's tragic fate was forgotten in the apprehension of what might happen when the Sioux discovered the significance of that surveying expedition.

"The Sioux could make the building of the U.P. impossible," said Henney, always nervous and pessimistic.

"No Indians—nothing can stop us!" declared his chief.

The troopers sent to follow Larry King came back to camp, saying that they had lost him and that they could not find any place where it was possible to get down into that gorge.

In the morning Larry King had not returned.

Detachments of troopers were sent in different directions to try again. And the engineers went out once more to attack their problem. Success did not attend the efforts of either party, and at sunset, when all had wearily returned to camp, Larry King was still absent. Then he was given up for lost.

But before dark the tall cowboy limped into camp, dusty and torn, carrying Neale's long tripod and surveying instrument. It looked the worse for a fall, but apparently was not badly damaged. King did not give the troopers any satisfaction. Limping on to the tents of the engineers, he set down the instrument and called. Boone was the first to come out, and his summons brought Henney, Baxter, and the younger members of the corps. General Lodge, sitting at his camp-fire some rods away, and bending over his drawings, did not see King's arrival.

No one detected any difference in the cowboy, except that he limped. Slow, cool, careless he was, yet somehow vital and impelling.

"Wal, we run the line around—four miles up the gorge whar the crossin' is easy. Only ninety-foot grade to the mile."

The engineers looked at him as if he were crazy.

"But Neale! He fell—he's dead!" exclaimed Henney.

"Daid? Wal, no, Neale ain't daid," drawled Larry.

"Where is he, then?"

"I reckon he's comin' along back heah."

"Is he hurt?"

"Shore. An' hungry, too, which is what I am," replied Larry, as he limped away.

Some of the engineers hurried out in the gathering dusk to meet Neale, while others went to General Lodge with the amazing story.

The chief received the good news quietly but with intent eyes. "Bring Neale and King here—as soon as their needs have been seen to," he ordered. Then he called after Baxter, "Ninety feet to the mile, you said?"

"Ninety-foot grade, so King reported."

"By all that's lucky!" breathed the chief, as if his load had been immeasurably lightened. "Send those boys to me."

Some of the soldiers had found Neale down along the trail and were helping him into camp. He was crippled and almost exhausted. He made light of his condition, yet he groaned when he dropped into a seat before the fire.

Some one approached Larry King to inform him that the general wanted to see him.

"Wal, I'm hungry—an' he ain't my boss," replied Larry, and went on with his meal. It was well known that the Southerner would not talk.

But Neale talked; he blazed up in eloquent eulogy of his lineman; before an hour had passed away every one in camp knew that Larry had saved Neale's life. Then the loquacious Casey, intruding upon the cowboy's reserve, got roundly cursed for his pains.

"G'wan out among thim Sooz Injuns an' be a dead hero, thin," retorted Casey, as the cowboy stalked off to be alone in the gloom. Evidently Casey was disappointed not to get another cursing, for he turned to his comrade, McDermott, an axman. "Say, Mac, phwot do you make of cowboys?"

"I tell ye, Pat, I make of thim thet you'll be full of bullet-holes before this railroad's built."

"Thin, b'gosh, I'll hould drink fer a long time yit," replied Casey.

Later General Lodge visited Neale and received the drawings and figures that made plain solution of what had been a formidable problem.

"It was easy, once I landed under that bulge of cliff," said Neale. "There's a slope of about forty-five degrees—not all rock. And four miles up the gorge peters out. We can cross. I got to where I could see the divide—and oh! there is where our troubles begin. The worst is all to come."

"You've said it," replied the chief, soberly. "We can't follow the trail and get the grade necessary. We've got to hunt up a pass."

"We'll find one," said Neale, hopefully.

"Neale, you're ambitious and you've the kind of spirit that never gives up. I've watched your work from the start. You'll make a big position for yourself with this railroad, if you only live through the building of it."

"Oh, I'll live through it, all right," replied Neale, laughing. "I'm like a cat—always land on my feet—and have nine lives besides."

"You surely must! How far did you fall this time?"

"Not far. I landed in a tree, where my instrument stuck. But I crashed down, and got a hard knock on the head. When Larry found me I was unconscious and sliding for another precipice."

"That Texan seems attached to you."

"Well, if he wasn't before he will be now," said Neale, feelingly. "I'll tell you, General, Larry's red-headed, a droll, lazy Southerner, and he's made fun of by the men. But they don't understand him. They certainly can't see how dangerous he is. Only I don't mean that. I do mean that he's true like steel."

"Yes, he showed that. When the rope snapped I made sure he'd pull a gun on us. . . . Neale, I would like to have had you and Larry Red King with me through the war."

"Thank you, General Lodge. . . . But I like the prospects now."

"Neale, you're hungry for wild life?"

"Yes," replied Neale, simply.

"I said as much. I felt very much the same way when I was your age. And you like our prospects? . . . Well, you've thought things out. Neale, the building of the U.P. will be hell!"

"General, I can see that. It sort of draws me—two ways—the wildness of it and then to accomplish something."

"My lad, I hope you will accomplish something big without living out all the wildness."

"You think I might lose my head?" queried Neale.

"You are excitable and quick-tempered. Do you drink?"

"Yes—a little," answered the young man. "But I don't care for liquor."

"Don't drink, Neale," said the chief, earnestly. "Of course it doesn't matter now, for we're only a few men out here in the wilds. But when our work is done over the divide, we must go back along the line. You know ground has been broken and rails laid west of Omaha. The work's begun. I hear that Omaha is a beehive. Thousands of idle men are flocking West. The work will be military. We must have the army to protect us, and we will hire all the soldiers who apply. But there will be hordes of others—the dregs of the war and all the bad characters of the frontier. They will flock to the construction camp. Millions of dollars will go along with the building. Gold! . . . Where it's all coming from I have no idea. The Government backs us with the army—that's all. But the gold will be forthcoming. I have that faith. . . . And think, lad, what it will mean in a year or two. Ten thousand soldiers in one camp out here in these wild hills. And thousands of others—honest merchants and dishonest merchants, whisky men, gamblers, desperadoes, bandits, and bad women. Niggers, Greasers, Indians, all together moving from camp to camp, where there can be no law."

"It will be great!" exclaimed Neale, with shining eyes.

"It will be terrible," muttered the elder man, gravely. Then, as he got up and bade his young assistant good night, the somberness had returned to his eyes and the weight to his shoulders. He did not underestimate his responsibility nor the nature of his task, and he felt the coming of nameless and unknown events beyond all divining.

Henney was Neale's next visitor. The old engineer appeared elated, but for the moment he apparently forgot everything else in his solicitation for the young man's welfare.

Presently, after he had been reassured, the smile came back to his face.

"The chief has promoted you," he said.

"What!" exclaimed Neale, starting up.

"It's a fact. He just talked it over with Baxter and me. This last job of yours pleased him mightily . . . and so you go up."

"Go up! . . . To what?" queried Neale, eagerly.

"Well, that's why he consulted us, I guess," laughed Henney. "You see, we sort of had to make something to promote you to, for the present."

"Oh, I see! I was wondering what job there could be," replied Neale, and he laughed, too. "What did the chief say?"

"He said a lot. Figured you'd land at the top if the U.P. is ever built. . . . Chief engineer! . . . Superintendent of maintenance of way!"

"Good Lord!" breathed Neale. "You're not in earnest?"

"Wal, I shore am, as your cowboy pard says," returned Henney. And then he spoke with real earnestness. "Listen, Neale. Here's the matter in a nutshell. You will be called upon to run these particular and difficult surveys, just as yesterday. But no more of the routine for you. Added to that, you will be sent forward and back, inspecting, figuring. You can make your headquarters with us or in the construction camps, as suits your convenience. All this, of course, presently, when we get farther on. So you will be in a way free—your own boss a good deal of the time. And fitting yourself for that 'maintenance of way' job. In fact, the chief said that—he called you Maintenance-of-Way Neale. Well, I congratulate you. And my advice is keep on as you've begun—go straight—look out for your wildness and temper. . . . That's all. Good night."

Then he went out, leaving Neale speechless.

Neale had many callers that night, and the last was Larry Red King. The cowboy stooped to enter the tent.

"Wal, how aboot you-all?" he drawled.

"Not so good, Red," replied Neale. "My head's hot and I've got a lot of pain. I think I'm going to be a little flighty. Would you mind getting your blankets and staying with me to-night?"

"I reckon I'd be glad," answered King. He put a hand on Neale's face. "You shore have fever." He left the tent, to return presently with a roll of blankets and a canteen. Then he awkwardly began to bathe Neale's face with cold water. There was a flickering camp-fire outside that threw shadows on the wall of the tent. By its light Neale saw that King's left hand was bandaged and that he used it clumsily.

"What's wrong with your hand?" he queried.

"I reckon nawthin'."

"Why is it bound up, then?"

"Wal, some one sent thet fool army doctor to me an' he said I had two busted bones in it."

"He did! I had no idea you were hurt. You never said a word. And you carried me and my instrument all day— with a broken hand!"

"Wal, I ain't so shore it's broke."

Neale swore at his friend and then he fell asleep. King watched beside him, ever and anon rewetting the hot brow.

The camp-fire died out, and at length the quietness of late night set in. The wind mourned and lulled by intervals; a horse thudded his hoofs now and then; there were the soft, steady footsteps of the sentry on guard, and the wild cry of a night bird.

CHAPTER V

Neale had not been wrong when he told the engineers that once they had a line surveyed across the gorge and faced the steep slopes of the other side their troubles would be magnified.

They found themselves deeper in the Wyoming hills, a range of mountains that had given General Lodge great difficulty upon former exploring trips, and over which a pass had not yet been discovered.

The old St. Vrain and Laramie Trail wound along the base of these slopes and through the valleys. But that trail was not possible for a railroad. A pass must be found—a pass that would give a grade of ninety feet to the mile. These mountains had short slopes, and they were high.

It turned out that the line as already surveyed through ravines and across the gorge had to be abandoned. The line would have to go over the hills. To that end the camp was moved east again to the first slopes of the Wyoming hills; from there the engineers began to climb. They reached the base of the mountains, where they appeared to be halted for good and all.

The second line, so far as it went, overlooked the Laramie

Trail, which fact was proof that the old trail-finders had as keen eyes as engineers.

With a large band of hostile Sioux watching their movements the engineer corps found it necessary to have the troops close at hand all the time. The surveyors climbed the ridges while the soldiers kept them in sight from below. Day after day this futile search for a pass went on. Many of the ridges promised well, only to end in impassable cliffs or breaks or ascents too steep. There were many slopes and they all looked alike. It took hard riding and hard climbing. The chief and his staff were in despair. Must their great project fail because of a few miles of steep ascent? They would not give up.

The vicinity of Cheyenne Pass seemed to offer encouragement. Camp was made in the valley on a creek. From here observations were taken. One morning the chief, with his subordinates and a scout, ascended the creek and then through the pass to the summit. Again the old St. Vrain and Laramie Trail lay in sight. And again the troops rode along it, with the engineers above.

The chief with his men rode on and up farther than usual; farther than they ought to have gone unattended. Once the scout halted and gazed intently across the valley.

"Smoke signals over thar," he said.

The engineers looked long, but none of them saw any smoke. They moved on. But the scout called them back.

"Thet bunch of redskins has split on us. Fust thing we'll run into some of them."

It was Neale's hawk eye that first sighted Indians. "Look! Look!" he cried, in great excitement, as he pointed with shaking finger.

Down a grassy slope of a ridge Indians were riding, evidently to head off the engineers, to get between them and the troops.

"Wal, we're in fer it now," declared the scout. "We can't get back the way we come up."

The chief gazed coolly at the Indians and then at the long ridge sloping away from the summit. He had been in tight places before.

"Ride!" was his order.

"Let's fight!" cried Neale.

The band of eight men were well armed and well mounted, and if imperative, could have held off the Sioux for a time. But General Lodge and the scout headed across a little valley and up a higher ridge, from which they expected to sight the troops. They rode hard and climbed fast, but it took a quarter of an hour to gain the ridge-top. Sure enough the troops were in sight, but far away, and the Sioux were cutting across to get in front.

It was a time for quick judgment. The scout said they could not ride down over the ridge, and the chief decided they must follow along it. The going got to be hard and rough. One by one the men dismounted to lead their horses. Neale, who rode a mettlesome bay, could scarcely keep up.

"Take mine," called Larry King, as he turned to Neale.

"Red, I'll handle this stupid beast or—"

"Wal, you ain't handlin' him," interrupted King. "Hosses is my job, you know."

Red took the bridle from Neale and in one moment the balky horse recognized a master arm.

"By Heaven! we've got to hurry!" called Neale.

It did seem that the Indians would head them off. Neale and King labored over the rocky ground as best they could, and by dint of hard effort came up with their party. The Indians were quartering the other ridge, riding as if on level ground. The going grew rougher. Baxter's horse slipped and lamed his right fore leg. Henney's saddle turned, and more valuable time was lost. All the men drew their rifles. At every dip of ground they expected to come to a break that would make a stand inevitable.

From one point on the ridge they had a good view of the troops.

"Signal!" ordered the chief.

They yelled and shot and waved hats and scarfs. No use—the soldiers kept moving on at a snail pace far below.

"On—down the ridge!" was the order.

"Wal, General, thet looks bad to me," objected the scout.

Red King shoved his lean, brown hand between them. There was a flame in his flashing, blue glance as it swept the slowly descending ridge.

"Judgin' the lay of land is my job," he said, in his cool way. "We'll git down heah or not at all."

Neale was sore, lame, and angry as well. He kept gazing across at the Sioux. "Let's stop—and fight," he panted. "We can—whip—that bunch."

"We may have to fight, but not yet," replied the chief. "Come on."

They scrambled on over rocky places, up and down steep banks. Here and there were stretches where it was possible to ride, and over these they made better time. The Indians fell out of sight under the side of the ridge, and this fact was disquieting, for no one could tell how soon they would show up again or in what quarter. This spurred the men to sterner efforts.

Meanwhile the sun was setting and the predicament of the engineers grew more serious. A shout from Neale, who held up the rear, warned all that the Indians had scaled the ridge behind them and now were in straightaway pursuit. Thereupon General Lodge ordered his men to face about with rifles ready. This move checked the Sioux. They halted out of range.

"They're waitin' fer dark to set in," said the scout.

"Come on! We'll get away yet," said the chief, grimly.

They went on, and darkness began to fall about them. This increased both the difficulty and the danger. On the other hand, it enabled them to try and signal the troops with fire. One of them would hurry ahead and build a fire while the others held back to check the Indians if they appeared. And at length their signals were answered by the troops. Thus encouraged, the little band of desperate men plunged on down the slope. And just when night set in black—the fateful hour that would have precipitated the Indian attack—the troops met the engineers on the slope. The Indians faded away into the gloom without firing a shot. There was a general rejoicing. Neale, however, complained that he would rather have fought them.

"Wal, I shore was achin' fer trouble," drawled his faithful ally, King.

The flagman, Casey, removed his black pipe to remark, "All thet cloimb without a foight!"

General Lodge's first word to Colonel Dillon was evidently inspired by Casey's remark.

"Colonel, did you have steep work getting up to us?"

"Yes, indeed, straight up out of the valley," was the rejoinder.

But General Lodge did not go back to camp by this short cut down the valley. He kept along the ridge, and it led for miles slowly down to the plain. There in the starlight he faced his assistants with singular fire and earnestness.

"Men, we've had a bad scare and a hard jaunt, but we've found our pass over the Wyoming hills. To-morrow we'll run a line up that long ridge. We'll name it Sherman Pass. . . . Thanks to those red devils!"

On the following morning Neale was awakened from a heavy, dreamless sleep by a hard dig in the ribs.

"Neale—air you daid?" Larry was saying. "Wake up! An' listen to thet."

Neale heard the clear, ringing notes of a bugle-call. He rolled out of his blankets. "What's up, Red?" he cried, reaching for his boots.

"Wal, I reckon them Injuns," drawled Red.

It was just daylight. They found the camp astir—troopers running for horses, saddles, guns.

"Red, you get our horses and I'll see what's up," cried Neale.

The cowboy strode off, hitching at his belt. Neale ran forward into camp. He encountered Lieutenant Leslie, whom he knew well, and who told him a scout had come in with news of a threatened raid; Colonel Dillon had ordered out a detachment of troopers.

"I'm going," shouted Neale. "Where's that scout?"

Neale soon descried a buckskin-clad figure, and he made toward it. The man, evidently a trapper or hunter, carried a long, brown rifle, and he had a powder-horn and bullet-pouch slung over his shoulder. There was a knife in his belt. Neale went directly up to the man.

"My name's Neale," he said. "Can I be of any help?"

He encountered a pair of penetrating gray eyes.

"My name's Slingerland," replied the other, as he offered his hand. "Are you an officer?"

"No. I'm a surveyor. But I can ride and shoot. I've a cowboy with me—a Texan. He'll go. What's happened?"

"Wal, I ain't sure yet. But I fear the wust. I got wind of some Sioux thet was trailin' some prairie-schooners up in the hills. I warned the boss—told him to break camp an' run. Then I come fer the troops. But the troops had changed camp an' I jest found them. Reckon we'll be too late."

"Was it a caravan?" inquired Neale, intensely interested.

"Six wagons. Only a few men. Two wimmen. An' one girl."

"Girl!" exclaimed Neale.

"Yes. I reckon she was about sixteen. A pretty girl with

big, soft eyes. I offered to take her up behind me on my hoss. An' they all wanted her to come. But she wouldn't. . . . I hate to think—"

Slingerland did not finish his thought aloud. Just then Larry rode up, leading Neale's horse. Slingerland eyed the lithe cowboy.

"Howdy!" drawled Larry. He did not seem curious or eager, and his cool, easy, reckless air was in sharp contrast to Neale's fiery daring.

"Red, you got the rifles, I see," said Neale.

"Sure, an' I rustled some biscuits."

In a few moments the troops were mounted and ready. Slingerland led them up the valley at a rapid trot and soon started to climb. When he reached the top he worked up for a mile, and then, crossing over, went down into another valley. Up and down he led, over ridge after ridge, until a point was reached where the St. Vrain and Laramie Trail could be seen in the valley below. From here he led them along the top of the ridge, and just as the sun rose over the hills he pointed down to a spot where the caravan had been encamped. They descended into this valley. There in the trail were fresh tracks of unshod horses.

"We ain't fur behind, but I reckon fur enough to be too late," said Slingerland. And he clenched a big fist.

On this level trail he led at a gallop, with the troops behind in a clattering roar. They made short work of that valley. Then rougher ground hindered speedy advance.

Presently Slingerland sighted something that made him start. It proved to be the charred skeleton of a prairie-schooner. The oxen were nowhere to be seen.

Then they saw that a little beyond blankets and camp utensils littered the trail. Still farther on the broad wheel-tracks sheered off the road, where the hurried drivers had missed the way in the dark. This was open, undulating ground, rock-strewn and overgrown with brush. A ledge of rock, a few scraggy trees, and more black, charred remains of wagons marked the final scene of the massacre.

Neale was the first man who dismounted, and Larry King was the second. They had outstripped the more cautious troopers.

"My Gawd!" breathed Larry.

Neale gripped his rifle with fierce hands and strode forward between two of the burned wagons. Naked, mutilated bodies, bloody and ghastly, lay in horrible positions. All had been scalped.

Slingerland rode up with the troops, and all dismounted, cursing and muttering.

Colonel Dillon ordered a search for anything to identify the dead. There was nothing. All had been burned or taken away. Of the camp implements, mostly destroyed, there were two shovels left, one with a burnt handle. These were used by the troopers to dig graves.

Neale had at first been sickened by the ghastly spectacle. He walked aside a little way and sat down upon a rock. His face was wet with clammy sweat. A gnawing rage seemed to affect him in the pit of the stomach. This was his first experience with the fiendish work of the savages. A whirl of thoughts filled his mind.

Suddenly he fancied he heard a low moan. He started violently. "Well, I'm hearing things," he muttered, soberly.

It made him so nervous that he got up and walked back to where the troopers were digging. He saw the body of a woman being lowered into a grave and the sight reminded him of what Slingerland had said. He saw the scout searching around and he went over to him.

"Have you found the girl?" he asked.

"Not yet. I reckon the devils made off with her. They'd take her, if she happened to be alive."

"God! I hope she's dead."

"Wal, son, so does Al Slingerland."

More searching failed to find the body of the girl. She was given up as lost.

"I'll find out if she was took captive," said Slingerland. "This Sioux band has been friendly with me."

"Man, they're on the war-path," rejoined Dillon.

"Wal, I've traded with them same Sioux when they was on the war-path. . . . This massacre sure is awful, an' the Sioux will hev to be extarminated. But they hev their wrongs. An' Injuns is Injuns."

Slabs of rock were laid upon the graves. Then the troopers rode away.

Neale and Slingerland and Larry King were the last to mount. And it was at this moment that Neale either remembered the strange, low moan or heard it again. He reined in his horse.

"I'm going back," he called.

"What fer?" Slingerland rejoined.

Larry King wheeled his mount and trotted back to Neale.

"Red, I'm not satisfied," said Neale, and told his friend what he thought he had heard.

"Boy, you're oot of yur haid!" expostulated Red.

"Maybe I am. But I'm going back. Are you coming?"

"Shore," replied Red, with his easy good nature.

Slingerland sat his horse and watched while he waited. The dust-cloud that marked the troops drew farther away.

Neale dismounted, threw his bridle, and looked searchingly around. But Larry, always more comfortable on horseback than on land, kept his saddle. Suddenly Neale felt inexplicably drawn in a certain direction—toward a rocky ledge. Still he heard nothing except the wind in the few scraggy trees. All the ground in and around the scene of the massacre had been gone over; there was no need to examine it again. Neale had nothing tangible upon which to base his strange feeling. Yet absurd or not, he refused to admit it was fancy or emotion. Some voice had called him. He swore it. If he did not make sure he would always be haunted. So with clear, deliberate eyes he surveyed the scene. Then he strode for the ledge of rock.

Tufts of sage grew close at its base. He advanced among them. The surface of the rock was uneven—and low down a crack showed. At that instant a slow, sobbing, gasping intake of breath electrified Neale.

"Red—come here!" he yelled, in a voice that made the cowboy jump.

Neale dropped to his knees and parted the tufts of sage. Lower down the crack opened up. On the ground, just inside that crack he saw the gleam of a mass of chestnut hair. His first flashing thought was that here was a scalp the red devils did not get.

Then Red King was kneeling beside him—bending forward. "It's a girl!" he ejaculated.

"Yes—the one Slingerland told me about—the girl with big eyes," replied Neale. He put a hand softly on her head. It was warm. Her hair felt silky, and the touch sent a quiver over him. Probably she was dying.

Slingerland came riding up. "Wal, boys, what hev you found?" he asked, curiously.

"That girl," replied Neale.

The reply brought Slingerland sliding out of his saddle.

Neale hesitated a moment, then reaching into the aperture, he got his hands under the girl's arms and carefully drew her out upon the grass. She lay face down, her hair a tumbled mass, her body inert. Neale's quick eye searched for blood-stains, but found none.

"I remember thet hair," said Slingerland. "Turn her over."

"I reckon we'll see then where she's hurt," muttered Red King.

Evidently Neale thought the same, for he was plainly afraid to place her on her back.

"Slingerland, she's not such a little girl," he said, irrelevantly. Then he slipped his hands under her arms again. Suddenly he felt something wet and warm and sticky. He pulled a hand out. It was blood-stained.

"Aw!" exclaimed Red.

"Son, what'd you expect?" demanded Slingerland. "She got shot or cut, an' in her fright she crawled in thar. Come, over with her. Let's see. She might live."

This practical suggestion acted quickly upon Neale. He turned the girl over so that her head lay upon his knees. The face thus exposed was deathly pale, set like stone in horror. The front of her dress was a bloody mass, and her hands were red.

"Stabbed in the breast!" exclaimed King.

"No," replied Slingerland. "If she'd been stabbed she'd been scalped, too. Mebbe thet blood comes from an arrow an' she might hev pulled it out."

Neale bent over her with swift scrutiny. "No cut or hole in her dress!"

"Boys, thar ain't no marks on her—only thet blood," added Slingerland, hopefully.

Neale tore open the front of her blouse and slipped his hand in upon her breast. It felt round, soft, warm under his touch, but quiet. He shook his head.

"Those moans I heard must have been her last dying breaths," he said.

"Mebbe. But she shore doesn't look daid to me," replied King. "I've seen daid people. Put your hand on her heart."

Neale had been feeling for heart pulsations on her right side. He shifted his hand. Instantly through the soft swell of her breast throbbed a beat—beat—beat. The beatings were regular and not at all faint.

"Good Lord, what a fool I am!" he cried. "She's alive! Her heart's going! There's not a wound on her!"

"Wal, we can't see any, thet's sure," replied Slingerland.

"She might hev a fatal hurt, all the same," suggested King.

"No!" exclaimed Neale. "That blood's from some one else—most likely her murdered mother. . . . Red, run for some water. Fetch it in your hat. Slingerland, ride after the troops."

Slingerland rose and mounted his horse. "Wal, I've an idee. Let's take the girl to my cabin. Thet's not fur from hyar. It's a long ride to the camp. An' if she needs the troop doctor we can fetch him to my place."

"But the Sioux?"

"Wal, she'd be safer with me. The Injuns an' me are friends."

"All right. Good. But you ride after the troops, anyhow, and tell Dillon about the girl—that we're going to your cabin."

Slingerland galloped away after the dust cloud down the trail.

Neale gazed strangely down at the face of the girl he had rescued. Her lips barely parted to make again the low moan. So that was what had called to him. No—not all! There was something more than this feeble cry that had brought him back to search; there had been some strong and nameless and inexplicable impulse. Neale believed in his impulses—in those strange ones which came to him at intervals. So far in his life girls had been rather nega-tive influences. But this girl, or the fact that he had saved her, or both impressions together, struck deep into him; life would never again be quite the same to Warren Neale.

Red King came striding back with a sombrero full of water.

"Take your scarf and wash that blood off her hands before she comes to and sees it," said Neale.

The cowboy was awkward at the task, but infinitely gentle. "Poor kid! I'll bet she's alone in the world now."

Neale wet his scarf and bathed the girl's face. "If she's only fainted she ought to be reviving now. But I'm afraid—"

Then suddenly her eyes opened. They were large, violet-hued, covered with a kind of veil or film, as though sleep had not wholly gone; and they were unseeingly, staringly set with horror. Her breast heaved with a sharply drawn breath; her hands groped and felt for something to hold; her body trembled. Suddenly she sat up. She was not weak. Her motions were violent. The dazed, horror-stricken eyes roved around, but did not fasten upon anything.

"Aw! Gone crazy!" muttered King, pityingly.

It did seem so. She put her hands to her ears as if to shut out a horrible sound. And she screamed. Neale grasped her shoulders, turned her round, and forced her into such a position that her gaze must meet his.

"You're safe!" he cried, sharply. "The Indians have gone! I'm a white man!"

It seemed as though his piercing voice stirred her reason. She stared at him. Her face changed. Her lips parted and her hand, shaking like a leaf, covered them, clutched at them. The other hand waved before her as if to brush aside some haunting terror.

Neale held that gaze with all his power—dominant, masterful, masculine. He repeated what he had said.

Then it became a wonderful and terrible sight to watch her, to divine in some little way the dark and awful state of her mind. The lines, the tenseness, the shade, the age faded out of her face; the deep-set frown smoothed itself out of her brow and it became young. Neale saw those staring eyes fix upon his; he realized a dull, opaque blackness of horror, hideous veils let down over the windows of a soul, images of hell limned forever on a mind. Then that film, that unseeing cold thing, like the shade of sleep or of death, passed from her eyes. Now they suddenly were alive, great dark-violet gulfs, full of shadows, dilating, changing into exquisite and beautiful lights.

"I'm a white man!" he said, tensely. "You're saved! The Indians are gone!"

She understood him. She realized the meaning of his words. Then, with a low, agonized, and broken cry she shut her eyes tight and reached blindly out with both hands; she screamed aloud. Shock claimed her again. Horror and fear convulsed her, and it must have been fear that was uppermost. She clutched Neale with fingers of steel, in a grip he could not have loosened without breaking her bones.

"Red, you saw—she was right in her mind for a moment— you saw?" burst out Neale.

"Shore I saw. She's only scared now," replied King. "It must hev been hell fer her."

At this juncture Slingerland came riding up to them. "Did she come around?" he inquired, curiously gazing at the girl as she clung to Neale.

"Yes, for a moment," replied Neale.

"Wal, thet's good. . . . I caught up with Dillon. Told him. He was mighty glad we found her. Cussed his troopers some. Said he'd explain your absence, an' we could send over fer anythin'."

"Let's go, then," said Neale. He tried to loosen the girl's hold on him, but had to give it up. Taking her in his arms, he rose and went toward his horse. King had to help him mount with his burden. Neale did not imagine he would ever forget that spot, but he took another long look to fix the scene indelibly on his memory. The charred wagons, the graves, the rocks over which the naked, gashed bodies had been flung, the three scraggy trees close together, and the ledge with the dark aperture at the base—he gazed at them all, and then turned his horse to follow Slingerland.

CHAPTER VI

Some ten miles from the scene of the massacre and perhaps fifteen from the line surveyed by the engineers, Slingerland lived in a wild valley in the heart of the Wyoming hills.

The ride there was laborsome and it took time, but Neale scarcely noted either fact. He paid enough attention to the trail to fix landmarks and turnings in his mind, so that he would remember how to find the way there again. He was, however, mostly intent upon the girl he was carrying.

Twice that he knew of her eyes opened during the ride. But it was to see nothing and only to grip him tighter, if that were possible. Neale began to imagine that he had been too hopeful. Her body was a dead weight and cold. Those two glimpses he had of her opened eyes hurt him. What should he do when she did come to herself? She would be frantic with horror and grief and he would be helpless. In a case like hers it might have been better if she had been killed.

The last mile to Slingerland's lay through a beautiful green valley with steep sides almost like a cañon—trees everywhere, and a swift, clear brook running over a bed of smooth rock. The trail led along this brook up to where the valley boxed and the water boiled out of a great spring in a green glade overhung by bushy banks and gray rocks above. A rude cabin with a red-stone chimney and clay-chinked cracks between the logs, stuffed to bursting with furs and pelts and horns and traps, marked the home of the trapper.

"Wal, we're hyar," sung out Slingerland, and in the cheery tones there was something which told that the place was indeed home to him.

"Shore is a likely-lookin' camp," drawled Red, throwing his bridle. "Been heah a long time, thet cabin."

"Me an' my pard was the first white men in these hyar hills," replied Slingerland. "He's gone now." Then he turned to Neale. "Son, you must be tired. Thet was a ways to carry a girl nigh onto dead. . . . Look how white! Hand her down to me."

The girl's hands slipped nervelessly and limp from their hold upon Neale. Slingerland laid her on the grass in a shady spot. The three men gazed down upon her, all sober, earnest, doubtful.

"I reckon we can't do nothin' but wait," said the trapper.

Red King shook his head as if the problem were beyond him.

Neale did not voice his thought, yet he wanted to be the first person her eyes should rest upon when she did return to consciousness.

"Wal, I'll set to work an' clean out a place fer her," said Slingerland.

"We'll help," rejoined Neale. "Red, you have a look at the horses."

"I'll slip the saddles an' bridles," replied King, "an' let 'em go. Hosses couldn't be chased out of heah."

Slingerland's cabin consisted really of two adjoining cabins with a door between, one part being larger and of later construction. Evidently he used the older building as a storeroom for his pelts. When all these had been removed the room was seen to be small, with two windows, a table, and a few other crude articles of home-made furniture. The men cleaned this room and laid down a carpet of deer hides, fur side up. A bed was made of a huge roll of buffalo skins, flattened and shaped, and covered with Indian blankets. When all this had been accomplished the trapper removed his fur cap, scratched his grizzled head, and appealed to Neale and King.

"I reckon you can fetch over some comfortable-like necessaries—fixin's fer a girl," he suggested.

Red King laughed in his cool, easy, droll way. "Shore, we'll rustle fer a lookin'-glass, an' hair-brush, an' such as girls hev to hev. Our camp is full of them things."

But Neale did not see any humor in Slingerland's perplexity or in the cowboy's facetiousness. It was the girl's serious condition that worried him, not her future comfort.

"Run out thar!" called Slingerland, sharply.

Neale, who was the nearest to the door, bolted outside, to see the girl sitting up, her hair disheveled, her manner wild in the extreme. At sight of him she gave a start, sudden and violent, and uttered a sharp cry. When Neale reached her it was to find her shaking all over. Terrible fear had never been more vividly shown, yet Neale believed she saw in him a white man, a friend. But the fear in her was still stronger than reason.

"Who are you?" she asked.

"My name's Neale—Warren Neale," he replied, sitting down beside her. He took one of the shaking hands in his. He was glad that she talked rationally.

"Where am I?"

"This is the home of a trapper. I brought you here. It was the best—in fact, the only place."

"You saved me—from—from those devils?" she queried, hoarsely, and again the cold and horrible shade veiled her eyes.

"Yes—yes—but don't think of them—they're gone," replied Neale, hastily. The look of her distressed and frightened him. He did not know what to say.

The girl fell back with a poignant cry and covered her eyes as if to shut out a hateful and appalling sight. "My—mother!" she moaned, and shuddered with agony. "They—murdered—her! . . . Oh! the terrible yells! . . . I saw—killed—every man—Mrs. Jones! My mother—she fell—she never spoke! Her blood was on me! . . . I crawled away—I hid! . . . The Indians—they tore—hacked—scalped—burned! . . . I couldn't die!—I saw! . . . Oh!—Oh!—Oh!" Then she fell to moaning in inarticulate fashion.

Slingerland and King came out and looked down at the girl.

"Wal, the life's strong in her," said the trapper. "I reckon I know when life is strong in any critter. She'll git over thet. All we can do now is to watch her an' keep her from doin' herself harm. Take her in an' lay her down."

For two days and nights Neale watched over her, except for the hours she slept, when he divided his vigil with King. She had periods of consciousness, in which she knew Neale, but most of the time she raved or tossed or moaned or lay like one dead. On the third day, however, Neale felt encouraged. She awoke weak and somber, but quiet and rational. Neale talked earnestly to her, in as sensible a way as he knew how, speaking briefly of the tragic fate that had been hers, bidding her force it out of her mind by taking interest in her new surroundings. She listened to him, but did not seem impressed. It was a difficult matter to get her to eat. She did not want to move. At length Neale told her that he must go back to the camp of the engineers, where he had work to do; he promised that he would return to see her soon and often. She did not speak or raise her eyes when he left her.

Outside, when Red brought up the horses, Slingerland said to Neale: "See hyar, son, I reckon you needn't worry. She'll come around all right."

"Shore she will," corroborated the cowboy. "Time'll cure her. I'm from Texas, whar sudden death is plentiful in all families."

Neale shook his head. "I'm not so sure," he said. "That girl's more sensitively and delicately organized than you fellows see. I doubt if she'll ever recover from the shock. It'll take a mighty great influence. . . . But let's hope for the best. Now, Slingerland, take care of her as best you can. Shut her in when you leave camp. I'll ride over as often as possible. If she gets so she will talk, then we can find out if she has any relatives, and if so I'll take her to them. If not I'll do whatever else I can for her."

"Wal, son, I like the way you're makin' yourself responsible fer thet kid," replied the trapper. "I never had no wife nor daughter. But I'm thinkin'—wouldn't it jest be hell to be a girl—tender an' young an' like Neale said— an' sudden hev all you loved butchered before your eyes?"

"It shore would," said Red, feelingly. "An' thet's what she sees all the time."

"Slingerland, do we run any chance of meeting Indians?" queried Neale.

"I reckon not. Them Sioux will git fur away from hyar after thet massacre. But you want to keep sharp eyes out, an' if you do meet any, jest ride an' shoot your way through. You've the best horses I've seen. Whar'd you git them?"

"They belong to King. He's a cowboy."

"Hosses was my job. An' we can shore ride away from any redskins," replied King.

"Wal, good luck, an' come back soon," was Slingerland's last word.

So they parted. The cowboy led the way with the steady, easy, trotting walk that saved a horse yet covered distance; in three hours they were hailed by a trooper outpost, and soon they were in camp.

Shortly after their arrival the engineers returned, tired, dusty, work-stained, and yet in unusually good spirits. They had run the line up over Sherman Pass, and now it seemed their difficulties were to lessen as the line began to descend from the summit of the divide. Neale's absence had been noticed, for his services were in demand. But all the men rejoiced in his rescue of the little girl, and were sympathetic and kind in their inquiries. It seemed to Neale that his chief looked searchingly at him, as if somehow the short absence had made a change in him. Neale himself grew conscious of a strange difference in his inner nature; he could not forget the girl, her helplessness, her pathetic plight.

"Well, it's curious," he soliloquized. "But—it's not so, either. I'm sorry for her."

And he remembered the strange change in her eyes when he had watched the shadow of horror and death and blood fade away before the natural emotions of youth and life and hope.

Next day Neale showed more than ever his value to the engineering corps, and again won a word of quiet praise from his chief. He liked the commendation of his superiors. He began to believe heart and soul in the coming greatness of the railroad. And that strenuous week drove his faithful lineman, King, to unwonted complaint.

Larry tugged at his boots and groaned as he finally pulled them off. They were full of holes, at which he gazed ruefully.

"Shore I'll be done with this heah job when they're gone," he said.

"Why do you work in high-heeled boots?" inquired

Neale. "You can't walk or climb in them. No wonder they're full of holes."

"Wal, I couldn't wear no boots like yours," declared Red.

"You'll have to. Another day will about finish them, and your feet, too."

Red eyed his boss with interest. "You-all cussed me today because I was slow," he complained.

"Larry, you always are slow, except with a horse or gun. And lately you've been—well, you don't move out of your tracks."

Neale often exaggerated out of a desire to tease his friend. Nobody else dared try and banter King.

"Wal, I didn't sign up with this heah outfit to run up hills all day," replied Red.

"I'll tell you what. I'll get Casey to be my lineman. No, I've a better idea. Casey is slow, too. I'll use one of the niggers."

Red King gave a hitch to his belt and a cold gleam chased away the lazy blue warmth from his eyes. "Go ahaid," he drawled, "an' they'll bury the nigger to-morrow night."

Neale laughed. He knew Red hated darkies—he suspected the Texan had thrown a gun on more than a few—and he knew there surely would be a funeral in camp if he changed his lineman.

"All right, Red. I don't want blood spilled," he said, cheerfully. "I'll be a martyr and put up with you. . . . What do you say to a day off? Let's ride over to Slingerland's."

The cowboy's red face slowly wrinkled into a smile. "Wal, I shore was wonderin' what in the hell made you rustle so lately. I reckon nothin' would suit me better. I've been wonderin', too, about our little girl."

"Red, let's wade through camp and see what we can get to take over."

"Man, you mean jest steal?" queried King, in mild surprise.

"No. We'll ask for things. But if we can't get what we want that way—why, we'll have to do the other thing," replied Neale, thoughtfully. "Slingerland did not have even a towel over there. Think of that girl! She's been used to comfort, if not luxury. I could tell. . . . Let's see. I've a mirror and an extra brush. . . . Red, come on."

Eagerly they went over their scant belongings, generously appropriating whatever might be made of possible use to an unfortunate girl in a wild and barren country. Then they fared forth into the camp. Every one in the corps contributed something. The chief studied Neale's heated face, and a smile momentarily changed his stern features—a wise smile, a little sad, and full of light.

"I suppose you'll marry her," he said.

Neale blushed like a girl. "It—that hadn't occurred to me, sir," he stammered.

Lodge laughed, but his glance was kind. "Sure you'll marry her," he said. "You saved her life. And, boy, you'll be a big man of the U.P. some day. Chief engineer or superintendent of maintenance of way or some other big job. What could be finer? Romance, boy. The little waif of the caravan—you'll send her back to Omaha to school; she'll grow into a beautiful woman! She'll have a host of admirers, but you'll be the king of the lot—sure."

Neale got out of the tent with tingling ears. He was used to the badinage of the men, and had always retaliated with a sharp and ready tongue. But this half-kind, half-humorous talk encroached upon what he felt to be the secret side of his nature—the romantic and the dreamful side—to which such fancies were unconsciously dear.

Early the next morning Neale and King rode out on the way to Slingerland's.

The sun was warm when they reached the valley through

which ran the stream that led up to the cabin. Spring was in the air. The leaves of cottonwood and willow added their fresh emerald to the darker green of the pine. Bluebells showed in the grass along the trail; there grew lavender and yellow flowers unfamiliar to Neale; trout rose and splashed on the surface of the pools; and the way was melodious with the humming of bees and the singing of birds.

Slingerland saw them coming and strode out to meet them with hearty greeting.

"Is she all right?" queried Neale, abruptly.

"No, she ain't," replied Slingerland, shaking his shaggy head. "She won't eat or move or talk. She's wastin' away. She jest sits or lays with that awful look in her eyes."

"Can't you make her talk?"

"Wal, she'll say no to 'most anythin'. There was three times she asked when you was comin' back. Then she quit askin'. I reckon she's forgot you. But she's never forgot thet bloody massacre. It's there in her eyes."

Neale dismounted, and, untying the pack from his saddle, he laid it down, removed saddle and bridle; then he turned the horse loose. He did this automatically while his mind was busy.

"Where is she?" he asked.

"Over thar under the pines whar the brook spills out of the spring. Thet's the only place she'll walk to. I believe she likes to listen to the water. An' she's always afraid."

"I've fetched a pack of things for her," said Neale. "Come on, Red."

"Shore you go alone," replied the cowboy, hanging back. "Girls is not my job."

So Neale approached alone. The spot was green, fragrant, shady, bright with flowers, musical with murmuring water. Presently he spied her—a drooping, forlorn little figure. The instant he saw her he felt glad and sad at once.

She started quickly at his step and turned. He remembered the eyes, but hardly the face. It had grown thinner and whiter than the one he had in mind.

"My Lord! she's going to die!" breathed Neale. "What can I do—what can I say to her?"

He walked directly but slowly up to her, aware of her staring eyes, and confused by them.

"Hello! little girl, I've brought you some things," he said, and tried to speak cheerfully.

"Oh—is—it you?" she said, brokenly.

"Yes, it's Neale. I hope you've not forgotten me."

There came a fleeting change over her, but not in her face, he thought, because not a muscle moved, and the white stayed white. It must have been in her eyes, though he could not certainly tell. He bent over to untie the pack.

"I've brought you a lot of things," he said. "Hope you'll find them useful. Here—"

She did not look at the open pack or pay any attention to him. The drooping posture had been resumed, together with the somber staring at the brook. Neale watched her in despair, and, watching, he divined that only the most infinite patience and magnetism and power could bring her out of her brooding long enough to give nature a chance. He recognized how unequal he was to the task. But the impossible or the unattainable had always roused Neale's spirit. Defeat angered him. This girl was alive; she was not hurt physically; he believed she could be made to forget that tragic night of blood and death. He set his teeth and swore he would display the tact of a woman, the patience of a saint, the skill of a physician, the love of a father— anything to hold back this girl from the grave into which she was fading. Reaching out, he touched her.

"Can you understand me?" he asked.

"Yes," she murmured. Her voice was thin, far away, an evident effort.

"I saved your life."

"I wish you had let me die." Her reply was quick with feeling, and it thrilled Neale because it was a proof that he could stimulate or aggravate her mind.

"But I *did* save you. Now you owe me something."

"What?"

"Why, gratitude—enough to want to live, to try to help yourself."

"No—no," she whispered, and relapsed into the somber apathy.

Neale could scarcely elicit another word from her; then by way of change he held out different articles he had brought—scarfs, a shawl, a mirror—and made her look at them. Her own face in the mirror did not interest her. He tried to appeal to a girl's vanity. She had none.

"Your hair is all tangled," he said, bringing forth comb and brush. "Here, smooth it out."

"No—no—no," she moaned.

"All right, I'll do it for you," he countered. Surprised at finding her passive when he had expected resistance, he began to comb out the tangled tresses. In his earnestness he did not perceive how singular his action might seem to an onlooker. She had a mass of hair that quickly began to smooth out and brighten under his hand. He became absorbed in his task and failed to see the approach of Larry King.

The cowboy was utterly amazed, and presently he grinned his delight. Evidently the girl was all right and no longer to be feared.

"Wal, shore thet's fine," he drawled. "Neale, I always knowed you was a lady's man." And Larry sat down beside them

The girl's face was half hidden under the mass of hair, and her head was lowered. Neale gave Larry a warning glance, meant to convey that he was not to be funny.

"This is my cowboy friend, Larry Red King," said Neale. "He was with me when I—I found you."

"Larry—Red—King," murmured the girl. "My name is—Allie."

Again Neale had penetrated into her close-locked mind. What she said astounded him so that he dropped the brush and stared at Larry. And Larry lost his grin; he caught a glimpse of her face, and his own grew troubled.

"Allie—I shore—am glad to meet you," he said, and there was more feeling in his voice than Neale had ever before heard. Larry was not slow of comprehension. He began to talk in his drawling way. Neale heard him with a smile he tried to hide, but he liked Larry the better for his simplicity. This gun-throwing cowboy had a big heart.

Larry, however, did not linger for long. His attempts to get the girl to talk grew weaker and ended; then, after another glance at the tragic, wan face he got up and thoughtfully slouched away.

"So your name is Allie," said Neale. "Well, Allie what?"

She did not respond to one out of a hundred questions, and this query found no lodgment in her mind.

"Will you braid your hair now?" he asked.

The answer was the low and monotonous negative, but, nevertheless, her hands sought her hair and parted it, and began to braid it mechanically. This encouraged Neale more than anything else; it showed him that there were habits of mind into which he could turn her. Finally he got her to walk along the brook and also to eat and drink.

At the end of that day he was more exhausted than he would have been after a hard climb. Yet he was encouraged to think that he could get some kind of passive unconscious obedience from her.

"Reckon you'd better stay over to-morrow," suggested Slingerland. His concern for the girl could not have been greater had she been his own daughter. "Allie—thet was her name, you said. Wal, it's pretty an' easy to say."

Next day Allie showed an almost imperceptible improvement. It might have been Neale's imagination leading him to believe that there were really grounds for hope. The trapper and the cowboy could not get any response from her, but there was certain proof that he could. The conviction moved him to deep emotion.

An hour before sunset Neale decided to depart, and told Larry to get the horses. Then he went to Allie, undecided what to say, feeling that he must have tortured her this day with his ceaseless importunities. How small the chance that he might again awaken the springs of life interest. Yet the desire was strong within him to try.

"Allie." He repeated her name before she heard him. Then she looked up. The depths—the tragic lonesomeness—of her eyes—haunted Neale.

"I'm going back. I'll come again soon."

She made a quick movement—seized his arm. He remembered the close, tight grip of her hands.

"Don't go!" she implored. Black fear stared out of her eyes.

Neale was thunderstruck at the suddenness of her speech—at its intensity. Also he felt an unfamiliar kind of joy. He began to explain that he must return to work, that he would soon come to see her again; but even as he talked she faded back into that dull and somber apathy.

Neale rode away with only one conviction gained from the developments of the two days; it was that he would be restless and haunted until he could go to her again. Something big and moving—something equal to his ambition for his work on the great railroad—had risen in him and would not be denied.

CHAPTER VII

Neale rode to Slingerland's cabin twice during the ensuing fortnight, but did not note any improvement in Allie's condition or demeanor. The trapper, however, assured Neale that she was gradually gaining a little and taking some slight interest in things; he said that if Neale could only spend enough time there the girl might recover. This made Neale thoughtful.

General Lodge and his staff had decided to station several engineers in camp along the line of the railroad for the purpose of studying the drift of snow. It was important that all information possible should be obtained during the next few winters. There would be severe hardship attached to this work, but Neale volunteered to serve, and the chief complimented him warmly. He was to study the action of the snow-drift along Sherman Pass.

Upon his next visit to Slingerland Neale had the project soberly in mind and meant to broach it upon the first opportunity.

This morning, when Neale and King rode up to the cabin, Allie did not appear as upon the last occasion of their arrival. Neale missed her.

Slingerland came out with his usual welcome.

"Where's Allie?" asked Neale.

"Wal, she went in jest now. She saw you comin' an' then run in to hide, I reckon. Girls is queer critters."

"She watched for me—for us—and then ran?" queried Neale, curiously.

"Wal, she 'ain't done nothin' but watch fer you since you went away last. An', son, thet's a new wrinkle fer Allie. An' run? Wal, like a skeered deer."

"Wonder what that means?" pondered Neale. Whatever it meant, it sent a little tingle of pleasure along his pulses. "Red, I want to have a serious talk with Slingerland," he announced, thoughtfully.

"Shore; go ahaid an' talk," drawled the Southerner, as he slipped his saddle and turned his horse loose with a slap on the flank. "I reckon I'll take a gun an' stroll off fer a while."

Neale led the trapper aside to a shady spot under the pines and there unburdened himself of his plan for the winter.

"Son, you'll freeze to death!" ejaculated the trapper.

"I must build a cabin, of course, and prepare for severe weather," replied Neale.

Slingerland shook his shaggy head. "I reckon you ain't knowin' these winters hyar as I know them. But thet long ridge you call Sherman Pass—it ain't so fur we couldn't get thar on snow-shoes except in the wust weather. I reckon you can stay with me hyar."

"Good!" exclaimed Neale. "And now about Allie."

"Wal, what about her?"

"Shall I leave her here or send her back to Omaha with the first caravan, or let her go to Fort Fetterman with the troops?"

"Son, she's your charge, but I say leave her hyar, 'specially now you can be with us. She'd die or go crazy if you sent her. Why, she won't even say if she's got a livin' relation. I reckon she hain't. She'd be better hyar. I've come to be fond of Allie. She's strange. She's like a spirit. But she's more human lately."

"I'm glad you say that, Slingerland," replied Neale. "What to do about her had worried me. I'll decide right now. I'll leave her with you, and I hope to Heaven I'm doing best by her."

"Wal, she ain't strong enough to travel fur. We didn't think of thet."

"That settles it, then," said Neale, in relief. "Time enough to decide when she is well again. . . . Tell me about her."

"Son, thar's nuthin' to tell. She's done jest the same, except fer thet takin' to watchin' fer you. Reckon thet means a good deal."

"What?"

"Wal, I don't figger girls as well as I do other critters," answered Slingerland, reflectively. "But I'd say Allie shows interest in you."

"Slingerland! You don't mean she—she cares for me?" demanded Neale.

"I don't know. Mebbe not. Mebbe she's beyond carin'. But I believe you an' thet red memory of bloody death air all she ever thinks of. An' mostly of it."

"Then it'll be a fight between me and that memory?"

"So I take it, son. But recollect I ain't no mind-doctor. I jest feel you could make her fergit thet hell if you tried hard enough."

"I'll try—hard as I can," replied Neale, resolutely, yet with a certain softness. "I'm sorry for her. I saved her. Why shouldn't I do everything possible?"

"Wal, she's alone."

"No, Allie has friends—you and King and me. That's three."

"Son, I reckon you don't figger me. Listen. You're a fine,

strappin' young feller an' good-lookin'. More 'n thet, you've got some—some quality like an Injun's—thet you can feel but can't tell about. You needn't be insulted, fer I know Injuns thet beat white men holler fer all thet's noble. Anyway, you attract. An' now if you keep on with all thet—thet—wal, usin' yourself to make Allie fergit the bloody murder of all she loved, to make her mind clear again—why, sooner or later she's a-goin' to breathe an' live through you. Jest as a flower lives offen the sun. Thet's all, I reckon."

Neale's bronze cheek had paled a little. "Well, if that's all, that's easy," he replied, with a cool, bright smile which showed the latent spirit in him. "If it's only that—why she can have me. . . . Slingerland, I've no ties now. The last one was broken when my mother died—not long ago. I'm alone, too. . . . I'd do as much for any innocent girl—but for this poor child Allie—whose life I saved—I'd do anything."

Slingerland shoved out a horny hand and made a giant grip express what evidently just then he could not express in speech.

Upon returning to the cabin they found Allie had left her room. From appearances Neale concluded that she had made little use of the things he had brought her. He was conscious of something akin to impatience. He was not sure what he did feel. The situation had subtly changed and grown, all in that brief talk with Slingerland. Neale slowly walked out toward the brook, where he expected to find her. It struck him suddenly that if she had watched for him all week and had run when he came, then she must have wanted to see him, but was afraid or shy or perverse. How like any girl! Possibly in the week past she had unconsciously grown a little away from her grief.

"I'll try something new on you, Allie," he muttered, and

the boy in him that would never grow into a man meant to be serious even in his fun.

Allie sat in the shady place under the low pine where the brook spilled out of the big spring. She drooped and appeared oblivious to her surroundings. A stray gleam of sunlight, touching her hair, made it shine bright. Neale's quick eye took note of the fact that she had washed the blood-stain from the front of her dress. He was glad. What hope had there been for her so long as she sat hour after hour with her hands pressed to that great black stain on her dress—that mark where her mother's head had rested? Neale experienced a renewal of hope. He began to whistle, and, drawing his knife, he went into the brush to cut a fishing-pole. The trout in this brook had long tempted his fisherman's eye, and upon this visit he had brought a line and hooks. He made a lot of noise all for Allie's benefit; then, tramping out of the brush, he began to trim the rod within twenty feet of where she sat. He whistled; he even hummed a song while he was rigging up the tackle. Then it became necessary to hunt for some kind of bait, and he went about this with pleasure, both because he liked the search and because, out of the corner of his eye, he saw that Allie was watching him. Therefore he redoubled his efforts at pretending to be oblivious of her presence and at keeping her continually aware of his. He found crickets, worms, and grubs under the dead pine logs, and with this fine variety of bait he approached the brook.

The first cast Neale made fetched a lusty trout, and right there his pretensions of indifference vanished, together with his awareness of Allie's proximity. Neale loved to fish. He had not yet indulged his favorite pastime in the West. He saw trout jumping everywhere. It was a beautiful little stream, rocky, swift here and eddying there, clear as crystal, murmurous with tiny falls, and bordered by a freshness of green and gold; there were birds singing in the trees, but over all seemed to hang the quiet of the lonely hills. Neale forgot Allie—forgot that he had meant to discover if she could be susceptible to a little neglect. The brook was full of trout, voracious and tame; they had never been angled for. He caught three in short order.

When his last bait, a large and luscious grub, struck the water there was a swirl, a splash, a tug. Neale excitedly realized that he had hooked a father of the waters. It leaped. That savage leap, the splash, the amazing size of the fish, inflamed in Neale the old boyish desire to capture, and, forgetting what little skill he possessed, he gave a mighty pull. The rod bent double. Out with a vicious splash lunged the huge, glistening trout, to dangle heavily for an instant in the air. Neale thought he heard a cry behind him. He was sitting down, in awkward posture. But he lifted and swung. The line snapped. The fish dropped in the grass and began to thresh. Frantically Neale leaped to prevent the escape of the hugest trout he had ever seen. There was a dark flash—a commotion before him. Then he stood staring in bewilderment at Allie, who held the wriggling trout by the gills.

"You don't know how to fish!" she exclaimed, with great severity.

"I don't, eh?" ejaculated Neale, blankly.

"You should play a big trout. You lifted him right out. He broke your line. He'd have—gotten—away—but for me."

She ended, panting a little from her exertion and quick speech. A red spot showed in each white cheek. Her eyes were resolute and flashing. It dawned upon Neale that he had never before seen a tinge of color in her face, nor any of the ordinary feelings of life glancing in her eyes. Now she seemed actually pretty. He had made a discovery— perhaps he had now another means to distract her from herself. Then the squirming trout drew his attention and he took it from her.

"What a whopper! Oh, say, Allie, isn't he a beauty? I could hug— I— You bet I'm thankful. You were quick. . . . He certainly is slippery."

Allie dropped to her knees and wiped her hands on the grass while Neale killed the fish and strung it upon a willow with the others he had caught. Then turning to Allie, he started to tell her how glad he was to see her again, to ask her if she were glad to see him. But upon looking at her he decided to try and keep her mind from herself. She was different now and he liked the difference. He feared he might frighten it away.

"Will you help me get more bait?" he asked.

Allie nodded and got up. Then Neale noticed her feet were bare. Poor child! She had no shoes and he did not know how to procure any suitable footwear in that wilderness.

"Have you ever fished for trout?" he asked, as he began to dig under a rotting log.

"Yes. In California," she replied, with sudden shadowing of her eyes.

"Let's go down the brook," said Neale, hastily, fearful that he had been tactless. "There are some fine holes below."

She walked beside him, careful of the sharp stones that showed here and there. Presently they came to a likely-looking pool.

"If you hook another big one don't try to pull him right out," admonished Allie.

Neale could scarcely conceal his delight, and in his effort to appear natural made a poor showing at this pool, losing two fish and scaring others so they would not rise.

"Allie, won't you try?" he asked, offering the rod.

"I'd rather look on. You like it so much."

"How do you know that?" he asked, more to hear her talk than from curiosity.

"You grow so excited," she said.

Thankfully he accepted the realization that after all these weeks of silence it was possible to make her speak. But he must exercise extreme caution. One wrong word might send her back into that apathy—that senseless, voiceless trance.

In every pool where Neale cast he caught or lost a trout. He was enjoying himself tremendously and at the same time feeling a warmth in his heart that was not entirely due to the exhilaration of fishing. Below the head of the valley, where the stream began and the cabin nestled, the ground was open, like a meadow, with grass and flowers growing to the edge of the water. There were deep, swirling pools running under the banks, and in these Neale hooked fish he could not handle with his poor tackle, and they broke away. But he did not care. There was a brightness, a beauty, a fragrance along the stream that seemed to enhance the farther down he went. Presently they came to a place where the water rushed over a rocky bed, and here Neale wanted to cross. He started to wade, curious and eager to see what Allie would do.

"I can't wade that," she called.

Neale returned to her side. "I'll carry you," he said. "You hold the rod. We'll leave the fish here." Then he lifted her in his arms. How light she was—how much lighter than upon that first occasion of his carrying her. He slipped in the middle of the brook and nearly fell with her. Allie squealed. The sound filled Neale with glee. After all, and whatever she had gone through, she was feminine—she was a girl—she was squeamish. Thereupon he slipped purposely and made a heroic effort to save himself. She clasped his neck convulsively with her free arm, and as he recovered his balance her head bumped into his and her hair got into his eyes. He laughed. This was great fun. But it could scarcely have been the exertion that made his heart beat out of time. At last he gained the opposite bank.

"You nearly fell with me," she said.

"Well, I'd have got wet, too," he replied, wondering if it were possible to make her laugh or even smile. If he could do that to-day, even in the smallest degree, he would be assured that happiness might come back to her.

Soon they met Larry, who came stooping along, burdened with a deer carcass on his shoulder. Relieving himself, he hailed them.

"How air you-all?" he drawled, addressing himself mostly to Allie.

"What's your name?" she asked.

"Allie, he's my friend and partner," replied Neale. "Larry King. But I call him Red—for obvious reasons."

"Wal, Miss Allie, I reckon no tall kick would be a-comin' if you was to call me Red," drawled Larry. "Or better—Reddy. No other lady ever had thet honor."

Allie looked at him steadily, as if this was the first time she had seen him, but she did not reply. And Larry, easily disconcerted, gathered up his burden and turned toward camp.

"Wal, I'm shore wishin' you-all good luck," he called, significantly.

Neale shot a quick glance at Allie to see if the cowboy's good-humored double meaning had occurred to her. But apparently she had not heard. She seemed to be tiring. Her lips were parted and she panted.

"Are you tired? Shall we go back?" he asked.

"No—I like it," she returned, slowly, as if the thought were strange to her.

They fished on, and presently came to a wide, shallow place with smooth rock bottom, where the trail crossed. Neale waded across alone. And he judged that the water in the middle might come up to Allie's knees.

"Come on," he called.

Allie hesitated. She gathered up her faded skirt, slowly waded in and halted, uncertain of her footing. She was not afraid, Neale decided, and neither did she seem aware that her slender, shapely legs gleamed white against the dark water.

"Won't you come and carry me?" she asked.

"Indeed I won't," replied Neale. "Carry a big girl like you!"

She took him seriously and moved a little farther. "My feet slip so," she said.

It became fascinating to watch her. The fun of it—the pleasure of seeing a girl wade a brook, innocently immodest, suddenly ceased for Neale. There was something else. He had only meant to tease; he was going to carry her; he started back. And then he halted. There was a strange earnestness in Allie's face—a deliberateness in her intent, out of all proportion to the exigency of the moment. It was as if she must cross that brook. But she kept halting. "Come on!" Neale called. And she moved again. Every time this happened she seemed to be compelled to go on. When she got into the swift water, nearly to her knees, then she might well have faltered. Yet she did not falter. All at once Neale discovered that she was weak. She did not have the strength to come on. It was that which made her slip and halt. What then made her try so bravely? How strange that she tried at all! Stranger than all was her peculiar attitude toward the task—earnest, sober, grave, forced.

Neale was suddenly seized with surprise and remorse. That which actuated this girl Allie was merely the sound of his voice—the answer to his demand. He plunged in and reached her just as she was slipping. He carried her back to the side from which she started. It cost him an effort not to hold her close. Whatever she was—orphan or waif, left alone in the world by a murdering band of Sioux—an unfortunate girl to be cared for, succored, pitied—none of these considerations accounted for the change that his power over her had wrought in him.

"You're not strong," he said, as he put her down.

"Was that it?" she asked, with just a touch of wonder. "I used to wade—anywhere."

He spoke little on the way back up the brook, for he hesitated to tell her that he must return to his camp so as to be ready for important work on the morrow, and not until they were almost at the cabin did he make up his mind. She received the intelligence in silence, and upon reaching the cabin she went to her room.

Neale helped Larry and Slingerland with the task of preparing a meal that all looked forward to having Allie share with them. However, when Slingerland called her there was no response.

Neale found her sunk in the old, hopeless, staring, brooding mood. He tried patience at first, and gentleness, but without avail. She would not come with him. The meal was eaten without her. Later Neale almost compelled her to take a little food. He felt discouraged again. Time had flown all too swiftly, and there was Larry coming with the horses and sunset not far off. It might be weeks, even months, before he would see her again.

"Allie, are you *ever* going to cheer up?" he demanded.

"No—no," she sighed.

He put his hand under her chin, and, forcing her face up, studied it earnestly. Strained, white, bloodless, thin, with drooping lips and tragic eyes, it was not a beautiful, not even a pretty face. But it might have been one—very easily. The veiled, mournful eyes did not evade his; indeed, they appeared to stare deeply, hopelessly, yearningly. If he could only say and do the right thing to kill that melancholia. She needed to be made to live. Suddenly he had the impulse to kiss her. That, no doubt, was owing to the proximity of her lips. But he must not kiss her. She might care for him some day—it was natural to imagine she would. But she did not care now, and that made kisses impossible.

"You just won't cheer up?" he went on.

"No—no."

"But you were so different out there by the brook."

She made no reply. The veil grew darker, more shadowy, over her eyes. Neale divined a deadness in her.

"I'm going away," he said, sharply.

"Yes."

"Do you care?" he went on, with greater intensity.

She only stared at him.

"You *must* care!" he exclaimed.

"Why?" she asked, dully.

"Why! . . . Because—because—" he stammered, angry with himself. After all, why should she care?

"I wish—you'd—left me—to die!" she moaned.

"Oh! Allie! Allie!" began Neale, in distress. Then he caught the different quality in her voice. It carried feeling. She was thinking again. He swore that he would overcome this malady of hers, and he grew keen, subtle, on fire with his resolve. He watched her. He put his hands on her shoulders and pulled her gently. She slid off the pile of buffalo robes to her knees before him. Then she showed the only hint of shyness he had ever noted in her. Perhaps it was fear. At any rate, she half averted her face, so that her loosened hair hid it.

"Allie! Allie! Listen! Have you nothing to *live* for?" he asked.

"No."

"Why, yes, you have."

"What?"

"Why, I— The thing is—Allie—you have *me!*" he said,

a little hoarsely. Then he laughed. How strange his laugh sounded! He would always remember that rude room of logs and furs and the kneeling girl in the dim light.

"*You!*"

"Yes, me," he replied, with a ring in his voice. Never before had she put wonder in a word. He had struck the right chord at last. Now it seemed that he held a live creature under his hands, as if the deadness and the dread apathy had gone away forever with the utterance of that one syllable. This was a big moment. If only he could make up to her for what she had lost! He felt his throat swell, and speech was difficult.

"Allie, do you understand me now? You—have something—to live for! . . . Do you hear?"

When his ear caught the faint "Yes" he suddenly grew glad and strong with what he felt to be a victory over her gloom and despair.

"Listen. I'm going to my work," he began, swiftly. "I'll be gone weeks—maybe more. *But I'll come back!* . . . Early in the fall. I'll be with you all winter. I'm to work here on the pass. . . . Then—then— Well, I'll be a big man on the U.P. some day. Chief engineer or superintendent of maintenance of way. . . . You're all alone—maybe you'll care for me some day. I'll work hard. It's a great idea— this railroad. When it's done—and I've my big job—will you—you'll marry me then?"

Neale heard her gasp and felt her quiver. He let go of her and stood up, for fear he might suddenly take her in his arms. His words had been shock enough. He felt remorse, anxiety, tenderness, and yet he was glad. Some delicate and fine consciousness in him told him he had not done wrong, even if he had been dominating. She was alone in the world; he had saved her life. His heart beat quick and heavy.

"Good-by, Allie. . . . I'll come back. Never forget!"

She stayed motionless on her knees with the mass of hair hiding her face, and she neither spoke nor made a sign.

Neale went out. The air seemed to wave in his face, cool and relieving. Larry was there with the horses. Slingerland stood by with troubled eyes. Both men stared at Neale. He was aware of that, and conscious of his agitation. And suddenly, as always at a climax of emotion, he swiftly changed and grew cool.

"Red, old pard, congratulate me! I'm engaged to marry Allie!" he said, with a low laugh that had pride in it.

"Wal, damn me!" ejaculated Larry King. Then he shot out the hand that was so quick with rope and gun. "Put her thar! Shore if you hadn't made up to her I'd have. . . . An', Neale, if you say Pard, I'm yours till I'm daid!"

"Pard!" replied Neale, as he met the outstretched hand.

Slingerland's hard and wrinkled face softened.

"Strange how we all cottoned to thet girl! No—I reckon it ain't so strange. Wal, it's as it oughter be. You saved her. May you both be happy, son!"

Neale slipped a ring from his little finger.

"Give Allie this. Tell her it's my pledge. I'll come back to her. And she must think of that."

CHAPTER VIII

That summer the engineers crossed the Wyoming hills and ran the line on into Utah, where they met the surveying party working in from the Pacific.

The initial step of the great construction work was done, the engineers with hardship and loss of life had proved that a railroad across the Rockies was a possibility. Only, they had little conception of the titanic labor involved in the building.

For Neale the months were hard, swift, full. It came to him that love of the open and the wild was incorporated in his ambition for achievement. He wondered if he would have felt the one without the other. Camp life and the daily climbing over the ridges made of him a lithe, strong, surefooted mountaineer. They made even the horse-riding cowboy a good climber, though nothing, Neale averred, would ever straighten Larry's bow legs.

Only two incidents or accidents marred the work and pleasure of those fruitful weeks.

The first happened in camp. There was a surly stakedriver by the name of Shurd who was lazy and otherwise offensive among hard-working men. Having been severely handled by Neale, he had nursed a grievance and only waited for an opportunity for revenge. Neale was quick-tempered, and prone to sharp language and action when irritated or angered. Shurd, passing through the camp, either drunk or unusually surly, had kicked Neale's instrument out of his way. Some one saw him do it and told Neale. Thereupon Neale, in high dudgeon, had sought out the fellow. Larry King, always Neale's shadow, came slouching after with his cowboy's gait. They found Shurd at the camp of the teamsters and other laborers. Neale did not waste many words. He struck Shurd a blow that staggered him, and would have followed it up with more had not the man, suddenly furious, plunged away to pick up a heavy stake with which he made at Neale to brain him.

Neale could not escape. He yelled at Shurd, trying to intimidate him.

Then came a shot from behind. It broke Shurd's arm. The stake fell and the man began to bawl curses.

"Get out of heah!" called Larry King, advancing slowly. The maddened Shurd tried to use the broken arm, perhaps to draw on King. Thereupon the cowboy, with gun low and apparently not aiming, shot again, this time almost tearing Shurd's arm off. Then he prodded Shurd with the cocked gun. The man turned ghastly. He seemed just now to have realized the nature of this gaunt flaming-eyed cowboy.

"Shore your mind ain't workin'," said Larry. "Get out of heah. Mozey over to thet camp doctor or you'll never need one."

Shurd backed away, livid and shaking, and presently he ran.

"Red! . . ." expostulated Neale. "You—you shot him all up! You nearly killed him."

"Why in hell don't you pack a gun?" drawled Larry.

"Red, you're—you're— I don't know what to call you. I'd have licked him, club and all."

"Mebbe," replied the cowboy, as he sheathed the big gun. "Neale, I'm used to what you ain't. Shore I can see death a-comin'. Wal, every day the outfit grows wilder. A little whisky'll burn hell loose along this heah U.P. line."

Larry strode on in the direction Shurd had taken. Neale pondered a moment, perplexed, and grateful to his comrade. He heard remarks among the laborers, and he saw the flagman Casey remove his black pipe from his lips—an unusual occurrence.

"Mac, it wus thot red-head cowboy wot onct p'inted his gun at me!" burst out Casey.

"Did yez see him shoot?" replied Mac, with round eyes. "Niver aimed an' yit he hit!"

Mike Shane, the third of the trio of Irish laborers in Neale's corps, was a little runt of a sandy-haired wizened man, and he spoke up: "Begorra, he's wan of thim Texas Jacks. He'd loike to kill yez, Pat Casey, an' if he ever throwed thot cannon at yez, why, runnin' 'd be slow to phwat yez 'd do."

"I niver run in me loife," declared Casey, doggedly.

Neale went his way. It was noted that from that day he always carried a gun, preferably a rifle when it was possible. In the use of the long gun he was an adept, but when it came to Larry's kind of a gun Neale needed practice. Larry could draw his gun and shoot twice before Neale could get his hand on his weapon.

It was through Neale's habit of carrying the rifle out on his surveying trips that the second incident came about.

One day in early summer Neale was waiting near a spring for Larry to arrive with the horses. On this occasion the cowboy was long in coming. Neale fell asleep in the shade of some bushes and was awakened by the thud of hoofs. He sat up to see Larry in the act of kneeling at the brook to drink. At the same instant a dark moving object above Larry attracted Neale's quick eye. It was an

Indian sneaking along with a gun ready to level. Quick as a flash Neale raised his own weapon and fired. The Indian fell and lay still.

Larry's drink was rudely disturbed by plunging horses. When he had quieted them he turned to Neale.

"So you-all was heah. Shore you scared me. What'd you shoot at?"

Neale stared and pointed. His hand shook. He felt cold, sick, hard, yet he held the rifle ready to fire again. Larry dropped the bridles and, pulling his gun, he climbed the bank with unusual quickness for him. Neale saw him stand over the Indian.

"Wal, plumb center!" he called, with a new note in his usually indolent voice. "Come heah!"

"No!" shouted Neale, violently. "Is he dead?"

"Daid! Wal, I should smile. . . . An' mebbe he ain't alone."

The cowboy ran down to his horse and Neale followed suit. They rode up on the ridge to reconnoiter, but saw no moving objects.

"I reckon thet redskin was shore a-goin' to plug me," drawled Larry, as they trotted homeward.

"He certainly was," replied Neale, with a shudder.

Larry reached a long hand to Neale's shoulder. He owed his life to his friend. But he did not speak of that. Instead he glanced wisely at Neale and laughed.

"Kinda weak in the middle, eh?" he said. "I felt thet way once. . . . Pard, if you ever get r'iled you'll be shore bad."

For Neale shooting at an Indian was strikingly different from boyish dreams of doing it. He had acted so swiftly that it seemed it must have been instinctive. Yet thinking back, slowly realizing the nature of the repellant feeling within him, he remembered a bursting gush of hot blood, a pantherish desire to leap, to strike—and then cool, stern watchfulness. The whole business had been most unpleasant.

Upon arriving at camp they reported the incident, and they learned Indians had showed up at various points along the line. Troopers had been fired upon. Orders were once more given that all work must be carried on under the protection of the soldiers, so that an ambush would be unlikely. Meanwhile a detachment of troops would be sent out to drive back the band of Sioux.

These two hard experiences made actuality out of what Neale's chief had told him would be a man's game in a wild time. This work on the U.P. was not play or romance. But the future unknown called alluringly to him. In his moments of leisure, by the camp-fire at night, he reflected and dreamed and wondered. And these reflections always turned finally to memory of Allie.

The girl he had saved seemed far away in mind as well as in distance. He tried to call up her face—to see it in the ruddy embers. But he could visualize only her eyes. They were unforgetable—the somber, haunting shadows of thoughts of death. Yet he remembered that once or twice they had changed, had become wonderful, with promise of exceeding beauty.

It seemed incredible that he had pledged himself. But he had no regrets. Time had not made any difference, only it had shown him that his pity and tenderness were not love. Still there had been another emotion connected with Allie—a strange thing too subtle and brief for him to analyze; when away from her he lost it. Could that have been love? He thought of the day she waded the brook, the feel of her as he carried her in his arms; and of that last sight of her, on her knees in the cabin, her face hidden, her slender form still as a statue. His own heart was touched. Yet this was not love. It was enough for Neale to feel that he had done what he would have applauded in another man, that he seemed the better for his pledge, that the next meeting with Allie was one he looked forward to with a strange, new interest.

September came and half sped by before Neale, with Larry and an engineer named Service, arrived at the head of Sherman Pass with pack-burros and supplies, ready to begin the long vigil of watching the snow drift over the line in winter.

They were to divide the pass between them, Service to range the upper half and Neale the lower. As there were but few trees up in that locality, and these necessary for a large supply of fire-wood, they decided not to attempt building a cabin for Service, but to dig a dugout. This was a hole hollowed out in a hillside and covered with roof of branches and earth.

No small job, indeed, was it to build a satisfactory dugout—one that was not conspicuous from every ridge for Indian eyes to spy out—and warm and dry and safe. They started several before they completed one.

"It'll be lonesomer for you—and colder," observed Neale.

"I won't mind that," replied the other.

"We'll see each other before the snow flies, surely."

"Not unless you come up. I'm no climber. I've got a bad leg."

"I'll come, then. We may have weeks of fine weather yet. I'm going to hunt some."

"Good luck to you."

So these comrades parted. They were only two of the intrepid engineers selected to brave the perils and hardships of that wild region in winter, to serve the great cause.

The golds and purples of autumn mingled with the predominating green of Slingerland's valley. In one place beaver had dammed the stream, forming a small lake, and here cranes and other aquatic birds had congregated. Neale saw beaver at work, and deer on the hillside.

"It's been three months," he soliloquized, as he paused at the ford which Allie had so bravely and weakly tried to cross at his bidding. "Three months! So much can have happened. But Slingerland is safe from Indians. I hope—I believe I'll find her well."

He was a prey to dread and yet he did not hurry. Larry, driving the pack-train, drew on ahead and passed out of sight in a green bend of the brook. At length Neale saw a column of blue smoke curling up above the trees, and that sight relieved him. If the trapper was there, the girl would be with him.

At this moment his horse shot up his long ears and snorted.

A gray form glided out of the green and began to run down the trail toward him—a lithe, swift girl in buckskin.

"An Indian girl!" ejaculated Neale.

But her face was white, her hair tawny and flying in the wind. Could that be Allie? It must be she. It was.

"Lord! I'm in for it!" muttered Neale, dismounting, and he gazed with eager eyes. She was approaching quickly.

"Neale! You've come!" she cried, and ran straight upon him.

He hardly recognized her face or her voice, but what she said proclaimed her to be Allie. She enveloped him. Her arms, strong, convulsive, clasped him. Up came her face, white, gleaming, joyous, strange to Neale, but he knew somehow that it was held up to be kissed. Dazedly he kissed her—felt cool sweet lips touch his lips again and then again.

"Allie! . . . I—I hardly knew you!" was his greeting. Now he was holding her, and he felt her press her head closely to his breast, felt the intensity of what must have been her need of physical contact to make sure he was here in the flesh. And as he held her, looking down upon her, he recognized the little head and the dull gold and ripple of chestnut hair. Yes—it was Allie. But this new Allie was taller—up to his shoulder—and lithe and full-bosomed and strong. This was not the frail girl he had left.

"I thought—you'd—never, never come," she murmured, clinging to him.

"It was—pretty long," he replied, unsteadily. "But I've come. . . . And I'm very glad to see you."

"You didn't know me," she said, shyly. "You looked—it."

"Well, no wonder. I left a thin, pale little girl, all eyes—and what do I find? . . . Let me look at you."

She drew back and stood before him, shy and modest, but without a trace of embarrassment, surely the sweetest and loveliest girl he had ever beheld. Some remembered trace he found in her features, perhaps the look, the shape of her eyes—all else was unfamiliar. And that all else was a white face, blue-veined, with rich blood slowly mantling to the broad brow, with sweet red lips haunting in their sadness, with glorious eyes, like violets drenched in dew, shadowy, exquisite, mournful and deep, yet radiant with beautiful light.

Neale recognized her beauty at the instant he realized her love, and he was so utterly astounded at the one, and overwhelmed with the other, that he was mute. A powerful reaction took place within him, so strong that it helped to free him from the other emotions. He found his tongue and controlled his glance.

"I took you for an Indian girl in all this buckskin," he said.

"Dress, leggings, moccasins, I made them all myself," she replied, sweeping a swift hand from fringe to beads. "Not a single button! Oh, it was hard—so much work! But they're more comfortable than any clothes I ever had."

"So you've not been—altogether idle since I left?"

"Since that day," and she blushed exquisitely at the words, "I've been doing everything under the sun except that grieving which you disliked—everything—cooking, sewing, fishing, bathing, climbing, riding, shooting—*and* watching for you."

"That accounts," he replied, musingly.

"For what?"

"Your—your improvement. You seem happy—and well."

"Do you mean the activity accounts for that—or my watching for you?" she queried, archly. She was quick, bright, roguish. Neale had no idea what qualities she might have possessed before that fateful massacre, but she was bewilderingly different from the sick-minded girl he had tried so hard to interest and draw out of her gloom. He was so amazed, so delighted with her, and so confused with his own peculiar state of mind, that he could not be natural. Then his mood shifted and a little heat at his own stupidity aroused his wits.

"Allie, I want to realize what's happened," he said. "Let's sit down here. We sat here once before, if you remember. Slingerland can wait to see me."

Neale's horse grazed along the green border of the brook. The water ran with low, swift rush; there were bees humming round the autumn flowers and a fragrance of wood-smoke wafted down from the camp; over all lay the dreaming quietness of the season and the wild.

Allie sat down upon the rock, but Neale, changing his mind, stood beside her. Still he did not trust himself to face her. He was unsettled, uncertain. All this was like a dream.

"So you watched for me?" he asked, gently.

"For hours and days and weeks," she sighed.

"Then you—cared—cared a little for me?"

She kept silence. And he, wanting intensely to look up, did not.

"Tell me," he insisted, with a hint of the old dominance. He remembered again the scene at the crossing of the brook. Could he control this wonderful girl now?

"Of course," she replied.

"But—how do you care?" he added, more forcibly. He felt ashamed, yet he could not resist it. What was happening to him?

"I—I love you." Her voice was low, almost faltering, rich with sweetness, and full of some unutterable emotion.

Neale sustained a shock. He never could have told how that affected him, except in his sudden fury at himself. Then he stole a glance at her. Her eyes were downcast, hidden under long lashes; her face was soft and sweet, dreaming and spiritual, singularly pure; her breast heaved under the beaded buckskin. Neale divined she had never dreamed of owing him anything except the maiden love which quivered on her tremulous lips and hovered in the exquisite light of her countenance. And now he received a great and impelling change in his spirit, an uplift, a splendid and beautiful consciousness of his good fortune. But what could he say to her? If only he could safely pass over this moment, so he could have time to think, to find himself. Another glance at her encouraged him. She expected nothing—not a word; she took all for granted. She was lost in dreams of her soul.

He looked down again to see her hand—small, shapely, strong and brown; and upon the third finger he espied his ring. He had forgotten to look to see if she wore it. Then softly he touched it and drew her hand in his.

"My ring. Oh, Allie!" he whispered.

The response was a wonderful purple blaze of her eyes. He divined then that his ring had been the tangible thing upon which she had reconstructed her broken life.

"You rode away—so quickly—I had no chance to—tell," she replied, haltingly and low-voiced. All was sweet shame about her now, and he had to fight himself to keep from gathering her to his breast. Verily this meeting between Allie and him was not what he had anticipated.

He kissed her hand.

"You've all the fall and all the winter to tell me such sweet things," he said. "Perhaps to-morrow I'll find my tongue and tell you something."

"Tell me now," she said, quickly.

"Well, you're beautiful," he replied, with strong feeling.

"Really?" she smiled, and that smile was the first he had ever seen upon her face. It brought out the sadness, the very soul of her great beauty. "I used to be pretty," she went on, naïvely. "But if I remember how I used to look I'm not pretty any more."

Neale laughed. He had begun to feel freer, and to accept this unparalleled situation with some composure.

"Tell me," he said, with gentle voice and touch—"tell me your name. Allie—what?"

"Didn't you ever know?" she asked.

"You said Allie. That was all."

He feared this call to her memory, yet he wanted to put her to a test. Her eyes dilated—the light shaded; they grew sad, dark, humid gulfs of thought. But the old, somber veil, the insane, brooding stare, did not return.

"Allie what?" he repeated.

Then the tears came, softening and dimming the pain. "Allie Lee," she said.

CHAPTER IX

lingerland appeared younger to Neale. The burden of loneliness did not weigh upon him, and the habit of silence had been broken. Neale guessed why, and was actually jealous.

"Wal, it's beyond my calculatin'," the trapper said, out by the spring, where Neale followed him. "She jest changed, thet's all. Not so much at first, though she sparked up after I give her your ring. I reckon it come little by little. An' one day, why, the cabin was full of sunshine! . . . Since then I've seen how she's growed an' brightened. Workin', runnin' after me—an' always watchin' fer you, Allie's changed to what she is now. Onct, fur back, I recollect she said she had you to live fer. Mebbe thet's the secret. Anyhow, she loves you as I never seen any man loved. . . . An', son, I reckon you oughter be somewhars near the kingdom of heaven!"

Neale stole off by himself and walked in the twilight. The air was warm and sultry, full of fragrance and the low chirp of crickets. Within his breast was a full uneasy sensation of imminent catastrophe. Something was rising in him—great—terrible—precious. It bewildered him to try to think of himself, of his strange emotions, when his mind seemed to hold only Allie.

What then had happened? After a long absence up in the mountains he had returned to Slingerland's valley home, and to the little girl he had rescued and left there. He had left her frail, sick-minded, silent, somber, a pale victim to a horrible memory. He had found her an amazing contrast to what she had been in the past. She had grown strong, active, swift. She was as lovely as a wild rose. No dream of his idle fancy, but a fact! Then last—stirring him even as he tried to clarify and arrange this magic, this mystery— had come the unbelievable, the momentous and dazzling assurance that she loved him. It was so plain that it seemed unreal. While near her he saw it, yet could not believe his eyes; he felt it, but doubted his sensibilities. But now, away from the distraction of her presence and with Slingerland's eloquent words ringing in his ears, he realized the truth. Love of him had saved the girl's mind and had made her beautiful and wonderful. He had heard of the infinite transforming power of love; here in Allie Lee was its manifestation. Whether or not he deserved such a blessing was not the question. It was his, and he felt unutterably grateful and swore he would be worthy of this great gift.

Darkness had set in when Neale returned to the cabin, the interior of which was lighted by blazing sticks in a huge stone fireplace.

Slingerland was in the shadow, busy as usual, but laughing at some sally of Larry's. The cowboy and Allie, however, were in plain sight. Neale needed only one look at Larry to divine what had come over that young man. Allie appeared perplexed.

"He objects to my calling him Mr. King and even Larry," she said.

Larry suddenly looked sheepish.

"Allie, this cowboy is a bad fellow with guns, ropes, horses—and I suspect with girls," replied Neale, severely.

"Neale, he doesn't look bad," she rejoined. "You're fooling me. . . . He wants me to call him Reddy."

"Ahuh!" grunted Neale. He laughed grimly at himself, for again he had felt a pang of jealousy. He knew what to expect from Larry or any other young man who ever had the wonderful good luck to get near Allie Lee. "All right, call him Reddy," he went on. "I guess I can allow my future wife so much familiarity with my pard."

This confused Allie out of her sweet gravity, and she blushed.

"Shore you're mighty kind," drawled Larry, recovering. "More 'n I reckoned on from a fellar who's shore lost his haid."

"I've lost more 'n that," retorted Neale, "and I'm afraid a certain wild young cowboy I know has lost as much."

"Wal, I reckon somethin' aboot this heah place of Slingerland's draws on a fellar," admitted Larry, resignedly.

Allie did not long stay embarrassed by their sallies.

"Neale, tell me—"

"See heah, Allie, if you call me Reddy an' him only Neale—why he's a-goin' to pitch into me," interrupted Larry, with twinkling eyes. "An' he's shore a bad customer when he's r'iled."

"Only Neale? What does he mean?" inquired Allie.

"Beyond human conjecture," replied Neale, laughing.

"Wal, don't you know his front name?" asked Larry.

"Neale. I call him that," she replied.

"Haw! Haw! But it ain't thet."

"Allie, my name is Warren," said Neale. "You've forgotten."

"Oh! . . . Well, it's always been Neale—and always will be."

Larry rose and stretched his long arms for the pipe on the rude stone chimney.

"Slingerland," he drawled, "these heah young people need to find out who they are. An' I reckon we'd do wal to go oot an' smoke an' talk."

The trapper came forth from the shadows, and as he filled his pipe his keen, bright gaze shifted from the task to his friends.

"It's good to see you an' hyar you," he said. "I was a youngster onct. I missed—but thet's no matter. . . . Live while you may! . . . Larry, come with me. I've got a trap to set yit."

Allie flashed a glance at them.

"It's not so. You never set traps after dark."

"Wal, child, any excuse is better 'n none. Neale wouldn't never git to hyar you say all thet sweet talk as is comin' to him—if two old fools hung round."

"Slingerland, I've throwed a gun fer less 'n thet," drawled Larry. "Aboot the fool part I ain't shore, but I was twenty-five yesterday—an' I'm sixteen to-day."

They lit their pipes with red embers scraped from the fire, and with wise nods at Neale and Allie passed out into the dark.

Allie's eyes were upon Neale, with shy, eloquent intent, and directly the others had departed she changed her seat to one close to Neale; she nestled against his shoulder, her face to the fire.

"They thought we wanted to make love, didn't they?" she said, dreamily.

"I guess they did," replied Neale.

He was intensely fascinated. Did she want him to make love to her? A look at her face was enough to rebuke him for the thought. The shadows from the flickering fire played over her.

"Tell me all about yourself," she said. "Then about your work."

Neale told all that he thought would interest her about his youth in the East with a widowed mother, the home that was broken up after she died, and his working his way through a course of civil engineering.

"I was twenty when I first read about this U.P. railroad project," he went on. "That was more than three years ago. It decided me on my career. I determined to be an engineer and be in the building of the road. No one had any faith in the railroad. I used to be laughed at. But I stuck. And—well, I had to steal some rides to get as far west as Omaha.

"That was more than a year ago. I stayed there—waiting. Nothing was sure, except that the town grew like a mushroom. It filled with soldiers—and the worst crowd I ever saw. You can bet I was shaky when I finally got an audience with General Lodge and his staff. They had an office in a big storehouse. The place was full of men—soldiers and tramps. It struck me right off what a grim and discouraged bunch those engineers looked. I didn't understand them, but I do now. . . . Well, I asked for a job. Nobody appeared to hear me. It was hard to make yourself heard. I tried again—louder. An old engineer, whom I know now—Henney—waved me aside. Just as if a job was unheard of!"

Neale quickened and warmed as he progressed, aware now of a little hand tight in his, of an interest that would have made any story-telling a pleasure.

"Well, I felt sick. Then mad. When I get mad I do things. I yelled at that bunch: 'Here, you men! I've walked and stole rides to get here. I'm a surveyor. You're going to build a railroad. I want a job and I'm going to get it.'

"My voice quieted the hubbub. The old engineer, Henney, looked queerly at me.

" 'Young man, there's not going to be any railroad.'

"Then I blurted out that there *was* going to be a railroad. Some one spoke up: 'Who said that? Fetch him here.' Pretty soon I was looking at Major-General Lodge. He was just from the war and he looked it. Stern and dark, with hard lines and keen eyes. He glanced me over.

"'There is going to be a railroad?' he questioned, sharply.

"'Of course there is,' I replied. I felt foolish, disappointed.

"'You're right,' he said, and I'll never forget his eyes. 'I can use a few more young fellows like you.' And that's how I got on the staff.

"Well, we ran a quick survey west to the bad lands—for it was out here that we must find success or failure. And Allie, it's all been like the biggest kind of an adventure. The troops and horses and camps and trails—the Indian country with its threats from out of the air—the wild places with their deer, buffalo, panthers, trappers like Slingerland, scouts, and desperadoes. It began to get such a hold on me that I was wild. That might have been bad for me but for my work. I did well. Allie, I ran lines for the U.P. that no other engineer could run."

Neale paused, as much from the squeeze Allie suddenly gave him as for an instant's rest to catch his breath.

"I mean I had the nerve to tackle cliffs and dangerous slopes," he went on. Then he told how Larry Red King had saved his life, and that recollection brought back his service to the cowboy; then naturally followed the two dominating incidents of the summer.

Allie lifted a blanched face and darkening eyes. "Neale! You were in danger."

"Oh, not much, I guess. But Red thought so."

"He saved you again! . . . I—I'll never forget that."

"Anyway, we're square, for he'd have got shot sure the day the Indian sneaked up on him." Allie shuddered and shrank back to Neale, while he hastily resumed his story. "We're great pards now, Red and I. He doesn't say much, but his acts tell. He will not let me alone. He follows me everywhere. It's a joke among the men. . . . Well, Allie, it seems unbelievable that we have crossed the mountains and the desert—grade ninety feet to the mile! The railroad can and will be built. I wish I could tell you how tremendously all this has worked upon me—upon all the engineers. But somehow I can't. It chokes me. The idea is big. But the work—what shall I call that? . . . Allie, if you can, imagine some spirit seizing hold of you and making you see difficulties as joys—impossible tasks as only things to strike fire from genius, perils of death as merely incidents of daring adventure to treasure in memory— well that's something like it. The idea of the U.P. has got me. I believe in it. I shall see it accomplished. . . . I'll live it all."

Allie moved her head on his shoulder, and, looking up at him with eyes that made him ashamed of his egotism, she said, "Then, when it's done you'll be chief of engineers or superintendent of maintenance of way?"

She had remembered his very words.

"Allie, I hope so," he replied, thrilling at her faith. "I'll work—I'll get some big position."

Next day ushered in for Neale a well-earned rest, and he proceeded to enjoy it to the full.

The fall had always been Neale's favorite season. Here, as elsewhere, the aspect of it was flaming and golden, but different from what he had known hitherto. Dreaming silence of autumn held the wildness and loneliness of the Wyoming hills. The sage shone gray and purple, the ridges yellow and gold; the valleys were green and amber and red. No dust, no heat, no wind—a clear, blue, cloudless sky, sweet odors in the still air—it was a beautiful time.

Days passed and nights passed, as if on wings. Every waking hour drew him closer to this incomparable girl who had arisen upon his horizon like a star. He knew the hour was imminent when he must read his heart. He fought it off; he played with his bliss. Allie was now his shadow instead of the faithful Larry, although the cowboy was often with them, adapting himself to the changed conditions, too big and splendid to be envious or jealous. They fished down the brook, and always at the never-to-be-forgotten ford he would cross first and turn to see her follow. She could never understand why Neale would delight in carrying her across at other points, yet made her ford this one by herself.

"It's such a bother to take off moccasins and leggings," she would say.

They rode horseback up and down the trails that Slingerland assured them were safe. And it was the cowboy Larry who lent his horse and taught her a flying mount; he said she would make a rider.

In the afternoons they would climb the high ridge, and on the summit sit in the long whitening grass and gaze out over the dim and purple vastness of the plains. In the twilight they walked under the pines. When night set in and the air grew cold they would watch the ruddy fire on the hearth and see pictures of the future there, and feel a warmth on hand and cheek that was not all from the cheerful blaze.

Neale found it strange to realize how his attachment for Larry had changed to love. All Neale's spiritual being was undergoing a great and vital change, but this was not the reason he loved Larry. It was because of Allie. The cowboy was a Texan and he had inherited the Southerner's fine and chivalric regard for women. Neale never knew whether Larry had ever had a sister or a sweetheart or a girl friend. But at sight Larry had become Allie's own; not a brother or a friend or a lover, but something bigger and higher. The man expanded under her smiles, her teasing, her playfulness, her affection. Neale had no pang in divining the love Larry bore Allie. Drifter, cowboy, gun-thrower, man-killer, whatever he had been, the light of this girl's beautiful eyes, her voice, her touch, had worked the last marvel in man—forgetfulness of self. And so Neale loved him.

It made Neale quake inwardly to think of the change being wrought in himself. It made him thoughtful of many things. There was much in life utterly new to him. He had listened to a moan in his keen ear; he had felt a call of something helpless; he had found a gleam of chestnut hair; he had stirred two other men to help him befriend a poor, broken-hearted, half-crazed orphan girl. And, lo! the world had changed, his friends had grown happier in their unloved lives, a strange strength had come to him, and, sweetest, most wonderful of all, in the place of the helpless and miserable waif appeared a woman, lovely of face and form, with only a ghost of sadness haunting her eyes, a woman adorable and bright, with the magic of love on her lips.

October came. In the early morning and late afternoon a keen cold breath hung in the air. Slingerland talked of a good prospect for fur. He chopped great stores of wood. Larry climbed the hills with his rifle. Neale walked the trails hand in hand with Allie.

He had never sought to induce her to speak of her past, though at times the evidence of refinement and education and mystery around her made strong appeal to him. She could tell her story whenever she liked or never—it did not greatly matter.

Then, one day, quite naturally, but with a shame she did

not try to conceal, she confided to him part of the story her mother had told her that dark night when the Sioux were creeping upon the caravan.

Neale was astounded, agitated, intensely concerned.

"Allie! . . . Your father lives!" he exclaimed.

"Yes."

"Then I must find him—take you to him."

"Do what you think best," she replied, sadly. "But I never saw him. I've no love for him. And he never knew I was born."

"Is it possible? How strange! . . . If any man could see you now! Allie, do you resemble your mother?"

"Yes, we were alike."

"Where is your father?" Neale went on, curiously.

"How should I know? It was in New Orleans that mother ran off from him. I—I never blamed her—since she said what she said. . . . Do you? Will this—make any difference to you?"

"My God, no! But I'm so—so thunderstruck. . . . This man—this Durade—tell me more of him."

"He was a Spaniard of high degree, an adventurer, a gambler. He was mad to gamble. He forced my mother to use her beauty to lure men to his gambling-hell. . . . Oh, it's terrible to remember. She said he meant to use me for that purpose. That's why she left him. But in a way he was good to me. I can see so many things now to prove he was wicked. . . . And mother said he would follow her—track her to the end of the world."

"Allie! If he should find you some day!" exclaimed Neale, hoarsely.

She put her arms up round his neck. And that, following a terrible pang of dread in Neale's breast, was too much for him. The tide burst. Love had long claimed him, but its utterance had been withheld. He had been happy in her happiness. He had trained himself to spare her.

"But some day—I'll be—your wife," she whispered.

"Soon? Soon?" he returned, trembling.

The scarlet fired her temples, her brow, darkening the skin under her bright hair.

"That's for you to say."

She held up her lips, tremulous and sweet.

Neale realized the moment had come. There had never been but the one kiss between them—that of the meeting upon his return in September.

"Allie, I love you!" He spoke thickly.

"And I love you," she replied, with sweet courage.

"This news you've told—this man Durade," he went on, hoarsely. "I'm suddenly alive—stinging—wild! . . . If I lost you!"

"Dear, you will never lose me—never in this world or any other," she replied, tenderly.

"My work, my hope, my life, they all get spirit now from you. . . . Allie! You're sweet—oh, so sweet! You're glorious!" he rang out, passionately.

Surprise momentarily checked the rising response of her feeling.

"Neale! You've never before said—such—things! . . . And the way you look!"

"How do I look?" he queried, seeing the joyousness of her surprise.

Then she laughed and that was new to him—a sound low, unutterably rich and full, sweet-toned like a bell, and all resonant of youth.

"Oh, you look like Durade when he was gambling away his soul. . . . You should see him!"

"Well, how's that?"

"So white—so terrible—so piercing!"

Neale drew her closer, slipped her arms farther up round his neck. "I'm gambling my soul away now," he said. "If I kiss you I lose it—and I must!"

"Must what?" she whispered, with all a woman's charm.

"I must kiss you!"

"Then hurry!"

So their lips met.

In the sweetness of that embrace, in the simplicity and answering passion of her kiss, in the overwhelming sense of her gift of herself, heart and soul, he found a strength, a restraint, a nobler fire that gave him peace.

Allie was to amaze Neale again before the sun set on that memorable day.

"I forgot to tell you about the gold!" she exclaimed, her face paling.

"Gold!" ejaculated Neale.

"Yes. He buried it—there—under the biggest of the three trees together. Near a rock! Oh, I can see him now!"

"Him! Who? Allie, what's this wild talk?"

She pressed his hand to enjoin silence.

"Listen! Horn had gold. How much I don't know. But it must have been a great deal. He owned the caravan with which we left California. Horn grew to like me. But he hated all the rest. . . . That night we ended the awful ride! The wagons stalled! . . . The grayness of dawn—the stillness—oh, I feel them now! . . . That terrible Indian yell rang out. All my life I'll hear it! . . . Then Horn dug a hole. He buried his gold. . . . And he said whoever escaped could have it. He had no hope."

"Allie, you're a mine of surprises. Buried gold! What next?"

"Neale, I wonder—did the Sioux find that gold?" she asked.

"It's not likely. There certainly wasn't any hole left open around that place. I saw every inch of ground under those trees. . . . Allie, I'll go there to-morrow and hunt for it."

"Let me go," she implored. "Ah! I forgot! No—no! . . . There must be my mother's grave."

"Yes, it's there. I saw. I will mark it. . . . Allie, how glad I am that you can speak of her—of her past—her grave there without weakening. You are brave! But forget. . . . Allie, if I find that gold it'll be yours."

"No. Yours."

"But I wasn't one of the caravan. He did not give it to any outsider. You escaped. Therefore it will belong to you."

"Dearest, I am yours."

Next day, without acquainting Slingerland or Larry with his purpose, Neale rode down the valley trail.

He expected the road to cross the old St. Vrain and Laramie Trail, but if it did cross he could not find the place. It was easy to lose bearings in these hills. Neale had to abandon the hunt for that day, and, turning back, with some annoyance at his failure, he decided that it would be best to take Larry and Slingerland into his confidence.

Allie was waiting for him at the brook ford.

"Oh, it was gone!" she cried.

"Allie, I couldn't find the place. Come, ride back and let me walk beside you. . . . We'll have fun telling Larry and Slingerland."

"Neale, let me tell them," she begged.

"Go ahead. Make a strong story. Larry always had leanings toward gold-strikes."

And that night, after supper, when the log fire had begun to blaze, and all were comfortable before it, Allie glanced demurely at Larry and said:

"Reddy, if you had known that I was heiress to great wealth, would you have proposed to me?"

Slingerland roared. Larry seemed utterly stricken.

"Wealth!" he echoed, feebly.

"Yes. Gold! Lots of gold!"

Slingerland's merry face suddenly grew curious and earnest.

Larry struggled with his discomfiture.

"I reckon I'd done thet anyhow—without knowin' you was rich—if it hadn't been fer this heah U.P. surveyor fellar."

And then the joke was on Allie, as her blushes proved. Neale came to her rescue and told the story of Horn's buried gold, and of his own search that day for the place.

"Shore I'll find it," declared Larry. "We'll go tomorrow. . . ."

Slingerland stroked his beard thoughtfully.

"If thar's gold been buried thar it's sure an' certain thar yet," he said. "But I'm afraid we won't git thar tomorrow."

"Why not? Surely you or Larry can find the place?"

"Listen."

Neale listened while he was watching Allie's parted lips and speaking eyes. A low, whining wind swept through the trees and over the roof of the cabin.

"Thet wind says snow," declared the trapper.

Neale went outside. The wind struck him cold and keen, with a sharp edge to it. The stars showed pale and dim through hazy atmosphere. Assuredly there was a storm brewing. Neale returned to the fire, shivering and holding his palms to the heat.

"Cold, you bet, with the wind rising," he said. "But, Slingerland, suppose it does snow. Can't we go, anyhow?"

"It ain't likely. You see, it snows up hyar. Mebbe we'll be snowed in fer a spell. An' thet valley is open down thar. In deep snow what could we find? We'll wait an' see?"

On the morrow a storm raged and all was dim through a ghostly, whirling pall. The season of drifting snow had come, and Neale's winter work had begun.

* * *

Five miles by short cut over the ridges curved the long survey over which Neale must keep watch; and the going and coming were Neale's hardest toil. It was laborsome to trudge up and down in soft snow.

That first snow of winter, however, did not last long, except in the sheltered places. Fortunately for Neale, almost all of his section of the survey ran over open ground. But this fact augured seriously for his task when the dry and powdery snow of midwinter began to fall and sweep before the wind and drift over the lee side of the ridge.

During the first week of tramping he thoroughly learned the lay of the land, the topography of his particular stretch of Sherman Pass. And one day, taking an early start from camp, he set forth to make his first call upon his nearest associate in this work, the engineer Service. Once high up on the pass he found the snow had not all melted, and still higher it lay white and unbroken as far as he could see. The air was keener up there. Neale gathered that Service would have a colder job than his own, if it was not so long and hard.

He found Service at home in his dugout, warm and comfortable and in excellent spirits. They compared notes, and even in this early work they decided it would be a wise plan for the engineering staff to study the problem of drifting snow.

Neale enjoyed a meal with Service, and then, early in the afternoon, he started back on his long tramp homeward. He gathered from his visit that Service did not mind the lonesomeness, but that he did suffer from the cold more than he had expected. Service was not an active, full-blooded man, and Neale had some misgivings. Judging from the trapper's remarks, winter high up in the Wyoming hills was something to dread.

November brought the real storms—the gray banks of

rolling cloud, the rain and sleet and snow and ice, and the wind. Neale concluded he had never before faced a real wind, and when, one day on a ridge-top, he was blown off his feet he was sure of it. Some days he could not go out at all. Other days it was not imperative, for it was only during and after snow-storms that he could make observations. He learned to travel on snow-shoes, and ten miles of such traveling up and down the steep slopes was the most killing hard toil he had ever attempted. After such trips he would reach the cabin utterly fagged out, too tired to eat, too weary to talk, almost too dead to hear the solicitations of his friends or to appreciate Allie's tender, anxious care. If he had not been strong and robust and in good training to begin with, he would have failed under the burden. Gradually he grew used to the strenuous toil, and became hardened, tough, and enduring.

Though Neale hated the cold and the wind, there were moments when an exceedingly keen exhilaration uplifted him. These experiences visited him while on the heights, looking far over the snowy ridges to the white, monotonous plain or up toward the shining peaks. All seemed barren and cold. He never saw a living creature or a track upon those slopes. When the sun shone all was so dazzlingly, glaringly white that his eyes were struck by temporary blindness.

Upon one of the milder days, which were getting rarer in mid-December, Neale again visited his comrade on the summit. He found Service in bad shape. In falling down a slippery ledge he had injured or broken his lame leg. Neale, with great concern, tried to ascertain the nature and extent of the harm done, but he was unable to do so. Service was practically helpless, although not suffering any great pain. The two of them decided, at length, that he had not broken any bones, but that it was necessary to move him to where he could be waited upon and treated, or else some one must be brought in to take care of him. Neale deliberated a moment.

"I'll tell you what," he said, finally. "You can be moved down to Slingerland's cabin without pain to you. I'll get Slingerland and his sled. You'll be more comfortable there. It'll be better all around."

So that was decided upon. And Neale, after doing all he could for Service, and assuring him that he would return in less than twenty-four hours, turned his steps for the valley.

The sunset that night struck him as singularly dull, pale, menacing. He understood its meaning later, when Slingerland said they were in for another storm. Before dark the wind began to moan through the trees like lost spirits. The trapper shook his shaggy head ominously.

"Reckon thet sounds bad to me," he said. And from moan it rose to wail, and from wail to roar.

That alarmed Neale. He went outside and Slingerland followed. Snow was sweeping down—light, dry, powdery. The wind was piercingly cold. Slingerland yelled something, but Neale could not distinguish what. When they got back inside the trapper said:

"Blizzard!"

Neale grew distressed.

"Wal, no use to worry about Service," argued the trapper. "If it is a blizzard we can't git up thar, thet's all. Mebbe this'll not be so bad. But I ain't bettin' on thet."

Even Allie couldn't cheer Neale that night. Long after she and the others had retired he kept up the fire and listened to the roar of the wind. When the fire died down a little the cabin grew uncomfortably cold, and this fact attested to a continually dropping temperature. But he hoped against hope and finally sought his blankets.

Morning came, but the cabin was almost as dark as by night. A blinding, swirling snow-storm obscured the sun.

A blizzard raged for forty-eight hours. When the snow finally ceased falling the cold increased until Neale guessed the temperature might be forty degrees below zero. The trapper claimed sixty. It was necessary to stay indoors till the weather moderated.

On the fifth morning Slingerland was persuaded to attempt the trip to aid Service. Larry wanted to accompany them, but Slingerland said he had better stay with Allie. So, muffled up, the two men set out on snow-shoes, dragging a sled. A crust had frozen on the snow, otherwise traveling would have been impossible. Once up on the slope the north wind hit them square in the face. Heavily clad as he was, Neale thought the very marrow in his bones would freeze. That wind blew straight through him. There were places where it took both men to hold the sled to keep it from getting away. They were blown back one step for every two steps they made. On the exposed heights they could not walk upright. At last, after hours of desperate effort, they got over the ridge to a sheltered side along which they labored up to Service's dugout.

Up there the snow had blown away in places, leaving bare spots, bleak, icy, barren, stark. No smoke appeared to rise above the dugout. The rude habitation looked as though no man had been there that winter. Neale glanced in swift dismay at Slingerland.

"Son, look fer the wust," he said. "An' we haint' got time to waste."

They pushed open the canvas framework of a door and, stooping low, passed inside. Neale's glance saw first the fireplace, where no fire had burned for days. Snow had sifted into the dugout and lay in little drifts everywhere. The blankets on the bunk covered Service, hiding his face.

Both men knew before they uncovered him what his fate had been.

"Frozen to death!" gasped Neale.

Service lay white, rigid, like stone, with no sign of suffering upon his face.

"He jest went to sleep—an' never woke up," declared Slingerland.

"Thank God for that!" exclaimed Neale. "Oh, why did I not stay with him!"

"Too late, son. An' many a good man will go to his death before thet damn railroad is done."

Neale searched for Service's notes and letters and valuables which could be turned over to the engineering staff.

Slingerland found a pick and shovel, which Neale remembered to have used in building the dugout; and with these the two men toiled at the frozen sand and gravel to open up a grave. It was like digging in stone. At length they succeeded. Then, rolling Service in the blankets and tarpaulin, they lowered him into the cold ground and hurriedly filled up his grave.

It was a grim, gruesome task. Another nameless grave! Neale had already seen nine graves. This one was up the slope not a hundred feet from the line of the survey.

"Slingerland," exclaimed Neale, "the railroad will run along there! Trains will pass this spot. In years to come travelers will look out of the train windows along here. Boys riding away to seek their fortunes! Bride and groom on their honeymoon! Thousands of people—going, coming, busy, happy at their own affairs, full of their own lives—will pass by poor Service's grave and never know it's there!"

"Wal, son, if people must hev railroads, they must kill men to build them," replied the trapper.

Neale conceived the idea that Slingerland did not welcome the coming of the steel rails. The thought shocked him. But then, he reflected, a trapper would not profit by the advance of civilization.

With the wind in their backs Neale and Slingerland were practically blown home. They made it up between them to keep knowledge of the tragedy from Allie. So ended the coldest and hardest and grimmest day Neale had ever known.

The winter passed, the snows melted, the winds quieted, and spring came.

Long since Neale had decided to leave Allie with Slingerland that summer. She would be happy there, and she wished to stay until Neale could take her with him. That seemed out of the question for the present. A construction camp full of troopers and laborers was no place for Allie. Neale dreaded the idea of taking her to Omaha. Always in his mind were haunting fears of this Spaniard, Durade, who had ruined Allie's mother, and of the father whom Allie had never seen. Neale instinctively felt that these men were to crop up somewhere in his life, and before they did appear he wanted to marry Allie. She was now little more than sixteen years old.

Neale's plans for the summer could not be wholly known until he had reported to the general staff, which might be at Fort Fetterman or North Platte or all the way back in Omaha. But it was probable that he would be set to work with the advancing troops and trains and laborers. Engineers had to accompany both the grading gangs and the rail gangs.

Neale, in his talks with Larry and Slingerland, had dwelt long and conjecturingly upon what life was going to be in the construction camps.

To Larry what might happen was of little moment. He lived in the present. But Neale was different. He had to be anticipating events; he lived in the future; his mind was centered on future work, achievement, and what he might go through in attaining his end. Slingerland was his appreciative listener.

"Wal," he would say, shaking his grizzled head, "I reckon I don't believe all your General Lodge says is goin' to happen."

"But, man, can't you imagine what it will be?" protested Neale. "Take thousands of soldiers—the riffraff of the war—and thousands of laborers of all classes, niggers, greasers, pigtailed chinks, and Irish. Take thousands of men who want to earn an honest dollar in trade, following the line. And thousands who want dollars, but not honestly. All the gamblers, outlaws, robbers, murderers, criminals, adventurers in the States, and perhaps many from abroad, will be on the trail. Think, man, of the money—the gold! Millions spilled out in these wilds! . . . And last and worst—the bad women!"

Slingerland showed his amazement at the pictures drawn by Neale, especially at the final one.

"Wal, I reckon thet's all guff too," he said. "A lot of bad women out in these wilds ain't to be feared. Supposing' that was a lot of them—which ain't likely—how'd they ever git out to the camps?"

"Slingerland, the trains—the trains will follow the laying of the rails!"

"Oho! An' you mean thar'll be towns grow up overnight—all full of bad people who ain't workin' on the railroad, but jest followin' the gold?"

"Exactly. Now listen. Remember all these mixed gangs—the gold—and the bad women—out here in the wild country—no law—no restraint—no fear, except of death—drinking-hells—gambling-hells—dancing-hells! What's going to happen?"

The trapper meditated awhile, stroking his beard, and then he said: "Wal, thar ain't enough gold to build thet railroad—an' if thar was it couldn't never be done!"

"Ah!" cried Neale, raising his head sharply. "It's a matter of gold first. Streams of gold! And then—*can* it be done?"

One day, as the time for Neale's departure grew closer, Slingerland's quiet and peaceful valley was violated by a visit from four rough-looking men.

They rode in without packs. It was significant to Neale that Larry swore at sight of them, and then in his cool, easy way sauntered between them and the cabin door, where Allie stood with astonishment fixed on her beautiful face. The Texan always packed his heavy gun, and certainly no Western men would mistake his quality. These visitors were civil enough, asked for a little tobacco, and showed no sign of evil intent.

"Way off the beaten track up hyar," said one.

"Yes. I'm a trapper," replied Slingerland. "Whar do you hail from?"

"Ogden. We're packin' east."

"Much travel on the trail?"

"Right smart fer wild country. An' all goin' east. We hain't met an outfit headin' west. Hev you heerd any talk of a railroad buildin' out of Omaha?"

Here Larry put a word in.

"Shore. We've had soldiers campin' around aboot all heah."

"Soldiers!" ejaculated one of the gang.

"Shore, the road's bein' built by soldiers."

The men made no further comment and turned away without any good-bys. Slingerland called out to them to have an eye open for Indians on the war-path.

"Wal, I don't like the looks of them fellars," he declared.

Neale likewise took an unfavorable view of the visit, but Larry scouted the idea of there being any danger in a gang like that.

"Shore they'd be afraid of a man," he declared.

"Red, can you look at men and tell whether or not there's danger in them?" inquired Neale.

"I shore can. One man could bluff thet outfit. . . . But I reckon I'd hate to have them find Allie aboot heah alone."

"I can take care of myself," spoke up Allie, spiritedly.

Neale and Slingerland, for all their respect for the cowboy's judgment, regarded the advent of these visitors as a forerunner of an evil time for lonely trappers.

"I'll hev to move back deeper in the mountains, away from the railroad," said Slingerland.

This incident also put a different light upon the intention Neale had of hunting for the buried gold. Just now he certainly did not want to risk being seen digging gold or packing it away; and Slingerland was just as loath to have it concealed in or near his cabin.

"Wal, seein' we're not sure it's really there, let's wait till you come back in summer or fall," he suggested. "If it's thar it'll stay thar."

All too soon the dawn came for Neale's departure with Larry. Allie was braver than he. At the last he was white and shaken. She kissed Larry.

"Reddy, you'll take care of yourself—and him," she said.

"Allie, I shore will. Good-by." Larry rode down the trail in the dim gray dawn.

"Watch sharp for Indians," she breathed, and her face whitened momentarily. Then the color returned. Her eyes welled full of sweet, soft light.

"Allie, I can't go," said Neale, hoarsely. The clasp of her arms unnerved him.

"You must. It's your work. Remember the big job! . . . Dearest! Dearest! Hurry—and—go!"

Neale could no longer see her face clearly. He did not know what he was saying.

"You'll—always—love me?" he implored.

"Do you need to ask? All my life! . . . I promise."

"Kiss me, then," he whispered, hoarsely, blindly leaning down. "It's hell—to leave you! . . . Wonderful girl—treasure—precious—Allie! . . . Kiss me—enough! . . . I—"

She held him with strong and passionate clasp and kissed him again and again.

"Good-by!" Her last word was low, choked, poignant, and had in it a mournful reminder of her old tragic woe.

Then he was alone. Mounting clumsily, with blurred eyes, he rode into the winding trail.

Neale and King traveled light, without pack-animals, and at sunrise they reached the main trail.

It bore evidence of considerable use and was no longer a trail, but a highroad. Fresh tracks of horses and oxen, wagon-wheel ruts, dead camp-fires, and scattered brush that had been used for wind-breaks—all these things attested to the growing impetus of that movement; soon it was to become extraordinary.

All this was Indian country. Neale and his companion had no idea whether or not the Sioux had left their winter quarters for the war-path. But it was a vast region, and the Indians could not be everywhere. Neale and King took chances, as had all these travelers, though perhaps the risk was not so great, because they rode fleet horses. They discovered no signs of Indians, and it appeared as if they were alone in a wilderness.

They covered sixty miles from early dawn to dark, with a short rest at noon, and reached Fort Fetterman safely without incident or accident. Troops were there, but none of the U.P. engineering staff. Neale did not meet any soldiers with whom he was acquainted. Orders were there for him, however, to report to North Platte as soon as it was possible to reach there. Troops were to be moving soon, so Neale learned, and the long journey could be made in comparative safety.

Here Neale received the tidings that forty miles of railroad had been built during the last summer, and trains had been run that distance west from Omaha. His heart swelled. Not for many a week had he heard anything favorable to the great U.P. project, and here was news of rails laid, trains run. Already this spring the graders were breaking ground far ahead of the rail-layers. Report and rumor at the fort had it that lively times had attended the construction. But the one absorbing topic was the Sioux Indians, who were expected to swarm out of the hills that summer and give the troops hot work.

I n due time Neale and Larry arrived at North Platte, which was little more than a camp. The construction gangs were not expected to reach there until late in the fall. Baxter was at North Platte, with a lame surveyor, and no other helpers; consequently he hailed Neale and Larry with open arms. A summer's work on the hot monotonous plains stared Neale in the face, but he must resign himself to the inevitable. He worked, as always, with that ability and energy which had made him invaluable to his superiors. Here, however, the labor was a dull, hot grind, without any thrills. Neale filled the long days with duty and seldom let his mind wander. In leisure hours, however, he dreamed of Allie and the future. He found no trouble in passing time that way. Also he watched eagerly for arrivals from the west, whom he questioned about Indians in the Wyoming hills; and from troops or travelers coming from the east he heard all the news of the advancing railroad construction. It was absorbingly interesting, yet Neale could credit so few of the tales.

The summer and early fall passed.

Neale was ordered to Omaha. The news stunned him. He had built all his hopes on another winter out in the Wyoming hills, and this disappointment was crushing. It made him ill for a day. He almost threw up his work. It did not seem possible to live that interminable stretch without seeing Allie Lee. The nature of his commission, however, brought once again to mind the opportunity that knocked at his door. Neale had run all the different surveys for bridges in the Wyoming hills and now he was needed in the office of the staff, where plans and drawings were being made. Again he bowed to the inevitable. But he determined to demand in the spring that he be sent ahead to the forefront of the construction work.

Another disappointment seemed in order. Larry King refused to go any farther back east. Neale was exceedingly surprised.

"Do you throw up your job?" he asked.

"Shore not. I can work heah," replied Larry.

"There won't be any outside work on these bleak plains in winter."

"Wal, I reckon I'll loaf, then," he drawled.

Neale could not change him. Larry vowed he would take his old place with Neale next spring, if it should be open to him.

"But why? Red, I can't figure you," protested Neale.

"Pard, I reckon I'm fur enough back east right heah," said Larry, significantly.

A light dawned upon Neale. "Red! You've done something bad!" exclaimed Neale, in genuine dismay.

"Wal, I don't know jest how bad it was, but it shore was hell," replied Larry, with a grin.

"Red, you aren't afraid," asserted Neale, positively.

The cowboy flushed and looked insulted. "If any one but you said thet to me he'd hev to eat it."

"I beg your pardon, old man. But I'm surprised. It doesn't seem like you. . . . And then—Lord! I'll miss you."

"No more 'n I'll miss you, pard," replied Larry.

Suddenly Neale had a happy thought. "Red, you go back to Slingerland's and help take care of Allie. I'd feel she was safer."

"Wal, she might be safer, but I wouldn't be," declared the cowboy, bluntly.

"You red-head! What do you mean?" demanded Neale.

"I mean this heah. If I stayed around another winter near Allie Lee—with her alone, fer thet trapper never set up before thet fire—I'd—why, Neale, I'd ambush you like an Injun when you come back!"

"You wouldn't," rejoined Neale. He wanted to laugh, but had no mirth.

Larry did not mean that, but neither did he mean to be funny. "I'll be hangin' round heah, waitin' fer you. It's only a few months. Go on to your work, pard. You'll be a big man on the road some day."

Neale left North Platte with a wagon-train. After a long, slow journey the point was reached where the graders had left off work for that year. Here had been a huge construction camp; and the bare and squalid place looked as if it once had been a town of crudest make, suddenly wrecked by a cyclone and burned by prairie fire. Fifty miles farther on, representing two more long, tedious, and unendurable days, and Neale heard the whistle of a locomotive. It came from far off. But it was a whistle. He yelled, and the men journeying with him joined in.

Smoke showed on the horizon, together with a wide, low, uneven line of shacks and tents.

Neale was all eyes when he rode into that construction camp. The place was a bedlam. A motley horde of men appeared to be doing everything under the sun but work, and most of them seemed particularly eager to board a long train of box-cars and little old passenger-coaches. Neale made a dive for the train, and his sojourn in that camp was a short and exciting one of ten minutes.

He felt unutterably proud. He had helped survey the line along which the train was now rattling and creaking and swaying. All that swiftly passed under his keen eyes was recorded in his memory—the uncouth crowd of laborers, the hardest lot he had ever seen; the talk, noise, smoke; the rickety old clattering coaches; the wayside dumps and heaps and wreckage. But they all seemed parts of a beautiful romance to him. Neale saw through the eyes of golden ambition and illimitable dreams.

And not for a moment of that endless ride, with interminable stops, did he weary of the two hundred and sixty miles of rails laid that year, and of the forty miles of the preceding year. Then came Omaha, a beehive—the making of a Western metropolis!

Neale plunged into the bewildering turmoil of plans, tasks, schemes, land-grants, politics, charters, inducements, liens and loans, Government and army and State and national interests, grafts and deals and bosses—all that mass of selfish and unselfish motives, all that wealth of cunning and noble aims, all that congested assemblage of humanity which went to make up the building of the Union Pacific.

Neale was a dreamer, like the few men whose minds had first given birth to the wonderful idea of a railroad from East to West. Neale found himself confronted by a singularly disturbing fact. However grand this project, its political and mercenary features could not be beautiful to him. Why could not all men be right-minded about a noble cause and work unselfishly for the development of the

West and the future generations? It was a melancholy thing to learn that men of sincere and generous purpose had spent their all trying to raise the money to build the Union Pacific; on the other hand, it was a satisfaction to hear that many capitalists with greedy claws had ruined themselves in like efforts.

The President of the United States and Congress had their own troubles at the close of the war, and the Government could do but little money-raising with land-grants and loans. But they offered a great bonus to the men who would build the railroad.

The first construction company subscribed over a million and a half dollars, and paid in one-quarter of that. The money went so swiftly that it opened the company's eyes to the insatiable gulf beneath that enterprise, and they quit.

Thereupon what was called the Credit Mobilier was inaugurated, and it became both famous and infamous.

It was a type of the construction company by which it was the custom to build railroads at that time. The directors, believing that whatever money was to be made out of the Union Pacific must be collected during the construction period, organized a clever system for just this purpose.

An extravagant sum was to be paid to the Credit Mobilier for the construction work, thus securing for stockholders of the Union Pacific, who now controlled the Credit Mobilier, the bonds loaned by the United States Government.

The operations of the Credit Mobilier finally gave rise to one of the most serious political scandals in the history of the United States Congress.

The cost of all material was high, and it rose with leaps and bounds until it was prodigious. Omaha had no railroad entering it from the east, and so all the supplies, materials, engines, cars, machinery, and laborers had to be transported from St. Louis up the swift Missouri on boats. This in itself was a work calling for the limit of practical management and energy. Out on the prairie-land, for hundreds of miles, were to be found no trees, no wood, scarcely any brush. The prairie-land was beautiful ground for buffalo, but it was a most barren desert for the exigencies of railroad men. Moreover, not only did wood and fuel and railroad-ties have to be brought from afar, but also stone for bridges and abutments. Then thousands of men had to be employed, and those who hired out for reasonable money soon learned that others were getting more; having the company at their mercy, they demanded exorbitant wages in their turn.

One of the peculiar features of the construction, a feature over which Neale grew impotently furious, was the law that when a certain section of so many miles had been laid and equipped the Government of the United States would send out expert commissioners, who would go over the line and pass judgment upon the finished work. No two groups of commissioners seemed to agree. These experts, who had their part to play in the bewildering and labyrinthine maze of men's contrary plans and plots, reported that certain sections would have to be done over again.

The particular fault found with one of these sections was the alleged steepness of the grade, and as Neale had been the surveyor in charge, he soon heard of his poor work. He went over his figures and notes with the result that he called on Henney and absolutely swore that the grade was right. Henney swore too, in a different and more forcible way, but he agreed with Neale and advised him to call upon the expert commissioners.

Neale did so, and found them, with one exception, open to conviction. The exception was a man named Allison Lee. The name Lee gave Neale a little shock. He was a gray-looking man, with lined face, and that concentrated air which Neale had learned to associate with those who were high in the affairs of the U.P.

Neale stated that his business was to show that his work had been done right, and he had the figures to prove it. Mr. Lee replied that the survey was poor and would have to be done over.

"Are you a surveyor?" queried Neale, sharply, with the blood beating in his temples.

"I have some knowledge of civil engineering," replied the commissioner.

"Well, it can't be very much," declared Neale, whose temper was up.

"Young man, be careful what you say," replied the other.

"But Mr.—Mr. Lee—listen to me, will you?" burst out Neale. "It's all here in my notes. You've hurried over the line and you just slipped up a foot or so in your observations of that section."

Mr. Lee refused to look at the notes and waved Neale aside.

"It'll hurt my chances for a big job," Neale said, stubbornly.

"You probably will lose your job, judging from the way you address your superiors."

That finished Neale. He grew perfectly white.

"All this expert-commissioner business is rot," he flung at Lee. "Rot! Lodge knows it. Henney knows it. We all do. And so do you. It's a lot of damn red tape! Every last man who can pull a stroke with the Government runs in here to annoy good efficient engineers who are building the road. It's an outrage. It's more. It's not honest. . . . That section has forty miles in it. Five miles you claim must be resurveyed—regarded—relaid. Forty-six thousand dollars a mile! . . . That's the secret—two hundred and thirty thousand dollars more for a construction company!"

Neale left the office and, returning to Henney, repeated

the interview to him word for word. Henney complimented Neale's spirit, but deplored the incident. It could do no good and might do harm. Many of these commissioners were politicians, working in close touch with the directors, and not averse to bleeding the Credit Mobilier.

All the engineers, including the chief, though he was noncommittal, were bitter about this expert-commissioner law. If a good road-bed had been surveyed, the engineers knew more about it than any one else. They were the pioneers of the work. It was exceedingly annoying and exasperating to have a number of men travel leisurely in trains over the line and criticize the labors of engineers who had toiled in heat and cold and wet, with brain and heart in the task. But it was so.

In May, 1866, a wagon-train escorted by troops rolled into the growing camp of North Platte, and the first man to alight was Warren Neale, strong, active, eager-eyed as ever, but older and with face pale from his indoor work and hope long deferred.

The first man to greet him was Larry King, in whom time did not make changes.

They met as long-separated brothers.

"Red, how're your horses?" was Neale's query, following the greeting.

"Wintered well, but cost me all I had. I'm shore busted," replied Larry.

"I've plenty of money," said Neale, "and what's mine is yours. Come on, Red. We'll get light packs and hit the trail for the Wyoming hills."

"Wal, I reckoned so. . . . Neale, it's shore goin' to be risky. The Injuns are on the rampage already. You see how this heah camp has growed. Men ridin' in all since winter broke. An' them from west tell some hard stories."

"I've got to go," replied Neale, with emotion. "It's nearly

a year since I saw Allie. Not a word between us in all that time! . . . Red, I can't stand it longer."

"Shore, I know," replied King, hastily. "You ain't reckonin' I wanted to crawfish? I'll go. We'll pack light, hit the trail at night, an' hide up in the daytime."

Neale had arrived in North Platte before noon, and before sunset he and King were far out on the swelling slopes of plain-land, riding toward the west.

Traveling by night, camping by day, they soon left behind them the monotonous plains of Nebraska. The Sioux had been active for two summers along the southern trails of Wyoming. The Texan's long training on the ranges stood them in good stead here. His keen eye for tracks and smoke and distant objects, his care in hiding trails and selecting camps, and his skill and judgment in all pertaining to the horses—these things made the journey possible. For they saw Indian signs more than once before the Wyoming hills loomed up in the distance. More than one flickering camp-fire they avoided by a wide detour.

Slingerland's valley showed all the signs of early summer. The familiar trail, however, bore no tracks of horses or man or beast. A heavy rain had fallen recently and it would have obliterated tracks.

Neale's suspense sustained the added burden of dread. In the oppressive silence of the valley he read some nameless reason for fear. The trail seemed the same, the brook flowed and murmured as of old, the trees shone soft and green, but Neale sensed a difference. He dared not look at Larry for confirmation of his fears. The valley had not of late been lived in!

Neale rode hard up the trail under the pines. A blackened heap lay where once the cabin had stood. Neale's heart gave a terrible leap and then seemed to cease beating. He could not breathe nor speak nor move. His eyes were fixed on the black remains of Slingerland's cabin.

"Gawd Almighty!" gasped Larry, and he put out a shaking hand to clutch Neale. "The Injuns! I always feared this—spite of Slingerland's talk."

The feel of Larry's fierce fingers, like hot, stinging arrows in his flesh, pierced Neale's mind and made him realize what his stunned faculties had failed to grasp. It seemed to loosen the vise-like hold upon his muscles, to liberate his tongue.

He fell off his horse.

"Red! Look—look around!"

Allie was gone! The disappointment at not seeing her was crushing, and the fear of utter loss was terrible. Neale lay on the ground, blind, sick, full of agony, with his fingers tearing at the grass. The evil presentiments that had haunted him for months had not been groundless fancies. Perhaps Allie had called to him again, in another hour of calamity, and this time he had not responded. She was gone! That idea struck him cold. It meant the most dreadful of all happenings. For a while he lay there, prostrate under the shock. He was dimly aware of Larry's coming and sitting down beside him.

"No sign of any one," he said, huskily. "Not even a track! . . . Thet fire must hev been about two weeks ago. Mebbe more, but not much. There's been a big rain an' the ground's all washed clean an' smooth. . . . Not a track!"

It was the cowboy's habit to calculate the past movements of people and horses by the nature of the tracks they left.

Then Neale awoke to violence. He sprang up and rushed to the ruins of the cabin, frantically tore and dug around the burnt embers, and did not leave off until he had overhauled the whole pile. There was nothing but ashes and embers. Whereupon he ran to the empty corrals, to the sheds, to the wood-pile, to the spring, and all around the space once so habitable. There was nothing to reward his fierce energy—nothing to scrutinize. Already grass was springing in the trails and upon spots that had once been bare.

Neale halted, sweating, hot, wild, before his friend. Larry avoided his gaze.

"She's gone! . . . She's gone!" Neale panted.

"Wal, mebbe Slingerland moved camp an' burned this place," suggested Larry. "He was sore after them four road-agents rustled in heah."

"No—no. He'd have left the cabin. In case he moved—Allie was to write me a note—telling me how to find them. I remember—we picked out the place to hide the note. . . . Oh! she's gone! She's gone!"

"Wal, then, mebbe Slingerland got away an' the cabin was burned after."

"I can't hope that. . . . I tell you—it means hell's opened up before me."

"Wal, it's tough, I know, Neale, but mebbe—"

Neale wheeled fiercely upon him. "You're only saying those things! You don't believe them! Tell me what you do really think."

"Lord, pard, it couldn't be no wuss," replied Larry, his lean face working. "I figger only one way. This heah. Slingerland had left Allie alone. . . . Then—she was made away with an' the cabin burned."

"Indians?"

"Mebbe. But I lean more to the idee of an outfit like thet one what was heah."

Neale groaned in his torture. "Not that, Reddy—not that! . . . The Indians would kill her—scalp her—or take her captive into their tribe. . . . But a gang of cutthroat ruffians like these. . . . My God! if I *knew* that had happened it'd kill me."

Larry swore at his friend. "It can't do no good to go to pieces," he expostulated. "Let's do somethin'."

"What—in Heaven's name!" cried Neale, in despair.

"Wal, we can rustle up every trail in these heah Black Hills. Mebbe we can find Slingerland."

Then began a search—frantic, desperate, and forlorn on the part of Neale; faithful and dogged and keen on the part of King. Neale was like a wild man. He heeded no advice or caution. Only the cowboy's iron arm saved Neale and his horse. It was imperative to find water and grass, and to eat, necessary things which Neale seemed to have forgotten. He seldom slept or rested or ate. They risked meeting the Sioux in every valley and on every ridge. Neale would have welcomed the sight of Indians; he would have rushed into peril in the madness of his grief. Still, there was hope! He lived all the hours in utter agony of mind, but his heart did not give up.

They coursed far and near, always keeping to the stream beds, for if Slingerland had made another camp it would be near water. More than one trail led nowhere; more than one horse track roused hopes that were futile. The Wyoming hills country was surely a lonely and a wild one, singularly baffling to the searchers, for in two weeks of wide travel it did not yield a sign or track of man. Neale and King used up all their scant supply of food, threw away all their outfit except a bag of salt, and went on, living on the meat they shot.

Then one day, unexpectedly, they came upon two trappers by a beaver-dam. Neale was overcome by his emotions; he sensed that from these men he would learn something. The first look from them told him that his errand was known.

"Howdy!" greeted Larry. "It shore is good to see you men—the fust we've come on in an awful hunt through these heah hills."

"Thar ain't any doubt thet you look it, friend," replied one of the trappers.

"We're huntin' fer Slingerland. Do you happen to know him?"

"Knowed Al fer years. He went through hyar a week ago—jest after the big rain, wasn't it, Bill?"

"Wal, to be exact it was eight days ago," replied the comrade Bill.

"Was—he—alone?" asked Larry, thickly.

"Sure, an' lookin' sick. He lost his girl not long since, he said, an' it broke him bad."

"Lost her! How?"

"Wal, he was sure it wasn't redskins," rejoined the trapper, reflectively. "Slingerland stood in with the Sioux—traded with 'em. He—"

"Tell me quick!" hoarsely interrupted Neale. "What happened to Allie Lee?"

"Fellars, my pard heah is hurt deep," said Larry. "The girl you spoke of was his sweetheart."

"Young man, we only know what Al told us," replied the trapper. "He said the only time he ever left the lass alone was the very day she was taken. Al come home to find the cabin red-hot ashes. Everythin' gone. No sign of the lass. No sign of murder. She was jest carried off. There was tracks—hoss tracks an' boot tracks, to the number of three or four men an' hosses. Al trailed 'em. But thet very night he had to hold up to keep from bein' drowned, as we had to hyar. Wal, next day he couldn't find any tracks. But he kept on huntin' fer a few days, an' then give up. He said she'd be dead by then—said she wasn't the kind thet could have lived more 'n a day with men like them. Some hard customers are driftin' by from the gold-fields. An' Bill an' I, hyar, ain't in love with this railroad idee. It'll ruin the country fer trappin' an' livin'."

Some weeks later a gaunt and ragged cowboy limped into North Platte, walking beside a broken horse, upon the back of which swayed and reeled a rider tied in the saddle.

It was not a sight to interest any except the lazy or the curious, for in that day such things were common in North Platte. The horse had bullet creases on his neck; the rider wore a bloody shirt; the gaunt pedestrian had a bandaged arm.

Neale lay ill of a deeper wound while the bullet-hole healed in his side. Day and night Larry tended him or sat by him or slept near him in a shack on the outskirts of the camp. Shock, grief, starvation, exhaustion, loss of blood and sleep—all these brought Warren Neale close to death. He did not care to live. It was the patient, loyal friend who fought fever and heartbreak and the ebbing tide of life.

Baxter and Henney visited North Platte and called to see him, and later the chief came and ordered Larry to take Neale to the tents of the corps. Every one was kind, solicitous, earnest. He had been missed. The members of his corps knew the strange story of Allie Lee; they guessed the romance and grieved over the tragedy. They did all they could do, and the troop doctor added his attention; but it was the nursing, the presence, and the spirit of Larry King that saved Neale.

He got well and went back to work with the cowboy for his helper.

In that camp of toil and disorder none but the few with whom Neale was brought in close touch noted anything singular about him. The engineers, however, observed that he did not work so well, nor so energetically, nor so accurately. His enthusiasm was lacking. The cowboy, always with him, was the one who saw the sudden spells of somber abstraction and the poignant, hopeless, sleepless pain, the eternal regret. And as Neale slackened in his duty Larry King grew more faithful.

Neale began to drink and gamble. For long the cowboy

fought, argued, appealed against this order of things, and then, failing to change or persuade Neale, he went to gambling and drinking with him. But then it was noted that Neale never got under the influence of liquor or lost materially at cards. The cowboy spilled the contents of Neale's glass and played the game into his hands.

Both of them shrank instinctively from the women of the camp. The sight of anything feminine hurt.

North Platte stirred with the quickening stimulus of the approach of the rails and the trains, and the army of soldiers whose duty was to protect the horde of toilers, and the army of tradesmen and parasites who lived off them.

The construction camp of the graders moved on westward, keeping ahead of the camps of the layers.

The first train that reached North Platte brought directors of the U.P.R.—among them Warburton and Rudd and Rogers; also Commissioners Lee and Dunn and a host of followers on a tour of inspection.

The five miles of Neale's section of road that the commissioners had judged at fault had been torn up, resurveyed, and relaid.

Neale rode back over the line with Baxter and surveyed the renewed part. Then, returning to North Platte, he precipitated consternation among directors and commissioners and engineers, as they sat in council, by throwing on the table figures of the new survey identical with his old data.

"Gentlemen, the five miles of track torn up and rebuilt had precisely the same grade, to an inch!" he declared, with ringing scorn.

Baxter corroborated his statement. The commissioners roared and the directors demanded explanations.

"I'll explain it," shouted Neale. "Forty-six thousand

dollars a mile! Five miles—two hundred and thirty thousand dollars! Spent twice! Taken twice by the same construction company!"

Warburton, a tall, white-haired man in a frock-coat, got up and pounded the table with his fist. "Who is this young engineer?" he thundered. "He has the nerve to back his work instead of sneaking to get a bribe. And he tells the truth. We're building twice—spending twice when once is enough!"

An uproar ensued. Neale had cast a bomb into the council. Every man there and all the thousands in camp knew that railroad ties cost several dollars each; that wages were abnormally high, often demanded in advance, and often paid twice; that parallel with the great spirit of the work ran a greedy and cunning graft. It seemed to be inevitable, considering the nature and proportions of the enterprise. An absurd law sent out the commissioners, the politicians appointed them, and both had fat pickings. The directors likewise played both ends against the middle; they received the money from the stock sales and loans; they paid it out to the construction companies; and as they employed and owned these companies the money returned to their own pockets. But more than one director was fired by the spirit of the project—the good to be done—the splendid achievement—the trade to come from across the Pacific. The building of the road meant more to some of them than a mere fortune.

Warburton was the lion of this group, and he roared down the dissension. Then with a whirl he grasped Neale round the shoulders and shoved him face to face with the others.

"Here's the kind of man we want on this job!" he shouted, with red face and bulging jaw. "His name's Neale. I've heard of some of his surveys. You've all seen him face this council. That only, gentlemen, is the spirit which can build the U.P.R. Let's push him up. Let's send him to Washington with those figures. Let's break this damned idiotic law for appointing commissioners to undo the work of efficient men."

Opportunity was again knocking at Neale's door.

Allison Lee arose in the flurry, and his calm, cold presence, the steel of his hard gray eyes, and the motion of his hand entitled him to a voice.

"Mr. Warburton—and gentlemen," he said, "I remember this young engineer Neale. When I got here to-day I inquired about him, remembering that he had taken severe exception to the judgment of the commissioners about that five miles of road-bed. I learned he is a strange, excitable young fellow, who leaves his work for long wild trips and who is a drunkard and a gambler. It seems to me somewhat absurd seriously to consider the false report with which he has excited this council."

"It's not false," retorted Neale, with flashing eyes. Then he appealed to Warburton and he was white and eloquent. "You directors know better. This man Lee is no engineer. He doesn't know a foot-grade from a forty-five-degree slope. Not a man in that outfit had the right or the knowledge to pass judgment on our work. It's political. It's a damned outrage. It's graft."

Another commissioner bounced up with furious gestures.

"We'll have you fired!" he shouted.

Neale looked at him and back at Allison Lee and then at Warburton.

"I quit," he declared, with scorn. "To hell with your rotten railroad!"

Another hubbub threatened in the big tent. Some one yelled for quiet.

And suddenly there was quiet, but it did not come from that individual's call. A cowboy had detached himself from the group of curious onlookers and had confronted the council with two big guns held low.

"Red! Hold on!" cried Neale.

It was Larry. One look at him blanched Neale's face.

"Everybody sit still an' let me talk," drawled Larry, with the cool, reckless manner that now seemed so deadly.

No one moved, and the silence grew unnatural. The cowboy advanced a few strides. His eyes, with a singular piercing intentness, were bent upon Allison Lee, yet seemed to hold all the others in sight. He held one gun in direct alignment with Lee, low down, and with the other he rapped on the table. The gasp that went up from round that table proved that some one saw the guns were both cocked.

"Did I understand you to say Neale lied aboot them surveyin' figgers?" he queried, gently.

Allison Lee turned as white as a corpse. The cowboy radiated some dominating force, but the chill in his voice was terrible. It meant that life was nothing to him—nor death. What was the U.P.R. to him, or its directors, or its commissioners, or the law? There was no law in that wild camp but the law in his hands. And he knew it.

"Did you say my pard lied?" he repeated.

Allison Lee struggled and choked over a halting, "No."

The cowboy backed away, slowly, carefully, with soft steps, and he faced the others as he moved.

"I reckon thet's aboot all," he said, and, slipping into the crowd, he was gone.

CHAPTER XI

After Neale and Larry left, Slingerland saw four seasons swing round, in which no visitors disturbed the loneliness of his valley.

All this while he did not leave Allie Lee alone, or at least out of hearing. When he went to tend his traps or to hunt, to chop wood or to watch the trail, Allie always accompanied him. She grew strong and supple; she could walk far and carry a rifle or pack; she was keen of eye and ear, and she loved the wilds; she not only was of help to him, but she made the time pass swiftly.

When a year passed after the departure of Neale and Larry King it seemed to Slingerland that they would never return. There was peril on the trails these days. He grew more and more convinced of some fatality, but he did not confide his fears to Allie. She was happy and full of trust; every day, almost every hour, she looked for Neale. The long wait did not drag her down; she was as fresh and hopeful as ever and the rich bloom mantled her cheek. Slingerland had not the heart to cast a doubt into her happiness. He let her live her dreams.

There came a day that spring when it was imperative for him to visit a distant valley, where he had left traps he now needed, and as the distance was long and time short he decided to go alone. Allie laughed at the idea of being unsafe at the cabin.

"I can take care of myself," she said. "I'm not afraid."

Slingerland scarcely doubted her. She had nerve, courage; she knew how to use a gun; and underneath her softness and tenderness was a spirit that would not flinch at anything. Still he did not feel satisfied with the idea of leaving her alone, and it was with a wrench that he did it now.

Moreover, he was longer at the journey than he had anticipated. The moment he turned his face homeward, a desire to hurry, an anxiety, a dread fastened upon him. A presentiment of evil gathered. But, encumbered as he was with heavy traps, he could not travel swiftly. It was late afternoon when he topped the last ridge between him and home.

What Slingerland saw caused him to drop his traps and gaze aghast. A heavy column of smoke rose above the valley. His first thought was of Sioux. But he doubted if the Indians would betray his friendship. The cabin had caught on fire by accident or else a band of wandering desperadoes had happened along to ruin him. He ran down the slope, stole down round to the group of pines, and under cover, cautiously, approached the spot where his cabin had stood.

It was a heap of smoking logs and probably had burned for hours. There was no sign of Allie or of any one. Then he ran into the glade. Almost at once he saw boot-tracks and hoof-tracks, while pelts and hides and furs lay scattered around, as if they had been discarded for choicer ones.

"Robbers!" muttered Slingerland. "An' they've got the lass!"

He shook under the roughest blow he had ever been

dealt; his conscience flayed him; his distress over Allie's fate was so keen and unfamiliar that, used as he was to prompt decision and action, he remained stock-still, staring at the ruins of his home.

Presently he roused himself. He had no hopes. He knew the nature of men who had done this deed. But it was possible that he might overtake them. In the dust he found four sizes of boot-tracks and he took the trail down the valley.

Then he became aware that a storm was imminent and that the air had become cold and raw. Rain began to fall, and darkness came quickly. Slingerland sought the shelter of a near-by ledge, and there, hungry, cold, wet, and unhappy, he waited for sleep that would not come.

It rained hard all night and by morning the brook had become a yellow flood and the trail was under water. Toward noon the rain turned to a drizzly snow, and finally ceased. Slingerland passed on down the valley, searching for tracks. The ground everywhere had been washed clean and smooth. When he reached the old St. Vrain and Laramie Trail it looked as though a horse had not passed there in months. He spent another wretched night, and next day awoke to the necessities of life. Except for his rifle, and his horses, and a few traps back up in the hills, he had nothing to show for years of hard and successful work. But that did not matter. He had begun with as little and he could begin again. He killed meat, satisfied his hunger, and cooked more that he might carry with him. Then he spent two more days in that locality, until he had crossed every outlet from his valley. Not striking a track, he saw nothing but defeat.

That moment was bitter. "If Neale'd happen along hyar now he'd kill me—an' sarve me right," muttered the trapper.

But he believed that Neale, too, had gone the way of so many who had braved these wilds. Slingerland saw in the fate of Neale and Allie the result of civilization marching westward. If before he had disliked the idea of the railroad entering his wild domain, he hated it now. Before that survey the Indians had been peaceful and no dangerous men rode the trails. What right had the Government to steal land from the Indians, to break treaties, to run a steam track across the plains and mountains? Slingerland foresaw the bloodiest period ever known in the West, before that work should be completed. It had struck him deep—this white-man movement across the Wyoming hills, and it was not the loss of all he had worked for that he minded. For years his life had been lonely, and then suddenly it had been full. Never again would it be either.

Slingerland turned his back to the trail made by the advancing march of the empire-builders, and sought the seclusion of the more inaccessible hills.

"Some day I'll work out with a load of pelts," he said, "an' then mebbe I'll hyar what become of Neale—an' her."

He found, as one of his kind knew how to find, the valleys where no white man had trod—where the game abounded and was tame—where if the red man came he was friendly—where the silent days and lonely nights slowly made more bearable his memory of Allie Lee.

CHAPTER XII

Allie Lee possessed a mind at once active and contemplative. While she dreamed of Neale and their future she busied herself with many tasks, and a whole year flew by without a lagging or melancholy hour.

Neale, she believed, had been detained or sent back to Omaha, or given more important work than formerly. She divined Slingerland's doubt, but she would not give it room in her consciousness. Her heart told her that all was well with Neale, and that sooner or later he would return to her.

In Allie love had worked magic. It had freed her from a horrible black memory. She had been alone; she had wanted to die so as to forget those awful yells and screams—the murder—the blood—the terror and the anguish; she had nothing to want to live for; she had almost hated those two kind men who tried so hard to make her forget. Then suddenly, she never quite remembered when, she had seen Neale with different eyes. A few words, a touch, a gift, and a pledge—and life had been transformed for Allie Lee. Like a flower blooming overnight, her heart had opened to love, and all the distemper in her blood and all the blackness in her mind were dispelled. The relief from pain and dread was so great that love became a beautiful and all-absorbing passion. Freed then, and strangely happy, she took to the life around her as naturally as if she had been born there, and she grew like a wild flower. Neale returned to her that autumn to make perfect the realization of her dreams. When he went away she could still be happy. She owed it to him to be perfect in joy, faith, love, and duty; and her adversity had discovered to her an inward courage and an indomitable will. She lived for Neale.

Summer, autumn, winter passed, short days full of solitude, beauty, thought, and anticipation, and always achievement, for she could not stay idle. When the first green brightened the cottonwoods and willows along the brook she knew that before their leaves had attained their full growth Neale would be on his way to her. A strange and inexplicable sense of the heart told her that he was coming.

More than once that spring had she bent over the mossy rock to peer down at her face mirrored in the crystal spring. Neale had made her aware of her beauty, and she was proud of it, since it seemed to be such a strange treasure to him.

On the May morning that Slingerland left her alone she was startled by the clip-clop of horses trotting up the trail a few hours after his departure.

Her first thought was that Neale and Larry had returned. All her being suddenly radiated with rapture. She flew to the door.

Four horsemen rode into the clearing, but Neale was not among them.

Allie's joy was short-lived, and the reaction to disappointment was a violent, agonizing wrench. She lost all control of her muscles for a moment, and had to lean against the cabin to keep from falling.

By this time the foremost rider had pulled in his horse

near the door. He was a young giant with hulking shoulders, ruddy-faced, bold-eyed, ugly-mouthed. He reminded Allie of some one she had seen in California. He stared hard at her.

"Hullo! Ain't you Durade's girl?" he asked, in gruff astonishment.

Then Allie knew she had seen him out in the goldfields.

"No, I'm not," she replied.

"A-huh! You look oncommon like her. . . . Anybody home round here?"

"Slingerland went over the hill," said Allie. "He'll be back presently."

The fellow brushed her aside and went into the cabin. Then the other three riders arrived.

"Mornin', miss," said one, a grizzled veteran, who might have been miner, trapper, or bandit. The other two reined in behind him. One wore a wide-brimmed black sombrero from under which a dark, sinister face gleamed. The last man had sandy hair and light roving eyes.

"Whar's Fresno?" he asked.

"I'm inside," replied the man called Fresno, and he appeared at the door. He stretched out a long arm and grasped Allie before she could avoid him. When she began to struggle the huge hand closed on her wrist until she could have screamed with pain.

"Hold on, girl! It won't do you no good to jerk, an' if you holler I'll choke you," he said "Fellers, get inside the cabin an' rustle around lively."

With one pull he hauled Allie toward his horse, and, taking a lasso off his saddle, he roped her arms to her sides and tied her to the nearest tree.

"Keep mum now or it'll be the wuss fer you," he ordered; then he went into the cabin.

They were a bad lot, and Slingerland's reason for worry

had at last been justified. Allie did not fully realize her predicament until she found herself bound to the tree. Then she was furious, and strained with all her might to slip free of the rope. But the efforts were useless; she only succeeded in bruising her arms for nothing. When she desisted she was ready to succumb to despair, until a flashing thought of Neale, of the agony that must be his if he lost her or if harm befell her, drew her up sharply, thrillingly. A girl's natural and instinctive fear was vanquished by her love.

She heard the robbers knocking things about in the cabin. They threw bales of beaver pelts out of the door. Presently Fresno reappeared carrying a buckskin sack in which Slingerland kept his money and few valuables, and the others followed, quarreling over a cane-covered demijohn in which there had once been liquor.

"Nary a drop!" growled the one who got possession of it. And with rage he threw the thing back into the cabin, where it crashed into the fire.

"Sandy, you've scattered the fire," protested the grizzled robber, as he glanced into the cabin. "Them furs is catchin'."

"Let 'em burn!" called Fresno. "We got all we want. Come on."

"But what's the sense burnin' the feller's cabin down?"

"Nuthin''ll burn," said the dark-faced man, "an' if it does it'll look like Indians' work. Savvy, Old Miles?"

They shuffled out together. Evidently Fresno was the leader, or at least the strongest force. He looked at the sack in his hand and then at Allie.

"You fellers fight over thet," he said, and, throwing the sack on the ground, he strode toward Allie.

The three men all made a rush for the sack and Sandy got it. The other two pressed round him, not threateningly, but aggressively, sure of their rights.

"I'll divide," said Sandy, as he mounted his horse. "Wait till we make camp. You fellers pack the beavers."

Fresno untied Allie from the tree, but he left the lasso round her; holding to it and her arm, he rudely dragged her to his horse.

"Git up, an' hurry," he ordered.

Allie mounted. The stirrups were too long.

"You fellers clear out," called Fresno, "an' ketch me one of them hosses we seen along the brook."

While he readjusted the stirrups Allie looked down upon him. He was an uncouth ruffian, and his touch gave her an insupportable disgust. He wore no weapons, but his saddle holster contained a revolver and the sheath a Winchester. Allie could have shot him and made a run for it, and she had the nerve to attempt it. The others, however, did not get out of sight before Fresno had the stirrups adjusted. He strode after them, leading the horse. Allie glanced back to see a thin stream of smoke coming out of the cabin door. Then she faced about, desperately resolved to take any chance to get away. She decided that she would not be safe among these men for very long. Whatever she was to do she must do that day, and she only awaited her opportunity.

At the ford Sandy caught one of Slingerland's horses—a mustang and a favorite of Allie's, and one she could ride. He was as swift as the wind. Once upon him, she could run away from any horse which these robbers rode. Fresno put the end of the lasso round the mustang's neck.

"Can you ride bareback?" he asked Allie.

Allied lied. Her first thought was to lead them astray as to her skill with a horse; and then it occurred to her that if she rode Fresno's saddle there might be an opportunity to use the gun.

Fresno leaped astride the mustang, and was promptly bucked off. The other men guffawed. Fresno swore and, picking himself up, tried again. This time the mustang behaved better, but it was plain he did not like the weight. Then Fresno started off, leading his own horse, and at a trot that showed he wanted to cover ground.

Allie heard the others quarreling over something, probably the gold Slingerland had been so many years in accumulating.

They rode on to where the valley opened into another, along which wound the old St. Vrain and Laramie Trail. They kept to this, traveling east for a few miles, and then entered an intersecting valley, where some distance up they had a camp. They had not taken the precaution to hide either packs or mules, and so far as Allie could tell they had no fear of Indians. Probably they had crossed from California, and, being dishonest and avoiding caravans and camps, they had not become fully acquainted with the perils of that region.

It was about noon when they arrived at this place. The sun was becoming blurred and a storm appeared brewing. Fresno dismounted, dropping the halter of the mustang. Then he let go his own bridle. The eyes he bent on Allie made her turn hers away as from something that could scorch and stain. He pulled her off the saddle, rudely, with coarse and meaning violence.

Allie pushed him back and faced him. In a way she had been sheltered all her life, yet she had lived among such men as this man, and she knew that resistance or pleadings were useless; they would only inflame him. She was not ready yet to court death.

"Wait," she said.

"A-huh!" he grunted, breathing heavily. He was an animal, slow-witted and brutal.

"Fresno, I am Durade's girl!" she went on.

"I thought I knowed you. But you're grown to be a woman an' a dam' pretty one."

Allie drew him aside, farther from the others, who had

renewed a loud altercation. "Fresno, it's gold you want," she affirmed, rather than asked.

"Sure. But no small stake like thet'd be my choice— ag'in' you," he leered, jerking a thumb back at his companions.

"You remember Horn?" went on Allie.

"Horn! The miner who made thet big strike out near Sacramento?"

"Yes, that's who I mean," replied Allie, hurriedly. "We—we left California in his caravan. He brought all his gold with him."

Fresno showed a growing interest.

"We were attacked by Sioux. . . . Horn buried all that gold—on the spot. All—all the others were killed— except me. . . . And I know where—" Allie shuddered with what the words brought up. But no memory could weaken her.

Fresno opened his large mouth to bawl this unexpected news to his comrades.

"Don't call them—don't tell them," Allie whispered. "There's only one condition. I'll take you—where that gold's hidden."

"Girl, I can make you tell," he replied, menacingly.

"No, you can't."

"You ain't so smart you think I'll let you go—jest fer some gold?" he queried. "Gold'll be cheap along this trail soon. An' girls like you are scarce."

"No, that's not what I meant. . . . Get rid of the others—and I'll take you where Horn buried his gold."

Fresno stared at her. He grinned. The idea evidently surprised and flattered him; yet it was perplexing.

"But Frank—he's my pard—thet one with the black hat," he protested. "I couldn't do no dirt to Frank. . . . What's your game, girl? I'll beat you into tellin' me where thet gold is."

"Beating won't make me tell," replied Allie, with intensity. "Nothing will—if I don't want to. My game is for my life. You know I've no chance among four men like you."

"Aw, I don't know about thet," he blustered. "I can take care of you. . . . But, say, if you'd stand fer Frank, mebbe I'll take you up. . . . Girl, are you lyin' about thet gold?"

"No."

"Why didn't the trapper dig it up? You must hev told him."

"Because he was afraid to keep it in or near his cabin. We meant to leave it until we were ready to get out of the country."

That appeared plausible to Fresno and he grew more thoughtful.

Meanwhile the altercation among the other three ruffians assumed proportions that augured a fight.

"I'll divide this sack when I git good an' ready," declared Sandy.

"But, pard, thet's no square deal," protested Old Miles. "I'm a-gittin' mad. I seen you meant to keep it all."

The dark-faced ruffian shoved a menacing fist under Sandy's nose. "When do I git mine?" he demanded.

Fresno wheeled and called, "Frank, you come here!"

The other approached sullenly. "Fresno, thet Sandy is whole hog or none!" he exclaimed.

"Let 'em fight it out," replied Fresno. "We've got a bigger game. . . . Besides, they'll shoot each other up. Then we'll hev it all. Come, give 'em elbow room."

He led Allie and his horse away a little distance.

"Fetch them packs, Frank," he called.

The mustang followed, and presently Frank came with one of the packs. Fresno slipped the saddle from his horse, and, laying it under a tree, he pulled gun and rifle from their sheaths. The gun he stuck in his belt; the rifle he leaned against a branch.

"Sandy'll plug Old Miles in jest another minnit," remarked Fresno.

"What's this other game?" queried Frank, curiously.

"It's gold, Frank—gold," replied Fresno; and in few words he told his comrade about Horn's buried treasure. But he did not mention the condition under which the girl would reveal its hiding-place. Evidently he had no doubt that he could force her to tell.

"Let's rustle," cried Frank, his dark face gleaming. "We want to git out of this country quick."

"You bet! An' I wonder when we'll be fetchin' up with them railroad camps we heerd about. . . . Camps full of gold an' whisky an' wimmen!"

"We've enough on our hands now," replied Frank. "Let's rustle fer thet—".

A gun-shot interrupted him. Then a hoarse curse rang out—and then two more reports from a different gun.

"Them last was Sandy's," observed Fresno, coolly. "An' of course they landed. . . . Go see if Old Miles hit Sandy."

Frank strode off under the trees.

Allie had steeled herself to anything, and those shots warned her that now she had two less enemies to contend with, and that she must be quick to seize the first opportunity to act. She could leap upon the mustang, and if she was lucky she could get away. She could jump for the Winchester and surely shoot one of these villains, perhaps both of them. But the spirit that gave her the nerve to attempt either plan bade her wait, not too long, but longer, in the hope of a more favorable moment.

Frank returned to Fresno, and he carried the sack of gold that had caused dissension. Fresno laughed.

"Sandy's plugged hard—low down," said Frank. "He can't live. An' Old Miles is croaked."

"A-huh! Frank, I'll go git the other packs. An' you see what's in this sack," said Fresno.

When he got out of sight, Allie slipped the lasso from her waist.

"I don't need that hanging to me," she said.

"Sure you don't, sweetheart," replied the ruffian Frank. "Thet man Fresno is rough with ladies. Now I'm gentle. . . . . Come an' let me spill this sack in your lap."

"I guess not," replied Allie.

"Wal, you're sure a cat. . . . Look at her eyes! . . . All right, don't git mad at me."

He spilled the contents of the sack out on the sand, and bent over it.

What had made Allie's eyes flash was the recognition of her opportunity. She did not hesitate an instant. First she looked to see just where the mustang stood. He was near, with the rope dragging, half coiled. Allie suddenly noticed the head and ears of the mustang. He heard something. She looked up the valley slope and saw a file of Indians riding down, silhouetted against the sky. They were coming fast. For an instant Allie's senses reeled. Then she rallied. Her situation was desperate—almost hopeless. But here was the issue of life or death, and she met it.

In one bound she had the rifle. Long before, she had ascertained that it was loaded. The man Frank heard the click of the raising hammer.

"What're you doin'?" he demanded, fiercely.

"Don't get up!" warned Allie. She stepped backward nearer the mustang. "Look up the slope! . . . Indians!"

But he paid no heed. He jumped up and strode toward her.

"Look, man!" cried Allie, piercingly. He came on.

Then Fresno appeared, running, white of face.

Allie, without leveling the rifle, fired at Frank, even as his clutching hands struck the weapon.

He halted, with sudden gasp, sank to his knees, fell against the tree, and then staggered up again.

Allie had to drop the rifle to hold the frightened mustang. She mounted him, urged him away, and hauled in the dragging lasso. Once clear of brush and stones, he began to run. Allie saw a clear field ahead, but there were steep rocky slopes boxing the valley. She would be hemmed in. She got the mustang turned, and ran among the trees, keeping far over to the left. She heard beating hoofs off to the right, crashings in brush, and then yells. An opening showed the slope alive with Indians riding hard. Some were heading down, and others up the valley to cut off her escape; the majority were coming straight for the clumps of trees.

Fresno burst out of cover mounted on Sandy's bay horse. He began to shoot. And the Indians fired in reply. All along the slopes rose white puffs of smoke, and bullets clipped dust from the ground in front of Allie. Fresno drew ahead. The bay horse was swift. Allie pulled her mustang more to the left, hoping to get over the ridge, which on that side was not high. To her dismay, Indians appeared there, too. She wheeled back to the first course and saw that she must attempt what Fresno was trying.

Then the robber Frank appeared, riding out of the cedars. The Indian riders closed rapidly in on him, shooting all the time. His horse was hit, and stumbling, it almost threw the rider. Then the horse ran wildly—could not be controlled. One Indian was speeding from among the others. He had a bow bent double, and suddenly it straightened. Allie saw dust fly from Frank's back. He threw up his arms and slid off under the horse, the saddle slipping with him. The horse, wounded and terrorized, began to plunge, dragging man and saddle.

Ahead, far to the right, Fresno was gaining on his pursuers. He was out of range now, but the Indians kept shooting. Then Allie's situation became so perilous that she saw only the Indians to the left, with their mustangs stretched out so as to intercept her before she got out into the wider valley.

Her mustang did not need to be goaded. The yells behind and on all sides, and the whistling bullets, drove him to his utmost. Allie had all she could do to ride him. She was nearly blinded by the stinging wind, yet she saw those lithe, half-naked savages dropping gradually back and she knew that she was gaining. Her hair became loose and streamed in the wind. She heard the yells then. No more rifles cracked. Her pursuers had discovered that she was a girl and were bent on her capture.

Fleet and strong the mustang ran, sure-footed, leaping the washes, and outdistancing the pursuers on the left. Allie thought she could turn into the big valley and go down the main trail before the Indians chasing Fresno discovered her. But vain hope! Across the width of the valley where it opened out, a string of Indians appeared, riding back to meet her.

A long dust line, dotted with bobbing objects, to the right. Behind a close-packed bunch of hard riders. In front an opening trap of yelling savages. She was lost. And suddenly she remembered the fate of her mother. Her spirit sank, her strength fled. Everything blurred around her. She lost control of the mustang. She felt him turning, slowing, the yells burst hideously in her ears. Like her mother's—her fate. A roar of speedy hoof-beats seemed to envelop her, and her nostrils were filled with dust. They were upon her. She prayed for a swift stroke—then for her soul. All darkened—her senses were failing. Neale's face glimmered there—in space—and again was lost. She was slipping—slipping— A rude and powerful hold fastened upon her. Then all faded.

CHAPTER XIII

When Allie Lee came back from that black gap in her consciousness she was lying in a circular tent of poles and hides.

For a second she was dazed. But the Indian designs and trappings in the tent brought swift realization—she had been brought a captive to the Sioux encampment. She raised her head. She was lying on a buffalo robe; her hands and feet were bound; the floor was littered with blankets and beaded buckskin garments. Through a narrow opening she saw that the day was far spent; Indians and horses passed to and fro; there was a bustle outside and jabber of Indian jargon; the wind blew hard and drops of rain pattered on the tent.

Allie could scarcely credit the evidence of her own senses. Here she was alive! She tried to see and feel if she had been hurt. Her arms and body appeared bruised, and they ached, but she was not in any great pain. Her hopes arose. If the Sioux meant to kill her they would have done it at once. They might intend to reserve her for torture, but more likely their object was to make her a captive in the tribe. In that case Slingerland would surely find her and get her freedom.

Rain began to fall more steadily. Allie smelled smoke and saw the reflection of fires on the wall of the tent. Presently a squaw entered. She was a huge woman, evidently old, very dark of face, and wrinkled. She carried a bowl and platter which she set down, and, grunting, she began to untie Allie's hands. Then she gave the girl a not ungentle shake. Allie sat up.

"Do you—do they mean—to harm and kill me?" asked Allie.

The squaw shook her head to indicate she did not understand, but her gestures toward the things she had brought were easy to interpret. Allie partook of the Indian food, which was coarse and unpalatable, but it satisfied her hunger. When she had finished the squaw laboriously tied the thongs round Allie's wrists, and, pushing her back on the robe, covered her up and left her.

After that it grew dark rapidly, and the rain increased to a torrent. Allie, hardly realizing how cold she had been, began to warm up under the woolly robe. The roar of the rain drowned all other sounds outside. She wondered if Slingerland had returned to his cabin, and, if so, what he had done. She felt sorry for him. He would take the loss hard. But he would trail her; he would hear of a white girl captive in the Sioux camp and she would soon be free. How fortunate she was! A star of Providence had watched over her. The prayer she had breathed had been answered. She thought of Neale. She would live for him; she would pray and fight off harm; she would find him if he could not find her. And lying there bound and helpless in an Indian camp, captive of the relentless Sioux, for all she knew in peril of death, with the roar of wind and rain around her, and the darkness like pitch, she yet felt her pulses throb and thrill and her spirit soar at remembrance of the man she loved. In the end she would find

Neale; and it was with his name trembling on her lips that she fell asleep.

More than once during the night she awoke in the pitchy darkness to hear the wind blow and the rain roar. The dawn broke cold and gray, and the storm gradually diminished. Allie lay alone for hours, beginning to suffer by reason of her bonds and cramped limbs. The longer she was left alone the more hopeful her case seemed.

In the afternoon she was visited by the squaw, released and fed as before. Allie made signs that she wanted to have her feet free, so that she could get up and move about. The squaw complied with her wishes. Allie could scarcely stand; she felt dizzy; a burning, aching sensation filled her limbs.

Presently the old woman led her out. Allie saw a great number of tents, many horses and squaws and children, but few braves. The encampment lay in a wide valley, similar to all the valleys of that country, except that it was larger. A stream in flood swept yellow and noisy along the edge of the encampment. The children ran at sight of Allie, and the women stared. It was easy to see that they disapproved of her. The few braves looked at her with dark, steady, unfathomable eyes. The camp appeared rich in color—in horses and trappings; evidently this tribe was not poor. Allie saw utensils, blankets, clothing—many things never made by Indians.

She was led to a big lodge with a tent adjoining. Inside an old Indian brave, grizzled and shrunken, smoked before a fire; and as Allie was pushed into the tent a young Indian squaw appeared. She was small, with handsome, scornful face and dark, proud eyes, gorgeously clad in elaborate beaded and fringed buckskin—evidently an Indian princess or a chief's wife. She threw Allie a venomous glance as she went out. Allie heard the old squaw's grunting voice, and the young one's quick and passionate answers.

There was nothing for Allie to do but await developments. She rested, rubbing her sore wrists and ankles, thankful she had been left unbound. She saw that she was watched, particularly by the young woman, who often walked to the opening to glance in. The interior of this tent presented a contrast to the other in which she had been confined. It was dry and clean, with floor of rugs and blankets; and all around hung beaded and painted and feathered articles, some for wear, and others for what purpose she could not guess.

The afternoon passed without further incident until the old squaw entered, manifestly to feed Allie, and tie her up as heretofore. The younger squaw came in to watch the latter process.

Allie spoke to her and held out her bound hands appealingly. This elicited no further response than an intent look.

Night came. Allie lay awake a good while, and then she fell asleep. Next morning she was awakened by an uproar. Whistling and trampling mustangs, whoops of braves, the babel of many voices, barking of dogs, movement, bustle, sound—all attested to the return of the warriors. Allie's heart sank for a moment; this would be the time of trial for her. But the clamor subsided without any disturbance near her tent. By and by the old squaw returned to attend to her needs. This time on the way out she dropped a blanket curtain between the tent and the lodge.

Soon Indians entered the lodge, quite a number, with squaws among them, judging by their voices. A harangue ensued, lasting an hour or more; it interested Allie, especially because at times she heard and recognized the quick, passionate utterance of the young squaw.

Soon Allie's old attendant shuffled in, lifting the curtain

and motioning Allie to come out. Allie went into the lodge. An early sun, shining into the wide door, lighted the place brightly. It was full of Indians. In the center stood a striking figure, probably a chief, tall and lean, with scars on his naked breast. His face was bronze, with deep lines, somber and bitter, and cruel thin lips, and eyes that glittered like black fire. His head had the poise of an eagle.

His piercing glance scarcely rested an instant upon Allie. He motioned for her to be taken away. Allie, as she was led back, got a glimpse of the young squaw. Sullen, with bowed head, and dark rich blood thick in her face, with heaving breast and clenched hands, she presented a picture of outraged pride and jealousy.

Probably the chief had decided to claim Allie as his captive, a decision which would be fiercely resented by the young Indian bride.

The camp quieted down after that. Allie peeped through a slit between the hides of which her tent was constructed, and she saw no one but squaws and children. The mustangs appeared worn out. Evidently the braves and warriors were resting after a hard ride or fight or foray.

Nothing happened. The hours dragged. Allie heard the breathing of heavy sleepers. About dark she was fed again and bound.

That night she was awakened by a gentle shake. A hand moved from her shoulder to her lips. The pale moonlight filtered into the tent. Allie saw a figure kneeling beside her and she heard a whispered "'Sh-s-s-sh!" Then her hands and feet were freed. She divined then that the young squaw had come to let her go, in the dead of night. Her heart throbbed high as her liberator held up a side of the tent. Allie crawled out. A bright moon soared in the sky. The camp was silent. The young woman slipped after her, and with a warning gesture to be silent she led Allie away toward the slope of the valley. It was a goodly distance. Not a sound disturbed the peace of the beautiful night. The air was cold and still. Allie shivered and trembled. This was the most exciting adventure of all. She felt a sudden tenderness and warmth for this Indian girl. Once the squaw halted, with ear intent, listening. Allie's heart stopped beating. But no bark of dog, no sound of pursuit, justified alarm. At last they reached the base of the slope.

The Indian pointed high toward the ridge-top. She made undulating motions of her hand, as if to picture the topography of the ridges, and the valleys between; then kneeling, she made a motion with her finger on the ground that indicated a winding trail. Whereupon she stealthily glided away—all without a spoken word.

Allie was left alone—free—with direction how to find the trail. But what use was it for her to find it in that wilderness? Still, her star kept drawing her spirit. She began to climb. The slope was grassy, and her light feet left little trace. She climbed and climbed until she thought her heart would burst. Once upon the summit, she fell in the grass and rested.

Far below in the moon-blanched valley lay the white tents and the twinkling camp-fires. The bay of a dog floated up to her. It was a tranquil, beautiful scene. Rising, she turned her back upon it, with a muttered prayer for the Indian girl whose jealousy and generosity had freed her, and again she faced the ridge-top and the unknown wilderness.

A wolf mourned, and the sound, clear and sharp, startled her. But remembering Slingerland's word that no beast would be likely to harm her in the warm season, she was reassured. Soon she had crossed the narrow back of the ridge, to see below another valley like the one she had left, but without the tents and fires. Descent was easy and she covered ground swiftly. She feared lest she should come upon a stream in flood. Again she mounted a slope, zig-zagging up, going slowly, reserving her strength, pausing often to rest and to listen, and keeping a straight line with the star she had marked. Climbing was hard work, how-ever slowly she went, just as going down was a relief to her wearied legs.

In this manner she climbed four ridges and crossed three valleys before a rest became imperative. Now dawn was near, as was evidenced by the paling stars and the gray in the east. It would be well for her to remain on high ground while day broke.

So she rested, but, soon cooling off, she suffered with the cold. Huddling down in the grass against a stone, and facing the east, she waited for dawn to break.

The stars shut their eyes; the dark blue of sky turned gray; a pale light seemed to suffuse itself throughout the east. The valley lay asleep in shadow, the ridges awoke in soft gray mist. Far down over the vastness and openness of the plains appeared a ruddy glow. It warmed, it changed, it brightened. A sea of cloudy vapors, serene and motion-less, changed to rose and pink; and a red curve slid up over the distant horizon. All that world of plain and cloud and valley and ridge quickened as with the soul of day, while it colored with the fire of sun. Red, radiant, glorious, the sun rose.

It was the dispeller of gloom, the bringer of hope. Allie Lee, lost on the heights, held out her arms to the east and the sun, and she cried: "Oh, God! . . . Oh, Neale—Neale!"

When she turned to look down into the valley below she saw the white winding ribbon-like trail, and with her eyes she followed it to where the valley opened wide upon the plains.

She must go down the slope to the cover of the trees and

brush, and there work along eastward, ever with eye alert. She must meet with travelers within a few days, or perish of starvation, or again fall into the hands of the Sioux. Thirst she did not fear, for the recent heavy rain had left water-holes everywhere.

With action her spirit lightened and the numbness of hands and feet left her. Time passed swiftly. The sun stood straight overhead before she realized she had walked miles; and it declined westward as she skulked like an Indian from tree to tree, from bush to bush, along the first bench of the valley floor.

Night overtook her at the gateway of the valley. The vast monotony of the plains opened before her like a gulf. She feared it. She found a mound of earth with a wind-worn shelf in its side and overgrown with sage; and into this she crawled, curled in the sand and prayed and slept.

Next day she took up a position a few hundred yards from the trail and followed its course, straining her eyes to see before and behind her, husbanding her strength with frequent rests, and drinking from every pool.

That day, like its predecessor, passed swiftly by and left her well out upon the huge, billowy bosom of the plains. Again she sought a hiding-place, but none offered. There was no warmth in the sand, and the night wind arose, cold and moaning. She could not sleep. The whole empty world seemed haunted. Rustlings of the sage, seepings of the sand, gusts of the wind, the night, the loneliness, the faithless stars and a treacherous moon that sank, the wailing of wolves—all these things worked upon her mind and spirit until she lost her courage. She feared to shut her eyes or cover her face, for then she could not see the stealthy forms stalking her out of the gloom. She prayed no more to her star.

"Oh, God, have you forsaken me?" she moaned.

How relentless the grip of the endless hours! The black

night held fast. And yet when she had grown nearly mad waiting for the dawn, it finally broke, ruddy and bright, with the sun, as always, a promise of better things to come.

Allie found no water that day. She suffered from the lack of it, but hunger appeared to have left her. Her strength diminished, yet she walked and plodded miles on miles, always gazing both hopelessly and hopefully along the winding trail.

At the close of the short and merciful day despair seized upon Allie's mind. With night came gloom and the memory of her mother's fate. She still clung to a strange faith that all would soon be well. But reason, fact, reality, these present things pointed to certain doom—starvation— death by thirst—or Indians! A thousand times she imagined she heard the fleet hoof-beating of many mustangs. Only the tiny pats of the broken sage leaves in the wind!

It was a dark and cloudy night, warmer and threatening rain. She kept continually turning round and round to see what it was that came creeping up behind her so stealthily. How horrible was the dark—the blackness that showed invisible things! A wolf sent up his hungry, lonely cry. She did not fear this reality so much as she feared the intangible. If she lived through this night, there would be another like it to renew the horror. She would rather not live. Like a creature beset by foes all around she watched; she faced every little sound; she peered into the darkness, instinctively unable to give up, to end the struggle, to lie down and die.

Neale seemed to be with her. He was alive. He was thinking of her at that very moment. He would expect her to overcome self and accident and calamity. He spoke to her out of the distance and his voice had the old power, stronger than fear, exhaustion, hopelessness, insanity. He could call her back from the grave.

And so the night passed.

In the morning, when the sun lit the level land, far down the trail westward gleamed a long white line of moving wagons.

Allie uttered a wild and broken cry, in which all the torture shuddered out of her heart. Again she was saved! That black doubt was shame to her spirit. She prayed her thanksgiving, and vowed in her prayers that no adversity, however cruel, could ever again shake her faith or conquer her spirit.

She was going on to meet Neale. Life was suddenly sweet again, unutterably full, blazing like the sunrise. He was there—somewhere to the eastward.

She waited. The caravan was miles away. But it was no mirage, no trick of the wide plain! She watched. If the hours of night had been long, what were these hours of day with life and the chance of happiness ever advancing?

At last she saw the scouts riding in front and alongside, and the plodding oxen. It was a large caravan, well equipped for defense.

She left the little rise of ground and made for the trail. How uneven the walking! She staggered. Her legs were weak. But she gained the trail and stood there. She waved. They were not so far away. Surely she would be seen. She staggered on—waved again.

There! The leading scout had halted. He pointed. Other riders crowded around him. The caravan came to a stop.

Allie heard voices. She waved her arms and tried to run. A scout dismounted, advanced to meet her, rifle ready. The caravan feared a Sioux trick. Allie descried a lean, gray old man; now he was rapidly striding toward her.

"It's a white gal!" she heard him shout.

Others ran forward as she staggered to meet them.

"I'm alone—I'm—lost!" she faltered.

"A white gal in Injun dress," said another.

And then kind hands were outstretched to her.

"I'm—running—away. . . . Indians!" panted Allie.

"Whar?" asked the lean old scout.

"Over the ridges—miles—twenty miles—more. They had me. I got—away . . . four—three days ago."

The group around Allie opened to admit another man.

"Who's this—who's this?" called a quick voice, soft and liquid, yet with a quality of steel in it.

Allie had heard that voice. She saw a tall man in long black coat and wide black hat and flowered vest and flowing tie. Her heart contracted.

"*Allie!*" rang the voice.

She looked up to see a dark, handsome face—a Spanish face with almond eyes, sloe-black and magnetic—a face that suddenly blazed.

She recognized the man with whom her mother had run away—the man she had long believed her father—the adventurer Durade! Then she fainted.

CHAPTER XIV

Allie recovered to find herself lying in a canvas-covered wagon, and being worked over by several sympathetic women.

She did not see Durade. But she knew she had not been mistaken. The wagon was rolling along as fast as oxen could travel. Evidently the caravan had been alarmed by the proximity of Sioux and was making as much progress as possible.

Allie did not answer many questions. She drank thirstily, but she was too exhausted to eat.

"Whose caravan?" was the only query she made.

"Durade's," replied one woman, and it was evident from the way she spoke that this was a man of consequence.

As Allie lay there, slowly succumbing to weariness and drowsiness, she thought of the irony of fate that had let her escape the Sioux only to fall into the hands of Durade. Still, there was hope. Durade was traveling toward the east. Out there somewhere he would meet Neale, and then blood would be spilled. She had always regarded Durade strangely, wondering that in spite of his kindness to her she could not really care for him. She understood now and hated him passionately. And if there was any one she feared it was Durade. Allie lost herself in the past, seeing the stream of mixed humanity that passed through Durade's gambling-halls. No doubt he was on his way, first to search for her mother, and secondly, to profit by the building of the railroad. But he would never find her mother. Allie was glad.

At length she fell asleep and slept long, then dozed at intervals. The caravan halted. Allie heard the familiar singsong calls to the oxen. Soon all was bustle about her, and this fully awakened her. In a moment or more she must expect to be face to face with Durade. What should she tell him? How much should she let him know? Not one word about her mother! He would be less afraid of her if he found out that the mother was dead. Durade had always feared Allie's mother.

The women with whom Allie had ridden helped her out of the wagon, and, finding her too weak to stand, they made a bed for her on the ground. The camp site appeared to be just the same as any other part of that monotonous plain-land, but evidently there was a stream or water-hole near by. Allie saw her companions were the only women in the caravan; they were plain persons, blunt, yet kind, used to hard, honest work, and probably wives of defenders of the wagon-train.

They could not conceal their curiosity in regard to Allie, nor their wonder. She had heard them whispering together whenever they came near.

Presently Allie saw Durade. He was approaching. How well she remembered him! Yet the lapse of time and the change between her childhood and the present seemed incalculable. He spoke to the women, motioning in her direction. His bearing and action were that of a man of education, and a gentleman. Yet he looked what her mother had called him—a broken man of class, an adventurer, a victim of base passions.

He came and knelt by Allie. "How are you now?" he asked. His voice was gentle and courteous, different from that of the other men.

"I can't stand up," replied Allie.

"Are you hurt?"

"No—only worn out."

"You escaped from Indians?"

"Yes—a tribe of Sioux. They intended to keep me captive. But a young squaw freed me—led me off."

He paused as if it was an effort to speak, and a long, thin, shapely hand went to his throat. "Your mother?" he asked, hoarsely. Suddenly his face had turned white.

Allie gazed straight into his eyes, with wonder, pain, suspicion. "My mother! I've not seen her for nearly two years."

"My God! What happened? You lost her? You became separated? . . . Indians—bandits? . . . Tell me!"

"I have—no—more to tell," said Allie. His pain revived her own. She pitied Durade. He had changed—aged—there were lines in his face that were new to her.

"I spent a year in and around Ogden, searching," went on Durade. "Tell me—more."

"No!" cried Allie.

"Do you know, then?" he asked, very low.

"I'm not your daughter—and mother ran off from you. Yes, I know that," replied Allie, bitterly.

"But I brought you up—took care of you—helped educate you," protested Durade, with agitation. "You were my own child, I thought. I was always kind to you. I—I loved the mother in the daughter."

"Yes, I know. . . . But you were wicked."

"If you won't tell me it must mean she's still alive," he replied, swiftly. "She's not dead! . . . I'll find her. I'll make her come back to me—or kill her. . . . After all these years—to leave me!"

He seemed wrestling with mingled emotions. The man was proud and strong, but defeat in life, in the crowning passion of life, showed in his white face. The evil in him was not manifest then.

"Where have you lived all this time?" he asked, presently.

"Back in the hills with a trapper."

"You have grown. When I saw you I thought it was the ghost of your mother. You are just as she was when we met."

He seemed lost in sad retrospection. Allie saw streaks of gray in his once jet-black hair.

"What will you do?" asked Allie.

He was startled. The softness left him. A blaze seemed to leap under skin and eyes, and suddenly he was different—he was Durade the gambler, instinct with the lust of gold and life.

"Your mother left me for *you*," he said, with terrible bitterness. "And the game has played you into my hands. I'll keep you. I'll hold you to get even with her."

Allie felt stir in her the fear she had had of him in her childhood when she disobeyed. "But you can't keep me against my will—not among people we'll meet eastward."

"I can, and I will!" he declared, softly, but implacably. "We're not going East. We'll be in rougher places than the gold-camps of California. There's no law but gold and guns out here. . . . But—if you speak of me to any one may your God have mercy on you!"

The blaze of him betrayed the Spaniard. He meant more than dishonor, torture, and death. The evil in him was rampant. The love that had been the only good in an abnormal and disordered mind had turned to hate.

Allie knew him. He was the first person who had ever dominated her through sheer force of will. Unless she abided by his command her fate would be worse than if she had stayed captive among the Sioux. This man was not an American. His years among men of later mold had not changed the Old World cruelty of his nature. She recognized the fact in utter despair. She had not strength left to keep her eyes open.

After a while Allie grew conscious that Durade had left her. She felt like a creature that had been fascinated by a deadly snake and then left to itself; in the mean time she could do nothing but wait. Shudderingly, mournfully, she resigned herself to the feeling that she must stay under Durade's control until a dominance stronger than his should release her. Neale seemed suddenly to have retreated far into the past, to have gone out of the realm of her consciousness. And yet the sound of his voice, the sight of his face, would make instantly that spirit of hers—his spirit— to leap like a tigress in her defense. But where was Neale? The habits of life were all-powerful; and all her habits had been formed under Durade's magnetic eye. Neale retreated and so did spirit, courage, hope. Love remained, despairing, yet unquenchable.

Allie's resignation established a return to normal feelings. She ate and grew stronger; she slept and was refreshed.

The caravan moved on about twenty-five miles a day. At the next camp Allie tried walking again, to find her feet were bruised, her legs cramped, and action awkward and painful. But she persevered, and the tingling of revived circulation was like needles pricking her flesh. She limped from one camp-fire to another; and all the rough men had a kind word or question or glance for her. Allie did not believe they were all honest men. Durade had employed a large force, and apparently he had taken on every one who applied. Miners, hunters, scouts, and men of no hall-mark except that of wildness composed the mixed caravan. It spoke much for Durade that they were under control. Allie well remembered hearing her mother say that he had a genius for drawing men to him and managing them.

Once during her walk, when every one appeared busy, a big fellow with hulking shoulders and bandaged head stepped beside her.

"Girl," he whispered, "if you want a knife slipped into Durade, tell him about me!"

Allie recognized the whisper before she did the heated, red face with its crooked nose and bold eyes and ugly mouth. Fresno! He must have escaped from the Sioux and fallen in with Durade.

Allie shrunk from him. Durade, compared with this kind of ruffian, was a haven of refuge. She passed on without a sign. But Fresno was safe from her. This meeting made her aware of an impulse to run back to Durade, instinctively, just as she had when a child. He had ruined her mother; he had meant to make a lure of her, the daughter; he had showed what his vengeance would be upon that mother, just as he had showed Allie her doom should she betray him. But notwithstanding all this, Durade was not Fresno, nor like any of those men whose eyes seemed to burn her.

She returned to the wagon and to the several women and men attached to it, with the assurance that there were at least some good persons in that motley caravan crew.

The women, naturally curious and sympathetic, questioned her in one way and another. Who was she, what had happened to her, where were her people or friends? How had she ever escaped robbers and Indians in that awful country? Was she really Durade's daughter?

Allie did not tell much about herself, and finally she was left in peace.

The lean old scout who had first seen Allie as she staggered into the trail told her it was over a hundred miles to the first camp of the railroad-builders.

"Down-hill all the way," he concluded. "An' we'll make it in a jiffy."

Nevertheless, it took nearly all of four days to sight the camp of the graders—the advance-guard of the great construction work.

In those four days Allie had recovered her bloom, her health, her strength—everything except the wonderful assurance which had been hers. Durade had spoken daily with her, and had been kind, watchful, like a guardian.

It was with a curious thrill that Allie gazed around as she rode into the construction camp—horses and men and implements all following the line of Neale's work. Could Neale be there? If so, how dead was her heart to his nearness?

The tents of the workers, some new and white, others soiled and ragged, stretched everywhere; large tents belched smoke and resounded with the ring of hammers on anvil; soldiers stood on guard; men, red-shirted and blue-shirted, swarmed as thick as ants; in a wide hollow a long line of horses, in double row, heads together, pulled hay from a rack as long as the line, and they pulled and snorted and bit at one another; a strong smell of hay and burning wood mingled with the odor of hot coffee and steaming beans; fires blazed on all sides; under another huge tent, or many tents without walls, stretched wooden tables and benches; on the scant sage and rocks and brush, and everywhere upon the tents, lay in a myriad of colors and varieties the lately washed clothes of the toilers; and through the wide street of the camp clattered teams and swearing teamsters, dragging plows with clanking chains and huge scoops turned upside down. Bordering the camp, running east as far as eye could see, stretched a high, flat, yellow lane, with the earth hollowed away from it, so that it stood higher than the level plain—and this was the work of the graders, the road-bed of the Union Pacific Railroad, the U.P. Trail.

This camp appeared to be Durade's destination. His caravan rode through and halted on the outskirts of the far side. Preparations began for what Allie concluded was to be a permanent halt. At once began a significant disintegration of Durade's party. One by one the scouts received payment from their employer, and with horse and pack disappeared toward the camp. The lean old fellow who had taken kindly interest in Allie looked in at the opening of the canvas over her wagon, and, wishing her luck, bade her good-by. The women likewise said good-by, informing her that they were going on home. Not one man among those left would Allie have trusted.

During the hurried settling of camp Durade came to Allie.

"Allie," he said, "you don't have to keep cooped up in there unless I tell you. But don't talk to any one—and don't go that way."

He pointed toward the humming camp. "That place beats any gold-diggings I ever saw," he concluded.

The tall, scant sage afforded Allie some little seclusion, and she walked there until Durade called her to supper. She ate alone on a wagon-seat, and when twilight fell she climbed into her wagon, grateful that it was high off the ground and so inclosed her from all except sound.

Darkness came; the fire died down; the low voices of Durade and his men, and of callers who visited them, flowed continuously.

Then, presently, there arose a strange murmur, unlike any sound Allie had ever heard. It swelled into a low, distant roar. She was curious about it. Peeping out of her wagon-cover she saw where the darkness flared to yellow with a line of lights—torches or lanterns or fires. Crossing and recrossing these lights were black objects, in twos and threes and dozens. And from this direction floated the strange, low roar. Suddenly she realized. It was the life of the camp. Hundreds and thousands of men were there together, and as the night advanced the low roar rose and fell, and lulled away to come again—strange, sad, hideous, mirthful. For a long time Allie could not sleep.

Next morning Durade called her. When she unlaced the canvas flaps, it was to see the sun high and to hear the bustle of work all about her.

Durade brought her breakfast and gave her instructions. While he was about in the daytime she might come out and do what she could to amuse herself; but when he was absent or at night she must be in her wagon-tent, laced in, and she was not to answer any call. She would be guarded by Stitt, one of his men, a deaf mute, faithful to his interests, and who had orders to handle her roughly should she disobey. Allie would not have been inclined to mutiny, even without the fear and abhorrence she felt of this ugly and deformed mute.

That day Durade caused to be erected tents, canopies, tables, benches, and last a larger tent, into which the tables and benches were carried. Fresno worked hard, as did all the men except Stitt, who had nothing to do but watch Allie's wagon.

Wearily the time passed for her. How many days must she spend thus, watching idly, because there was nothing else to do? Still, back in her consciousness there was a vague and growing thought. Sooner or later Neale would appear in the flesh, as he now came to her in her dreams.

That night Allie, peeping out, saw by the fire and torchlight a multitude of men drawn to Durade's large tent. Mexicans, negroes, Irishmen—all kinds of men passed, loud and profane, careless and reckless, quarrelsome and loquacious. Soon there arose in her ears the long-forgotten but now familiar sounds of a gambling-hell in full blast. The rolling rattle of the wheel, sharp, strident, and keen, intermingled with the strange rich false clink of gold.

It needed only a few days and nights for Allie Lee to divine Durade's retrogression. Before this he had been a gambler for the sake of gambling, even a sportsman in his evil way; now he seemed possessed of an unscrupulous intent, a strange, cold, devouring passion to get gold and more gold—always more gold. Allie divined evidence of this, saw it, heard it. The man had struck the descent, and he was all the more dangerous for his lapse from his former standards, poor as they had been.

Not a week had elapsed before the gambling-hell roared all night. Allie got most of her sleep during the day. She tried to shut out what sound she could, and tried to be deaf to the rest. But she had to hear the angry bawls, pistol-shots, and shrill cries; yes, and the trample of heavy boots as men dragged a dead gamester out to the ditch.

Day was a relief, a blessing. Allie was frequently cooped up in her narrow canvas-covered wagon, but she saw from there the life of the grading camp.

There were various bosses—the boarding boss, who fed the laborers; the stable boss, who had charge of the teams; the grading boss, who ruled the diggers and scrapers; and the time-keeper boss, who kept track of the work of all.

In the early morning a horde of hungry men stampeded the boarding-tents where the cooks and waiters made mad haste to satisfy loud and merry demands. At sunset the same horde dropped in, dirty and hot and lame, and fought for seats while others waited for their turn.

Out on the level plain stretched the hundreds of teams, moving on and returning, the drivers shouting, the horses bending. The hot sun glared, the wind whipped up the dust, the laborers speeded up to the shout of the boss. And ever westward crept the low, level, yellow bank of sand and gravel—the road-bed of the first transcontinental railway.

Thus the daytime had its turmoil, too, but this last was splendid, like the toil of heroes united to gain some common end. And the army of soldiers waited, ever keen-eyed, for the skulking Sioux.

Mull, the boss of the camp, became a friend of Durade's. The wily Spaniard could draw to him any class of men. This Mull had been a driver of truck-horses in New York, and now he was a driver of men.

He was huge, like a bull, heavy-lipped and red-cheeked, hairy and coarse, with big sunken eyes. A brute—a caveman. He drank; he gambled. He was at once a bully and a pirate. Responsible to no one but his contractor, he hated the contractor and he hated his job. He was great in his place, brutal with fist and foot, a gleaner of results from hard men at a hard time.

He won gold from Durade, or, as Fresno guffawed to a comrade, he had been allowed to win it. Durade picked his man. He had big schemes and he needed Mull.

Benton was Durade's objective point—Benton, the great and growing camp-city, where gold and blood were spilled in the dusty streets and life roared like a blast from hell.

All that Allie heard of Benton increased her dread, and at last she determined that she would run any risk rather than be taken there. And so one night, as soon as it grew dark, she slipped out of the wagon and, under cover of darkness, made her escape.

CHAPTER XV

The building of the U.P.R. as it advanced westward caused many camps and towns to spring up and flourish, like mushrooms, in a single night; and trains were run as far as the rails were laid.

Therefore strange towns and communities were born, like to nothing that the world had ever seen before.

Warren Neale could not get away from the fascination of the work and life, even though he had lost all his ambition and was now nothing more than an ordinary engineer, insignificant and idle. He began to drink and gamble in North Platte, more in a bitter defiance to fate than from any real desire; then with Larry King he drifted out to Kearney.

At Kearney, Larry got into trouble—characteristic trouble. In a quarrel with a construction boss named Smith, Larry accused Smith of being the crooked tool of the crooked commissioners who had forced Neale to quit his job. Smith grew hot and profane. The cowboy promptly slapped his face. Then Smith, like the fool he was, went after his gun. He never got it out.

It distressed Neale greatly that Larry had shot up a man—and a railroad man at that. No matter what Larry said, Neale knew the shooting was on his account. This deed made the cowboy a marked man. It changed him, also, toward Neale, inasmuch as that he saw his wildness was making small Neale's chances of returning to work. Larry never ceased importuning Neale to go back to his job. After shooting Smith the cowboy made one more eloquent appeal to Neale and then left for Cheyenne. Neale followed him.

Cheyenne was just sobering up after its brief and tempestuous reign as headquarters town, and though depleted and thin, it was now making a bid for permanency. But the sting and wildness of life had departed with the construction operations, and now Benton had become the hub of the railway universe.

Neale boarded a train for Benton and watched with bitterness the familiar landmarks he had learned to know so well while surveying the line. He was no longer connected with the great project—no more a necessary part of the great movement.

Beyond Medicine Bow the grass and the green failed and the immense train of freight-cars and passenger-coaches, loaded to capacity, clattered on into arid country. Gray and red, the drab and fiery colors of the desert lent the ridges character—forbidding and barren.

From a car window Neale got his first glimpse of the wonderful terminus city, and for once his old thrills returned. He recalled the distance—seven hundred—no, six hundred and ninety-eight miles from Omaha. So far westward was Benton.

It lay in the heart of barrenness, alkali, and desolation, on the face of the windy desert, alive with dust-devils, sweeping along, yellow and funnel-shaped—a huge blocked-out town, and set where no town could ever live. Benton was prey for sun, wind, dust, drought, and the wind was terribly and insupportably cold. No sage, no cedars, no grass, not even a cactus-bush, nothing green or living to relieve the eye, which swept across the gray and the white, through the dust, to the distant bare and desolate hills of drab.

The hell that was reported to abide at Benton was in harmony with its setting.

The immense train clattered and jolted to a stop. A roar of wind, a cloud of powdery dust, a discordant and unceasing din of voices, came through the open windows of the car. The heterogeneous mass of humanity with which Neale had traveled jostled out, struggling with packs and bags.

Neale, carrying his bag, stepped off into half a foot of dust. He saw a disintegrated crowd of travelers that had just arrived, and of travelers ready to depart—soldiers, Indians, Mexicans, negroes, loafers, merchants, tradesmen, laborers, an ever-changing and ever-remarkable spectacle of humanity. He saw stage-coaches with hawkers bawling for passengers bound to Salt Lake, Ogden, Montana, Idaho; he saw a wide white street—white with dust where it was not thronged with moving men and women, and lined by tents and canvas houses and clapboard structures, together with the strangest conglomeration of painted and printed signs that ever advertised anything in the world.

A woman, well clad, young, not uncomely, but with hungry eyes like those of a hawk, accosted Neale. He drew away. In the din he had not heard what she said. A boy likewise spoke to him; a greaser tried to take his luggage; a man jostling him felt of his pocket; and as Neale walked on he was leered at, importuned, jolted, accosted, and all but mobbed.

So this was Benton.

A pistol-shot pierced the din. Some one shouted. A wave of the crowd indicated commotion somewhere; and then the action and noise went on precisely as before. Neale crossed five intersecting streets; evidently the wide street he was on must be the main one.

In that walk of five blocks he saw thousands of persons, but they were not the soldiers who protected the line, nor the laborers who made the road. These were the travelers, the business people, the stragglers, the nondescripts, the parasites, the criminals, the desperadoes, and the idlers— all who must by hook or crook live off the builders.

Neale was conscious of a sudden exhilaration. The spirit was still in him. After all, his defeated ambition counted for nothing in the great sum of this work. How many had failed! He thought of the nameless graves already dotting the slopes along the line and already forgotten. It would be something to live through the heyday of Benton.

Under a sign, "Hotel," he entered a door in a clapboard house. The place was as crude as an unfinished barn. Paying in advance for lodgings, he went to the room shown him—a stall with a door and a bar, a cot and a bench, a bowl and a pitcher. Through cracks he could see out over an uneven stretch of tents and houses. Toward the edge of town stood a long string of small tents and several huge ones, which might have been the soldiers' quarters.

Neale went out in search of a meal and entered the first restaurant. It was merely a canvas house stretched over poles, with compartments at the back. High wooden benches served as tables, low benches as seats. The floor was sand. At one table sat a Mexican, an Irishman, and a negro. The Irishman was drunk. The negro came to wait on Neale, and, receiving an order, went to the kitchen. The Irishman sidled over to Neale.

"Say, did yez hear about Casey?" he inquired, in very friendly fashion.

"No, I didn't," replied Neale. He remembered Casey, the flagman, but probably there were many Caseys in that camp.

"There wus a foight, out on the line, yisteddy," went on the fellow, "an' the dom' redskins chased the gang to the troop-train. Phwat do you think? A bullet knocked Casey's pipe out of his mouth, as he wus runnin', an' b'gorra, Casey sthopped fer it an' wus all shot up."

"Is he dead?" inquired Neale.

"Not yit. No bullets can't kill Casey."

"Was his pipe a short, black one?"

"It wus thot."

"And did Casey have it everlastingly in his mouth?"

"He shlept in it."

Neale knew that particular Casey, and he examined this loquacious Irishman more closely. He recognized him as Pat Shane, one of the trio he had known during the survey in the hills two years ago. The recognition was like a stab to Neale. Memory of the Wyoming hills—of the lost Allie Lee—cut him to the quick. Shane had aged greatly. There were scars on his face that Neale had not seen before.

"Mister, don't I know yez?" leered Shane, studying Neale with bleary eyes.

Neale did not care to be remembered. The waiter brought his dinner, which turned out to be a poor one at a high price. After eating, Neale went out and began to saunter along the walk. The sun had set and the wind had gone down. There was no flying dust. The street was again crowded with men, but nothing like it had been after the arrival of the train. No one paid much attention to Neale. On that walk he counted nineteen saloons, and probably some of the larger places were of like nature, but not so wide open to the casual glance.

Neale strolled through the town from end to end, and across the railroad outside the limits, to a high bank, where he sat down. The desert was beautiful away to the west, with its dull, mottled hues backed by gold and purple, with its sweep and heave and notched horizon. Near at hand it seemed drab and bare. He watched a long train of flat and box cars come in, and saw that every car swarmed with soldiers and laborers. The train discharged its load of thousands, and steamed back for more.

Twilight fell. All hours were difficult for Neale, but twilight was the most unendurable, for it had been the hour Allie Lee loved best, and during which she and Neale had walked hand in hand along the brook, back there in the lovely and beautiful valley in the hills. Neale could not sit still long; he could not rest, nor sleep well, nor work, nor indeed be of any use to himself or to any one, and all because he was haunted and driven by the memory of Allie Lee. And at such quiet hours as this, in the midst of the turmoil he had sought for weeks, a sadness filled his soul, and an eternal remorse. The love that had changed him and the life that had failed him seemed utterly misrelated.

To and fro he paced on the bare ridge while twilight shadowed. A star twinkled in the west, a night wind began to seep the sand. The desert, vast, hidden, mysterious, yet so free and untrammeled, darkened.

Lights began to flash up along the streets of Benton, and presently Neale became aware of a low and mounting hum, like a first stir of angry bees.

The loud and challenging strains of a band drew Neale toward the center of the main street, where men were pouring into a big tent.

He halted outside and watched. This strident, business-like, quick-step music and the sight of the men and women attracted thereby made Neale realize that Benton had arisen in a day and would die out in a night; its life would be swift, vile, and deadly.

When the band ceased a sudden roar came from inside

the big tent, a commingling of the rough voices of men and the humming of wheels, the clinking of glasses and gold, the rattling of dice, the hoarse call of a dealer, the shuffling of feet—a roar pierced now and then by the shrill, vacant, soundless laugh of a woman.

It was that last sound which almost turned Neale away from the door. He shunned women. But this place fascinated him. He went in under the flaming lamps.

The place was crowded—a huge tent stretched over a framework of wood, and it was full of people, din, smoke, movement. The floor was good planking covered with sand. Walking was possible only round the narrow aisles between groups at tables.

Neale's sauntering brought him to the bar. It had to him a familiar look, and afterward he learned that it had been brought complete from St. Louis, where he had seen it in a saloon. It seemed a huge, glittering, magnificent monstrosity in that coarse, bare setting. Wide mirrors, glistening bottles, paintings of nude women, row after row of polished glasses, a brawny, villanous barkeeper, with three attendants, all working fast, a line of rough, hoarse men five deep before the counter—all these things constituted a scene that had the aspects of a city and yet was redolent with an atmosphere no city ever knew. The drinkers were not all rough men. There were elegant black-hatted, frock-coated men of leisure in that line—not directors and commissioners and traveling guests of the U.P.R., but gentlemen of chance. Gamblers!

The band now began a different strain of dance music. Neale slowly worked his way around. At the end of the big tent a wide door opened into another big room—a dance-hall, full of dancers.

Neale had seen nothing like this in the other construction camps.

A ball was in progress. Just now it was merry, excited,

lively. Neale got inside and behind the row of crowded benches; he stood up against a post to watch. Probably two-hundred people were in the hall, most of them sitting. How singular, it struck Neale, to see good-looking, bare-armed and bare-necked young women dancing there, and dancing well! There were other women—painted, hollow-eyed—sad wrecks of womanhood. The male dancers were young men, as years counted, mostly unfamiliar with the rhythmic motion of feet to a tune, and they bore the rough stamp of soldiers and laborers. But there were others, as there had been before the bar, who wore their clothes differently, who had a different poise and swing—young men, like Neale, whose earlier years had known some of the graces of society. They did not belong there; the young women did not belong there. The place seemed unreal. This was a merry scene, apparently with little sign, at that moment, of what it actually meant. Neale sensed its un-dercurrent.

He left the dance-hall. Of the gambling games, he liked best both to watch and to play poker. It had interest for him. The winning or losing of money was not of great moment. Poker was not all chance or luck, such as the roll of a ball, the turn of a card, or the facing up of dice. Pres-ently he became one of an interested group round a table watching four men play poker.

One, a gambler in black, immaculate in contrast to his companions, had a white, hard, expressionless face, with eyes of steel and thin lips. His hands were wonderful. Probably they never saw the sunlight, certainly no labor. They were as swift as light, too swift for the glance of an eye. But when he dealt the cards he was slow, careful, de-liberate. The stakes were gold, and the largest heap lay in front of him. One of his opponents was a giant of a fellow, young, with hulking shoulders, heated face, and broken nose—a desperado if Neale ever saw one. The other two players called this strapping brute Fresno. The little man with a sallow face like a wolf was evidently too intent on the game to look up. He appeared to be losing. Beside his small pile of gold stood an empty tumbler. The other and last player was a huge, bull-necked man whom Neale had seen before. It was difficult to place him, but after studying the red cheeks and heavy, drooping mustache, and hearing the loud voice, he recognized him as a boss of graders—a head boss. Presently the sallow-faced player called him Mull, and then Neale remembered him well.

Several of the watchers round this table lounged away, leaving a better vantage-place for Neale.

"May I sit in the game?" he inquired, during a deal.

"Certainly," replied the gambler.

"Naw. We gotta nough," said the sallow man, and he glanced from Neale to the gambler as if he suspected them. Gamblers often worked in pairs.

"I just came to Benton," added Neale, reading the man's thought. "I never saw the gentleman in black before."

"What th' hell!" rumbled Mull, grabbing up his cards. Fresno leered.

The gambler leaned back and his swift white hands flashed. Neale believed he had a derringer up each sleeve. A wrong word now would precipitate a fight.

"Excuse me," said Neale, hastily. "I don't want to make trouble. I just said I never saw this gentleman before."

"Nor I him," returned the gambler, courteously. "My name is Place Hough and my word is not doubted."

Neale had heard of this famous Mississippi River gambler. So, evidently, had the other three players. The game proceeded, and when it came to Hough's deal Mull bet hard and lost all. His big, hairy hands shook. He looked at Fresno and the other fellow, but not at Hough.

"I'm broke," he said, gruffly, and got up from the bench. He strode past Hough, and behind him; then as if suddenly, instinctively, answering to fury, he whipped out a gun.

Neale, just as instinctively, grasped the rising hand.

"Hold on, there!" he called. "Would you shoot a man in the back?"

And Neale, whose grip was powerful, caused the other to drop the gun. Neale kicked it aside. Fresno got up.

"Whar's your head, Mull?" he growled. "Git out of this!"

Attention had been attracted to Mull. Some one picked up the gun. The sallow-faced man rose, holding out his hand for it. Hough did not even turn around.

"I was goin' to hold him up," said Mull. He glared fiercely at Neale, wrenched his hand free, and with his comrades disappeared in the crowd.

The gambler rose and shook down his sleeves. The action convinced Neale that he had held a little gun in each hand.

"I saw him draw," he said. "You saved his life! . . . Nevertheless, I appreciate your action. My name is Place Hough. Will you drink with me?"

"Sure. . . . My name is Neale."

They approached the bar and drank together.

"A railroad man, I take it?" asked Hough.

"I was. I'm foot-loose now."

A fleeting smile crossed the gambler's face. "Benton is bad enough, without you being foot-loose."

"All these camps are tough," replied Neale.

"I was in North Platte, Kearney, Cheyenne, and Medicine Bow during their rise," said Hough. "They were tough. But they were not Benton. And the next camp west, which will be the last—it will be Roaring Hell. What will be its name?"

"Why is Benton worse?" inquired Neale.

"The big work is well under way now, with a tremendous push from behind. There are three men for every man's work. That lays off two men each day. Drunk or dead. The place is wild—far off. There's gold—hundreds of thousands of dollars in gold dumped off the trains. Benton has had one pay-day. That day was the sight of my life! . . . Then . . . there are women."

"I saw a few in the dance-hall," replied Neale.

"Then you haven't looked in at Stanton's?"

"Who's he?"

"Stanton is not a man," replied Hough.

Neale glanced inquiringly over his glass.

"Beauty Stanton, they call her," went on Hough. "I saw her in New Orleans years ago when she was a very young woman—notorious then. She had the beauty and she led the life . . . did Beauty Stanton."

Neale made no comment, and Hough, turning to pay for the drinks, was accosted by several men. They wanted to play poker.

"Gentlemen, I hate to take your money," he said. "But I never refuse to sit in a game. Neale, will you join us?"

They found a table just vacated. Neale took two of the three strangers to be prosperous merchants or ranchers from the Missouri country. The third was a gambler by profession. Neale found himself in unusually sharp company. He did not have a great deal of money. So in order to keep clear-headed he did not drink. And he began to win, not by reason of excellent judgment, but because he was lucky. He had good cards all the time, and part of the time very strong ones. It struck him presently that these remarkable hands came during Hough's deal, and he wondered if the gambler was deliberately manipulating the cards to his advantage. At any rate, he won hundreds of dollars.

"Mr. Neale, do you always hold such cards?" asked one of the men.

"Why, sure," replied Neale. He could not help being excited and elated.

"Well, he can't be beat," said the other.

"Lucky at cards, unlucky in love," remarked the third of the trio. "I pass."

Hough was looking straight at Neale when this last remark was made. And Neale suddenly lost his smile, his flush. The gambler dropped his glance.

"Play the game and don't get personal in your remarks," he said. "This is poker."

Neale continued to win, but his excitement did not return, nor his elation. A random word from a strange man had power to sting him. Unlucky in love! Alas! What was luck, gold—anything to him any more!

By the time the game was ended Neale felt a friendly interest in Hough that was difficult to define or explain; and the conviction gained upon him that the gambler had deliberately dealt him those remarkable cards.

"Let's see," said Hough, consulting his watch. "Twelve o'clock! Stanton's will be humming. We'll go in."

Neale did not want to show his reluctance, yet he did not know just what to say. After all, he was drifting. So he went.

It seemed that all the visitors who had been in the gambling-hell had gravitated to this other dance-hall. The entrance appeared to be through a hotel. At least Neale saw the hotel sign. The building was not made of canvas, but painted wood in sections, like the scenes of a stage. Men were coming and going; the hum of music and gaiety came from the rear; there were rugs, pictures, chairs; this place, whatever its nature, made pretensions. Neale did not see any bar.

They entered a big room full of people, apparently doing nothing. From the opposite side, where the dance-hall opened, came a hum that seemed at once music and discordance, gaiety and wildness, with a strange, carrying undertone raw and violent.

Hough led Neale across the room to where he could look into the dance-hall.

Neale saw a mad, colorful flash and whirl of dancers.

Hough whispered in Neale's ear: "Stanton throws the drunks out of here."

No, it appeared the dancers were not drunk with liquor. But there was evidence of other drunkenness than that of the bottle. The floor was crowded. Looking at the mass, Neale could only see whirling, heated faces, white, clinging arms, forms swaying round and round, a wild rhythm without grace, a dance in which music played no real part, where men and women were lost. Neale had never seen a sight like that. He was stunned. There were no souls here. Only beasts of men, and women for whom there was no name. If death stalked in that camp, as Hough had intimated, and hell was there, then the two could not meet too soon.

If the mass and the spirit and the sense of the scene dismayed Neale, the living beings, the creatures, the women—for the men were beyond him—confounded him with pity, consternation, and stinging regret. He had loved two women—his mother and Allie—so well that he ought to love all women because they were of the same sex. Yet how impossible! Had these creatures any sex? Yet they were—at least many were—young, gay, pretty, wild, full of life. They had swift suppleness, smiles, flashing eyes, a look at once intent and yet vacant. But few onlookers would have noticed that. The eyes for which the dance was meant saw the mad whirl, the bare flesh, the brazen glances, the close embrace.

The music ended, the dancers stopped, the shuffling ceased. There were no seats unoccupied, so the dancers walked around or formed in groups.

"Well, I see Ruby has spotted you," observed Hough.

Neale did not gather exactly what the gambler meant, yet he associated the remark with a girl dressed in red who had paused at the door with others and looked directly at Neale. At that moment some one engaged Hough's attention.

The girl would have been striking in any company. Neale thought her neither beautiful nor pretty, but he kept on looking. Her arms were bare, her dress cut very low. Her face offered vivid contrast to the carmine on her lips. It was a round, soft face, with narrow eyes, dark, seductive, bold. She tilted her head to one side and suddenly smiled at Neale. It startled him. It was a smile with the shock of a bullet. It held Neale, so that when she crossed to him he could not move. He felt rather than saw Hough return to his side. The girl took hold of the lapels of Neale's coat. She looked up. Her eyes were dark, with what seemed red shadows deep in them. She had white teeth. The carmined lips curled in a smile—a smile, impossible to believe, of youth and sweetness, that disclosed a dimple in her cheek. She was pretty. She was holding him, pulling him a little toward her.

"I like you!" she exclaimed.

The suddenness of the incident, the impossibility of what was happening, made Neale dumb. He felt her, saw her as he were in a dream. Her face possessed a peculiar fascination. The sleepy, seductive eyes; the provoking half-smile, teasing, alluring; the red lips, full and young through the carmine paint; all of her seemed to breathe a different kind of a power than he had ever before experienced—unspiritual, elemental, strong as some heady wine. She represented youth, health, beauty, terribly linked with evil wisdom, and a corrupt and irresistible power, possessing a base and mysterious affinity for man.

The breath and the charm and the pestilence of her passed over Neale like fire.

"Sweetheart, will you dance with me?" she asked, with her head tilted to one side and her half-open veiled eyes on his.

"No," replied Neale. He put her from him, gently but coldly.

She showed slow surprise. "Why not? Can't you dance? You don't look like a gawk."

"Yes, I can dance," replied Neale.

"Then will you dance with me?" she retorted, and red spots showed through the white on her cheeks.

"I told you no," replied Neale.

His reply transported her into a sudden fury. She swung her hand viciously. Hough caught it, saving Neale from a sounding slap in the face.

"Ruby, don't lose your temper," remonstrated the gambler.

"He insulted me!" she cried, passionately.

"He did not. Ruby, you're spoiled—"

"Spoiled—hell! . . . Didn't he look at me, flirt with me? That's why I asked him to dance. Then he insulted me. I'll make Cordy shoot him up for it."

"No, you won't," replied Hough, and he pulled her toward his companion, a tall woman with golden hair. "Stanton, shut her up."

The woman addressed spoke a few words in Ruby's ear. Then the girl flounced away. But she spoke with withering scorn to Neale.

"What in hell did you come in here for, you big handsome stiff?"

With that she was lost amid her mirthful companions.

Hough turned to Neale. "The girl's a favorite. You ruffled her vanity . . . you see. That's Benton. If you had happened to be alone you would have had gunplay. Be careful after this."

"But I didn't flirt with her," protested Neale. "I only looked at her—curiously, of course. And I said I wouldn't dance."

Hough laughed. "You're young in Benton. Neale, let me introduce to you the lady who saved you from some inconvenience. . . . Miss Stanton—Mr. Neale."

And that was how Neale met Beauty Stanton. It seemed she had done him a service. He thanked her. Neale's manner with women was courteous and deferential. It showed strangely here by contrast. The Stanton woman was superb, not more than thirty years old, with a face that must have been lovely once and held the haunting ghost of beauty still. Her hair was dead gold; her eyes were large and blue, with dark circles under them; and her features had a clear-cut classic regularity.

"Where's Ancliffe?" asked Hough, addressing Stanton. She pointed, and Hough left them.

"Neale, you're new here," affirmed the woman, rather curiously.

"Didn't I look like it? I can't forget what that girl said," replied Neale.

"Tell me."

"She asked me what in the hell I came here for. And she called me—"

"Oh, I heard what Ruby called you. It's a wonder it wasn't worse. She can swear like a trooper. The men are mad over Ruby. It'd be just like her to fall in love with you for snubbing her."

"I hope she doesn't," replied Neale, constrainedly.

"May I ask—what did you come here for?"

"You mean here to your dance-hall? Why, Hough brought me. I met him. We played cards and—"

"No. I mean what brought you to Benton?"

"I just drifted here. . . . I'm looking for a—a lost friend," said Neale.

"No work? But you're no spiker or capper or boss. I know that sort. And I can spot a gambler a mile. The whole world meets out here in Benton. But not many young men like you wander into my place."

"Like me? How so?"

"The men here are wolves on the scent for flesh; like bandits on the trail of gold. . . . But you—you're like my friend Ancliffe."

"Who is he?" asked Neale, politely.

"*Who* is he? God only knows. But he's an Englishman and a gentleman. It's a pity men like Ancliffe and you drift out here."

She spoke seriously. She had the accent and manner of breeding.

"Why, Miss Stanton?" inquired Neale. He was finding another woman here and it was interesting to him.

"Because it means wasted life. You don't work. You're not crooked. You can't do any good. And only a knife in the back or a bullet from some drunken bully's gun awaits you."

"That isn't a very hopeful outlook, I'll admit," replied Neale, thoughtfully.

At this point Hough returned with a pale, slender man whose clothes and gait were not American. He introduced him as Ancliffe. Neale felt another accession of interest. Benton might be hell, but he was meeting new types of men and women. Ancliffe was fair; he had a handsome face that held a story, and tired blue eyes that looked out upon the world wearily and mildly, without curiosity and without hope. An Englishman of broken fortunes.

"Just arrived, eh?" he said to Neale. "Rather jolly here, don't you think?"

"A fellow's not going to stagnate in Benton," replied Neale.

"Not while he's alive," interposed Stanton.

"Miss Stanton, that idea seems to persist with you—the brevity of life," said Neale, smiling. "What are the average days for a mortal in this bloody Benton?"

"Days! You mean hours. I call the night blessed that some one is not dragged out of my place. And I don't sell drinks. . . . I've saved Ancliffe's life nine times I know of. Either he hasn't any sense or he wants to get killed."

"I assure you it's the former," said the Englishman.

"But, my friends, I'm serious," she returned, earnestly. "This awful place is getting on my nerves. . . . Mr. Neale here, he would have had to face a gun already but for me."

"Miss Stanton, I appreciate your kindness," replied Neale. "But it doesn't follow that if I had to face a gun I'd be sure to go down."

"You can throw a gun?" questioned Hough.

"I had a cowboy gun-thrower for a partner for years, out on the surveying of the road. He's the friend I mentioned."

"Boy, you're courting death!" exclaimed Stanton.

Then the music started up again. Conversation was scarcely worth while during the dancing. Neale watched as before. Twice as he gazed at the whirling couples he caught the eyes of the girl Ruby bent upon him. They were expressive of pique, resentment, curiosity. Neale did not look that way any more. Besides, his attention was drawn elsewhere. Hough yelled in his ear to watch the fun. A fight had started. A strapping fellow wearing a belt containing gun and bowie-knife had jumped upon a table just as the music stopped. He was drunk. He looked like a young workman ambitious to be a desperado.

"Ladies an' gennelmen," he bawled, "I been—requested t' sing."

Yells and hoots answered him. He glared ferociously

around, trying to pick out one of his insulters. Trouble was brewing. Something was thrown at him from behind and it struck him. He wheeled, unsteady upon his feet. Then several men, bareheaded and evidently attendants of the hall, made a rush for him. The table was upset. The would-be singer went down in a heap, and he was pounced upon, handled like a sack, and thrown out. The crowd roared its glee.

"The worst of that is those fellows always come back drunk and ugly," said Stanton. "Then we all begin to run or dodge."

"Your men didn't lose time with that rowdy," remarked Neale.

"I've hired all kinds of men to keep order," she replied. "Laborers, ex-sheriffs, gunmen, bad men. The Irish are the best on the job. But they won't stick. I've got eight men here now, and they are a tough lot. I'm scared to death of them. I believe they rob my guests. But what can I do? Without some aid I couldn't run the place. It'll be the death of me."

Neale did not doubt that. A shadow surely hovered over this strange woman, but he was surprised at the serious-ness with which she spoke. Evidently she tried to preserve order, to avert fights and bloodshed, so that licentiousness could go on unrestrained. Neale believed they must go hand in hand. He did not see how it would be possible for a place like this to last long. It could not. The life of the place brought out the worst in men. It created opportuni-ties. Neale watched them pass, seeing the truth in the red eyes, the heavy lids, the open mouths, the look and gait and gesture. A wild frenzy had fastened upon their minds. He found an added curiosity in studying the faces of An-cliffe and Hough. The Englishman had run his race. Any place would suit him for the end. Neale saw this and mar-veled at the man's ease and grace and amiability. He reminded Neale of Larry Red King—the same cool, easy, careless air. Ancliffe would die game. Hough was not affected by this sort of debauched life any more than he would have been by any other kind. He preyed on men. He looked on with cold, gray, expressionless face. Possibly he, too, would find an end in Benton sooner or later.

These reflections, passing swiftly, made Neale think of himself. What was true for others must be true for him. The presence of any of these persons—of Hough and Ancliffe, of himself, in Beauty Stanton's gaudy resort was sad proof of a disordered life.

Some one touched him, interrupted his thought.

"You've had trouble?" asked Stanton, who had turned from the others.

"Yes," he said.

"Well, we've all had that. . . . You seem young to me."

Hough turned to speak to Stanton. "Ruby's going to make trouble."

"No!" exclaimed the woman, with eyes lighting.

Neale then saw that the girl Ruby, with a short, bold-looking fellow who packed a gun, and several companions of both sexes, had come in from the dance-hall and had taken up a position near him. Stanton went over to them. She drew Ruby aside and talked to her. The girl showed none of the passion that had marked her manner a little while before. Presently Stanton returned.

"Ruby's got over her temper," she said, with evident relief, to Neale. "She asked me to say that she apologized. It's just what I told you. She'll fall madly in love with you for what you did. . . . She's of good family, Neale. She has a sister she talks much of, and a home she could go back to if she wasn't ashamed."

"That so?" replied Neale, thoughtfully. "Let me talk to her."

At a slight sign from Stanton, Ruby joined the group.

"Ruby, you've already introduced yourself to this gentleman, but not so nicely as you might have done," said Beauty.

"I'm sorry," replied Ruby. A certain wistfulness showed in her low tones.

"Maybe I was rude," said Neale. "I didn't intend to be. I couldn't dance with any one here—or anywhere. . . ." Then he spoke to her in a lower tone. "But I'll tell you what I will do. I won a thousand dollars to-night. I'll give you half of it if you'll go home."

The girl shrank as if she had received a stab. Then she stiffened.

"Why don't you go home?" she retorted. "We're all going to hell out here, and the gamest will get there soonest."

She glared at Neale an instant, white-faced and hard, and then, rejoining her companions, she led them away.

Beauty Stanton seemed to have received something of the check that had changed the girl Ruby.

"Gentlemen, you are my only friends in Benton. But these are business hours."

Presently she leaned toward Neale and whispered to him: "Boy, you're courting death. Some one—something has hurt you. But you're young. . . . *Go home!*"

Then she bade him good night and left the group.

He looked on in silence after that. And presently, when Ancliffe departed, he was glad to follow Hough into the street. There the same confusion held. A loud throng hurried by, as if bent on cramming into a few hours the life that would not last long.

Neale was interested to inquire more about Ancliffe. And the gambler replied that the Englishman had come from no one knew where; that he did not go to extremes in drinking or betting; that evidently he had become attached to Beauty Stanton; that surely he must be a ruined man of class who had left all behind him, and had become like so many out there—a leaf in the storm.

"Stanton took to you," went on Hough. "I saw that. . . . And poor Ruby! I'll tell you, Neale, I'm sorry for some of these women."

"Who wouldn't be?"

"Women of this class are strange to you, Neale. But I've mixed with them for years. Of course Benton sets a pace no man ever saw before. Still, even the hardest and vilest of these scullions sometimes shows an amazing streak of good. And women like Ruby and Beauty Stanton, whose early surroundings must have been refined—they are beyond understanding. They will cut your heart out for a slight, and sacrifice their lives for sake of a courteous word. It was your manner that cut Ruby and won Beauty Stanton. They meet with neither coldness nor courtesy out here. It must be bitter as gall for a woman like Stanton to be treated as you treated her—with respect. Yet see how it got her."

"I didn't see anything in particular," replied Neale.

"You were too excited and disgusted with the whole scene," said Hough as they reached the roaring lights of the gambling-hell. "Will you go in and play again? There are always open games."

"No, I guess not—unless you think—"

"Boy, I think nothing except that I liked your company and that I owed you a service. Good night."

Neale walked to his lodgings tired and thoughtful and moody. Behind him the roar lulled and swelled. It was three o'clock in the morning. He wondered when these night-hawks slept. He wondered where Larry was. As for himself, he found slumber not easily gained. Dawn was lighting the east when he at last fell asleep.

CHAPTER XVI

Neale slept until late the next day and awoke with the pang that a new day always gave him now. He arose slowly, gloomily, with the hateful consciousness that he had nothing to do. He had wanted to be alone, and now loneliness was bad for him.

"If I were half a man I'd get out of here, quick!" he muttered, in scorn. And he thought of the broken Englishman, serene and at ease, settled with himself. And he thought of the girl Ruby who had flung the taunt at him. Not for a long time would he forget that. Certainly this abandoned girl was not a coward. She was lost, but she was magnificent.

"I guess I'll leave Benton," he soliloquized. But the place, the wildness, fascinated him. "No! I guess I'll stay."

It angered him that he was ashamed of himself. He was a victim of many moods, and underneath every one of them was the steady ache, the dull pain, the pang in his breast, deep in the bone.

As he left his lodgings he heard the whistle of a train. The scene down the street was similar to the one which had greeted him the day before, only the dust was not blowing so thickly. He went into a hotel for his meal and fared better, watching the hurry and scurry of men. After he had finished he strolled toward the station.

Benton had two trains each day now. This one, just in, was long and loaded to its utmost capacity. Neale noticed an Indian arrow sticking fast over a window of one of the coaches. There were flat cars loaded with sections of houses, and box-cars full of furniture. Benton was growing every day. At least a thousand persons got off that train, adding to the dusty, jostling mêlée.

Suddenly Neale came face to face with Larry King.

"Red!" he yelled, and made at the cowboy.

"I'm shore glad to see you," drawled Larry. "What 'n hell busted loose round heah?"

Neale drew Larry out of the crowd. He carried a small pack done up in a canvas covering.

"Red, your face looks like home to a man in a strange land," declared Neale. "Where are your horses?"

Larry looked less at his ease.

"Wal, I sold them."

"Sold them! Those great horses? Oh, Red, you didn't!"

"Hell! It costs money to ride on this heah U.P.R. thet we built, an' I had no money."

"But what did you sell them for? I—I cared for those horses."

"Will you keep quiet aboot my hosses?"

Neale had never before seen the tinge of gray in that red-bronze face.

"But I told you to straighten up!"

"Wal, who hasn't?" retorted Larry.

"You haven't! Don't lie."

"If you put it thet way, all right. Now what're you-all goin' to do aboot it?"

"I'll lick you good," declared Neale, hotly. He was angry with Larry, but angrier with himself that he had been the cause of the cowboy's loss of work and of his splendid horses.

"Lick me!" ejaculated Larry. "You mean beat me up?"

"Yes. You deserve it."

Larry took him in earnest and seemed very much concerned. Neale could almost have laughed at the cowboy's serious predicament.

"Wal, I reckon I ain't much of a fighter with my fists," said Larry, soberly. "So come an' get it over."

"Oh, damn you, Red! . . . I wouldn't lay a hand on you. And I am sick, I'm so glad to see you! . . . I thought you got here ahead of me."

Neale's voice grew full and trembling.

Larry became confused, his red face grew redder, and the keen blue flash of his eyes softened.

"Wal, I heerd what a tough place this heah Benton was—so I jest come."

Larry ended this speech lamely, but the way he hitched at his belt was conclusive.

"Wal, by Gawd! Look who's heah!" he suddenly exclaimed.

Neale wheeled with a start. He saw a scout, in buckskin, a tall form with the stride of a mountaineer, strangely familiar.

"Slingerland!" he cried.

The trapper bounded at them, his tanned face glowing, his gray eyes glad.

"Boys, it's come at last! I knowed I'd run into you some day," he said, and he gripped them with horny hands.

Neale tried to speak, but a terrible cramp in his throat choked him. He appealed with his hands to Slingerland. The trapper lost his smile and the iron set returned to his features.

Larry choked over his utterance. "Al-lie! What aboot—her?"

"Boys, it's broke me down!" replied Slingerland, hoarsely. "I swear to you I never left Allie alone fer a year—an' then—the fust time—when she made me go—I come back an' finds the cabin burnt. . . . She's gone! Gone! . . . No redskin job. That damned riffraff out of Californy. I tracked 'em. Then a hell of a storm comes up. No tracks left! All's lost! An' I goes back to my traps in the mountains."

"What—became—of—her?" whispered Neale.

Slingerland looked away from him.

"Son! You remember Allie. She'd die, quick! . . . Wouldn't she, Larry?"

"Shore. Thet girl—couldn't—hev lived a day," replied Larry, thickly.

Neale plunged blindly away from his friends. Then the torture in his breast seemed to burst. The sobs came, heavy, racking. He sank upon a box and bowed his head. There Larry and Slingerland found him.

The cowboy looked down with helpless pain. "Aw, pard—don't take it—so hard," he implored.

But he knew and Slingerland knew that sympathy could do no good here. There was no hope, no help. Neale was stricken. They stood there, the elder man looking all the sadness and inevitableness of that wild life, and the younger, the cowboy, slowly changing to iron.

"Slingerland, you-all said some Californy outfit got Allie?" he queried.

"I'm sure an' sartin," replied the trapper. "Them days there wasn't any travelin' west, so early after winter. You recollect them four bandits as rode in on us one day? They was from Californy."

"Wal, I'll be lookin' fer men with thet Californy brand," drawled King, and in his slow, easy, cool speech there was a note deadly and terrible.

Neale slowly ceased his sobbing. "My nerve's gone," he said, shakily.

"No. It jest broke you all up to see Slingerland. An' it shore did me, too," replied Larry.

"It's hard, but—" Slingerland could not finish his thought.

"Slingerland, I'm glad to see you, even if it did cut me," said Neale, more rationally. "I'm surprised, too. Are you here with a load of pelts?"

"No. Boys, I hed to give up trappin'. I couldn't stand the loneliness—after—after . . . An' now I'm killin' buffalo meat for the soldiers an' the construction gangs. Jest got in on thet train with a car-load of fresh meat."

"Buffalo meat," echoed Neale. His mind wandered.

"Son, how's your work goin'?"

Neale shook his head.

The cowboy, answering for him, said, "We kind of chucked the work, Slingerland."

"What? Are you hyar in Benton, doin' nothin'?"

"Shore. Thet's the size of it."

The trapper made a vehement gesture of disapproval and he bent a scrutinizing gaze upon Neale.

"Son, you've not gone an'—an'—"

"Yes," replied Neale, throwing out his hands. "I quit. I couldn't work. I *can't* work. I *can't* rest or stand still!"

A spasm of immense regret contracted the trapper's face. And Larry King, looking away over the sordid, dusty passing throng, cursed under his breath. Neale was the first to recover his composure.

"Let's say no more. What's done is done," he said. "Suppose you take us on one of your buffalo-hunts."

Slingerland grasped at straws. "Wal, now, thet ain't a bad idee. I can use you," he replied, eagerly. "But it's hard an' dangerous work. We git chased by redskins often. An' you'd hev to ride. I reckon, Neale, you're good enough on a hoss. But our cowboy friend hyar, he can't ride, as I recollect your old argyments."

"My job was hosses," drawled Larry.

"An' besides, you've got to shoot straight, which Reddy hasn't hed experience of," went on Slingerland, with a broader smile.

"I seen you was packin' a Winchester all shiny an' new," replied Larry. "Shore I'm in fer anythin' with ridin' an' shootin'."

"You'll both go, then?"

Neale and Larry accepted the proposition then and there.

"You'll need to buy rifles an' shells, thet's all," said Slingerland. "I've hosses an' outfit over at the workcamp, an' I've been huntin' east of thar. Come on, we'll go to a store. Thet train's goin' back soon."

"Wal, I come in on thet train an' now I'm leavin' on it," drawled Larry. "Shore is funny. Without even lookin' over this heah Benton."

On the ride eastward Slingerland inquired if Neale and Larry had ever gone back to the scene of the massacre of the caravan where Horn had buried his gold.

Neale had absolutely forgotten the buried gold. Probably when he and Larry had scoured the wild hills for trace of Allie they had passed down the valley where the treasure had been hidden. Slingerland gave the same reason for his oversight. They talked about the gold and planned, when the railroad reached the foot-hills, to go after it.

Both Indians and buffalo were sighted from the train before the trio got to the next camp.

"I reckon I don't like thet," declared Slingerland. "I was friendly with the Sioux. But now thet I've come down hyar to kill off their buffalo fer the whites they're ag'in' me. I know thet. An' I allus regarded them buffalo as Injun property. If it wasn't thet I seen this railroad means the end of the buffalo, an' the Indians, too, I'd never hev done it. Thet I'll swar."

It was night when they reached their destination. How quiet and dark after Benton! Neale was glad to get there. He wondered if he could conquer his unrest. Would he go on wandering again? He doubted himself and dismissed the thought. Perhaps the companionship of his old friends and the anticipation of action would effect a change in him.

Neale and Larry spent the night in Slingerland's tent. Next morning the trapper was ready with horses at an early hour, but, owing to the presence of Sioux in the vicinity, it was thought best to wait for the work-train and ride out on the plains under its escort.

By and by the train, with its few cars and half a hundred workmen, was ready, and the trapper and his comrades rode out alongside. Some few miles from camp the train halted at a place where stone-work and filling awaited the laborers. Neale was again interested, in spite of himself. Yet his love for that railroad was quite as hopeless as other things in his life.

These laborers were picked men, all soldiers, and many Irish; they stacked their guns before taking up shovels and bars.

"Dom me if it ain't me ould fri'nd Neale!" exclaimed a familiar voice.

And there stood Casey, with the same old grin, the same old black pipe.

Neale's first feeling of pleasure at seeing the old flagman was counteracted by one of dismay at the possibility of coming in contact with old acquaintances. It would hurt him to meet General Lodge or any of the engineers who had predicted a future for him.

Shane and McDermott were also in this gang, and they slouched forward.

"It's thot gun-throwin' cowboy as wuz onct goin' to kill Casey!" exclaimed McDermott, at sight of Larry.

Neale, during the few moments of reunion with his old comrades of the survey, received a melancholy insight into himself and a clearer view of them. The great railroad had gone on, growing, making men change. He had been passed by. He was no longer a factor. Along with many, many other men, he had retrograded. The splendid spirit of the work had not gone from him, but it had ceased to govern his actions. He had ceased to grow. But these uncouth Irishmen, they had changed. In many ways they were the same slow, loquacious, quarreling trio as before, but they showed the effect of toil, of fight, of growth under the great movement and its spirit—the thing which great minds had embodied; and these laborers were no longer ordinary men. Something shone out of them. Neale saw it. He felt an inexplicable littleness in their presence. They had gone on; he had been left. They would toil and fight until they filled nameless graves. He, too, would find a nameless grave, he thought, but he would not lie in it as one of these. The moment was poignant for Neale, exceedingly bitter, and revealing.

Slingerland was not long in sighting buffalo. After making a careful survey of the rolling country for lurking Indians he rode out with Neale, Larry, and two other men—Brush and an Irishman named Pat—who were to skin the buffalo the hunters killed, and help load the meat into wagons which would follow.

"It ain't no trick to kill buffalo," Slingerland was saying to his friends. "But I don't want old bulls an' old cows killed. An' when you're ridin' fast an' the herd is bunched it's hard to tell the difference. You boys stick close to me an' watch me first. An' keep one eye peeled fer Injuns!"

Slingerland approached the herd without alarming it, until some little red calves on the outskirts of the herd became frightened. Then the herd lumbered off, raising a cloud of dust. The roar of hoofs was thunderous.

"Ride!" yelled Slingerland.

Not the least interesting sight to Neale was Larry riding away from them. He was whacking the buffalo on the rumps with his bare hand before Slingerland and Neale got near enough to shoot.

At the trapper's first shot the herd stampeded. Thereafter it took fine riding to keep up, to choose the level ground, and to follow Slingerland's orders. Neale got up in the thick of the rolling din and dust. The pursuit liberated something fierce within him which gave him a measure of freedom from his constant pain. All before spread the great bobbing herd. The wind whistled, the dust choked him, the gravel stung his face, the strong, even action of his horse was exhilarating. He lost track of Larry, but he stayed close to Slingerland. The trapper kept shooting at intervals. Neale saw the puffs of smoke, but in the thundering din he could not hear a report. It seemed impossible for him to select the kind of buffalo Slingerland wanted shot. Neale could not tell one from the other. He rode right upon their flying heels. Unable, finally, to restrain himself from shooting, he let drive and saw a beast drop and roll over. Neale rode on.

Presently out of a lane in the dust he thought he saw Slingerland pass. He reined toward the side. Larry was riding furiously at him, and Slingerland's horse was stretched out, heading straight away. The trapper madly waved his arms. Neale spurred toward them. Something was amiss. Larry's face flashed in the sun. He whirled his horse to take Neale's course and then he pointed.

Neale thrilled as he looked. A few hundred rods in the rear rode a band of Sioux, coming swiftly. A cloud of dust rose behind them. They had, no doubt, been hiding in the vicinity of the grazing buffalo, lying in wait.

As Neale closed in on Larry he saw the cowboy's keen glance measuring distance and speed.

"We shore got to ride!" was what Larry apparently yelled, though the sound of words drifted as a faint whisper to Neale. But the roar of buffalo hoofs was rapidly diminishing.

Then Neale realized what it meant to keep close to the cowboy. Every moment Larry turned round both to watch the Indians and to have a glance at his comrade. They began to gain on Slingerland. Brush was riding for dear life off to the right, and the Irishman, Pat, still farther in that direction, was in the most perilous situation of all. Already the white skipping streaks of dust from bullets whipped up in front of him. The next time Neale looked back the Sioux had split up; some were riding hard after Brush and Pat; the majority were pursuing the other three hunters, cutting the while a little to the right, for Slingerland was working round toward the work-train. Neale saw the smoke of the engine and then the train. It seemed far away. And he was sure the Indians were gaining. What incomparable riders! They looked half naked, dark, gleaming, low over their mustangs, feathers and trappings flying in the wind—a wild and panic-provoking sight.

"Don't ride so close!" yelled Larry. "They're spreadin'!"

Neale gathered that the Indians were riding farther apart because they soon expected to be in range of bullets; and Larry wanted Neale to ride farther from him for the identical reason.

Neale saw the first white puff of smoke from a rifle of the leader. The bullet hit far behind. More shots kept raising the dust, the last time still a few yards short.

"Gawd! Look!" yelled Larry. "The devils hit Pat's hoss!"

Neale saw the Irishman go down with his horse, plunge in the dust, and then roll over and lie still.

"They got him!" he yelled at Larry.

"Ride thet hoss!" came back grimly and appealingly from the cowboy.

Neale rode as he had never before ridden. Fortunately his horse was fresh and fast, and that balanced the driving the cowboy was giving his mount. For a long distance they held their own with the Sioux. They had now gained a straightaway course for the work-train, so that with the Sioux behind they had only to hold out for a few miles. Brush appeared as well off as they were. Slingerland led by perhaps a hundred feet, far over to the left, and he was wholly out of range.

It took a very short time at that pace to cover a couple of miles. And then the Indians began to creep up closer and closer. Again they were shooting. Neale heard the reports and each one made him flinch in expectation of feeling the burn of a bullet. Brush was now turning to fire his rifle.

Neale bethought himself of his own Winchester, which he was carrying in his hand. Dropping the rein over the horn of his saddle, he turned half round. How close, how red, how fierce these Sioux were! He felt his hair rise stiff under his hat. And at the same instant a hot wrath rushed over him, madness to fight, to give back blow for blow. Just then several of the Indians fired. He heard the sharp cracks, then the spats of bullets striking the ground; he saw the little streaks of dust in front of him. Then the whistle of lead. That made him shoot in return. His horse lunged forward, almost throwing him, and ran the faster for his fright. Neale heard Larry begin to shoot. It became a running duel now, with the Indians scattering wide, riding low, yelling like demons, and keeping up a continuous volley. They were well armed with white men's guns. Neale worked the lever of his rifle while he looked ahead for an instant to see where his horse was running; then he wheeled quickly and took a snap shot at the nearest Indian, no more than three hundred yards distant now. He saw where his bullet, going wide, struck up the dust. It was desperately hard to shoot from the back of a scared horse. Neale did not notice that Larry's shots were any more effective than his own. He grew certain that the Sioux were gaining faster now. But the work-train was not far away. He saw the workmen on top of the cars waving their arms. Rougher ground, though, on this last stretch.

Larry was drawing ahead. He had used all the shells in his rifle and now with hand and spur was goading his horse.

Suddenly Neale heard the soft thud of lead striking flesh. His horse leaped with a piercing snort of terror, and Neale thought he was going down. But he recovered, and went plunging on, still swift and game, though with uneven gait. Larry yelled. His red face flashed back over his shoulder. He saw something was wrong with Neale's horse and he pulled his own.

"Save your own life!" yelled Neale, fiercely. It enraged him to see the cowboy holding back to let him come up. But he could not prevent it.

"He's hit!" shouted Larry.

"Yes, but not badly," shouted Neale, in reply. "Spread out!"

The cowboy never swerved a foot. He watched Neale's horse with keen, sure eyes.

"He's breakin'! Mebbe he can't last!"

Bullets whistled all around Neale now. He heard them strike the stones on the ground and sing away; he saw them streak through the scant grass; he felt the tug at his shoulder where one cut through his coat, stinging the skin. That touch, light as it was, drove the panic out of him. The strange darkness before his eyes, hard to see through, passed away. He wheeled to shoot again, and with deliberation he aimed as best he could. Yet he might as well have tried to hit flying birds. He emptied the Winchester.

Then, hunching low in the saddle, Neale hung on. Slingerland was close to the train; Brush on his side appeared to be about out of danger; the pursuit had narrowed down to Neale and Larry. The anger and the grimness faded from Neale. He did not want to go plunging down in front of those lean wild mustangs, to be ridden over and trampled and mutilated. The thought sickened him. The roar of pursuing hoofs grew distinct, but Neale did not look back.

Another roar broke on his ear—the clamor of the Irish soldier-laborers as they yelled and fired.

"Pull him! Pull him!" came the piercing cry from Larry.

Neale was about to ride his frantic horse straight into the work-train. Desperately he hauled the horse up and leaped off. Larry was down, waiting, and his mount went plunging away. Bullets were pattering against the sides of the cars, from which puffed streaks of flame and smoke.

"Up wid yez, lads!" sang out a cheery voice. Casey's grin and black pipe appeared over the rim of the car, and his big hands reached down.

One quick and straining effort and Neale was up, over the side, to fall on the floor in a pile of sand and gravel. All whirled dim round him for a second. His heart labored. He was wet and hot and shaking.

"Shure yez ain't hit now!" exclaimed Casey.

Larry's nervous hands began to slide and press over Neale's quivering body.

"No—I'm—all—safe!" panted Neale.

The engine whistled shrilly, as if in defiance of the Indians, and with a jerk and rattle the train started.

Neale recovered to find himself in a novel and thrilling

situation. The car was of a gondola type, being merely a flat-car, with sides about four feet high, made of such thick oak planking that bullets did not penetrate it. Besides himself and Larry there were half a dozen soldiers, all kneeling at little port-holes. Neale peeped over the rim. In a long thinned-out line the Sioux were circling round the train, hiding on the off sides of their mustangs, and shooting from these difficult positions. They were going at full speed, working in closer. A bullet, striking the rim of the car and showering splinters in Neale's face, attested to the fact that the Sioux were still to be feared, even from a moving fort. Neale dropped back and, reloading his rifle, found a hole from which to shoot. He emptied his magazine before he realized it. But what with his trembling hands, the jerking of the train, and the swift motion of the Indians, he did not do any harm to the foe.

Suddenly, with a jolt, the train halted.

"Blocked ag'in, b'gorfa," said Casey, calmly. "Me pipe's out. Sandy, gimme a motch."

The engine whistled two shrill blasts.

"What's that for?" asked Neale, quickly.

"Them's for the men in the foist car to pile over the engine an' remove obstruchtions from the track," replied Casey.

Neele dared to risk a peep over the top of the car. The Sioux were circling closer to the front of the train. All along the half-dozen cars ahead of Neale puffs of smoke and jets of flame shot out. Heavy volleys were being fired. The attack of the savages seemed to be concentrating forward, evidently to derail the engine or kill the engineer.

Casey pulled Neale down. "Risky fer yez," he said. "Use a port-hole an' foight."

"My shells are gone," replied Neale.

He lay well down in the car then, and listened to the uproar, and watched the Irish trio. When the volleys and the fiendish yells mingled he could not hear anything else. There were intervals, however, when the uproar lulled for a moment.

Casey got his black pipe well lit, puffed a cloud of smoke, and picked up his rifle.

"Drill, ye terriers, drill!" he sang, and shoved his weapon through a port-hole. He squinted over the breech.

"Mac, it's the same bunch as attackted us day before yisteddy," he observed.

"It shure ain't," replied McDermott. "There's a million of thim to-day."

He aimed his rifle as if following a moving object, and fired.

"Mac, you git excited in a foight. Now I niver do. An' I've seen thot pinto hoss an' thot dom' redskin a lot of times. I'll kill him yit."

Casey kept squinting and aiming, and then, just as he pressed the trigger, the train started with a sudden lurch.

"Sp'iled me aim! Thot engineer's savin' of the Sooz tribe! . . . Drill, ye terriers, drill! Drill, ye terriers, drill! . . . Shane, I don't hear yez shootin'."

"How'n hell can I shoot whin me eye is full of blood?" demanded Shane.

Neale then saw blood on Shane's face. He crawled quietly to the Irishman.

"Man, are you shot? Let me see."

"Jist a bullet hit me, loike," replied Shane.

Neale found that a bullet, perhaps glancing from the wood, had cut a gash over Shane's eye, from which the blood poured. Shane's hands and face and shirt were crimson. Neale bound a scarf tightly over the wound.

"Let me take the rifle now," he said.

"Thanks, lad. I ain't hurted. An' hev Casey make me loife miserable foriver? Not much. He's a harrd mon, thot Casey."

Shane crouched back to his port-hole, with his bloody bandaged face and his bloody hands. And just then the train stopped with a rattling crash.

"Whin we git beyond thim ties as was scattered along here mebbe we'll go on in," remarked McDermott.

"Mac, yez looks on the gloomy side," replied Casey. Then quickly he aimed the shot. "I loike it better whin we ain't movin'," he soliloquized, with satisfaction. "Thot redskin won't niver scalp a soldier of the U.P.R. . . . Drill, ye terriers! Drill, ye terriers, drill!"

The engine whistle shrieked out and once more the din of conflict headed to the front. Neale lay there, seeing the reality of what he had so often dreamed. These old soldiers, these toilers with rail and sledge and shovel, these Irishmen with the rifles, they were the builders of the great U.P.R. Glory might never be theirs, but they were the battle-scarred heroes. They were as used to fighting as to working. They dropped their sledges or shovels to run for their guns.

Again the train started up and had scarcely gotten under way when with jerk and bump it stopped once more. The conflict grew fiercer as the Indians became more desperate. But evidently they were kept from closing in, for during the thick of the heaviest volleying the engine again began to puff and the wheels to grind. Slowly the train moved on. Like hail the bullets pattered against the car. Smoke drifted away on the wind.

Neale lay there, watching these cool men who fought off the savages. No doubt Casey and Shane and McDermott were merely three of many thousands engaged in building and defending the U.P.R. This trio liked the fighting, perhaps better than the toiling. Casey puffed his old black pipe, grinned and aimed, shot and reloaded, sang his quaint song, and joked with his comrades, all in the same cool, quiet way. If he knew that the shadow of death hung over the train, he did not show it. He was not a thinker. Casey was a man of action. Only once he yelled, and that was when he killed the Indian on the pinto mustang.

Shane grew less loquacious and he dropped and fumbled over his rifle, but he kept on shooting. Neale saw him feel the hot muzzle of his gun and shake his bandaged head. The blood trickled down his cheek.

McDermott plied his weapon, and ever and anon he would utter some pessimistic word, or presage dire disaster, or remind Casey that his scalp was destined to dry in a Sioux's lodge, or call on Shane to hit something to save his life, or declare the engine was off the track. He rambled on. But it was all talk. The man had gray hairs and he was a born fighter.

This time the train gained more headway, and evidently had passed the point where the Indians could find obstructions to place on the track. Neale saw through a port-hole that the Sioux were dropping back from the front of the train and were no longer circling. Their firing had become desultory. Medicine Bow was in sight. The engine gathered headway.

"We'll git the rest of the day off," remarked Casey, complacently. "Shane, yez are dom' quiet betoimes. An' Mac, I shure showed yez up to-day."

"Ye *did* not," retorted McDermott. "I kilt jist twinty-nine Sooz!"

"Jist thorty wus moine. An', Mac, as they wus only about fifthy of thim, yez must be a liar."

The train drew on toward Medicine Bow. Firing ceased. Neale stood up to see the Sioux riding away. Their ranks did not seem noticeably depleted.

"Drill, ye terriers, drill!" sang Casey, as he wiped his sweaty and begrimed rifle. "Mac, how many Sooz did Shane kill?"

"B'gorra, he ain't said yit," replied McDermott. "Say, Shane. . . . *Casey!*"

Neale whirled at the sharp change of tone.

Shane lay face down on the floor of the car, his bloody hands gripping his rifle. His position was inert, singularly expressive.

Neale strode toward him. But Casey reached him first. He laid a hesitating hand on Shane's shoulder.

"Shane, old mon!" he said, but the cheer was not in his voice.

Casey dropped his pipe! Then he turned his comrade over. Shane had done his best and his last for the U.P.R.

CHAPTER XVII

Neale and Larry and Slingerland planned to go into the hills late in the fall, visit Slingerland's old camp, and then try to locate the gold buried by Horn. For the present Larry meant to return to Benton, and Neale, though vacillating as to his own movements, decided to keep an eye on the cowboy.

The trapper's last words to Neale were interesting. "Son," he said, "there's a feller hyar in Medicine Bow who says as how he thought your pard Larry was a bad cow-puncher from the Pan Handle of Texas."

"Bad?" queried Neale.

"Wal, he meant a gun-throwin' bad man, I take it."

"Don't let Reddy overhear you say it," replied Neale, "and advise your informant to be careful. I've always had a hunch that Reddy was really somebody."

"Benton'll work on the cowboy," continued Slingerland, earnestly. "An', son, I ain't so all-fired sure of you."

"I'll take what comes," returned Neale, shortly. "Good-by, old friend. And if you can use us for buffalo-hunting without the 'dom' Sooz,' as Casey says, why, we'll come."

After Slingerland departed Neale carried with him a memory of the trapper's reluctant and wistful good-by. It made Neale think—where were he and Larry going? Friendships in this wild West were stronger ties than he had known elsewhere.

The train arrived at Benton after dark. And the darkness seemed a windy gulf out of which roared yellow lights and excited men. The tents, with the dim lights through the canvas, gleamed pale and obscure, like so much of the life they hid. The throngs hurried, the dust blew, the band played, the barkers clamored for their trade.

Neale found the more pretentious hotels overcrowded, and he was compelled to go to his former lodgings, where he and Larry were accommodated.

"Now we're here, what'll we do?" queried Neale, more to himself. He felt as if driven. And the mood he hated and feared was impinging upon his mind.

"Shore we'll eat," replied Larry.

"Then what?"

"Wal, I reckon we'll see what's goin' on in this heah Benton."

As a matter of fact, Neale reflected, there was nothing to do that he wanted to do.

"You-all air gettin' the blues," said Larry, with solicitude.

"Red, I'm never free of them."

Larry put his hands on Neale's shoulder. Demonstration of this kind was rare in the cowboy.

"Pard, are we goin' to see this heah Benton, an' then brace, an' go back to work?"

"No. I can't hold a job," replied Neale, bitterly.

"You're showin' a yellow streak? You're done, as you told Slingerland? Nothin' ain't no good? . . . Life's over, fer all thet's sweet an' right? Is thet your stand?"

"Yes, it must be, Reddy," said Neale, with scorn of himself. "But you—it needn't apply to you."

"I reckon I'm sorry," rejoined Larry, ignoring Neale's

last words. "I always hoped you'd get over Allie's loss. . . . You had so much to live fer."

"Reddy, I wish the bullet that hit Shane to-day had hit me instead. . . . You needn't look like that. I mean it. To-day when the Sioux chased us my hair went stiff and my heart was in my mouth. I ran for my life as if I loved it. But that was my miserable cowardice. . . . I'm sick of the game."

"Are you in daid earnest?" asked Larry, huskily.

Neale nodded gloomily. He did not even regret the effect of his speech upon the cowboy. He divined that somehow the moment was critical and fateful for Larry, but he did not care. The black spell was enfolding him. All seemed hard, cold, monstrous within his breast. He could not love anything. He was lost. He realized the magnificent loyalty of this simple Texan, who was his true friend.

"Reddy, for God's sake don't make me ashamed to look you in the eyes," appealed Neale. "I want to go on. *You* know!"

"Wal, I reckon there ain't anythin' to hold me now," drawled Larry. He had changed as he spoke. He had aged. The dry humor of the cowboy, the amiable ease, were wanting.

"Oh, forgive my utter selfishness!" burst out Neale. "I'm not the man I was. But don't think I don't love you."

They went out together, and the hum of riotous Benton called them; the lights beckoned and the melancholy night engulfed them.

Next morning late, on the way to breakfast, Neale encountered a young man whose rough, bronzed face somehow seemed familiar.

At sight of Neale this young fellow brightened and he lunged forward.

"Neale! Lookin' for you was like huntin' for a needle in a haystack."

Neale could not place him, and he did not try hard for recognition, for that surely would recall his former relations to the railroad.

"I don't remember you," replied Neale.

"I'll bet Larry does," said the stranger, with a grin at the cowboy.

"Shore. Your name's Campbell an' you was a lineman for Baxter," returned Larry.

"Right you are," said Campbell, offering his hand to Neale, and then to Larry. He appeared both glad and excited.

"I guess I recall you now," said Neale, thoughtfully. "You said—you were hunting me?"

"Well, I should smile!" returned Campbell, and handed Neale a letter.

Neale tore it open and hastily perused its contents. It was a brief, urgent request from Baxter that Neale should return to work. The words, almost like an order, made Neale's heart swell for a moment. He stood there staring at the paper. Larry read the letter over his shoulder.

"Pard, shore I was expectin' jest thet there, an' I say go!" exclaimed Larry.

Neale slowly shook his head.

Campbell made a quick, nervous movement. "Neale, I was to say—tell— There's more 'n your old job waitin' for you."

"What do you mean?" queried Neale.

"That's all, except the corps have struck a snag out here west of Benton. It's a bad place. You an' Henney were west in the hills when this survey was made. It's a deep wash— bad grade an' curves. The gang's stuck. An' Baxter swore, 'We've got to have Neale back on the job!' "

"Where's Henney?" asked Neale, rather thickly. Campbell's words affected him powerfully.

"Henney had to go to Omaha. Boone is sick at Fort Fetterman. Baxter has only a new green hand out there, an' they've sure struck a snag."

"That's too bad," replied Neale, still thoughtfully. "Is—the chief—is General Lodge there?"

"Yes. There's a trooper camp. Colonel Dillon an' some of the officers have their wives out on a little visit to see the work. They couldn't stand Benton."

"Well—you thank Baxter and tell him I'm sorry I must refuse," said Neale.

"You won't come!" ejaculated Campbell.

Neale shook his head. Larry reached out with big, eager hand.

"See heah, pard, I reckon you will go."

Campbell acted strangely, as if he wanted to say more, but did not have authority to do so. He looked dismayed. Then he said: "All right, Neale. I'll take your message. But you can expect me back."

And he went on his way.

"Neale, shore there's somethin' in the wind," said Larry. "Wal, it jest tickles me. They can't build the railroad without you."

"Would you go back to work?" queried Neale.

"Shore I would if they'd have me. But I reckon thet little run-in of mine with Smith has made bad feelin'. An' come to think of thet, if I did go back I'd only have to fight some of Smith's friends. An' I reckon I'd better not go. It'd only make trouble for you."

"Me! . . . You heard me refuse."

"Shore I heerd you," drawled Larry, softly, "but you're goin' back if I have to hawg-tie you an' pack you out there on a hoss."

Neale said no more. If he had said another word he would have betrayed himself to his friend. He yearned for his old work. To think that the engineer corps needed him filled him with joy. But at the same time he knew what an effort it would take to apply himself to any task. He hated to attempt it. He doubted himself. He was morbid. All that day he wandered around at Larry's heels, half oblivious of what was going on. After dark he slipped away from his friend to be alone. And being alone in the dark quietness brought home to him the truth of a strange, strong growth, out of the depths of him, that was going to overcome his morbid craving to be idle, to drift, to waste his life on a haunting memory.

He could not sleep that night, and so was awake when Larry lounged in, slow and heavy. The cowboy was half-drunk. Neale took him to task, and they quarreled. Finally Larry grew silent and fell asleep. After that Neale likewise dropped into slumber.

In the morning Larry was again his old, cool, easy, reckless self, and had apparently forgotten Neale's sharp words. Neale, however, felt a change in himself. This was the first morning for a long time that he had not hated the coming of daylight.

When he and Larry went out the sun was high. For Neale there seemed something more than sunshine in the air. At sight of Campbell, waiting in the same place in which they had encountered him yesterday, Neale's pulses quickened.

Campbell greeted them with a bright smile. "I'm back," he said.

"So I see," replied Neale, constrainedly.

"I've a message for you from the chief," announced Campbell.

"The chief!" exclaimed Neale.

Larry edged closer to them, with the characteristic hitch at his belt, and his eyes flashed.

"He asks as a personal favor that you come out to see him," replied Campbell.

Neale flushed. "General Lodge asks that!" he echoed. There was a slow heat stirring all through him.

"Yes. Will you go?"

"I—I guess I'll have to," replied Neale. He did not feel that he was deciding. He had to go. But this did not prove that he must take up his old work.

Larry swung his hand on Neale's shoulder, almost staggering him. The cowboy beamed.

"Go in to breakfast," he said. "Order for me, too. I'll be back."

"You want to hurry," rejoined Campbell. "We've only a half-hour to eat an' catch the work-train."

Larry strode back toward the lodging-house. And it was Campbell who led Neale into the restaurant and ordered the meal. Neale's mind was not in a whirl, nor dazed, but he did not get much further in thought than the remarkable circumstance of General Lodge sending for him personally. Meanwhile Campbell rapidly talked about masonry, road-beds, washouts, and other things that Neale heard but did not clearly understand. Then Larry returned. He carried Neale's bag, which he deposited carefully on the bench.

"I reckon you might as well take it along," he drawled.

Neale felt himself being forced along an unknown path.

They indulged in little further conversation while hurriedly eating breakfast. That finished, they sallied forth toward the station. Campbell clambered aboard the work-train.

"Come on, Larry," he said.

And Neale joined in the request. "Yes, come," he said.

"Wal, seein' as how I want you-all to get on an' the railroad built, I reckon I'd better not go," drawled Larry. His blue eyes shone warm upon his friend.

"Larry, I'll be back in a day or so," said Neale.

"Aw, now, pard, you stay. Go back on the job an' stick," appealed the cowboy.

"No. I quit and I'll stay quit. I might help out—for a day—just as a favor. But—" Neale shook his head.

"I reckon, if you care anythin' aboot me, you'll shore stick."

"Larry, you'll go to the bad if I leave you here alone," protested Neale.

"Wal, if you stay we'll both go," replied Larry, sharply. He had changed subtly. "It's in me to go to hell—I reckon I've gone—but that ain't so for you."

"Two's company," said Neale, with an attempt at lightness. But it was a pretense. Larry worried him.

"Listen. If you go back on the job—then it'll be all right for you to run in heah to see me once in a while. But if you throw up this chance I'll—"

Larry paused. His ruddy tan had faded slightly.

Neale eyed him, aware of a hard and tense contraction of the cowboy's throat.

"Well, what'll you do?" queried Neale, shortly.

Larry threw back his head, and the subtle, fierce tensity seemed to leave him.

"Wal, the day you come back I'll clean out Stanton's place—jest to start entertainin' you," he replied, with his slow drawl as marked as ever it was.

A stir of anger in Neale's breast subsided with the big, warm realization of this wild cowboy's love for him and the melancholy certainty that Larry would do exactly as he threatened.

"Suppose I come back and beat you all up?" suggested Neale.

"Wal, thet won't make a dam' bit difference," replied Larry, seriously.

Whereupon Neale soberly bade his friend good-by and boarded the train.

The ride appeared slow and long, dragged out by innumerable stops. All along the line laborers awaited the train to unload supplies. At the end of the line there was a congestion Neale had not observed before in all the work. Freight-cars, loaded with stone and iron beams and girders for bridge-work, piles of ties and piles of rails, and gangs of idle men attested to the delay caused by an obstacle to progress. The sight aggressively stimulated Neale. He felt very curious to learn the cause of the setback, and his old scorn of difficulties flashed up.

The camp Neale's guide led him to was back some distance from the construction work. It stood in a little valley through which ran a stream. There was one large building, low and flat, made of boards and canvas, adjoining a substantial old log cabin; and clustered around, though not close together, were a considerable number of tents. Troopers were in evidence, some on duty and many idle. In the background, the slopes of the valley were dark green with pine and cedar.

At the open door of the building Neale met Baxter face to face, and that worthy's greeting left Neale breathless and aghast, yet thrilling with sheer gladness.

"What're you up against?" asked Neale.

"The boss'll talk to you. Get in there!" Baxter replied, and pushed Neale inside. It was a big room, full of smoke, noise, men, tables, papers. There were guns stacked under port-holes. Some one spoke to Neale, but he did not see who it was. All the faces he saw so swiftly appeared vague, yet curious and interested. Then Baxter halted him at a table. Once again Neale faced his chief. Baxter announced something. Neale did not hear the words plainly.

General Lodge looked older, sterner, more worn. He stood up.

"Hello, Neale!" he said, offering his hand, and the flash of a smile went over his grim face.

"Come in here," continued the chief, and he led Neale into another room, of different aspect. It was small; the walls were of logs; new boards had been recently put in the floor; new windows had been cut; and it contained Indian blankets, chairs, a couch.

Here General Lodge bent a stern and piercing gaze upon his former lieutenant.

"Neale, you failed me when you quit your job," he said. "You were my right-hand man. You quit me in my hour of need."

"General, I—I was furious at that rotten commissioner deal," replied Neale, choking. What he had done now seemed an offense to his chief. "My work was ordered done over!"

"Neale, that was nothing to what I've endured. You should have grit your teeth—and gone on. That five miles of reconstruction was nothing—nothing."

In his chief's inflexible voice, in the worn, shadowed face, Neale saw the great burden, and somehow he was reminded of Lincoln, and a passion of remorse seized him. Why had he not been faithful to this steadfast man who had needed him!

"It seemed—so much to me," faltered Neale.

"Why did you not look at that as you have looked at so many physical difficulties—the running of a survey, for instance?"

"I—I guess I have a yellow streak."

"Why didn't you come to me?" went on the chief. Evidently he had been disappointed in Neale.

"I might have come—only Larry, my friend—he got into it, and I was afraid he'd kill somebody," replied Neale.

"That cowboy—he was a great fellow, but gone wrong. He shot one of the bosses—Smith."

"Yes, I know. Did—did Smith die?"

"No, but he'll never be any more good for the U.P.R., that's certain. . . . Where is your friend now?"

"I left him in Benton."

"Benton!" exclaimed the chief, bitterly. "I am responsible for Benton. This great work of my life is a hell on wheels, moving on and on. . . . Your cowboy friend has no doubt found his place—and his match—in Benton."

"Larry has broken loose from me—from any last restraint."

"Neale, what have you been doing?"

And at that Neale dropped his head.

"Idling in the camps—drifting from one place to the next—drinking, gambling, eh?"

"I'm ashamed to say, sir, that of late I have been doing just those things," replied Neale, and he raised his gaze to his chief's.

"But you haven't been associating with those camp women!" exclaimed General Lodge, with his piercing eyes dark on Neale.

"No!" cried Neale. The speech had hurt him.

"I'm glad to hear that—gladder than you can guess. I was afraid— But no matter. . . . What you did do is bad enough. You ought to be ashamed. A young man with your intelligence, your nerve, your gifts! I have not had a single man whose chances compared with yours. If you had stuck you'd be at the head of my engineer corps right now. Baxter is played out. Boone is ill. Henney had to take charge of the shops in Omaha. . . . And you, with fortune

and fame awaiting you, throw up your job to become a
bum, . . . to drink and gamble away your life in these rotten camps!"

General Lodge's scorn flayed Neale.

"Sir, you may not know I—I lost some one—very dear
to me. After that I didn't seem to care." Neale turned to
the window. He was ashamed of what blurred his eyes. "If
it hadn't been for that—I'd never have failed you."

The chief strode to Neale and put a hand on his shoulder. "Son, I believe you. Maybe I've been a little hard. Let's
forget it." His tone softened and there was a close pressure
of his hand. "The thing is now—will you come back on
the job?"

"Baxter's note—Campbell said they'd struck a snag
here. You mean help them get by that?"

"Snag! I guess it is a snag. It bids fair to make all our
labor and millions of dollars—wasted. . . . But I'm not asking you to come back just to help us over this snag. I mean
will you come back for good—and stick?"

Neale was lifted out of the gloom into which memory
had plunged him. He turned to his chief and found him
another person. There was a light on his face and eagerness on his lips, and the keen, stern eyes were soft.

"Son, will you come back—stand by me till the finish?"
repeated General Lodge, his voice deep and full. There
was more here than just the relation of employer to his lieutenant.

"Yes, sir, I'll come back," replied Neale, in low voice.

Their hands met.

"Good!" exclaimed the chief.

Then he deliberately took out his watch and studied it.
His hand trembled slightly. He did not raise his eyes again
to Neale's face.

"I'll call you—later," he said. "You stay here. I'll send
some one in."

With that he went out.

Neale remained standing, his eyes fixed on the gray-green slope, seen through the window. He seemed a trifle unsteady on his feet, and he braced himself with a knee against the couch. His restraint, under extreme agitation, began to relax. A flooding splendid thought filled his mind—his chief had called him back to the great work.

Presently the door behind him opened and closed very softly. Then he heard a low, quick gasp. Some one had entered. Suddenly the room seemed strange, full, charged with terrible portent. And he turned as if a giant hand had heavily swung him around.

It was not light at the other end of the room, yet he saw a slight figure of a girl backed against the door. Her outline was familiar. Haunting ghost of his dreams! Bewildered and speechless, he stared, trembling all over. The figure moved, swayed. A faint, sweet voice called, piercing his heart like a keen blade. All of a sudden he had gone mad, he thought; this return to his old work had disordered his mind. The tremor of his body succeeded to a dizziness; his breast seemed about to burst.

"Neale!" called the sweet voice. She was coming toward him swiftly. *"It's Allie—alive and well!"*

Neale felt lifted, as if by invisible wings. His limbs were useless—had lost strength and feeling. The room whirled around him, and in that whirl appeared Allie Lee's face. Alive—flushed—radiant! Recognition brought a maddening check—a shock—and Neale's sight darkened. Tender, fluttering hands caught him; soft strong arms enfolded him convulsively.

CHAPTER XVIII

Neale seemed to come into another world—a paradise. His eyes doubted the exquisite azure blue—the fleecy cloud—the golden sunshine.

There was a warm, wet cheek pressed close to his, bright chestnut strands of hair over his face, tight little hands clutching his breast. He scarcely breathed while he realized that Allie Lee lived. Then he felt so weak that he could hardly move.

"Allie—you're not dead?" he whispered.

With a start she raised her head. It was absolutely the face of Allie Lee.

"I'm the livest girl you ever saw," she replied, with a little low laugh of joy.

"Allie—then you're actually alive—safe—here!" he exclaimed, in wild assurance.

"Yes—yes. . . . With you again! Isn't it glorious? But, oh! I gave you a shock. You frightened me so. Neale, are you well?"

"I wasn't—but I am now."

He trembled as he gazed at her. Yes, it was Allie's face—incomparable, unforgettable. She might have been a little thin and strained. But time and whatever she had endured had only enhanced her loveliness. No harm had befallen her—that was written in the white glow of her face, in the violet eyes, dark and beautiful, with the brave soul shining through their haunting shadows, in the perfect lips, tremulous and tender with love.

"Neale, they told me you gave up your work—were going to the bad," she said, with an eloquence of distress changing her voice and expression.

"Yes. Allie Lee, I loved you so well—that after I lost you—I cared for nothing."

"You gave up—"

"Allie," he interrupted, passionately, "don't talk of *me!* . . . You haven't kissed me!"

Allie blushed. "I haven't? . . . That's all you know!"

"Have you?"

"Yes I have—I have. . . . I was afraid I'd strangled you!"

"I never felt it. I lost all sense of feeling. . . . Kiss me now! Prove you're alive and love me still!"

A nd then presently, when Neale caught his breath again, it was to whisper, "Precious Allie!"

"Am I alive? Do I love you?" she whispered, her eyes like purple stars, her face flooded with a dark rose color.

"I'm forced to believe it, but you must prove it often," he replied. Then he drew her to a seat beside him. "I've had many dreams of you, yet not one like this. . . . How is it you *are* alive? By what Providence? . . . I shall pray to Providence all my life. How do you come to be here? Tell me, quick."

She leaned close against him. "That's easy," she replied. "Only sometime I want to tell you all—everything. . . . Do you remember the four ruffians who visited Slingerland's cabin one day when we were all there? Well, they came back one day, the first time Slingerland ever left me alone. They fired the cabin and carried me off. Then they fought among themselves. Two were killed. I made up my mind to get on a horse and run. Just as I was ready I spied Indians riding down. I had to shoot the ruffian Frank. But I didn't kill him. Then I got on a horse and tried to ride away. The Indians captured me—took me to their camp. There an Indian girl freed me—led me away at night. I found a trail and walked—oh, nights and days it seemed. Then I fell in with a caravan. I thought I was saved. But the leader of that caravan turned out to be Durade."

"Durade!" echoed Neale, intensely.

"Yes. He was traveling east. He treated me well, but threatened me. When we reached the construction camp, somewhere back there, he started his gambling-place. One night I escaped. I walked all that night—all the next day. And I was about ready to drop when I found this camp. It was night again. I saw the lights. They took me in. Mrs. Dillon and the other women were so kind, so good to me. I told them very little about myself. I only wanted to be hidden here and have them send for you. Then they brought General Lodge, your chief, to see me. He was kind, too. He promised to get you here. It has been a whole terrible week of waiting. . . . But now—"

"Allie," burst out Neale, "they never told me a word about you—never gave me a hint. They sent for me to come back to my job. I could have come a day sooner—the day Campbell found me. . . . Oh!"

"I know they did not find you at once. And I learned yesterday they had located you. That eased my mind. A day more or less—what was that? . . . But they were somehow strange about you. Then Mrs. Dillon told me how the chief had been disappointed in you—how he had needed you—how he must have you back."

"Good Lord! Getting me back would have been easy enough if they had only told me!" exclaimed Neale, impatiently.

"Dear, maybe that was just it. I suspect General Lodge cared enough for you to want you to come back to your job for your sake—for his sake—for sake of the railroad. And not for me."

"Aha!" breathed Neale, softly. "I wonder! . . . Allie, how cheap, how little I felt awhile ago, when he talked to me. I never was so ashamed in my life. He called me. . . . But that's over. . . . You said Durade had you. Allie, that scares me to death."

"It scares me, too," she replied. "For I'm in more danger hidden here than when he had me."

"Oh no! How can that be?"

"He would kill me for running away," she shuddered, paling. "But while I was with him, obedient—I don't think he would have done me harm. I'm more afraid now than when I was his prisoner."

"I'll take a bunch of soldiers and go after Durade," said Neale, grimly.

"No. Don't do that. Let him alone. Just get me away safely, far out of his reach."

"But, Allie, that's not possible now," declared Neale. "I'm certainly not going to lose sight of you, now I've got you again. And I must go back to work. I promised."

"I can stay here—or go along with you to other camps, and be careful to veil myself and hide."

"But that's not safe—not the best plan," protested Neale. Then he gave a start; his face darkened. "I'll put Larry King on Durade's trail."

"Oh no, Neale! Don't do that! Please don't do that! Larry would kill him."

"I rather guess Larry would. And why not?"

"I don't want Durade killed. It would be dreadful. He never hurt me. Let him alone. After all, he seems to be the only father I ever knew. Oh, I don't care for him. I despise him. . . . But let him live. . . . He will soon forget me. He is mad to gamble. This railroad of gold is a rich stake for him. He will not last long, nor will any of his kind."

Neale shook his head doubtfully. "It doesn't seem wise to me—letting him go. . . . Allie, does he use his right name—Durade?"

"No."

"What does he look like? You described him once to me, but I've forgotten."

Allie resolutely refused to tell him and once more entreated Neale to let well enough alone, to keep her hidden from the mob, and not to seek Durade.

"He has a bad gang," she added. "They might kill you. And do you—you think I'd—ever be—able to live longer without you?"

Whereupon Neale forgot all about Durade and vengeance, and everything but the nearness and sweetness of this girl.

"When shall we get married?" he asked, presently.

This simple question caused Allie to avert her face, and just at that moment there came a knock on the door. Allie made a startled movement.

"Come in," called Neale.

It was his chief who entered. General Lodge's face wore the smile that softened it. Then it showed surprise.

"Neale, you're transfigured!"

Neale's laugh rang out. "Behold cause—even for that," he replied, indicating the blushing Allie.

"Son, I didn't have to play my trump card to fetch you back to work," said the general.

"If you only had!" exclaimed Neale.

Allie got up, shyly and with difficulty disengaged her hand from Neale's.

"You—you must want to talk," she said, and then she fled.

"A wonderful girl, Neale. We're all in love with her," declared the chief. "She dropped down on us one night—asked for protection and you. She does not talk much. All we know is that she is the girl you saved back in the hills and has been kept a prisoner. Here she hides, by day and night. She will not talk. But we know she fears some one."

"Yes, indeed she does," replied Neale, seriously. And then briefly he told General Lodge Allie's story as related by her.

"Well!" ejaculated the chief. "If that doesn't beat me! . . . What are you going to do?"

"I'll keep her close. Surely she will be safe here—hidden—with the soldiers about."

"Of course. But you can never tell what's going to happen. If she could be gotten to Omaha—now—"

"No—no," replied Neale, almost violently. He could not bear the thought of parting with Allie, now just when he had found her. Then the chief's suggestion had reminded Neale of the possibility of Allie's father materializing. And the idea was attended by a vague dread.

"I appreciate how you feel. Don't worry about it, Neale."

"What's this snag the engineers are up against?" queried Neale, abruptly changing the subject.

"We're stuck. It's an engineering problem that I hope—and expect you to solve."

"Who ran this survey in the first place?"

"It's Baxter's work—with the men he had under him then," replied the chief. "Somebody blundered. His later surveys make over one hundred feet grade to the mile. That won't do. We've got to get down to ninety feet. Baxter's stuck. The new surveyor is floundering. Oh, it's bad business. Neale . . . I don't sleep of nights."

"No wonder," returned Neale, and he felt suddenly the fiery grip of his old state of mind toward all the engineering obstacles. "I'm going out to look over the ground."

"I'll send Baxter and some of the men with you."

"No, thanks," replied Neale. "I'd rather—take up my job all alone out there."

The chief's acquiescence was silent and eloquent.

Neale strode outdoors. The color of things, the feel of wind, the sounds of men and horses all about him, had remarkably changed, just as he himself had incalculably changed; General Lodge had said—transfigured!

He walked down to the construction line and went among the idle men and the strings of cars, the piles of rails and the piles of ties. He seemed to absorb in them again. Then he walked down the loose, unspiked ties to where they ended, and so on along the graded road-bed to the point where his quick eyes recognized the trouble. They swiftly took in what had been done and what had been attempted. How much needless work begun and completed in the building of the railroad! He clambered around in the sand, up and down the ravine, over the rocks, along the stream for half a mile, and it was laborious work. But how good to pant and sweat once more! He retraced his steps. Then he climbed the long slope of the hill. The wind up there blew him a welcome, and the sting and taste of dust were sweet. His step was swift. And then again he loitered, with keen, roving glance studying the lay of the ground. Neale's was the deductive method of arriving at conclusions. To-day he was inspired. And at length there blazed suddenly his solution to the problem.

Then he gazed over the rolling hills with contemplative and dreamy vision. They were beautiful, strong, changeless—and he divined now how they might have helped him if he had only looked with seeing eyes.

Late that afternoon, tired and dusty, he tramped into the big office-room. General Lodge was pacing the floor, chewing at his cigar; Baxter sat over blue-print papers, and his face was weary; Colonel Dillon, Campbell, and several other young men were there.

Neale saw that his manner of entrance, or the look of him, or both together, struck these men singularly. He laughed.

"It was great—going back to my job!" he exclaimed.

Baxter sat up. General Lodge threw away his cigar with an action that suggested a sudden vitalizing of a weary but indomitable spirit.

"Did you find the snag we've struck?" asked Baxter, slowly.

"No," replied Neale.

"Aha! Well, I'll have to take you out to-morrow and show you."

The chief's keen eyes began to shine as they studied Neale.

"No, couldn't find any snag, Baxter, old boy, . . . and the reason is because there's no snag to find."

Baxter stared and his worn face reddened. "Boy, somethin's gone to your head," he retorted.

"Wal, I should smile, as Larry would say."

Baxter pounded the table. "Neale, it's no smiling matter," he said, harshly. "You come back here, your eye and mind fresh, but even so, it can't be you make light of this difficulty. You can't—you can't—"

"But I do!" cried Neale, his manner subtly changing.

Baxter got up. His shaking hand rustled a paper he held. "I know you—of old. You've tormented me often. You're a boy. . . . But here—this—this thing has stumped me. I've had no one to help . . . and I'm getting old—this damned railroad has made me old. If—if you saw a way out—tell me—"

Baxter faltered. Indeed he had aged. Neale saw the growth of the great railroad with its problems in the face and voice of the old engineer.

"Listen," said Neale, swiftly. "A half-mile down from where you struck your snag we'll change the course of that stream. . . . We'll change the line—set a compound curve by intersections—and we'll get much less than a ninety-foot grade to the mile."

Then he turned to General Lodge. "Chief, Baxter had so many problems—so much on his mind—that he couldn't think. . . . The work will go on to-morrow."

"But, Neale, you went out without any instrument," protested the chief.

"I didn't need one."

"Son, are you sure? This has been a stumper. What you say—seems too good—too—"

"Am I sure?" cried Neale, gaily. "Look at Baxter's face!"

Indeed, one look at the old engineer was confirmation enough.

N eale was made much of that night. The chief and his engineers, the officers and their wives, all vied with one another in their efforts to celebrate Neale's return to work. The dinner party was merry, yet earnest, too. Baxter made a speech, his fine old face alight with gladness as he extolled youth and genius and the inspiring power of bright eyes. Neale had to answer. His voice was deep and full as he said that Providence had returned him to his work and to a happiness he had believed lost. He denied the genius attributed to him, but not the inspiring power of bright eyes. And he paid a fine tribute to Baxter.

Through all this gaiety and earnestness Allie's lips were mute, and her cheeks flushed and paled by turns. It was an ordeal for her, both confusing and poignant. At last she and Neale got away alone to the cabin room where they had met earlier in the day.

* * *

They stood at the open window, close together, hands locked, gazing out over the quiet valley. The moon was full, and broad belts of silver light lay in strong contrast to black shadows. The hour was late. The sentries paced their beats.

Allie stirred and lifted her face to Neale's. "What they said about you makes me almost as happy as to see you again," she said.

"They said! Who? What?" asked Neale, dreamily.

"Oh, I heard, I remember! . . . For instance, Mr. Baxter said you had genius."

"He was just eulogizing me," replied Neale. "What he said about your bright eyes was more to the point, I think."

"It's sweet to believe I could inspire you. But I know— and you know—that if I had not been here you would have seen through the engineering problem just the same. . . . Now, be honest."

"Yes, I would," replied Neale, frankly. "Though perhaps not so swiftly. I could see through stone to-day."

"And that proves your worth. Your duty it always has been—to stand by your chief. Oh, I love him! . . . He seems so much younger to-day. You have encouraged them all. . . . Oh, dear Neale, there is something noble in what you can do for him. Can't you see it?"

"Yes, Allie, indeed I do."

"Promise me—never to fail him again."

"I promise."

"No matter what happens to me. I am alive, safe, well . . . and I'm yours. But something might happen—you can never tell, and I don't refer particularly to Durade and his gang. I mean life and everything is uncertain out here. So promise me, no matter what happens, that you'll stand by your work."

"I promise that, too," replied Neale, huskily. "But you frighten me. You fear—for yourself?"

"No, I don't," she protested.

"Fate could not be so brutal—to take you from me. Anyway, I'll not think of it."

"Do not. Nor will I. . . . I wouldn't have asked you—only this night has shown me your opportunity. I'm so proud—so proud. You'll be great some day."

"Well, if you're so proud—if you think I'm so wonderful—why haven't you rewarded me for that little job to-day?"

"Reward you! . . . How?"

"How do you suppose?"

She was pale, eloquent, grave. But he was low-voiced, gay, intense.

"Dear Neale—what—what can I do? . . . I have nothing . . . so big a thing as you did to-day!"

"Child! You can kiss me."

Allie's sweet gravity changed. She smiled. "I shore can, as Larry used to say. That's my privilege. But you spoke of a reward. My kisses—they are yours—and as many as the—the grains of sand out there. But they are not reward."

"No? . . . Listen. For just one kiss—if I had to earn it so—I would dig that road-bed out there, carry every tie and rail with my bare hands, drive every spike—"

"Neale, you talk like a boy. Something, indeed, has gone to your head."

"Yes, indeed, it has. It's your face—in the moonlight."

She hid her blushes for a moment on his breast.

"I—I want to be serious," she whispered. "I want to thank God for my good fortune. To think of you and your work! . . . The future! And you—you only want kisses."

"Well, since your future must be largely made up of kisses, suppose you begin *your* work—right now."

"Oh, you're teasing! Yet when you ask of me—whatever you ask—I have no mind—no will. Something drags at me . . . I feel it now—as I used to—when you made me wade the brook."

"Oh! That's my sweetest memory of you. How it haunted me!"

They stood silent for a while. Out in the moon-blanched space the sentries trod monotonously. A coyote yelped, sharp and wild. The wind moaned low. Suddenly Neale shook himself, as if awakening.

"Allie, it grows late. We must say good night. . . . To-day has been blessed. I am grateful to the depths of my heart. . . . But I won't let you go—until my reward—"

She raised her face, white and noble in the moonlight.

CHAPTER XIX

Neale slept in a tent, and when he was suddenly awakened it was bright daylight. His ears vibrated to a
piercing blast. For an instant he could not distinguish the
sound. But when it ceased he knew it had been a ringing
bugle-call. Following that came the voices and movements
of excited troopers.

He rolled from his blankets to get into boots and coat
and rush out. The troopers appeared all around him in hurried orderly action. Neale asked a soldier what was up.

"Redskins, b'gorra—before brikfast!" was the disgusted
reply.

Neale thought of Allie and his heart contracted. A swift
glance on all sides, however, failed to see any evidence
of attack on the camp. He espied General Lodge and
Colonel Dillon among a group before the engineers'
quarters. Neale hurried up.

"Good morning, Neale," said the chief, grimly. "You're
back on the job, all right."

And Colonel Dillon added, "A little action to celebrate
your return, Neale!"

"What's happened?" queried Neale, shortly.

"We just got a telegraph message: 'Big force—Sioux.'

That's all. The operator says the wire was cut in the middle of the message."

"Big force—Sioux!" repeated Neale. "Between here and Benton?"

"Of course. We sent a scout on horseback down along the line."

"Neale, you'll find guns inside. Help yourself," said General Lodge. "You'll take breakfast with us in the cabin. We don't know what's up yet. But it looks bad for us—having the women here. This cabin is no fort."

"General, we can have all those railroad ties hustled here and throw up defenses," suggested the officer.

"That's a good idea. But the troopers will have to carry them. That work-train won't get out here to-day."

"It's not likely. But we can use the graders from the camp up the line. . . . Neale, go in and get guns and a bite to eat. I'll have a horse here ready for you. I want you to ride out after those graders."

"All right," replied Neale, rapidly. "Have you told—Do the women know yet what's up?"

"Yes. And that girl of yours has nerve. Hurry, Neale."

Neale rode away on his urgent errand without having seen Allie. His orders had been to run the horse. It was some distance to the next grading camp—how far he did not know. And the possibility of his return being cut off by Indians had quickened Neale into a realization of the grave nature of the situation.

He had difficulty climbing down and up the gorge, but, once across it, there was the graded road-bed, leading straight to the next camp. This road-bed was soft, and not easy going for a horse. Neale found better ground along the line, on hard ground, and here he urged the fresh horse to a swift and steady gait.

The distance was farther than he had imagined, and

probably exceeded ten miles. He rode at a gallop through a wagon-train camp, which, from its quiet looks, was not connected with the work on the railroad, straight on into the midst of two hundred or more graders just about to begin the day's work. His advent called a halt to everything. Sharply and briefly Neale communicated the orders given him. Then he wheeled his horse for the return trip.

When he galloped through the wagon-train camp several rough-appearing men hailed him curiously.

"Indians!" yelled Neale, as he swept on.

He glanced back once to see a tall, dark-faced man wearing a frock-coat speak to the others and then wildly fling out his arms.

It was down-hill on the way back, and the horse, now thoroughly heated and excited, ran his swiftest. Far down the line Neale saw columns of smoke rolling upward. They appeared farther on than his camp, yet they caused him apprehension. His cheek blanched at the thought that the camp containing Allie Lee might be surrounded by Indians. His fears, however, were groundless, for soon he saw the white tents and the cabins, with the smoke columns rising far below.

Neale rode into camp from the west in time to see Dillon's scout galloping hard up from the east. Neale dismounted before the waiting officers to give his report.

"Good!" replied Dillon. "You certainly made time. We can figure on those graders in an hour or so?"

"Yes. There were horses enough for half the gang," answered Neale.

"Now for Anderson's report," muttered the officer.

Anderson was the scout. He rode up on a foam-lashed mustang, and got off, dark and grimy with dust. His report was that he had been unable to get in touch with any soldiers or laborers along the line, but he had seen enough with his own eyes. Half-way between the camp and Benton a large force of Sioux had torn up the track, halted and fired the work-train. A desperate battle was being fought, with the odds against the workmen, for the reason that the train of box-cars was burning. Troops must be rushed to the rescue.

Colonel Dillon sent a trooper with orders to saddle the horses.

This sent a cold chill through Neale. "General, if the Sioux rounded us up here in this camp we'd be hard put to it," he said, forcibly.

"Right you are, Neale. The high slopes, rocks, and trees would afford cover. Whoever picked out this location for a camp wasn't thinking of Indians. . . . But we need scarcely expect an attack here."

"Suppose we get the women away—to the hills," suggested Neale.

Anderson shook his head. "They might be worse off. Here you've shelter, water, food, and men coming. That's a big force of Sioux. They'll have lookouts on all the hills."

It was decided to leave a detachment of soldiers under Lieutenant Brady, who was to remain in camp until the arrival of the graders, and then follow hard on Colonel Dillon's trail.

Besides Allie Lee there were five other women in camp, and they all came out to see the troops ride away. Neale heard Colonel Dillon assure his wife that he did not think there was any danger. But the color failed to return to her face. The other women, excepting Allie, were plainly frightened. Neale found new pride in Allie. She showed little fear of the Sioux.

General Lodge rode beside Colonel Dillon at the head of the troops. They left camp on a trot, raising a cloud of dust, and quickly disappeared round the curve of the hill. The troopers who were left behind stacked their guns and sallied out after railroad ties with which to build defenses.

Anderson, the scout, rode up the slope to a secluded point from which he was to keep watch. The women were instructed to stay inside the log cabin that adjoined the flimsy quarters of the engineers. Baxter, with his assistants, overhauled the guns and ammunition left; and Neale gathered up all the maps and plans and drawings and put them in a bag close at hand.

Time passed swiftly, and in another half-hour the graders began to arrive. They came riding in bareback, sometimes two on one horse, flourishing their guns—a hundred or more red-faced Irishmen spoiling for a fight. Their advent eased Neale's dread. Still, a strange feeling weighed upon him and he could not understand it or shake it. He had no optimism for the moment. He judged it to be overemotion, a selfish and rather exaggerated fear for Allie's safety.

Lieutenant Brady then departed with his soldiers, leaving the noisy laborers to carry ties and erect bulwarks. The Irish, as ever, growled and voiced their complaints at finding work instead of fighting.

"Hurry an' fetch on yez dim Sooz!" was the cry sent after Brady, and that request voiced the spirit of the gang.

In an hour they had piled a fence of railroad ties, six feet high, around the engineers' quarters. This task had scarcely been done when Anderson was discovered riding recklessly down the slope. Baxter threw up his hands.

"We're going to have it," he said. "Neale, I'm not so young as I was."

Anderson rode in behind the barricade and dismounted. "Sioux!"

The graders greeted this information with loud hurrahs. But when Anderson pointed out a large band of Sioux filing down from the hilltop the enthusiasm was somewhat checked. It was the largest hostile force of Sioux that Neale

Neale sustained a strange surprise. That face had been familiar, but he could not recall where he had ever seen it. The red, leering, evil visage, with its prominent, hard features, grew more vivid in memory as Neale's mind revolved closer to discovery.

"Inside with you, Neale," yelled Baxter.

Baxter and Neale, with the four young engineers, took to the several rooms of the log cabin, where each selected an aperture between the logs or a window through which to fire upon the Indians. But Neale soon ascertained that there was nothing to shoot at, outside of some white puffs of smoke rising from behind rocks on the slope. There was absolutely not a sign of an Indian. The graders were firing, but Neale believed they would have done better to save their powder. Bullets pattered against the logs; now and then a leaden pellet sang through a window, to thud into the wall. Neale shut the heavy door leading from the cabin into the engineers' quarters, for bullets were ripped through from one side to the other of this canvas-and-clapboard structure. Then Neale passed from room to room, searching for Allie. Two of the engineers were kneeling at a chink between the logs, aiming and firing in great excitement. Campbell had sustained a slight wound and looked white with rage and fear. Baxter was peeping from behind the rude jamb of a window.

"Nothin' to shoot at, boy," he said, in exasperation.

"Wait. Listen to that bunch of Irish shoot. They're wasting powder."

"We've plenty of ammunition. Let 'em shoot. They may not hit any redskins, but they'll scare 'em."

"We can hold out here—if the troopers hurry back," said Neale.

"Sure. But maybe they're hard at it, too. I've no hope this is the same bunch of Sioux that held up the work-train."

"Neither have I. And if the troops [   ] dark—"

Neale halted, and Baxter shook hi[   ]

"That would be bad," he said. "Bu[   ] of narrow places before, buildin' this[   ]

Neale found the women in the lar[   ] corner of the walls and a huge stone[   ] quiet. Allie leaped at sight of Neale.[   ] as she grasped him.

"Neale!" she whispered. "I saw Fr[   ]

"Who's he?" queried Neale, blank[   ]

"He's one of Durade's gang."

"No!" exclaimed Neale. He drew[   ] scared."

"I'd never forget Fresno," she rep[   ] was one of the four ruffians who [   ] cabin and made off with me."

Then Neale shook with a violent [   ] lie tight.

"I saw him, too. Just before I cam[   ] men that visited us at Slingerland[   ] fellow—red, ugly face—bad look."

"That's Fresno. He and the gang m[   ] with those graders you brought here.[   ] of Fresno's gang than of the Indians.[   ]

"But, Allie—they don't know you[   ] The troops will be back soon, and [   ] away."

Allie clung to Neale, and again [   ] the terror these ruffians had inspired[   ] her, assuming a confidence he was [   ] cautioned her to stay in that protec[   ] went in the other room to his statio[   ] and alarmed him, that another per[   ] Allie. And he prayed for the return [   ]

[   ] he
[   ] pa[   ]
the par[   ]
all afte[   ]
from p[   ]
wise so[   ]
shots fr[   ]

It de[   ]
ery arr[   ]
curve o[   ]
to be a [   ]
ceased [   ]
of little [   ]
paring [   ]
camp.

Ande[   ]
rounde[   ]
burnin'[   ]

"Wh[   ]
Ande[   ]

On th[   ]
ing the [   ]
a long, [   ]

"Tha[   ]

The [   ]
neers' [   ]
dotted [   ]
showed[   ]
streak [   ]
clear o[   ]

"Soo[   ]
Anders[   ]

Nea[   ]
in the i[   ]

Those fiends had ground her to ... He believed now all that she had said; and there was something of hope in the thought that if Durade had found her again she would at least not bear the misery of ... like finding her this ... a low voice. Still, ... aghast hope and determined him to seek ... during the days in which his work did not occupy him. ...

And thus it came about ... watched through his work-along the ditch, the day, and late in the after-noon, going back with the laborers to Benton. If Allie Lee lived she must be in Benton.

CHAPTER XX

Neale took up lodgings with his friend Larry. He did not at first tell the cowboy about his recovery of Allie Lee and then her loss for the second time; and when finally he could not delay the revelation any longer he regretted that he had been compelled to tell.

Larry took the news hard. He inclined to the idea that she had fallen again into the hands of the Indians. Nevertheless, he showed himself terribly bitter against men of the Fresno stamp, and in fact against all the outlaw, ruffianly, desperado class so numerous in Benton.

Neale begged Larry to be cautious, to go slow, to ferret out things, and so help him, instead of making it harder to locate Allie through his impetuosity.

"Pard, I reckon Allie's done for," said Larry, gloomily.

"No—no! Larry, I feel she's alive—well. If she were dead or—or—well, wouldn't I know?" protested Neale.

But Larry was not convinced. He had seen the hard side of border life; he knew the odds against Allie.

"Reckon I'll look fer that Fresno," he said.

And deeper than before he plunged into Benton's wild life.

One evening Neale, on returning from work to his lodg-

had ever seen. The sight of the lean, wild figures stirred Neale's blood, and then again sent that cold chill over him. The Indians rode down the higher slope and turned off at the edge of the timber out of rifle-range. Here they got off their mustangs and apparently held a council. Neale plainly saw a befeathered chieftain point with long arm. Then the band moved, disintegrated, and presently seemed to have melted into the ground.

"Men, we're in for a siege!" yelled old Baxter.

At this juncture the women came running out, badly frightened.

"The Indians! The Indians!" cried Mrs. Dillon. "We saw them—behind the cabin—creeping down through the rocks."

"Get inside—stay in the cabin!" ordered Baxter.

Allie was the last one crowded in. Neale, as he half forced her inside, was struck with a sudden wild change in her expression.

"There! There!" she whispered, trying to point.

Just then rifle-shots and the spattering of bullets made quick work urgent.

"Go—get inside the log walls," said Neale, as he shoved Allie in.

Excitement prevailed among the graders. They began to run under cover of the inclosure and some began to shoot aimlessly.

"Anderson, take some men! Go to the back of the cabin!" shouted Baxter.

The scout called for men to follow him and ran out. So many of the graders essayed to follow that they blocked the narrow opening between the inclosure and house. Suddenly one of them in the rear sheered round so that he looked at Neale. It was but a momentary glance, but Neale sensed recognition there. Then the man was gone and

Neale sustained a strange surprise. That face had been familiar, but he could not recall where he had ever seen it. The red, leering, evil visage, with its prominent, hard features, grew more vivid in memory as Neale's mind revolved closer to discovery.

"Inside with you, Neale," yelled Baxter.

Baxter and Neale, with the four young engineers, took to the several rooms of the log cabin, where each selected an aperture between the logs or a window through which to fire upon the Indians. But Neale soon ascertained that there was nothing to shoot at, outside of some white puffs of smoke rising from behind rocks on the slope. There was absolutely not a sign of an Indian. The graders were firing, but Neale believed they would have done better to save their powder. Bullets pattered against the logs; now and then a leaden pellet sang through a window, to thud into the wall. Neale shut the heavy door leading from the cabin into the engineers' quarters, for bullets were ripped through from one side to the other of this canvas-and-clapboard structure. Then Neale passed from room to room, searching for Allie. Two of the engineers were kneeling at a chink between the logs, aiming and firing in great excitement. Campbell had sustained a slight wound and looked white with rage and fear. Baxter was peeping from behind the rude jamb of a window.

"Nothin' to shoot at, boy," he said, in exasperation.

"Wait. Listen to that bunch of Irish shoot. They're wasting powder."

"We've plenty of ammunition. Let 'em shoot. They may not hit any redskins, but they'll scare 'em."

"We can hold out here—if the troopers hurry back," said Neale.

"Sure. But maybe they're hard at it, too. I've no hope this is the same bunch of Sioux that held up the work-train."

"Neither have I. And if the troops don't get here before dark—"

Neale halted, and Baxter shook his gray head.

"That would be bad," he said. "But we've squeezed out of narrow places before, buildin' this U.P.R."

Neale found the women in the large room, between the corner of the walls and a huge stone fireplace. They were quiet. Allie leaped at sight of Neale. Her hands trembled as she grasped him.

"Neale!" she whispered. "I saw Fresno!"

"Who's he?" queried Neale, blankly.

"He's one of Durade's gang."

"No!" exclaimed Neale. He drew Allie aside. "You're scared."

"I'd never forget Fresno," she replied, positively. "He was one of the four ruffians who burned Slingerland's cabin and made off with me."

Then Neale shook with a violent start. He grasped Allie tight.

"I saw him, too. Just before I came in. I saw one of the men that visited us at Slingerland's. . . . Big, hulking fellow—red, ugly face—bad look."

"That's Fresno. He and the gang must have been camped with those graders you brought here. Oh, I'm more afraid of Fresno's gang than of the Indians."

"But, Allie—they don't know you're here. You're safe. The troops will be back soon, and drive these Indians away."

Allie clung to Neale, and again he felt something of the terror these ruffians had inspired in her. He reassured her, assuming a confidence he was far from feeling, and cautioned her to stay in that protected corner. Then he went in the other room to his station. It angered Neale, and alarmed him, that another peril perhaps menaced Allie. And he prayed for the return of the troops.

* * *

The day passed swiftly, in intense watchfulness on the part of the defenders, and in a waiting game on the part of the besiegers. They kept up a desultory firing all afternoon. Now and then a reckless grader running from post to post drew a volley from the Sioux; and likewise something that looked like an Indian would call forth shots from the defenses. But there was no real fighting.

It developed that the Sioux were waiting for night. A fiery arrow, speeding from a bow in the twilight, left a curve of sparks in the air, like a falling rocket. It appeared to be a signal for demoniacal yells on all sides. Rifle-shots ceased to come from the slopes. As darkness fell gleams of little fires shot up from all around. The Sioux were preparing to shoot volleys of burning arrows down into the camp.

Anderson hurried in to consult with Baxter. "We're surrounded," he said, tersely. "The redskins are goin' to try burnin' us out. We're in a mighty tight place."

"What's to be done?" asked Baxter.

Anderson shook his head.

On the instant there was a dull spat of an object striking the roof over their heads. This sound was followed by a long, shrill yell.

"That was a burnin' arrow," declared Anderson.

The men, as of one accord, ran out through the engineers' quarters to the open. It was now dark. Little fires dotted the hillsides. A dull red speck, like an ember, showed over the roof, darkened, and disappeared. Then a streak of fire shot out from the black slope and sped on clear over the camp.

"Sooner or later they'll make a go of that," muttered Anderson.

Neale heard the scout's horse, that had been left there in the inclosure.

"Anderson, suppose I jump your horse. It's dark as pitch. I could run through—reach the troops. I'll take a chance."

"I had that idee myself," replied Anderson. "But it seems to me if them troopers wasn't havin' hell they'd been here long ago. I'm lookin' for them every minnit. They'll come. An' we've got to fight fire now till they get here."

"But there's no fire yet," said Baxter.

"There will be," replied Anderson. "But mebbe we can put it out as fast as they start it. Plenty of water here. An' it's dark. What I'm afraid of is they'll fire the tents out there, an' then it'll be light as day. We can't risk climbin' over the roofs."

"Neale, go inside—call the boys out," said Baxter.

Neale had to feel his way through the rooms. He called to his comrades, and then to the women to keep up their courage—that surely the troops would soon return.

When he went out again the air appeared full of fiery streaks. Shouts of the graders defiantly answered the yells of the savages. Showers of sparks were dropping upon the camp. The Sioux had ceased shooting their rifles for the present, and, judging from their yells, they had crawled down closer under the cover of night.

Presently a bright light flared up outside of the inclosure. One of the tents had caught fire. The Indians yelled triumphantly. Neale and his companions crouched back in the shadow. The burning tent set fire to the tent adjoining. They blazed up like paper, lighting the camp and slopes. But not an Indian was visible. They stopped yelling. Then Neale heard the thudding of arrows. Almost at once the roof of the engineers' quarters, which was merely strips of canvas over a wooden frame, burst into flames. In a single moment the roof of the cabin was blazing. More tents ignited, flared up, and the scene became almost as light as day. Rifles again began to crack. The crafty Indians poured a hail of bullets into the inclosure and the walls of the buildings. Still not an Indian was visible for the defenders to shoot at.

Anderson, Neale, and Baxter were in grim consultation. They agreed on the scout's dictum: "Reckon the game's up. Hustle the women out."

Neale crawled along the inclosure to the opening. On that side of the buildings there was dark shadow. But it was lifting. He ran along the wall, and he heard the whistle of bullets. Back of the cabin the Indians appeared to have gathered in force. Neale got to the corner and peered round. The blazing tents lighted up this end. He saw the graders break and run, some on his side of the cabin, some on the other, while others crowded into the door and window. Neale ran back to the window on the dark side of the cabin. He clambered in. A door of this room was open, and through it Neale saw the roof of the engineers' quarters blazing. He heard the women screaming. Evidently they too were running out to the inclosure. Neale hurried into the room where he had left Allie. He called. There was no answer, but a growing roar outside apparently drowned his voice. It was dark in this room. He felt along the wall, the fireplace, the corner. Allie was not there. The room was empty. His hands groping low along the floor came in contact with the bag he had left in Allie's charge. It contained the papers he had taken the precaution to save. Probably in her flight to escape from the burning cabin she had dropped it. But that was not like Allie: she would have clung to the bag while strength and sense were hers. Perhaps she had gotten out of the cabin. Neale searched again, growing more and more aware of the strife outside. He heard the crackling of wood over his head. Evidently the cabin was burning like tinder. There were men in the back room, fighting, yelling, crowding. Neale could see only dim, burly forms and the flashes of guns. Smoke floated thickly there. Some one, on the inside or outside, was beating out the door with an axe.

He decided quickly that whatever Allie might have done she would not have gone into that room. He retraced his steps, groping, feeling everywhere in the dark.

Suddenly the crackling, the shots, the yells ceased, or were drowned in a volume of greater sound. Neale ran to the window. The flare from the burning tents was dying down. But into the edge of the circle of light he saw loom a line of horsemen.

"Troopers!" he cried, joyfully. A great black pressing weight seemed lifted off his mind. The troops would soon rout that band of sneaking Sioux.

Neale ran to the back room, where, above the din outside, he made himself heard. But for all he could see or hear his tidings of rescue did not at once affect the men there. Then he forgot them and the fight outside in his search for Allie. The cabin was on fire, and he did not mean to leave it until he was absolutely sure she was not hidden or lying in a faint in some corner. And he had not made sure of that until the burning roof began to fall in. Then he leaped out the window and ran back to the inclosure.

The blaze here was no longer bright, but Neale could see distinctly. Some of the piles of ties were burning. The heat had begun to drive the men out. Troopers were everywhere. And it appeared the rattle of rifles was receding up the valley. The Sioux had retreated.

Here Neale continued his search for Allie. He found Mrs. Dillon and her companions, but Allie was not with them. All he could learn from the frightened women was that Allie had been in their company when they started to run from the cabin. They had not seen her since.

Still Neale did not despair, though his heart sank. Allie was hiding somewhere. Frantically he searched the inclosure, questioned every man he met, rushed back to the burning cabin, where the fire drove him out. But there was no trace of Allie.

Then the conviction of calamity settled upon him. While the cabin burned, and the troopers and graders watched, Neale now searched for the face of the man he had recognized—the ruffian Allie called Fresno. This search was likewise fruitless.

The following hours were a hideous, slow nightmare for Neale. He had left one hope—that daylight would disclose Allie somewhere.

Day eventually dawned. It disclosed many facts. The Sioux had departed, and if they had suffered any loss there was no evidence of it. The engineers' quarters, cabin, and tents had burned to the ground. Utensils, bedding, food, grain, tools, and instruments—everything of value except the papers Neale had saved—had gone up in smoke. The troopers who had rescued the work-train must now depend upon that train for new supplies. Many of the graders had been wounded, some seriously, but none fatally. Nine of them were missing, as was Allie Lee.

The blow was terrible for Neale. Yet he did not sink under it. He did not consider the opinion of his sympathetic friends that Allie had wildly run out of the burning cabin to fall into the hands of the Sioux. He returned with the graders to their camp; and it was no surprise to him to find the wagon-train, that had tarried near, gone in the night. He trailed that wagon-train to the next camp, where on the busy road he lost the wheel-tracks. Next day he rode horseback all the way in to Benton. But all his hunting and questioning availed nothing. Gloom, heartsickness, and despair surged in upon him, but he did not think of giving up. He remembered all Allie had told him.

Those fiends had gotten her again. He believed now all that she had said; and there was something of hope in the thought that if Durade had found her again she would at least not be at the mercy of ruffians like Fresno. But this was a forlorn hope. Still, it upheld Neale and determined him to seek her during the time in which his work did not occupy him.

And thus it came about that Neale plodded through his work along the line during the day, and late in the afternoon rode back with the laborers to Benton. If Allie Lee lived she must be in Benton.

CHAPTER XX

Neale took up lodgings with his friend Larry. He did not at first tell the cowboy about his recovery of Allie Lee and then her loss for the second time; and when finally he could not delay the revelation any longer he regretted that he had been compelled to tell.

Larry took the news hard. He inclined to the idea that she had fallen again into the hands of the Indians. Nevertheless, he showed himself terribly bitter against men of the Fresno stamp, and in fact against all the outlaw, ruffianly, desperado class so numerous in Benton.

Neale begged Larry to be cautious, to go slow, to ferret out things, and so help him, instead of making it harder to locate Allie through his impetuosity.

"Pard, I reckon Allie's done for," said Larry, gloomily.

"No—no! Larry, I feel she's alive—well. If she were dead or—or—well, wouldn't I know?" protested Neale.

But Larry was not convinced. He had seen the hard side of border life; he knew the odds against Allie.

"Reckon I'll look fer that Fresno," he said.

And deeper than before he plunged into Benton's wild life.

One evening Neale, on returning from work to his lodgings, found the cowboy there. In the dim light Larry looked strange. He had his gun-belt in his hands. Neale turned up the lamp.

"Hello, Red! What's the matter? You look pale and sick," said Neale.

"They wanted to throw me out of thet dance-hall," said Larry.

"Which one?"

"Stanton's."

"Well, *did* they?" inquired Neale.

"Wal, I reckon not. I walked. An' some night I'll shore clean out thet hall."

Neale did not know what to make of Larry's appearance. The cowboy seemed to be relaxing. His lips, that had been tight, began to quiver, and his hands shook. Then he swung the heavy gun-belt with somber and serious air, as if he were undecided about leaving it off even when about to go to bed.

"Red, you've thrown a gun!" exclaimed Neale.

Larry glanced at him, and Neale sustained a shock.

"Shore," drawled Larry.

"By Heaven! I knew you would," declared Neale, excitedly, and he clenched his fist. "Did you—you kill some one?"

"Pard, I reckon he's daid," mused the cowboy. "I didn't look to see. . . . Fust gun I've throwed fer long. . . . It'll come back now, shorer 'n hell!"

"What'll come back?" queried Neale.

Larry did not answer this.

"Who'd you shoot?" Neale went on.

"Pard, I reckon it ain't my way to gab a lot," replied Larry.

"But you'll tell *me,*" insisted Neale, passionately. He jerked the gun and belt from Larry, and threw them on the bed.

"All-l right," drawled Larry, taking a deep breath. "I went into Stanton's hall the other night, an' a pretty girl made eyes at me. Wal, I shore asked her to dance. I reckon we'd been good pards if we'd been let alone. But there's a heap of fellers runnin' her an' some of them didn't cotton to me. One they called Cordy—he shore did get offensive. He's the four-flush, loud kind. I didn't want to make any trouble for the girl Ruby—thet's her name—so I was mighty good-natured. . . . I dropped in Stanton's to-day. Ruby spotted me fust off, an' *she* asked me to dance. Shore I'm no dandy dancer, but I tried to learn. We was gettin' along powerful nice when in comes Cordy, hoppin' mad. He had a feller with him. An' both had been triflin' with red liquor. You oughter seen the crowd get back. Made me think Cordy an' his pard had blowed a lot round heah an' got a rep. Wal, I knowed they was bluff. Jest mean, ugly four-flushers. Shore they didn't an' couldn't know nothin' of me. I reckon I was only thet long-legged, red-headed galoot from Texas. Anyhow, I was made to understand it might get hot sudden-like if I didn't clear out. I left it to the girl. An' some of them girls is full of hell. Ruby jest stood there scornful an' sassy, with her haid leanin' to one side, her eyes half-shut, an' a little smile on her face. I'd call her more 'n hell. A nice girl gone wrong. Them kind shore is the dangerest. . . . Wal, she says: 'Reddy, are you goin' to let them run you out of heah? They haven't any strings on me.' So I slapped Cordy's face an' told him to shut up. He let out a roar an' got wild with his hands, like them four-flush fellers do who wants to look real bad. I says, pretty sharp-like, 'Don't make any moves now!' An' the darned fool went fer his gun! . . . Wal, I caught his hand, twisted the gun away from him, poked him in the ribs with it, an' then shoved it back in his belt. He was crazy, but pretty pale an' surprised. Shore I acted sudden-like. Then I says, 'My festive gent, if you *think* of thet move again you'll be stiff before you start it.' . . . Guess he believed me."

Larry paused in his narrative, wiped his face, and moistened his lips. Evidently he was considerably shaken.

"Well, go on," said Neale, impatiently.

"Thet was all right so far as it went," resumed Larry. "But the pard of Cordy's—he was half-drunk an' a big brag, anyhow. He took up Cordy's quarrel. He hollered so he stopped the music an' drove 'most everybody out of the hall. They was peepin' in at the door. But Ruby stayed. There's a game kid, an' I'm goin' to see her to-morrow."

"You are not," declared Neale. "Hurry up. Finish your story."

"Wal, the big bloke swaggered all over me, an' I seen right off thet he didn't have sense enough to be turned. Then I got cold. I always used to. . . . He says, 'Are you goin' to keep away from Ruby?'

"An' I says, very polite, 'I reckon not.'

"Then he throws hisself in shape, like he meant to leap over a hoss, an' hollers, 'Pull yer gun!'

"I asks, very innocent, 'What for, mister?'

"An' he bawls fer the crowd, ' 'Cause I'm a-goin' to bore you, an' I never kill a man till he goes fer his gun.'

"To thet I replies, more considerate: 'But it ain't fair. You'd better get the fust shot.'

"Then the fool hollers, 'Redhead!'

"Thet settled him. I leaps over *quick,* slugged him one—left-handed. He staggered, but he didn't fall. . . . Then he straightens up an' goes fer his gun."

Larry halted again. He looked as if he had been insulted, and a bitter irony sat upon his lips.

"I seen, when he dropped, thet he never got his hand to his gun at all. . . . Jest as I'd reckoned. . . . Wal, what made me sick was that my bullet went through him an' then some of them thin walls—an' hit a girl in another house.

She's bad hurt. . . . . They ought to have walls thet'd stop a bullet."

Neale heard the same narrative from the lips of Ancliffe, and it differed only in the essential details of the cowboy's consummate coolness. Ancliffe, who was an eye-witness of the encounter, declared that drink or passion or bravado had no part in determining Larry's conduct. Ancliffe talked at length about the cowboy. Evidently he had been struck with Larry's singular manner and look and action. Ancliffe had all an Englishman's intelligent observing powers, and the conclusion he drew was that Larry had reacted to a situation familiar to him.

Neale took more credence in what Slingerland had told him at Medicine Bow. That night Hough and then many other acquaintances halted Neale to gossip about Larry Red King.

The cowboy had been recognized by Texans visiting Benton. They were cattle barons and they did not speak freely of King until ready to depart from the town. Larry's right name was Fisher. He had a brother—a famous Texas outlaw called King Fisher. Larry had always been Red Fisher, and when he left Texas he was on the way to become as famous as his brother. Texas had never been too hot for Red until he killed a sheriff. He was a born gunfighter, and was well known on all the ranches from the Pan Handle to the Rio Grande. He had many friends, he was a great horseman, a fine cowman. He had never been notorious for bad habits or ugly temper. Only he had an itch to throw a gun and he was unlucky in always running into trouble. Trouble gravitated to him. His red head was a target for abuse, and he was sensitive and dangerous because of that very thing. Texas, the land of gun-fighters, had seen few who were equal to him in cool nerve and keen eye and swift hand.

Neale did not tell Larry what he had heard. The cowboy changed subtly, but not in his attitude toward Neale. Benton and its wildness might have been his proper setting. So many rough and bad men, inspired by the time and place, essayed to be equal to Benton. But they lasted a day and were forgotten. The great compliment paid to Larry King was the change in the attitude of this wild camp. He had been one among many—a stranger. The time came when the dance-halls grew quiet as he entered and the gambling-hells suspended their games. His fame increased as from lip to lip his story passed, always gaining something. Jealousy, hatred, and fear grew with his fame. It was hinted that he was always seeking some man or men from California. He had been known to question new arrivals: "Might you-all happen to be from California? Have you ever heard of an outfit that made off with a girl out heah in the hills?"

Neale, not altogether in the interest of his search for Allie, became a friend and companion of Place Hough. Ancliffe sought him, also, and he was often in the haunts of these men. They did not take so readily to Larry King. The cowboy had become a sort of nervous factor in any community; his presence was not conducive to a comfortable hour. For Larry, though he still drawled his talk and sauntered around, looked the name the Texan visitors had left him. His flashing blue eyes, cold and intent and hard in his flaming red face, his blazing red hair, his stalking form, and his gun swinging low—these characteristics were so striking as to make his presence always felt. Beauty Stanton insisted the cowboy had ruined her business and that she had a terror of him. But Neale doubted the former statement. All business, good and bad, grew in Benton.

It was strange that as this attractive and notorious

woman conceived a terror of Larry, she formed an infatuation for Neale. He would have been blind to it but for the
dry humor of Placé Hough, and the amiable indifference
of Ancliffe, who had anticipated a rival in Neale. Their
talk, like most talk, drifted through Neale's ears. What did
he care? Both Hough and Ancliffe began to loom large to
Neale. They wasted every day, every hour; and yet, underneath the one's cold, passionless pursuit of gold, and the
other's serene and gentle quest for effacement there was
something finer left of other years. Benton was full of
gamblers and broken men who had once been gentlemen.
Neale met them often—gambled with them, watched
them. He measured them all. They had given life up, but
within him there was a continual struggle. He swore to
himself, as he had to Larry, that life was hopeless without
Allie Lee—yet there was never a sleeping or a waking
hour that he gave up hope. The excitement and allurement
of the dance-halls, though he admitted their power, were
impossible for him; and he frequented them, as he went
everywhere else, only in search of a possible clue.

Gambling, then, seemed the only excuse open to him
for his presence in Benton's sordid halls. And he had to
bear as best he could the baseness of his associates; of
course, women had free run of all the places in Benton.

At first Neale was flirted with and importuned. Then he
was scorned. Then he was let alone. Finally, as time went
on, always courteous, even considerate of the women who
happened in his way, but blind and cold to the meaning of
their looks and words, he was at last respected and admired.

There was always a game in the big gambling-place, and
in fact the greatest stakes were played for by gamblers like
Hough, pitted against each other. But most of the time was
reserved for the fleecing of the builders of the U.P.R., the
wage-earners whose gold was the universal lure and
the magnet. Neale won money in those games in which

he played with Place Hough. His winnings he scattered or lost in games where he was outpointed or cheated.

One day a number of Eastern capitalists visited Benton. The fame of the town drew crowds of the curious and greedy. And many of these transient visitors wanted to have their fling at the gambling-hells and dancing-halls. There was a contagion in the wildness that affected even the selfish. It would be something to remember and boast of when Benton with its wild life should be a thing of the past.

Place Hough met old acquaintances among some St. Louis visitors, who were out to see the road and Benton, and perhaps to find investments; and he assured them blandly that their visit would not be memorable unless he relieved them of their surplus cash. So a game with big stakes was begun. Neale, with Hough and five of the visitors, made up the table.

Eastern visitors worked upon Neale's mood, but he did not betray it. He was always afraid he would come face to face with some of the directors, whom he did not care to meet in such surroundings. And so, while gambling, he seldom looked up from his cards. The crowd came and went, but he never saw it.

This big game attracted watchers. The visitors were noisy; they drank a good deal; they lost with an equanimity that excited interest, even in Benton. The luck for Neale seesawed back and forth. Then he lost steadily until he had to borrow from Hough.

About this time Beauty Stanton, with Ruby and another woman, entered the room, and were at once attracted by the game, to the evident pleasure of the visitors. And then, unexpectedly, Larry Red King stalked in and lounged forward, cool, easy, careless, his cigarette half smoked, his blue eyes keen.

"Hey! is that *him!*" whispered one of the visitors, indicating Larry.

"That's Red," replied Hough. "I hope he's not looking for one of you gentlemen."

They laughed, but not spontaneously.

"I've seen his like in Dodge City," said one.

"Ask him to sit in the game," said another.

"No. Red's a card-sharp," replied Hough. "And I'd hate to see him catch one of you pulling a crooked deal."

They lapsed back into the intricacies and fascination of poker.

Neale, however, found the game unable to hold his undivided attention. Larry was there, looking and watching, and he made Neale's blood run cold. The girl Ruby stood close at hand, with her half-closed eyes, mysterious and sweet, upon him, and Beauty Stanton came up behind him.

"Neale, I'll bring you luck," she said, and put her hand on his shoulder.

Neale's luck did change. Fortune faced about abruptly, with its fickle inconsistency, and Neale had a run of cards that piled the gold and bills before him and brought a crowd ten deep around the table. When the game broke up Neale had won three thousand dollars.

"See! I brought you luck," whispered Beauty Stanton in his ear. And across the table Ruby smiled hauntingly and mockingly.

Neale waved the crowd toward the bar. Only the women and Larry refused the invitation. Ruby gravitated irresistibly toward the cowboy.

"Aren't you connected with the road?" inquired one of the visitors, drinking next to Neale.

"Yes," replied Neale.

"Saw you in Omaha at the office of the company. My name's Blair. I sell supplies to Commissioner Lee. He has growing interests along the road."

Neale's lips closed and he set down his empty glass. Excusing himself, he went back to the group he had left.

Larry sat on the edge of the table; Ruby stood close to him and she was talking; Stanton and the other woman had taken chairs.

"Wal, I reckon you made a rake-off," drawled Larry, as Neale came up. "Lend me some money, pard."

Neale glanced at Larry and from him to the girl. She dropped her eyes.

"Ruby, do you like Larry?" he queried.

"Sure do," replied the girl.

"Reddy, do you like Ruby?" went on Neale.

Beauty Stanton smiled her interest. The other woman came back from nowhere to watch Neale. Larry regarded his friend in mild surprise.

"I reckon it was a turrible case of love at fust sight," he drawled.

"I'll call your bluff!" flashed Neale. "I've just won three thousand dollars. I'll give it to you. Will you take it and leave Benton—go back—no! go west—begin life over again?"

"Together, you mean!" exclaimed Beauty Stanton, as she rose with a glow on her faded face. No need to wonder why she had been named Beauty.

"Yes, together," replied Neale, in swift steadiness. "You've started bad. But you're young. It's never too late. With this money you can buy a ranch—begin all over again."

"Pard, haven't you seen too much red liquor?" drawled Larry.

The girl shook her head. "Too late!" she said, softly.

"Why?"

"Larry is bad, but he's honest. I'm both bad and dishonest."

"Ruby, I wouldn't call you dishonest," returned Neale, bluntly. "Bad—yes. And wild! But if you had a chance?"

"No," she said.

"You're both slated for hell. What's the sense of it?"

"I don't see that you're slated for heaven," retorted Ruby.

"Wal, I shore say echo," drawled Larry, as he rolled a cigarette. "Pard, you're drunk this heah minnit."

"I'm not drunk. I appeal to you, Miss Stanton," protested Neale.

"You certainly are not drunk," she replied. "You're just—"

"Crazy," interrupted Ruby.

They laughed.

"Maybe I do have queer impulses," replied Neale, as he felt his face grow white. "Every once in a while I see a flash—of—of I don't know what. *I* could do something big—even now—if my heart wasn't dead."

"Mine's in its grave," said Ruby, bitterly. "Come, Stanton, let's get out of this. Find me men who talk of drink and women."

Neale deliberately reached out and stopped her as she turned away. He faced her.

"You're no four-flush," he said. "You're game. You mean to play this out to a finish. . . . But you're no—no maggot like the most. You can think. You're afraid to talk to me."

"I'm afraid of no man. But you—you're a fool—a sky-pilot. You're—"

"The thing is—it's not too late."

"It is too late!" she cried, with trembling lips.

Neale saw and felt his dominance over her.

"It is *never* too late!" he responded, with all his force. "I can prove that."

She looked at him mutely. The ghost of another girl stood there instead of the wild Ruby of Benton.

"Pard, you're drunk shore!" ejaculated Larry, as he towered over them and gave his belt a hitch. The cowboy sensed events.

"I've annoyed you more than once," said Neale. "This's

the last. . . . So tell me the truth. . . . Could *I* take you away from this life?"

"Take me? . . . How—man?"

"I—I don't know. But somehow. . . . I'd hold it—as worthy—to save a girl like you—*any* girl—from hell."

"But—how?" she faltered. The bitterness, the irony, the wrong done by her life, was not manifest now.

"You refused my plan with Larry. . . . Come, let me find a home for you—with good people."

"My God—he's not in earnest!" gasped the girl to her women friends.

"I am in earnest," said Neale.

Then the tension of the girl relaxed. Her face showed a rebirth of soul.

"I can't accept," she replied. If she thanked him it was with a look. Assuredly her eyes had never before held that gaze for Neale. Then she left the room, and presently Stanton's companion followed her. But Beauty Stanton remained. She appeared amazed, even dismayed.

Larry lighted his cigarette. "Shore I'd call thet a square kid," he said. "Neale, if you get any drunker you'll lose all thet money."

"I'll lose it anyhow," replied Neale, absent-mindedly.

"Wal, stake me right heah an' now."

At that Neale generously and still absent-mindedly delivered to Larry a handful of gold and notes that he did not count.

"Hell! I ain't no bank," protested the cowboy.

Hough and Ancliffe joined them and with amusement watched Larry try to find pockets enough for his small fortune.

"Easy come, easy go in Benton," said the gambler, with a smile. Then his glance, alighting upon the quiet Stanton, grew a little puzzled. "Beauty, what ails you?" he asked.

She was pale and her expressive eyes were fixed upon Neale. Hough's words startled her.

"What ails me? . . . Place, I've had a forgetful moment—a happy one—and I'm deathly sick!"

Ancliffe stared in surprise. He took her literally.

Beauty Stanton looked at Neale again. "Will you come to see me?" she asked, with sweet directness.

"Thank you—no," replied Neale. He was annoyed. She had asked him that before, and he had coldly but courteously repelled what he thought were her advances. This time he was scarcely courteous.

The woman flushed. She appeared about to make a quick and passionate reply, in anger and wounded pride, but she controlled the impulse. She left the room with Ancliffe.

"Neale, do you know Stanton is infatuated with you?" asked Hough, thoughtfully.

"Nonsense!" replied Neale.

"She is, though. These women can't fool me. I told you days ago I suspected that. Now I'll gamble on it. And you know how I play my cards."

"She saw me win a pile of money," said Neale, with scorn.

"I'll bet you can't make her take a dollar of it. Any amount you want and any odds."

Neale would not accept the wager. What was he talking about, anyway? What was this drift of things? His mind did not seem clear. Perhaps he had drunk too much. The eyes of both Ruby and Beauty Stanton troubled him. What had he done to these women?

"Neale, you're more than usually excited to-day," observed Hough. "Probably was the run of luck. And then you spouted to the women."

Neale confessed his offer to Ruby and Larry, and then his own impulse.

"Ruby called me a fool—crazy—a sky-pilot. Maybe I am."

"Sky-pilot! Well, the little devil!" laughed Hough. "I'll gamble she called you that before you declared yourself."

"Before, yes. I tell you, Hough, I have crazy impulses. They've grown on me out here. They burst like lightning out of a clear sky. I would have done just that thing for Ruby. . . . Mad, you say? . . . Why, man, she's not hopeless! There was something deep behind that impulse. Strange— not understandable! I'm at the mercy of every hour I spend here. Benton has got into my blood. And I see how Benton is a product of this great advance of progress—of civilization—the U.P.R. We're only atoms in a force no one can understand. . . . Look at Reddy King. That cowboy was set—fixed like stone in his character. But Benton has called to the worst and wildest in him. He'll do something terrible. Mark what I say. We'll all do something terrible. You, too, Place Hough, with all your cold, implacable control. The moment will come, born out of this abnormal time. I can't explain, but I feel. There's a work-shop in this hell of Benton. Invisible, monstrous, and nameless! . . . Nameless like the new graves dug every day out here on the desert. . . . How few of the honest toilers dream of the spirit that is working on them. That Irishman, Shane, think of him. He fought while his brains oozed from a hole in his head. I saw, but I didn't know then. I wanted to take his place. He said, no, he wasn't hurt, and Casey would laugh at him. Aye, Casey would have laughed! . . . They are men. There are thousands of them. The U.P.R. goes on. It can't be stopped. It has the momentum of a great nation pushing it on from behind. . . . And I, who have lost all I cared for, and you, who are a drone among the bees, and Ruby and Stanton with their kind, poor creatures sucked into the vortex; yes, and that mob of leeches, why we all are so stung by that nameless spirit that we are stirred beyond ourselves and dare both height and depth of impossible things."

"You must be drunk," said Place, gravely, "and yet what you say hits me hard. I'm a gambler. But sometimes— there are moments when I might be less or more. There's mystery in the air. This Benton is a chaos. Those hairy toilers of the rails! I've watched them hammer and lift and dig and fight. By day they sweat and they bleed, they sing and joke and quarrel—and go on with the work. By night they are seized by the furies. They fight among themselves while being plundered and murdered by Benton's wolves. Heroic by day—hellish by night. . . . And so, spirit or what—they set the pace."

Next afternoon, when parasitic Benton awoke, it found the girl Ruby dead in her bed.

Her door had to be forced. She had not been murdered. She had destroyed much of the contents of a trunk. She had dressed herself in simple garments that no one in Benton had ever seen. It did not appear what means she had employed to take her life. She was only one of many. More than one girl of Benton's throng had sought the same short road and cheated life of further pain.

When Neale heard about it, upon his return to Benton, late that afternoon, Ruby was in her grave. It suited him to walk out in the twilight and stand awhile in the silence beside the bare sandy mound. No stone—no mark. Another nameless grave! She had been a child once, with dancing eyes and smiles, loved by some one, surely, and perhaps mourned by some one living. The low hum of Benton's awakening night life was borne faintly on the wind. The sand seeped; the coyotes wailed; and yet there was silence. Twilight lingered. Out on the desert the shadows deepened.

By some chance the grave of the scarlet woman adjoined

that of a laborer who had been killed by a blast. Neale remembered the spot. He had walked out there before. A morbid fascination often drew him to view that ever-increasing row of nameless graves. As the workman had given his life to the road, so had the woman. Neale saw a significance in the parallel.

Neale returned to the town troubled in mind. He remembered the last look Ruby had given him. Had he awakened conscience in her? Upon questioning Hough, he learned that Ruby had absented herself from the dancing-hall and had denied herself to all on that last night of her life.

There was to be one more incident relating to this poor girl before Benton in its mad rush should forget her.

Neale divined the tragedy before it came to pass, but he was as powerless to prevent it as any other spectator in Beauty Stanton's hall.

Larry King reacted in his own peculiar way to the news of Ruby's suicide, and the rumored cause. He stalked into that dancing-hall, where his voice stopped the music and the dancers.

"Come out heah!" he shouted to the pale Cordy.

And King spun the man into the center of the hall, where he called him every vile name known to the camp, scorned and slapped and insulted him, shamed him before that breathless crowd, goaded him at last into a desperate reaching for his gun, and killed him as he drew it.

CHAPTER XXI

Benton slowed and quieted down a few days before pay-day, to get ready for the great rush. Only the saloons and dance-halls and gambling-hells were active, and even here the difference was manifest.

The railroad-yard was the busiest place in the town, for every train brought huge loads of food, merchandise, and liquor, the transporting of which taxed the teamsters to their utmost.

The day just before pay-day saw the beginning of a singular cycle of change. Gangs of laborers rode in on the work-trains from the grading-camps and the camps at the head of the rails, now miles west of Benton. A rest of several days inevitably followed the visit of the pay-car. It was difficult to keep enough men at work to feed and water the teams, and there would have been sorry protection from the Indians had not the troops been on duty. Pay-days were not off-days for the soldiers.

Steady streams of men flowed toward Benton from east and west; and that night the hum of Benton was merry, subdued, waiting.

Bright and early the town with its added thousands

awoke. The morning was clear, rosy, fresh. On the desert the colors changed from soft gray to red and the whirls of dust, riding the wind, resembled little clouds radiant with sunset hues. Silence and solitude and unbroken level reigned outside in infinite contrast to the seething town. Benton resembled an ant-heap at break of day. A thousand songs arose, crude and coarse and loud, but full of joy. Payday and vacation were at hand!

> Then drill, my Paddies, drill!
> Drill, my heroes, drill!
> Drill all day,
> No sugar in your tay,
> Workin' on the U.P. Railway.

Casey was one Irish trooper of thousands who varied the song and tune to suit his taste. The content alone they all held. Drill! They were laborers who could turn into regiments at a word.

They shaved their stubby beards and donned their best—a bronzed, sturdy, cheery army of wild boys. The curse rested but lightly upon their broad shoulders.

Strangely enough, the morning began without the gusty wind so common to that latitude, and the six inches of powdery white dust did not rise. The wind, too, waited. The powers of heaven smiled in the clear, quiet morning, but the powers of hell waited—for the hours to come, the night and the darkness.

At nine o'clock a mob of five thousand men had congregated around the station, most of them out in the open, on the desert side of the track. They were waiting for the pay-train to arrive. This hour was the only orderly one that Benton ever saw. There were laughter, profanity, play—a continuous hum, but compared to Benton's usual turmoil, it was pleasant. The workmen talked in groups, and, like all crowds of men sober and unexcited, they were given largely to badinage and idle talk.

"Wot was ut I owed ye, Moike?" asked a strapping garder.

Moike scratched his head. "Wor it thorty dollars this toime?"

"It wor," replied the other. "Moike, yez hev a mimory."

A big negro pushed out his huge jaw and blustered at his fellows.

"I's a-gwine to bust thet yaller nigger's haid," he declared.

"Bill, he's your fr'en'. Cool down, man, cool down," replied a comrade.

A teamster was writing a letter in lead-pencil, using a board over his knees.

"Jim, you goin' to send money home?" queried a fellow-laborer.

"I am that, an' first thing when I get my pay," was the reply.

"Reminds me I owe for this suit I'm wearin'. I'll drop in an' settle."

A group of spikers held forth on a little bank above the railroad track, at a point where a few weeks before they had fastened those very rails with lusty blows.

"Well, boys, I think I see the smoke of our pay-dirt, way down the line," said one.

"Bandy, your eyes are pore," replied another.

"Yep, she's comin'," said another. "'Bout time, for I haven't two-bits to my name."

"Boys, no buckin' the tiger for me to-day," declared Bandy.

He was laughed at by all except one quiet comrade who gazed thoughtfully eastward, back over the vast and rolling country. This man was thinking of home, of wife and little girl, of what pay-day meant for them.

Bandy gave him a friendly slap on the shoulder.

"Frank, you got drunk an' laid out all night, last pay-day."

Frank remembered, but he did not say what he had forgotten that last pay-day.

A long and gradual slope led from Benton down across the barren desert toward Medicine Bow. The railroad track split it and narrowed to a mere thread upon the horizon. The crowd of watching, waiting men saw smoke rise over that horizon line, and a dark, flat, creeping object. Through the big throng ran a restless murmur. The train was in sight. It might have been a harbinger of evil, for a subtle change, nervous, impatient, brooding, visited that multitude. A slow movement closed up the disintegrated crowd and a current of men worked forward to encounter resistance and opposing currents. They had begun to crowd for advantageous positions closer to the pay-car so as to be the first in line.

A fight started somewhere, full of loud curses and dull blows; and then a jostling mass tried the temper of the slow-marching men. Some boss yelled an order from a box-car, and he was hooted. There was no order. When the train whistled for Benton a hoarse and sustained shout ran through the mob, not from all lips, nor from any massed group, but taken up from man to man—a strange sound, the first note of calling Benton.

The train arrived. Troops alighting preserved order near the pay-car; and out of the dense mob a slow stream of men flowed into the car at one end and out again at the other.

Bates, a giant digger and a bully, was the first man in the line, the first to get his little share of the fortunes in gold passing out of the car that day.

Long before half of that mob had received its pay Bates lay dead upon a sanded floor, killed in a drunken brawl.

And the Irishman Mike had received his thirty dollars.

And the big negro had broken the head of his friend.

And the teamster had forgotten to send money home.

And his comrade had neglected to settle for the suit of clothes he was wearing.

And Bandy, for all his vows, had gone straight for bucking the tiger.

And Frank, who had gotten drunk last pay-day, had been mindful of wife and little girl far away and had done his duty.

As the spirit of the gangs changed with the coming of the gold, so did that of the day.

The wind began to blow, the dust began to fly, the sun began to burn; and the freshness and serenity of the morning passed.

Main street in Benton became black-streaked with men, white-sheeted with dust. There was a whining whistle in the wind as it swooped down. It complained; it threatened; it strengthened; and from the heating desert it blew in stiflingly hot. A steady tramp, tramp, tramp rattled the loose boards as the army marched down upon Benton. It moved slowly, the first heave of a great mass getting under way. Stores and shops, restaurants and hotels and saloons, took toll from these first comers. Benton swallowed up the builders as fast as they marched from the pay-train. It had an insatiable maw. The bands played martial airs, and soldiers who had lived through the Rebellion felt the thrill and the quick-step and the call of other days.

Toward afternoon Benton began to hurry. The hour was approaching when crowded halls and tents must make room for fresh and unspent gangs. The swarms of men still marched up the street. Benton was gay and noisy and busy then. White shirts and blue and red plaid held their brightness despite the dust. Gaudily dressed women passed in and out of the halls. All was excitement, movement, color, merriment, and dust and wind and heat. The crowds moved on because they were pushed on. Music, laughter, shuffling feet and clinking glass, a steady tramp, voices low and voices loud, the hoarse brawl of the barker—all these varying elements merged into a roar—a roar that started with a merry note and swelled to a nameless din.

The sun set, the twilight fell, the wind went down, the dust settled, and night mantled Benton. The roar of the day became subdued. It resembled the purr of a gorging hyena. The yellow and glaring torches, the bright lamps, the dim, pale lights behind tent walls, all accentuated the blackness of the night and filled space with shadows, like specters. Benton's streets were full of drunken men, staggering back along the road upon which they had marched in. No woman now showed herself. The darkness seemed a cloak, cruel yet pitiful. It hid the flight of a man running from fear; it softened the sounds of brawling and deadened the pistol-shot. Under its cover soldiers slunk away sobered and ashamed, and murderous bandits waited in ambush, and brawny porters dragged men by the heels, and young gamblers in the flush of success hurried to new games, and broken wanderers sought some place to rest, and a long line of the vicious, of mixed dialect, and of different colors, filed down in the dark to the tents of lust.

Life indoors that night in Benton was monstrous, wonderful, and hideous.

Every saloon was packed, and every dive and room filled with a hoarse, violent mob of furious men: furious with mirth, furious with drink, furious with wildness—insane and lecherous, spilling gold and blood.

The gold that did not flow over the bars went into the greedy hands of the cold, swift gamblers or into the clutching fingers of wild-eyed women. The big gambling-hell had extra lights, extra attendants, extra tables; and there round the great glittering mirror-blazing bar struggled and laughed and shouted a drink-sodden mass of humanity. And all through the rest of the big room groups and knots of men stood and sat around tables, intent, absorbed, obsessed, listening with strained ears, watching with wild eyes, reaching with shaking hands—only to gasp and throw down their cards and push rolls of gold toward cold-faced gamblers, with a muttered curse. This was the night of golden harvest for the black-garbed, steel-nerved, cold-eyed card-sharps. They knew the brevity of time, and of hour, and of life.

In the dancing-halls there was a maddening whirl, an immense and incredible hilarity, a wild fling of unleashed, burly men, an honest drunken spree. But there was also the hideous, red-eyed drunkenness that did not spring from drink; the unveiled passion, the brazen lure, the raw, corrupt, and terrible presence of bad women in absolute license at a wild and baneful hour.

That was the last pay-day Beauty Stanton's dancing-hall ever saw. Likewise it was to be the last she should ever see. In the madness of that night there was written finality— the end. Benton had reached its greatest, wildest, blackest, vilest. But not its deadliest! That must come—later—as an aftermath. But the height or the depth was reached.

The scene at midnight was unreal, livid, medieval. Dance of cannibals, dance of sun-worshipers, dance of Apaches on the war-path, dance of cliff-dwellers wild over the massacre of a dreaded foe—only these orgies might have been comparable to that whirl of gold and lust in Beauty Stanton's parlors.

Benton seemed breathing hard, laboring under its load of evil, dancing toward its close.

Night wore on and the hour of dawn approached.

The lamps were dead; the tents were dark; the music was stilled; and the low, soft roar was but a hollow mockery of its earlier strength.

Like specters men staggered slowly and wanderingly through the gray streets. Gray ghosts! All was gray. A vacant laugh pealed out and a strident curse, and then again the low murmur prevailed. Benton was going to rest. Weary, drunken, spent nature sought oblivion—on disordered beds, on hard floors, and in dusty corners. An immense and hovering shadow held the tents and halls and streets. Through this opaque gloom the silent and the mumbling revelers reeled along. Louder voices broke the spell only for an instant. Death lay in the middle of the main street, in the dust—and no passing man halted. It lay as well down the side streets, in sandy ditches, and on tent floors, and behind the bar of the gambling-hell, and in a corner of Beauty Stanton's parlor. Likewise death had his counterpart in hundreds of prostrate men, who lay in drunken stupor, asleep, insensible to the dust in their faces. No one answered the low moans of the man who, stabbed and robbed, had crawled so far and could crawl no farther.

But the dawn would not stay back in order to hide Benton's hideousness. The gray lifted out of the streets, the shadows lightened, the east kindled, and the sweet, soft freshness of a desert dawn came in on the gentle breeze.

And when the sun arose, splendid and golden, with its promise and beauty, it shone upon a ghastly, silent, motionless sleeping Benton.

CHAPTER XXII

To Allie Lee, again a prisoner in the clutches of Durade, the days in Benton had been mysterious, the nights dreadful. In fear and trembling she listened with throbbing ears to footsteps and low voices, ceaseless, as of a passing army, and a strange, muffled roar, rising and swelling and dying.

Durade's caravan had entered Benton in the dark. Allie had gotten an impression of wind and dust, lights and many noisy hurried men, and a crowded jumble of tents. She had lived in the back room of a canvas house. A door opened out into a little yard, fenced high with many planks, over or through which she could not see. Here she had been allowed to walk. She had seen Durade once, the morning after Fresno and his gang had brought her to Benton, when he had said that meals would be sent her, and that she must stay there until he had secured better quarters. He threatened to kill her if he caught her in another attempt to escape. Allie might have scaled the high fence, but she was more afraid of the unknown peril outside than she was of him.

She listened to the mysterious life of Benton, wondering and fearful; and through the hours there came to her the nameless certainty of something tremendous and terrible that was to happen to her. But spirit and hope were unquenchable. Not prayer nor reason nor ignorance was the source of her sustained and inexplicable courage. A star shone over her destiny or a good angel hovered near. She sensed in a vague and perplexing way that she must be the center of a mysterious cycle of events. The hours were fraught with strain and suspense, yet they passed fleetingly. A glorious and saving moment was coming—a meeting that would be as terrible as sweet. Benton held her lover Neale and her friend Larry. They were searching for her. She felt their nearness. It was that which kept her alive. She knew the truth with her heart. And while she thrilled at the sound of every step, she also shuddered, for there was Durade with his desperadoes. Blood would be spilled. Somewhere, somehow, that meeting would come. Neale would rush to her. And the cowboy! . . . Allie remembered the red blaze of his face, the singular, piercing blue of his eye, his cool, easy, careless air, his drawling speech—and underneath all his lazy gentleness a deadliness of blood and iron.

So Allie Lee listened to all sounds, particularly to all footsteps, waiting for that one which was to make her heart stand still.

Some one had entered the room adjoining hers and was now fumbling at the rude door which had always been barred from the other side. It opened. Stitt, the mute who attended and guarded her, appeared, carrying bundles. Entering, he deposited these upon Allie's bed. Then he made signs for her to change from the garb she wore to the clothes contained in the bundles. Further, he gave her to understand that she was to hurry, that she was to be taken away. With that he went out, shutting and barring the door after him.

Allie's hands shook as she opened the packages. That

very hour might bring her freedom. She was surprised to find a complete outfit of woman's apparel, well made and of fine material. Benton, then, had stores and women. Hurriedly she made the change, which was very welcome. The dress did not fit her as well as it might have done, but the bonnet and cloak were satisfactory, as were also the little boots. She found a long, dark veil and wondered if she was expected to put that on.

A knocking at the door preceded a call, "Allie, are you ready?"

"Yes," she replied.

The door opened. Durade entered. He appeared thinner than she had ever seen him, with more white in or beneath his olive complexion, and there were marks of strain and of passion on his face. Allie knew he labored under some strong, suppressed excitement. More and more he seemed to lose something of his old character—of the stately Spanish manner.

"Put that veil on," he said. "I'm not ready for Benton to see you."

"Are you—taking me away?" she asked.

"Only down the street. I've a new place," he replied. "Come. Stitt will bring your things."

Allie could not see very well through the heavy veil and she stumbled over the rude threshold. Durade took hold of her arm and presently led her out into the light. The air was hot, windy, dusty. The street was full of hurrying and lounging men. Allie heard different snatches of speech as she and Durade went on. Some stared and leered at her, at which times Durade's hold tightened on her arm and his step quickened. She was certain no one looked at Durade. Some man jostled her, another pinched her arm. Her ears tingled with unfamiliar and coarse speech.

They walked through heavy sand and dust, then along a board walk, to turn aside before what was apparently a new brick structure, but a closer view proved it to be only painted wood. The place rang hollow with a sound of hammers. It looked well, but did not feel stable underfoot. Durade led her through two large hall-like rooms into a small one, light and newly furnished.

"The best Benton afforded," said Durade, waving his hand. "You'll be comfortable. There are books—newspapers. Here's a door opening into a little room. It's dark, but there's water, towel, soap. And you've a mirror. . . . Allie, this is luxury to what you've had to put up with."

"It is, indeed," she replied, removing her veil, and then the cloak and bonnet. "But—am I to be shut up here?"

"Yes. Sometimes at night early I'll take you out to walk. But Benton is—"

"What?" she asked, as he paused.

"Benton will not last long," he finished, with a shrug of his shoulders. "There'll be another one of these towns out along the line. We'll go there. And then to Omaha."

More than once he had hinted at going on eastward.

"I'll find your mother—some day," he added, darkly. "If I didn't believe that I'd do differently by you."

"Why?"

"I want her to see you as good as she left you. Then! . . . Are you ever going to tell me how she gave me the slip?"

"She's dead, I told you."

"Allie, that's a lie. She's hiding in some trapper's cabin or among the Indians. I should have hunted all over that country where you met my caravan. But the scouts feared the Sioux. The Sioux! We had to run. And so I never got the truth of your strange appearance on that trail."

Allie had learned that reiteration of the fact of her mother's death only convinced Durade the more that she must be living. While he had this hope she was safe so long as she obeyed him. A dark and sinister meaning lay covert in his words. She doubted not that he had the nature and the power to use her in order to be revenged upon her mother. That passion and gambling appeared to be all for which he lived.

Suddenly he seized her fiercely in his arms. "You're the picture of *her!*"

Then slowly he released her and the corded red of his neck subsided. His action had been that of a man robbed of all he loved, who remembered, in a fury of violent longing, hate, and despair, what he had lost in life.

Allie was left alone.

She gazed around the room that she expected to be her prison for an indefinite length of time. Walls and ceiling were sections, locking together, and in some places she could see through the cracks. One side opened upon a tent wall; the other into another room; the small glass windows upon a house of canvas. When Allie put her hand against any part of her room she found that it swayed and creaked. She understood then that this house had been made in sections, transported to Benton by train, and hurriedly thrown together.

She looked next at the newspapers. How strange to read news of the building of the U.P.R.! The name of General Lodge, chief engineer, made Allie tremble. He had predicted a fine future for Warren Neale. She read that General Lodge now had a special train and that he contemplated an inspection trip out as far as the rails were laid. She read that the Pacific Construction Company was reputed to be crossing the Sierra Nevada, that there were ten thousand Chinamen at work on the road, that the day when East and West were to meet was sure to come. Eagerly she searched, her heart thumping, for the name of Neale, but she did not find it. She read in one paper that the Sioux were active along the line between Medicine Bow and Kearney. Every day the workmen would sight a band of

Indians, and, growing accustomed to the sight, they would become careless, and so many lost their lives. A massacre had occurred out on the western end of the road, where the construction gangs were working. Day after day the Sioux had prowled around, without attacking, until the hardy and reckless laborers lost fear and caution. Then, one day, a grading gang working a mile from the troops was set upon by a band of swiftly riding warriors, and before they could raise a gun in defense were killed and scalped in their tracks.

Allie read on. She devoured the news. Manifestly the world was awakening to the reality of the great railroad. How glad Neale must be! Always he had believed in the greatness and the reality of the U.P.R. Somewhere along that line he was working—perhaps every night he rode into Benton. Her emotions overwhelmed her as she thought of him so near, and for a moment she could not see the print. Neale would never again believe she was dead. And indeed she did live! She breathed—she was well, strong, palpitating. She was sitting here in Benton, reading about the building of the railroad. She wondered with a pang what her disappearance would mean to Neale. He had said his life would be over if he lost her again. She shivered.

Suddenly her eye rested on printed letters, familiar and startling. Allison Lee!

"Allison Lee!" she breathed, very low. *"My father!"*

And she read that Allison Lee, commissioner of the U.P.R. and contractor for big jobs along the line, would shortly leave his home in Council Bluffs, to meet some of the directors in New York City in the interests of the railroad.

"If Durade and he ever meet!" she whispered.

And in that portent she saw loom on the gambler's horizon another cloud. In his egotism and passion and despair he was risking more than he knew. He could not hope to keep her a prisoner for very long. Allie felt again the gathering surety of an approaching climax.

"My danger is, he may harm me, use me for his gambling lure, or kill me," she murmured. And her prevision of salvation contended with the dark menace of the hour. But, as always, she rose above hopelessness.

Her thoughts were interrupted by the entrance of the mute, Stitt, who brought her a few effects left at the former place, and then a tray holding her dinner.

That day passed swiftly.

Darkness came, bringing a strange augmentation of the sounds with which Allie had become familiar. She did not use her lamp, for she had become accustomed to being without one, and she seemed to be afraid of a light. Only a dim, pale glow came in at her window. But the roar of Benton—that grew as night fell. She had heard something similar in the gold-camps of California and in the grading-camps where Durade had lingered; this was at once the same and yet vastly different. She lay listening and thinking. The low roar was that of human beings, and any one of its many constituents seemed difficult to distinguish. Voices—footsteps—movement—music—mirth—dancing—clink of gold and glasses—the high, shrill laugh of a woman—the loud, vacant laugh of a man—sudden gust of dust-laden wind sweeping overhead . . . all these blended in the mysterious sound that voiced the strife and agony of Benton. For hours it kept her awake; and when she did fall asleep it was so late in the night that, upon awakening next day, she thought it must be noon or later.

That day passed and another night came. It brought a change in that the house she was in became alive and roaring. Durade had gotten his establishment under way. Allie lay in sleepless suspense. Rough, noisy, thick-voiced men appeared to be close to her, in one of the rooms adjoining hers, and outside in the tents. The room, however, into which hers opened was not entered. Dawn had come before Allie fell asleep.

Thus days passed during which she saw only the attendant, Stitt, and Allie began to feel a strain that she believed would be even harder on her than direct contact with Benton life. While she was shut up there, what chance had she of ever seeing Neale or Larry even if they were in Benton? Durade had said he would take her outdoors occasionally, but she had not seen him. Restlessness and gloom began to weigh upon her and she was in continual conflict with herself. She began to think of disobeying Durade. Something would happen to him sooner or later, and in that event what was she to do? Why not try and escape? Whatever the evil of Benton, it was possible that she might not fall into bad hands. Anything would be better than her confinement here, with no sight of the sun, with no one to speak to, with nothing to do but brood and fight her fancies and doubts, and listen to that ceaseless, soft, mysterious din. Allie believed she could not long bear that. Now and then occurred a change in her mind which frightened her. It was a regurgitation of the old tide of somber horror which had submerged her after the murder of her mother.

She was working herself into a frenzied state when unexpectedly Durade came to her room. At first glance she hardly knew him. He looked thin and worn; his eyes glittered; his hands shook; and the strange radiance that emanated from him when his passion for gambling had been crowned with success shone stronger than Allie had ever seen it.

"Allie, the time's come," he said. He seemed to be looking back into the past.

"What time?" she asked.

"For you to do for me—as your mother did before you."

"I—I—don't understand."

"Make yourself beautiful!"

"Beautiful! . . . How?" Allie had an inkling of what he meant, but all her mind repudiated the horrible suggestion.

Durade laughed. He had indeed changed. He seemed a weaker man. Benton was acting powerfully upon him.

"How little vanity you have! . . . Allie, you are beautiful now or at any time. You'll be so when you're old or dead. . . . I mean for you to show more of your beauty. . . . Let down your hair. Braid it a little. Put on a white waist. Open it at the neck. . . . You remember how your mother did."

Allie stared at him, slowly paling. She could not speak. It had come—the crisis that she had dreaded.

"You look like a ghost!" Durade exclaimed. "Like she did, years ago when I told her—this same thing—the first time!"

"You mean to use me—as you used her?" faltered Allie.

"Yes. But you needn't be afraid or sick. I'll pick the men who are to see you. You'll only be looked at. I'll always be with you."

"What am I to do?"

"Be ready in the afternoon when I call you."

"I know now why my mother hated you," burst out Allie. For the first time she too hated him, and felt the stronger for it.

"She'll pay for that hate, and so will you," he replied, passionately. His physical action seemed involuntary—a shrinking as if from a stab. Then followed swift violence. He struck Allie across the mouth with his open hand, a hard blow, almost knocking her down.

"Don't let me hear that from you again!" he continued, furiously.

With that he left the room, closing but not barring the door.

Allie put her hand to her lips. They were bleeding. She tasted her own warm and salty blood. Then there was born in her something that burned and throbbed and swelled and drove out all her vacillations. That blow was what she had needed. There was a certainty now as to her peril, just as there was imperious call for her to help herself and save herself.

"Neale or Larry will visit Durade's," she soliloquized, with her pulses beating fast. "And if they do not come— some one else will . . . some man I can trust."

Therefore she welcomed Durade's ultimatum. She paid more heed to the brushing and arranging of her hair, and to her appearance, than ever before in her life. The white of her throat and neck mantled red as she exposed them, intentionally, for the gaze of men. Her beauty was to be used as had been her mother's. But there would be some one who would understand, some one to pity and help her.

She had not long to meditate and wait. She heard the heavy steps and voices of men entering the room next hers.

Presently Durade called her. With a beating heart Allie rose and pushed open the door. From that moment there never would be any more monotony for her—nor peace—nor safety. Yet she was glad, and faced the room bravely, for Neale or Larry might be there.

Durade had furnished this larger place luxuriously, and evidently intended to use it for a private gambling-den, where he would bring picked gamesters. Allie saw about eight or ten men who resembled miners or laborers.

Durade led her to a table that had been placed under some shelves which were littered with bottles and glasses. He gave her instructions what to do when called upon, saying that Stitt would help her; then motioning her to a chair, he went back to the men. It was difficult for her to raise her eyes, and she could not at once do so.

"Durade, who's the girl?" asked a man.

The gambler vouchsafed for reply only a mysterious smile.

"Bet she's from California," said another. "They bloom like that out there."

"Now, ain't she your daughter?" queried a third.

But Durade chose to be mysterious. In that he left his guests license for covert glances without the certainty which would permit of brutal boldness.

They gathered around a table to play faro. Then Durade called for drinks. This startled Allie and she hastened to comply with his demand. When she lifted her eyes and met the glances of these men she had a strange feeling that somehow recalled the California days. Her legs were weak under her; a hot anger labored under her breast; she had to drag her reluctant feet across the room. Her spirit sank, and then leaped. It whispered that looks and words and touches could only hurt and shame her for this hour of her evil plight. They must rouse her resistance and cunning wit. It was a fact that she was helpless for the present. But she still lived, and her love was infinite.

Fresno was there, throwing dice with two soldiers. To his ugliness had been added something that had robbed his face of the bronze tinge of outdoor life and had given it red and swollen lines and shades of beastly greed. Benton had made a bad man worse.

Mull was there, heavier than when he had ruled the grading-camp, sodden with drink, thick-lipped and red-cheeked, burly, brutal, and still showing in every action and loud word the bully. He was whirling a wheel and rolling a ball and calling out in his heavy voice. With him was a little, sallow-faced man, like a wolf, with sneaky, downcast eyes and restless hands. He answered to the name of Andy. These two were engaged in fleecing several blue-shirted, half-drunken spikers.

Durade was playing faro with four other men, or at least there were that number seated with him. One, whose back was turned toward Allie, wore black, and looked and seemed different from the others. He did not talk nor drink. Evidently his winning aggravated Durade. Presently Durade addressed the man as Jones.

Then there were several others standing around, dividing their attention between Allie and the gamblers. The door opened occasionally, and each time a different man entered, held a moment's whispered conversation with Durade, and then went out. These men were of the same villainous aspect that characterized Fresno. Durade had surrounded himself with lieutenants and comrades who might be counted upon to do anything.

Allie was not long in gathering this fact, nor that there were subtle signs of suspicion among the gamesters. Most of them had gotten under the influence of drink that Durade kept ordering. Evidently he furnished this liquor free and with a purpose.

The afternoon's play ended shortly. So far as Allie could see, Jones, the man in black, a pale, thin-lipped, cold-eyed gambler, was the only guest to win. Durade's manner was not pleasant while he paid over his debts. Durade always had been a poor loser.

"Jones, you'll sit in to-morrow," said Durade.

"Maybe," replied the other.

"Why not? You're winner," retorted Durade, hotheaded in an instant.

"Winners are choosers," returned Jones, with an enigmatic smile. His hard, cold eyes shifted to Allie and seemed to pierce her, then went back to Durade and Mull and Fresno. Plain it was to Allie, with her woman's intuition, that if Jones returned it would not be because he trusted that trio. Durade apparently made an effort to swallow his resentment, but the gambling pallor of his face had never been more marked. He went out with Jones, and the others slowly followed.

Fresno approached Allie.

"Hullo, gurly! You sure look purtier than in thet buckskin outfit," he leered.

Allie got up, ready for flight or defense. Durade had forgotten her.

Fresno saw her glance at the door.

"He's goin' to the bad," he went on, with his big hand indicating the door. "Benton's too hot fer his kind. He'll not git up some fine mornin'. . . . An' you'd better cotton to me. You ain't his kin—an' he hates you an' you hate him. I seen thet. I'm no fool. I'm sorta gone on you. I wish I hadn't fetched you back to him."

"Fresno, I'll tell Durade," replied Allie, forcing her lips to be firm. If she expected to intimidate him she was disappointed.

Fresno leered wisely. "You'd better not. Fer I'll kill him, an' then you'll be a sweet little chunk of meat among a lot of wolves!"

He laughed and his large frame lurched closer. He wore a heavy gun and a knife in his belt. Also there protruded the butt of a pistol from the inside of his open vest. Allie felt the heat from his huge body, and she smelled the whisky upon him, and sensed the base, faithless, malignant animalism of the desperado. Assuredly, if he had any fear, it was not of Durade.

"I'm sorta gone on you myself," repeated Fresno. "An' Durade's a greaser. He's runnin' a crooked game. All these games are crooked. But Benton won't stand for a polite greaser who talks sweet an' gambles crooked. Mebbe no one's told you what this place Benton is."

"I haven't heard. Tell me," replied Allie. She might learn from any one.

Fresno appeared at fault for speech. "Benton's a bee-hive," he replied, presently. "An' when the bees come home with their honey, why, the red ants an' scorpions an' centipedes an' rattlesnakes git busy. I've seen some places in my time, but Benton beats 'em all. . . . Say, I'll sneak you out at nights to see what's goin' on, an' I'll treat you handsome. I'm sorta—"

The entrance of Durade cut short Fresno's further speech.

"What are you saying to her?" demanded Durade, in anger.

"I was jest tellin' her about what a place Benton is," replied Fresno.

"Allie, is that true?" queried Durade, sharply.

"Yes," she replied.

"Fresno, I did not like your looks."

"Boss, if you don't like 'em you know what you can do," rejoined Fresno, impudently, and he lounged out of the room.

"Allie, these men are all bad," said Durade. "You must avoid them when my back's turned. I cannot run my place without them, so I am compelled to endure much."

Allie's attendant came in with her supper and she went to her room.

Thus began Allie Lee's life as an unwilling and inno-cent accomplice of Durade in his retrogression from the status of a gambler to that of a criminal. In California he had played the game, diamond cut diamond. But he had broken. His hope, spirit, luck, nerve were gone. The bottle and Benton had almost destroyed his skill at professional gambling.

The days passed swiftly. Every afternoon Durade intro-duced a new company to his private den. Few ever came twice. In this there was a grain of hope, for if all the men in Benton, or out on the road, could only pass through

Durade's hall, the time would come when she would meet Neale or Larry. She lived for that. She was constantly on the lookout for a man she could trust with her story. Honest-faced laborers were not wanting in the stream of visitors Durade ushered into her presence, but either they were drunk or obsessed by gambling, or she found no opportunity to make her appeal.

These afternoons grew to be hideous for Allie. She had been subjected to every possible attention, annoyance, indignity, and insult, outside of direct violence. She could only shut her eyes and ears and lips. Fresno found many opportunities to approach her, sometimes in Durade's presence, the gambler being blind to all but the cards and gold. At such times Allie wished she was sightless and deaf and feelingless. But after she was safely in her room again she told herself nothing had happened. She was still the same as she had always been. And sleep obliterated quickly what she had suffered. Every day was one nearer to that fateful and approaching moment. And when that moment did come what would all this honor amount to? It would fade—be as nothing. She would not let words and eyes harm her. They were not tangible—they had no substance for her. They made her sick with rage and revolt at the moment, but they had no power, no taint, no endurance. They were evil passing winds.

As she saw Durade's retrogression, so she saw the changes in all about him. His winnings were large and his strange passion for play increased with them. The free gold that enriched Fresno and Mull and Andy only augmented their native ferocity. There were also Durade's other helpers—Black, his swarthy doorkeeper, a pallid fellow called Dayss, who always glanced behind him, and Grist, a short, lame, bullet-headed, silent man—all of them under the spell of the green cloth.

With Durade's success had come the craze for bigger

stakes, and these could only be played for with other gamblers. So the black-frocked, cold-faced sharps became frequent visitors at Durade's. Jones, the professional, won on that second visit—a fatal winning for him. Allie saw the giant Fresno suddenly fling himself upon Jones and bear him to the floor. Then Allie fled to her room. But she heard curses—a shot—a groan—Durade's loud voice proclaiming that the gambler had cheated—and then the scraping of a heavy body being dragged out.

This murder horrified Allie, yet sharpened her senses. Providence had protected her. Durade had grown rich—wild—vain—mad to pit himself against the coolest and most skilful gamblers in Benton—and therefore his end was imminent. Allie lay in the dark, listening to Benton's strange wailing roar, sad, yet hideous, and out of what she had seen and heard, and from the mournful message on the night wind, she realized how closely associated were gold and evil and men, and how inevitably they must lead to lawlessness and to bloodshed and to death.

CHAPTER XXIII

Neale conceived an idea that he was in line for the long-looked-for promotion. Neither the chief nor Baxter gave any suggestion of a hint of such possibility, but more and more, as the work rapidly progressed, Neale had been intrusted with important inspections.

Long since he had discovered his talent for difficult engineering problems, and with experience had come confidence in his powers. He had been sent from place to place, in each case with favorable results. General Lodge consulted him, Baxter relied upon him, the young engineers learned from him. And when Baxter and his assistants were sent on ahead into the hills Neale had an enormous amount of work on his hands. Still he usually managed to get back to Benton at night.

Whereupon he became a seeker, a searcher; he believed there was not a tent or a hut or a store or a hall in the town that he had not visited. But he found no clue of Allie; he never encountered the well-remembered face of the bandit Fresno. He saw more than one Spaniard and many Mexicans, not one of whom could have been the gambler Durade.

But Benton was too full, too changeful, too secret to be thoroughly searched in little time. Neale bore his burden, although it grew heavier each day. And his growing work on the railroad was his salvation.

One morning he went to the telegraph station, expecting orders from General Lodge. He found the chief's special train at the station, headed east.

"Neale, I'm off for Omaha," said Lodge. "Big powwow. The directors roaring again!"

"What about?" queried Neale, always alive to interest of that nature.

"Cost of the construction. What else? Neale, there are two kinds of men building the U.P.R.—men who see the meaning of the great work, and men who see only the gold in it."

"And they conflict! . . . That's what you mean?"

"Exactly. We've been years on the job now, and the nearer the meeting of rails from west to east the harder become our problems. Henney is played out, Boone is ill, and Baxter won't last much longer. If I were not an old soldier, I would be done up now."

"Chief, I can see only success," replied Neale, with spirit.

"Assuredly. We see with the same eyes," said General Lodge, smiling. "Neale, I've a job for you that will make you gray-headed."

"Hardly that," returned Neale, laughing.

"Do you remember the survey we made out here in the hills for Number Ten Bridge? Made over two years ago."

"I'm not likely to forget it."

"Well, the rails are within twenty miles of Number Ten. They'll be there presently—and no piers to cross on."

"How's that?"

"I don't know. The report came in only last night. It's a queer document. Here it is. Study it at your leisure. . . . It seems a big force of men have been working there for months. Piers have been put in—only to sink."

"Sink!" ejaculated Neale. "*Whew!* That's a stumper! . . .

Chief, the survey is mine. I'll never forget how I worked on it."

"Could you have made a mistake?"

"Of course," replied Neale, readily. "But I'd never believe that unless I saw it. A tough job it was—but just the kind of work I eat up."

"Well, you can go out and eat it up some more."

"That means I'll have to camp out there. I can't get back to Benton."

"No, you can't. And isn't that just as well?" queried the chief, with his keen, dark glance on Neale. "Son, I've heard your name coupled with gamblers—and that Stanton woman."

"No doubt. I know them. I've been—seeking some trace of—Allie."

"You still hope to find her? You still imagine some of this riffraff Benton gang made off with her?"

"Yes."

"Son, it's scarcely possible," said Lodge, earnestly. "Anderson claims the Sioux got her. We all incline to that. . . . Oh, it's hard, Neale. . . . Love and life are only atoms under the iron heel of the U.P.R. . . . It's too late now. You can't forget—no—but you must not risk your life—your opportunities—your reputation."

Neale turned away his face for a moment and was silent. An engine whistled; a bell began to ring; some train official called to General Lodge. The chief held up his hand for a little more delay.

"I'm off," he said, rapidly. "Neale, you'll go out to Number Ten and take charge."

That surprised and thrilled Neale into eagerness.

"Who are the engineers?"

"Blake and Coffee. I don't know them. Henney sent them out from Omaha. They're well recommended. But that's no matter. Something is wrong. You're to have full charge of engineers, bosses, masons. In fact, I've sent word out to that effect."

"Who's the contractor?" asked Neale.

"I don't know. But whoever he is he has made a pile of money out of this job. And the job's not done. That's what galls me."

"Well, chief, it *will* be done," said Neale, sharp with determination.

"Good! Neale, I'll start east with another load off my shoulders. . . . And, son, if you throw up a bridge so there'll be no delay, something temporary for the rails and the work-train, and then plan piers right for Number Ten— well—you'll hear from it, that's all."

They shook hands.

"I may be gone a week or a month—I can't tell," went on the chief. "But when I do come I'll probably have a train-load of directors, commissioners, stockholders."

"Bring them on," said Neale. "Maybe if they saw more of what we're up against they wouldn't holler so."

"Right. . . . Remember, you've full charge and that I trust you implicitly. Good-by and good luck!"

The chief boarded his train as it began to move. Neale watched it leave the station, and with a swelling heart he realized that he had been placed high, that his premonition of advancement had not been without warrant.

The work-train was backing into the station and would depart westward in short order. Neale hurried to his lodgings to pack his few belongings. Larry was lying on his cot, fully dressed and asleep. Neale shook him.

"Wake up, you lazy son-of-a-gun!" shouted Neale.

Larry opened his eyes. "Wal, what's wrong? Is it last night or to-morrow?"

"Larry, I'm off. Got charge of a big job."

"Is thet all?" drawled Larry, sleepily. "Why, shore I always knowed you'd be chief engineer some day."

"Pard—sit up," said Neale, unsteadily. "Will you stay sober—and watch—and listen for some news of Allie? . . . Till I come back to Benton?"

"Neale, air you still dreamin'?" asked Larry, incredulously.

"Will you do that much for me?"

"Shore."

"Thank you, old friend. Good-by now. I've got to rustle."

He left Larry sitting on his cot, staring at nothing. On the way to the station Neale encountered the gambler, Place Hough, who, despite his nocturnal habits, was an early riser. In the excitement of the hour Neale gave way to an impulse. Briefly he told Hough about Allie—her disappearance and probable hidden presence in Benton, and he asked the gambler to keep his eyes and ears open. Hough seemed both surprised and pleased with the confidence, and he said he would go out of his way to help Neale.

Neale had to run to catch the train. A brawny Irishman extended a red-sleeved arm to help him up.

"Up wid yez. Thor!"

Neale found himself with bag and rifle and blanket sprawling on the gravel-covered floor of a flat-car. Casey, the old lineman, grinned at him over the familiar short, black pipe.

"B'gorra, it's me ould fri'nd Neale!"

"It sure is. How're you, Casey?"

"Pretty good fur an ould soldier. . . . An' it's news I hear of yez, me boy."

"What news?"

"Shure yez hed a boost. Gineral Lodge hisself wor tellin' Grady, the boss, that yez had been given charge of Number Ten."

"Yes, that's correct."

"I'm dom' glad to hear ut," declared the Irishman. "But yez hev a hell of a job in thot Number Ten."

"So I've been told. What do you know about it, Casey?"

"Shure ut ain't much. A fri'nd of mine was muxin' mortor over there. An' he sez whin the crick was dry ut hed a bottom, but whin wet ut shure hed none."

"Then I have got a job on my hands," replied Neale, grimly.

Those days it took the work-train several hours to reach the end of the rails. Neale rode by some places with a profound satisfaction in the certainty that but for him the track would not yet have been spiked there. Construction was climbing fast into the hills. He wondered when and where would be the long-looked-for meeting of the rails connecting East with West. Word had drifted over the mountains that the Pacific division of the construction was already in Utah.

At the camp Colonel Dillon offered Neale an escort of troopers out to Number Ten, but Neale decided he could make better time alone. There had been no late sign of the Indians in that locality and he knew both the road and the trail.

Early next morning, mounted on a fast horse, he set out. It was a melancholy ride. Several times he had been over that ground, once traveling west with Larry, full of ardor and joy at the prospect of soon seeing Allie Lee, and again on the return, in despair at the loss of her.

He rode the twenty miles in three hours. The camp of dirty tents was clustered in a hot valley surrounded by hills sparsely fringed with trees. Neale noted the timber as a lucky augury to his enterprise. It was an idle camp full of lolling laborers.

As Neale dismounted a Mexican came forward.

"Look after the horse," said Neale, and, taking his

luggage, he made for a big tent with a fly extended in front. Several men sat on camp-chairs round a table. One of them got up and stepped out.

"Where's Blake and Coffee?" inquired Neale.

"I'm Blake," was the reply, "and there's Coffee. Are you Mr. Neale?"

"Yes."

"Coffee, here's our new boss," called Blake as he took part of Neale's baggage.

Coffee appeared to be a sunburnt, middle-aged man, rather bluff and hearty in his greeting. The younger engineer, Blake, was a tanned, thin-faced individual, with a shifty gaze and constrained manner. The third fellow they introduced as a lineman named Somers. Neale had not anticipated a cordial reception and felt disposed to be generous.

"Have you got quarters for me here?" he inquired.

"Sure. There's lots of room and a cot," replied Coffee.

They carried Neale's effects inside the tent. It was large and spare, containing table and lamp, boxes for seats, several cots, and bags.

"It's hot. Got any drinking-water?" asked Neale, taking off his coat. Next he opened his bag to take things out, then drank thirstily of the water offered him. He did not care much for this part of his new task. These engineers might be sincere and competent, but he had been sent on to judge their work, and the situation was not pleasant. Neale had observed many engineers come and go during his experience on the road; and that fact, together with the authority given him and his loyalty to the chief, gave him cause for worry. He hoped, and he was ready to believe, that these engineers had done their best on an extremely knotty problem.

"We got Lodge's telegram last night," said Coffee. "Kinda sudden. It jarred us."

"No doubt. I'm sorry. What was the message?"

"Lodge never wastes words," replied the engineer, shortly. But he did not vouchsafe the information for which Neale had asked.

Neale threw his note-book upon the dusty table and, sitting down on a box, he looked up at the men. Both engineers were studying him intently, almost eagerly, Neale imagined.

"Number Ten's a tough nut to crack, eh?" he inquired.

"We've been here three months," replied Blake.

"Wait till you see that quicksand hole," added Coffee.

"Quicksand! It was a dry, solid stream-bed when I ran the line through here and drew the plans for Number Ten," declared Neale.

Coffee and Blake stared blankly at him. So did the lineman Somers.

"You? Did *you* draw the plans we—we've been working on?" asked Coffee.

"Yes, I did," answered Neale, slowly. It struck him that Blake had paled slightly. Neale sustained a slight shock of surprise and antagonism. He bent over his note-book, opening it to a clean page. Fighting his first impressions, he decided they had arisen from the manifest dismay of the engineers and their consciousness of a blunder.

"Let's get down to notes," Neale went on, taking up his pencil. "You've been here three months?"

"Yes."

"With what force?"

"Two hundred men on and off."

"Who's the gang boss?"

"Colohan. He's had some of the biggest contracts along the line."

Neale was about to inquire the name of the contractor, but he refrained, governed by one of his peculiar impulses.

"Anybody working when you got here?" he went on.

"Yes. Masons had been cutting stone for six weeks."

"What's been done?"

Coffee laughed harshly. "We got the three piers in— good and solid on dry bottom. Then along comes the rain—and our work melts into the quicksand. Since then we've been trying to do it over."

"But why did this happen in the first place?"

Coffee spread wide his arms. "Ask me something easy. Why was the bottom dry and solid? Why did it rain? Why did solid earth turn into quicksand?"

Neale slapped the note-book shut and rose to his feet. "Gentlemen, that is not the talk of engineers," he said, de-liberately.

"The hell you say! What is it, then?" burst out Coffee, his face flushing redder.

"I'll inform you later," replied Neale, turning to the line-man. "Somers, tell this gang boss, Colohan, I want him."

Then Neale left the tent. He had started to walk away when he heard Blake speak in a fierce undertone.

"Didn't I tell you? We're up against it!"

And Coffee growled a reply Neale could not understand. But the tone of it was conclusive. These men had made a serious blunder and were blaming each other, hating each other for it. Neale was conscious of anger. This section of line came under his survey, and he had been proud to be given such important and difficult work. Incompetent or careless engineers had bungled Number Ten. Neale strode on among the idle and sleeping laborers, between the tents, and then past the blacksmith's shop and the feed corrals down to the river.

A shallow stream of muddy water came murmuring down from the hills. It covered the wide bed that Neale remembered had been a dry, sand-and-gravel waste. On each side the abutment piers had been undermined and washed out. Not a stone remained in sight. The banks were hollowed inward and shafts of heavy boards were sliding down. In the middle of the stream stood a coffer-dam in course of building, and near it another that had collapsed. These frameworks almost hid the tip of the middle pier, which had evidently slid over and was sinking on its side. There was no telling what had been sunk in that hole. All the surroundings—the tons of stone, cut and uncut, the piles of muddy lumber, the platforms and rafts, the crevices in the worn shores up and down both sides—all attested to the long weeks of fruitless labor and to the engulfing mystery of that shallow, murmuring stream.

Neale returned thoughtfully to camp. Blake and Coffee were sitting under the fly in company with a stalwart Irishman.

"Fine sink-hole you picked out for Number Ten, don't you think?" queried Blake.

Neale eyed his interrogator with somewhat of a penetrating glance. Blake did not meet that gaze frankly.

"Yes, it's a sink-hole, all right, and no mistake," replied Neale. "It's just what I calculated when I ran the plans. . . . Did you follow those plans?"

Blake appeared about to reply when Coffee cut him short. "Certainly we did," he snapped.

"Then where are the breakwaters?" asked Neale, sharply.

"Breakwaters?" ejaculated Coffee. His surprise was sincere.

"Yes, breakwaters," retorted Neale. "I drew plans for breakwaters to be built up-stream so that in high water the rapid current would be directed equally between the piers, and not against them."

"Oh yes! Why—we must have got—it mixed," replied Coffee. "Thought they were to be built last. Wasn't that it, Blake?"

"Sure," replied his colleague, but his tone lacked something.

"Ah—I see," said Neale, slowly.

Then the big Irishman got up to extend a huge hand. "I'm Colohan," he boomed.

Neale liked the bronzed, rough face, good-natured and intelligent. And he was aware of a shrewd pair of gray eyes taking his measure. Why these men seemed to want to look through Neale might have been natural enough, but somehow it struck him strangely. He had come there to help them, not to discharge them. Colohan, however, did not rouse Neale's antagonism as the others had done.

"Colohan, are you sick of this job?" queried Neale, after greeting the boss.

"Yes—an' no," replied Colohan.

"You want to quit, then?" went on Neale, bluntly.

The Irishman evidently took this curt query as a foreword of the coming dismissal. He looked shamed, crest fallen, at a loss to reply.

"Don't misunderstand me," continued Neale. "I'm not going to fire you. But if you are sick of the job you can quit. I'll boss the gang myself. . . . The rails will be here in ten days, and I'm going to have a trestle over that hole so the rails can cross. No holding up the work at this stage of the game. . . . There's near five thousand men in the gangs back along the line—coming fast. They've all got just one idea—success. The U.P.R. is going through. Soon out here the rails will meet. . . . Colohan, make it a matter of your preference. Will you stick?"

"You bet!" he replied, heartily. A ruddy glow emanated from his face. Neale was quick to sense that this Irishman, like Casey, had an honest love for the railroad, whatever he might feel for the labor.

"Get on the job, then," ordered Neale, cheerily. "We'll hustle while there's daylight. We'll have that trestle ready when the rails get here."

Coffee laughed scornfully. "Neale, that sounds fine, but

it's impossible until the trains get here with piles and timbers, iron, and other stuff. We meant to run up a trestle then."

"I dare say," replied Neale. "But the U.P.R. did not start that way, and never would finish that way."

"Well, you'll have your troubles," declared Coffee.

"Troubles! . . . Do you imagine I'm going to think of *myself*?" retorted Neale. These fellows were beginning to get on his nerves. Coffee grew sullen, Blake shifted uneasily from foot to foot, Colohan beamed upon Neale.

"Come on with them orders," he said.

"Right! . . . Send men up on the hills to cut and trim trees for piles and beams. . . . Find a way or make one for horses to snake down these timbers. Haul that pile-driver down to the river and set it up. . . . Have the engineer start up steam and try out. . . . Look the blacksmith shop over to see if there's iron enough. If not, telegraph Benton for more—for whatever you want—and send wagons back to the end of the rails. . . . That's all for this time, Colohan."

"All right, chief," replied the boss, and he saluted. Then he turned sneeringly to Blake and Coffee. "Did you hear them orders? I'm not takin' none from you again. They're from the chief."

Colohan's manner or tone or the word chief amazed Coffee. He looked nasty.

"Go on and work, then, you big Irish Paddy," he said, violently. "Your chief-blarney doesn't fool us. You're only working to get on the right side of your new boss. . . . Let me tell you—you're in this Number Ten deal as deep—as deep as we are."

It had developed that there was hatred between these men. Colohan's face turned fiery red, and, looming over Coffee, he looked the quick-tempered and dangerous nature of his class.

"Coffee, I'm sayin' this to your face right now. I ain't

deep in this Number Ten deal. . . . I obeyed orders—an' damn strange ones, some of them."

Neale intervened and perhaps prevented a clash. "Don't quarrel, men. Sure there's bound to be a little friction for a day or so. But we'll soon get to working."

Colohan strode away without another word. His brawny shoulders were expressive of a doubt.

"Get me my plans for Number Ten construction," said Neale, pleasantly, for he meant to do his share at making the best of it.

Blake brought the plans and spread them out on the table.

"Will you both go over them with me?" inquired Neale.

"What's the use?" returned Coffee, disgustedly. "Neale, you're thick-headed."

"Yes, I guess so," rejoined Neale, constrainedly. "That's why General Lodge sent me up here—over your clear heads."

No retort was forthcoming from the two disgruntled engineers. Neale went into the tent and drew a seat up to the table. He wanted to be alone—to study his plans—to think about the whole matter. He found his old figures and drawings as absorbing as a good story; still, there came breaks in his attention. Blake walked into the tent several times, as if to speak, and each time he retired silently. Again, some messenger brought a telegram to one of the engineers outside, and it must have caused the whispered colloquy that followed. Finally they went away, and Neale, getting to work in earnest, was not disturbed until called for supper.

Neale ate at a mess-table with the laborers, and enjoyed his meal. The Paddies always took to him. One thing he gathered early was the fact that Number Ten bridge was a joke with the men. This sobered Neale and he left the cheery, bantering company for a quiet walk alone.

It was twilight down in the valley, while still daylight

up on the hilltops. A faint glow remained from the sunset, but it faded as Neale looked. He walked a goodly distance from camp, so as to be out of earshot. The cool night air was pleasant after the hot day. It fanned his face. And the silence, the darkness, the stars calmed him. A lonely wolf mourned from the heights, and the long wail brought to mind Slingerland's cabin. Then it was only a quick step to memory of Allie Lee; and Neale drifted from the perplexities and problems of his new responsibility to haunting memories, hopes, doubts, fears.

When he returned to the tent he espied a folded paper on the table in the yellow lamplight. It was a telegram addressed to him. It said that back salaries and retention of engineers were at his discretion, and was signed Lodge. This message nonplussed Neale. The chief must mean that Blake and Coffee would not be paid for past work nor kept for future work unless Neale decided otherwise. While he was puzzling over this message the engineers came in.

"Say, what do you make of this?" demanded Neale, and he shoved the telegram across the table toward them.

Both men read it. Coffee threw his coat over on his cot and then lit his pipe.

"What I make of that is—I lose three months' back pay . . . nine hundred dollars," he replied, puffing a cloud of smoke.

"And I lose six hundred," supplemented Blake.

Neale leaned back and gazed up at his subordinates. He felt a subtle change in them. They had arrived at some momentous decision.

"But this message reads at my discretion," said Neale. "It's a plain surprise to me. I've no intention of making you lose your back pay, or of firing you, either."

"You'll probably do both—unless we can get together," asserted Coffee.

"Well, can't we get together?"

"That remains to be seen," was the enigmatic reply.

"I'll need you both," went on Neale, thoughtfully. "We've a big job. We've got to put a force of men on the piers while we're building the trestle. . . . Maybe I'll fall down myself. Heavens! I've made blunders myself. I can't condemn you fellows. I'm willing to call off all talk about past performances and begin over again."

Neale felt that this proposition should have put another light on the question, that it should have been received appreciatively if not enthusiastically. But he was somewhat taken back by the fact that it was not.

"Ahem! Well, we can talk it over to-morrow," yawned Coffee.

Neale made no more overtures, busied himself with his notes for an hour, and then sought his cot.

Next morning, bright and early, Neale went down to the river to make his close inspection of what had been done toward building Number Ten. From Colohan he ascertained the number of shafts and coffer-dams sunk; from the masons he learned the amount of stone cut to patterns. And he was not only amazed and astounded, but overwhelmed, and incensed beyond expression. The labor had been prodigious. Hundreds of tons of material had been sunk there; and that meant that hundreds of thousands of dollars also had been sunk.

Upon investigation Neale found that, although many cribbings had been sunk for the piers, they had never been put deep enough. And there were coffer-dams that did not dam at all—useless, senseless wastes of time and material, not to say wages. His plans called for fifty thirty-foot piles driven to bedrock, which, according to the excavations he had had made at the time of survey, was forty feet below the surface. Not a pile had been driven! There had been no solid base for any of the cribbings! No foundations for the piers!

At the discovery the blood burned hot in Neale's face and neck.

"No blunder! No incompetence! No misreading of my plans! But a rotten, deliberate deal! . . . Work done over and over again! Oh, I see it all now! General Lodge knew it without ever coming here. The same old story! That black stain—that dishonor on the great work! . . . Graft! Graft!"

He clambered out of the wet and muddy hole and up the bank. Then he saw Blake sauntering across the flat toward him. Neale sat down abruptly to hide his face and fury, giving himself the task of scraping mud from his boots. When Blake got there Neale had himself fairly well in hand.

"Hello, Neale!" said Blake, suavely. "Collected some mud, I see. It's sure a dirty job."

"Yes, it's been dirty in more ways than mud, I guess," replied Neale. The instant his voice sounded in his ears it unleashed his temper.

"Sure has been a pile of money—dirty government money—sunk in there," rejoined Blake. He spoke with assurance that surprised Neale into a desire to see how far he would go.

"Blake, it's an ill wind that blows nobody good."

A moment of silence passed before Blake spoke again. "Sure. And it'll blow you good, too," he said, breathing hard.

"Every man has his price," replied Neale, lightly.

Then he felt a big, soft roll of bills stuffed into his hand. He took it, trembling all over. He wanted to spring erect, to fling that bribe in its giver's face. But he could control himself a moment longer.

"Blake, who's the contractor on this job?" he queried, rapidly.

"Don't you know?"

"I don't."

"Well, we supposed you knew. It's Lee."

Neale started as if he had received a stab; the name hurt him in one way and was a shock in another.

"Allison Lee—the commissioner?" he asked, thickly.

"Sure. Oh, we're in right, Neale," replied Blake, with a laugh of relief.

Swift as an Indian, and as savagely, Neale sprang up. He threw the roll of bills into Blake's face.

"You try to bribe me! *Me!*" burst out Neale, passionately. "You think I'll take your dirty money—cover up your crooked job! Why, you sneak! You thief! You dog!"

He knocked Blake down. "Hold—on—Neale!" gasped Blake. He raised himself on his elbow, half stunned.

"Pick up that money," ordered Neale, and he threatened Blake again. "Hurry! . . . Now march for camp!"

Neale walked the young engineer into the presence of his superior. Coffee sat at his table under the fly, with Somers and another man. Colohan appeared on the moment, and there were excited comments from others near by. Coffee stood up. His face turned yellow. His lips snarled.

"Coffee, here's your side partner," called Neale, and his voice was biting. "I've got you both dead to rights, you liars! . . . You never even tried to work on my plans for Number Ten."

"Neale, what in the hell do you suppose we're out here for?" demanded Coffee, harshly. "They're all getting a slice of this money. There's barrels of it. The directors of the road are crooked. They play both ends against the middle. They borrow money from the government and then pay it out to themselves. You're one of these dreamers. You're Lodge's pet. But you can't scare me."

"Coffee, if there was any law out here for stealing you'd go to jail," declared Neale. "You're a thief, same as this pup who tried to bribe me. You're worse. You've held up the line. You've ordered your rotten work done over and over again. This is treachery to General Lodge—to Henney, who sent you out here. And to me it's—it's—there's no name low enough. I surveyed the line through here. I drew the plans for Number Ten. And I'm going to prove you both cheats. You and your contractor."

"Neale, there's more than us in the deal," said Coffee, sullenly.

Colohan strode close, big and formidable. "If you mean me, you're a liar," he declared. "An' don't say it!" Coffee was plainly intimidated, and Colohan turned to Neale. "Boss, I swear I wasn't in on this deal. Lately I guessed it was all wrong. But all I could do was obey orders."

"Neale, you can't prove anything," sneered Coffee. "If you have any sense you'll shut up. I tell you this is only a *little* deal. I'm on the inside. I know financiers, commissioners, Congressmen, and Senators—and I told you before the directors are all in on this U.P.R. pickings. You're a fool!"

"Maybe. But I'm no thief," retorted Neale.

"Shut up, will you?" shouted Coffee, who plainly did not take kindly to that epithet before the gathering crowd. "I'm no thief. . . . Men get shot out here for saying less than that."

Neale laughed. He read Coffee's mind. That worthy, responding to the wildness of the time and place, meant to cover his tracks one way or another. And Neale had not lived long with Larry Red King for nothing.

"Coffee, you *are* a thief," declared Neale, striding forward. "The worst kind. Because you stole without risk. You can't be punished. But I'll carry this deal higher than you." And quick as a flash Neale snatched some telegrams from Coffee's vest pocket. The act infuriated Coffee. His face went purple.

"Hand 'em back!" he yelled, his arm swinging back to his hip.

"I'll bet there's a telegram here from Lee, and I'm entitled to keep it," responded Neale, coolly and slowly.

Then as Coffee furiously jammed his hand back for his gun Neale struck him. Coffee fell with the overturned table out in the sand. His gun dropped as he dropped. Neale was there light and quick. He snatched up the gun.

"Coffee, you and Blake are to understand you're fired," said Neale. "Fired off the job and out of camp, just as you are."

Fifteen days later the work-train crossed Number Ten on a trestle and the construction progressed with new impetus.

Not many days later a train of different character crept slowly foot by foot over that temporary bridge. It carried passenger-coaches, a private car containing the directors of the railroad, and General Lodge's special car. The engine was decorated with flags and the engineer whistled a piercing blast as he rolled out upon the structure. Number Ten had been the last big obstacle.

As fortune would have it, Neale happened on the moment to be standing in a significant and thrilling position, for himself and for all who saw him. And that happened to be in the middle of the stream opposite the trestle on the masonry of the middle pier, now two feet above the coffer-dam. He was as wet and muddy as the laborers with him.

Engineer, fireman, brakemen, and passengers cheered him. For Neale the moment was unexpected and simply heart-swelling. Never in his life had he felt so proud. And yet, stinging among these sudden sweet emotions was a nameless pang.

Presently Neele espied General Lodge leaning out of a

window of his car. He was waving. Neale pointed down at his feet, at the solid masonry; and then, circling his mouth with his hands, he yelled with all his might:

"Bed-rock!"

His chief yelled back, "You're a soldier!"

That perhaps in the excitement and joy of the moment was the greatest praise the army officer could render. Nothing could have pleased Neale more.

The train passed over the trestle and on out of sight. Upon its return, about the middle of the afternoon, it stopped in camp. A messenger came with word for Neale to report at once to the directors. He hurried to his tent to secure his papers, and then, wet and muddy, he entered the private car of the directors.

It contained only four men—General Lodge, and Warburton, Rogers, and Rudd. All except the tall, white-haired Warburton were comfortable in shirt-sleeves, smoking with a table between them. The instant Neale entered their presence he divined that he faced a big moment in his life.

The chief's manner, like Larry King's when there was something in the wind, seemed quiet, easy, potential. His searching glance held warmth and a gleam that thrilled Neale. But he was ceremonious, not permitting himself his old familiarity before these dignitaries of the great railroad.

"Gentlemen, you remember Mr. Neale," said Lodge.

They were cordial—pleasant.

Warburton vigorously shook Neale's hand, and leaned back, after the manner of matured men, to look Neale over.

"Young man, I'm glad to meet you again," he declared, in his big voice. "Remember him! Well, I do—though he's thinner, older."

"Small wonder," interposed the chief. "He's been doing a man's work."

"Neale, back there in Omaha you got sore—you quit

us," went on Warburton, reprovingly. "That was bad business. I cottoned to you—and I might have—But no matter. You're with us again."

"Mr. Warburton, I'm ashamed of that," replied Neale, hastily. "But I was hot-headed . . . am so still, I fear."

"So am I. So is Lodge. So is any man worth a damn," replied the director.

"Mr. Neale, you look cool enough now," observed Rogers, smiling. "Wish I was as wet and cool as you are. It's hot—in this desert."

Warburton took off his frock-coat. "You gentlemen aren't going to have any the best of me. . . . And now, Neale, tell us things."

Neale looked at his papers and then at his chief. "For instance," said Lodge, "tell us about Blake and Coffee."

"Haven't you seen them—heard from them?" inquired Neale.

"No. Henney has not, either. And they were his men."

"Gentlemen, I'm afraid I lost my head in regard to them."

"Explain, please," said Warburton. "We will judge your conduct."

It was a rather difficult moment for Neale, because his actions regarding the two engineers now appeared to have been the result of violent temper, rather than a dignified exercise of authority. But then as he remembered Blake's offer and Coffee's threat the heat thrilled along his nerves; and that stirred him to forceful expression.

"I drove them both out of this camp."

"Why?" queried Warburton, sharply.

"Blake tried to bribe me, and Coffee—"

"One at a time," interrupted Warburton, and he thrust a strong hand through his hair, ruffling it. He began to scent battle. "What did Blake try to bribe you to do?"

"He didn't say. But he meant me to cover their tracks."

"So! . . . And what did Coffee do?"

"He tried to pull a gun on me."

"Why? Be explicit, please."

"Well, he threatened me. And I laughed at him—called him names."

"What names?"

"Quite a lot, if I remember. The one he objected to was thief. . . . I repeated that, and snatched some telegrams from his pocket. He tried to draw his gun on me—and then I drove them both out of camp. They got through safely, for they were seen in Benton."

"Sir, it appears to me you lost your head to good purpose," said Warburton. "Now just what were the tracks they wanted you to cover?"

"I drew the original plans for Number Ten. They had not followed them. To be exact, they did not drive piles to hold the cribbings for the piers. They did not go deep enough. They sank shafts, they built coffer-dams, they put in piers over and over again. There was forty feet of quicksand under all their work and of course it slipped and sank."

Warburton slowly got up. He was growing purple in the face. His hair seemed rising. He doubled a huge fist. "Over and over again!" he roared, furiously. "Over and over again! Lodge, do you hear that?"

"Yes. Sounds kind of familiar to me," replied the chief, with one of his rare smiles. He was beyond rage now. He saw the end. He alone, perhaps, had realized the nature of that great work. And that smile had been sad as well as triumphant.

Warburton stamped up and down the car aisle. Manifestly he wanted to smash something or to take out his anger upon his comrades. That was not the quick rage of a moment; it seemed the bursting into flame of a smoldering fire. He used language more suited to one of Benton's dance-halls than the private car of the directors of the

Union Pacific Railroad. Once he stooped over Lodge, pounded the table.

"Three hundred thousand dollars sunk in that quicksand hole!" he thundered. "Over and over again! That's what galls me. Work done over and over—unnecessary—worse than useless—all for dirty gold! Not for the railroad, but for gold! . . . God! what a band of robbers we've dealt with! . . . Lodge, why in hell didn't you send Neale out here at the start?"

A shadow lay dark in the chief's lined face. Why had he not done a million other things? Why, indeed! He did not answer the irate director.

"Three hundred thousand dollars sunk in that hole—for nothing!" shouted Warburton, in a final explosion.

The other two directors laughed. "Pooh!" exclaimed Rogers, softly. "What is that? A drop in the bucket! Consult your note-book, Warburton."

And that speech cooled the fighting director. It contained volumes. It evidently struck home. Warburton growled, he mopped his red face, he fell into a seat.

"Lodge, excuse me," he said, apologetically. "What our fine young friend here told me was like someone stepping on my gouty foot. I've been maybe a little too zealous— too exacting. Then I'm old and testy. . . . What does it matter? How could it have been prevented? Alas! it's black like that hideous Benton. . . . But we're coming out into the light. Lodge, didn't you tell me this Number Ten bridge was the last obstacle?"

"I did. The rails will go down now fast and straight till they meet out there in Utah! Soon!"

Warburton became composed. The red died out of his face. He looked at Neale.

"Young man, can *you* put permanent piers in that sink hole?"

"Yes. They are started, on bed-rock," replied Neale.

"Bed-rock!" he repeated, and remained gazing at Neale fixedly. Then he turned to Lodge. "Do you remember that wild red-head cowboy—Neale's friend—when he said, 'I reckon thet's aboot all?' . . . I'll never forget him. . . . Lodge, say we have Lee and his friend Senator Dunn come in, and get it over. An' thet'll be aboot all!"

"Thank Heaven!" replied the chief, fervently. He called to his porter, but as no one replied, General Lodge rose and went into the next car.

Neale had experienced a disturbing sensation in his breast. Lee! Allison Lee! The mere name made him shake. He could not understand, but he felt there was more reason for its effect on him than his relation to Allison Lee as a contractor. Somewhere there was a man named Lee who was Allie's father, and Neale knew he would meet him some day.

Then when the chief walked back into the car with several frock-coated individuals, Neale did recognize in the pale face of one a resemblance to the girl he loved.

There were no greetings. This situation had no formalities. Warburton faced them and he seemed neither cold nor hot.

"Mr. Lee, as a director of the road I have to inform you that, following the reports of our engineer here, your present contracts are void and you will not get any more."

A white radiance of rage swiftly transformed Allison Lee. His eyes seemed to blaze purple out of his white face.

And Neale knew him to be Allie's father—saw the beauty and fire of her eyes in his.

"Warburton! You'll reconsider. I have great influence—"

"To hell with your influence!" retorted Warburton, the lion in him rising. "The builders—the directors—the owners of the U.P.R. are right here in this car. Do you understand that? Do you demand that I call a spade a spade?"

"I have been appointed by Congress. I will—"

"Congress or no Congress, you will never rebuild a foot of this railroad," thundered Warburton. He stood there glaring, final, assured. "For the sake of your—your government connections, let us say—let well enough alone."

"This upstart boy of an engineer!" burst out Lee, in furious resentment. "Who is he? How dare he accuse or report against me?"

"Mr. Lee, your name has never been mentioned by him," replied the director.

Lee struggled for self-control. "But, Warburton, it's preposterous!" he protested. "This wild boy—the associate of desperadoes—his report, whatever it is—absurd! Absurd as opposed to my position! A cub surveyor—slick with tongue and figures—to be thrown in my face! It's outrageous! I'll have him—"

Warburton held up a hand that impelled Lee to silence. In that gesture Neale read what stirred him to his soul. It was coming. He saw it again in General Lodge's fleeting, rare smile. He held his breath. The old pang throbbed in his breast.

"Lee, pray let me enlighten you and Senator Dunn," said Warburton, sonorously, "and terminate this awkward interview. . . . When the last spike is driven out here—presently—Mr. Neale will be chief engineer of maintenance of way of the Union Pacific Railroad."

CHAPTER XXIV

So for Neale the wonderful dream had come to pass, and but for the memory that made all hours of life bitter his cup of joy would have been full.

He made his headquarters in Benton and spent his days riding east or west over the line, taking up the great responsibility he had long trained for—the maintaining of the perfect condition of the railroad.

Toward the end of that month Neale was summoned to Omaha.

The message had been signed Warburton. Upon arriving at the terminus of the road Neale found a marvelous change even in the short time since he had been there. Omaha had become a city. It developed that Warburton had been called back to New York, leaving word for Neale to wait for orders.

Neale availed himself of this period to acquaint himself with the men whom he would deal with in the future. Among them, and in the roar of the railroad shops and the bustle of the city, he lost, perhaps temporarily, that haunting sense of pain and gloom. Despite himself the deference shown him was flattering, and his old habit of making friends reasserted itself. His place was assured now. There were rumors in the air of branch lines for the Union Pacific. He was consulted for advice, importuned for positions, invited here and there. So that the days in Omaha were both profitable and pleasurable.

Then came a telegram from Warburton calling him to Washington, D.C.

It took more than two days to get there, and the time dragged slowly for Neale. It seemed to him that his importance grew as he traveled, a fact which was amusing to him. All this resembled a dream.

When he reached the hotel designated in the telegram it was to receive a warm greeting from Warburton.

"It's a long trip to make for nothing," said the director. "And that's what it amounts to now. I thought I'd need you to answer a few questions for me. But you'll not be questioned officially, and so you'd better keep a close mouth. . . . We've raised the money. The completion of the U.P.R. is assured."

Neale could only conjecture what those questions might have been, for the director offered no explanation. And this circumstance recalled to mind his former impression of the complexity of the financial and political end of the construction. Warburton took him to dinner and later to a club, and introduced him to many men.

For this alone Neale was glad that he had been summoned to the capital. He met Senators, Congressmen, and other government officials, and many politicians and prominent men, all of whom, he was surprised to note, were well informed regarding the Union Pacific. He talked with them, but answered questions guardedly. And he listened to discussions and talks covering every phase of the work, from the Credit Mobilier to the Chinese coolies that were advancing from the west to meet the Paddies of his own division.

How strange to realize that the great railroad had its

nucleus, its impetus, and its completion in such a center as this! Here were the frock-coated, soft-voiced, cigar-smoking gentlemen among whom Warburton and his directors had swung the colossal enterprise. What a vast difference between these men and the builders! With the handsome white-haired Warburton, and his associates, as they smoked their rich cigars and drank their wine, Neale contrasted Casey and McDermott and many another burly spiker or teamster out on the line. Each class was necessary to this task. These Easterners talked of money, of gold, as a grade foreman might have talked of gravel. They smoked and conversed at ease, laughing at sallies, gossiping over what was a tragedy west of North Platte; and about them was an air of luxury, of power, of importance, and a singular grace that Neale felt rather than saw.

Strangest of all to him was the glimpse he got into the labyrinthine plot built around the stock, the finance, the gold that was constructing the road. He was an engineer, with a deductive habit of mind, but he would never be able to trace the intricacy of this monumental aggregation of deals. Yet he was hugely interested. Much of the scorn and disgust he had felt out on the line for the mercenaries connected with the work he forgot here among these frock-coated gentlemen.

An hour later Neale accompanied Warburton to the station where the director was to board a train for his return to New York.

"You'll start back to-morrow," said Warburton. "I'll see you soon, I hope—out there in Utah where the last spike is to be driven. That will be *the* day—*the* hour! . . . It will be celebrated all over the United States."

Neale returned to his hotel, trying to make out the vital thing that had come to him on this hurried and apparently useless journey. His mind seemed in a whirl. Yet as he pondered, there gradually loomed up the reflection that in the eastern, or constructive, end of the great plan there were the same spirits of evil and mystery as existed in the western, or building, end. Here big men were interested, involved; out there bigger men sweat and burned and aged and died. The difference was that these toilers gave all for an ideal while the directors and their partners thought only of money, of profits.

Neale restrained what might have been contempt, but he thought that if these financiers could have seen the life of the diggers and spikers as he knew it they might be actuated by a nobler motive. Before he dropped to sleep that night he concluded that his trip to Washington, and the recognition accorded him by Warburton's circle, had fixed a new desire in his heart to heave some more rails and drive some more spikes for the railroad he loved so well. To him the work had been something for which he had striven with all his might and for which he had risked his life. Not only had his brain been given to the creation, but his muscles had ached from the actual physical toil attendant upon this biggest of big jobs.

When Neale at last reached Benton it was night. Benton and night! And he had forgotten. A mob of men surged down and up on the train. Neale had extreme difficulty in getting off at all. But the excitement, the hurry, the discordant and hoarse medley of many voices, were unusual at that hour around the station, even for strenuous Benton. All these men were carrying baggage. Neale shouted questions into passing ears, until at length some fellow heard and yelled a reply.

The last night of Benton!

He understood then. The great and vile construction camp had reached the end of its career. It was being torn down—moved away—depopulated. There was an exodus. In another forty-eight hours all that had been Benton, with its accumulated life and gold and toil, would be incorporated in another and a greater and a last camp—Roaring City.

The contrast to the beautiful Washington, the check to his half-dreaming memory of what he had experienced there, the sudden plunge into this dim-lighted, sordid, and roaring hell, all brought about in Neale a revulsion of feeling.

And with the sinking of his spirit there returned the old haunting pangs—the memory of Allie Lee, the despairing doubts of life or death for her. Beyond the camp loomed the dim hills, mystical, secretive, and unchangeable. If she were out there among them, dead or alive, to know it would be a blessed relief. It was this horror of Benton that he feared.

He walked the street, up and down, up and down, until the hour was late and he was tired. All the halls and saloons were blazing in full blast. Once he heard low, hoarse cries and pistol-shots—and then again quick, dull, booming guns. How strange they should make him shiver! But all seemed strange. From these sounds he turned away, not knowing what to do or where to go, since sleep or rest was impossible. Finally he went into a gambling-den and found a welcome among players whose faces he knew.

It was Benton's last night, and there was something in the air, menacing, terrible.

Neale gave himself up to the spirit of the hour and the game. He had almost forgotten himself when a white, jeweled hand flashed over his shoulder, to touch it softly. He heard his name whispered. Looking up, he saw the flushed and singularly radiant face of Beauty Stanton.

CHAPTER XXV

The afternoon and night of pay-day in Benton, during which Allie Lee was barred in her room, were hideous, sleepless, dreadful hours. Her ears were filled with Benton's roar—whispers and wails and laughs; thick shouts of drunken men; the cold voices of gamblers; clink of gold and clink of glasses; a ceaseless tramp and shuffle of boots; pistol-shots muffled and far away, pistol-shots ringing and near at hand; the angry hum of brawling men; and strangest of all this dreadful roar were the high-pitched, piercing voices of women, in songs without soul, in laughter without mirth, in cries wild and terrible and mournful.

Allie lay in the dark, praying for the dawn, shuddering at this strife of sound, fearful that any moment the violence of Benton would burst through the flimsy walls of her room to destroy her. But the roar swelled and subsided and died away; the darkness gave place to gray light and then dawn; the sun arose, the wind began to blow. Now Benton slept, the sleep of sheer exhaustion.

Her mirror told Allie the horror of that night. Her face was white; her eyes were haunted by terrors, with great dark shadows beneath. She could not hold her hands steady.

Late that afternoon there were stirrings and sounds in Durade's hall. The place had awakened. Presently Durade himself brought her food and drink. He looked haggard, worn, yet radiant. He did not seem to note Allie's condition or appearance.

"That deaf and dumb fool who waited on you is gone," said Durade. "Yesterday was pay-day in Benton. . . . Many are gone. . . . Allie, I won fifty thousand dollars in gold!"

"Isn't that enough?" she asked.

He did not hear her, but went on talking of his winnings, of gold, of games, and of big stakes coming. His lips trembled, his eyes glittered, his fingers clawed at the air.

For Allie it was a relief when Durade left her. He had almost reached the apex of his fortunes and the inevitable end. Allie realized that if she were ever to lift a hand to save herself she must do so at once.

This was a fixed and desperate thought in her mind when Durade called her to her work.

Allie always entered that private den of Durade's with eyes cast down. She had been scorched too often by the glances of men. As she went in this time she felt the presence of gamblers, but they were quieter than those to whom she had become accustomed. Durade ordered her to fetch drinks, then he went on talking, rapidly, in excitement, elated, boastful, almost gay.

Allie did not look up. As she carried the tray to the large table she heard a man whisper low: "By jove! . . . Hough, that's the girl!"

Then she heard a slight, quick intake of breath, and the exclamation, "Good God!"

Both voices thrilled Allie. The former seemed the low, well-modulated, refined, and drawling speech of an Englishman; the latter was keen, quick, soft, and full of genuine emotion.

Allie returned to her chair by the sideboard before she

ventured to look up. Durade was playing cards with four men, three of whom were black-garbed, after the manner of professional gamblers. The other player wore gray, and a hat of unusual shape, with wide, loose, cloth band. He removed his hat as he caught Allie's glance, and she associated the act with the fact of her presence. She thought that this must be the man whose voice had proclaimed him English. He had a fair face, lined and shadowed and dissipated, with tired blue eyes and a blond mustache that failed to altogether hide a well-shaped mouth. It was the kindest and saddest face Allie had ever seen there. She read its story. In her extremity she had acquired a melancholy wisdom in the judgment of the faces of the men drifting through Durade's hall. What Allie had heard in this Englishman's voice she saw in his features. He did not look at her again. He played cards wearily, carelessly, indifferently, with his mind plainly on something else.

"Ancliffe, how many cards?" called one of the black-garbed men.

The Englishman threw down his cards. "None," he said.

The game was interrupted by a commotion in the adjoining room, which was the public gambling-hall of Durade's establishment.

"Another fight!" exclaimed Durade, impatiently. "And only Mull and Fresno showed up to-day."

Harsh voices and heavy stamps were followed by a pistol-shot. Durade hurriedly arose.

"Gentlemen, excuse me," he said, and went out. One of the gamblers also left the room, and another crossed it to peep through the door.

This left the Englishman sitting at the table with the last gambler, whose back was turned toward Allie. She saw the Englishman lean forward to speak. Then the gambler arose and, turning, came directly toward her.

"My name is Place Hough," he said, speaking rapidly

and low. "I am a gambler—but a gentleman. I've heard strange rumors about you, and now I see for myself. Are you Allie Lee?"

Allie's heart seemed to come to her throat. She shook all over, and she gazed with piercing intensity at the man. When he had arisen from the table he had appeared the same black-garbed, hard-faced gambler as any of the others. But looked at closely, he was different. Underneath the cold, expressionless face worked something mobile and soft. His eyes were of crystal clearness and remarkable for a penetrating power. They shone with wonder, curiosity, sympathy.

Allie instinctively trusted the voice and then consciously trusted the man. "Oh, sir, I am—distressed—ill from fright!" she faltered. "If I only dared—"

"You dare tell me," he interrupted, swiftly. "Be quick. Are you here willingly with this man?"

"Oh no!"

"What then?"

"Oh, sir—you do not think—I—"

"I knew you were good, innocent—the moment I laid eyes on you, . . . Who are you?"

"Allie Lee. My father is Allison Lee."

"Whew!" The gambler whistled softly and, turning, glanced at the door, then beckoned Ancliffe. The Englishman arose. In the adjoining rooms sounds of strife were abating.

"Ancliffe, this girl is Allie Lee—daughter of Allison Lee—a big man of the U.P.R. . . . Something terribly wrong here." And he whispered to Ancliffe.

Allie became aware of the Englishman's scrutiny, doubtful, sad, yet kind and curious. Indeed these men had heard of her.

"Hough, you must be mistaken," he said.

Allie felt a sudden rush of emotion. Her opportunity had

come. "I am Allie Lee. My mother ran off with Durade—to California. He used her as a lure to draw men to his gambling-hells—as he uses me now. . . . Two years ago we escaped—started east with a caravan. The Indians attacked us. I crawled under a rock—escaped the massacre. I—"

"Never mind all your story," interrupted Hough. "We haven't time for that. I believe you. . . . You are held a close prisoner?"

"Oh yes—locked and barred. I never get out. I have been threatened so—that until now I feared to tell anyone. But Durade—he is going mad. I—I can bear it no longer."

"Miss Lee, you shall not bear it," declared Ancliffe. "We'll take you out of here."

"How?" queried Hough, shortly.

Ancliffe was for walking right out with her, but Hough shook his head.

"Listen," began Allie, hurriedly. "He would kill me the instant I tried to escape. He loved my mother. He does not believe she is dead. He lives only to be revenged upon her. . . . He has a desperate gang here. Fresno, Mull, Stitt, Black, Grist, Dayss, a greaser called Mex, and others—all the worst of bad men. You cannot get me out of here alive except by some trick."

"How about bringing the troops?"

"Durade would kill me the first thing."

"Could we steal you out at night?"

"I don't see how. They are awake all night. I am barred in, watched. . . . Better work on Durade's weakness. Gold! He's mad for gold. When the fever's on him he might gamble me away—or sell me for gold."

Hough's cold eyes shone like fire in ice. He opened his lips to speak—then quickly motioned Ancliffe back to the table. They had just seated themselves when the two gamblers returned, followed by Durade. He was rubbing his hands in satisfaction.

"What was the fuss about?" queried Hough, tipping the ashes off his cigar.

"Some drunks after money they had lost."

"And got thrown out for their pains?" inquired Ancliffe.

"Yes. Mull and Fresno are out there now."

The game was taken up again. Allie sensed a different note in it. The gambler Hough now faced her in his position at the table; and behind every card he played there seemed to be intense purpose and tremendous force. Ancliffe soon left the game. But he appeared fascinated where formerly he had been indifferent. Soon it developed that Hough, by his spirit and skill, was driving his opponents, inciting their passion for play, working upon their feelings. Durade seemed the weakest gambler, though he had the best luck. Good luck balanced his excited play. The two other gamblers pitted themselves against Hough.

The shadows of evening had begun to darken the room when Durade called for lights. A slim, sloe-eyed, pantherish-moving Mexican came in to execute the order. He wore a belt with a knife in it and looked like a brigand. When he had lighted the lamps he approached Durade and spoke in Spanish. Durade replied in the same tongue. Then the Mexican went out. One of the gamblers lost and arose from the table.

"Gentlemen, may I go out for more money and return to the game?" he asked.

"Certainly," replied Hough.

Durade assented with bad grace.

The game went on and grew in interest. Probably the Mexican had reported the fact of its possibilities, or perhaps Durade had sent out word of some nature. For one by one his villainous lieutenants came in, stepping softly, gleaming-eyed.

"Durade, have you stopped play outside?" queried Hough.

"Supper-time. Not much going on," replied Mull.

Hough watched this speaker with keen coolness.

"I did not address you," he said.

Durade, catching the drift, came out of his absorption of play long enough to say that with a big game at hand he did not want to risk any interruption. He spoke frankly, but he did not look sincere.

Presently the second gambler announced that he would consider it a favor to be allowed to go out and borrow money. Then he left hurriedly. Durade and Hough played alone; and the luck seesawed from one to the other until both the other players returned. They did not come alone. Two more black-frocked, black-sombreroed, cold-faced individuals accompanied them.

"May we sit in?" they asked.

"With pleasure," replied Hough.

Durade frowned and the glow left his face. Though the luck was still with him, it was evident that he did not favor added numbers. Yet the man's sensitiveness to any change immediately manifested itself when he won the first large stake. His radiance returned and also his vanity.

Hough interrupted the game by striking the table with his hand. The sound seemed hard, metallic, yet his hand was empty. Any attentive observer would have become aware that Hough had a gun up his sleeve. But Durade did not catch the significance.

"I object to that man leaning over the table," said Hough, and he pointed to the lounging Fresno.

"Thet so?" leered the ugly giant. He looked bold and vicious.

"Do not address me," ordered Hough.

Fresno backed away silently from the cold-faced gambler.

"Don't mind him, Hough," protested Durade. "They're all excited. Big stakes always work them up."

"Send them out so we can play without annoyance."

"No," replied Durade, sharply. "They can watch the game."

"Ancliffe," called Hough, just as sharply, "fetch some of my friends to watch this game. Don't forget Neale and Larry King."

Allie, who was watching and listening with strained faculties, nearly fainted at the sudden mention of her lover Neale and her friend Larry. She went blind for a second; the room turned round and round; she thought her heart would burst with joy.

The Englishman hurried out.

Durade looked up with a passionate and wolfish swiftness.

"What do you mean?"

"I want some of my friends to watch the game," replied Hough.

"But I don't allow that red-headed cowboy gun-fighter to come into my place."

"That is regrettable, for you will make an exception this time. . . . Durade, you don't stand well in Benton. I do."

The Spaniard's eyes glittered. "You insinuate—*Señor*—"

"Yes," interposed Hough, and his cold, deliberate voice dominated the explosive Durade. "Do you remember a gambler named Jones? . . . He was shot in this room. . . . If I should happen to be shot here—in the same way—you and your gang would not last long in Benton!"

Durade's face grew livid with rage and fear. And in that moment the mask was off. The nature of the Spaniard stood forth. Another manifest fact was that Durade had not before matched himself against a gambler of Hough's caliber.

"Well, are you only a bluff or do we go on with the game?" inquired Hough.

Durade choked back his rage and signified with a motion of his hand that play should be resumed.

Allie fastened her eyes upon the door. She was in a tumult of emotion. Despite that, her mind revolved wild and intermittent ideas as to the risk of letting Neale see and recognize her there. Yet her joy was so overpowering that she believed if he entered the door she would rush to him and trust in God to save her. In God and Reddy King! She remembered the cowboy, and a thrill linked all her emotions. Durade and his gang would face a terrible reckoning if Reddy King ever entered to see her there.

Moments passed. The gambling went on. The players spoke low; the spectators were silent. Discordant sounds from outside disturbed the quiet.

Allie stared fixedly at the door. Presently it opened. Ancliffe entered with several men, all quick in movement, alert of eye. But Neale and Larry King were not among them. Allie's heart sank like lead. The revulsion of feeling, the disappointment, was sickening. She saw Ancliffe shake his head, and divined in the action that he had not been able to find the friends Hough wanted particularly. Then Allie felt the incredible strangeness of being glad that Neale was not to find her there—that Larry was not to throw his guns on Durade's crowd. There might be a chance of her being liberated without violence.

This reaction left her weak and dazed for a while. Still she heard the low voices of the gamesters, the slap of cards and clink of gold. Her wits had gone from her ever since the mention of Neale. She floundered in a whirl of thoughts and fears until gradually she recovered self-possession. Whatever instinct or love or spirit had guided her had done so rightly. She had felt Neale's presence in Benton. It was stingingly sweet to realize that. Her heart swelled with pangs of fullest measure. Surely he again believed her dead. Soon he would come upon her—face to face—somewhere. He would learn she was alive—unharmed—true to him with all her soul. Indians, renegade Spaniards, Benton with its terrors, a host of evil men, not these nor anything else could keep her from Neale forever. She had believed that always, but never as now, in the clearness of this beautiful spiritual insight. Behind her belief was something unfathomable and great. Not the movement of progress as typified by those men who had dreamed of the railroad, nor the spirit of the unconquerable engineers as typified by Neale, nor the wildness of wild youth like Larry King, nor the heroic labor and simplicity and sacrifice of common men, nor the inconceivable passion of these gamblers for gold, nor the mystery hidden in the mad laughter of these fallen women, strange and sad on the night wind—not any of these things nor all of them, wonderful and incalculable as they were, loomed so great as the spirit that upheld Allie Lee.

When she raised her head again the gambling scene had changed. Only three men played—Hough, Durade, and another. And even as Allie looked this third player threw his cards into the deck and with silent gesture rose from the table to take a position with the other black-garbed gamblers standing behind Hough. The blackness of their attire contrasted strongly with the whiteness of their faces. They had lost gold, which fact meant little to them. But there was something big and significant in their presence behind Hough. Gamblers leagued against a crooked gambling-hell! Durade had lost a fortune, yet not all his fortune. He seemed a haggard, flaming-eyed wreck of the once debonair Durade. His hair was wet and dishevelled, his collar was open, his hand wavered. Blood trickled down from his lower lip. He saw nothing except the gold, the cards, and that steel-nerved, gray-faced, implacable Hough. Behind him lined up his gang, nervous, strained, frenzied, with eyes on the gold—hate-filled, murderous eyes.

Allie slipped into her room, leaving the door ajar so she could peep out, and there she paced the floor, waiting, listening for what she dared not watch. The gambler Hough would win all that Durade had, and then stake it against her. That was what Allie believed. She had no doubts of Hough's winning her, too, but she doubted if he could take her away. There would be a fight. And if there was a fight, then that must be the end of Durade. For this gambler, Hough, with his unshakable nerve, his piercing eyes, his wonderful white hands, swift as light—he would at the slightest provocation kill Durade.

Suddenly Allie was arrested by a loud, long suspiration—a heave of heavy breaths in the room of the gamblers. A chair scraped, noisily breaking the silence, which instantly clamped down again.

"Durade, you're done!" It was the cold, ringing voice of Hough.

Allie ran to the door, peeped through the crack. Durade sat there like a wild beast bound. Hough stood erect over a huge golden pile on the table. The others seemed stiff in their tracks.

"There's a fortune here," went on Hough, indicating the gold. "All I had—all our gentlemen opponents had— all *you* had. . . . I have won it all!"

Durade's eyes seemed glued to that dully glistening heap. He could not even look up at the coldly passionate Hough.

"All! All!" echoed Durade.

Then Hough, like a striking hawk, bent toward the Spaniard. "Durade, have you anything more to bet?"

Durade was the only man who moved. Slowly he arose, shaking in every limb, and not till he became erect did he unrivet his eyes from that yellow heap on the table.

"*Señor*—do you—mock me?" he gasped, hoarsely.

"I offer you my winnings—*all*—*for the girl you have here!*"

"You are crazy!" ejaculated the Spaniard.

"Certainly. . . . But hurry! Do you accept?"

"*Señor*, I would not sell that girl for all the gold of the Indies," replied Durade, instantly. No vacillation—no indecision in him here. Hough's offer held no lure for this Spaniard who had committed many crimes for gold.

"*But you'll gamble her!*" asserted Hough, and now indeed his words were mockery. In one splendid gesture he swept his winnings into the middle of the table, and the gold gave out a ringing clash. As a gambler he read the soul of his opponent.

Durade's jaw worked convulsively, as if he had difficulty in holding it firm enough for utterance. What he would not sell for any price he would risk on a gambler's strange faith in chance.

"All my winnings against this girl," went on Hough, relentlessly. Scorn and a taunting dare and an insidious persuasion mingled with the passion of his offer. He knew how to inflame. Durade, as a gambler, was a weakling in the grasp of a giant. "Come! . . . Do you accept?"

Durade's body leaped, as if an irresistible current had been shot into it.

"*Si, Señor!*" he cried, with power and joy in his voice. In that moment, no doubt the greatest in his life of gambling, he unconsciously went back to the use of his mother tongue.

Actuated by one impulse, Hough and Durade sat down at the table. The others crowded around. Fresno lurched close, with a wicked gleam in his eyes.

"I was onto Hough," he said to his nearest ally. "It's the girl he's after!"

The gamblers cut the cards for who should deal. Hough

won. For him victory seemed to exist in the suspense of the very silence, in the charged atmosphere of the room. He began to shuffle the cards. His hands were white, shapely, perfect, like a woman's, and yet not beautiful. The spirit, the power, the ruthless nature in them had no relation to beauty. How marvelously swift they moved—too swift for the gaze to follow. And the incomparable dexterity with which he manipulated the cards gave forth the suggestion as to what he could do with them. In those gleaming hands, in the flying cards, in the whole intenseness of the gambler there showed the power and the intent to win. The crooked Durade had met his match, a match who toyed with him. If there were an element of chance in this short game it was that of the uncertainty of life, not of Durade's chance to win. He had no chance. No eye, no hand could have justly detected Hough in the slightest deviation from honesty. Yet all about the man in that tense moment proved what a gambler really was.

Durade called in a whisper for two cards, and he received them with trembling fingers. Terrible hope and exultation transformed his face.

"I'll take three," said Hough, calmly. With deliberate care and slowness, in strange contrast to his former motions, he took, one by one, three cards from the deck. Then he looked at them, and just as calmly dropped all his cards, face up, on the table, disclosing what he knew to be an unbeatable hand.

Durade stared. A thick cry escaped him.

Swiftly Hough rose. "Durade, I have won." Then he turned to his friends. "Gentlemen, please pocket this gold."

With that he stepped to Allie's door. He saw her peering out. "Come, Miss Lee," he said.

Allie stepped out, trembling and unsteady on her feet.

The Spaniard now seemed compelled to look up from the gold Hough's comrades were pocketing. When he saw

Allie another slow and remarkable transformation came over him. At first he started slightly at Hough's hand on Allie's arm. The radiance of his strange passion for gold, that had put a leaping glory into his haggard face, faded into a dark and mounting surprise. A blaze burned away the shadows. His eyes betrayed an unsupportable sense of loss and the spirit that repudiated it. For a single instant he was magnificent—and perhaps in that instant race and blood spoke; then, with bewildering suddenness, surely with the suddenness of a memory, he became a black, dripping-faced victim of unutterable and unquenchable hate.

Allie recoiled in the divination that Durade saw her mother in her. No memory, no love, no gold, no wager, could ever thwart the Spaniard.

"*Señor*, you tricked me!" he whispered.

"I beat you at your own game," said Hough. "My friends and your men heard the stake—saw the game."

"*Señor*, I would not—bet—that girl—for any stake!"

"You have *lost* her. . . . Let me warn you, Durade. Be careful, once in your life! . . . You're welcome to what gold is left there."

Durade shoved back the gold so fiercely that he upset the table, and its contents jangled on the floor. The spill and the crash of a scattered fortune released Durade's men from their motionless suspense. They began to pick up the coins.

The Spaniard was halted by the gleam of a derringer in Hough's hand. Hissing like a snake, Durade stood still, momentarily held back by a fear that quickly gave place to insane rage.

"Shoot him!" said Ancliffe, with a coolness which proved his foresight.

One of Hough's friends swung a cane, smashing a lamp; then with like swift action he broke the other lamp, instantly plunging the room into darkness. This appeared to be the signal for Durade's men to break loose into a mad scramble for the gold. Durade began to scream and rush forward.

Allie felt herself drawn backward, along the wall, through her door. It was not so dark in there. She distinguished Hough and Ancliffe. The latter closed the door. Hough whispered to Allie, though the din in the other room made such caution needless.

"Can we get out this way?" he asked.

"There's a window," replied Allie.

"Ancliffe, open it and get her out. I'll stop Durade if he comes in. Hurry!"

While the Englishman opened the window Hough stood in front of the door with both arms extended. Allie could just see his tall form in the pale gloom. Pandemonium had begun in the other room, with Durade screaming for lights, and his men yelling and fighting for the gold, and Hough's friends struggling to get out. But they did not follow Hough into this room and evidently must have thought he had escaped through the other door.

"Come," said Ancliffe, touching Allie.

He helped her get out, and followed laboriously. Then he softly called to Hough. The gambler let himself down swiftly and noiselessly.

"Now what?" he muttered.

They appeared to be in a narrow alley between a house of boards and a house of canvas. Excited voices sounded inside this canvas structure and evidently alarmed Hough, for with a motion he enjoined silence and led Allie through the dark passage out into a gloomy square surrounded by low, dark structures. Ancliffe followed close behind.

The night was dark, with no stars showing. A cool wind blew in Allie's face, refreshing her after her long confinement. Hough began groping forward. This square had a rough board floor and a skeleton framework. It had been a house of canvas. Some of the partitions were still standing.

"Look for a door—any place to get out," whispered Hough to Ancliffe, as they came to the opposite side of this square space. Hough, with Allie close at his heels, went to the right while Ancliffe went to the left. Hough went so far, then muttering, drew Allie back again to the point whence they had started. Ancliffe was there.

"No place! All boarded up tight," he whispered.

"Same on this side. We'll have to—"

"Listen!" exclaimed Ancliffe, holding up his hand.

There appeared to be noise all around, but mostly on the other side of the looming canvas house, behind which was the alleyway that led to Durade's hall. Gleams of light flashed through the gloom. Durade's high, quick voice mingled with hoarser and deeper tones. Some one in the canvas house was talking to Durade, who apparently must have been in Allie's room and at her window.

"See hyar, Greaser, we ain't harborin' any of your outfit, an' we'll plug the fust gent we see," called a surly voice.

Durade's staccato tones succeeded it. "Did you see them?"

"We heerd them gettin' out the winder."

Durade's voice rose high in Spanish curses. Then he called: "Fresno—Mull—take men—go around the street. They can't get away. . . . You, Mex, get down in there with the gang."

Lower voices answered, questioning, eager, but indistinct.

"Kill him—bring her back—and you can have the gold," shouted Durade.

Following that came the heavy tramp of boots and the low roar of angry men.

Hough leaned toward Ancliffe. "They've got us penned in."

"Yes. But it's pretty dark here. And they'll be slow. You watch while I tear a hole through somewhere," replied Ancliffe.

He was perfectly cool and might have been speaking of some casual incident. He extinguished his cigarette, dropped it, then put on his gloves.

Hough loomed tall and dark. His face showed pale in the shadow. He stood with his elbows stiff against his sides, a derringer in each hand.

"I wish I had heavier guns," he said.

Allie's thrill of emotion spent itself in a shudder of realization. Calmly and chivalrously these two strangers had taken a stand against her enemies and with a few cool words and actions had accepted whatever might betide.

"I must tell you—oh, I must!" she whispered, with her hand on Hough's arm. "I heard you send for Neale and Larry King. . . . It made my heart stop! . . . Neale—Warren Neale is my sweetheart. See, I wear his ring! . . . Reddy King is my dearest friend—my brother! . . ."

Hough bent low to peer into Allie's face—to see her ring. Then he turned to Ancliffe.

"How things work out! . . . I always suspected what was wrong with Neale. Now I know—after seeing his girl."

"By Jove!" exclaimed Ancliffe.

"Well, I'll block Durade's gang. Will you save the girl?"

"Assuredly," answered the imperturbable Englishman. "Where shall I take her?"

"Where *can* she be safe? The troop camp? No, too far. . . . Aha! take her to Stanton. Tell Stanton the truth. Stanton will hide her. Then find Neale and King."

Hough turned to Allie. "I'm glad you spoke—about Neale," he said, and there was a curious softness in his voice. "I owe him a great deal. I like him. . . . Ancliffe will get you out of here—and safely back to Neale."

Allie knew somehow—from something in his tone, his

presence—that he would never leave this gloomy inclosure. She heard Ancliffe ripping a board off the wall or fence, and that sound seemed alarmingly loud. The voices no longer were heard behind the canvas house. The wind whipped through the bare framework. Somewhere at a distance were music and revelry. Benton's night roar had begun. Over all seemed to hang a menacing and ponderous darkness.

Suddenly a light appeared moving slowly from the most obscure corner of the square, perhaps fifty paces distant.

Hough drew Allie closer to Ancliffe. "Get behind me," he whispered.

A sharp ripping and splitting of wood told of Ancliffe's progress; also it located the fugitives for Durade's gang. The light vanished; quick voices rasped out; then stealthy feet padded over the boards.

Allie saw or imagined she saw gliding forms black against the pale gloom. She was so close to Ancliffe that he touched her as he worked. Turning, she beheld a ray of light through an aperture he had made.

Suddenly the gloom split to a reddish flare. It revealed dark forms. A gun cracked. Allie heard the heavy thud of a bullet against the wall. Then Hough shot. His derringer made a small, spiteful report. It was followed by a cry—a groan. Other guns cracked. Bullets pattered on the wood. Allie heard the spat of lead striking Hough. It had a sickening sound. He moved as if from a blow. A volley followed and Allie saw the bright flashes. All about her bullets were whistling and thudding. She knew with a keen horror every time Hough was struck. Hoarse yells and strangling cries mixed with the diminishing shots.

Then Ancliffe grasped her and pushed her through a vent he had made. Allie crawled backward and she could see Hough still standing in front. It seemed that he swayed. Then as she rose further view was cut off. Although she had not looked around, she was aware of a dimly lighted storeroom. Outside the shots had ceased. She heard something heavy fall suddenly; then a patter of quick, light footsteps.

Ancliffe essayed to get through the opening feet first. It was a tight squeeze, or else some one held him back. There came a crashing of wood; Ancliffe's body whirled in the aperture and he struggled violently. Allie heard hissing, sibilant Spanish utterances. She stood petrified, certain that Durade had attacked Ancliffe. Suddenly the Englishman crashed through, drawing a supple, twisting, slender man with him. He held this man by the throat with one hand and by the wrist with the other. Allie recognized Durade's Mexican ally. He gripped a knife and the blade was bloody.

Once inside, where Ancliffe could move, he handled the Mexican with deliberate and remorseless ease. Allie saw him twist and break the arm which held the knife. Not that sight, but the eyes of the Mexican made Allie close her own. When she opened them, at a touch, Ancliffe stood beside her and the Mexican lay quivering. Ancliffe held the bloody knife; he hid it under his coat.

"Come," he said. His voice seemed thin.

"But Hough! We must—"

Ancliffe's strange gesture froze Allie's lips. She followed him—clung close to him. There were voices near—and persons. All seemed to fall back before the Englishman. He strode on. Indeed, his movements appeared unnatural. They went down a low stairway, out into the dark. Lights were there to the right, and hurrying forms. Ancliffe ran with her in the other direction. Only dim, pale lamps shone through tents. Down this side street it was quiet and dark. Allie stumbled, would have fallen but for Ancliffe. Yet sometimes he stumbled, too. He turned a corner and proceeded rapidly toward bright lights. The houses loomed big. Down that way many people passed to and fro. Allie's senses recognized a new sound—a confusion of music, dancing, hilarity, all distinct, near at hand. She could scarcely keep up with Ancliffe. He did not speak nor look to right or left.

At the corner of a large house—a long structure which sent out gleams of light—Ancliffe opened a door and pulled Allie into a hallway, dark near at hand, but brilliant at the other end. He drew her along this passage, striding slower now and unsteadily. He turned into another hall lighted by lamps. Music and gaiety seemed to sweep stunningly into Allie's face. But Allie saw only one person there—a negress. As Ancliffe halted, the negress rose from her seat. She was frightened.

"Call Stanton—quick!" he panted. He thrust gold at her. "Tell no one else!"

Then he opened a door, pushed Allie into a handsomely furnished parlor, and, closing the door, staggered to a couch, upon which he fell. His face wore a singular look, remarkable for its whiteness. All its weary, careless indifference had vanished.

As he lay back his hands loosed their hold of his coat and fell away all bloody. The knife slid to the floor. A crimson froth flecked his lips.

"Oh—Heaven! You were—stabbed!" gasped Allie, sinking to her knees.

"If Stanton doesn't come in time—tell her what happened—ask her to fetch Neale to you," he said. He spoke with extreme difficulty and a fluttering told of blood in his throat.

Allie could not speak. She could not pray. But her sight and her perception were abnormally keen. Ancliffe's strange, clear gaze rested upon her, and it seemed to Allie that he smiled, not with lips or face, but in spirit. How strange and beautiful!

Then Allie heard a rush of silk at the door. It opened—closed. A woman of fair face, bare of arm and neck, glittering with diamonds, swept into the parlor. She had great, dark-blue eyes full of shadows and they flashed from Ancliffe to Allie and back again.

"What's happened? You're pale as death! . . . Ancliffe! Your hands—your breast! . . . *My God!*"

She bent over him. "Stanton, I've been—cut up—and Hough is—dead."

"Oh, this horrible Benton!" cried the woman.

"Don't faint. . . . Hear me. You remember we were curious about a girl—Durade had in his place. This is she—Allie Lee. She is innocent. Durade held her for revenge. He had loved—then hated her mother. . . . Hough won all Durade's gold—and then the girl. . . . But we had to fight. . . . Stanton, this Allie Lee is Neale's sweetheart. . . . He believes her dead. . . . You hide her—bring Neale to her."

Quickly she replied, "I promise you, Ancliffe, I promise. . . . How strange—what you tell! . . . But not strange for Benton! . . . Ancliffe! Speak to me!—Oh, he is going!"

With her first words a subtle change passed over Ancliffe. It was the release of his will. His whole body sank. Under the intense whiteness of his face a cold gray shade began to creep. His last conscious instant spent itself in the strange gaze Allie had felt before, and now she had a vague perception that in some way it expressed a blessing and a deliverance. The instant the beautiful light turned inward, as if to illumine the darkness of his soul, she divined what he had once been, his ruin, his secret and eternal remorse—and the chance to die that had made him great.

So, forgetful of the other beside her, Allie Lee watched Ancliffe, sustained by a nameless spirit, feeling with tragic pity her duty as a woman—to pray for him, to stay beside him, that he might not be alone when he died.

And while she watched, with the fading of that singular radiance, there returned to his face a slow, careless weariness.

"He's gone!" murmured Stanton, rising. A dignity had come to her. "Dead! And we knew nothing of him—not his real name—nor his place. . . . But even Benton could not keep him from dying like an English gentleman."

She took Allie by the hand, led her out of the parlor and across the hall into a bedroom. Then she faced Allie, wonderingly, with all a woman's sympathy, and something else that Allie sensed as a sweet and poignant wistfulness.

"Are you—Neale's sweetheart?" she asked, very low.

"Oh—please—find him—for me!" sobbed Allie.

The tenderness in this woman's voice and look and touch was what Allie needed more than anything, and it made her a trembling child. How strangely, hesitatingly, with closing eyes, this woman reached to fold her in gentle arms. What a tumult Allie felt throbbing in the full breast where she laid her head.

"Allie Lee! . . . and he thinks you dead," she murmured, brokenly. "I will bring him—to you."

When she released Allie years and shadows no longer showed in her face. Her eyes were tear-wet and darkening; her lips were tremulous. At that moment there was something beautiful and terrible about her.

But Allie could not understand.

"You stay here," she said. "Be very quiet . . . I will bring Neale."

Opening the door, she paused on the threshold, to glance down the hall first, and then back at Allie. Her smile was beautiful. She closed the door and locked it. Allie heard the soft swish of silk dying away.

CHAPTER XXVI

Beauty Stanton threw a cloak over her bare shoulders and, hurriedly leaving the house by the side entrance, she stood a moment, breathless and excited, in the dark and windy street.

She had no idea why she halted there, for she wanted to run. But the instant she got out into the cool night air a check came to action and thought. Strange sensations poured in upon her—the darkness, lonesome and weird; the wailing wind with its weight of dust; the roar of Benton's main thoroughfare; and the low, strange murmur, neither musical nor mirthful, behind her, from that huge hall she called her home. Stranger even than these emotions were the swelling and aching of her heart, the glow and quiver of her flesh, thrill on thrill, deep, like bursting pangs of joy never before experienced, the physical sense of a touch, inexplicable in its power.

On her bare breast a place seemed to flush and throb and glow. "Ah!" murmured Beauty Stanton. "That girl laid her face here—over my heart! What was I to do?" she murmured. "Oh yes—to find her sweetheart—Neale!"

Then she set off rapidly, but if she had possessed wings

or the speed of the wind she could not have kept pace with her thoughts.

She turned the corner of the main street and glided among the hurrying throng. Men stood in groups, talking excitedly. She gathered that there had been fights. More than once she was addressed familiarly, but she did not hear what was said. The wide street seemed strange, dark, dismal, the lights yellow and flaring, the wind burdened, the dark tide of humanity raw, wild, animal, unstable. Above the lights and the throngs hovered a shadow—not the mantle of night nor the dark desert sky.

Her steps took familiar ground, yet she seemed not to know this Benton.

"Once I was like Allie Lee!" she whispered. "Not so many years ago."

And the dark tide of men, the hurry and din, the wind and dust, the flickering lights, all retreated spectral-like to the background of a mind returned to youth, hope, love, home. She saw herself at eighteen—yes, Beauty Stanton even then, possessed of a beauty that was her ruin; at school, the favorite of a host of boys and girls; at home, where the stately oaks were hung with silver moss and the old Colonial house rang with song of sister and sport of brother, where a sweet-faced, gentle-voiced mother—

"*Ah! . . . Mother!*" And at that word the dark tide of men seemed to rise and swell at her, to trample her sacred memory as inevitably and brutally as it had used her body.

Only the piercing pang of that memory remained with Beauty Stanton. She was a part of Benton. She was treading the loose board-walk of the great and vile construction camp. She might draw back from leer and touch, but none the less was she there, a piece of this dark, bold, obscure life. She was a cog in the wheel, a grain of dust in the whirlwind, a morsel of flesh and blood for the hungry maw of a wild and passing monster of progress.

Her hurried steps carried her on with her errand. Neale! She knew where to find him. Often she had watched him play, always regretfully, conscious that he did not fit there. His indifference had baffled her as it had piqued her professional vanity. Men had never been indifferent to her; she had seen them fight for her mocking smiles. But Neale! He had been stone to her charm, yet kind, gracious, deferential. Always she had felt strangely shamed when he stood bareheaded before her. Beauty Stanton had foregone respect. Yet respect was what she yearned for. The instincts of her girlhood, surviving, made a whited sepulcher of her present life. She could not bear Neale's indifference and she had failed to change it. Her infatuation, born of that hot-bed of Benton life, had beaten and burned itself to destruction against a higher and better love—the only love of her womanhood. She would have slaved for him. But he had passed her by, absorbed with his own secret, working toward some fateful destiny, lost, perhaps, like all the others there.

And now she learned that the mystery of him—his secret—was the same old agony of love that sent so many on endless, restless roads—Allie Lee! and he believed her dead!

After all the bitterness, life had moments of sweetest joy. Fate was being a little kind to her—Beauty Stanton. It would be from her lips Neale would hear that Allie Lee was alive—innocent—unharmed—faithful to him—waiting for him. Beauty Stanton's soul seemed to soar with the realization of how that news would uplift Neale, craze him with happiness, change his life, save him. He was going to hear the blessed tidings from a woman whom he had scorned. Always afterward, then, he would think of Beauty Stanton with a grateful heart. She was to be the instrument of his salvation. Hough and Ancliffe had died to save Allie Lee from the vile clutch of Benton; but to Beauty Stanton, the woman of ill-fame, had been given the power. She gloried in it. Allie Lee was safely hidden in her house. Those tigers of Durade's, on the scent of gold, would tear down all places in Benton before they would dare to attack her house. The iniquity of her establishment furnished a haven for the body and life and soul of innocent Allie Lee. Beauty Stanton marveled at the strange ways of life. If she could have prayed, if she had ever dared to hope for some splendid duty, some atonement to soften the dark, grim ending of her dark career, it would not have been for so much as fate had now dealt to her. She was overwhelmed with her opportunity.

All at once she reached the end of the street. On each side the wall of lighted tents and houses ceased. Had she missed her way—gone down a side street to the edge of the desert? No. The rows of lights behind assured her this was the main street. Yet she was far from the railroad station. The crowds of men hurried by, as always. Before her reached a leveled space, dimly lighted, full of moving objects, and noise of hammers and wagons, and harsh voices. Then suddenly she remembered.

Benton was being evacuated. Tents and houses were being taken down and loaded on trains to be hauled to the next construction camp. Benton's day was done! This was the last night. She had forgotten that the proprietor of her hall, from whom she rented it, had told her that early on the morrow he would take it down section by section, load it on the train, and put it together again for her in the next town. In forty-eight hours Benton would be a waste place of board floors, naked frames, debris and sand, ready to be reclaimed by the desert. It would be gone like a hideous nightmare, and no man would believe what had happened there.

The gambling-hell where she had expected to find Neale

had vanished, in a few hours, as if by magic. Beauty Stanton retraced her steps. She would find Neale in one of the other places—the Big Tent, perhaps.

This hall was unusually crowded, and the scene had the number of men, though not the women and the hilarity and the gold, that was characteristic of pay-day in Benton. All the tables in the gambling-room were occupied.

Beauty Stanton stepped into this crowded room, her golden head uncovered, white and rapt and strangely dark-eyed, with all the beauty of her girlhood returned, and added to it that of a woman transformed, supreme in her crowning hour. As a bad woman, infatuated and piqued, she had failed to allure Neale to baseness; now as a good woman, with pure motive, she would win his friendship, his eternal gratitude.

Stanton had always been a target for eyes, yet never as now, when she drew every gaze like a dazzling light in a dark room.

As soon as she saw Neale she forgot every one else in that hall. He was gambling. He did not look up. His brow was somber and dark. She approached—stood behind him. Some of the players spoke to her, familiarly, as was her bitter due. Then Neale turned apparently to bow with his old courtesy. Thrill on thrill coursed over her. Always he had showed her respect, deference.

Her heart was full. She had never before enjoyed a moment like this. She was about to separate him from the baneful and pernicious life of the camps—to tender him a gift of unutterable happiness—to give all of him back to the work of the great railroad.

She put a trembling hand on his shoulder—bent over him. "Neale—come with me," she whispered.

He shook his head.

"Yes! Yes!" she returned, her voice thrilling with emotion.

Wearily, with patient annoyance, he laid down his cards and looked up. His dark eyes held faint surprise and something that she thought might be pity.

"Miss Stanton—pardon me—but please understand—No!"

Then he turned and, picking up his cards, resumed the game.

Beauty Stanton suffered a sudden vague check. It was as if a cold thought was trying to enter a warm and glowing mind. She found speech difficult. She could not get off the track of her emotional flight. Her woman's wit, tact, knowledge of men, would not operate.

"Neale! . . . Come with—me!" she cried, brokenly. "There's—"

Some man laughed coarsely. That did not mean anything to Stanton until she saw how it affected Neale. His face flushed red and his hands clenched the cards.

"Say, Neale," spoke up this brutal gamester, with a sneer, "never mind us. Go along with your lady friend. . . . You're ahead of the game—as I reckon she sees."

Neale threw the cards in the man's face; then, rising, he bent over to slap him so violently as to knock him off his chair.

The crash stilled the room. Every man turned to watch.

Neale stood up, his right arm down, menacingly. The gambler arose, cursing, but made no move to draw a weapon.

Beauty Stanton could not, to save her life, speak the words she wanted to say. Something impeding, totally unexpected, seemed to have arisen.

"Neale—come with—me!" was all she could say.

"No!" he declared, vehemently, with a gesture of disgust and anger.

That, following the coarse implication of the gambler, conveyed to Stanton what all these men imagined. The fools! The fools! A hot vibrating change occurred in her emotion, but she controlled it. Neale turned his back upon her. The crowd saw and many laughed. Stanton felt the sting of her pride, the leap of her blood. She was misunderstood, but what was that to her? As Neale stepped away she caught his arm—held him while she tried to get close to him so she could whisper. He shook her off. His face was black with anger. He held up one hand in a gesture that any woman would have understood and hated. It acted powerfully upon Beauty Stanton. Neale believed she was importuning him. To him her look, whisper, touch had meant only the same as to these coarse human animals gaping and grinning as they listened. The sweetest and best and most exalted moment she had ever known was being made bitter as gall, sickening, hateful. She must speak openly, she must make him understand.

"Allie Lee! . . . At my house!" burst out Stanton, and then, as if struck by lightning she grew cold, stiff-lipped.

The change in Neale was swift, terrible. Not comprehension, but passion transformed him into a gray-faced man, amazed, furious, agonized, acting in seeming righteous and passionate repudiation of a sacrilege.

"——!" His voice hurled out a heinous name, the one epithet that could inflame and burn and curl Beauty Stanton's soul into hellish revolt. Gray as ashes, fire-eyed, he appeared about to kill her. He struck her—hard—across the mouth.

"Don't breathe that name!"

Beauty Stanton's fear suddenly broke. Blindly she ran out into the street. She fell once—jostled against a rail. The lights blurred; the street seemed wavering; the noise about her filtered through deadened ears; the stalking figures before her were indistinct and unreal.

"He struck me! He called me——!" she gasped. And the exaltation of the last hour vanished as if it had never been. All the passion of her stained and evil years leaped into ascendency. "Hell—hell! I'll have him knifed—I'll see him dying! I'll wet my hands in his blood! I'll spit in his face as he dies!"

So she gasped out, staggering along the street toward her house. There is no flame of hate so sudden and terrible and intense as that of the lost woman. Beauty Stanton's blood had turned to vitriol. Men had wronged her, ruined her, dragged her down into the mire. One by one, during her dark career, the long procession of men she had known had each taken something of the good and the virtuous in her, only to leave behind something evil in exchange. She was what they had made her. Her soul was a bottomless gulf, black and bitter as the Dead Sea. Her heart was a volcano, seething, turgid, full of contending fires. Her body was a receptacle into which Benton had poured its dregs. The weight of all the iron and stone used in the construction of the great railroad was the burden upon her shoulders. These dark streams of humanity passing her in the street, these beasts of men, these hairy-breasted toilers, had found in her and her kind the strength or the incentive to endure, to build, to go on. And one of them, stupid, selfish, merciless, a man whom she had really loved, who could have made her better, to whom she had gone with only hope for him and unselfish abnegation for herself— he had put a vile interpretation upon her appeal, he had struck her before a callous crowd, he had called her the name for which there was no pardon from her class, a name that evoked all the furies and the powers of hell.

"Oh, to cut him—to torture him—to burn him alive. . . . But it would not be enough!" she panted.

And into the mind that had been lately fixed in happy consciousness of her power of good there flashed a thousand scintillating, corruscating gleams of evil thought. And then came a crowning one, an inspiration straight from hell.

"By God! I'll make of Allie Lee the thing I am! The thing he struck—the thing he named!"

The woman in Beauty Stanton ceased to be. All that breathed, in that hour, was what men had made her. Revenge, only a word! Murder, nothing! Life, an implacable, inexplicable, impossible flux and reflux of human passion! Reason, intelligence, nobility, love, womanhood, motherhood—all the heritage of her sex—had been warped by false and abnormal and terrible strains upon her physical and emotional life. No tigress, no cannibal, no savage, no man, no living creature except a woman of race who knew how far she had fallen could have been capable of Beauty Stanton's deadly and immutable passion to destroy. Thus life and nature avenged her. Her hate was immeasurable. She who could have walked naked and smiling down the streets of Benton or out upon the barren desert to die for the man she loved had in her the inconceivable and mysterious passion of the fallen woman; she could become a flame, a scourge, a fatal wind, a devastation. She was fire to man; to her own sex, ice.

Stanton reached her house and entered. Festivities in honor of the last night of Benton were already riotously in order. She placed herself well back in the shadow and watched the wide door.

"The first man who enters I'll give him this key!" she hissed.

She was unsteady on her feet. All her frame quivered. The lights in the hall seemed to have a reddish tinge. She watched. Several men passed out. Then a tall, stalking form appeared, entering.

A ball of fire in Stanton's breast leaped and burst. She had recognized in that entering form the wildest, the most violent, and the most dangerous man in Benton—Larry Red King.

Stanton stepped forward and for the first time in the

cowboy's presence she did not experience that singular chill of gloom which he was wont to inspire in her.

Her eyes gloated over King. Tall, lean, graceful, easy, with his flushed, ruddy face and his flashing blue eyes and the upstanding red hair, he looked exactly what he was—a handsome red devil, fearing no man or thing, hell-bent in his cool, reckless wildness.

He appeared to be half-drunk. Stanton was trained to read the faces of men who entered there; and what she saw in King's added the last and crowning throb of joy to her hate. If she had been given her pick of the devils in Benton she would have selected this stalking, gun-packing cowboy.

"Larry, I've a new girl here," she said. "Come."

"Evenin', Miss—Stanton," he drawled. He puffed slightly, after the manner of men under the influence of liquor, and a wicked, boyish, heated smile crossed his face.

She led him easily. But his heavy gun bumped against her, giving her little cold shudders. The passage opened into a wide room, which in turn opened into her dancing-hall. She saw strange, eager, dark faces among the men present, but in her excitement she did not note them particularly. She led Larry across the wide room, up a stairway to another hall, and down this to the corner of an intersecting passageway.

"Take—this—key!" she whispered. Her hand shook. She felt herself to be a black and monstrous creature. All of Benton seemed driving her. She was another woman. This was her fling at a rotten world, her slap in Neale's face. But she could not speak again; her lips failed. She pointed to a door.

She waited long enough to see the stalking, graceful cowboy halt in front of the right door. Then she fled.

CHAPTER XXVII

For many moments after the beautiful barearmed woman closed and locked the door Allie Lee sat in ecstasy, in trembling anticipation of Neale.

Gradually, however, in intervals of happy mind-wanderings, other thoughts intruded. This little bedroom affected her singularly and she was at a loss to account for the fact. It did not seem that she was actually afraid to be there, for she was glad. Fear of Durade and his gang recurred, but she believed that the time of her deliverance was close at hand. Possibly Durade, with some of his men, had been killed in the fight with Hough. Then she remembered having heard the Spaniard order Fresno and Mull to go round by the street. They must be on her trail at this very moment. Ancliffe had been seen, and not much time could elapse before her whereabouts would be discovered. But Allie bore up bravely. She was in the thick of grim and bloody and horrible reality. Those brave men, strangers to her, had looked into her face, questioned her, then had died for her. It was all so unbelievable. In another room, close to her, lay Ancliffe, dead. Allie tried not to think of him; of the remorseless way in which he had killed the Mexican; of the contrast between this action and his gentle voice

and manner. She tried not to think of the gambler Hough—
the cold iron cast of his face as he won Durade's gold, the
strange, intent look which he gave her a moment before the
attack. There was something magnificent in Ancliffe's
bringing her to a refuge while he was dying; there was
something magnificent in Hough's standing off the gang.
Allie divined that through her these two men had fought
and died for something in themselves as well as for her
honor and life.

The little room seemed a refuge for Allie, yet it was
oppressive, as had been the atmosphere of the parlor
where Ancliffe lay. But this oppressiveness was not death.
Allie had become familiar with death near at hand. This
refuge made her flesh creep.

The room was not the home of any one—it was not in-
habited, it was not livable. Yet it contained the same kind
of furniture Durade had bought for her and it was clean
and comfortable. Still, Allie shrank from touching
anything. Through the walls came the low, strange, discordant din to which she had become accustomed—an
intense, compelling blend of music, song, voice, and step
actuated by one spirit. Then at times she imagined she
heard distant hammering and the slap of a falling board.

Probably Allie had not stayed in this room many moments when she began to feel that she had been there hours.
Surely the woman would return soon with Neale. And the
very thought drove all else out of her mind, leaving her
palpitating with hope, sick with longing.

Footsteps outside distracted her from the nervous,
dreamy mood. Some one was coming along the hall. Her
heart gave a wild bound—then sank. The steps passed by
her door. She heard the thick, maudlin voice of a man and
the hollow, trilling laugh of a girl.

Allie's legs began to grow weak under her. The strain,
the suspense, the longing grew to be too much for her and

occasioned a revulsion of feeling. She had let her hopes carry her too high.

Suddenly the door-handle rattled and turned. Allie was brought to a stifling expectancy, motionless in the center of the room. Some one was outside at the door. Could it be Neale? It must be! Her sensitive ears caught short, puffing breaths—then the click of a key in the lock. Allie stood there in an anguish of suspense, with the lift of her heart almost suffocating her. Like a leaf in the wind she quivered.

Whoever was out there fumbled at the key. Then the lock rasped, the handle turned, the door opened. A tall man swaggered in, with head bent sideways, his hand removing the key from the lock. Before he saw Allie he closed the door. With that he faced around.

Allie recognized the red face, the flashing eyes, the flaming hair.

"Larry!" she cried, with bursting heart.

She took a quick step, ready to leap into his arms, but his violent start checked her. Larry staggered back—put a hand out. His face was heated and flushed as Allie had never seen it. A stupid surprise showed there. Slowly his hand moved up to cross his lips, to brush through his red hair; then with swifter movement it swept back to feel the door, as if he wanted the touch of tangible things.

"Reckon I'm seein' 'em again!" he muttered to himself.

"Oh, Larry—I'm Allie Lee!" she cried, holding out her hands.

She saw the color fade out of his face. A shock seemed to go over his body. He took a couple of dragging strides toward her. His eyes had the gaze of a man who did not believe what he saw. The hand he reached out shook.

"I'm no ghost! Larry, don't—you—know me?" she faltered.

Indeed he must have thought her a phantom. Great, clammy drops stood out upon his brow.

"Dear old—redhead!" she whispered, brokenly, with a smile of agony and joy. He would know her when she spoke that way—called him the name she had tormented him with—the name no one else would have dared to use.

Then she saw he believed in her reality. His face began to work. She threw her arms about him—she gave up to a frenzy of long-deferred happiness. Where Larry was there would Neale be.

"Allie—it ain't—you?" he asked, hoarsely, as he hugged her close.

"Oh, Larry—yes—yes—and I'll die of joy!" she whispered.

"Then you shore ain't—daid?" he went on, incredulously.

How sweet to Allie was the old familiar Southern drawl!

"Dead? Never. . . . Why, I've kissed you! . . . and you haven't kissed me back."

She felt his breast heave as he lifted her off her feet to kiss her awkwardly, boyishly.

"Shore—the world's comin' to an end! . . . But mebbe I'm only drunk!"

He held her close, towering over her, while he gazed around him and down at her, shaking his head, muttering again in bewilderment.

"Reddy dear—where, oh, where is Neale?" she breathed, all her heart in her voice.

As he released her Allie felt a difference. His whole body seemed to gather, to harden, then vibrate, as if he had been stung.

"My Gawd!" he whispered, in hoarse accents of amaze and horror. "Is it you—Allie—*here?*"

"Of course it's I," replied Allie, blankly.

His face turned white to the lips.

"Reddy, what in the world is wrong?" she gasped, beginning to wring her hands.

Suddenly he leaped at her. With rude, iron grasp he forced her back, under the light, and fixed piercing eyes upon hers. He bent closer. Allie was frightened, yet fascinated. His gaze hurt with its intensity, its strange, penetrating power. Allie could not bear it.

"Allie, look at me," he said, low and hard. "Fer I reckon you mayn't hev very long to live!"

Allie struggled weakly. He looked so gray, grim, and terrible. But she could resist neither his strength nor his spirit. She lay quiet and met the clear, strange fire of his eyes. In a few swift moments he had changed utterly.

"Larry—aren't—you—drunk?" she faltered.

"I was, but now I'm sober. . . . Girl, kiss me again!"

In wonder and fear Allie complied, now flushing scarlet.

"I—I was never so happy," she whispered. "But Larry—you—you frighten me. . . . I—"

"Happy!" ejaculated Larry. Then he let her go and stood up, breathing hard. "There's a hell of a lie heah somewheres—but it ain't in you."

"Larry, talk sense. I'm weak from long waiting. Oh, tell me of Neale!"

What a strange, curious, incomprehensible glance he gave her!

"Allie—Neale's heah in Benton. I can take you to him in ten minutes. Do you want me to?"

"*Want you to!* . . . Reddy! I'll die if you don't take me—at once!" she cried, in anguish.

Again Larry loomed over her. This time he took her hands. "How long had you been heah—before I came?" he asked.

"Half an hour, perhaps; maybe less. But it seemed long."

"Do you—know—what kind of a house you're in—this

heah room—what it means?" he went on, very low and huskily.

"No, I don't," she replied, instantly, with sudden curiosity. Questions and explanations rushed to her lips. But this strangely acting Larry dominated her.

"No other man—came in heah? I—was the first?"

"Yes."

Then Larry King seemed to wrestle with himself—with the hold drink had upon him—with that dark and sinister oppression so thick in the room. Allie thrilled to see his face grow soft and light up with the smile she remembered. How strange to feel in Larry King a spirit of gladness, of gratefulness for something beyond her understanding! Again he drew her close. And Allie, keen to read and feel him, wondered why he seemed to want to hide the sight of his face.

"Wal—I reckon—I was nigh onto bein' drunk," he said, haltingly. "Shore is a bad habit of mine—Allie. . . . Makes me think a lot of—guff—jest the same as it makes me see snakes—an' things. . . . I'll quit drinkin', Allie. . . . Never will touch liquor again—now if you'll jest forgive."

He spoke gently, huskily, with tears in his voice, and he broke off completely.

"Forgive! Larry, boy, there's nothing to forgive—except your not hurrying me to—to *him!*"

She felt the same violent start in him. He held her a moment longer. Then, when he let go of her and stepped back Allie saw the cowboy as of old, cool and easy, yet somehow menacing, as he had been that day the strangers rode into Slingerland's camp.

"Allie—thet woman Stanton locked you in heah?" queried Larry.

"Yes. Then she—"

Larry's quick gesture enjoined silence. Stealthy steps sounded out in the hall. They revived Allie's fear of Durade and his men. It struck her suddenly that Larry must be ignorant of the circumstances that had placed her there.

The cowboy unlocked the door—peeped out. As he turned, how clear and cold his blue eyes flashed!

"I'll get you out of heah," he whispered. "Come."

They went out. The passage was empty. Allie clung closely to him. At the corner, where the halls met, he halted to listen. Only the low hum of voices came up.

"Larry, I must tell you," whispered Allie. "Durade and his gang are after me. Fresno—Mull—Black—Dayss—you know them?"

"I—reckon," he replied, swallowing hard. "My Gawd! you poor little girl! With that gang after you! An' Stanton! I see all now. . . . She says to me, 'Larry, I've a new girl heah'. . . . Wal, Beauty Stanton, thet was a bad deal for you—damn your soul!"

Trembling, Allie opened her lips to speak, but again the cowboy motioned her to be quiet. He need not have done it, for he suddenly seemed terrible, wild, deadly, rendering her mute.

"Allie, if I call to you, duck behind me an' hold on to me. I'll take you out of heah."

Then he put her on his left side and led her down the right-hand passage toward the wide room Allie remembered. She looked on into the dance-hall. Larry did not hurry. He sauntered carelessly, yet Allie felt how intense he was. They reached the head of the stairway. The room was full of men and girls. The woman Stanton was there and, wheeling, she uttered a cry that startled Allie. Was this white, glaring-eyed, drawn-faced woman the one who had gone for Neale? Allie began to shake. She saw and heard with startling distinctness. The woman's cry had turned every face toward the stairway, and the buzz of voices ceased.

Stanton ran to the stairway, started up, and halted, raising a white arm in passionate gesture.

"Where are you taking that girl?" she called, stridently.

Larry stepped down, drawing Allie with him. "I'm takin' her to Neale."

Stanton shrieked and waved her arms. Indeed, she seemed another woman from the one upon whose breast Allie had laid her head just a little while before.

"No, you won't take her to Neale!" cried Stanton.

The cowboy stepped down slowly, guardedly, but he kept on. Allie saw men run out of the crowded dance-hall into the open space behind Stanton. Dark, hateful, well-remembered faces of Fresno—Mull—Black! Allie pressed the cowboy's arm to warn him, and he, letting go of her, appeared to motion her behind him.

"Stanton! Get out of my way!" yelled Larry. His voice rang with a wild, ruthless note; it carried far and stiffened every figure except that of the frantic woman. With convulsed face, purple in its fury, and the hot eyes of a beast of prey she ran right up at the cowboy, heedless of the gun he held leveled low down.

He shot her. She swayed backward, uttering a low and horrible cry, and even as she swayed her face blanched and her eyes changed. She fell heavily, with her golden hair loosening and her bare white arms spreading wide. Then in the horror-stricken silence she lay there, still conscious, but with an awful hunted realization in the eyes fixed upon the cowboy, a great growing splotch of blood darkening the white of her dress.

Larry King did not look at Stanton and he kept moving down the steps; he was walking faster now, and he drew Allie behind him. The first of that stunned group to awake to action was the giant Fresno, as, with blind, unreasoning passion, he attempted to draw upon the cowboy. The boom of Larry's big gun and the crash of Fresno as he fell woke the spellbound crowd into an uproar. Screaming women and shouting men rushed madly back into the dance-hall.

Larry turned toward the hallway leading to the street. Mull and Black began shooting as he turned, and hit him, for Allie, holding fast to him, felt the vibrating shock of his body. With two swift shots Larry killed both men. Mull fell across the width of the hall. And as Allie stumbled over his body she looked down to see his huge head, his ruddy face, and the great ox-eyes, rolling and ghastly. In that brief glance she saw him die.

The cowboy strode fast now. Allie, with hands clenched in his coat, clung desperately to him. Hollow booms of guns filled the passageway, and hoarse shouts of alarmed men sounded from the street. Burned powder smoke choked Allie. The very marrow of her bones seemed curdled. She saw the red belches of fire near and far; she passed a man floundering and bellowing on the floor; she felt Larry jerk back as if struck, and then something hot grazed her shoulder. A bullet had torn clear through him, from breast to back. He staggered, but he went on. Another man lay on the threshold of the wide door, his head down the step, and his pallid face blood-streaked. A smoking gun lay near his twitching hand. That pallid face belonged to Dayss.

Larry King staggered out into an empty street, looking up and down. "Wal, I reckon—thet's—aboot—all!" he drawled, with low, strangled utterance.

Then swaying from side to side he strode swiftly, almost falling forward, holding tight to Allie. They drew away from the brighter lights. Allie was dimly aware of moving forms ahead and across the street. Once, fearfully, she looked back, to see if they were followed.

The cowboy halted, tottering against a house. He seemed pale and smiling.

"Run—Allie!" he whispered.

"No—no—no!" she replied, clinging to him. "You're shot! . . . Oh, Larry—come on!"

"Tell—my pard—Neale—"

His head fell back hard against the wood and his body, sagging, lodged there. Life had passed out of the gray face. Larry Red King died standing, with a gun in each hand, and the name of his friend the last word upon his lips.

"Oh, Larry—Larry!" moaned Allie.

She could not run. She could scarcely walk. Dark forms loomed up. Her strength failed, and as she reeled, sinking down, rude hands grasped her. Above her bent the gleaming face and glittering eyes of Durade.

CHAPTER XXVIII

Beauty Stanton opened her eyes to see blue sky through the ragged vents of a worn-out canvas tent. An unusual quietness all around added to the strange unreality of her situation. She heard only a low, mournful seeping of wind-blown sand. Where was she? What had happened? Was this only a vivid, fearful dream?

She felt stiff, unable to move. Did a ponderous weight hold her down? Her body seemed immense, full of dull, horrible ache, and she had no sensation of lower limbs except a creeping cold.

Slowly she moved her eyes around. Yes, she was in a tent—an abandoned tent, old, ragged, dirty; and she lay on the bare ground. Through a wide tear in the canvas she saw a stretch of flat ground covered with stakes and boards and denuded frameworks and piles of debris. Then grim reality entered her consciousness. Benton was evacuated. Benton was depopulated. Benton—houses, tents, people—had moved away.

During her unconsciousness, perhaps while she had been thought dead, she had been carried to this abandoned tent. A dressing-gown covered her, the one she always put on in the first hours after arising. The white dress she had worn last night—was it last night?—still adorned her, but all her jewelry had been taken. Then she remembered being lifted to a couch and cried over by her girls, while awestruck men came to look at her and talk among themselves. But she had heard how the cowboy's shot had doomed her—how he had fought his way out, only to fall dead in the street and leave the girl to be taken by Durade.

Now Beauty Stanton realized that she had been left alone in an abandoned tent of an abandoned camp—to die. She became more conscious then of dull physical agony. But neither fear of death nor thought of pain occupied her mind. That suddenly awoke to remorse. With the slow ebbing of her life evil had passed out. If she had been given a choice between the salvation of her soul and to have Neale with her in her last moments, to tell him the truth, to beg his forgiveness, to die in his arms, she would have chosen the latter. Would not some trooper come before she died, some one to whom she could intrust a message? Some grave-digger! For the great U.P.R. buried the dead it left in its bloody tracks!

With strange, numb hands Stanton searched the pockets of her dressing-gown, to find, at length, a little account-book with pencil attached. Then, with stiffened fingers, but acute mind, she began to write to Neale. As she wrote into each word went something of the pang, the remorse, the sorrow, the love she felt; and when that letter was ended she laid the little book on her breast and knew for the first time in many years—peace.

She endured the physical agony; she did not cry out, or complain, or repent, or pray. Most of the spiritual emotion and life left in her had gone into the letter. Memory called up only the last moments of her life—when she saw Ancliffe die; when she folded innocent Allie Lee to the breast that had always yearned for a child; when Neale in his monstrous stupidity had misunderstood her; when he had struck her before the grinning crowd, and in burning words branded her with the one name unpardonable to her class; when at the climax of a morbid and all-consuming hate, a hate of the ruined woman whose body and mind had absorbed the vile dregs, the dark fire and poison, of lustful men, she had inhumanly given Allie Lee to the man she had believed the wildest, most depraved, and most dangerous brute in all Benton; when this Larry King, by some strange fatality, becoming as great as he was wild, had stalked out to meet her like some red and terrible death.

She remembered now that strange, icy gloom and shudder she had always felt in the presence of the cowboy. Within her vitals now was the same cold, deadly, sickening sensation, and it was death. Always she had anticipated it, but vaguely, unrealizingly.

Larry King had lifted the burden of her life. She would have been glad—if only Neale had understood her! That was her last wavering conscious thought.

Now she drifted from human consciousness to the instinctive physical struggle of the animal to live, and that was not strong. There came a moment, the last, between life and death, when Beauty Stanton's soul lingered on the threshold of its lonely and eternal pilgrimage, and then drifted across into the gray shadows, into the unknown, out to the great beyond.

Casey leaned on his spade while he wiped the sweat from his brow and regarded his ally McDermott. Between them yawned a grave they had been digging and near at hand lay a long, quiet form wrapped in old canvas.

"Mac, I'll be domned if I loike this job," said Casey, drawing hard at his black pipe.

"Yez want to be a directhor of the U.P.R., huh?" replied McDermott.

"Shure an' I've did iviry job but run an ingine. . . . It's

imposed on we are, Mac. Thim troopers niver work. Why couldn't they plant these stiffs?"

"Casey, I reckon no wan's bossin' us. Benton picked up an' moved yisteday. An' we'll be goin' soon wid the gravel-train. It's only dacent of us to bury the remains of Benton. An' shure yez ought to be glad to see that orful red-head cowboy go under the ground."

"An' fer why?" queried Casey.

"Didn't he throw a gun on yez onct an' scare the day-lights out of yez?"

"Mac, I wuz as cool as a coocumber. An' as to buryin' Larry King, I'm proud an' sorry. He wuz Neale's fri'nd."

"My Gawd! but he wor chain lightnin', Casey. They said he shot the woman Stanton, too."

"Mac, thet wor a dorn' lie, I bet," replied Casey. "He shot up Stanton's hall, an' a bullet from some of thim wot was foightin' him must hev hit her."

"Mebbe. But it wor bad bizness. That cowboy hit iviry wan of thim fellars in the same place. Shure, they niver blinked afther."

"An' Mac, the best an' dirtiest job we've had on this U.P. was the plantin' of thim fellars."

Casey's huge hand indicated a row of freshly filled graves over which the desert sand was seeping. Then drop-ping his spade, he bent to the quiet figure.

"Lay hold, Mac," he said.

They lowered the corpse into the hole. Casey stood up, making a sign of the cross before him.

"He wor a man!"

Then they filled the grave.

"Mac, wouldn't it be dacent to mark where Larry King's buried? A stone or wooden cross with his name?"

McDermott wrinkled his red brow and scratched his sandy beard. Then he pointed. "Casey, wot's the use? See, the blowin' sand's kivered all the graves."

"Mac, yez wor always hell at shirkin' worrk. Come on, now. Drill, ye terrier, drill!"

They quickly dug another long, narrow hole. Then, taking a rude stretcher, they plodded away in the direction of a dilapidated tent that appeared to be the only structure left of Benton. Casey entered ahead of his comrade.

"Thot's sthrange!"

"Wot?" queried McDermott.

"Didn't yez kiver her face whin we laid her down here?"

"Shure an' I did, Casey."

"An' that face has a different look now! . . . Mac, see here!"

Casey stooped to pick up a little book from the woman's breast. His huge fingers opened it with difficulty.

"Mac, there's wroitin' in ut!" he exclaimed.

"Wal, rade, ye baboon."

"Oh, I kin rade ut, though I ain't much of a wroiter meself," replied Casey, and then laboriously began to decipher the writing. He halted suddenly and looked keenly at McDermott.

"Wot the divil! . . . B'gorra, ut's to me fri'nd Neale—an' a love letter—an'—"

"Wal, kape it, thin, fer Neale an' be dacent enough to rade no more."

Lifting Beauty Stanton, they carried her out into the sunlight. Her white face was a shadowed and tragic record.

"Mac, she wor shure a handsome woman," said Casey, "an' a loidy."

"Casey, yez are always sorry fer somebody. . . . Thot Stanton wuz a beauty an' she mebbe wuz a loidy. But she wuz dom' bad."

"Mac, I knowed long ago thot the milk of human kindness hed curdled in yez. An' yez hev no brains."

"I'm as intilligint as yez any day," retorted McDermott.

"Thin why hedn't yez seen thot this poor woman was alive whin we packed her out here? She come to an' writ thot letter to Neale—thin she doied!"

"My Gawd! Casey, yez ain't meanin' ut!" ejaculated McDermott, aghast.

Casey nodded grimly, and then he knelt to listen at Stanton's breast. "Stone dead now—thot's shure."

For her shroud these deliberate men used strippings of canvas from the tent, and then, carrying her up the bare and sandy slope, they lowered her into the grave next to the one of the cowboy.

Again Casey made a sign of the cross. He worked longer at the filling in than his comrade, and patted the mound of sand hard and smooth. When he finished, his pipe was out. He relighted it.

"Wal, Beauty Stanton, shure yez hev a cleaner grave than yez hed a bed. . . . Nice white desert sand. . . . An' prisintly no man will ivir know where yez come to lay."

The laborers shouldered their spades and plodded away.

The wind blew steadily in from the desert, seeping the sand in low, thin sheets. Afternoon waned, the sun sank, twilight crept over the barren waste. There were no sounds but the seep of sand, the moan of wind, the mourn of wolf. Loneliness came with the night that mantled Beauty Stanton's grave. Shadows trooped in from the desert and the darkness grew black. On that slope the wind always blew, and always the sand seeped, dusting over everything, imperceptibly changing the surface of the earth. The desert was still at work. Nature was no respecter of graves. Life was nothing. Radiant, cold stars blinked pitilessly out of the vast blue-black vault of heaven. But there hovered a spirit beside this woman's last resting-place—a spirit like the night, sad, lonely, silent, mystical, immense.

And as it hovered over hers so it hovered over other nameless graves.

In the eternal workshop of nature, the tenants of these unnamed and forgotten graves would mingle dust of good with dust of evil, and by the divinity of death resolve equally into the elements again.

The place that had known Benton knew it no more. Coyotes barked dismally down what had been the famous street of the camp and prowled in and out of the piles of debris and frames of wood. Gone was the low, strange roar that had been neither music nor mirth nor labor. Benton remained only a name.

The sun rose upon a squalid scene—a wide flat area where stakes and floors and frames mingled with all the flotsam and jetsam left by a hurried and profligate populace, moving on to another camp. Daylight found no man there nor any living creature. And all day the wind blew the dust and sheets of sand over the place where had reigned such strife of toil and gold and lust and blood and death. A train passed that day, out of which engineer and fireman gazed with wondering eyes at what had been Benton. Like a mushroom it had arisen, and like a duststorm on the desert wind it had roared away, bearing its freight of labor, of passion, and of evil. Benton had become a name—a fabulous name.

But nature seemed more merciful than life. For it began to hide what men had left—the scars of habitations where hell had held high carnival. Sunset came, then night and the starlight. The lonely hours were winged, as if in hurry to resolve back into the elements the flimsy remains of that great camp.

And that spot was haunted.

CHAPTER XXIX

Casey left Benton on the work-train. It was composed of a long string of box and flat cars loaded with stone, iron, gravel, ties—all necessaries for the up-keep of the road. The engine was at the rear end, pushing instead of pulling; and at the extreme front end there was a flat-car loaded with gravel. A number of laborers rode on this car, among whom was Casey. In labor or fighting this Irishman always gravitated to the fore.

All along the track, from outside of Benton to the top of a long, slow rise of desert were indications of the fact that Indians had torn up the track or attempted to derail trains.

The signs of Sioux had become such an every-day matter in the lives of the laborers that they were indifferent and careless. Thus isolated, unprotected groups of men, out some distance from the work-train, often were swooped down upon by Indians and massacred.

The troopers had gone on with the other trains that carried Benton's inhabitants and habitations.

Casey and his comrades had slow work of it going westward, as it was necessary to repair the track and at the same time to keep vigilant watch for the Sioux. They expected the regular train from the east to overtake them, but did not even see its smoke. There must have been a wreck or telegraph messages to hold it back at Medicine Bow.

Toward sunset the work-train reached the height of desert land that sloped in long sweeping lines down to the base of the hills.

At this juncture a temporary station had been left in the shape of several box-cars where the telegraph operators and a squad of troopers lived.

As the work-train lumbered along to the crest of this heave of barren land Casey observed that some one at the station was excitedly waving a flag. Thereupon Casey, who acted as brakeman, signaled the engineer.

"Dom' coorious thet," remarked Casey to his comrade McDermott. "Thim operators knowed we'd stop, anyway."

"Injins!" exclaimed McDermott.

That was the opinion of the several other laborers on the front car. And when the work-train halted, that car had run beyond the station a few rods. Casey and his comrades jumped off.

A little group of men awaited them. The operator, a young fellow named Collins, was known to Casey. He stood among the troopers, pale-faced and shaking.

"Casey, who's in charge of the train?" he asked, nervously.

The Irishman's grin enlarged, making it necessary for him to grasp his pipe.

"Shure the engineer's boss of the train an' I'm boss of the gang."

More of the work-train men gathered round the group, and the engineer with his fireman approached.

"You've got to hold up here," said Collins.

Casey removed his pipe to refill it. "Ah-huh!" he grunted.

"Wire from Medicine Bow—order to stop General Lodge's train—three hundred Sioux in ambush near this station—Lodge's train between here and Roaring City," breathlessly went on the operator.

"An' the message come from Medicine Bow!" ejaculated Casey, while his men gaped and muttered.

"Yes. It must have been sent here last night. But O'Neil, the night operator, was dead. Murdered by Indians while we slept."

"Thot's hell!" replied Casey, seriously, as he lit his pipe.

"The message went through to Medicine Bow. Stacey down there sent it back to me. I tried to get Hills at Roaring City. No go! The wire's cut!"

"An' shure the gineral's train has left—wot's that new camp—Roarin' wot?"

"Roaring City. . . . General Lodge went through two days ago with a private train. He had soldiers, as usual. But no force to stand off three hundred Sioux, or even a hundred."

"Wal, the gineral must hev lift Roarin' Camp—else thot message niver would hev come."

"So I think. . . . Now what on earth can we do? The engineer of his train can't stop for orders short of this station, for the reason that there are no stations."

"An' thim Sooz is in ambush near here?" queried Casey, reflectively. "Shure thot could only be in wan place. I rimimber thot higher, narrer pass."

"Right. It's steep up-grade coming east. Train can be blocked. General Lodge with his staff and party—and his soldiers—would be massacred without a chance to fight. That pass always bothered us for fear of ambush. Now the Sioux have come west far enough to find it. . . . No chance on earth for a train there—not if it carried a thousand soldiers."

"Wal, if the gineral an' company was sthopped some-where beyond thot pass?" queried Casey, shrewdly, as he took a deep pull at his pipe.

"Then at least they could fight. They have stood off attacks before. They might hold out for the train following, or even run back."

"Thin, Collins, we've only got to sthop the gineral's train before it reaches thot dom' trap."

"But we can't!" cried Collins. "The wire is cut. It wouldn't help matters if it weren't. I thought when I saw your train we might risk sending the engine on alone. But your engine is behind all these loaded cars. No switch. Oh, it is damnable!"

"Collins, there's more domnable things than yez ever heerd of. . . . I'll sthop Gineral Lodge!"

The brawny Irishman wheeled and strode back toward the front car of the train. All the crowd, to a man, muttering and gaping, followed him. Casey climbed up on the gravel-car.

"Casey, wot in hell would yez be afther doin'?" demanded McDermott.

Casey grinned at his old comrade. "Mac, yez do me a favor. Uncouple the car."

McDermott stepped between the cars and the rattle and clank of iron told that he had complied with Casey's request.

Collins, with all the men on the ground, grasped Casey's idea.

"By God! Casey, *can* you do it? There's down-grade for twenty miles. Once start this gravel-car and she'll go clear to the hills. But—but—"

"Collins, it'll be aisy. I'll slip through thot pass loike oil. Thim Sooz won't be watchin' this way. There's a curve. They won't hear till too late. An' shure they don't niver obsthruct a track till the last minute."

"But, Casey, once through the pass you can't control that gravel-car. The brakes won't hold. You'll run square into the general's train—wreck it!"

"Naw! I've got a couple of ties, an' if thot wreck threatens I'll heave a tie off on the track an' derail me private car."

"Casey, it's sure death!" exclaimed Collins. His voice and the pallor of his face and the beads of sweat all proclaimed him new to the U.P.R.

"Me boy, nuthin's shure whin yez are drillin' with the Paddies."

Casey was above surprise and beyond disdain. He was a huge, toil-hardened, sun-reddened, hard-drinking soldier of the railroad, a loquacious Irishman whose fixed grin denied him any gravity, a foreman of his gang. His chief delight was to outdo his bosom comrade, McDermott. He did not realize that he represented an unconquerable and unquenchable spirit. Neither did his comrade know. But under Casey's grin shone something simple, radiant, hard as steel.

"Put yer shoulders ag'in' an' shove me off," he ordered.

Like automatons the silent laborers started the car.

"Drill, ye terriers, drill! Drill, ye terriers, drill!" sang Casey, as he stood at the wheel-brake.

The car gathered momentum. McDermott was the last to let go.

"Good luck to yez!" he shouted, hoarsely.

"Mac, tell thim yez saw me!" called Casey. Then he waved his hand in good-by to the crowd. Their response was a short, ringing yell. They watched the car glide slowly out of sight.

For a few moments Casey was more concerned with the fact that a breeze had blown out his pipe than with anything else. Skilful as years had made him, he found unusual difficulty in relighting it, and he would not have been beyond stopping the car to accomplish that imperative need. When he had succeeded and glanced back the station was out of sight.

Casey fixed his eyes upon the curve of the track ahead where it disappeared between the sage-covered sandy banks. Here the grade was scarcely perceptible to any but experienced eyes. And the gravel-car crept along as if it would stop any moment. But Casey knew that it was not likely to stop, and if it did he could start it again. A heavy-laden car like this, once started, would run a long way on a very little grade. What worried him was the creaking and rattle of wheels, sounds that from where he stood were apparently very loud.

He turned the curve into a stretch of straight track where there came a perceptible increase in the strength of the breeze against his face. While creeping along at this point he scooped out a hole in the gravel mound on the car, making a place that might afford some protection from Indian bullets and arrows. That accomplished, he had nothing to do but hold on to the wheel-brake, and gaze ahead.

It seemed a long time before the speed increased sufficiently to insure him against any danger of a stop. The wind began to blow his hair and whip away the smoke of his pipe. And the car began to cover distance. Several miles from the station he entered the shallow mouth of a gully where the grade increased. His speed accelerated correspondingly until he was rolling along faster than a man could run. The track had been built on the right bank of the gully which curved between low bare hills, and which grew deeper and of a rougher character. Casey had spiked many of the rails over which he passed.

He found it necessary to apply the brake so that he would not take the sharp curves at dangerous speed. The brake did not work well and gave indications that it would not stand a great deal. With steady, rattling creak, and an occasional clank, the car rolled on.

If Casey remembered the lay of the land, there was a long, straight stretch of track, ending in several curves, the last of which turned sharply into the narrow cut where the Sioux would ambush and obstruct the train. At this point it was Casey's intention to put off the brake and let his car run wild.

It seemed an endless time before he reached the head of that stretch. Then he let go of the wheel. And the gravel-car began to roll on faster.

Casey appeared to be grimly and conscientiously concerned over his task, and he was worried about the outcome. He must get his car beyond that narrow cut. If it jumped the track or ran into an obstruction, or if the Sioux spied him in time, then his work would not be well done. He welcomed the gathering momentum, yet was fearful of the curve he saw a long distance ahead. When he reached that he would be going at a high rate of speed—too fast to take the curve safely.

A little dimness came to Casey's eyes. Years of hot sun and dust and desert wind had not made his eyes any stronger. The low gray walls, the white bleached rocks, the shallow stream of water, the fringe of brush, and the long narrowing track—all were momentarily indistinct in his sight. His breast seemed weighted. Over and over in his mind revolved the several possibilites that awaited him at the cut, and every rod of the distance now added to his worry. It grew to be dread. Chances were against him. The thing intrusted to him was not in his control. Casey resented this. He had never failed at a job. The U.P.R. had to be built—and who could tell?—if the chief engineer and all his staff and the directors of the road were massacred by the Sioux, perhaps that might be a last and crowning catastrophe.

Casey had his first cold thrill. And his nerves tightened for the crisis, while his horny hands gripped on the brake. The car was running wild, with a curve just ahead. It made an unearthly clatter. The Indians would hear that. But they would have to be swift, if he stayed on the track. Almost before he realized it the car lurched at the bend. Casey felt the off-side wheels leave the rail, heard the scream of the inside wheels grinding hard. But for his grip on the wheel he would have been thrown. The wind whistled in his ears. With a sudden lurch the car seemed to rise. Casey thought it had jumped the track. But it banged back, righted itself, rounded the curve.

Here the gully widened—sent off branches. Casey saw hundreds of horses—but not an Indian. He rolled swiftly on, crossed a bridge, and saw more horses. His grim anticipation became a reality. The Sioux were in the ambush. What depended on him and his luck! Casey's red check blanched, but it was not with fear for himself. Not yet on this ride had he entertained one thought concerning his own personal relation to its fragile possibilities.

To know the Sioux were there made a tremendous difference. A dark and terrible sternness actuated Casey. He projected his soul into that clattering car of iron and wood. And it was certain he prayed. His hair stood straight up. There! the narrow cut in the hill! the curve of the track! He was pounding at it. The wheels shrieked. Looking up, he saw only the rocks and gray patches of brush and the bare streak of earth. No Indian showed.

His gaze strained to find an obstruction on the track. The car rode the curve on two wheels. It seemed alive. It entered the cut with hollow, screeching roar. The shade of the narrow place was gloomy. Here! It must happen! Casey's heart never lifted its ponderous weight. Then, shooting round the curve, he saw an open track and bright sunlight beyond.

Above the roar of wheels sounded spatting reports of rifles. Casey forgot to dodge into his gravel shelter. He was living a strange, dragging moment—an age. Out shot the car into the light. Likewise Casey's dark blankness of mind ended. His heart lifted with a mighty throb. There shone the gray endless slope, stretching out and down to the black hills in the distance. Shrill wild yells made Casey wheel. The hillside above the cut was colorful and spotted with moving objects. Indians! Puffs of white smoke arose. Casey felt the light impact of lead. Glancing bright streaks darted down. They were arrows. Two thudded into the gravel, one into the wood. Then something tugged at his shoulder. Another arrow! Suddenly the shaft was there in his sight, quivering in his flesh. It bit deep. With one wrench he tore it out and shook it aloft at the Sioux.

"Oi bate yez dom' Sooz!" he yelled, in fierce defiance. The long screeching clamor of baffled rage and the scattering volley of rifle-shots kept up until the car passed out of range.

Casey faced ahead. The Sioux were behind him. He had a free track. Far down the gray valley, where the rails disappeared, were low streaks of black smoke from a locomotive. The general's train was coming.

The burden of worry and dread that had been Casey's was now no more—vanished as if by magic. His job had not yet been completed, but he had won. He never glanced back at the Sioux. They had failed in their first effort at ambushing the cut, and Casey knew the troops would prevent a second attempt. Casey faced ahead. The whistle of wind filled his ears, the dry, sweet odor of the desert filled his nostrils. His car was on a straight track, rolling along down-grade, half a mile a minute. And Casey, believing he might do well to slow up gradually, lightly put on the brake. But it did not hold. He tried again. The brake had broken.

He stood at the wheel, his eyes clear now, watching ahead. The train down in the valley was miles away, not yet even a black dot in the gray. The smoke, however, began to lift.

Casey was suddenly struck by a vague sense that something was wrong with him.

"Phwat the hell!" he muttered. Then his mind, strangely absorbed, located the trouble. His pipe had gone out! Casey stooped in the hole he had made in the gravel, and there, knocking his pipe in his palm, he found the ashes cold. When had that ever happened before? Casey wagged his head. For his pipe to go cold and he not to know! Things were happening on the U.P.R. these days. Casey refilled the pipe, and, with the wind whistling over him, he relit it. He drew deep and long, stood up, grasped the wheel, and felt all his blood change.

"Me poipe goin' cold—that wor funny!" soliloquized Casey.

The phenomenon appeared remarkable to him. Indeed, it stood alone. He measured the nature of this job by that forgetfulness. And memories thrilled him. With his eye clear on the track that split the gray expanse, with his whole being permeated by the soothing influence of smoke, with his task almost done, Casey experienced an unprecedented thing for him—he lived over past performances and found them vivid, thrilling, somehow sweet. Battles of the Civil War; the day he saved a flag; and, better, the night he saved Pat Shane, who had lived only to stop a damned Sioux bullet; many and many an adventure with McDermott, who, just a few minutes past, had watched him with round, shining eyes; and the fights he had seen and shared—all these things passed swiftly through Casey's mind and filled him with a lofty and serene pride.

He was pleased with himself; more pleased with what McDermott would think. Casey's boyhood did not return to him, but his mounting exhilaration and satisfaction were boyish. It was great to ride this way! . . . There! he saw a long, black dot down in the gray. The train! . . . General Lodge had once shaken hands with Casey.

Somebody had to do these things, since the U.P.R. must reach across to the Pacific. A day would come when a splendid passenger-train would glide smoothly down this easy grade where Casey jolted along on his gravel-car. The fact loomed large in the simplicity of the Irishman's mind. He began to hum his favorite song. Facing westward, he saw the black dot grow into a long train. Likewise he saw the beauty of the red-gold sunset behind the hills. Casey gloried in the wildness of the scene—in the meaning of his ride—particularly in his loneliness. He seemed strangely alone there on that vast gray slope—a man and somehow accountable for all these things. He felt more than he understood. His long-tried nerve and courage and strength had never yielded this wonderful buoyancy and sense of loftiness. He was Casey—Casey who had let all the gang run for shelter from the Sioux while he had remained for one last and final drive at a railroad spike. But the cool, devil-may-care indifference, common to all his comrades as well as to himself, was not the strongest factor in the Casey of to-day. Up out of the rugged and dormant soul had burst the spirit of a race embodied in one man. Casey was his own audience, and the light upon him was the glory of the setting sun. A nightingale sang in his heart, and he realized that this was his hour. Here the bloody, hard years found their reward. Not that he had ever wanted one or thought of one, but it had come—out of the toil, the pain, the weariness. So his nerves tingled, his pulses beat, his veins glowed, his heart throbbed; and all the new, sweet, young sensations of a boy wildly reveling in the success of his first great venture, all the vague, strange, deep, complex emotions of a man who has become conscious of what he is giving to the world—these shook Casey by storm, and life had no more to give. He knew that, whatever he was, whatever this incomprehensible driving spirit in him, whatever his unknown relation to man and to duty, there had been given him in the peril just passed, in this wonderful ride, a gift splendid and divine.

Casey rolled on, and the train grew plain in his sight. When perhaps several miles of track lay between him and the approaching engine, he concluded it was time to get ready. Lifting one of the heavy ties, he laid it in front where he could quickly shove it off with his foot.

Then he stood up. It was certain that he looked backward, but at no particular thing—just an instinctive glance. With his foot on the tie he steadied himself so that he could push it off and leap instantly after.

And at that moment he remembered the little book he had found on Beauty Stanton's breast, and which contained the letter to his friend Neale. Casey deliberated in spite of the necessity for haste. Then he took the book from his pocket.

"B'gorra, yez niver can tell, an' thim U.P.R. throopers hev been known to bury a mon widout searchin' his pockets," he said.

And he put the little book between the teeth that held his pipe. Then he shoved off the tie and leaped.

CHAPTER XXX

Neale, aghast and full of bitter amaze and shame at himself, fled from the gambling-hall where he had struck Beauty Stanton. How beside himself with rage and torture he had been! That woman to utter Allie Lee's name! Inconceivable! Could she know his story?

He tramped the dark streets, and the exercise and the cool wind calmed him. Then the whistle of an engine made him decide to leave Benton at once, on the first train out. Hurriedly he got his baggage and joined the throng which even at that late hour was making for the station.

A regret that was pain burned deep in him—somehow inexplicable. He, like other men, had done things that must be forgotten. What fatality in the utterance of a single name—what power to flay!

From a window of an old coach he looked out upon the dim lights and pale tent shapes.

"The last—of Benton! . . . Thank God!" he murmured, brokenly. Well he realized how Providence had watched over him there. And slowly the train moved out upon the dark, windy desert.

It took Neale nearly forty-eight hours to reach the new camp—Roaring City. A bigger town than Benton had arisen, and more was going up—tents and clapboard houses, sheds and cabins—the same motley jumble set under beetling red Utah bluffs.

Neale found lodgings. Being without food or bed or wash for two days and nights was not helpful to the task he must accomplish—the conquering of his depression. He ate and slept long, and the following day he took time to make himself comfortable and presentable before he sallied forth to find the offices of the engineer corps. Then he walked on as directed, and heard men talking of Indian ambushes and troops.

When at length he reached the headquarters of the engineer corps he was greeted with restraint by his old officers and associates; was surprised and at a loss to understand their attitude.

Even in General Lodge there was a difference. Neale gathered at once that something had happened to put out of his chief's mind the interest that officer surely must have in Neale's trip to Washington. And after greeting him, the first thing General Lodge said gave warrant to the rumors of trouble with Indians.

"My train was to have been ambushed at Deep Cut," he explained. "Big force of Sioux. We were amazed to find them so far west. It would have been a massacre—but for Casey. . . . We have no particulars yet, for the wire is cut. But we know what Casey did. He ran the gantlet of the Indians through that cut. . . . He was on a gravel-car running wild down-hill. You know the grade, Neale. . . . Of course his intention was to hold up my train—block us before we reached the ambushed cut. There must have been a broken brake, for he derailed the car not half a mile ahead of us. My engineer saw the runaway flat-car and feared a collision. . . . Casy threw a railroad tie—on the track—in front of him. . . . We found him under the car—crushed—dying—"

General Lodge's voice thickened and slowed a little. He looked down. His face appeared quite pale.

Neale began to quiver in the full presaging sense of a revelation.

"My engineer, Tom Daley, reached Casey's side just the instant before he died," said General Lodge, resuming his story. "In fact, Daley was the only one of us who did see Casey alive. . . . Casey's last words were 'ambush— Sooz—Deep Cut,' and then 'me fri'nd Neale!' . . . We were at a loss to understand what he meant—that is, at first. We found Casey with this little note-book and his pipe tight between his teeth."

The chief gave the note-book to Neale, who received it with a trembling hand.

"You can see the marks of Casey's teeth in the leather. It was difficult to extract the book. He held on like grim death. Oh! Casey *was* grim death. . . . We could not pull his black pipe out at all. We left it between his set jaws, where it always had been—where it belonged. . . . I ordered him interred that way. . . . So they buried him out there along the track."

The chief's low voice ceased, and he stood motionless a moment, his brow knotted, his eyes haunted, yet bright with a glory of tribute to a hero.

Neale heard the ticking of a watch and the murmur of the street outside. He felt the soft little note-book in his hand. And the strangest sensation shuddered over him. He drew his breath sharply.

When General Lodge turned again to face him, Neale saw him differently—aloof, somehow removed, indistinct.

"Casey meant the note-book for you," said the general. "It belonged to the woman, Beauty Stanton. It contained a letter, evidently written while she was dying. . . . This developed when Daley began to read aloud. We all heard. The instant I understood it was a letter intended for you I took the book. No more was read. We were all crowded round Daley—curious, you know. There were visitors on my train—and your enemy Lee. I'm sorry—but, no matter. You see it couldn't be helped. . . . That's all. . . ."

Neale was conscious of calamity. It lay in his hand. "Poor old Casey!" he murmured. Then he remembered. Stanton dying! What had happened? He could not trust himself to read that message before Lodge, and, bowing, he left the room.

But he had to grope his way through the lobby, so dim had become his sight. By the time he reached the street he had lost his self-control. Something burnt his hand. It was the little leather note-book. He had not the nerve to open it. What had been the implication in General Lodge's strange words?

He gazed with awe at the tooth-marks on the little book. How had Casey come by anything of Beauty Stanton's? Could it be true that she was dead?

Then again he was accosted in the street. A heavy hand, a deep voice arrested his progress. His eyes, sweeping up from the path, saw fringed and beaded buckskin, a stalwart form, a bronzed and bearded face, and keen, gray eyes warm with the light of gladness. He was gripped in hands of iron.

"Son! hyar you air—an' it's the savin' of me!" exclaimed a deep, familiar voice.

"*Slingerland!*" cried Neale, and he grasped his old friend as a drowning man at an anchor-rope. "My God! What will happen next? . . . Oh, I'm glad to find you! . . . All these years! Slingerland, I'm in trouble!"

"Son, I reckon I know," replied the other.

Neale shivered. Why did men look at him so? This old trapper had too much simplicity, too big a heart, to hide his pity.

"Come! Somewhere—out of the crowd!" cried Neale,

dragging at Slingerland. "Don't talk. Don't tell me anything. Wait! . . . I've a letter here—that's going to be hell!"

Neale stumbled along out of the crowded street, he did not know where, and with death in his soul he opened Beauty Stanton's book. And he read:

You called me that horrible name. You struck me. You've killed me. I lie here dying. Oh, Neale! I'm dying—and I loved you. I came to you to prove it. If you had not been so blind—so stupid! My prayer is that some one will see this I'm writing—and take it to you.

Ancliffe brought your sweetheart, Allie Lee, to me—to hide her from Durade. He told me to find you and then he died. He had been stabbed in saving her from Durade's gang. And Hough, too, was killed.

Neale, I looked at Allie Lee, and then I understood your ruin. You fool! She was not dead, but alive. Innocent and sweet like an angel. Ah! the wonder of it in Benton! Neale, she did not know—did not feel the kind of a woman I am. She changed me—crucified me. She put her face on my breast. And I have that touch with me now, blessed, softening.

I locked her in a room and hurried out to find you. For the first time in years I had a happy moment. I understood why you had never cared for me. I respected you. Then I would have gone to hell for you. It was my joy that you must owe your happiness to me—that I would be the one to give you back Allie Lee and hope, and the old, ambitious life. Oh, I gloried in my power. It was sweet. You would owe every kiss of hers, every moment of pride, to the woman you had repulsed. That was to be my revenge.

And I found you, and in the best hour of my bitter life—when I had risen above the woman of shame, above thought of self—then you, with hellish stupidity, imagined I was seeking you—*you* for myself! Your annoyance, your scorn, robbed me of my wits. I could not tell you. I could only speak her name and bid you come.

You branded me before that grinning crowd, you struck me! And the fires of hell—*my* hell—burst in my heart. I ran out of there—mad to kill your soul—to cause you everlasting torment. I swore I would give that key of Allie Lee's room to the first man who entered my house.

The first man was Larry Red King. He was drunk. He looked wild. I welcomed him. I sent him to her room.

But Larry King was your friend. I had forgotten that. He came out with her. He was sober and terrible. Like the mad woman that I was I rushed at him to tear her away. He shot me. I see his eyes now. But oh, thank God, he shot me! It was a deliverance.

I fell on the stairs, but I saw that flaming-faced devil kill four of Durade's men. He got Allie Lee out. Later I heard he had been killed and that Durade had caught the girl.

Neale, hurry to find her. Kill that Spaniard. No man could tell why he has spared her, but I tell you he will not spare her long.

Don't ever forget Hough or Ancliffe or that terrible cowboy. Ancliffe's death was beautiful. I am cold. It's hard to write. All is darkening. I hear the moan of wind. Forgive me! Neale, the difference between me and Allie Lee—is a good man's love. Men are blind to woman's agony. She laid her cheek here—on my breast. I—who always wanted a child. I shall die alone. No—I think God is here. There is some one! After all, I was a woman. Neale forgive—

CHAPTER XXXI

"**W**or I there?" echoed McDermott, as he wiped the clammy sweat from his face. B'gosh, I wor!"

It was half-past five. There appeared to be an unusual number of men on the street, not so hurried and business-like and merry as generally, and given to collecting in groups, low-voiced and excited.

General Lodge drew McDermott inside. "Come. You need a bracer. Man, you look sick," he said.

At the bar McDermott's brown and knotty hand shook as he lifted a glass and gulped a drink of whisky.

"Gineral, I ain't the mon I wuz," complained McDermott. "Casey's gone! An' we had hell wid the Injuns gittin' here. An' thin jest afther I stepped off the train—it happened."

"What happened? I've heard conflicting reports. My men are out trying to get news. Tell me, Sandy," replied the general, eagerly.

"Afther hearin' of Casey's finish I was shure needin' stimulants," began the Irishman. "An' prisintly I drhopped into that Durade's Palace. I had my drink, an' thin went into the big room where the moosic wuz. It shure wuz a palace. A lot of thim swells with frock-coats wuz there. B'gorra they ain't above buckin' the tiger. Some of thim I knew. That Misther Lee, wot wuz once a commissioner of the U.P., he wor there with a party of friends.

"An' I happened to be close by thim whin a gurl come out. She was shure purty. But thot sad! Her eyes wor turrible hauntin', an' roight off I wanted to start a foight. She wor lookin' fer Durade, as I seen afterwards.

"Wal, the minnit that Lee seen the gurl he acted strange. I wuz standin' close an' I went closer. 'Most exthraordinary rezemblance,' he kept sayin'. An' thin he dug into his vest fer a pocket-book, an' out of that he took a locket. He looked at it—thin at the little gurl who looked so sad. Roight off he turned the color of a sheet. 'Gintlemen, look!' he sez. They all looked, an' shure wuz sthruck with somethin'.

"'Gintlemen,' sez Lee, 'me wife left me years ago—ran off West wid a gambler. If she iver hed a child—thot gurl is thot child. Fer she's the livin' image of me wife nineteen years ago!'

"Some of thim laughed at him—some of thim stared. But Lee wuz dead in earnest an' growin' more excited ivery minnit. I heerd him mutter low: 'My Gawd! it can't be! Her child! . . . In a gamblin' hell! But that face! . . . Ah! where else could I expect the child of such a mother?'

"An' Lee went closer to where the gurl was waitin'. His party follered an' I follered too. . . . Jest whin the moosic sthopped an' the gurl looked up—thin she seen Lee. Roight out he sthepped away from the crowd. He wuz whiter 'n a ghost. An' the gurl she seemed paralyzed. Sthrange it wor to see how she an' him looked alike thin.

"The crowd seen somethin' amiss, an' went quiet, starin' an' nudgin'. . . . Gineral, dom' me if the gurl's face didn't blaze. I niver seen the loike. An' she sthepped an' come straight fer Lee. An' whin she sthopped she wuz close enough to touch him. Her eyes wor great burnin' holes an' her face shone somethin' wonderful.

"Lee put up a shakin' hand.

" 'Gurl,' he sez, 'did yez iver hear of Allison Lee?'

"An' all her body seemed to lift.

" 'He is my father!' she cried. 'I am Allie Lee!'

"An' thin that crowd wuz split up by a mon wot hurried through. He wuz a greaser—one of thim dandies on dress an' diamonds—a handsome, wicked-lookin' gambler. Seein' the gurl, he snarled, 'Go back there!' an' he pointed. She niver even looked at him.

"Some wan back of me sez thot's Durade. Wal, it was! An' sudden he seen who the gurl wuz watchin'—Lee.

"Thot Durade turned green an' wild-eyed an' stiff. But thot couldn't hould a candle to Lee. Shure he turned into a fiend. He bit out a Spanish name, nothin' loike Durade.

"An' loike a hissin' snake Durade sez, 'Allison Lee!'

"Thin there wuz a dead-lock between thim two men, wid the crowd waitin' fer hell to pay. Life-long inimies, sez I, to meself, an' I hed the whole story.

"Durade began to limber up. Any wan what knows a greaser would have been lookin' fer blood. 'She—wint—back—to yez!' panted Durade.

" 'No—thief—Spanish dog! I have not seen her for nineteen years,' sez Lee.

"The gurl spoke up: 'Mother is dead! Killed by Injuns!'

"Thin Lee cried out, 'Did she leave *him?*'

" 'Yes, she did,' sez the gurl. 'She wuz goin' back. Home! Takin' me home. But the caravan wuz attacked by Injuns. An' all but me wor massacred.'

"Durade cut short the gurl's spache. If I iver seen a reptoile it wuz thin.

" 'Lee, they both left me,' he hisses. 'I tracked them. I lost the mother, but caught the daughter.'

"Thin thot Durade lost his spache fer a minnit, foamin'

at the mouth wid rage. If yez niver seen a greaser mad thin yez niver seen the rale thin'. His face changed yaller an' ould an' wrinkled, wid spots of red. His lip curled up loike a wolf's, an' his eyes—they wint down to little black points of hell's fire. He wuz crazy.

" 'Look at her!' he yelled. 'Allie Lee! Flesh an' blood yez can't deny! Her baby! . . . An' she's been my slave—my dog to beat an' kick! She's been through Benton! A toy fer the riff-raff of the camps! . . . She's as vile an' black an' lost as her treacherous mother!'

"Allison Lee shrunk under thot shame. But the gurl! Lord! she niver looked wot she was painted by thot devil. She stood white an' still, loike an angel above judgment.

"Durade drew one of thim little derringers. An' sudden he hild it on Lee, hissin' now in his greaser talk. I niver seen sich hellish joy on a human face. Murder was nothin' to thot look.

"Jist thin I seen Neale an' Slingerland, an', by Gawd! I thought I'd drop. They seemed to loom up. The girl screamed wild-loike an' she swayed about to fall. Neale leaped in front of Lee.

" 'Durade!' he split out, an' dom' me if I didn't expect to see the roof fly off.'"

McDermott wiped his moist face and tipped his empty glass to his lips, and swallowed hard. His light-blue eyes held a glint.

"Gineral," he went on, "yez know Neale. How big he is! Wot nerve he's got! There niver wor a mon his equal on the U.P. 'ceptin' Casey. . . . But me, nor any wan, nor yez, either, ever seen Neale loike he wuz thin. He niver hesitated an inch, but wint roight fer Durade. Any dom' fool, even a crazy greaser, would hev seen his finish in Neale. Durade changed quick from hot to cold. An' he shot Neale.

"Neale laughed. Funny ringin' sort of laugh, full of thot

same joy Durade hed sung out to Lee. Hate an' love of blood it wor. Yez would hev thought Neale felt wonderful happy to sthop a bullet.

"Thin his hand shot out an' grabbed Durade. . . . He jerked him off his feet an' swung him round. The little der-ringer flew, an' Sandy McDermott wuz the mon who picked it up. It'll be Neale's whin I see him. . . . Durade jabbered fer help But no wan come. Thot big trapper Sling-erland stood there with two guns, an' shure he looked bad. Neale slung Durade around, spillin' some fellers who didn't dodge quick, an' thin he jerked him up backwards.

"An' Durade come up with a long knife in the one hand he had free.

"Neale yelled, 'Lee, take the gurl out!'

"I seen thin she hed fainted in Lee's arms. He lifted her—moved away—an' thin I seen no more of thim.

"Durade made wild an' wicked lunges at Neale, only to be jerked off his balance. I heerd the bones crack in the arm Neale held. The greaser screamed. Sudden he wuz turned agin, an' swung backwards so thot Neale grabbed the other arm—the wan wot held the knife. It wuz a child in the grasp of a giant. Neale shure looked beautiful. I niver wished so much in me loife fer Casey as thin. He would hev enjoyed thot foight, fer he bragged of his friend-ship fer Neale. An'—"

"Go on, man, end your story!" ordered the general, breathlessly.

"Wal, b'gorra, there wuz more crackin' of bones, an' sich screams as I niver heerd from a mon. Turrible, blood-curdlin'! . . . Neale held both Durade's hands an' wuz squeezin' thot knife-handle so the greaser couldn't let go.

"Thin Neale drew out thot hand of Durade's—the wan wot held the knife—an' made Durade jab himself, low down! . . . My Gawd! how thot jenteel Spaniard howled! I seen the blade go in an' come out red. Thin Slingerland

tore thim apart, an' the greaser fell. He warn't killed.
Mebbe he ain't goin' to croak. But he'll shure hev to l'ave
Roarin' City, an' he'll shure be a cripple fer loife."

McDermott looked at the empty glass.

"Thot's all, Gineral. An' if it's jist the same to yez I'll
hev another drink."

CHAPTER XXXII

The mere sight of Warren Neale had transformed life for Allie Lee. The shame of being forced to meet degraded men, the pain from Durade's blows, the dread that every hour he would do the worst by her or kill her, the sudden and amazing recognition between her and her father—these became dwarfed and blurred in the presence of the glorious truth that Neale was there.

She had recognized him with reeling senses and through darkening eyes. She had seen him leap before her father to confront that glittering-eyed Durade. She had neither fear for him nor pity for the Spaniard.

Sensations of falling, of being carried, of the light and dust and noise of the street, of men around her, of rooms and the murmur of voices, of being worked over and spoken to by a kindly woman, of swallowing what was put to her mouth, of answering questions, of letting other clothes be put upon her; she was as if in a trance, aware of all going on about her, but with consciousness riveted upon one stunning fact—his presence. When she was left alone this state gradually wore away, and there remained a throbbing, quivering suspense of love. Her despair had ended.

The spirit that had upheld her through all the long, dark hours had reached its fulfilment.

She lay on a couch in a small room curtained off from another, the latter large and light, and from which came a sound of low voices. She heard the quick tread of men; a door opened.

"Lee, I congratulate you. A narrow escape!" exclaimed a deep voice, with something sharp, authoritative in it.

"General Lodge, it was indeed a narrow shave for me," replied another voice, low and husky.

Allie slowly sat up, with the dreamy waiting abstraction less strong. Her father, Allison Lee, and General Lodge, Neale's old chief, were there in the other room.

"Neale almost killed Durade! Broke him! Cut him all up!" said the general, with agitation. "I had it from McDermott, one of my spikers—a reliable man. . . . Neale was shot—perhaps cut, too. . . . But he doesn't seem to know it."

Allie sprang up, transfixed and thrilling.

"Neale almost killed—him!" echoed Allison Lee, hoarsely. Then followed a sound of a chair falling.

"Indeed, Allison, it's true," broke in a strange voice. "The street's full of men—all talking—all stirred up."

Other men entered the room.

"Is Neale here?" queried General Lodge, sharply.

"They're trying to hold him up—in the office. The boys want to pat him on the back. . . . Durade was not liked," replied some one.

"Is Neale badly hurt?"

"I don't know. He looked it. He was all bloody."

"Colonel Dillon, did you see Neale?" went on the sharp, eager voice.

"Yes. He seemed dazed—wild. Probably badly hurt. Yet he moved steadily. No one could stop him," answered another strange voice.

"Ah! here comes McDermott!" exclaimed General Lodge.

Allie's ears throbbed to a slow, shuffling, heavy tread. Her consciousness received the fact of Neale's injury, but her heart refused to accept it as perilous. God could not mock her faith by a last catastrophe.

"Sandy—you've seen Neale?"

Allie loved this sharp, keen voice for its note of dread.

"Shure. B'gorra, yez couldn't hilp seein' him. He's as big as a hill an' his shirt's as red as Casey's red wan. I wint to give him the little gun wot Durade pulled on him. Dom' me! he looked roight at me an' niver seen me," replied the Irishman.

"Lee, you will see Neale?" queried General Lodge.

There was a silence.

"No," presently came a cold reply. "It is not necessary. He saved me—injury perhaps. I am grateful. I'll reward him."

"How?" rang General Lodge's voice.

"Gold, of course. Neale was a gambler. Probably he had a grudge against this Durade. . . . I need not meet Neale, it seems. I am somewhat—overwrought. I wish to spare myself further excitement."

"Lee—listen!" returned General Lodge, violently. "Neale is a splendid young man—the nerviest, best engineer I ever knew. I predicted great things for him. They have come true."

"That doesn't interest me."

"You'll hear it, anyhow. He saved the life of this girl who has turned out to be your daughter. He took care of her. He loved her—was engaged to marry her. . . . Then he lost her. And after that he was half mad. It nearly ruined him."

"I do not credit that. It was gambling, drink—and bad women that ruined him."

"No!"

"But, pardon me, General. If—as you intimate—there was an attachment between him and my unfortunate child, would he have become an associate of gamblers and vicious women?"

"He would not. The nature of his fury, the retribution he visited upon this damned Spaniard, prove the manner of man he is."

"Wild indeed. But hardly from a sense of loyalty. These camps breed blood-spillers. I heard you say that."

"You'll hear me say something more, presently," retorted the other, with heat scarcely controlled. "But we're wasting time. I don't insist that you see Neale. That's your affair. It seems to me the least you could do would be to thank him. I certainly advise you not to offer him gold. I do insist, however, that you let him see the girl."

"No!"

"But, man. . . . Say, McDermott, go fetch Neale in here."

Allie Lee heard all this strange talk with consternation. An irresistible magnet drew her toward those curtains, which she grasped with trembling hands, ready, but not able, to part them and enter the room. It seemed that in there was a friend of Neale's whom she was going to love, and an enemy whom she was going to hate. As for Neale seeing her—at once—only death could rob her of that.

"General Lodge, I have no sympathy for Neale," came the cold voice of Allison Lee.

There was no reply. Some one coughed. Footsteps sounded in the hallway, and a hum of distant voices.

"You forget," continued Lee, "what happened not many hours ago when your train was saved by that dare-devil Casey—the little book held tight in his locked teeth—the letter meant for this Neale from one of Benton's camp-women. . . . Your engineer read enough. You heard. I heard. . . . A letter from a dying woman. She accused Neale of striking her—of killing her. . . . She said she was dying, but she loved him. . . . Do you remember that, General Lodge?"

"Yes, alas! . . . Lee, I don't deny that. But—"

"There are no buts."

"Lee, you're hard, hard as steel. Appearances seem against Neale. I don't seek to extenuate them. But I know men. Neale might have fallen—it seems he must have. These are terrible times. In anger or drink Neale might have struck this woman. . . . But kill her— No!"

A gleam pierced Allie Lee's dark bewilderment. They meant Beauty Stanton, that beautiful, fair woman with such a white, soft bosom and such sad eyes—she whom Larry King had shot. What a tangle of fates and lives! She could tell them why Beauty Stanton was dying. Then other words, like springing fire, caught Allie's thought, and a sickening ripple of anguish convulsed her. They believed Beauty Stanton had loved Neale—had— Allie would have died before admitting that last thought to her consciousness. For a second the room turned black. Her hold on the curtains kept her from falling. With frantic and terrible earnestness—the old dominance Neale had acquired over her—she clung to the one truth that mattered. She loved Neale—belonged to him—and he was there! That they were about to meet again was as strange and wonderful a thing as had ever happened. What had she not endured? What must he have gone through? The fiery, stinging nature of her new and sudden pain she could not realize.

Again the strong speech became distinct to her.

". . . You'll stay here—and you, Dillon. . . . Don't any one leave this room. . . . Lee, you can leave, if you want. But we'll see Neale, and so will Allie Lee."

Allie spread the curtains and stood there. No one saw her. All the men faced the door through which sounded slow, heavy tread of boots. An Irishman entered. Then a tall man. Allie's troubled soul suddenly calmed. She saw Neale.

Slowly he advanced a few steps. Another man entered, and Allie knew him by his buckskin garb. Neale turned, his face in the light. And a poignant cry leaped up from Allie's heart to be checked on her lips. Was this her young and hopeful and splendid lover? She recognized him, yet now did not know him. He stood bareheaded, and her swift, all-embracing glance saw the gray over his temples, and the eyes that looked out from across the border of a dark hell, and a face white as death and twitching with spent passion.

"Mr.—Lee," he panted, very low, and the bloody patch on his shirt heaved with his breath, "my only—regret—is—I didn't—think to make—Durade—tell the truth. . . . He lied. . . . He wanted to—revenge himself—on Allie's mother—through Allie. . . . What he said—about Allie—was a lie—as black as his heart. He meant evil—for her. But—somehow she was saved. He was a tiger—playing—and he waited—too long. You must realize—her innocence—and understand. God has watched over Allie Lee! It was not luck—nor accident. But innocence! . . . Hough died to save her! Then Ancliffe! Then my old friend—Larry King! These men—broken—gone to hell—out here—felt an innocence that made them—mad—as I have just been. . . . That is proof—if you need it. . . . Men of ruined lives—could not rise—and die—as they did—victims of a false impression—of innocence. . . . *They knew!*"

Neale's voice sank to a whisper, his eyes intent to read belief in the cold face of Allison Lee.

"I thank you, Neale, for your service to me and your defense of her," he said. "What can I do for you?"

"Sir—I—I—"

"Can I reward you in any way?"

The gray burned out of Neale's face. "I ask—nothing—except that you believe me."

Lee did not grant this, nor was there any softening of his cold face.

"I would like to ask you a few questions," he said. "General Lodge here informed me that you saved my—my daughter's life long ago. . . . Can you tell me what became of her mother?"

"She was in the caravan—massacred by Sioux," replied Neale. "I saw her buried. Her grave is not so many miles from here."

Then a tremor changed Allison Lee's expression. He turned away an instant; his hand closed tight; he bit his lips. This evidence of feeling in him relaxed the stony scrutiny of the watchers, and they shifted uneasily on their feet.

Allie stood watching—waiting, with her heart at her lips.

"Where did you take my daughter?" queried Lee, presently.

"To the home of a trapper. My friend—Slingerland," replied Neale, indicating the buckskin-clad figure. "She lived there—slowly recovering. You don't know that she lost her mind—for a while. But she recovered. . . . And during an absence of Slingerland's—she was taken away."

"Were you and she—sweethearts?"

"Yes."

"And engaged to marry?"

"Of course," replied Neale, dreamily.

"That cannot be now."

"I understand. I didn't expect—I didn't think. . . ."

Allie Lee had believed many times that her heart was breaking, but now she knew it had never broken till then. Why did he not turn to see her waiting there—stricken motionless and voiceless, wild to give the lie to those cold, strange words?

"Then, Neale—if you will not accept anything from me, let us terminate this painful interview," said Allison Lee.

"I'm sorry. I only wanted to tell you—and ask to see—Allie—a moment," replied Neale.

"No. It might cause a breakdown. I don't want to risk anything that might prevent my taking the next train with her."

"Going to take her—back East?" asked Neale, as if talking to himself.

"Certainly."

"Then—I—won't see her!" Neale murmured, dazedly.

At this juncture General Lodge stepped out. His face was dark, his mouth stern.

His action caused a breaking of the strange, vise-like clutch—the mute and motionless spell—that had fallen upon Allie. She felt the gathering of tremendous forces in her; in an instant she would show these stupid men the tumult of a woman's heart.

"Lee, be generous," spoke up General Lodge, feelingly. "Let Neale see the girl."

"I said no!" snapped Lee.

"But why not, in Heaven's name?"

"Why? I told you why," declared Lee, passionately.

"But, Lee—that implication may not be true. We didn't read all that letter," protested General Lodge.

"Ask him?"

Then the general turned to Neale. "Boy—tell me—did this Stanton woman love you—did you strike her? Did you—" The general's voice failed.

Neale faced about with a tragic darkening of his face. "To my shame—it is true," he said, clearly.

Then Allie Lee swept forward. *"Oh, Neale!"*

He seemed to rise and leap at once. And she ran straight into his arms. No man, no trouble, no mystery, no dishonor, no barrier—nothing could have held her back the instant she saw how the sight of her, how the sound of her voice, had transformed Neale. For one tumultuous, glorious, terrible moment she clung to his neck, blind, her heart bursting. Then she fell back with hands seeking her breast.

"I heard!" she cried. "I know nothing of Beauty Stanton's letter. . . . But you didn't shoot her. It was Larry. I saw him do it."

"Allie!" he whispered.

At last he had realized her actual presence, the safety of her body and soul; and all that had made him strange and old and grim and sad vanished in a beautiful transfiguration.

"You know Larry did it!" implored Allie. "Tell them so."

"Yes, I know," he replied. "But I did worse. I—"

She saw him shaken by an agony of remorse; and that agony was communicated to her.

"Neale! she loved you?"

He bowed his head.

"Oh!" Her cry was almost mute, full of an unutterable realization of tragic fatality for her. *"And you—you—"*

Allison Lee strode between them facing Neale. "See! She knows . . . and if you would spare her—go!" he exclaimed.

"She knows—what?" gasped Neale, in a frenzy between doubt and certainty.

Allie felt a horrible, nameless, insidious sense of falsity—a nightmare unreality—an intangible Neale, fated, drifting away from her.

"Good-by—Allie! . . . Bless you! I'll be—happy—knowing—you're—" He choked, and the tears streamed down his face. It was a face convulsed by renunciation, not by guilt. Whatever he had done, it was not base.

"Don't let me—go! . . . I—forgive you!" she burst out. She held out her arms. *"There's no one in the world but you!"*

But Neale plunged away, upheld by Slingerland, and Allie's world grew suddenly empty and black.

The train swayed and creaked along through the night with that strain and effort which told of up-grade. The oil-lamps burned dimly in corners of the coach. There were soldiers at open windows looking out. There were passengers asleep sitting up and lying down and huddled over their baggage.

But Allie Lee was not asleep. She lay propped up with pillows and blankets, covered by a heavy coat. Her window was open, and a cool desert wind softly blew her hair. She stared out into the night, and the wheels seemed to be grinding over her crushed heart.

It was late. An old moon, misshapen and pale, shone low down over a dark, rugged horizon. Clouds hid the stars. The desert void seemed weirdly magnified by the wan light, and all that shadowy waste, silent, lonely, bleak, called out to Allie Lee the desolation of her soul. For what had she been saved? The train creaked on, and every foot added to her woe. Her unquenchable spirit, pure as a white flame that had burned so wonderfully through the months of her peril, flickered now that her peril ceased to be. She had no fount of emotion left to draw on, else she would have hated this creaking train.

It moved on. And there loomed bold outlines of rock and ridge familiar to her. They had been stamped upon her memory by the strain of her lonely wanderings along that very road. She knew every rod of the way, dark, lonely, wild as it was. In the midst of that stark space lay the spot where Benton had been. A spot lost in the immensity of the desert. If she had been asleep she would have awakened while passing there. There was not a light. Flat patches and pale gleams, a long, wan length of bare street, shadows everywhere—these marked Benton's grave.

Allie stared with strained eyes. They were there—in the blackness—those noble men who had died for her in vain. No—not in vain! She breathed a prayer for them—a word of love for Larry. Larry, the waster of life, yet the faithful, the symbol of brotherhood. As long as she lived she would see him stalk before her with his red, blazing fire, his magnificent effrontery, his supreme will. He, who had been the soul of chivalry, the meekest of men before a woman, the inheritor of a reverence for womanhood, had ruthlessly shot out of his way that wonderful white-armed Beauty Stanton.

She, too, must lie there in the shadow. Allie shivered with the cool desert wind that blew in her face from the shadowy spaces. She shut her eyes to hide the dim passing traces of terrible Benton and the darkness that hid the lonely graves.

The train moved on and on, leaving what had been Benton far behind; and once more Allie opened her weary eyes to the dim, obscure reaches of the desert. Her heart beat very slowly under its leaden weight, its endless pang. Her blood flowed at low ebb. She felt the long-forgotten recurrence of an old, morbid horror, like a poison lichen fastening upon the very spring of life. It passed and came again, and left her once more. Her thoughts wandered back along the night track she had traversed, until again her ears were haunted by that strange sound which had given Roaring City its name. She had been torn away from hope, love, almost life itself. Where was Neale? He had turned from her, obedient to Allison Lee and the fatal complexity and perverseness of life. The vindication of her spiritual faith and the answer to her prayers lay in the fact that she had been saved; but rather than to be here in this car, daughter of a rich father, but separated from Neale, she would have preferred to fill one of the nameless graves in Benton.

CHAPTER XXXIII

The sun set pale-gold and austere as Neale watched the train bear Allie Lee away. No thought of himself entered into that solemn moment of happiness. Allie Lee—alive—safe—her troubles ended—on her way home with her father! The long train wound round the bold bluff and at last was gone. For Neale the moment held something big, final. A phase—a part of his life ended there.

"Son, it's over," said Slingerland, who watched with him. "Allie's gone home—back to whar she belongs—to come into her own. Thank God! An' you—why this day turns you back to whar you was once. . . . Allie owes her life to you an' her father's life. Think, son, of these hyar times—how much wuss it might hev been."

Neale's sense of thankfulness was unutterable. Passively he went with Slingerland, silent and gentle. The trapper dressed his wounds, tended him, kept men away from him, and watched by him as if he were a sick child.

Neale suffered only the weakness following the action and stress of great passion. His mind seemed full of beautiful solemn bells of blessing, resonant, ringing the wonder of an everlasting unchangeable truth. Night fell—the darkness thickened—the old trapper kept his vigil—and

Neale sank to sleep, and the sweet, low-toned bells claimed him in his dreams.

How strange for Neale to greet a dawn without hatred! He and Slingerland had breakfast together.

"Son, will you go into the hills with me?" asked the old trapper.

"Yes, some day, when the railroad's built," replied Neale, thoughtfully.

Slingerland's keen eyes quickened. "But the railroad's about done—an' you need a vacation," he insisted.

"Yes," Neale answered, dreamily.

"Son, mebbe you ought to wait awhile. You're packin' a bullet somewhar in your carcass."

"It's here," said Neale, putting his hand to his breast, high up toward the shoulder. "I feel it—a dull, steady, weighty pain. . . . But that's nothing. I hope I always have it."

"Wal, I don't. . . . An', son, you ain't never goin' back to drink an' cards—an' all thet hell? . . . Not now!"

Neale's smile was a promise, and the light of it was instantly reflected on the rugged face of the trapper.

"Reckon I needn't asked thet. Wal, I'll be sayin' goodby. . . . You kin expect me back some day. . . . To see the meetin' of the rails from east an' west—an' to pack you off to my hills."

Neale rode out of Roaring City on the work-train, sitting on a flat-car with a crowd of hairy-breasted, red-shirted laborers.

That train carried hundreds of men, tons of steel rails, thousands of ties; and also it was equipped to feed the workers and to fight Indians. It ran to the end of the rails, about forty miles out of Roaring City.

Neale sought out Reilly, the boss. This big Irishman was

in the thick of the start of the day—which was like a battle. Neale waited in the crowd, standing there in his shirt-sleeves, with the familiar bustle and color strong as wine to his senses. At last Reilly saw him and shoved out a huge paw.

"Hullo, Neale! I'm glad to see ye. . . . They tell me ye did a dom' foine job."

"Reilly, I need work," said Neale.

"But, mon—ye was shot!" ejaculated the boss.

"I'm all right."

"Ye look thot an' no mistake. . . . Shure, now, ye ain't serious about work? You—that's chafe of all thim engineer jobs?"

"I want to work with my hands. Let me heave ties or carry rails or swing a sledge—for just a few days. I've explained to General Lodge. It's a kind of vacation for me."

Reilly gazed with keen, twinkling eyes at Neale. "Ye can't be drunk an' look sober."

"Reilly, I'm sober—and in dead earnest," appealed Neale. "I want to go back—be in the finish—to lay some rails—drive some spikes."

The boss lost his humorous, quizzing expression. "Shure—shure," replied Reilly, as if he saw, but failed to comprehend. "Ye're on. . . . An' more power to ye!"

He sent Neale out with the gang detailed to heave rail-road ties.

A string of flat-cars, loaded with rails and ties, stood on the track where the work of yesterday had ended. Beyond stretched the road-bed, yellow, level, winding as far as eye could see. The sun beat down hot; the dry, scorching desert breeze swept down from the bare hills, across the waste; dust flew up in puffs; uprooted clumps of sage, like balls, went rolling along; and everywhere the veils of heat rose from the sun-baked earth.

"Drill, ye terriers, drill!" rang out a cheery voice. And Neale remembered Casey.

Neale's gang was put to carrying ties. Neale got hold of the first tie thrown off the car.

"Phwat the hell's ye're hurry!" protested his partner. This fellow was gnarled and knotted, brick-red in color, with face a network of seams, and narrow, sun-burnt slits for eyes. He answered to the name of Pat.

They carried the tie out to the end of the rails and dropped it on the level road-bed. Men there set it straight and tamped the gravel around it. Neale and his partner went back for another, passing a dozen couples carrying ties forward. Behind these staggered the rows of men burdened with the heavy iron rails.

So the day's toil began.

Pat had glanced askance at Neale, and then had made dumb signs to his fellow-laborers, indicating his hard lot in being yoked to this new wild man on the job. But his ridicule soon changed to respect. Presently he offered his gloves to Neale. They were refused.

"But, fri'nd, ye ain't tough loike me," he protested.

"Pat, they'll put you to bed to-night—if you stay with me," replied Neale.

"The hell ye say! Come on, thin!"

At first Neale had no sensations of heat, weariness, thirst, or pain. He dragged the little Irishman forward to drop the ties—then strode back ahead of him. Neale was obsessed by a profound emotion. This was a new beginning for him. For him the world and life had seemed to cease when yesternight the sun sank and Allie Lee passed out of sight. His motive in working there, he imagined, was to lay a few rails, drive a few spikes along the last miles of the road that he had surveyed. He meant to work this way only a little while, till the rails from east met those from west.

This profound emotion seemed accompanied by a procession of thoughts, each thought in turn, like a sun with satellites, reflecting its radiance upon them and rousing strange, dreamy, full-hearted fancies. . . . Allie lived—as good, as innocent as ever, incomparably beautiful—sad-eyed, eloquent, haunting. From that mighty thought sprang both Neale's exaltation and his activity. He had loved her so well that conviction of her death had broken his heart, deadened his ambition, ruined his life. But since, by the mercy of God and the innocence that had made men heroic, she had survived all peril, all evil, then had begun a colossal overthrow in Neale's soul of the darkness, the despair, the hate, the indifference. He had been flung aloft, into the heights, and he had seen into heaven. He asked for nothing in the world. All-satisfied, eternally humble, grateful with every passionate drop of blood throbbing through his heart, he dedicated all his spiritual life to memory. And likewise there seemed a tremendous need in him of sustained physical action, even violence. He turned to the last stages of the construction of the great railroad.

What fine comrades these hairy-breasted toilers made! Neale had admired them once; now he loved them. Every group seemed to contain a trio like that one he had known so well—Casey, Shane, and McDermott. Then he divined that these men were all alike. They all toiled, swore, fought, drank, gambled. Hundreds of them went to nameless graves. But the work went on—the great, driving, united heart beat on.

Neale was under its impulse, in another sense.

When he lifted a tie and felt the hard, splintering wood, he wondered where it had come from, what kind of a tree it was, who had played in its shade, how surely birds had nested in it and animals had grazed beneath it. Between him and that square log of wood there was an affinity. Somehow his hold upon it linked him strangely to a long-past, intangible spirit of himself. He must cling to it, lest he might lose that illusive feeling. Then when he laid it down he felt regret fade into a realization that the yellow-gravel road-bed also inspirited him. He wanted to feel it, work in it, level it, make it somehow his own.

When he strode back for another load his magnifying eyes gloated over the toilers in action—the rows of men carrying and laying rails, and the splendid brawny figures of the spikers, naked to the waist, swinging the heavy sledges. The blows rang out *spang—spang—spang!* Strong music, full of meaning! When his turn came to be a spiker, he would love that hardest work of all.

The engine puffed smoke and bumped the cars ahead, little by little as the track advanced; men on the train carried ties and rails forward, filling the front cars as fast as they were emptied; long lines of laborers on the ground passed to and fro, burdened going forward, returning empty-handed; the rails and the shovels and the hammers and the picks all caught the hot gleam from the sun; the dust swept up in sheets; the ring, the crash, the thump, the scrape of iron and wood and earth in collision filled the air with a sound rising harshly above the song and laugh and curse of men.

A shifting, colorful, strenuous scene of toil!

Gradually Neale felt that he was fitting into this scene, becoming a part of it, an atom once more in the great whole. He doubted while he thrilled. Clearly as he saw, keenly as he felt, he yet seemed bewildered. Was he not gazing out at this construction work through windows of his soul, once more painted, colored, beautiful, because the most precious gift he might have prayed for had been given him—life and hope for Allie Lee?

He did not know. He could not think.

His comrade, Pat, wiped floods of sweat from his scarlet face. "I'll be domned if ye ain't a son-of-a-gun fer worrk!" he complained.

"Pat, we've been given the honor of pace-makers. They've got to keep up with us. Come on," replied Neale.

"Be gad! there ain't a mon in the gang phwat'll trade fer me honor, thin," declared Pat. "Fri'nd, I'd loike to live till next pay-day."

"Come on, then, work up an appetite," rejoined Neale.

"Shure I'll die. . . . An' I'd loike to ask, beggin' ye're pardon, hevn't ye got some Irish in ye?"

"Yes, a little."

"I knowed thot. . . . All roight, I'll die with ye, thin."

In half an hour Pat was in despair again. He had to rest.

"Phwat's—ye're—name?" he queried.

"Neale."

"It ought to be Casey. Fer there was niver but wan loike ye—an' he was Casey. . . . Mon, ye're sweatin' blood roight now!"

Pat pointed at Neale's red, wet shirt. Neale slapped his breast, and drops of blood and sweat spattered from under his hand.

"An' shure ye're hands are bladin', too!" ejaculated Pat.

They were, indeed, but Neale had not noted that.

The boss, Reilly, passing by, paused to look and grin.

"Pat, yez got some one to kape up with to-day. We're half a mile ahead of yestidy this time."

Then he turned to Neale.

"I've seen one in yer class—Casey by name. An' thot's talkin'."

He went his way. And Neale, plodding on, saw the red face of the great Casey, with its set grin and the black pipe. Swiftly then he saw it as he had heard of it last, and a shadow glanced fleetingly across the singular radiance of his mind.

The shrill whistle of the locomotive halted the work and called the men to dinner and rest. Instantly the scene changed. The slow, steady, rhythmic motions of labor gave place to a scramble back to the long line of cars. Then the horde of sweaty toilers sought places in the shade, and ate and drank and smoked and rested. As the spirit of work had been merry, so was that of rest, with always a dry, grim earnestness in the background.

Neale slowed down during the afternoon, to the un-concealed thankfulness of his partner. The burn of the sun, the slippery sweat, the growing ache of muscles, the never-ending thirst, the lessening of strength—these sensations impinged upon Neale's emotion and gradually wore to the front of his consciousness. His hands grew raw, his back stiff and sore, his feet crippled. The wound in his breast burned and bled and throbbed. At the end of the day he could scarcely walk.

He rode in with the laborers, slept twelve hours, and awoke heavy-limbed, slow, and aching. But he rode out to work, and his second day was one of agony.

The third was a continual fight between will and body, between spirit and pain. But so long as he could step and lift he would work on. From that time he slowly began to mend.

Then came his siege with the rails. That was labor which made carrying ties seem light. He toiled on, sweating thin, wearing hard, growing clearer of mind. As pain subsided, and weariness of body no longer dominated him, slowly thought and feeling returned until that morning dawned when, like a flash of lightning illuminating his soul, the profound and exalted emotion again possessed him. Soon he came to divine that the agony of toil and his victory over weak flesh had added to his strange happiness. Hour after hour he bent his back and plodded beside his comrades, doing his share, burdened as they were, silent, watchful, listening, dreaming, keen to note the progress of the road, yet deep in his own intense abstraction. He seemed to have two minds. He saw every rod of the ten miles of track laid every day, knew, as only an engineer could know, the wonder of such progress; and, likewise, always in his sight, in his mind, shone a face, red-lipped, soulful, lovely like a saint's, with mournful violet eyes, star-sweet in innocence. Life had given Allie Lee back to him—to his love and his memory; and all that could happen to him now must be good. At first he had asked for nothing, so grateful was he to fate, but now he prayed for hours and days and nights to remember.

The day came when Neale graduated into the class of spikers. This division of labor to him had always represented the finest spirit of the building. The drivers—the spikers—the men who nailed the rails—who riveted the last links—these brawny, half-naked wielders of the sledges, bronzed as Indians, seemed to embody both the romance and the achievement. Neale experienced a subtle perception with the first touch and lift and swing of the great hammer. And there seemed born in him a genius for the stroke. He had a free, easy swing, with tremendous power. He could drive so fast that his comrade on the opposite rail, and the carriers and layers, could not keep up with him. Moments of rest seemed earned. During these he would gaze with glinting eyes back at the gangs and the trains, at the smoke, dust, and movement; and beyond toward the east.

One day he drove spikes for hours, with the gangs in uninterrupted labor around him, while back a mile along the road the troopers fought the Sioux; and all this time, when any moment he might be ordered to drop his sledge for a rifle, he listened to the voice in his memory and saw the face.

Another day dawned in which he saw the grading gangs return from work ahead. They were done. Streams of horses, wagons, and men on the return! They had met the graders from the west, and the two lines of roadbed had been connected. As these gangs passed, cheer on cheer greeted them from the rail-layers. It was a splendid moment.

From lip to lip then went the word that the grading-gangs from east and west had passed each other in plain sight, working on, grading on for a hundred miles farther than necessary. They had met and had passed on, side by side, doubling the expense of construction.

This knowledge gave Neale a melancholy reminder of the dishonest aspect of the road-building. And he thought of many things. The spirit of the work was grand, the labor heroic, but, alas! side by side with these splendid and noble attributes stalked the specters of greed and gold and lust of blood and of death.

But neither knowledge such as this, nor peril from Indians, nor the toil-pangs of a galley slave had power to change Neale's supreme state of joy.

He gazed back toward the east, and then with mighty swing he drove a spike. He loved Allie Lee beyond all conception, and next he loved the building of the railroad.

When such thoughts came he went back to pure sensations, the great, bold peaks looming dark, the winding, level road-bed, the smoky desert-land, reflecting heat, the completed track and gangs of moving men like bright ants in the sunlight, and the exhaust of the engines, the old song, "Drill, ye terriers, drill!" the ring and crash and thud and scrape of labor, the whistle of the seeping sand on the wind, the feel of the heavy sledge that he could wield as a toy, the throb of pulse, the smell of dust and sweat, the sense of his being there, his action, his solidarity, his physical brawn—once more manhood.

But at last human instincts encroached upon Neale's superlative detachment from self. It seemed all of a sudden that he stepped toward an east-bound train. When he reached the coach something halted him—a thought— where was he going? The west-bound work-train was the one he wanted. He laughed, a little grimly. Certainly he had grown absent-minded. And straightway he became thoughtful, in a different way. Not many moments of reflection were needed to assure him that he had moved toward the east-bound train with the instinctive idea of going to Allie Lee. The thing amazed him.

"But she—she's gone out of my life," he soliloquized. "And I am—I *was* glad!"

The lightning-swift shift to past tense enlightened Neale.

He went out to work. That work still loomed splendid to him, but it seemed not the same. He saw and felt the majesty of common free men, sweating and bleeding and groaning over toil comparable to the building of the Pyramids; he felt the best that had ever been in him quicken and broaden as he rubbed elbows with these simple, elemental toilers; with them he had gotten down to the level of truth. His old genius for achievement, the practical and scientific side of him, still thrilled with the battle of strong hands against the natural barriers of the desert. He saw the thousands of plodding, swearing, fighting, blaspheming, joking laborers on the field of action—saw the picture they made, red and bronzed and black, dust-begrimed; and how here with the ties and the rails and the road-bed was the heart of that epical turmoil. What approach could great and rich engineers and directors have made to that vast enterprise without these sons of brawn? Neale now saw what he had once dreamed, and that was the secret of his longing to get down to the earth with these men.

He loved to swing that sledge, to hear the *spang* of the

steel ring out. He had a sheer physical delight in the power of his body, long since thinned-out, hardened, tough as the wood into which he drove the spikes. He loved his new comrade, Pat, the gnarled and knotted little Irishman who cursed and complained of his job and fought his fellow-workers, yet who never lagged, never shirked, and never failed, though his days of usefulness must soon be over. Soon Pat would drop by the roadside, a victim to toil and whisky and sun. And he was great in his obscurity. He wore a brass tag with a number; he signed his wage receipt with a cross; he cared only for drink and a painted hag in a squalid tent; yet in all the essentials that Neale now called great his friend Pat reached up to them—the spirit to work, to stand his share, to go on, to endure, to fulfil his task.

Neale might have found salvation in this late-developed and splendid relation to labor and to men. But there was a hitch in his brain. He would see all that was beautiful and strenuous and progressive around him; and then, in a flash, that hiatus in his mind would operate to make him hopeless.

Then he would stand as in a trance, with far-away gaze in his eyes, until his fellow-spiker would recall him to his neglected work. These intervals of abstraction grew upon him until he would leave off in the act of driving a spike.

And sometimes in these strange intervals he longed for his old friend, brother, shadow—Larry Red King. He held to Larry's memory, though with it always would return that low, strange roar of Benton's gold and lust and blood and death. Neale did not understand the mystery of what he had been through. It had been a phase of wildness never to be seen again by his race. His ambition and effort, his fall, his dark siege with hell, his friendship and loss, his agony and toil, his victory, were all symbolical of the progress of a great movement. In his experience lay hid all that development.

The coming of night was always a relief now, for with the end of the day's work he need no longer fight his battle. It was a losing battle—that he knew. Shunning everybody, he paced to and fro out on the dark, windy desert, under the lonely, pitiless stars.

His longing to see Allie Lee grew upon him. While he had believed her dead he had felt her spirit hovering near him, in every shadow, and her voice whispered on the wind. She was alive now, but gone away, far distant, over mountains and plains, out of his sight and reach, somewhere to take up a new life alien to his. What would she do? Could she bear it? Never would she forget him— be faithless to his memory! Yet she was young and her life had been hard. She might yield to that cold Allison Lee's dictation. In happy surroundings her beauty and sweetness would bring a crowd of lovers to her.

"But that's all—only natural," muttered Neale, in perplexity. "I want her to forget—to be happy—to find a home. . . . For her to grow old—alone! No! She must love some man—marry—"

And with the spoken words Neale's heart contracted. He knew that he lied to himself. If she ever cared for another man, that would be the end of Warren Neale. But then, he was ended, anyhow. Jealousy, strange, new, horrible, added to Neale's other burdens, finished him. He had the manhood to try to fight selfishness, but he had failed to subdue it; and he had nothing left to fight his consuming love and hatred of life and terrible loneliness and that fierce thing— jealousy. He had saved Allie Lee! Why had he given her up? He had stained his hands with blood for her sake. And that awful moment came back to him when, maddened by the sting of a bullet, he had gloried in the cracking of Durade's bones, in the ghastly terror and fear of death upon the Spaniard's face, in the feel of the knife-blade as he forced Durade to stab himself. Always Neale had been haunted by this final scene of his evil life in the construction camps. A somber and spectral shape, intangible, gloomy-faced, often attended him in the shadow. He justified his deed, for Durade would have killed Allison Lee. But that fact did not prevent the haunting shape, the stir in the dark air, the nameless step upon Neale's trail.

And jealousy, stronger than all except fear, wore Neale out of his exaltation, out of his dream, out of his old disposition to work. He could persist in courage if not in joy. But jealous longing would destroy him—he felt that. It was so powerful, so wonderful that it brought back to him words and movements which until then he had been unable to recall.

And he lived over the past. Much still baffled him, yet gradually more and more of what had happened became clear specifically in his memory. He could not think from the present back over the past. He had to ponder the other way.

One day, leaning on his sledge, Neale's torturing self, morbid, inquisitive, growing by what it fed on, whispered another question to his memory.

"What were some of the last words she spoke to me?"

And there, limned white on the dark background of his mind, the answer appeared, *"Neale, I forgive you!"*

He recalled her face, the tragic eyes, the outstretched arms.

"Forgive me! For what?" Neale muttered, dazed and troubled. He dropped his sledge and remained standing there, though the noon whistle called the gang to dinner. Looking out across the hot, smoky, arid desert he saw again that scene where he had appealed to Allison Lee.

The picture was etched out vividly, and again he lived through those big moments of emotion.

The room full of men—Lee's cold acceptance of fact—his thanks, his offer, his questions, his refusal—General Lodge's earnest solicitation—the rapid exchange of passionate words between them—the query put to Neale and his answer—the sudden appearance of Allie, shocking his heart with rapture—her sweet, wild words—and so the end! How vivid now—how like flashes of lightning in his mind!

"Lee thought I'd killed Stanton," muttered Neale, in intense perplexity. "But she—she told them Larry did it. . . . What a strange idea Lee had—and General Lodge, too. He defended me. . . . *Ah!*"

Suddenly Neale drew from his pocket the little leather note-book that had been Stanton's, and which contained her letter to him. With trembling hands he opened it. Again this letter was to mean a revelation.

General Lodge had said his engineer had read aloud only the first of that message to Neale; and from this Allison Lee and all the listeners had formed their impressions.

Neale read these first lines.

"No wonder they imagined I killed her!" he exclaimed. "She accuses me. But she never meant what they imagined she meant. Why, that evidence could hang me! . . . Allie told them she saw Larry do it. And it's common knowledge now—I've heard it here. . . . What, then, had Allie to forgive—to forgive with eyes that will haunt me to my grave?"

Then the truth burst upon him with merciless and stunning force.

"My God! Allie believed what they all believed—*what I must have blindly made seem true! . . . That I was Beauty Stanton's lover!"*

CHAPTER XXXIV

The home to which Allie Lee was brought stood in the outskirts of Omaha upon a wooded bank above the river.

Allie watched the broad, yellow Missouri swirling by. She liked best to be alone outdoors in the shade of the trees. In the weeks since her arrival there she had not recovered from the shock of meeting Neale only to be parted from him.

But the comfort, the luxury of her home, the relief from constant dread, such as she had known for years, the quiet at night—these had been so welcome, so saving, that her burden of sorrow seemed endurable. Yet in time she came to see that the finding of a father and a home had only added to her bitterness.

Allison Lee's sister, an elderly woman of strong character, resented the home-bringing of this strange, lost daughter. Allie had found no sympathy in her. For a while neighbors and friends of the Lees flocked to the house and were kind, gracious, attentive to Allie. Then somehow her story, or part of it, became gossip. Her father, sensitive, cold, embittered by the past, suffered intolerable shame at the disgrace of a wife's desertion and a daughter's notoriety.

Allie's presence hurt him; he avoided her as much as possible; the little kindnesses that he had shown, and his feelings of pride in her beauty and charm, soon vanished. There was no love between them. Allie had tried hard to care for him, but her heart seemed to be buried in that vast grave of the West. She was obedient, dutiful, passive, but she could not care for him. And there came a day when she realized that he did not believe she had come unscathed through the wilds of the gold-fields and the vileness of the construction camps. She bore this patiently, though it stung her. But the loss of respect for her father did not come until she heard men in his study, loud-voiced and furious, wrangle over contracts and accuse him of double-dealing.

Later he told her that he had become involved in financial straits, and that unless he could raise a large sum by a certain date he would be ruined.

And it was this day that Allie sat on a bench in the little arbor and watched the turbulent river. She was sorry for her father, but she could not help him. Moreover, alien griefs did not greatly touch her. Her own grief was deep and all-enfolding. She was heart-sick, and always yearning—yearning for that she dared not name.

The day was hot, sultry; no birds sang, but the locusts were noisy; the air was full of humming bees.

Allie watched the river. She was idle because her aunt would not let her work. She could only remember and suffer. The great river soothed her. Where did it come from and where did it go? And what was to become of her? Almost it would have been better—

A servant interrupted her. "Missy, heah's a gennel-man to see yo'," announced the negro girl.

Allie looked. She thought she saw a tall, buckskin-clad man carrying a heavy pack. Was she dreaming or had she lost her mind? She got up, shaking in every limb. This tall man moved; he seemed real; his bronzed face beamed. He approached; he set the pack down on the bench. Then his keen, clear eyes pierced Allie.

"Wal, lass," he said, gently.

The familiar voice was no dream, no treachery of her mind. Slingerland! She could not speak. She could hardly see. She swayed into his arms. Then when she felt the great, strong clasp and the softness of buckskin on her face and the odor of pine and sage and desert dust, she believed in his reality.

Her heart seemed to collapse. All within her was riot.

"Neale!" she whispered, in anguish.

"All right an' workin' hard. He sent me," replied Slingerland, swift to get his message out.

Allie quivered and closed her eyes and leaned against him. A beautiful something pervaded her soul. Slowly the tumult within her breast subsided. She recovered.

"Uncle Al!" she called him, tenderly.

"Wal, I should smile! An' glad to see you—why Lord! I'd never tell you! . . . You're white an' shaky, lass. . . . Set down hyar—on the bench—beside me. Thar! . . . Allie, I've a powerful lot to tell you."

"Wait! To see you—and to hear—of *him*—almost killed me with joy," she panted. Her little hands, once so strong and brown, but now thin and white, fastened tight in the fringe of his buckskin hunting-coat.

"Lass, sight of you sort of makes me young agin—but— Allie, those are not the happy eyes I remember."

"I—am very unhappy," she whispered.

"Wal, if thet ain't too bad! Shore it's natural you'd be downhearted, losin' Neale thet way."

"It's not all—that," she murmured, and then she told him.

"Wal, wal!" ejaculated the trapper, stroking his beard in thoughtful sorrow. "But I reckon thet's natural, too. You're strange hyar, an' thet story will hang over you. . . .

Lass, with all due respect to your father, I reckon you'd better come back to me an' Neale."

"Did *he* tell you—to say that?" she whispered, tremulously.

"Lord, no!" ejaculated Slingerland.

"Does he—care—for me still?"

"Lass, he's dyin' fer you—an' I never spoke a truer word."

Allie shuddered close to him, blinded, stormed by an exquisite bitter-sweet fury of love. She seemed rising, uplifted, filled with rich, strong joy.

"I forgave him," she murmured, dreamily low to herself.

"Wal, mebbe you'll be right glad you did—presently," said Slingerland, with animation. "'Specially when thar wasn't nothin' much to forgive."

Allie became mute. She could not lift her eyes.

"Lass, listen!" began Slingerland. "After you left Roarin' City Neale went at hard work. Began by heavin' ties an' rails, an' now he's slingin' a sledge. . . . This was amazin' to me. I seen him only onct since, an' thet was the other day. But I heerd about him. I rode over to Roarin' City several times. An' I made it my bizness to find out about Neale. . . . He never came into the town at all. They said he worked like a slave thet first day, bleedin' hard. But he couldn't be stopped. An' the work didn't kill him, though thar was some as swore it would. They said he changed, an' when he toughened up thar was never but one man as could equal him, an' thet was an Irish feller named Casey. I heerd it was somethin' worth while to see him sling a sledge. . . . Wal, I never seen him do it, but mebbe I will yet.

"A few days back I met him gettin' off a train at Roarin' City. Lord! I hardly knowed him! He stood like an Injun, with the big muscles bulgin', an' his face was clean an' dark, his eye like fire. . . . He nearly shook the daylights out of me. 'Slingerland, I want you!' he kept yellin' at me. An' I said, 'So it 'pears, but what fer?' Then he told me he was goin' after the gold thet Horn had buried along the old Laramie Trail. Wal, I took my outfit, an' we rode back into the hills. You remember them. Wal, we found the gold, easy enough, an' we packed it back to Roarin' City. Thar Neale sent me off on a train to fetch the gold to you. An' hyar I am an' thar's the gold."

Allie stared at the pack, bewildered by Slingerland's story. Suddenly she sat up and she felt the blood rush to her cheeks.

"Gold! Horn's gold! But it's not mine! Did Neale send it to me?"

"Every ounce," replied the trapper, soberly. "I reckon it's yours. Thar was no one else left—an' you recollect what Horn said. Lass, it's yours—an' I'm goin' to make you keep it."

"How much is there?" queried Allie, with thrills of curiosity. How well she remembered Horn! He had told her he had no relatives. Indeed, the gold was hers.

"Wal, Neale an' me couldn't calkilate how much, hevin' nothin' to weigh the gold. But it's a fortune."

Allie turned from the pack to the earnest face of the trapper. There had been many critical moments in her life, but never one with the suspense, the fullness, the inevitableness of this.

"Did Neale send anything else?" she flashed.

"Wal, yes, an' I was comin' to thet," replied Slingerland, as he unlaced the front of his hunting-frock. Presently he drew forth a little leather note-book, which he handed to Allie. She took it while looking up at him. Never had she seen his face radiate such strange emotion. She divined it to be the supreme happiness inherent in the power to give happiness.

Allie trembled. She opened the little book. Surely it

would contain a message that would be as sweet as life to dying eyes. She read a name, written in ink, in a clear script: "Beauty Stanton."

Her pulses ceased to beat, her blood to flow, her heart to throb. All seemed to freeze within her except her mind. And that leaped fearfully over the first lines of a letter—then feverishly on to the close—only to fly back and read again.

Then she dropped the book. She hid her face on Slingerland's breast. She clutched him with frantic hands. She clung there, her body all held rigid, as if some extraordinary strength or inspiration or joy had suddenly inhibited weakness.

"Wal, lass, hyar you're takin' it powerful hard—an' I made sure—"

"Hush!" whispered Allie, raising her face. She kissed him. Then she sprang up like a bent sapling released. She met Slingerland's keen gaze—saw him start—then rise as if the better to meet a shock.

"I am going back West with you," she said, coolly.

"Wal, I knowed you'd go."

"Divide that gold. I'll leave half for my father."

Slingerland's great hands began to pull at the pack.

"Thar's a train soon. I calkilated to stay over a day. But the sooner the better. . . . Lass, will you run off or tell him?"

"I'll tell him. He can't stop me, even if he would. . . . The gold will save him from ruin. . . . He will let me go."

She stooped to pick up the little leather note-book and placed it in her bosom. Her heart seemed to surge against it. The great river rolled on—rolled on—magnified in her sight. A thick, rich, beautiful light shone under the trees. What was this dance of her blood while she seemed so calm, so cool, so sure?

"Does he have any idea—that I might return to him?" she asked.

"None, lass, none! Thet I'll swear," declared Slingerland. "When I left him at Roarin' City the other day he was—wal, like he used to be. The boy come out in him again, not jest the same, but brave. Sendin' thet gold an' thet little book made him happy. . . . I reckon Neale found his soul then. An' he never expects to see you again in this hyar world."

CHAPTER XXXV

uilding a railroad grew to be an exact and wonderful
science with the men of the Union Pacific, from engineers down to the laborers who ballasted and smoothed
the road-bed.

Wherever the work-trains stopped there began a hum
like a bee-hive. Gangs loaded rails on a flat-car, and the
horses or mules were driven at a gallop to the front. There
two men grasped the end of a rail and began to slide it off.
In couples, other laborers of that particular gang laid hold,
and when they had it off the car they ran away with it to
drop it in place. While they were doing this other gangs
followed with more rails. Four rails laid to the minute!
When one of the cars was empty it was tipped off the track
to make room for the next one. And as that next one passed
the first was levered back again on the rails to return for
another load.

Four rails down to the minute! It was Herculean toil.
The men who fitted the rails were cursed the most frequently, because they took time, a few seconds, when there
was no time.

Then the spikers! These brawny, half-naked, sweaty
giants—what a grand spanging music of labor rang from

under their hammers! Three strokes to a spike for most spikers! Only two strokes for such as Casey or Neale! Ten spikes to a rail—four hundred rails to a mile! . . . How many million times had brawny arms swung and sledges clanged!

Forward every day the work-trains crept westward, closer and closer to that great hour when they would meet the work-trains coming east.

The momentum now of the road-laying was tremendous. The spirit that nothing could stop had become embodied in a scientific army of toilers, a mass, a machine, ponderous, irresistible, moving on to the meeting of the rails.

Every day the criss-cross of ties lengthened out along the winding road-bed, and the lines of glistening rails kept pace with them. The sun beat down hot—the dust flew in sheets and puffs—the smoky veils floated up from the desert. Red-shirted toilers, blue-shirted toilers, half-naked toilers, sweat and bled, and laughed grimly, and sucked at their pipes, and bent their broad backs. The pace had quickened to the limit of human endurance. Fury of sound filled the air. Its rhythmical pace was the mighty gathering impetus of a last heave, a last swing.

Promontory Point was the place destined to be famous as the meeting of the rails.

On that summer day in 1869, which was to complete the work, special trains arrived from west and east. The Governor of California, who was also president of the western end of the line, met the Vice-President of the United States and the directors of the Union Pacific. Mormons from Utah were there in force. The Government was represented by officers and soldiers in uniform; and these, with their military band, lent the familiar martial air to the last scene of the great enterprise. Here mingled the Irish and negro laborers from the east with the Chinese and

Mexican from the west. Then the eastern paddies laid the last rails on one end, while the western coolies laid those on the other. The rails joined. Spikes were driven, until the last one remained.

The Territory of Arizona had presented a spike of gold, silver, and iron; Nevada had given one of silver, and a railroad tie of laurel wood; and the last spike of all—of solid gold—was presented by California.

The driving of the last spike was to be heard all over the United States. Omaha was the telegraphic center. The operator here had informed all inquirers, "When the last spike is driven at Promontory Point we will say, 'Done!'"

The magic of the wire was to carry that single message abroad over the face of the land.

The President of the United States was to be congratulated, as were the officers of the army, and the engineers of the work. San Francisco had arranged a monster celebration marked by the booming of cannon and enthusiastic parades. Free railroad tickets into Sacramento were to fill that city with jubilant crowds. At Omaha cannons were to be fired, business abandoned, and the whole city given over to festivity. Chicago was to see a great parade and decoration. In New York a hundred guns were to boom out the tidings. Trinity Church was to have special services, and the famous chimes were to play "Old Hundred." In Philadelphia a ringing of the Liberty Bell in Independence Hall would initiate a celebration. And so it would be in all prominent cities of the Union.

Neale was at Promontory Point that summer day. He stood aloof from the crowd, on a little bank, watching with shining eyes.

To him the scene was great, beautiful, final.

Only a few hundreds of that vast army of laborers were present at the meeting of the rails, but enough were there to represent the whole. Neale's glances were swift and gathering. His comrades, Pat and McDermott, sat near, exchanging lights for their pipes. They seemed reposeful, and for them the matter was ended. Broken hulks of toilers of the rails! Neither would labor any more. A burly negro, with crinkly, bullet-shaped head, leaned against a post; a brawny spiker, naked to the waist, his wonderful shoulders and arms brown, shiny, knotted, scarred, stood near, sledge in hand; a group of Irishmen, red- and blue-shirted, puffed their black pipes and argued; swarthy, sloe-eyed Mexicans, with huge sombreros on their knees, lolled in the shade of a tree, talking low in their mellow tones and fingering cigarettes; Chinamen, with long pigtails and foreign dress, added strangeness and colorful contrast.

Neale heard the low murmur of voices of the crowd, and the slow puffing of the two engines, head on, only a few yards apart, so strikingly different in shape. Then followed the pounding of hoofs and tread of many feet, the clang of iron as the last rail went down. How clear, sweet, spanging the hammer blows! And there was the old sighing sweep of the wind. Then came a gun-shot, the snort of a horse, a loud laugh.

Neale heard all with sensitive, recording ears.

"Mac, yez are so dom' smart—now tell me who built the U.P.?" demanded Pat.

"Thot's asy. Me fri'nd Casey did, b'gorra," retorted McDermott.

"Loike hell he did! It was the Irish."

"Shure, thot's phwat I said," McDermott replied

"Wal, thin, *phwat* built the U.P.? Tell me thot. Yez knows so much."

McDermott scratched his sun-blistered, stubble-field of a face, and grinned. "Whisky built the eastern half, an' cold tay built the western half."

Pat regarded his comrade with considerable respect. "Mac, shure yez is intilligint," he granted. "The Irish lived on whisky an' the Chinamons on tay. . . . Wal, yez is so dom' orful smart, mebbe yez can tell me who got the money for thot worrk."

"B'gorra, I know where ivery dollar wint," replied Mc-Dermott.

And so they argued on, oblivious to the impressive last stage.

Neale sensed the rest, the repose in the attitude of all the laborers present. Their hour was done. And they accepted that with the equanimity with which they had met the toil, the heat and thirst, the Sioux. A splendid, rugged, loquacious, crude, elemental body of men, unconscious of heroism. Those who had survived the five long years of toil and snow and sun, and the bloody Sioux, and the roaring camps, bore the scars, the furrows, the gray hairs of great and wild times.

A lane opened up in the crowd to the spot where the rails had met.

Neale got a glimpse of his associates, the engineers, as they stood near the frock-coated group of dignitaries and directors. Then Neale felt the stir and lift of emotion, as if he were on a rising wave. His blood began to flow fast and happily. He was to share their triumph. The moment had come. Some one led him back to his post of honor as the head of the engineer corps.

A silence fell then over that larger, denser multitude. It grew impressive, charged, waiting.

Then a man of God offered up a prayer. His voice floated dreamily to Neale. When he had ceased there were slow, dignified movements of frock-coated men as they placed in position the last spike.

The silver sledge flashed in the sunlight and fell. The

sound of the driving-stroke did not come to Neale with the familiar spang of iron; it was soft, mellow, golden.

A last stroke! The silence vibrated to a deep, hoarse acclaim from hundreds of men—a triumphant, united hurrah, simultaneously sent out with that final message, *"Done!"*

A great flood of sound, of color seemed to wave over Neale. His eyes dimmed with salt tears, blurring the splendid scene. The last moment had passed—that for which he had stood with all faith, all spirit—and the victory was his. The darkness passed out of his soul.

Then, as he stood there, bareheaded, at the height of this all-satisfying moment, when the last echoing melody of the sledge had blended in the roar of the crowd, a strange feeling of a presence struck Neale. Was it spiritual—was it divine—was it God? Or was it only baneful, fateful—the specter of his accomplished work—a reminder of the long, gray future?

A hand slipped into his—small, soft, trembling, exquisitely thrilling. Neale became still as a stone—transfixed. He knew that touch. No dream, no fancy, no morbid visitation! He felt warm flesh—tender, clinging fingers; and then the pulse of blood that beat of hope—love—life—Allie Lee!

CHAPTER XXXVI

Slingerland saw Allie Lee married to Neale by that minister of God whose prayer had followed the joining of the rails.

And to the old trapper had fallen the joy and the honor of giving the bride away and of receiving her kiss, as though he had been her father. Then the happy congratulations from General Lodge and his staff; the merry dinner given the couple, and its toasts warm with praise of the bride's beauty and the groom's luck and success; Neale's strange, rapt happiness and Allie's soul shining through her dark-blue eyes—this hour was to become memorable for Slingerland's future dreams.

Slingerland's sight was not clear when, as the train pulled away, he waved a last good-by to his young friends. Now he had no hope, no prayer left unanswered, except to be again in his beloved hills.

Abruptly he hurried away to the corrals where his pack-train was all in readiness to start. He did not speak to a man.

He had packed a dozen burros—the largest and completest pack-train he had ever driven. The abundance of carefully selected supplies, tools, and traps should last him many years—surely all the years that he would live.

Slingerland did not intend to return to civilization, and he never even looked back at that blotch on the face of the bluff—that hideous Roaring City.

He drove the burros at a good trot, his mind at once busy and absent, happy with the pictures of that last hour, gloomy with the undefined, unsatisfied cravings of his heart. Friendship with Neale, affection for Allie, acquainted him with the fact that he had missed something in life—not friendship, for he had had hunter friends, but love, perhaps of a sweetheart, surely love of a daughter.

For the rest the old trapper was glad to see the last of habitations, and of men, and of the railroad. Slingerland hated that great, shining steel band of progress connecting East and West. Every ringing sledge-hammer blow had sung out the death-knell of the trapper's calling. This railroad spelled the end of the wilderness. What one group of greedy men had accomplished others would imitate; and the grass of the plains would be burned, the forests blackened, the fountains dried up in the valleys, and the wild creatures of the mountains driven and hunted and exterminated. The end of the buffalo had come—the end of the Indian was in sight—and that of the fur-bearing animal and his hunter must follow soon with the hurrying years.

Slingerland hated the railroad, and he could not see as Neale did, or any of the engineers or builders. This old trapper had the vision of the Indian—that far-seeing eye cleared by distance and silence, and the force of the great, lonely hills. Progress was great, but nature undespoiled was greater. If a race could not breed all stronger men, through its great movements, it might better not breed any, for the bad over-multiplied the good, and so their needs magnified into greed. Slingerland saw many shining bands of steel across the plains and mountains, many stations and hamlets and cities, a growing and marvelous prosperity from timber, mines, farms, and in the distant end—a gutted West.

He made his first camp on a stream watering a valley twenty miles from the railroad. There were Indian tracks on the trails. But he had nothing to fear from Indians. That night, though all was starry and silent around him as he lay, he still held the insupportable feeling.

Next day he penetrated deeper into the foothills, and soon he had gained the fastnesses of the mountains. No longer did he meet trails except those of deer and lion and bear. And so day after day he drove his burros, climbing and descending the rocky ways, until he had penetrated to the very heart of the great wild range.

In all his roaming over untrodden lands he had never come into such a wild place. No foot, not even an Indian's, had ever desecrated this green valley with its clear, singing stream, its herds of tame deer, its curious beaver, its pine-covered slopes, its looming, gray, protective peaks. And at last he was satisfied to halt there—to build his cabin and his corral.

Discontent and longing, and then hate, passed into oblivion. These useless passions could not long survive in such an environment. By and by the old trapper's only link with the past was memory of a stalwart youth, and of a girl with violet eyes, and of their sad and wonderful romance, in which he had played a happy part.

The rosy dawn, the days of sun and cloud, the still, windy nights, the solemn stars, the moon-blanched valley with its grazing herds, the beautiful wild mourn of the hunting wolf and the whistle of the stag, and always and ever the murmur of the stream—in these, and in the solitude and loneliness of their haunts, he found his goal, his serenity, the truth and best of remaining life for him.

CHAPTER XXXVII

A band of Sioux warriors rode out upon a promontory of the hills, high above the great expanse of plain. Long, lean arms were raised and pointed.

A chief dismounted and strode to the front of his band. His war-bonnet trailed behind him; there were unhealed scars upon his bronze body; his face was old, full of fine, wavy lines, stern, craggy, and inscrutable; his eyes were dark, arrowy lightnings.

They beheld, far out and down upon the plain, a long, low, moving object leaving a trail of smoke. It was a train on the railroad. It came from the east and crept toward the west. The chief watched it, and so did his warriors. No word was spoken, no sign made, no face changed.

But what was in the mind and the heart and the soul of that great chief?

This beast that puffed smoke and spat fire and shrieked like a devil of an alien tribe; that split the silence as hideously as the long track split the once smooth plain; that was made of iron and wood; this thing of the white man's, coming from out of the distance where the Great Spirit lifted the dawn, meant the end of the hunting-grounds and the doom of the Indian. Blood had flowed; many warriors lay in their last sleep under the trees; but the iron monster that belched fire had gone only to return again. Those white men were many as the needles of the pines. They fought and died, but always others came.

This chief was old and wise, taught by sage and star and mountain and wind and the loneliness of the prairie-land. He recognized a superior race, but not a nobler one. White men would glut the treasures of water and earth. The Indian had been born to hunt his meat, to repel his red foes, to watch the clouds and serve his gods. But these white men would come like a great flight of grasshoppers to cover the length and breadth of the prairie-land. The buffalo would roll away, like a dust-cloud, in the distance, and never return. No meat for the Indian—no grass for his mustang—no place for his home. The Sioux must fight till he died or be driven back into waste places where grief and hardship would end him.

Red and dusky, the sun was setting beyond the desert. The old chief swept aloft his arm, and then in his acceptance of the inevitable bitterness he stood in magnificent austerity, somber as death, seeing in this railroad train creeping, fading into the ruddy sunset, a symbol of the destiny of the Indian—vanishing—vanishing—vanishing—

THE CALL
OF THE
CANYON

CHAPTER I

What subtle strange message had come to her out of the West? Carley Burch laid the letter in her lap and gazed dreamily through the window.

It was a day typical of early April in New York, rather cold and gray, with steely sunlight. Spring breathed in the air, but the women passing along Fifty-seventh Street wore furs and wraps. She heard the distant clatter of an L train and then the hum of a motor car. A hurdy-gurdy jarred into the interval of quiet.

"Glenn has been gone over a year," she mused, "three months over a year—and of all his strange letters this seems the strangest yet."

She lived again, for the thousandth time, the last moments she had spent with him. It had been on New-Year's Eve, 1918. They had called upon friends who were staying at the McAlpin, in a suite on the twenty-first floor overlooking Broadway. And when the last quarter hour of that eventful and tragic year began slowly to pass with the low swell of whistles and bells, Carley's friends had discreetly left her alone with her lover, at the open window, to watch and hear the old year out, the new year in.

Glenn Kilbourne had returned from France early that

fall, shell-shocked and gassed, and otherwise incapacitated for service in the army—a wreck of his former sterling self and in many unaccountable ways a stranger to her. Cold, silent, haunted by something, he had made her miserable with his aloofness. But as the bells began to ring out the year that had been his ruin Glenn had drawn her close, tenderly, passionately, and yet strangely, too.

"Carley, look and listen!" he had whispered.

Under them stretched the great long white flare of Broadway, with its snow-covered length glittering under a myriad of electric lights. Sixth Avenue swerved away to the right, a less brilliant lane of blanched snow. The L trains crept along like huge fire-eyed serpents. The hum of the ceaseless moving line of motor cars drifted upward faintly, almost drowned in the rising clamor of the street. Broadway's gay and thoughtless crowds surged to and fro, from that height merely a thick stream of black figures, like contending columns of ants on the march. And everywhere the monstrous electric signs flared up vivid in white and red and green; and dimmed and paled, only to flash up again.

Ring out the Old! Ring in the New! Carley had poignantly felt the sadness of the one, the promise of the other. As one by one the siren factory whistles opened up with deep, hoarse bellow, the clamor of the street and the ringing of the bells were lost in a volume of continuous sound that swelled on high into a magnificent roar. It was the voice of a city—of a nation. It was the voice of a people crying out the strife and the agony of the year—pealing forth a prayer for the future.

Glenn had put his lips to her ear: "It's like the voice in my soul!" Never would she forget the shock of that. And how she had stood spell-bound, enveloped in the mighty volume of sound no longer discordant, but full of great, pregnant melody, until the white ball burst upon the tower of the Times Building, showing the bright figures 1919.

The new year had not been many minutes old when Glenn Kilbourne had told her he was going West to try to recover his health.

Carley roused out of her memories to take up the letter that had so perplexed her. It bore the postmark, Flagstaff, Arizona. She reread it with slow pondering thoughtfulness.

WEST FORK,
March 25.

DEAR CARLEY:

It does seem my neglect in writing you is unpardonable. I used to be a pretty fair correspondent, but in that as in other things I have changed.

One reason I have not answered sooner is because your letter was so sweet and loving that it made me feel an ungrateful and unappreciative wretch. Another is that this life I now lead does not induce writing. I am outdoors all day, and when I get back to this cabin at night I am too tired for anything but bed.

Your imperious questions I must answer—and that *must,* of course, is a third reason why I have delayed my reply. First, you ask, "Don't you love me any more as you used to?" . . . Frankly, I do not. I am sure my old love for you, before I went to France, was selfish, thoughtless, sentimental, and boyish. I am a man now. And my love for you is different. Let me assure you that it has been about all left to me of what is noble and beautiful. Whatever the changes in me for the worse, my love for you, at least, has grown better, finer, purer.

And now for your second question, "Are you coming home as soon as you are well again?" . . . Carley, I *am* well. I have delayed telling you this because I knew you

would expect me to rush back East with the telling.
But—the fact is, Carley, I am not coming—just yet. I
wish it were possible for me to make you understand.
For a long time I seem to have been frozen within. You
know when I came back from France I couldn't talk. It's
almost as bad as that now. Yet all that I was then seems
to have changed again. It is only fair to you to tell you
that, as I feel now, I hate the city, I hate people, and
particularly I hate that dancing, drinking, lounging set
you chase with. I don't want to come East until I am
over that, you know. . . . Suppose I never get over it?—
Well, Carley, you can free yourself from me by one
word that I could never utter. I could never break our
engagement. During the hell I went through in the war
my attachment to you saved me from moral ruin, if it
did not from perfect honor and fidelity. This is another
thing I despair of making you understand. And in the
chaos I've wandered through *since* the war my love
for you was my only anchor. You never guessed, did
you, that I lived on your letters until I got well. And now
the fact that I might get along without them is no dis-
credit to their charm or to you.

It is all so hard to put in words, Carley. To lie down
with death and get up with death was nothing. To face
one's degradation was nothing. But to come home—an
incomprehensibly changed man—and to see my old life
as strange as if it were the new life of another planet—
to try to slip into the old groove—well, no words of mine
can tell you how utterly impossible it was.

My old job was not open to me, even if I had been
able to work. The government that I fought for left me
to starve, or to die of my maladies like a dog, for all it
cared. I could not live on your money, Carley. My people
are poor, as you know. So there was nothing for me to
do but to borrow a little money from my friends and to

come West. I'm glad I had the courage to come. What this West is I'll never try to tell you, because, loving the luxury and excitement and glitter of the city as you do, you'd think I was crazy.

Getting on here, in my condition, was as hard as trench life. But now, Carley—something has come to me out of the West. That, too, I am unable to put into words. Maybe I can give you an inkling of it. I'm strong enough to chop wood all day. No man or woman passes my cabin in a month. But I am never lonely. I love these vast red canyon walls towering above me. And the silence is so sweet. Think of the hellish din that filled my ears. Even now—sometimes, the brook here changes its babbling murmur to the roar of war. I never understood anything of the meaning of nature until I lived under these looming stone walls and whispering pines.

So, Carley, try to understand me, or at least be kind. You know they came very near writing, "Gone west!" after my name, and considering *that,* this "Out West" signifies for me a very fortunate difference. A tremendous difference! For the present I'll let well enough alone.

Adios. Write soon. Love from

GLENN.

Carley's second reaction to the letter was a sudden up-flashing desire to see her lover—to go out West and find him. Impulses with her were rather rare and inhibited, but this one made her tremble. If Glenn was well again he must have vastly changed from the moody, stone-faced, and haunted-eyed man who had so worried and distressed her. He had embarrassed her, too, for sometimes, in her home, meeting young men there who had not gone into the service, he had seemed to retreat into himself, singularly aloof, as if his world was not theirs.

Again, with eager eyes and quivering lips, she read the letter. It contained words that lifted her heart. Her starved love greedily absorbed them. In them she had excuse for any resolve that might bring Glenn closer to her. And she pondered over this longing to go to him.

Carley had the means to come and go and live as she liked. She did not remember her father, who had died when she was a child. Her mother had left her in the care of a sister, and before the war they had divided their time between New York and Europe, the Adirondacks and Florida. Carley had gone in for Red Cross and relief work with more of sincerity than most of her set. But she was really not used to making any decision as definite and important as that of going out West alone. She had never been farther west than Jersey City; and her conception of the West was a hazy one of vast plains and rough mountains, squalid towns, cattle herds, and uncouth ill-clad men.

So she carried the letter to her aunt, a rather slight woman with a kindly face and shrewd eyes, and who appeared somewhat given to old-fashioned garments.

"Aunt Mary, here's a letter from Glenn," said Carley. "It's more of a stumper than usual. Please read it."

"Dear me! you look upset," replied the aunt, mildly, and, adjusting her spectacles, she took the letter.

Carley waited impatiently for the perusal, conscious of inward forces coming more and more to the aid of her impulse to go West. Her aunt paused once to murmur how glad she was that Glenn had gotten well. Then she read on to the close.

"Carley, that's a fine letter," she said, fervently. "Do you see through it?"

"No, I don't," replied Carley. "That's why I asked you to read it."

"Do you still love Glenn as you used to—before—"

"Why, Aunt Mary!" exclaimed Carley, in surprise.

"Excuse me, Carley, if I'm blunt. But the fact is young women of modern times are very different from my kind when I was a girl. You haven't acted as though you pined for Glenn. You gad around almost the same as ever."

"What's a girl to do?" protested Carley.

"You are twenty-six years old, Carley," retorted Aunt Mary.

"Suppose I am. I'm as young—as I ever was."

"Well, let's not argue about modern girls and modern times. We never get anywhere," returned her aunt, kindly. "But I can tell you something of what Glenn Kilbourne means in that letter—if you want to hear it."

"I do—indeed."

"The war did something horrible to Glenn aside from wrecking his health. Shell-shock, they said! I don't understand that. Out of his mind, they said! But that never was true. Glenn was as sane as I am, and, my dear, that's pretty sane, I'll have you remember. But he must have suffered some terrible blight to his spirit—some blunting of his soul. For months after he returned he walked as one in a trance. Then came a change. He grew restless. Perhaps that change was for the better. At least it showed he'd roused. Glenn saw you and your friends and the life you lead, and all the present, with eyes from which the scales had dropped. He saw what was *wrong*. He never said so to me, but I knew it. It wasn't only to get well that he went West. It was to get *away*. . . . And, Carley Burch, if your happiness depends on him you had better be up and doing—or you'll *lose* him!"

"Aunt Mary!" gasped Carley.

"I mean it. That letter shows how near he came to the Valley of the Shadow—and how he has become a man. . . . If I were you I'd go out West. Surely there must be a place where it would be all right for you to stay."

"Oh, yes," replied Carley, eagerly. "Glenn wrote me

there was a lodge where people went in nice weather—right down in the canyon not far from his place. Then, of course, the town—Flagstaff—isn't far. . . . Aunt Mary, I think I'll go."

"I would. You're certainly wasting your time here."

"But I could only go for a visit," rejoined Carley, thoughtfully. "A month, perhaps six weeks, if I could stand it."

"Seems to me if you can stand New York you could stand that place," said Aunt Mary, dryly.

"The idea of staying away from New York—any length of time—why, I couldn't do it! . . . But I can stay out there long enough to bring Glenn back with me."

"That may take you longer than you think," replied her aunt, with a gleam in her shrewd eyes. "If you want my advice you will surprise Glenn. Don't write him—don't give him a chance to—well—to suggest courteously that you'd better not come just yet. I don't like his words 'just yet.'"

"Auntie, you're—rather—more than blunt," said Carley, divided between resentment and amaze. "Glenn would be simply wild to have me come."

"Maybe he would. Has he ever asked you?"

"No-o—come to think of it, he hasn't," replied Carley, reluctantly. "Aunt Mary, you hurt my feelings."

"Well, child, I'm glad to learn your feelings are hurt," returned the aunt. "I'm sure, Carley, that underneath all this—this blasé ultra something you've acquired, there's a real heart. Only you must hurry and listen to it—or—"

"Or what?" queried Carley.

Aunt Mary shook her gray head sagely. "Never mind what. Carley, I'd like your idea of the most significant thing in Glenn's letter."

"Why, his love for me, of course!" replied Carley.

"Naturally you think that. But I don't. What struck me

most were his words, 'out of the West.' . . . Carley, you'd
do well to ponder over them."

"I will," rejoined Carley, positively. "I'll do more. I'll
go out to his wonderful West and see what he meant by
them."

Carley Burch possessed in full degree the prevailing
modern craze for speed. She loved a motor-car ride at sixty
miles an hour along a smooth, straight road, or, better, on
the level seashore of Ormond, where on moonlight nights
the white blanched sand seemed to flash toward her. Therefore quite to her taste was the Twentieth Century Limited
which was hurtling her on the way to Chicago. The un-
ceasingly smooth and even rush of the train satisfied something in her. An old lady sitting in an adjoining seat with
a companion amused Carley by the remark: "I wish we
didn't go so fast. People nowadays haven't time to draw a
comfortable breath. Suppose we should run off the track!"

Carley had no fear of express trains, or motor cars, or
transatlantic liners; in fact, she prided herself in not being
afraid of anything. But she wondered if this was not the
false courage of association with a crowd. Before this enterprise at hand she could not remember anything she had
undertaken alone. Her thrills seemed to be in abeyance
to the end of her journey. That night her sleep was permeated with the steady low whirring of the wheels.
Once, roused by a jerk, she lay awake in the darkness
while the thought came to her that she and all her fellow
passengers were really at the mercy of the engineer. Who
was he, and did he stand at his throttle keen and vigilant,
thinking of the lives intrusted to him? Such thoughts
vaguely annoyed Carley, and she dismissed them.

A long half-day wait in Chicago was a tedious prelimi-
nary to the second part of her journey. But at last she found
herself aboard the California Limited, and went to bed
with a relief quite a stranger to her. The glare of the sun

under the curtain awakened her. Propped up on her pillows, she looked out at apparently endless green fields or pastures, dotted now and then with little farmhouses and tree-skirted villages. This country, she thought, must be the prairie-land she remembered lay west of the Mississippi.

Later, in the dining car, the steward smilingly answered her question: "This is Kansas, and those green fields out there are the wheat that feeds the nation."

Carley was not impressed. The color of the short wheat appeared soft and rich, and the boundless fields stretched away monotonously. She had not known there was so much flat land in the world, and she imagined it might be a fine country for automobile roads. When she got back to her seat she drew the blinds down and read her magazines. Then tiring of that, she went back to the observation car. Carley was accustomed to attracting attention, and did not resent it, unless she was annoyed. The train evidently had a full complement of passengers, who, as far as Carley could see, were people not of her station in life. The glare from the many windows, and the rather crass interest of several men, drove her back to her own section. There she discovered that some one had drawn up her window shades. Carley promptly pulled them down and settled herself comfortably. Then she heard a woman speak, not particularly low: "I thought people traveled west to see the country." And a man replied, rather dryly, "Wal, not always." His companion went on: "If that girl was mine I'd let down her skirt." The man laughed and replied: "Martha, you're shore behind the times. Look at the pictures in the magazines."

Such remarks amused Carley, and later she took advantage of an opportunity to notice her neighbors. They appeared a rather quaint old couple, reminding her of the natives of country towns in the Adirondacks. She was not amused, however, when another of her woman neighbors, speaking low, referred to her as a "lunger." Carley appreciated the fact that she was pale, but she assured herself that there ended any possible resemblance she might have to a consumptive. And she was somewhat pleased to hear this woman's male companion forcibly voice her own convictions. In fact, he was nothing if not admiring.

Kansas was interminably long to Carley, and she went to sleep before riding out of it. Next morning she found herself looking out at the rough gray and black land of New Mexico. She searched the horizon for mountains, but there did not appear to be any. She received a vague, slow-dawning impression that was hard to define. She did not like the country, though that was not the impression which eluded her. Bare gray flats, low scrub-fringed hills, bleak cliffs, jumble after jumble of rocks, and occasionally a long vista down a valley, somehow compelling—these passed before her gaze until she tired of them. Where was the West Glenn had written about? One thing seemed sure, and it was that every mile of this crude country brought her nearer to him. This recurring thought gave Carley all the pleasure she had felt so far in this endless ride. It struck her that England or France could be dropped down into New Mexico and scarcely noticed.

By and by the sun grew hot, the train wound slowly and creakingly upgrade, the car became full of dust, all of which was disagreeable to Carley. She dozed on her pillow for hours, until she was stirred by a passenger crying out, delightedly: "Look! Indians!"

Carley looked, not without interest. As a child she had read about Indians, and memory returned images both colorful and romantic. From the car window she espied dusty flat barrens, low squat mud houses, and queer-looking little people, children naked or extremely ragged and dirty, women in loose garments with flares of red, and men in white man's garb, slovenly and motley. All these strange individuals stared apathetically as the train slowly passed.

"Indians," muttered Carley, incredulously. "Well, if they are the noble red people, my illusions are dispelled." She did not look out of the window again, not even when the brakeman called out the remarkable name of Albuquerque.

Next day Carley's languid attention quickened to the name of Arizona, and to the frowning red walls of rock, and to the vast rolling stretches of cedar-dotted land. Nevertheless, it affronted her. This was no country for people to live in, and so far as she could see it was indeed uninhabited. Her sensations were not, however, limited to sight. She became aware of unfamiliar disturbing little shocks or vibrations in her ear drums, and after that a disagreeable bleeding of the nose. The porter told her this was owing to the altitude. Thus, one thing and another kept Carley most of the time away from the window, so that she really saw very little of the country. From what she had seen she drew the conviction that she had not missed much. At sunset she deliberately gazed out to discover what an Arizona sunset was like. Just a pale yellow flare! She had seen better than that above the Palisades. Not until reaching Winslow did she realize how near she was to her journey's end and that she would arrive at Flagstaff after dark. She grew conscious of nervousness. Suppose Flagstaff were like these other queer little towns!

Not only once, but several times before the train slowed down for her destination did Carley wish she had sent Glenn word to meet her. And when, presently, she found herself standing out in the dark, cold, windy night before a dim-lit railroad station she more than regretted her decision to surprise Glenn. But that was too late and she must make the best of her poor judgment.

Men were passing to and fro on the platform, some of whom appeared to be very dark of skin and eye, and were probably Mexicans. At length an expressman approached Carley, soliciting patronage. He took her bags and, depositing them in a wagon, he pointed up the wide street: "One block up an' turn. Hotel Wetherford." Then he drove off. Carley followed, carrying her small satchel. A cold wind, driving the dust, stung her face as she crossed the street to a high sidewalk that extended along the block. There were lights in the stores and on the corners, yet she seemed impressed by a dark, cold, windy bigness. Many people, mostly men, were passing up and down, and there were motor cars everywhere. No one paid any attention to her. Gaining the corner of the block, she turned, and was relieved to see the hotel sign. As she entered the lobby a clicking of pool balls and the discordant rasp of a phonograph assailed her ears. The expressman set down her bags and left Carley standing there. The clerk or proprietor was talking from behind his desk to several men, and there were loungers in the lobby. The air was thick with tobacco smoke. No one paid any attention to Carley until at length she stepped up to the desk and interrupted the conversation there.

"Is this a hotel?" she queried, brusquely.

The shirt-sleeved individual leisurely turned and replied, "Yes, ma'am."

And Carley said: "No one would recognize it by the courtesy shown. I have been standing here waiting to register."

With the same leisurely ease and a cool, laconic stare the clerk turned the book toward her. "Reckon people round here ask for what they want."

Carley made no further comment. She assuredly recognized that what she had been accustomed to could not be expected out here. What she most wished to do at the moment was to get close to the big open grate where a cheery red-and-gold fire cracked. It was necessary, however, to follow the clerk. He assigned her to a small drab room which contained a bed, a bureau, and a stationary washstand with one spigot. There was also a chair. While Carley removed her coat and hat the clerk went downstairs for the rest of her luggage. Upon his return Carley learned that a stage left the hotel for Oak Creek Canyon at nine o'clock next morning. And this cheered her so much that she faced the strange sense of loneliness and discomfort with something of fortitude. There was no heat in the room, and no hot water. When Carley squeezed the spigot handle there burst forth a torrent of water that spouted up out of the washbasin to deluge her. It was colder than any ice water she had ever felt. It was piercingly cold. Hard upon the surprise and shock Carley suffered a flash of temper. But then the humor of it struck her and she had to laugh.

"Serves you right—you spoiled doll of luxury!" she mocked. "This is out West. Shiver and wait on yourself!"

Never before had she undressed so swiftly nor felt grateful for thick woollen blankets on a hard bed. Gradually she grew warm. The blackness, too, seemed rather comforting.

"I'm only twenty miles from Glenn," she whispered. "How strange! I wonder will he be glad." She felt a sweet, glowing assurance of that. Sleep did not come readily. Excitement had laid hold of her nerves, and for a long time she lay awake. After a while the chug of motor cars, the click of pool balls, the murmur of low voices all ceased. Then she heard a sound of wind outside, an intermittent, low moaning, new to her ears, and somehow pleasant. Another sound greeted her—the musical clanging of a clock that struck the quarters of the hour. Some time late sleep claimed her.

Upon awakening she found she had overslept, necessitating haste upon her part. As to that, the temperature of the room did not admit of leisurely dressing. She had no adequate name for the feeling of the water. And her fingers grew so numb that she made what she considered a disgraceful matter of her attire.

Downstairs in the lobby another cheerful red fire burned in the grate. How perfectly satisfying was an open fireplace! She thrust her numb hands almost into the blaze, and simply shook with the tingling pain that slowly warmed out of them. The lobby was deserted. A sign directed her to a dining room in the basement, where of the ham and eggs and strong coffee she managed to partake a little. Then she went upstairs into the lobby and out into the street.

A cold, piercing air seemed to blow right through her. Walking to the near corner, she paused to look around. Down the main street flowed a leisurely stream of pedestrians, horses, cars, extending between two blocks of low buildings. Across from where she stood lay a vacant lot, beyond which began a line of neat, oddly constructed houses, evidently residences of the town. And then lifting her gaze, instinctively drawn by something obstructing the sky line, she was suddenly struck with surprise and delight.

"Oh! how perfectly splendid!" she burst out.

Two magnificent mountains loomed right over her, sloping up with majestic sweep of green and black timber, to a ragged tree-fringed snow area that swept up cleaner and whiter, at last to lift pure glistening peaks, noble and sharp, and sunrise-flushed against the blue.

Carley had climbed Mont Blanc and she had seen the Matterhorn, but they had never struck such amaze and admiration from her as these twin peaks of her native land.

"What mountains are those?" she asked a passer-by.

"San Francisco Peaks, ma'am," replied the man.

"Why, they can't be over a mile away!" she said.

"Eighteen miles, ma'am," he returned, with a grin. "Shore this Arizonie air is deceivin'."

"How strange," murmured Carley. "It's not that way in the Adirondacks."

She was still gazing upward when a man approached her and said the stage for Oak Creek Canyon would soon be ready to start, and he wanted to know if her baggage was ready. Carley hurried back to her room to pack.

She had expected the stage would be a motor bus, or at least a large touring car, but it turned out to be a two-seated vehicle drawn by a team of ragged horses. The driver was a little wizen-faced man of doubtful years, and he did not appear obviously susceptible to the importance of his passenger. There was considerable freight to be hauled, besides Carley's luggage, but evidently she was the only passenger.

"Reckon it's goin' to be a bad day," said the driver. "These April days high up on the desert are windy an' cold. Mebbe it'll snow, too. Them clouds hangin' around the peaks ain't very promisin'. Now, miss, haven't you a heavier coat or somethin'?"

"No, I have not," replied Carley. "I'll have to stand it. Did you say this was desert?"

"I shore did. Wal, there's a hoss blanket under the seat, an' you can have that," he replied, and, climbing to the seat in front of Carley, he took up the reins and started the horses off at a trot.

At the first turning Carley became specifically acquainted with the driver's meaning of a bad day. A gust of wind, raw and penetrating, laden with dust and stinging sand, swept full in her face. It came so suddenly that she was scarcely quick enough to close her eyes. It took considerable clumsy effort on her part with a handkerchief, aided by relieving tears, to clear her sight again. Thus uncomfortably Carley found herself launched on the last lap of her journey.

All before her and alongside lay the squalid environs of the town. Looked back at, with the peaks rising behind, it was not unpicturesque. But the hard road with its sheets of flying dust, the bleak railroad yards, the round pens she took for cattle corrals, and the sordid debris littering the approach to a huge sawmill—these were offensive in Carley's sight. From a tall domelike stack rose a yellowish smoke that spread overhead, adding to the lowering aspect of the sky. Beyond the sawmill extended the open country sloping somewhat roughly, and evidently once a forest, but now a hideous bare slash, with ghastly burned stems of trees still standing, and myriads of stumps attesting to denudation.

The bleak road wound away to the southwest, and from this direction came the gusty wind. It did not blow regularly so that Carley could be on her guard. It lulled now and then, permitting her to look about, and then suddenly again whipping dust into her face. The smell of the dust was as unpleasant as the sting. It made her nostrils smart. It was penetrating, and a little more of it would have been suffocating. And as a leaden gray bank of broken clouds rolled up the wind grew stronger and the air colder. Chilled before, Carley now became thoroughly cold. There appeared to be no end to the devastated forest land, and the farther she rode the more barren and sordid grew the landscape. Carley forgot about the impressive mountains behind her. And as the ride wore into hours, such was her discomfort and disillusion that she forgot about Glenn Kilbourne. She did not reach the point of regretting her adventure, but she grew mightily unhappy. Now and then she espied dilapidated log cabins and surroundings even more squalid than the ruined forest. What wretched abodes!

Could it be possible that people had lived in them? She imagined men had but hardly women and children. Somewhere she had forgotten an idea that women and children were extremely scarce in the West.

Straggling bits of forest—yellow pines, the driver called the trees—began to encroach upon the burned-over and arid barren land. To Carley these groves, by reason of contrast and proof of what once was, only rendered the landscape more forlorn and dreary. Why had these miles and miles of forest been cut? By money grubbers, she supposed, the same as were devastating the Adirondacks. Presently, when the driver had to halt to repair or adjust something wrong with the harness, Carley was grateful for a respite from cold inaction. She got out and walked. Sleet began to fall, and when she resumed her seat in the vehicle she asked the driver for the blanket to cover her. The smell of this horse blanket was less endurable than the cold. Carley huddled down into a state of apathetic misery. Already she had enough of the West.

But the sleet storm passed, the clouds broke, the sun shone through, greatly mitigating her discomfort. By and by the road led into a section of real forest, unspoiled in any degree. Carley saw large gray squirrels with tufted ears and white bushy tails. Presently the driver pointed out a flock of huge birds, which Carley, on second glance, recognized as turkeys, only these were sleek and glossy, with flecks of bronze and black and white, quite different from turkeys back East. "There must be a farm near," said Carley, gazing about.

"No, ma'am. Them's wild turkeys," replied the driver, "an' shore the best eatin' you ever had in your life."

A little while afterwards, as they were emerging from the woodland into more denuded country, he pointed out to Carley a herd of gray white-rumped animals that she took to be sheep.

"An' them's antelope," he said. "Once this desert was overrun by antelope. Then they nearly disappeared. An' now they're increasin' again."

More barren country, more bad weather, and especially an exceedingly rough road reduced Carley to her former state of dejection. The jolting over roots and rocks and ruts was worse than uncomfortable. She had to hold on to the seat to keep from being thrown out. The horses did not appreciably change their gait for rough sections of the road. Then a more severe jolt brought Carley's knee in violent contact with an iron bolt on the forward seat, and it hurt her so acutely that she had to bite her lips to keep from screaming. A smoother stretch of road did not come any too soon for her.

It led into forest again. And Carley soon became aware that they had at last left the cut and burned-over district of timberland behind. A cold wind moaned through the treetops and set the drops of water pattering down upon her. It lashed her wet face. Carley closed her eyes and sagged in her seat, mostly oblivious to the passing scenery. "The girls will never believe this of me," she soliloquized. And indeed she was amazed at herself. Then thought of Glenn strengthened her. It did not really matter what she suffered on the way to him. Only she was disgusted at her lack of stamina, and her appalling sensitiveness to discomfort.

"Wal, hyar's Oak Creek Canyon," called the driver.

Carley, rousing out of her weary preoccupation, opened her eyes to see that the driver had halted at a turn of the road, where apparently it descended a fearful declivity.

The very forest-fringed earth seemed to have opened into a deep abyss, ribbed by red rock walls and choked by steep mats of green timber. The chasm was a V-shaped split and so deep that looking downward sent at once a chill and a shudder over Carley. At that point it appeared narrow and ended in a box. In the other direction, it widened and deepened, and stretched farther on between tremendous walls of red, and split its winding floor of green with glimpses of a gleaming creek, bowlder-strewn and ridged by white rapids. A low mellow roar of rushing waters floated up to Carley's ears. What a wild, lonely, terrible place! Could Glenn possibly live down there in that ragged rent in the earth? It frightened her—the sheer sudden plunge of it from the heights. Far down the gorge a purple light shone on the forested floor. And on the moment the sun burst through the clouds and sent a golden blaze down into the depths, transforming them incalculably. The great cliffs turned gold, the creek changed to glancing silver, the green of trees vividly freshened, and in the clefts rays of sunlight burned into the blue shadows. Carley had never gazed upon a scene like this. Hostile and prejudiced, she yet felt wrung from her an acknowledgment of beauty and grandeur. But wild, violent, savage! Not livable! This insulated rift in the crust of the earth was a gigantic burrow for beasts, perhaps for outlawed men— not for a civilized person—not for Glenn Kilbourne.

"Don't be scart, ma'am," spoke up the driver. "It's safe if you're careful. An' I've druv this manys the time."

Carley's heartbeats thumped at her side, rather denying her taunted assurance of fearlessness. Then the rickety vehicle started down at an angle that forced her to cling to her seat.

CHAPTER II

Carley, clutching her support, with abated breath and prickling skin, gazed in fascinated suspense over the rim of the gorge. Sometimes the wheels on that side of the vehicle passed within a few inches of the edge. The brakes squeaked, the wheels slid; and she could hear the scrape of the iron-shod hoofs of the horses as they held back stiff legged, obedient to the wary call of the driver.

The first hundred yards of that steep road cut out of the cliff appeared to be the worst. It began to widen, with descents less precipitous. Tips of trees rose level with her gaze, obstructing sight of the blue depths. Then brush appeared on each side of the road. Gradually Carley's strain relaxed, and also the muscular contraction by which she had braced herself in the seat. The horses began to trot again. The wheels rattled. The road wound around abrupt corners, and soon the green and red wall of the opposite side of the canyon loomed close. Low roar of running water rose to Carley's ears. When at length she looked out instead of down she could see nothing but a mass of green foliage crossed by tree trunks and branches of brown and gray. Then the vehicle bowled under dark cool shade, into a tunnel with mossy wet cliff on one side, and close-standing trees on the other.

"Reckon we're all right now, onless we meet somebody comin' up," declared the driver.

Carley relaxed. She drew a deep breath of relief. She had her first faint intimation that perhaps her extensive experience of motor cars, express trains, transatlantic liners, and even a little of airplanes, did not range over the whole of adventurous life. She was likely to meet something entirely new and striking out here in the West.

The murmur of falling water sounded closer. Presently Carley saw that the road turned at the notch in the canyon, and crossed a clear swift stream. Here were huge mossy bowlders, and red walls covered by lichens, and the air appeared dim and moist, and full of mellow, hollow roar. Beyond this crossing the road descended the west side of the canyon, drawing away and higher from the creek. Huge trees, the like of which Carley had never seen, began to stand majestically up out of the gorge, dwarfing the maples and white-spotted sycamores. The driver called these great trees yellow pines.

At last the road led down from the steep slope to the floor of the canyon. What from far above had appeared only a green timber-choked cleft proved from close relation to be a wide winding valley, up and down, densely forested for the most part, yet having open glades and bisected from wall to wall by the creek. Every quarter of a mile or so the road crossed the stream; and at these fords Carley again held on desperately and gazed out dubiously, for the creek was deep, swift, and full of bowlders. Neither driver nor horses appeared to mind obstacles. Carley was splashed and jolted not inconsiderably. They passed through groves of oak trees, from which the creek manifestly derived its name; and under gleaming walls, cold, wet, gloomy, and silent; and between lines of solemn wide-spreading pines. Carley saw deep, still green pools eddying under huge massed jumble of cliffs, and stretches of white water, and then, high above the treetops, a wild line of canyon rim, cold against the sky. She felt shut in from the world, lost in an unscalable rut of the earth. Again the sunlight had failed, and the gray gloom of the canyon oppressed her. It struck Carley as singular that she could not help being affected by mere weather, mere heights and depths, mere rock walls and pine trees, and rushing water. For really, what had these to do with her? These were only physical things that she was passing. Nevertheless, although she resisted sensation, she was more and more shot through and through with the wildness and savageness of this canyon.

A sharp turn of the road to the right disclosed a slope down the creek, across which showed orchards and fields, and a cottage nestling at the base of the wall. The ford at this crossing gave Carley more concern than any that had been passed, for there was greater volume and depth of water. One of the horses slipped on the rocks, plunged up and on with great splash. They crossed, however, without more mishap to Carley than further acquaintance with this iciest of waters. From this point the driver turned back along the creek, passed between orchards and fields, and drove along the base of the red wall to come suddenly upon a large rustic house that had been hidden from Carley's sight. It sat almost against the stone cliff, from which poured a white foamy sheet of water. The house was built of slabs with the bark on, and it had a lower and upper porch running all around, at least as far as the cliff. Green growths from the rock wall overhung the upper porch. A column of blue smoke curled lazily upward from a stone chimney. On one of the porch posts hung a sign with rude lettering: "Lolomi Lodge."

"Hey, Josh, did you fetch the flour?" called a woman's voice from inside.

"Hullo! Reckon I didn't forgit nothin'," replied the man, as he got down. "An' say, Mrs. Hutter, hyar's a young lady from Noo Yorrk."

That latter speech of the driver's brought Mrs. Hutter out on the porch. "Flo, come here," she called to some one evidently near at hand. And then she smilingly greeted Carley.

"Get down an' come in, miss," she said. "I'm sure glad to see you."

Carley, being stiff and cold, did not very gracefully disengage herself from the high muddy wheel and step. When she mounted to the porch she saw that Mrs. Hutter was a woman of middle age, rather stout, with strong face full of fine wavy lines, and kind dark eyes.

"I'm Miss Burch," said Carley.

"You're the girl whose picture Glenn Kilbourne has over his fireplace," declared the woman, heartily. "I'm sure glad to meet you, an' my daughter Flo will be, too."

That about her picture pleased and warmed Carley. "Yes, I'm Glenn Kilbourne's fiancée. I've come West to surprise him. Is he here . . . Is—is he well?"

"Fine. I saw him yesterday. He's changed a great deal from what he was at first. Most all the last few months. I reckon you won't know him. . . . But you're wet an' cold an' you look fagged. Come right in to the fire."

"Thank you; I'm all right," returned Carley.

At the doorway they encountered a girl of lithe and robust figure, quick in her movements. Carley was swift to see the youth and grace of her; and then a face that struck Carley as neither pretty nor beautiful, but still wonderfully attractive.

THE CALL OF THE CANYON ★ 465

"Flo, here's Miss Burch," burst out Mrs. Hutter, with cheerful importance. "Glenn Kilbourne's girl come all the way from New York to surprise him!"

"Oh, Carley, I'm shore happy to meet you!" said the girl, in a voice of slow drawling richness. "I know you. Glenn has told me all about you."

If this greeting, sweet and warm as it seemed, was a shock to Carley, she gave no sign. But as she murmured something in reply she looked with all a woman's keenness into the face before her. Flo Hutter had a fair skin generously freckled; a mouth and chin too firmly cut to suggest a softer feminine beauty; and eyes of clear light hazel, penetrating, frank, fearless. Her hair was very abundant, almost silver-gold in color, and it was either rebellious or showed lack of care. Carley liked the girl's looks and liked the sincerity of her greeting; but instinctively she reacted antagonistically because of the frank suggestion of intimacy with Glenn. But for that she would have been spontaneous and friendly rather than restrained.

They ushered Carley into a big living room and up to a fire of blazing logs, where they helped divest her of the wet wraps. And all the time they talked in the solicitous way natural to women who were kind and unused to many visitors. Then Mrs. Hutter bustled off to make a cup of hot coffee while Flo talked.

"We'll shore give you the nicest room—with a sleeping porch right under the cliff where the water falls. It'll sing you to sleep. Of course you needn't use the bed outdoors until it's warmer. Spring is late here, you know, and we'll have nasty weather yet. You really happened on Oak Creek at its least attractive season. But then it's always—well, just Oak Creek. You'll come to know."

"I dare say I'll remember my first sight of it—and the ride down that cliff road," said Carley, with a wan smile.

"Oh, that's nothing to what you'll see and do," returned

Flo, knowingly. "We've had Eastern tenderfeet here before. And never was there a one of them who didn't come to love Arizona."

"Tenderfoot! It hadn't occurred to me. But of course—" murmured Carley.

Then Mrs. Hutter returned, carrying a tray, which she set upon a chair, and drew to Carley's side. "Eat an' drink," she said, as if these actions were the cardinally important ones of life. "Flo, you carry her bags up to that west room we always give to some particular person we want to love Lolomi." Next she threw sticks of wood upon the fire, making it crackle and blaze; then seated herself near Carley and beamed upon her.

"You'll not mind if we call you Carley?" she asked, eagerly.

"Oh, indeed no! I—I'd like it," returned Carley, made to feel friendly and at home in spite of herself.

"You see it's not as if you were just a stranger," went on Mrs. Hutter. "Tom—that's Flo's father—took a likin' to Glenn Kilbourne when he first came to Oak Creek over a year ago. I wonder if you all know how sick that soldier boy was. . . . Well, he lay on his back for two solid weeks— in the room we're givin' you. An' I for one didn't think he'd ever get up. But he did. An' he got better. An' after a while he went to work for Tom. Then six months an' more ago he invested in the sheep business with Tom. He lived with us until he built his cabin up West Fork. He an' Flo have run together a good deal, an' naturally he told her about you. So you see you're not a stranger. An' we want you to feel you're with friends."

"I thank you, Mrs. Hutter," replied Carley, feelingly. "I never could thank you enough for being good to Glenn. I did not know he was so—so sick. At first he wrote but seldom."

"Reckon he never wrote you or told you what he did in the war," declared Mrs. Hutter.

"Indeed he never did!"

"Well, I'll tell you some day. For Tom found out all about him. Got some of it from a soldier who came to Flagstaff for lung trouble. He'd been in the same company with Glenn. We didn't know this boy's name while he was in Flagstaff. But later Tom found out. John Henderson. He was only twenty-two, a fine lad. An' he died in Phœnix. We tried to get him out here. But the boy wouldn't live on charity. He was always expectin' money—a war bonus, whatever that was. It didn't come. He was a clerk at the El Tovar for a while. Then he came to Flagstaff. But it was too cold an' he stayed there too long."

"Too bad," rejoined Carley, thoughtfully. This information as to the suffering of American soldiers had augmented during the last few months, and seemed to possess strange, poignant power to depress Carley. Always she had turned away from the unpleasant. And the misery of unfortunates was as disturbing almost as direct contact with disease and squalor. But it had begun to dawn upon Carley that there might occur circumstances of life, in every way affronting her comfort and happiness, which it would be impossible to turn her back upon.

At this juncture Flo returned to the room, and again Carley was struck with the girl's singular freedom of movement and the sense of sure poise and joy that seemed to emanate from her presence.

"I've made a fire in your little stove," she said. "There's water heating. Now won't you come up and change those traveling clothes. You'll want to fix up for Glenn, won't you?"

Carley had to smile at that. This girl indeed was frank and unsophisticated, and somehow refreshing. Carley rose.

"You are both very good to receive me as a friend," she said. "I hope I shall not disappoint you. . . . Yes, I do want to improve my appearance before Glenn sees me. . . . Is there any way I can send word to him—by some one who has not seen me?"

"There shore is. I'll send Charley, one of our hired boys."

"Thank you. Then tell him to say there is a lady here from New York to see him, and it is very important."

Flo Hutter clapped her hands and laughed with glee. Her gladness gave Carley a little twinge of conscience. Jealously was an unjust and stifling thing.

Carley was conducted up a broad stairway and along a boarded hallway to a room that opened out on the porch. A steady low murmur of falling water assailed her ears. Through the open door she saw across the porch to a white tumbling lacy veil of water falling, leaping, changing, so close that it seemed to touch the heavy pole railing of the porch.

This room resembled a tent. The sides were of canvas. It had no ceiling. But the roughhewn shingles of the roof of the house sloped down closely. The furniture was home made. An Indian rug covered the floor. The bed with its woolly clean blankets and the white pillows looked inviting.

"Is this where Glenn lay—when he was sick?" queried Carley.

"Yes," replied Flo, gravely, and a shadow darkened her eyes. "I ought to tell you all about it. I will some day. But you must not be made unhappy now. . . . Glenn nearly died here. Mother or I never left his side—for a while there—when he was so bad."

She showed Carley how to open the little stove and put the short billets of wood inside and work the damper; and cautioning her to keep an eye on it so that it would not get too hot, she left Carley to herself.

Carley found herself in unfamiliar mood. There came a leap of her heart every time she thought of the meeting with Glenn, so soon now to be, but it was not that which was unfamiliar. She seemed to have difficult approach to undefined and unusual thoughts. All this was so different from her regular life. Besides she was tired. But these explanations did not suffice. There was a pang in her breast which must owe its origin to the fact that Glenn Kilbourne had been ill in this little room and some other girl than Carley Burch had nursed him. "Am I jealous?" she whispered. "No!" But she knew in her heart that she lied. A woman could no more help being jealous, under such circumstances, than she could help the beat and throb of her blood. Nevertheless, Carley was glad Flo Hutter had been there, and always she would be grateful to her for that kindness.

Carley disrobed and, donning her dressing gown, she unpacked her bags and hung her things upon pegs under the curtained shelves. Then she lay down to rest, with no intention of slumber. But there was a strange magic in the fragrance of the room, like the piny tang outdoors, and in the feel of the bed, and especially in the low, dreamy hum and murmur of the waterfall. She fell asleep. When she awakened it was five o'clock. The fire in the stove was out, but the water was still warm. She bathed and dressed, not without care, yet as swiftly as was her habit at home; and she wore white because Glenn had always liked her best in white. But it was assuredly not a gown to wear in a country house where draughts of cold air filled the unheated rooms and halls. So she threw round her a warm sweater-shawl, with colorful bars becoming to her dark eyes and hair.

All the time that she dressed and thought, her very being seemed to be permeated by that soft murmuring sound of falling water. No moment of waking life there at Lolomi

Lodge, or perhaps of slumber hours, could be wholly free of that sound. It vaguely tormented Carley, yet was not uncomfortable. She went out upon the porch. The small alcove space held a bed and a rustic chair. Above her the peeled poles of the roof descended to within a few feet of her head. She had to lean over the rail of the porch to look up. The green and red rock wall sheered ponderously near. The waterfall showed first at the notch of a fissure, where the cliff split; and down over smooth places the water gleamed, to narrow in a crack with little drops, and suddenly to leap into a thin white sheet.

Out from the porch the view was restricted to glimpses between the pines, and beyond to the opposite wall of the canyon. How shut-in, how walled in this home!

"In summer it might be good to spend a couple of weeks here," soliloquized Carley. "But to *live* here? Heavens! A person might as well be buried."

Heavy footsteps upon the porch below accompanied by a man's voice quickened Carley's pulse. Did they belong to Glenn? After a strained second she decided not. Nevertheless, the acceleration of her blood and an unwonted glow of excitement, long a stranger to her, persisted as she left the porch and entered the boarded hall. How gray and barnlike this upper part of the house! From the head of the stairway, however, the big living room presented a cheerful contrast. There were warm colors, some comfortable rockers, a lamp that shed a bright light, and an open fire which alone would have dispelled the raw gloom of the day.

A large man in corduroys and top boots advanced to meet Carley. He had a clean-shaven face that might have been hard and stern but for his smile, and one look into his eyes revealed their resemblance to Flo's.

"I'm Tom Hutter, an' I'm shore glad to welcome you to Lolomi, Miss Carley," he said. His voice was deep and slow. There were ease and force in his presence, and the grip he gave Carley's hand was that of a man who made no distinction in hand-shaking. Carley, quick in her perceptions, instantly liked him and sensed in him a strong personality. She greeted him in turn and expressed her thanks for his goodness to Glenn. Naturally Carley expected him to say something about her fiancé, but he did not.

"Well, Miss Carley, if you don't mind, I'll say you're prettier than your picture," said Hutter. "An' that is shore sayin' a lot. All the sheep herders in the country have taken a peep at your picture. Without permission, you understand."

"I'm greatly flattered," laughed Carley.

"We're glad you've come," replied Hutter, simply. "I just got back from the East myself. Chicago an' Kansas City. I came to Arizona from Illinois over thirty years ago. An' this was my first trip since. Reckon I've not got back my breath yet. Times have changed, Miss Carley. Times an' people!"

Mrs. Hutter bustled in from the kitchen, where manifestly she had been importantly engaged. "For the land's sakes!" she exclaimed, fervently, as she threw up her hands at sight of Carley. Her expression was indeed a compliment, but there was a suggestion of shock in it. Then Flo came in. She wore a simple gray gown that reached the top of her high shoes.

"Carley, don't mind mother," said Flo. "She means your dress is lovely. Which is my say, too. . . . But, listen. I just saw Glenn comin' up the road."

Carley ran to the open door with more haste than dignity. She saw a tall man striding along. Something about him appeared familiar. It was his walk—an erect swift carriage, with a swing of the march still visible. She recognized Glenn. And all within her seemed to become unstable. She watched him cross the road, face the house. How changed! No—this was not Glenn Kilbourne. This was a bronzed man, wide of shoulder, roughly garbed, heavy limbed, quite different from the Glenn she remembered. He mounted the porch steps. And Carley, still unseen herself, saw his face. Yes—Glenn! Hot blood seemed to be tingling liberated in her veins. Wheeling away, she backed against the wall behind the door and held up a warning finger to Flo, who stood nearest. Strange and disturbing then, to see something in Flo Hutter's eyes that could be read by a woman in only one way!

A tall form darkened the doorway. It strode in and halted.

"Flo!—who—where?" he began, breathlessly.

His voice, so well remembered, yet deeper, huskier, fell upon Carley's ears as something unconsciously longed for. His frame had so filled out that she did not recognize it. His face, too, had unbelievably changed—not in the regularity of feature that had been its chief charm, but in contour of cheek and vanishing of pallid hue and tragic line. Carley's heart swelled with joy. Beyond all else she had hoped to see the sad fixed hopelessness, the havoc, gone from his face. Therefore the restraint and nonchalance upon which Carley prided herself sustained eclipse.

"Glenn! Look—who's—here!" she called, in voice she could not have steadied to save her life. This meeting was more than she had anticipated.

Glenn whirled with an inarticulate cry. He saw Carley. Then—no matter how unreasonable or exacting had been Carley's longings, they were satisfied.

"You!" he cried, and leaped at her with radiant face.

Carley not only did not care about the spectators of this meeting, but forgot them utterly. More than the joy of seeing Glenn, more than the all-satisfying assurance to her woman's heart that she was still beloved, welled up a deep, strange, profound something that shook her to her depths. It was beyond selfishness. It was gratitude to God and to the West that had restored him.

"Carley! I couldn't believe it was you," he declared, releasing her from his close embrace, yet still holding her.

"Yes, Glenn—it's I—all you've left of me," she replied, tremulously, and she sought with unsteady hands to put up her dishevelled hair. "You—you big sheep herder! You Goliath!"

"I never was so knocked off my pins," he said. "A lady to see me—from New York! . . . Of course it had to be you. But I couldn't believe. Carley, you were good to come."

Somehow the soft, warm look of his dark eyes hurt her. New and strange indeed it was to her, as were other things about him. Why had she not come West sooner? She disengaged herself from his hold and moved away, striving for the composure habitual with her. Flo Hutter was standing before the fire, looking down. Mrs. Hutter beamed upon Carley.

"Now let's have supper," she said.

"Reckon Miss Carley can't eat now, after that hug Glenn gave her," drawled Tom Hutter. "I was some worried. You see Glenn has gained seventy pounds in six months. An' he doesn't know his strength."

"Seventy pounds!" exclaimed Carley, gayly. "I thought it was more."

"Carley, you must excuse my violence," said Glenn. "I've been hugging sheep. That is, when I shear a sheep I have to hold him."

They all laughed, and so the moment of readjustment passed. Presently Carley found herself sitting at table, directly across from Flo. A pearly whiteness was slowly warming out of the girl's face. Her frank clear eyes met

Carley's and they had nothing to hide. Carley's first requisite for character in a woman was that she be a thoroughbred. She lacked it often enough herself to admire it greatly in another woman. And that moment saw a birth of respect and sincere liking in her for this Western girl. If Flo Hutter ever was a rival she would be an honest one.

Not long after supper Tom Hutter winked at Carley and said he "reckoned on general principles it was his hunch to go to bed." Mrs. Hutter suddenly discovered tasks to perform elsewhere. And Flo said in her cool sweet drawl, somehow audacious and tantalizing, "Shore you two will want to spoon."

"Now, Flo, Eastern girls are no longer old-fashioned enough for that," declared Glenn.

"Too bad! Reckon I can't see how love could ever be old-fashioned. . . . Good night, Glenn. Good night, Carley."

Flo stood an instant at the foot of the dark stairway where the light from the lamp fell upon her face. It seemed sweet and earnest to Carley. It expressed unconscious longing, but no envy. Then she ran up the stairs to disappear.

"Glenn, is that girl in love with you?" asked Carley, bluntly.

To her amaze, Glenn laughed. When had she heard him laugh? It thrilled her, yet nettled her a little.

"If that isn't like you!" he ejaculated. "Your very first words after we are left alone! It brings back the East, Carley."

"Probably recall to memory will be good for you," returned Carley. "But tell me. Is she in love with you?"

"Why, no, certainly not!" replied Glenn. "Anyway, how could I answer such a question? It just made me laugh, that's all."

"Humph! I can remember when you were not above making love to a pretty girl. You certainly had me worn to a frazzle—before we became engaged," said Carley.

"Old times! How long ago they seem! . . . Carley, it's sure wonderful to see you."

"How do you like my gown?" asked Carley, pirouetting for his benefit.

"Well, what little there is of it is beautiful," he replied, with a slow smile. "I always liked you best in white. Did you remember?"

"Yes. I got the gown for you. And I'll never wear it except for you."

"Same old coquette—same old eternal feminine," he said, half sadly. "You know when you look stunning. . . . But, Carley, the cut of that—or rather the abbreviation of it—inclines me to think that style for women's clothes has not changed for the better. In fact, it's worse than two years ago in Paris and later in New York. Where will you women draw the line?"

"Women are slaves to the prevailing mode," rejoined Carley. "I don't imagine women who dress would ever draw a line, if fashion went on dictating."

"But would they care so much—if they had to work—plenty of work—and children?" inquired Glenn, wistfully.

"Glenn! Work and children for modern women? Why, you are dreaming!" said Carley, with a laugh.

She saw him gaze thoughtfully into the glowing embers of the fire, and as she watched him her quick intuition grasped a subtle change in his mood. It brought a sternness to his face. She could hardly realize she was looking at the Glenn Kilbourne of old.

"Come close to the fire," he said, and pulled up a chair for her. Then he threw more wood upon the red coals. "You must be careful not to catch cold out here. The altitude makes a cold dangerous. And that gown is no protection."

"Glenn, one chair used to be enough for us," she said, archly, standing beside him.

But he did not respond to her hint, and, a little affronted, she accepted the proffered chair. Then he began to ask questions rapidly. He was eager for news from home—from his people—from old friends. However he did not inquire of Carley about her friends. She talked unremittingly for an hour, before she satisfied his hunger. But when her turn came to ask questions she found him reticent.

He had fallen upon rather hard days at first out here in the West; then his health had begun to improve; and as soon as he was able to work his condition rapidly changed for the better; and now he was getting along pretty well. Carley felt hurt at his apparent disinclination to confide in her. The strong cast of his face, as if it had been chiseled in bronze; the stern set of his lips and the jaw that protruded lean and square cut; the quiet masked light of his eyes; the coarse roughness of his brown hands, mute evidence of strenuous labors—these all gave a different impression from his brief remarks about himself. Lastly there was a little gray in the light-brown hair over his temples. Glenn was only twenty-seven, yet he looked ten years older. Studying him so, with the memory of earlier years in her mind, she was forced to admit that she liked him infinitely more as he was now. He seemed proven. Something had made him a man. Had it been his love for her, or the army service, or the war in France, or the struggle for life and health afterwards? Or had it been this rugged, uncouth West? Carley felt insidious jealousy of this last possibility. She feared this West. She was going to hate it. She had womanly intuition enough to see in Flo Flutter a girl somehow to be reckoned with. Still, Carley would not acknowledge to herself that this simple, unsophisticated Western girl could possibly be a rival. Carley did not need to consider the fact that she had been spoiled by the attention of men. It was not her vanity that precluded Flo Hutter as a rival.

Gradually the conversation drew to a lapse, and it suited

Carley to let it be so. She watched Glenn as he gazed thoughtfully into the amber depths of the fire. What was going on in his mind? Carley's old perplexity suddenly had rebirth. And with it came an unfamiliar fear which she could not smother. Every moment that she sat there beside Glenn she was realizing more and more a yearning, passionate love for him. The unmistakable manifestation of his joy at sight of her, the strong, almost rude expression of his love, had called to some responsive, but hitherto unplumbed deeps of her. If it had not been for these undeniable facts Carley would have been panic-stricken. They reassured her, yet only made her state of mind more dissatisfied.

"Carley, do you still go in for dancing?" Glenn asked, presently, with his thoughtful eyes turning to her.

"Of course. I like dancing, and it's about all the exercise I get," she replied.

"Have the dances changed—again?"

"It's the music, perhaps, that changes the dancing. Jazz is becoming popular. And about all the crowd dances now is an infinite variation of fox-trot."

"No waltzing?"

"I don't believe I waltzed once this winter."

"Jazz? That's a sort of tinpanning, jiggly stuff, isn't it?"

"Glenn, it's the fever of the public pulse," replied Carley. "The graceful waltz, like the stately minuet, flourished hack in the days when people rested rather than raced."

"More's the pity," said Glenn. Then after a moment, in which his gaze returned to the fire, he inquired rather too casually, "Does Morrison still chase after you?"

"Glenn, I'm neither old—nor married," she replied, laughing.

"No, that's true. But if you were married it wouldn't make any difference to Morrison."

Carley could not detect bitterness or jealousy in his voice. She would not have been averse to hearing either.

She gathered from his remark, however, that he was going to be harder than ever to understand. What had she said or done to make him retreat within himself, aloof, impersonal, unfamiliar? He did not impress her as loverlike. What irony of fate was this that held her there yearning for his kisses and caresses as never before, while he watched the fire, and talked as to a mere acquaintance, and seemed sad and far away? Or did she merely imagine that? Only one thing could she be sure of at the moment, and it was that pride would never be her ally.

"Glenn, look here," she said, sliding her chair close to his and holding out her left hand, slim and white, with its glittering diamond on the third finger.

He took her hand in his and pressed it, and smiled at her. "Yes, Carley, it's a beautiful, soft little hand. But I think I'd like it better if it were strong and brown, and coarse on the inside—from useful work."

"Like Flo Hutter's?" queried Carley.

"Yes."

Carley looked proudly into his eyes. "People are born in different stations. I respect your little Western friend, Glenn, but could I wash and sweep, milk cows and chop wood, and all that sort of thing?"

"I suppose you couldn't," he admitted, with a blunt little laugh.

"Would you want me to?" she asked.

"Well, that's hard to say," he replied, knitting his brows. "I hardly know. I think it depends on you. . . . But if you did do such work wouldn't you be happier?"

"Happier! Why Glenn, I'd be miserable! . . . But listen. It wasn't my beautiful and useless hand I wanted you to see. It was my engagement ring."

"Oh!—Well?" he went on, slowly.

"I've never had it off since you left New York," she said, softly. "You gave it to me four years ago. Do you remember? It was on my twenty-second birthday. You said it would take two months' salary to pay the bill."

"It sure did," he retorted, with a hint of humor.

"Glenn, during the war it was not so—so very hard to wear this ring as an engagement ring should be worn," said Carley, growing more earnest. "But after the war—especially after your departure West—it was terribly hard to be true to the significance of this betrothal ring. There was a let-down in all women. Oh, no one need tell *me!* There was. And men were affected by that and the chaotic condition of the times. New York was wild during the year of your absence. Prohibition was a joke.—Well, I gadded, danced, dressed, drank, smoked, motored, just the same as the other women in our crowd. Something drove me to. I never rested. Excitement seemed to be happiness.—Glenn, I am not making any plea to excuse all that. But I want you to know—how under trying circumstances—I was absolutely true to you. Understand me. I mean true as regards love. Through it all I loved you just the same. And now I'm with you, it seems, oh, so much more! . . . Your last letter hurt me. I don't know just how. But I came West to see you—to tell you this—and to ask you. . . . Do you want this ring back?"

"Certainly not," he replied, forcibly, with a dark flush spreading over his face.

"Then—you love me?" she whispered.

"Yes—I love you," he returned, deliberately. "And in spite of all you say—very probably more than you love me. . . . But you, like all women, make love and its expression the sole object of life. Carley, I have been concerned with keeping my body from the grave and my soul from hell."

"But—dear—you're well now?" she returned, with trembling lips.

"Yes, I've almost pulled out."

"Then what is wrong?"

"Wrong?—With me or you?" he queried, with keen, enigmatical glance upon her.

"What is wrong between us? There is something."

"Carley, a man who has been on the verge—as I have been—seldom or never comes back to happiness. But perhaps—"

"You frighten me," cried Carley, and, rising, she sat upon the arm of his chair and encircled his neck with her arms. "How can I help if I do not understand? Am I so miserably little? . . . Glenn, *must* I tell you? No woman can live without love. I need to be loved. That's all that's wrong with *me*."

"Carley, you are still an imperious, mushy girl," replied Glenn, taking her into his arms. "I need to be loved, too. But that's not what is wrong with me. You'll have to find it out yourself."

"You're a dear old Sphinx," she retorted.

"Listen, Carley," he said, earnestly. "About this love-making stuff. Please don't misunderstand me. I love you. I'm starved for your kisses. But—is it right to ask them?"

"Right! Aren't we engaged? And don't I want to give them?"

"If I were only *sure* we'd be married!" he said, in low, tense voice, as if speaking more to himself.

"Married!" cried Carley, convulsively clasping him. "Of course we'll be married. Glenn, you wouldn't jilt me?"

"Carley, what I mean is that you might never really marry me," he answered, seriously.

"Oh, if that's all you need be sure of, Glenn Kilbourne, you may begin to make love to me now."

It was late when Carley went up to her room. And she was in such a softened mood, so happy and excited and yet disturbed in mind, that the coldness and the darkness did not matter in the least. She undressed in pitchy blackness, stumbling over chair and bed, feeling for what she needed. And in her mood this unusual proceeding was fun. When ready for bed she opened the door to take a peep out. Through the dense blackness the waterfall showed dimly opaque. Carley felt a soft mist wet her face. The low roar of the falling water seemed to envelop her. Under the cliff wall brooded impenetrable gloom. But out above the treetops shone great stars, wonderfully white and radiant and cold, with a piercing contrast to the deep clear blue of sky. The waterfall hummed into an absolutely dead silence. It emphasized the silence. Not only cold was it that made Carley shudder. How lonely, how lost, how hidden this canyon!

Then she hurried to bed, grateful for the warm woolly blankets. Relaxation and thought brought consciousness of the heat of her blood, the beat and throb and swell of her heart, of the tumult within her. In the lonely darkness of her room she might have faced the truth of her strangely renewed and augmented love for Glenn Kilbourne. But she was more concerned with her happiness. She had won him back. Her presence, her love had overcome his restraint. She thrilled in the sweet consciousness of her woman's conquest. How splendid he was! To hold back physical tenderness, the simple expressions of love, because he had feared they might unduly influence her! He had grown in many ways. She must be careful to reach up to his ideals. That about Flo Hutter's toil-hardened hands! Was that significance somehow connected with the rift in the lute? For Carley admitted to herself that there was something amiss, something incomprehensible, something intangible that obtruded its menace into her dream of future happiness. Still, what had she to fear, so long as she could be with Glenn?

And yet there were forced upon her, insistent and

perplexing, the questions—was her love selfish? was she considering him? was she blind to something he could see? Tomorrow and next day and the days to come held promise of joyous companionship with Glenn, yet likewise they seemed full of a portent of trouble for her, of fight and ordeal, of lessons that would make life significant for her.

CHAPTER III

Carley was awakened by rattling sounds in her room. The raising of sleepy eyelids disclosed Flo on her knees before the little stove, in the act of lighting a fire.

"Mawnin', Carley," she drawled. "It's shore cold. Reckon it'll snow to-day, worse luck, just because you're here. Take my hunch and stay in bed till the fire burns up."

"I shall do no such thing," declared Carley, heroically.

"We're afraid you'll take cold," said Flo. "This is desert country with high altitude. Spring is here when the sun shines. But it's only shinin' in streaks these days. That means winter, really. Please be good."

"Well, it doesn't require much self-denial to stay here awhile longer," replied Carley, lazily.

Flo left with a parting admonition not to let the stove get red-hot. And Carley lay snuggled in the warm blankets, dreading the ordeal of getting out into that cold bare room. Her nose was cold. When her nose grew cold, it being a faithful barometer as to temperature, Carley knew there was frost in the air. She preferred summer. Steam-heated rooms with hothouse flowers lending their perfume had certainly not trained Carley for primitive conditions. She had a spirit, however, that was waxing a little rebellious to all this intimation as to her susceptibility to colds and her probable weakness under privation. Carley got up. Her bare feet landed upon the board floor instead of the Navajo rug, and she thought she had encountered cold stone. Stove and hot water notwithstanding, by the time she was half dressed she was also half frozen. "Some actor fellow once said w-when you w-went West you were c-camping out," chattered Carley. "Believe me, he said something."

The fact was Carley had never camped out. Her set played golf, rode horseback, motored and house-boated, but they had never gone in for uncomfortable trips. The camps and hotels in the Adirondacks were as warm and luxurious as Carley's own home. Carley now missed many things. And assuredly her flesh was weak. It cost her effort of will and real pain to finish lacing her boots. As she had made an engagement with Glenn to visit his cabin, she had donned an outdoor suit. She wondered if the cold had anything to do with the perceptible diminishing of the sound of the waterfall. Perhaps some of the water had frozen, like her fingers.

Carley went downstairs to the living room, and made no effort to resist a rush to the open fire. Flo and her mother were amused at Carley's impetuosity. "You'll like that stingin' of the air after you get used to it," said Mrs. Hutter. Carley had her doubts. When she was thoroughly thawed out she discovered an appetite quite unusual for her, and she enjoyed her breakfast. Then it was time to sally forth to meet Glenn.

"It's pretty sharp this mawnin'," said Flo. "You'll need gloves and sweater."

Having fortified herself with these, Carley asked how to find West Fork Canyon.

"It's down the road a little way," replied Flo. "A great narrow canyon opening on the right side. You can't miss it."

Flo accompanied her as far as the porch steps. A queer-looking individual was slouching along with ax over his shoulder.

"There's Charley," said Flo. "He'll show you." Then she whispered: "He's sort of dotty sometimes. A horse kicked him once. But mostly he's sensible."

At Flo's call the fellow halted with a grin. He was long, lean, loose jointed, dressed in blue overalls stuck into the tops of muddy boots, and his face was clear olive without beard or line. His brow bulged a little, and from under it peered out a pair of wistful brown eyes that reminded Carley of those of a dog she had once owned.

"Wal, it ain't a-goin' to be a nice day," remarked Charley, as he tried to accommodate his strides to Carley's steps.

"How can you tell?" asked Carley. "It looks clear and bright."

"Naw, this is a dark mawnin'. Thet's a cloudy sun. We'll hev snow on an' off."

"Do you mind bad weather?"

"Me? All the same to me. Reckon, though, I like it cold so I can loaf round a big fire at night."

"I like a big fire, too."

"Ever camped out?" he asked.

"Not what you'd call the real thing," replied Carley.

"Wal, thet's too bad. Reckon it'll be tough fer you," he went on, kindly. "There was a gurl tenderfoot heah two years ago an' she had a hell of a time. They all joked her, 'cept me, an' played tricks on her. An' on her side she was always puttin' her foot in it. I was shore sorry fer her."

"You were very kind to be an exception," murmured Carley.

"You look out fer Tom Hutter, an' I reckon Flo ain't so darn above layin' traps fer you. 'Specially as she's sweet on your beau. I seen them together a lot."

"Yes?" interrogated Carley, encouragingly.

"Kilbourne is the best fellar thet ever happened along Oak Creek. I helped him build his cabin. We've hunted some together. Did you ever hunt?"

"No."

"Wal, you've shore missed a lot of fun," he said. "Turkey huntin'. Thet's what fetches the gurls. I reckon because turkeys are so good to eat. The old gobblers hev begun to gobble now. I'll take you gobbler huntin' if you'd like to go."

"I'm sure I would."

"There's good trout fishin' along heah a little later," he said, pointing to the stream. "Crick's too high now. I like West Fork best. I've ketched some lammin' big ones up there."

Carley was amused and interested. She could not say that Charley had shown any indication of his mental peculiarity to her. It took considerable restraint not to lead him to talk more about Flo and Glenn. Presently they reached the turn in the road, opposite the cottage Carley had noticed yesterday, and here her loquacious escort halted.

"You take the trail heah," he said, pointing it out, "an' foller it into West Fork. So long, an' don't forget we're goin' huntin' turkeys."

Carley smiled her thanks, and, taking to the trail, she stepped out briskly, now giving attention to her surroundings. The canyon had widened, and the creek with its deep thicket of green and white had sheered to the left. On her right the canyon wall appeared to be lifting higher and higher. She could not see it well, owing to intervening treetops. The trail led her through a grove of maples and sycamores, out into an open parklike bench that turned to the right toward the cliff. Suddenly Carley saw a break in the red wall. It was the intersecting canyon, West Fork. What a narrow red-walled gateway! Huge pine trees spread wide gnarled branches over her head. The wind made soft rush in their tops, sending the brown needles lightly on the air. Carley turned the bulging corner, to be halted by a magnificent spectacle. It seemed a mountain wall loomed over her. It was the western side of this canyon, so lofty that Carley had to tip back her head to see the top. She swept her astonished gaze down the face of this tremendous red mountain wall and then slowly swept it upward again. This phenomenon of a cliff seemed beyond the comprehension of her sight. It looked a mile high. The few trees along its bold rampart resembled short spear-pointed bushes outlined against the steel gray of sky. Ledges, caves, seams, cracks, fissures, beetling red brows, yellow crumbling crags, benches of green growths and niches choked with brush, and bold points where single lonely pine trees grew perilously, and blank walls a thousand feet across their shadowed faces—these features gradually took shape in Carley's confused sight, until the colossal mountain front stood up before her in all its strange, wild, magnificent ruggedness and beauty.

"Arizona! Perhaps this is what he meant," murmured Carley. "I never dreamed of anything like this. . . . But, oh! it overshadows me—bears me down! I could never have a moment's peace under it."

It fascinated her. There were inaccessible ledges that haunted her with their remote fastnesses. How wonderful would it be to get there, rest there, if that were possible! But only eagles could reach them. There were places, then, that the desecrating hands of man could not touch. The dark caves were mystically potent in their vacant staring out at the world beneath them. The crumbling crags, the toppling ledges, the leaning rocks all threatened to come thundering down at the breath of wind. How deep and soft the red color in contrast with the green! How splendid the sheer bold uplift of gigantic steps! Carley found herself marveling at the forces that had so rudely, violently, and grandly left this monument to nature.

"Well, old Fifth Avenue gadder!" called a gay voice. "If the back wall of my yard so halts you—what will you ever do when you see the Painted Desert, or climb Sunset Peak, or look down into the Grand Canyon?"

"Oh, Glenn, where are you?" cried Carley, gazing everywhere near at hand. But he was farther away. The clearness of his voice had deceived her. Presently she espied him a little distance away, across a creek she had not before noticed.

"Come on," he called. "I want to see you cross the stepping stones."

Carley ran ahead, down a little slope of clean red rock, to the shore of the green water. It was clear, swift, deep in some places and shallow in others, with white wreathes or ripples around the rocks evidently placed there as a means to cross. Carley drew back aghast.

"Glenn, I could never make it," she called.

"Come on, my Alpine climber," he taunted. "Will you let Arizona daunt you?"

"Do you want me to fall in and catch cold?" she cried, desperately.

"Carley, big women might even cross the bad places of modern life on stepping stones of their dead selves!" he went on, with something of mockery. "Surely a few physical steps are not beyond you."

"Say, are you mangling *Tennyson* or just kidding me?" she demanded slangily.

"My love, Flo could cross here with her eyes shut."

That thrust spurred Carley to action. His words were

jest, yet they held a hint of earnest. With her heart at her throat Carley stepped on the first rock, and, poising, she calculated on a running leap from stone to stone. Once launched, she felt she was falling downhill. She swayed, she splashed, she slipped; and clearing the longest leap from the last stone to shore she lost her balance and fell into Glenn's arms. His kisses drove away both her panic and her resentment.

"By Jove! I didn't think you'd even attempt it!" he declared, manifestly pleased. "I made sure I'd have to pack you over—in fact, rather liked the idea."

"I wouldn't advise you to employ any such means again—to dare me," she retorted.

"That's a nifty outdoor suit you've on," he said, admiringly. "I was wondering what you'd wear. I like short outing skirts for women, rather than trousers. The service sort of made the fair sex dippy about pants."

"It made them dippy about more than that," she replied. "You and I will never live to see the day that women recover their balance."

"I agree with you," replied Glenn.

Carley locked her arm in his. "Honey, I want to have a good time to-day. Cut out all the *other* women stuff. . . . Take me to see your little gray home in the West. Or is it gray?"

He laughed. "Why, yes, it's gray, just about. The logs have bleached some."

Glenn led her away up a trail that climbed between bowlders, and meandered on over piny mats of needles under great, silent, spreading pines; and closer to the impondering mountain wall, where at the base of the red rock the creek murmured strangely with hollow gurgle, where the sun had no chance to affect the cold damp gloom; and on through sweet-smelling woods, out into the sunlight again, and across a wider breadth of stream; and up a slow slope covered with stately pines, to a little cabin that faced the west.

"Here we are, sweetheart," said Glenn. "Now we shall see what you are made of."

Carley was noncommittal as to that. Her intense interest precluded any humor at this moment. Not until she actually saw the log cabin Glenn had erected with his own hands had she been conscious of any great interest. But sight of it awoke something unaccustomed in Carley. As she stepped into the cabin her heart was not acting normally for a young woman who had no illusions about love in a cottage.

Glenn's cabin contained one room about fifteen feet wide by twenty long. Between the peeled logs were lines of red mud, hard dried. There was a small window opposite the door. In one corner was a couch of poles, with green tips of pine boughs peeping from under the blankets. The floor consisted of flat rocks laid irregularly, with many spaces of earth showing between. The open fireplace appeared too large for the room, but the very bigness of it, as well as the blazing sticks and glowing embers, appealed strongly to Carley. A rough-hewn log formed the mantel, and on it Carley's picture held the place of honor. Above this a rifle lay across deer antlers. Carley paused here in her survey long enough to kiss Glenn and point to her photograph.

"You couldn't have pleased me more."

To the left of the fireplace was a rude cupboard of shelves, packed with boxes, cans, bags, and utensils. Below the cupboard, hung upon pegs, were blackened pots and pans, a long-handled skillet, and a bucket. Glenn's table was a masterpiece. There was no danger of knocking it over. It consisted of four poles driven into the ground, upon which had been nailed two wide slabs. This table showed considerable evidence of having been scrubbed scrupulously clean. There were two low stools, made out of boughs, and the seats had been covered with woolly sheep hide. In the right-hand corner stood a neat pile of firewood, cut with an ax, and beyond this hung saddle and saddle blanket, bridle and spurs. An old sombrero was hooked upon the pommel of the saddle. Upon the wall, higher up, hung a lantern, resting in a coil of rope that Carley took to be a lasso. Under a shelf upon which lay a suit case hung some rough wearing apparel.

Carley noted that her picture and the suit case were absolutely the only physical evidences of Glenn's connection with his Eastern life. That had an unaccountable effect upon Carley. What had she expected? Then, after another survey of the room, she began to pester Glenn with questions. He had to show her the spring outside and the little bench with basin and soap. Sight of his soiled towel made her throw up her hands. She sat on the stools. She lay on the couch. She rummaged into the contents of the cupboard. She threw wood on the fire. Then, finally, having exhausted her search and inquiry, she flopped down on one of the stools to gaze at Glenn in awe and admiration and incredulity.

"Glenn—you've actually lived here!" she ejaculated.

"Since last fall before the snow came," he said, smiling.

"Snow! Did it snow?" she inquired.

"Well, I guess. I was snowed in for a week."

"Why did you choose this lonely place—way off from the Lodge?" she asked, slowly.

"I wanted to be by myself," he replied, briefly.

"You mean this is a sort of camp-out place?"

"Carley, I call it my home," he replied, and there was a low, strong sweetness in his voice she had never heard before.

That silenced her for a while. She went to the door and

gazed up at the towering wall, more wonderful than ever, and more fearful, too, in her sight. Presently tears dimmed her eyes. She did not understand her feeling; she was ashamed of it; she hid it from Glenn. Indeed, there was something terribly wrong between her and Glenn, and it was not in him. This cabin he called home gave her a shock which would take time to analyze. At length she turned to him with gay utterance upon her lips. She tried to put out of her mind a dawning sense that this close-to-the-earth habitation, this primitive dwelling, held strange inscrutable power over a self she had never divined she possessed. The very stones in the hearth seemed to call out from some remote past, and the strong sweet smell of burnt wood thrilled to the marrow of her bones. How little she knew of herself! But she had intelligence enough to understand that there was a woman in her, the female of the species; and through that the sensations from logs and stones and earth and fire had strange power to call up the emotions handed down to her from the ages. The thrill, the queer heartbeat, the vague, haunting memory of something, as of a dim childhood adventure, the strange prickling sense of dread—these abided with her and augmented while she tried to show Glenn her pride in him and also how funny his cabin seemed to her.

Once or twice he hesitatingly, and somewhat appealingly, she imagined, tried to broach the subject of his work there in the West. But Carley wanted a little while with him free of disagreeable argument. It was a foregone conclusion that she would not like his work. Her intention at first had been to begin at once to use all persuasion in her power toward having him go back East with her, or at the latest some time this year. But the rude log cabin had checked her impulse. She felt that haste would be unwise.

"Glenn Kilbourne, I told you why I came West to see you," she said, spiritedly. "Well, since you still swear allegiance to your girl from the East, you might entertain her a little bit before getting down to business talk."

"All right, Carley," he replied, laughing. "What do you want to do? The day is at your disposal. I wish it were June. Then if you didn't fall in love with West Fork you'd be no good."

"Glenn, I love people, not places," she returned.

"So I remember. And that's one thing I don't like. But let's not quarrel. What'll we do?"

"Suppose you tramp with me all around, until I'm good and hungry. Then we'll come back here—and you can cook dinner for me."

"Fine! Oh, I know you're just bursting with curiosity to see how I'll do it. Well, you may be surprised, miss."

"Let's go," she urged.

"Shall I take my gun or fishing rod?"

"You shall take nothing but *me*," retorted Carley. "What chance has a girl with a man, if he can hunt or fish?"

So they went out hand in hand. Half of the belt of sky above was obscured by swiftly moving gray clouds. The other half was blue and was being slowly encroached upon by the dark storm-like pall. How cold the air! Carley had already learned that when the sun was hidden the atmosphere was cold. Glenn led her down a trail to the brook, where he calmly picked her up in his arms, quite easily, it appeared, and leisurely packed her across, kissing her half a dozen times before he deposited her on her feet.

"Glenn, you do this sort of thing so well that it makes me imagine you have practice now and then," she said.

"No. But you are pretty and sweet, and like the girl you were four years ago. That takes me back to those days."

"Thank you. That's dear of you. I think I am something of a cat. . . . I'll be glad if this walk leads us often to the creek."

Spring might have been fresh and keen in the air, but it

had not yet brought much green to the brown earth or to the trees. The cotton-woods showed a light feathery verdure. The long grass was a bleached white, and low down close to the sod fresh tiny green blades showed. The great fern leaves were sear and ragged, and they rustled in the breeze. Small gray sheath-barked trees with clumpy foliage and snags of dead branches, Glenn called cedars; and, grotesque as these were, Carley rather liked them. They were approachable, not majestic and lofty like the pines, and they smelled sweetly wild, and best of all they afforded some protection from the bitter wind. Carley rested better than she walked. The huge sections of red rock that had tumbled from above also interested Carley, especially when the sun happened to come out for a few moments and brought out their color. She enjoyed walking on the fallen pines, with Glenn below, keeping pace with her and holding her hand. Carley looked in vain for flowers and birds. The only living things she saw were rainbow trout that Glenn pointed out to her in the beautiful clear pools. The way the great gray bowlders trooped down to the brook as if they were cattle going to drink; the dark caverns under the shelving cliffs, where the water murmured with such hollow mockery; the low spear-pointed gray plants, resembling century plants, and which Glenn called mescal cactus, each with its single straight dead stalk standing on high with fluted head; the narrow gorges, perpendicularly walled in red, where the constricted brook plunged in amber and white cascades over fall after fall, tumbling, rushing, singing its water melody—these all held singular appeal for Carley as aspects of the wild land, fascinating for the moment, symbolic of the lonely red man and his forbears, and by their raw contrast making more necessary and desirable and elevating the comforts and conventions of civilization. The cave man theory interested Carley only as mythology.

Lonelier, wilder, grander grew Glenn's canyon. Carley was finally forced to shift her attention from the intimate objects of the canyon floor to the aloof and unattainable heights. Singular to feel the difference! That which she could see close at hand, touch if she willed, seemed to become part of her knowledge, could be observed and so possessed and passed by. But the gold-red ramparts against the sky, the crannied cliffs, the crags of the eagles, the lofty, distant blank walls, where the winds of the gods had written their wars—these haunted because they could never be possessed. Carley had often gazed at the Alps as at celebrated pictures. She admired, she appreciated—then she forgot. But the canyon heights did not affect her that way. They vaguely dissatisfied, and as she could not be sure of what they dissatisfied, she had to conclude that it was in herself. To see, to watch, to dream, to seek, to strive, to endure, to find! Was that what they meant? They might make her thoughtful of the vast earth, and its endless age, and its staggering mystery. But what more!

The storm that had threatened blackened the sky, and gray scudding clouds buried the canyon rims, and long veils of rain and sleet began to descend. The wind roared through the pines, drowning the roar of the brook. Quite suddenly the air grew piercingly cold. Carley had forgotten her gloves, and her pockets had not been constructed to protect hands. Glenn drew her into a sheltered nook where a rock jutted out from overhead and a thicket of young pines helped break the onslaught of the wind. There Carley sat on a cold rock, huddled up close to Glenn, and wearing to a state she knew would be misery. Glenn not only seemed content; he was happy. "This is great," he said. His coat was open, his hands uncovered, and he watched the storm and listened with manifest delight. Carley hated to betray what a weakling she was, so she resigned herself to her fate, and imagined she felt her fingers numbing into ice, and her sensitive nose slowly and painfully freezing.

The storm passed, however, before Carley sank into abject and open wretchedness. She managed to keep pace with Glenn until exercise warmed her blood. At every little ascent in the trail she found herself laboring to get her breath. There was assuredly evidence of abundance of air in this canyon, but somehow she could not get enough of it. Glenn detected this and said it was owing to the altitude. When they reached the cabin Carley was wet, stiff, cold, exhausted. How welcome the shelter, the open fireplace! Seeing the cabin in new light, Carley had the grace to acknowledge to herself that, after all, it was not so bad.

"Now for a good fire and then dinner," announced Glenn, with the air of one who knew his ground.

"Can I help?" queried Carley.

"Not to-day. I do not want you to spring any domestic science on me now."

Carley was not averse to withholding her ignorance. She watched Glenn with surpassing curiosity and interest. First he threw a quantity of wood upon the smoldering fire.

"I have ham and mutton of my own raising," announced Glenn, with importance. "Which would you prefer?"

"Of your own raising. What do you mean?" queried Carley.

"My dear, you've been so steeped in the fog of the crowd that you are blind to the homely and necessary things of living. I mean I have here meat of both sheep and hog that I raised myself. That is to say, mutton and ham. Which do you like?"

"Ham!" cried Carley, incredulously.

Without more ado Glenn settled to brisk action, every move of which Carley watched with keen eyes. The usurping of a woman's province by a man was always an amusing thing. But for Glenn Kilbourne—what more would it be? He evidently knew what he wanted, for every movement was quick, decisive. One after another he placed bags, cans, sacks, pans, utensils on the table. Then he kicked at the roaring fire, settling some of the sticks. He strode outside to return with a bucket of water, a basin, towel, and soap. Then he took down two queer little iron pots with heavy lids. To each pot was attached a wire handle. He removed the lids, then set both the pots right on the fire or in it. Pouring water into the basin, he proceeded to wash his hands. Next he took a large pan, and from a sack he filled it half full of flour. To this he added baking powder and salt. It was instructive for Carley to see him run his skillful fingers all through that flour, as if searching for lumps. After this he knelt before the fire and, lifting off one of the iron pots with a forked stick, he proceeded to wipe out the inside of the pot and grease it with a piece of fat. His next move was to rake out a pile of the red coals, a feat he performed with the stick, and upon these he placed the pot. Also he removed the other pot from the fire, leaving it, however, quite close.

"Well, all eyes?" he bantered, suddenly staring at her. "Didn't I say I'd surprise you?"

"Don't mind me. This is about the happiest—and most bewildered moment—of my life," replied Carley.

Returning to the table, Glenn dug at something in a large red can. He paused a moment to eye Carley.

"Girl, do you know how to make biscuits?" he queried.

"I might have known in my school days, but I've forgotten," she replied.

"Can you make apple pie?" he demanded, imperiously.

"No," rejoined Carley.

"How do you expect to please your husband?"

"Why—by marrying him, I suppose," answered Carley, as if weighing a problem.

"That has been the universal feminine point of view for a good many years," replied Glenn, flourishing a flour-whitened hand. "But it never served the women of the Revolution or the pioneers. And they were the builders of the nation. It will never serve the wives of the future, if we are to survive."

"Glenn, you rave!" ejaculated Carley, not knowing whether to laugh or be grave. "You were talking of humble housewifely things."

"Precisely. The humble things that were the foundation of the great nation of Americans. I meant work and children."

Carley could only stare at him. The look he flashed at her, the sudden intensity and passion of his ringing words, were as if he gave her a glimpse into the very depths of him. He might have begun in fun, but he had finished otherwise. She felt that she really did not know this man. Had he arraigned her in judgment? A flush, seemingly hot and cold, passed over her. Then it relieved her to see that he had returned to his task.

He mixed the shortening with the flour, and, adding water, he began a thorough kneading. When the consistency of the mixture appeared to satisfy him he took a handful of it, rolled it into a ball, patted and flattened it into a biscuit, and dropped it into the oven he had set aside on the hot coals. Swiftly he shaped eight or ten other biscuits and dropped them as the first. Then he put the heavy iron lid on the pot, and with a rude shovel, improvised from a flattened tin can, he shoveled red coals out of the fire, and covered the lid with them. His next move was to pare and slice potatoes, placing these aside in a pan. A small black coffee-pot half full of water, was set on a glowing part of the fire. Then he brought into use a huge, heavy knife, a murderous-looking implement it appeared to Carley, with which he cut slices of ham. These he dropped into the second pot, which he left uncovered. Next he removed the flour sack and other inpedimenta from the table, and proceeded to set places for two—blue-enamel plate and cup, with plain, substantial-looking knives, forks, and spoons. He went outside, to return presently carrying a small crock of butter. Evidently he had kept the butter in or near the spring. It looked dewy and cold and hard. After that he peeped under the lid of the pot which contained the biscuits. The other pot was sizzling and smoking, giving forth a delicious savory odor that affected Carley most agreeably. The coffee-pot had begun to steam. With a long fork Glenn turned the slices of ham and stood a moment watching them. Next he placed cans of three sizes upon the table; and these Carley conjectured contained sugar, salt, and pepper. Carley might not have been present, for all the attention he paid to her. Again he peeped at the biscuits. At the edge of the hot embers he placed a tin plate, upon which he carefully deposited the slices of ham. Carley had not needed sight of them to know she was hungry; they made her simply ravenous. That done, he poured the pan of sliced potatoes into the pot. Carley judged the heat of that pot to be extreme. Next he removed the lid from the other pot, exposing biscuits slightly browned; and evidently satisfied with these, he removed them from the coals. He stirred the slices of potatoes round and round; he emptied two heaping tablespoonfuls of coffee into the coffee-pot.

"Carley," he said, at last turning to her with a warm smile, "out here in the West the cook usually yells, 'Come and get it!' Draw up your stool."

And presently Carley found herself seated across the crude table from Glenn, with the background of chinked logs in her sight, and the smart of wood smoke in her eyes. In years past she had sat with him in the soft, subdued, gold-green shadows of the Astor, or in the sumptuous atmosphere of the St. Regis. But this event was so different, so striking, that she felt it would have limitless significance. For one thing, the look of Glenn! When had he ever seemed like this, wonderfully happy to have her there, consciously proud of this dinner he had prepared in half an hour, strangely studying her as one on trial? This might have had its effect upon Carley's reaction to the situation, making it sweet, trenchant with meaning, but she was hungry enough and the dinner was good enough to make this hour memorable on that score alone. She ate until she was actually ashamed of herself. She laughed heartily, she talked, she made love to Glenn. Then suddenly an idea flashed into her quick mind.

"Glenn, did this girl Flo teach you to cook?" she queried, sharply.

"No. I always was handy in camp. Then out here I had the luck to fall in with an old fellow who was a wonderful cook. He lived with me for a while. . . . Why, what difference would it have made—had Flo taught me?"

Carley felt the heat of blood in her face. "I don't know that it would have made a difference. Only—I'm glad she didn't teach you. I'd rather no girl could teach you what I couldn't."

"You think I'm a pretty good cook, then?" he asked.

"I've enjoyed this dinner more than any I've ever eaten."

"Thanks, Carley. That'll help a lot," he said, gayly, but his eyes shone with earnest, glad light. "I hoped I'd surprise you. I've found out here that I want to do things well. The West stirs something in a man. It must be an unwritten law. You stand or fall by your own hands. Back East you know meals are just occasions—to hurry through—to dress for—to meet somebody—to eat because you have to eat. But out here they are different. I don't know how. In the city, producers, merchants, waiters serve you for money. The meal is a transaction. It has no significance. It is money that keeps you from starvation. But in the West money doesn't mean much. You must work to live."

Carley leaned her elbows on the table and gazed at him curiously and admiringly. "Old fellow, you're a wonder. I can't tell you how proud I am of you. That you could come West weak and sick, and fight your way to health, and learn to be self-sufficient! It is a splendid achievement. It amazes me. I don't grasp it. I want to think. Nevertheless I—"

"What?" he queried, as she hesitated.

"Oh, never mind now," she replied, hastily, averting her eyes.

The day was far spent when Carley returned to the Lodge—and in spite of the discomfort of cold and sleet, and the bitter wind that beat in her face as she struggled up the trail—it was a day never to be forgotten. Nothing had been wanting in Glenn's attention or affection. He had been comrade, lover, all she craved for. And but for his few singular words about work and children there had been no serious talk. Only a play day in his canyon and his cabin! Yet had she appeared at her best? Something vague and perplexing knocked at the gate of her consciousness.

CHAPTER IV

Two warm sunny days in early May inclined Mr. Hutter to the opinion that pleasant spring weather was at hand and that it would be a propitious time to climb up on the desert to look after his sheep interests. Glenn, of course, would accompany him.

"Carley and I will go too," asserted Flo.

"Reckon that'll be good," said Hutter, with approving nod.

His wife also agreed that it would be fine for Carley to see the beautiful desert country round Sunset Peak. But Glenn looked dubious.

"Carley, it'll be rather hard," he said. "You're soft, and riding and lying out will stove you up. You ought to break in gradually."

"I rode ten miles to-day," rejoined Carley. "And didn't mind it—much." This was a little deviation from stern veracity.

"Shore Carley's well and strong," protested Flo. "She'll get sore, but that won't kill her."

Glenn eyed Flo with rather penetrating glance. "I might drive Carley round about in the car," he said.

"But you can't drive over those lava flats, or go round,

either. We'd have to send horses in some cases miles to meet you. It's horseback if you go at all."

"Shore we'll go horseback," spoke up Flo. "Carley has got it all over that Spencer girl who was here last summer."

"I think so, too. I am sure I hope so. Because you remember what the ride to Long Valley did to Miss Spencer," rejoined Glenn.

"What?" inquired Carley.

"Bad cold, peeled nose, skinned shin, saddle sores. She was in bed two days. She didn't show much pep the rest of her stay here, and she never got on another horse."

"Oh, is that all, Glenn?" returned Carley, in feigned surprise. "Why, I imagined from your tone that Miss Spencer's ride must have occasioned her discomfort . . . See here, Glenn. I may be a tenderfoot, but I'm no mollycoddle."

"My dear, I surrender," replied Glenn, with a laugh. "Really, I'm delighted. But if anything happens—don't you blame me. I'm quite sure that a long horseback ride, in spring, on the desert, will show you a good many things about yourself."

That was how Carley came to find herself, the afternoon of the next day, astride a self-willed and unmanageable little mustang, riding in the rear of her friends, on the way through a cedar forest toward a place called Deep Lake.

Carley had not been able yet, during the several hours of their journey, to take any pleasure in the scenery or in her mount. For in the first place there was nothing to see but scrubby little gnarled cedars and drab-looking rocks; and in the second this Indian pony she rode had discovered she was not an adept horsewoman and had proceeded to take advantage of the fact. It did not help Carley's predicament to remember that Glenn had decidedly advised her against riding this particular mustang. To be sure, Flo had approved of Carley's choice, and Mr. Hutter, with a hearty laugh, had fallen in line: "Shore. Let her ride one of the broncs, if she wants." So this animal she bestrode must have been a bronc, for it did not take him long to elicit from Carley a muttered, "I don't know what bronc means, but it sounds like this pony acts."

Carley had inquired the animal's name from the young herder who had saddled him for her.

"Wal, I reckon he ain't got much of a name," replied the lad, with a grin, as he scratched his head. "For us boys always called him Spillbeans."

"Humph! What a beautiful cognomen!" ejaculated Carley. "But according to Shakespeare any name will serve. I'll ride him or—or—"

So far there had not really been any necessity for the completion of that sentence. But five miles of riding up into the cedar forest had convinced Carley that she might not have much farther to go. Spillbeans had ambled along well enough until he reached level ground where a long bleached grass waved in the wind. Here he manifested hunger, then a contrary nature, next insubordination, and finally direct hostility. Carley had urged, pulled, and commanded in vain. Then when she gave Spillbeans a kick in the flank he jumped stiff legged, propelling her up out of the saddle, and while she was descending he made the queer jump again, coming up to meet her. The jolt she got seemed to dislocate every bone in her body. Likewise it hurt. Moreover, along with her idea of what a spectacle she must have presented, it quickly decided Carley that Spillbeans was a horse that was not to be opposed. Whenever he wanted a mouthful of grass he stopped to get it. Therefore Carley was always in the rear, a fact which in itself did not displease her. Despite his contrariness, however, Spillbeans had apparently no intention of allowing the other horses to get completely out of sight.

Several times Flo waited for Carley to catch up. "He's

loafing on you, Carley. You ought to have on a spur. Break off a switch and beat him some." Then she whipped the mustang across the flank with her bridle rein, which punishment caused Spillbeans meekly to trot on with alacrity. Carley had a positive belief that he would not do it for her. And after Flo's repeated efforts, assisted by chastisement from Glenn, had kept Spillbeans in a trot for a couple of miles Carley began to discover that the trotting of a horse was the most uncomfortable motion possible to imagine. It grew worse. It became painful. It gradually got unendurable. But pride made Carley endure it until suddenly she thought she had been stabbed in the side. This strange piercing pain must be what Glenn had called a "stitch" in the side, something common to novices on horseback. Carley could have screamed. She pulled the mustang to a walk and sagged in ther saddle until the pain subsided. What a blessed relief! Carley had keen sense of the difference between riding in Central Park and in Arizona. She regretted her choice of horses. Spillbeans was attractive to look at, but the pleasure of riding him was a delusion. Flo had said his gait resembled the motion of a rocking chair. This Western girl, according to Charley, the sheep herder, was not above playing Arizona jokes. Be that as it might, Spillbeans now manifested a desire to remain with the other horses, and he broke out of a walk into a trot. Carley could not keep him from trotting. Hence her state soon wore into acute distress.

Her left ankle seemed broken. The stirrup was heavy, and as soon as she was tired she could no longer keep its weight from drawing her foot in. The inside of her right knee was as sore as a boil. Besides, she had other pains, just as severe, and she stood momentarily in mortal dread of that terrible stitch in her side. If it returned she knew she would fall off. But, fortunately, just when she was growing weak and dizzy, the horses ahead slowed to a walk on a descent. The road wound down into a wide deep canyon. Carley had a respite from her severest pains. Never before had she known what it meant to be so grateful for relief from anything.

The afternoon grew far advanced and the sunset was hazily shrouded in gray. Hutter did not like the looks of those clouds. "Reckon we're in for weather," he said. Carley did not care what happened. Weather or anything else that might make it possible to get off her horse! Glenn rode beside her, inquiring solicitously as to her pleasure. "Ride of my life!" she lied heroically. And it helped some to see that she both fooled and pleased him.

Beyond the canyon the cedared desert heaved higher and changed its aspect. The trees grew larger, bushier, greener, and closer together, with patches of bleached grass between, and russet-lichened rocks everywhere. Small cactus plants bristled sparsely in open places; and here and there bright red flowers—Indian paintbrush, Flo called them—added a touch of color to the gray. Glenn pointed to where dark banks of cloud had massed around the mountain peaks. The scene to the west was somber and compelling.

At last the men and the pack-horses ahead came to a halt in a level green forestland with no high trees. Far ahead a chain of soft gray round hills led up to the dark heaved mass of mountains. Carley saw the gleam of water through the trees. Probably her mustang saw or scented it, because he started to trot. Carley had reached a limit of strength, endurance, and patience. She hauled him up short. When Spillbeans evinced a stubborn intention to go on Carley gave him a kick. Then it happened.

She felt the reins jerked out of her hands and the saddle propel her upward. When she descended it was to meet that before-experienced jolt.

"Look!" cried Flo. "That bronc is going to pitch."

"Hold on, Carley!" yelled Glenn.

Desperately Carley essayed to do just that. But Spill beans jolted her out of the saddle. She came down on his rump and began to slide back and down. Frightened and furious, Carley tried to hang to the saddle with her hands and to squeeze the mustang with her knees. But another jolt broke her hold, and then, helpless and bewildered, with her heart in her throat and a terrible sensation of weakness, she slid back at each upheave of the muscular rump until she slid off and to the ground in a heap. Whereupon Spillbeans trotted off toward the water.

Carley sat up before Glenn and Flo reached her. Manifestly they were concerned about her, but both were ready to burst with laughter. Carley knew she was not hurt and she was so glad to be off the mustang that, on the moment, she could almost have laughed herself.

"That beast is well named," she said. "He spilled me, all right. And I presume I resembled a sack of beans."

"Carley—you're—not hurt?" asked Glenn, choking, as he helped her up.

"Not physically. But my feelings are."

Then Glenn let out a hearty howl of mirth, which was seconded by a loud guffaw from Hutter. Flo, however, appeared to be able to restrain whatever she felt. To Carley she looked queer.

"Pitch! You called it that," said Carley.

"Oh, he didn't really pitch. He just humped up a few times," replied Flo, and then when she saw how Carley was going to take it she burst into a merry peal of laughter. Charley, the sheep herder was grinning, and some of the other men turned away with shaking shoulders.

"Laugh, you wild and woolly Westerners!" ejaculated Carley. "It must have been funny. I hope I can be a good sport. . . . But I bet you I ride him to-morrow."

"Shore—you—will," replied Flo.

Evidently the little incident drew the party closer together. Carley felt a warmth of good nature that overcame her first feeling of humiliation. They expected such things from her, and she should expect them, too, and take them, if not fearlessly or painlessly, at least without resentment.

Carley walked about to ease her swollen and sore joints, and while doing so she took stock of the camp ground and what was going on. At second glance the place had a certain attraction difficult for her to define. She could see far, and the view north toward those strange gray-colored symmetrical hills was one that fascinated while it repelled her. Near at hand the ground sloped down to a large rock-bound lake, perhaps a mile in circumference. In the distance, along the shore she saw a white conical tent, and blue smoke, and moving gray objects she took for sheep.

The men unpacked and unsaddled the horses, and, hobbling their forefeet together, turned them loose. Twilight had fallen and each man appeared to be briskly set upon his own task. Glenn was cutting around the foot of a thickly branched cedar where, he told Carley, he would make a bed for her and Flo. All that Carley could see that could be used for such purpose was a canvas-covered roll. Presently Glenn untied a rope from round this, unrolled it, and dragged it under the cedar. Then he spread down the outer layer of canvas, disclosing a considerable thickness of blankets. From under the top of these he pulled out two flat little pillows. These he placed in position, and turned back some of the blankets.

"Carley, you crawl in here, pile the blankets up, and the tarp over them," directed Glenn. "If it rains pull the tarp up over your head—and let it rain."

This direction sounded in Glenn's cheery voice a good deal more pleasurable than the possibilities suggested. Surely that cedar tree could not keep off rain or snow.

"Glenn, how about—about animals—and crawling things, you know?" queried Carley.

"Oh, there are a few tarantulas and centipedes, and sometimes a scorpion. But these don't crawl around much at night. The only thing to worry about are the hydrophobia skunks."

"What on earth are they?" asked Carley, quite aghast.

"Skunks are polecats, you know," replied Glenn, cheerfully. "Sometimes one gets bitten by a coyote that has rabies, and then he's a dangerous customer. He has no fear and he may run across you and bite you in the face. Queer how they generally bite your nose. Two men have been bitten since I've been here. One of them died, and the other had to go to the Pasteur Institute with a well-developed case of hydrophobia."

"Good heavens!" cried Carley, horrified.

"You needn't be afraid," said Glenn. "I'll tie one of the dogs near your bed."

Carley wondered whether Glenn's casual, easy tone had been adopted for her benefit or was merely an assimilation from this Western life. Not improbably Glenn himself might be capable of playing a trick on her. Carley endeavored to fortify herself against disaster, so that when it befell she might not be wholly ludicrous.

With the coming of twilight a cold, keen wind moaned through the cedars. Carley would have hovered close to the fire even if she had not been too tired to exert herself. Despite her aches, she did justice to the supper. It amazed her that appetite consumed her to the extent of overcoming a distaste for this strong, coarse cooking. Before the meal ended darkness had fallen, a windy raw darkness that enveloped heavily like a blanket. Presently Carley edged closer to the fire, and there she stayed, alternately turning back and front to the welcome heat. She seemingly roasted hands, face, and knees while her back froze. The wind blew the smoke in all directions. When she groped around with blurred, smarting eyes to escape the hot smoke, it followed her. The other members of the party sat comfortably on sacks or rocks, without much notice of the smoke that so exasperated Carley. Twice Glenn insisted that she take a seat he had fixed for her, but she preferred to stand and move around a little.

By and by the camp tasks of the men appeared to be ended, and all gathered near the fire to lounge and smoke and talk. Glenn and Hutter engaged in interested conversation with two Mexicans, evidently sheep herders. If the wind and cold had not made Carley so uncomfortable she might have found the scene picturesque. How black the night! She could scarcely distinguish the sky at all. The cedar branches swished in the wind, and from the gloom came a low sound of waves lapping a rocky shore. Presently Glenn held up a hand.

"Listen, Carley!" he said.

Then she heard strange wild yelps, staccato, piercing, somehow infinitely lonely. They made her shudder.

"Coyotes," said Glenn. "You'll come to love that chorus. Hear the dogs bark back."

Carley listened with interest, but she was inclined to doubt that she would ever become enamoured of such wild cries.

"Do coyotes come near camp?" she queried.

"Shore. Sometimes they pull your pillow out from under your head," replied Flo, laconically.

Carley did not ask any more questions. Natural history was not her favorite study and she was sure she could dispense with any first-hand knowledge of desert beasts. She thought, however, she heard one of the men say, "Big varmint prowlin' round the sheep." To which Hutter replied, "Reckon it was a bear." And Glenn said, "I saw his fresh track by the lake. Some bear!"

The heat from the fire made Carley so drowsy that she could scarcely hold up her head. She longed for bed even if it was out there in the open. Presently Flo called her: "Come. Let's walk a little before turning in."

So Carley permitted herself to be led to and fro down an open aisle between some cedars. The far end of that aisle, dark, gloomy, with the bushy secretive cedars all around, caused Carley apprehension she was ashamed to admit. Flo talked eloquently about the joys of camp life, and how the harder any outdoor task was and the more endurance and pain it required, the more pride and pleasure one had in remembering it. Carley was weighing the import of these words when suddenly Flo clutched her arm. "What's that?" she whispered, tensely.

Carley stood stockstill. They had reached the furthermost end of that aisle, but had turned to go back. The flare of the camp fire threw a wan light into the shadows before them. There came a rustling in the brush, a snapping of twigs. Cold tremors chased up and down Carley's back.

"Shore it's a varmint, all right. Let's hurry," whispered Flo.

Carley needed no urging. It appeared that Flo was not going to run. She walked fast, peering back over her shoulder, and, hanging to Carley's arm, she rounded a large cedar that had obstructed some of the firelight. The gloom was not so thick here. And on the instant Carley espied a low, moving object, somehow furry, and gray in color. She gasped. She could not speak. Her heart gave a mighty throb and seemed to stop.

"What do you see?" cried Flo, sharply, peering ahead. "Oh! . . . Come, Carley. *Run!*"

Flo's cry showed she must nearly be strangled with terror. But Carley was frozen in her tracks. Her eyes were riveted upon the gray furry object. It stopped. Then it came faster. It magnified. It was a huge beast. Carley had no control over mind, heart, voice, or muscle. Her legs gave way. She was sinking. A terrible panic, icy, sickening, rending, possessed her whole body.

The huge gray thing came at her. Into the rushing of her ears broke thudding sounds. The thing leaped up. A horrible petrifaction suddenly made stone of Carley. Then she saw a gray mantlelike object cast aside to disclose the dark form of a man. Glenn!

"Carley, dog-gone it! you don't scare worth a cent," he laughingly complained.

She collapsed into his arms. The liberating shock was as great as had been her terror. She began to tremble violently. Her hands got back a sense of strength to clutch. Heart and blood seemed released from that ice-banded vise.

"Say, I believe you were scared," went on Glenn, bending over her.

"Scar-ed!" she gasped. "Oh—there's no word—to tell—what I was!"

Flo came running back, giggling with joy. "Glenn, she shore took you for a bear. Why, I felt her go stiff as a post! . . . Ha! Ha! Ha! Ha! Carley, now how do you like the wild and woolly?"

"Oh! You put up—a trick on me!" ejaculated Carley. "Glenn, how could you? . . . Such a terrible trick! I wouldn't have minded—something reasonable. But that! Oh, I'll never forgive you!"

Glenn showed remorse, and kissed her before Flo in a way that made some little amends. "Maybe I overdid it," he said. "But I thought you'd have a momentary start, you know, enough to make you yell, and then you'd see through it. I only had a sheepskin over my shoulders as I crawled on hands and knees."

"Glenn, for me you were a prehistoric monster—a dinosaur, or something," replied Carley.

It developed, upon their return to the campfire circle, that everybody had been in the joke; and they all derived hearty enjoyment from it.

"Reckon that makes you one of us," said Hutter, genially. "We've all had our scares."

Carley wondered if she were not so constituted that such trickery alienated her. Deep in her heart she resented being made to show her cowardice. But then she realized that no one had really seen any evidence of her state. It was fun to them.

Soon after this incident Hutter sounded what he called the roll-call for bed. Following Flo's instructions, Carley sat on their bed, pulled off her boots, folded coat and sweater at her head, and slid down under the blankets. How strange and hard a bed! Yet Carley had the most delicious sense of relief and rest she had ever experienced. She straightened out on her back with a feeling that she had never before appreciated the luxury of lying down.

Flo cuddled up to her in quite sisterly fashion, saying: "Now don't cover your head. If it rains I'll wake and pull up the tarp. Good night, Carley." And almost immediately she seemed to fall asleep.

For Carley, however, sleep did not soon come. She had too many aches; the aftermath of her shock of fright abided with her; and the blackness of night, the cold whip of wind over her face, and the unprotected helplessness she felt in this novel bed, were too entirely new and disturbing to be overcome at once. So she lay wide eyed, staring at the dense gray shadow, at the flickering lights upon the cedar. At length her mind formed a conclusion that this sort of thing might be worth the hardship once in a lifetime, anyway. What a concession to Glenn's West! In the secret seclusion of her mind she had to confess that if her vanity had not been so assaulted and humiliated she might have enjoyed herself more. It seemed impossible, however, to have thrills and pleasures and exaltations in the face of discomfort, privation, and an uneasy half-acknowledged fear. No woman could have either a good or a profitable time when she was at her worst. Carley thought she would not be averse to getting Flo Hutter to New York, into an atmosphere wholly strange and difficult, and see how she met situation after situation unfamiliar to her. And so Carley's mind drifted on until at last she succumbed to drowsiness.

A voice pierced her dreams of home, of warmth and comfort. Something sharp, cold, and fragrant was scratching her eyes. She opened them. Glenn stood over her, pushing a sprig of cedar into her face.

"Carley, the day is far spent," he said, gayly. "We want to roll up your bedding. Will you get out of it?"

"Hello, Glenn! What time is it?" she replied.

"It's nearly six."

"What! . . . Do you expect me to get up at that ungodly hour?"

"We're all up. Flo's eating breakfast. It's going to be a bad day, I'm afraid. And we want to get packed and moving before it starts to rain."

"Why do girls leave home?" she asked, tragically.

"To make poor devils happy, of course," he replied, smiling down upon her.

That smile made up to Carley for all the clamoring sensations of stiff, sore muscles. It made her ashamed that she could not fling herself into this adventure with all her heart. Carley essayed to sit up. "Oh, I'm afraid my anatomy has become disconnected! . . . Glenn, do I look a sight?" She never would have asked him that if she had not known she could bear inspection at such an inopportune moment.

"You look great," he asserted, heartily. "You've got

color. And as for your hair—I like to see it mussed that way. You were always one to have it dressed—just so. . . . Come, Carley, rustle now."

Thus adjured, Carley did her best under adverse circumstances. And she was gritting her teeth and complimenting herself when she arrived at the task of pulling on her boots. They were damp and her feet appeared to have swollen. Moreover, her ankles were sore. But she accomplished getting into them at the expense of much pain and sundry utterances more forcible than elegant. Glenn brought her warm water, a mitigating circumstance. The morning was cold and thought of that biting desert water had been trying.

"Shore you're doing fine," was Flo's greeting. "Come and get it before we throw it out."

Carley made haste to comply with the Western mandate, and was once again confronted with the singular fact that appetite did not wait upon the troubles of a tenderfoot. Glenn remarked that at least she would not starve to death on the trip.

"Come, climb the ridge with me," he invited. "I want you to take a look to the north and east."

He led her off through the cedars, up a slow red-earth slope, away from the lake. A green moundlike eminence topped with flat red rock appeared near at hand and not at all a hard climb. Nevertheless, her eyes deceived her, as she found to the cost of her breath. It was both far away and high.

"I like this location," said Glenn. "If I had the money I'd buy this section of land—six hundred and forty acres— and make a ranch of it. Just under this bluff is a fine open flat bench for a cabin. You could see away across the desert clear to Sunset Peak. There's a good spring of granite water. I'd run water from the lake down into the lower flats, and I'd sure raise some stock."

"What do you call this place?" asked Carley, curiously.

"Deep Lake. It's only a watering place for sheep and cattle. But there's fine grazing, and it's a wonder to me no one has ever settled here."

Looking down, Carley appreciated his wish to own the place; and immediately there followed in her a desire to get possession of this tract of land before anyone else discovered its advantages, and to hold it for Glenn. But this would surely conflict with her intention of persuading Glenn to go back East. As quickly as her impulse had been born it died.

Suddenly the scene gripped Carley. She looked from near to far, trying to grasp the illusive something. Wild lonely Arizona land! She saw ragged dumpy cedars of gray and green, lines of red earth, and a round space of water, gleaming pale under the lowering clouds; and in the distance isolated hills, strangely curved, wandering away to a black uplift of earth obscured in the sky.

These appeared to be mere steps leading her sight farther and higher to the cloud-navigated sky, where rosy and golden effulgence betokened the sun and the east. Carley held her breath. A transformation was going on before her eyes.

"Carley, it's a stormy sunrise," said Glenn.

His words explained, but they did not convince. Was this sudden-bursting glory only the sun rising behind storm clouds? She could see the clouds moving while they were being colored. The universal gray surrendered under some magic paint brush. The rifts widened, and the gloom of the pale-gray world seemed to vanish. Beyond the billowy, rolling, creamy edges of clouds, white and pink, shone the soft exquisite fresh blue sky. And a blaze of fire, a burst of molten gold, sheered up from behind the rim of cloud and suddenly poured a sea of sunlight from east to west. It transfigured the round foothills. They seemed bathed in ethereal light, and the silver mists that overhung them faded while Carley gazed, and a rosy flush crowned the symmetrical domes. Southward along the horizon line, down-dropping veils of rain, just touched with the sunrise tint, streamed in drifting slow movement from cloud to earth. To the north the range of foothills lifted toward the majestic dome of Sunset Peak, a volcanic upheaval of red and purple cinders, bare as rock, round as the lower hills, and wonderful in its color. Full in the blaze of the rising sun it flaunted an unchangeable front. Carley understood now what had been told her about this peak. Volcanic fires had thrown up a colossal mound of cinders burned forever to the hues of the setting sun. In every light and shade of day it held true to its name. Farther north rose the bold bulk of the San Francisco Peaks, that, half lost in the clouds, still dominated the desert scene. Then as Carley gazed the rifts began to close. Another transformation began, the reverse of what she watched. The golden radiance of sunrise vanished, and under a gray, lowering, coalescing pall of cloud the round hills returned to their bleak somberness, and the green desert took again its cold sheen.

"Wasn't it fine, Carley?" asked Glenn. "But nothing to what you will experience. I hope you stay till the weather gets warm. I want you to see a summer dawn on the Painted Desert, and a noon with the great white clouds rolling up from the horizon, and a sunset of massed purple and gold. If *they* do not get you then I'll give up."

Carley murmured something of her appreciation of what she had just seen. Part of his remark hung on her ear, thought-provoking and disturbing. He hoped she would stay until summer! That was kind of him. But her visit must be short and she now intended it to end with his return East with her. If she did not persuade him to go he might not want to go for a while, as he had written—"just

yet." Carley grew troubled in mind. Such mental disturbance, however, lasted no longer than her return with
Glenn to camp, where the mustang Spillbeans stood ready
for her to mount. He appeared to put one ear up, the other
down, and to look at her with mild surprise, as if to say:
"What—hello—tenderfoot! Are you going to ride me
again?"

Carley recalled that she had avowed she would ride him.
There was no alternative, and her misgivings only made
matters worse. Nevertheless, once in the saddle, she
imagined she had the hallucination that to ride off so, with
the long open miles ahead, was really thrilling. This remarkable state of mind lasted until Spillbeans began to
trot, and then another day of misery beckoned to Carley
with gray stretches of distance.

She was to learn that misery, as well as bliss, can swallow up the hours. She saw the monotony of cedar trees, but
with blurred eyes; she saw the ground clearly enough, for
she was always looking down, hoping for sandy places or
rocky places where her mustang could not trot.

At noon the cavalcade ahead halted near a cabin and
corral, which turned out to be a sheep ranch belonging to
Hutter. Here Glenn was so busy that he had no time to devote to Carley. And Flo, who was more at home on a
horse than on the ground, rode around everywhere with
the men. Most assuredly Carley could not pass by the
chance to get off Spillbeans and to walk a little. She found,
however, that what she wanted most was to rest. The cabin
was deserted, a dark, damp place with a rank odor. She
did not stay long inside.

Rain and snow began to fall, adding to what Carley felt
to be a disagreeable prospect. The immediate present,
however, was cheered by a cup of hot soup and some bread
and butter which the herder Charley brought her. By and

by Glenn and Hutter returned with Flo, and all partook of some lunch.

All too soon Carley found herself astride the mustang again. Glenn helped her don the slicker, an abominable sticky rubber coat that bundled her up and tangled her feet round the stirrups. She was glad to find, though, that it served well indeed to protect her from raw wind and rain.

"Where do we go from here?" Carley inquired, ironically.

Glenn laughed in a way which proved to Carley that he knew perfectly well how she felt. Again his smile caused her self-reproach. Plain indeed was it that he had really expected more of her in the way of complaint and less of fortitude. Carley bit her lips.

Thus began the afternoon ride. As it advanced the sky grew more threatening, the wind rawer, the cold keener, and the rain cut like little bits of sharp ice. It blew in Carley's face. Enough snow fell to whiten the open patches of ground. In an hour Carley realized that she had the hardest task of her life to ride to the end of the day's journey. No one could have guessed her plight. Glenn complimented her upon her adaptation to such unpleasant conditions. Flo evidently was on the lookout for the tenderfoot's troubles. But as Spillbeans had taken to lagging at a walk, Carley was enabled to conceal all outward sign of her woes. It rained, hailed, sleeted, snowed, and grew colder all the time. Carley's feet became lumps of ice. Every step the mustang took sent acute pains ramifying from bruised and raw places all over her body.

Once, finding herself behind the others and out of sight in the cedars, she got off to walk awhile, leading the mustang. This would not do, however, because she fell too far in the rear. Mounting again, she rode on, beginning to feel that nothing mattered, that this trip would be the end of

Carley Burch. How she hated that dreary, cold, flat land
the road bisected without end. It felt as if she rode hours
to cover a mile. In open stretches she saw the whole party
straggling along, separated from one another, and each
for himself. They certainly could not be enjoying themselves. Carley shut her eyes, clutched the pommel of the
saddle, trying to support her weight. How could she endure
another mile? Alas! there might be many miles. Suddenly
a terrible shock seemed to rack her. But it was only that
Spillbeans had once again taken to a trot. Frantically she
pulled on the bridle. He was not to be thwarted. Opening
her eyes, she saw a cabin far ahead which probably was
the destination for the night. Carley knew she would never
reach it, yet she clung on desperately. What she dreaded
was the return of that stablike pain in her side. It came,
and life seemed something abject and monstrous. She rode
stiff legged, with her hands propping her stiffly above the
pommel, but the stabbing pain went right on, and in deeper.
When the mustang halted his trot beside the other horses
Carley was in the last extremity. Yet as Glenn came to her,
offering a hand, she still hid her agony. Then Flo called
out gayly: "Carley, you've done twenty-five miles on as rotten a day as I remember. Shore we all hand it to you. And
I'm confessing I didn't think you'd ever stay the ride out.
Spillbeans is the meanest nag we've got and he has the
hardest gait."

CHAPTER V

Later Carley leaned back in a comfortable seat, before a blazing fire that happily sent its acrid smoke up the chimney, pondering ideas in her mind.

There could be a relation to familiar things that was astounding in its revelation. To get off a horse that had tortured her, to discover an almost insatiable appetite, to rest weary, aching body before the genial warmth of a beautiful fire—these were experiences which Carley found to have been hitherto unknown delights. It struck her suddenly and strangely that to know the real truth about anything in life might require infinite experience and understanding. How could one feel immense gratitude and relief, or the delight of satisfying acute hunger, or the sweet comfort of rest, unless there had been circumstances of extreme contrast? She had been compelled to suffer cruelly on horseback in order to make her appreciate how good it was to get down on the ground. Otherwise she never would have known. She wondered, then, how true that principle might be in all experience. It gave strong food for thought. There were things in the world never before dreamed of in her philosophy.

Carley was wondering if she were narrow and dense to

circumstances of life differing from her own when a remark of Flo's gave pause to her reflections.

"Shore the worst is yet to come," Flo had drawled.

Carley wondered if this distressing statement had to do in some way with the rest of the trip. She stifled her curiosity. Painful knowledge of that sort would come quickly enough.

"Flo, are you girls going to sleep here in the cabin?" inquired Glenn.

"Shore. It's cold and wet outside," replied Flo.

"Well, Felix, the Mexican herder, told me some Navajos had been bunking here."

"Navajos? You mean Indians?" interposed Carley, with interest.

"Shore do," said Flo. "I knew that. But don't mind Glenn. He's full of tricks, Carley. He'd give us a hunch to lie out in the wet."

Hutter burst into his hearty laugh. "Wal, I'd rather get some things anyday than a bad cold."

"Shore I've had both," replied Flo, in her easy drawl, "and I'd prefer the cold. But for Carley's sake—"

"Pray don't consider me," said Carley. The rather crude drift of the conversation affronted her.

"Well, my dear," put in Glenn, "it's a bad night outside. We'll all make our beds here."

"Glenn, you shore are a nervy fellow," drawled Flo.

Long after everybody was in bed Carley lay awake in the blackness of the cabin, sensitively fidgeting and quivering over imaginative contact with creeping things. The fire had died out. A cold air passed through the room. On the roof pattered gusts of rain. Carley heard a rustling of mice. It did not seem possible that she could keep awake, yet she strove to do so. But her pangs of body, her extreme fatigue soon yielded to the quiet and rest of her bed, engendering a drowsiness that proved irresistible.

Morning brought fair weather and sunshine, which helped to sustain Carley in her effort to brave out her pains and woes. Another disagreeable day would have forced her to humiliating defeat. Fortunately for her, the business of the men was concerned with the immediate neighborhood, in which they expected to stay all morning.

"Flo, after a while persuade Carley to ride with you to the top of this first foothill," said Glenn. "It's not far, and it's worth a good deal to see the Painted Desert from there. The day is clear and the air free from dust."

"Shore. Leave it to me. I want to get out of camp, anyhow. That conceited *hombre*, Lee Stanton, will be riding in here," answered Flo, laconically.

The slight knowing smile on Glenn's face and the grinning disbelief on Mr. Hutter's were facts not lost upon Carley. And when Charley, the herder, deliberately winked at Carley, she conceived the idea that Flo, like many women, only ran off to be pursued. In some manner Carley did not seek to analyze, the purported advent of this Lee Stanton pleased her. But she did admit to her consciousness that women, herself included, were both as deep and mysterious as the sea, yet as transparent as an inch of crystal water.

It happened that the expected newcomer rode into camp before anyone left. Before he dismounted he made a good impression on Carley, and as he stepped down in lazy, graceful action, a tall lithe figure, she thought him singularly handsome. He wore black sombrero, flannel shirt, blue jeans stuffed into high boots, and long, big-roweled spurs.

"How are you-all?" was his greeting.

From the talk that ensued between him and the men, Carley concluded that he must be overseer of the sheep hands. Carley knew that Hutter and Glenn were not interested in cattle raising. And in fact they were, especially Hutter, somewhat inimical to the dominance of the range land by cattle barons of Flagstaff.

"When's Ryan goin' to dip?" asked Hutter.

"To-day or to-morrow," replied Stanton.

"Reckon we ought to ride over," went on Hutter. "Say, Glenn, do you reckon Miss Carley could stand a sheep-dip?"

This was spoken in a low tone, scarcely intended for Carley, but she had keen ears and heard distinctly. Not improbably this sheep-dip was what Flo meant as the worst to come. Carley adopted a listless posture to hide her keen desire to hear what Glenn would reply to Hutter.

"I should say not!" whispered Glenn, fiercely. "Cut out that talk. She'll hear you and want to go."

Whereupon Carley felt mount in her breast an intense and rebellious determination to see a sheep-dip. She would astonish Glenn. What did he want, anyway? Had she not withstood the torturing trot of the hardest-gaited horse on the range? Carley realized she was going to place considerable store upon that feat. It grew on her.

When the consultation of the men ended, Lee Stanton turned to Flo. And Carley did not need to see the young man look twice to divine what ailed him. He was caught in the toils of love. But seeing through Flo Hutter was entirely another matter.

"Howdy, Lee!" she said, coolly, with her clear eyes on him. A tiny frown knitted her brow. She did not, at the moment, entirely approve of him.

"Shore am glad to see you, Flo," he said, with rather a heavy expulsion of breath. He wore a cheerful grin that in no wise deceived Flo, or Carley either. The young man had a furtive expression of eye.

"Ahuh!" returned Flo.

"I was shore sorry about—about that—" he floundered, in low voice.

"About what?"

"Aw, you know, Flo."

Carley strolled out of hearing, sure of two things—that she felt rather sorry for Stanton, and that his course of love did not augur well for smooth running. What queer creatures were women! Carley had seen several million coquettes, she believed; and assuredly Flo Hutter belonged to the species.

Upon Carley's return to the cabin she found Stanton and Flo waiting for her to accompany them on a ride up the foothill. She was so stiff and sore that she could hardly mount into the saddle; and the first mile of riding was something like a nightmare. She lagged behind Flo and Stanton, who apparently forgot her in their quarrel.

The riders soon struck the base of a long incline of rocky ground that led up to the slope of the foothill. Here rocks and gravel gave place to black cinders out of which grew a scant bleached grass. This desert verdure was what lent the soft gray shade to the foothill when seen from a distance. The slope was gentle, so that the ascent did not entail any hardship. Carley was amazed at the length of the slope, and also to see how high over the desert she was getting. She felt lifted out of a monotonous level. A green-gray league-long cedar forest extended down toward Oak Creek. Behind her the magnificent bulk of the mountains reached up into the stormy clouds, showing white slopes of snow under the gray pall.

The hoofs of the horses sank in the cinders. A fine choking dust assailed Carley's nostrils. Presently, when there appeared at least a third of the ascent still to be accomplished and Flo dismounted to walk, leading their horses. Carley had no choice but to do likewise. At first walking was a relief. Soon, however, the soft yielding cinders began to drag at her feet. At every step she slipped back a few inches, a very annoying feature of climbing. When her legs seemed to grow dead Carley paused for a little rest. The last of the ascent, over a few hundred yards of looser cinders, taxed her remaining strength to the limit. She grew hot and wet and out of breath. Her heart labored. An unreasonable antipathy seemed to attend her efforts. Only her ridiculous vanity held her to this task. She wanted to please Glenn, but not so earnestly that she would have kept on plodding up this ghastly bare mound of cinders. Carley did not mind being a tenderfoot, but she hated the thought of these Westerners considering her a weakling. So she bore the pain of raw blisters and the miserable sensation of staggering on under a leaden weight.

Several times she noted that Flo and Stanton halted to face each other in rather heated argument. At least Stanton's red face and forceful gestures attested to heat on his part. Flo evidently was weary of argument, and in answer to a sharp reproach she retorted, "Shore I was different after he came." To which Stanton responded by a quick passionate shrinking as if he had been stung.

Carley had her own reaction to this speech she could not help hearing; and inwardly, at least, her feeling must have been similar to Stanton's. She forgot the object of this climb and looked off to her right at the green level without really seeing it. A vague sadness weighed upon her soul. Was there to be a tangle of fates here, a conflict of wills, a crossing of loves? Flo's terse confession could not be taken lightly. Did she mean that she loved Glenn? Carley began to fear it. Only another reason why she must persuade Glenn to go back East! But the closer Carley came to what she divined must be an ordeal the more she dreaded it. This raw, crude West might have confronted her with a situation beyond her control. And as she dragged her weighted feet through the cinders, kicking up little puffs of black dust, she felt what she admitted to be an unreasonable resentment toward these Westerners and their barren, isolated, and boundless world.

"Carley," called Flo, "come—looksee, as the Indians

say. Here is Glenn's Painted Desert, and I reckon it's shore worth seeing."

To Carley's surprise, she found herself upon the knob of the foothill. And when she looked out across a suddenly distinguishable void she seemed struck by the immensity of something she was unable to grasp. She dropped her bridle; she gazed slowly, as if drawn, hearing Flo's voice.

"That thin green line of cottonwoods down there is the Little Colorado River," Flo was saying. "Reckon it's sixty miles, all down hill. The Painted Desert begins there and also the Navajo Reservation. You see the white strips, the red veins, the yellow bars, the black lines. They are all desert steps leading up and up for miles. That sharp black peak is called Wildcat. It's about a hundred miles. You see the desert stretching away to the right, growing dim—lost in distance? We don't know that country. But that north country we know as landmarks, anyway. Look at that saw-tooth range. The Indians call it Echo Cliffs. At the far end it drops off into the Colorado River. Lee's Ferry is there—about one hundred and sixty miles. That ragged black rent is the Grand Canyon. Looks like a thread, doesn't it? But Carley, it's some hole, believe me. Away to the left you see the tremendous wall rising and turning to come this way. That's the north wall of the Canyon. It ends at the great bluff—Greenland Point. See the black fringe above the bar of gold. That's a belt of pine trees. It's about eighty miles across this ragged old stone washboard of a desert. . . . Now turn and look straight and strain your sight over Wildcat. See the rim-purple dome. You must look hard. I'm glad it's clear and the sun is shining. We don't often get this view. . . . That purple dome is Navajo Mountain, two hundred miles and more away!"

Carley yielded to some strange drawing power and slowly walked forward until she stood at the extreme edge of the summit.

What was it that confounded her sight? Desert slope—down and down—color—distance—space! The wind that blew in her face seemed to have the openness of the whole world back of it. Cold, sweet, dry, exhilarating, it breathed of untainted vastness. Carley's memory pictures of the Adirondacks faded into pastorals; her vaunted images of European scenery changed to operetta settings. She had nothing with which to compare this illimitable space.

"Oh!—America!" was her unconscious tribute.

Stanton and Flo had come on to places beside her. The young man laughed. "Wal, now Miss Carley, you couldn't say more. When I was in camp trainin' for service overseas I used to remember how this looked. An' it seemed one of the things I was goin' to fight for. Reckon I didn't like the idea of the Germans havin' my Painted Desert. I didn't get across to fight for it, but I shore was willin'."

"You see, Carley, this is our America," said Flo, softly.

Carley had never understood the meaning of the word. The immensity of the West seemed flung at her. What her vision beheld, so far-reaching and boundless, was only a dot on the map.

"Does any one live—out there?" she asked, with slow sweep of hand.

"A few white traders and some Indian tribes," replied Stanton. "But you can ride all day an' next day an' never see a livin' soul."

What was the meaning of the gratification in his voice? Did Westerners court loneliness? Carley wrenched her gaze from the desert void to look at her companions. Stanton's eyes were narrowed; his expression had changed; lean and hard and still, his face resembled bronze. The careless humor was gone, as was the heated flush of his quarrel with Flo. The girl, too, had subtly changed, had responded to an influence that had subdued and softened her. She was mute; her eyes held a light, comprehensive and all-embracing; she was beautiful then. For Carley, quick to read emotion, caught a glimpse of a strong, steadfast soul that spiritualized the brown freckled face.

Carley wheeled to gaze out and down into this incomprehensible abyss, and on to the far up-flung heights, white and red and yellow, and so on to the wonderful mystic haze of distance. The significance of Flo's designation of miles could not be grasped by Carley. She could not estimate distance. But she did not need that to realize her perceptions were swallowed up by magnitude. Hitherto the power of her eyes had been unknown. How splendid to see afar! She could see—yes—but what did she see? Space first, annihilating space, dwarfing her preconceived images, and then wondrous colors! What had she known of color? No wonder artists failed adequately and truly to paint mountains, let alone the desert space. The toiling millions of the crowded cities were ignorant of this terrible beauty and sublimity. Would it have helped them to see? But just to breathe that untainted air, just to see once the boundless open of colored sand and rock—to realize what the freedom of eagles meant—would not that have helped anyone?

And with the thought there came to Carley's quickened and struggling mind a conception of freedom. She had not yet watched eagles, but she now gazed out into their domain. What then must be the effect of such environment on people whom it encompassed? The idea stunned Carley. Would such people grow in proportion to the nature with which they were in conflict? Hereditary influence could not be comparable to such environment in the shaping of character.

"Shore I could stand here all day," said Flo. "But it's beginning to cloud over and this high wind is cold. So we'd better go, Carley."

"I don't know what I am, but it's not cold," replied Carley.

"Wal, Miss Carley, I reckon you'll have to come again

an' again before you get a comfortable feelin' here," said Stanton.

It surprised Carley to see that this young Westerner had hit upon the truth. He understood her. Indeed she was uncomfortable. She was oppressed, vaguely unhappy. But why? The thing there—this infinitude of open sand and rock—was beautiful, wonderful, even glorious. She looked again.

Steep black-cindered slope, with its soft gray patches of grass, sheered down and down, and out in rolling slope to merge upon a cedar-dotted level. Nothing moved below, but a red-tailed hawk sailed across her vision. How still— how gray the desert floor as it reached away, losing its black dots, and gaining bronze spots of stone! By plain and prairie it fell away, each inch of gray in her sight magnifying into its league-long roll, on and on, and down across dark lines that were steppes, and at last blocked and changed by the meandering green thread which was the verdure of a desert river. Beyond stretched the white sand, where whirlwinds of dust sent aloft their funnel-shaped spouts; and it led up to the horizon-wide ribs and ridges of red and walls of yellow and mountains of black, to the dim mound of purple so ethereal and mystic against the deep-blue cloud-curtained band of sky.

And on the moment the sun was obscured and that world of colorful flame went out, as if a blaze had died.

Deprived of its fire, the desert seemed to retreat, to fade coldly and gloomily, to lose its great landmarks in dim obscurity. Closer, around to the north, the canyon country yawned with innumerable gray jaws, ragged and hard, and the riven earth took on a different character. It had no shadows. It grew flat and, like the sea, seemed to mirror the vast gray cloud expanse. The sublime vanished, but the desolate remained. No warmth—no movement—no life! Dead stone it was, cut into a million ruts by ruthless ages. Carley felt that she was gazing down into chaos.

At this moment, as before, a hawk had crossed her vision, so now a raven sailed by, black as coal, uttering a hoarse croak.

"Quoth the raven—" murmured Carley, with a half-bitter laugh, as she turned away shuddering in spite of an effort of self-control. "Maybe he meant this wonderful and terrible West is never for such as I. . . . Come, let us go."

Carley rode all that afternoon in the rear of the caravan, gradually succumbing to the cold raw wind and the aches and pains to which she had subjected her flesh. Nevertheless, she finished the day's journey, and, sorely as she needed Glenn's kindly hand, she got off her horse without aid.

Camp was made at the edge of the devastated timber zone that Carley had found so dispiriting. A few melancholy pines were standing, and everywhere, as far as she could see southward, were blackened fallen trees and stumps. It was a dreary scene. The few cattle grazing on the bleached grass appeared as melancholy as the pines. The sun shone fitfully at sunset, and then sank, leaving the land to twilight and shadows.

Once in a comfortable seat beside the camp fire, Carley had no further desire to move. She was so far exhausted and weary that she could no longer appreciate the blessing of rest. Appetite, too, failed her this meal time. Darkness soon settled down. The wind moaned through the pines. She was indeed glad to crawl into bed, and not even the thought of skunks could keep her awake.

Morning disclosed the fact that gray clouds had been blown away. The sun shone bright upon a white-frosted land. The air was still. Carley labored at her task of rising, and brushing her hair, and pulling on her boots; and

it appeared her former sufferings were as naught compared
with the pangs of this morning. How she hated the cold,
the bleak, denuded forest land, the emptiness, the roughness, the crudeness! If this sort of feeling grew any worse
she thought she would hate Glenn. Yet she was none the
less set upon going on, and seeing the sheep-dip, and riding that fiendish mustang until the trip was ended.

Getting in the saddle and on the way this morning was
an ordeal that made Carley actually sick. Glenn and Flo
both saw how it was with her, and they left her to herself.
Carley was grateful for this understanding. It seemed to
proclaim their respect. She found further matter for satisfaction in the astonishing circumstance that after the first
dreadful quarter of an hour in the saddle she began to feel
easier. And at the end of several hours of riding she was
not suffering any particular pain, though she was weaker.

At length the cut-over land ended in a forest of straggling pines, through which the road wound southward, and
eventually down into a wide shallow canyon. Through the
trees Carley saw a stream of water, open fields of green,
log fences and cabins, and blue smoke. She heard the chug
of a gasoline engine and the baa-baa of sheep. Glenn
waited for her to catch up with him, and he said: "Carley,
this is one of Hutter's sheep camps. It's not a—a very
pleasant place. You won't care to see the sheep-dip. So I'm
suggesting you wait here—"

"Nothing doing, Glenn," she interrupted. "I'm going to
see what there is to see."

"But, dear—the men—the way they handle sheep—
they'll—really it's no sight for you," he floundered.

"Why not?" she inquired, eying him.

"Because, Carley—you know how you hate the—the
seamy side of things. . . . And the stench—why, it'll make
you sick!"

"Glenn, be on the level," she said. "Suppose it does. Wouldn't you think more of me if I could stand it?"

"Why, yes," he replied, reluctantly, smiling at her, "I would. But I wanted to spare you. This trip has been hard. I'm sure proud of you. And, Carley—you can overdo it. Spunk is not everything. You simply couldn't stand this."

"Glenn, how little you know a woman!" she exclaimed. "Come along and show me your old sheep-dip."

They rode out of the woods into an open valley that might have been picturesque if it had not been despoiled by the work of man. A log fence ran along the edge of open ground and a mud dam held back a pool of stagnant water, slimy and green. As Carley rode on the baa-baa of sheep became so loud that she could scarcely hear Glenn talking.

Several log cabins, rough hewn and gray with age, stood down inside the inclosure; and beyond there were large corrals. From the other side of these corrals came sounds of rough voices of men, a trampling of hoofs, heavy splashes, the beat of an engine, and the incessant baaing of the sheep.

At this point the members of Hutter's party dismounted and tied their horses to the top log of the fence. When Carley essayed to get off Glenn tried to stop her, saying she could see well enough from there. But Carley got down and followed Flo. She heard Hutter call to Glenn: "Say, Ryan is short of men. We'll lend a hand for a couple of hours."

Presently Carley reached Flo's side and the first corral that contained sheep. They formed a compact woolly mass, rather white in color, with a tinge of pink. When Flo climbed up on the fence the flock plunged as one animal and with a trampling roar ran to the far side of the corral.

Several old rams with wide curling horns faced around; and some of the ewes climbed up on the densely packed mass. Carley rather enjoyed watching them. She surely could not see anything amiss in this sight.

The next corral held a like number of sheep, and also several Mexicans who were evidently driving them into a narrow lane that led farther down. Carley saw the heads of men above other corral fences, and there was also a thick yellowish smoke rising from somewhere.

"Carley, are you game to see the dip?" asked Flo, with good nature that yet had a touch of taunt in it.

"That's my middle name," retorted Carley, flippantly.

Both Glenn and this girl seemed to be bent upon bringing out Carley's worst side, and they were succeeding. Flo laughed. The ready slang pleased her.

She led Carley along that log fence, through a huge open gate, and across a wide pen to another fence, which she scaled. Carley followed her, not particularly overanxious to look ahead. Some thick odor had begun to reach Carley's delicate nostrils. Flo led down a short lane and climbed another fence, and sat astride the top log. Carley hurried along to clamber up to her side, but stood erect with her feet on the second log of the fence.

Then a horrible stench struck Carley almost like a blow in the face, and before her confused sight there appeared to be drifting smoke and active men and running sheep, all against a background of mud. But at first it was the odor that caused Carley to close her eyes and press her knees hard against the upper log to keep from reeling. Never in her life had such a sickening nausea assailed her. It appeared to attack her whole body. The forerunning qualm of seasickness was as nothing to this. Carley gave a gasp, pinched her nose between her fingers so she could not smell, and opened her eyes.

Directly beneath her was a small pen open at one end

into which sheep were being driven from the larger corral. The drivers were yelling. The sheep in the rear plunged into those ahead of them, forcing them on. Two men worked in this small pen. One was a brawny giant in undershirt and overalls that appeared filthy. He held a cloth in his hand and strode toward the nearest sheep. Folding the cloth round the neck of the sheep, he dragged it forward, with an ease which showed great strength, and threw it into a pit that yawned at the side. Souse went the sheep into a murky, muddy pool and disappeared. But suddenly its head came up and then its shoulders. And it began half to walk and half swim down what appeared to be a narrow boxlike ditch that contained other floundering sheep. Then Carley saw men on each side of this ditch bending over with poles that had crooks at the end, and their work was to press and pull the sheep along to the end of the ditch, and drive them up a boarded incline into another corral where many other sheep huddled, now a dirty muddy color like the liquid into which they had been emersed. Souse! Splash! In went sheep after sheep. Occasionally one did not go under. And then a man would press it under with the crook and quickly lift its head. The work went on with precision and speed, in spite of the yells and trampling and baa-baas, and the incessant action that gave an effect of confusion.

Carley saw a pipe leading from a huge boiler to the ditch. The dark fluid was running out of it. From a rusty old engine with big smokestack poured the strangling smoke. A man broke open a sack of yellow powder and dumped it into the ditch. Then he poured an acid-like liquid after it.

"Sulphur and nicotine," yelled Flo up at Carley. "The dip's poison. If a sheep opens his mouth he's usually a goner. But sometimes they save one."

Carley wanted to tear herself away from this disgusting spectacle. But it held her by some fascination. She saw

Glenn and Hutter fall in line with the other men, and work like beavers. These two pacemakers in the small pen kept the sheep coming so fast that every worker below had a task cut out for him. Suddenly Flo squealed and pointed.

"There! that sheep didn't come up," she cried. "Shore he opened his mouth."

Then Carley saw Glenn energetically plunge his hooked pole in and out and around until he had located the sub-merged sheep. He lifted its head above the dip. The sheep showed no sign of life. Down on his knees dropped Glenn, to reach the sheep with strong brown hands, and to haul it up on the ground, where it flopped inert. Glenn pummeled it and pressed it, and worked on it much as Carley had seen a life-guard work over a half-drowned man. But the sheep did not respond to Glenn's active administrations.

"No use, Glenn," yelled Hutter, hoarsely. "That one's a goner."

Carley did not fail to note the state of Glenn's hands and arms and overalls when he returned to the ditch work. Then back and forth Carley's gaze went from one end to the other of that scene. And suddenly it was arrested and held by the huge fellow who handled the sheep so bru-tally. Every time he dragged one and threw it into the pit he yelled: "Ho! Ho!" Carley was impelled to look at his face, and she was amazed to meet the rawest and bold-est stare from evil eyes that had ever been her misfortune to incite. She felt herself stiffen with a shock that was un-familiar. This man was scarcely many years older than Glenn, yet he had grizzled hair, a seamed and scarred visage, coarse, thick lips, and beetling brows, from under which peered gleaming light eyes. At every turn he flashed them upon Carley's face, her neck, the swell of her bosom. It was instinct that caused her hastily to close her riding coat. She felt as if her flesh had been burned. Like a snake he fascinated her. The intelligence in his bold gaze made the beastliness of it all the harder to endure, all the stronger to arouse.

"Come, Carley, let's rustle out of this stinkin' mess," cried Flo.

Indeed, Carley needed Flo's assistance in clambering down out of the choking smoke and horrid odor.

"*Adios*, pretty eyes," called the big man from the pen.

"Well," ejaculated Flo, when they got out, "I'll bet I call Glenn good and hard for letting you go down there."

"It was—my—fault," panted Carley. "I said I'd stand it."

"Oh, you're game, all right. I didn't mean the dip. . . . That sheep-slinger is Haze Ruff, the toughest *hombre* on this range. Shore, now, wouldn't I like to take a shot at him? . . . I'm going to tell dad and Glenn."

"Please don't," returned Carley, appealingly.

"I shore am. Dad needs hands these days. That's why he's lenient. But Glenn will cowhide Ruff and I want to see him do it."

In Flo Hutter then Carley saw another and a different spirit of the West, a violence unrestrained and fierce that showed in the girl's even voice and in the piercing light of her eyes.

They went back to the horses, got their lunches from the saddlebags, and, finding comfortable seats in a sunny, protected place, they ate and talked. Carley had to force herself to swallow. It seemed that the horrid odor of dip and sheep had permeated everything. Glenn had known her better than she had known herself, and he had wished to spare her an unnecessary and disgusting experience. Yet so stubborn was Carley that she did not regret going through with it.

"Carley, I don't mind telling you that you've stuck it out better than any tenderfoot we ever had here," said Flo.

"Thank you. That from a Western girl is a compliment I'll not soon forget," replied Carley.

"I shore mean it. We've had rotten weather. And to end

the little trip at this sheep-dip hole! Why, Glenn certainly wanted you to stack up against the real thing!"

"Flo, he did not want me to come on the trip, and especially here," protested Carley.

"Shore I know. But he *let* you."

"Neither Glenn nor any other man could prevent me from doing what I wanted to do."

"Well, if you'll excuse me," drawled Flo, "I'll differ with you. I reckon Glenn Kilbourne is not the man you knew before the war."

"No, he is not. But that does not alter the case."

"Carley, we're not well acquainted," went on Flo, more carefully feeling her way, "and I'm—not your kind. I don't know your Eastern ways. But I know what the West does to a man. The war ruined your friend—both his body and mind . . . How sorry mother and I were for Glenn—those days when it looked he'd sure 'go west,' for good! . . . Did you know he'd been gassed and that he had five hemorrhages?"

"Oh! I knew his lungs had been weakened by gas. But he never told me about having hemorrhages."

"Well, he shore had them. The last one I'll never forget. Every time he'd cough it would fetch the blood, I could tell! . . . Oh, it was awful. I begged him *not* to cough. He smiled—like a ghost smiling—and he whispered, 'I'll quit.' . . . And he did. The doctor came from Flagstaff and packed him in ice. Glenn sat propped up all night and never moved a muscle. Never coughed again! And the bleeding stopped. After that we put him out on the porch where he could breathe fresh air all the time. There's something wonderfully healing in Arizona air. It's from the dry desert and here it's full of cedar and pine. Anyway Glenn got well. And I think the West has cured his mind, too."

"Of what?" queried Carley, in an intense curiosity she could scarcely hide.

"Oh, God only knows!" exclaimed Flo, throwing up her gloved hands. "I never could understand. But I *hated* what the war did to him."

Carley leaned back against the log, quite spent. Flo was unwittingly torturing her. Carley wanted passionately to give in to jealousy of this Western girl, but she could not do it. Flo Hutter deserved better than that. And Carley's baser nature seemed in conflict with all that was noble in her. The victory did not yet go to either side. This was a bad hour for Carley. Her strength had about played out and her spirit was at low ebb.

"Carley, you're all in," declared Flo. "You needn't deny it. I'm shore you've made good with me as a tenderfoot who stayed the limit. But there's no sense in your killing yourself, nor in me letting you. So I'm going to tell dad we want to go home."

She left Carley there. The word home had struck strangely into Carley's mind and remained there. Suddenly she realized what it was to be homesick. The comfort, the ease, the luxury, the rest, the sweetness, the pleasure, the cleanliness, the gratification to eye and ear— to all the senses—how these thoughts came to haunt her! All of Carley's will power had been needed to sustain her on this trip to keep her from miserably failing. She had not failed. But contact with the West had affronted, disgusted, shocked, and alienated her. In that moment she could not be fair minded; she knew it; she did not care.

Carley gazed around her. Only one of the cabins was in sight from this position. Evidently it was a home for some of these men. On one side the peaked rough roof had been built out beyond the wall, evidently to serve as a kind of porch. On that wall hung the motliest assortment of things Carley had ever seen—utensils, sheep and cow hides, saddles, harness, leather clothes, ropes, old sombreros, shovels, stove pipe, and many other articles for which she could find no name. The most striking characteristic manifest in this collection was that of service. How they had been used! They had enabled people to live under primitive conditions. Somehow this fact inhibited Carley's sense of repulsion at their rude and uncouth appearance. Had any of her forefathers ever been pioneers? Carley did not know, but the thought was disturbing. It was thought-provoking. Many times at home, when she was dressing for dinner, she had gazed into the mirror at the graceful lines of her throat and arms, at the proud poise of her head, at the alabaster whiteness of her skin, and wonderingly she had asked of her image: "Can it be possible that I am a descendant of cavemen?" She had never been able to realize it, yet she knew it was true. Perhaps somewhere not far back along her line there had been a great-great-grandmother who had lived some kind of a primitive life, using such implements and necessaries as hung on this cabin wall, and thereby helped some man to conquer the wilderness, to live in it, and reproduce his kind. Like flashes Glenn's words came back to Carley—"Work and children!"

Some interpretation of his meaning and how it related to this hour held aloof from Carley. If she would ever be big enough to understand it and broad enough to accept it the time was far distant. Just now she was sore and sick physically, and therefore certainly not in a receptive state of mind. Yet how could she have keener impressions than these she was receiving? It was all a problem. She grew tired of thinking. But even then her mind pondered on, a stream of consciousness over which she had no control. This dreary woods was deserted. No birds, no squirrels, no creatures such as fancy anticipated! In another direction, across the canyon, she saw cattle, gaunt, ragged, lumbering, and stolid. And on the moment the scent of sheep came on the breeze. Time seemed to stand still here, and what Carley wanted most was for the hours and days to fly, so that she would be home again.

At last Flo returned with the men. One quick glance at Glenn convinced Carley that Flo had not yet told him about the sheep dipper, Haze Ruff.

"Carley, you're a real sport," declared Glenn, with the rare smile she loved. "It's a dreadful mess. And to think you stood it! . . . Why, old Fifth Avenue, if you needed to make another hit with me you've done it!"

His warmth amazed and pleased Carley. She could not quite understand why it would have made any difference to him whether she had stood the ordeal or not. But then every day she seemed to drift a little farther from a real understanding of her lover. His praise gladdened her, and fortified her to face the rest of this ride back to Oak Creek.

Four hours later, in a twilight so shadowy that no one saw her distress, Carley half slipped and half fell from her horse and managed somehow to mount the steps and enter the bright living room. A cheerful red fire blazed on the hearth, Glenn's hound, Moze, trembled eagerly at sight of her and looked up with humble dark eyes; the white-clothed dinner table steamed with savory dishes. Flo stood before the blaze, warming her hands. Lee Stanton leaned against the mantel, with eyes on her, and every line of his lean, hard face expressed his devotion to her. Hutter was taking his seat at the head of the table. "Come an' get it— you-all," he called, heartily. Mrs. Hutter's face beamed with the spirit of that home. And lastly, Carley saw Glenn waiting for her, watching her come, true in this very moment to his stern hope for her and pride in her, as she dragged her weary, spent body toward him and the bright fire.

By these signs, or the effect of them, Carley vaguely realized that she was incalculably changing, that this Carley Burch had become a vastly bigger person in the sight of her friends, and strangely in her own a lesser creature.

CHAPTER VI

If spring came at all to Oak Creek Canyon it warmed into summer before Carley had time to languish with the fever characteristic of early June in the East.

As if by magic it seemed the green grass sprang up, the green buds opened into leaves, the bluebells and primroses bloomed, the apple and peach blossoms burst exquisitely white and pink against the blue sky. Oak Creek fell to a transparent, beautiful brook, leisurely eddying in the stone-walled nooks, hurrying with murmur and babble over the little falls. The mornings broke clear and fragrantly cool, the noon hours seemed to lag under a hot sun, the nights fell like dark mantles from the melancholy star-sown sky.

Carley had stubbornly kept on riding and climbing until she killed her secret doubt that she was really a thorough-bred, until she satisfied her own insistent vanity that she could train to a point where this outdoor life was not too much for her strength. She lost flesh despite increase of appetite; she lost her pallor for a complexion of gold-brown she knew her Eastern friends would admire; she wore out the blisters and aches and pains; she found herself growing firmer of muscle, lither of line, deeper of chest. And in addition to these physical manifestations there were subtle intimations of a delight in a freedom of body she had never before known, of an exhilaration in action that made her hot and made her breathe, of a sloughing off of numberless petty and fussy and luxurious little superficialities which she had supposed were necessary to her happiness. What she had undertaken in vain conquest of Glenn's pride and Flo Hutter's Western tolerance she had found to be a boomerang. She had won Glenn's admiration; she had won the Western girl's recognition. But her passionate, stubborn desire had been ignoble, and was proved so by the rebound of her achievement, coming home to her with a sweetness she had not the courage to accept. She forced it from her. This West with its rawness, its ruggedness, she hated.

Nevertheless, the June days passed, growing dreamily swift, growing more incomprehensibly full; and still she had not broached to Glenn the main object of her visit—to take him back East. Yet a little while longer! She hated his work and had not talked of that. Yet an honest consciousness told her that as time flew by she feared more and more to tell him that he was wasting his life there and that she could not bear it. Still—was he wasting it? Once in a while a timid and unfamiliar Carley Burch voiced a pregnant query. Perhaps what held Carley back most was the happiness she achieved in her walks and rides with Glenn. She lingered because of them. Every day she loved him more, and yet—there was something. Was it in her or in him? She had a woman's assurance of his love and sometimes she caught her breath—so sweet and strong was the tumultuous emotion it stirred. She preferred to enjoy while she could, to dream instead of think. But it was not possible to hold a blank, dreamy, lulled consciousness all the time. Thought would return. And not always could she drive away a feeling that Glenn would never be her slave. She divined something in his mind that kept him gentle and kindly, restrained always, sometimes melancholy and aloof, as if he were an impassive destiny waiting for the iron consequences he knew inevitably must fall. What was this that he knew which she did not know? The idea haunted her. Perhaps it was that which compelled her to use all her woman's wiles and charms on Glenn. Still, though it thrilled her to see she made him love her more as the days passed, she could not blind herself to the truth that no softness or allurement of hers changed this strange restraint in him. How that baffled her! Was it resistance or knowledge or nobility or doubt?

Flo Hutter's twentieth birthday came along the middle of June, and all the neighbors and range hands for miles around were invited to celebrate it.

For the second time during her visit Carley put on the white gown that had made Flo gasp with delight, and had stunned Mrs. Hutter, and had brought a reluctant compliment from Glenn. Carley liked to create a sensation. What were exquisite and expensive gowns for, if not that?

It was twilight on this particular June night when she was ready to go downstairs, and she tarried a while on the long porch. The evening star, so lonely and radiant, so cold and passionless in the dusky blue, had become an object she waited for and watched, the same as she had come to love the dreaming, murmuring melody of the waterfall. She lingered there. What had the sights and sounds and smells of this wild canyon come to mean to her? She could not say. But they had changed immeasurably.

Her soft slippers made no sound on the porch, and as she turned the corner of the house, where shadows hovered thick, she heard Lee Stanton's voice:

"But, Flo, you loved me before Kilbourne came."

The content, the pathos, of his voice chained Carley to the spot. Some situations, like fate, were beyond resisting.

"Shore I did," replied Flo, dreamily. This was the voice

of a girl who was being confronted by happy and sad thoughts on her birthday.

"Don't you—love me—still?" he asked, huskily.

"Why, of course, Lee! I don't change," she said.

"But then, why—" There for the moment his utterance or courage failed.

"Lee, do you want the honest to God's truth?"

"I reckon—I do."

"Well, I love you just as I always did," replied Flo, earnestly. "But, Lee, I love—him more than you or anybody."

"My Heaven! Flo—you'll ruin us all!" he exclaimed, hoarsely.

"No, I won't either. You can't say I'm not level headed. I hated to tell you this, Lee, but you made me."

"Flo, you love me an' him—two men?" queried Stanton, incredulously.

"I shore do," she drawled, with a soft laugh. "And it's no fun."

"Reckon I don't cut much of a figure alongside Kilbourne," said Stanton, disconsolately.

"Lee, you could stand alongside any man," replied Flo, eloquently. "You're Western, and you're steady and loyal, and you'll—well, some day you'll be like dad. Could I say more? . . . But, Lee, this man is different. He is wonderful. I can't explain it, but I feel it. He has been through hell's fire. Oh! will I ever forget his ravings when he lay so ill? He means more to me than just one man. He's American. You're American, too, Lee, and you trained to be a soldier, and you would have made a grand one—if I know old Arizona. But you were not called to France. . . . Glenn Kilbourne went. God only knows what that means. But he went. And there's the difference. I saw the wreck of him. I did a little to save his life and his mind. I wouldn't be an American girl if I didn't love him. . . . Oh, Lee, can't you understand?"

"I reckon so. I'm not begrudging Glenn what—what you care. I'm only afraid I'll lose you."

"I never promised to marry you, did I?"

"Not in words. But kisses ought to—"

"Yes, kisses mean a lot," she replied. "And so far I stand committed. I suppose I'll marry you some day and be blamed lucky. I'll be happy, too—don't you overlook that hunch. . . . You needn't worry. Glenn is in love with Carley. She's beautiful, rich—and of his class. How could he ever see me?"

"Flo, you can never tell," replied Stanton, thoughtfully. "I didn't like her at first. But I'm comin' round. The thing is, Flo, does she love him as you love him?"

"Oh, I think so—I hope so," answered Flo, as if in distress.

"I'm not so shore. But then I can't savvy her. Lord knows I hope so, too. If she doesn't—if she goes back East an' leaves him here—I reckon my case—"

"Hush! I know she's out here to take him back. Let's go downstairs now."

"Aw, wait—Flo," he begged. "What's your hurry? . . . Come—give me—"

"There! That's all you get, birthday or no birthday," replied Flo, gayly.

Carley heard the soft kiss and Stanton's deep breath, and then footsteps as they walked away in the gloom toward the stairway. Carley leaned against the log wall. She felt the rough wood—smelled the rusty pine rosin. Her other hand pressed her bosom where her heart beat with unwonted vigor. Footsteps and voices sounded beneath her. Twilight had deepened into night. The low murmur of the waterfall and the babble of the brook floated to her strained ears.

Listeners never heard good of themselves. But Stanton's subtle doubt of any depth to her, though it hurt, was not so conflicting as the ringing truth of Flo Hutter's love for Glenn. This unsought knowledge powerfully affected Carley. She was forewarned and forearmed now. It saddened her, yet did not lessen her confidence in her hold on Glenn. But it stirred to perplexing pitch her curiosity in regard to the mystery that seemed to cling round Glenn's transformation of character. This Western girl really knew more about Glenn than his fiancée knew. Carley suffered a humiliating shock when she realized that she had been thinking of herself, of her love, her life, her needs, her wants instead of Glenn's. It took no keen intelligence or insight into human nature to see that Glenn needed her more than she needed him.

Thus unwontedly stirred and upset and flung back upon pride of herself, Carley went downstairs to meet the assembled company. And never had she shown to greater contrast, never had circumstance and state of mind contrived to make her so radiant and gay and unbending. She heard many remarks not intended for her far-reaching ears. An old grizzled Westerner remarked to Hutter: "Wall, she's shore an unbroke filly." Another of the company—a woman—remarked: "Sweet an' pretty as a columbine. But I'd like her better if she was dressed decent." And a gaunt range rider, who stood with others at the porch door, looking on, asked a comrade: "Do you reckon that's style back East?" To which the other replied: "Mebbe, but I'd gamble they're short on silk back East an' likewise sheriffs."

Carley received some meed of gratification out of the sensation she created, but she did not carry her craving for it to the point of overshadowing Flo. On the contrary, she contrived to have Flo share the attention she received. She taught Flo to dance the fox-trot and got Glenn to dance with her. Then she taught it to Lee Stanton. And when Lee danced with Flo, to the infinite wonder and delight of the onlookers, Carley experienced her first sincere enjoyment of the evening.

Her moment came when she danced with Glenn. It reminded her of days long past and which she wanted to return again. Despite war tramping and Western labors Glenn retained something of his old grace and lightness. But just to dance with him was enough to swell her heart, and for once she grew oblivious to the spectators.

"Glenn, would you like to go to the Plaza with me again, and dance between dinner courses, as we used to?" she whispered up to him.

"Sure I would—unless Morrison knew you were to be there," he replied.

"Glenn! . . . I would not even see him."

"Any old time you wouldn't see Morrison!" he exclaimed, half mockingly.

His doubt, his tone grated upon her. Pressing closer to him, she said, "Come back and I'll prove it."

But he laughed and had no answer for her. At her own daring words Carley's heart had leaped to her lips. If he had responded, even teasingly, she could have burst out with her longing to take him back. But silence inhibited her, and the moment passed.

At the end of that dance Hutter claimed Glenn in the interest of neighboring sheep men. And Carley, crossing the big living room alone, passed close to one of the porch doors. Some one, indistinct in the shadow, spoke to her in low voice: "Hello, pretty eyes!"

Carley felt a little cold shock go tingling through her. But she gave no sign that she had heard. She recognized the voice and also the epithet. Passing to the other side of the room and joining the company there, Carley presently took a casual glance at the door. Several men were lounging there. One of them was the sheep dipper, Haze

Ruff. His bold eyes were on her now, and his coarse face wore a slight, meaning smile, as if he understood something about her that was a secret to others. Carley dropped her eyes. But she could not shake off the feeling that wherever she moved this man's gaze followed her. The unpleasantness of this incident would have been nothing to Carley had she at once forgotten it. Most unaccountably, however, she could not make herself unaware of this ruffian's attention. It did no good for her to argue that she was merely the cynosure of all eyes. This Ruff's tone and look possessed something heretofore unknown to Carley. Once she was tempted to tell Glenn. But that would only cause a fight, so she kept her counsel. She danced again, and helped Flo entertain her guests, and passed that door often; and once stood before it, deliberately, with all the strange and contrary impulse so inscrutable in a woman, and never for a moment wholly lost the sense of the man's boldness. It dawned upon her, at length, that the singular thing about this boldness was its difference from any which had ever before affronted her. The fool's smile meant that he thought she saw his attention, and, understanding it perfectly, had secret delight in it. Many and various had been the masculine egotisms which had come under her observation. But quite beyond Carley was this brawny sheep dipper, Haze Ruff. Once the party broke up and the guests had departed, she instantly forgot both man and incident.

Next day, late in the afternoon, when Carley came out on the porch, she was hailed by Flo, who had just ridden in from down the canyon.

"Hey Carley, come down. I shore have something to tell you," she called.

Carley did not lose any time pattering down that rude porch stairway. Flo was dusty and hot, and her chaps carried the unmistakable scent of sheep-dip.

"Been over to Ryan's camp an' shore rode hard to beat Glenn home," drawled Flo.

"Why?" queried Carley, eagerly.

"Reckon I wanted to tell you something Glenn swore he wouldn't let me tell. . . . He makes me tired. He thinks you can't stand things."

"Oh! Has he been—hurt?"

"He's skinned an' bruised up some, but I reckon he's not hurt."

"Flo—what happened?" demanded Carley, anxiously.

"Carley, do you know Glenn can fight like the devil?" asked Flo.

"No, I don't. But I remember he used to be athletic. Flo, you make me nervous. Did Glenn fight?"

"I reckon he did," drawled Flo.

"With whom?"

"Nobody else but that big *hombre*, Haze Ruff."

"Oh!" gasped Carley, with a violent start. "That—that ruffian! Flo, did you see—were you there?"

"I shore was, an' next to a horse race I like a fight," replied the Western girl. "Carley, why didn't you tell me Haze Ruff insulted you last night?"

"Why, Flo—he only said, 'Hello, pretty eyes,' and I let it pass!" said Carley, lamely.

"You never want to let anything pass, out West. Because next time you'll get worse. This turn your other cheek doesn't go in Arizona. But we shore thought Ruff said worse than that. Though from him that's aplenty."

"How did you know?"

"Well, Charley told it. He was standing out here by the door last night an' he heard Ruff speak to you. Charley thinks a heap of you an' I reckon he hates Ruff. Besides, Charley stretches things. He shore riled Glenn, an' I want to say, my dear, you missed the best thing that's happened since you got here."

"Hurry—tell me," begged Carley, feeling the blood come to her face.

"I rode over to Ryan's place for dad, an' when I got there I knew nothing about what Ruff said to you," began Flo, and she took hold of Carley's hand. "Neither did dad. You see, Glenn hadn't got there yet. Well, just as the men had finished dipping a bunch of sheep Glenn came riding down, lickety cut.

"'Now what the hell's wrong with Glenn?' said dad, getting up from where we sat.

"Shore I knew Glenn was mad, though I never before saw him that way. He looked sort of grim an' black. . . . Well, he rode right down on us an' piled off. Dad yelled at him an' so did I. But Glenn made for the sheep pen. You know where we watched Haze Ruff an' Lorenzo slinging the sheep into the dip. Ruff was just about to climb out over the fence when Glenn leaped up on it.

"'Say, Ruff,' he said, sort of hard, 'Charley an' Ben tell me they heard you speak disrespectfully to Miss Burch last night.'

"Dad an' I ran to the fence, but before we could catch hold of Glenn he'd jumped down into the pen.

"'I'm not carin' much for what them herders say,' replied Ruff.

"'Do you deny it?' demanded Glenn.

"'I ain't denyin' nothin', Kilbourne,' growled Ruff. 'I might argue against me bein' disrespectful. That's a matter of opinion.'

"'You'll apologize for speaking to Miss Burch or I'll beat you up an' have Hutter fire you.'

"'Wal, Kilbourne, I never eat my words,' replied Ruff.

"Then Glenn knocked him flat. You ought to have heard that crack. Sounded like Charley hitting a steer with a club. Dad yelled: 'Look out, Glenn. He packs a gun!'—Ruff got up mad clear through I reckon. Then they mixed it. Ruff got in some swings, but he couldn't reach Glenn's face. An' Glenn batted him right an' left, every time in his ugly mug. Ruff got all bloody an' he cussed something awful. Glenn beat him against the fence an' then we all saw Ruff reach for a gun or knife. All the men yelled. An' shore I screamed. But Glenn saw as much as we saw. He got fiercer. He beat Ruff down to his knees an' swung on him hard. Deliberately knocked Ruff into the dip ditch. What a splash! It wet all of us. Ruff went out of sight. Then he rolled up like a huge hog. We were all scared now. That dip's rank poison, you know. Reckon Ruff knew that. He floundered along an' crawled up at the end. Anyone could see that he had mouth an' eyes tight shut. He began to grope an' feel around, trying to find the way to the pond. One of the men led him out. It was great to see him wade in the water an' wallow an' souse his head under. When he came out the men got in front of him an' stopped him. He shore looked bad. . . . An' Glenn called to him, 'Ruff, that sheep-dip won't go through your tough hide, but a bullet will!' "

Not long after this incident Carley started out on her usual afternoon ride, having arranged with Glenn to meet her on his return from work.

Toward the end of June Carley had advanced in her horsemanship to a point where Flo lent her one of her own mustangs. This change might not have had all to do with a wonderful difference in riding, but it seemed so to Carley. There was as much difference in horses as in people. This mustang she had ridden of late was of Navajo stock, but he had been born and raised and broken at Oak Creek. Carley had not yet discovered any objection on his part to do as she wanted him to. He liked what she liked, and most of all he liked to go. His color resembled a pattern of calico, and in accordance with Western ways his name was therefore Calico. Left to choose his own gait, Calico always dropped into a gentle pace which was so easy and comfortable and swinging that Carley never tired of it. Moreover, he did not shy at things lying in the road or rabbits darting from bushes or at the upwhirring of birds. Carley had grown attached to Calico before she realized she was drifting into it; and for Carley to care for anything or anybody was a serious matter, because it did not happen often and it lasted. She was exceedingly tenacious of affection.

June had almost passed and summer lay upon the lonely land. Such perfect and wonderful weather had never before been Carley's experience. The dawns broke cool, fresh, fragrant, sweet, and rosy, with a breeze that seemed of heaven rather than earth, and the air seemed tremulously full of the murmur of falling water and the melody of mocking birds. At the solemn noontides the great white sun glared down hot—so hot that it burned the skin, yet strangely was a pleasant burn. The waning afternoons were Carley's especial torment, when it seemed the sounds and winds of the day were tiring, and all things were seeking repose, and life must soften to an unthinking happiness. These hours troubled Carley because she wanted them to last, and because she knew for her this changing and transforming time could not last. So long as she did not think she was satisfied.

Maples and sycamores and oaks were in full foliage, and their bright greens contrasted softly with the dark shine of the pines. Through the spaces between brown tree trunks and the white-spotted boles of the sycamores gleamed the amber water of the creek. Always there was murmur of little rills and the musical dash of little rapids. On the surface of still, shady pools trout broke to make ever-widening ripples. Indian paintbrush, so brightly carmine in color, lent touch of fire to the green banks, and under the oaks, in cool dark nooks where mossy bowlders lined the stream, there were stately nodding yellow columbines. And high on the rock ledges shot up the wonderful mescal stalks, beginning to blossom, some with tints of gold and others with tones of red.

Riding along down the canyon, under its looming walls, Carley wondered that if unawares to her these physical aspects of Arizona could have become more significant than she realized. The thought had confronted her before. Here, as always, she fought it and denied it by the simple defense of elimination. Yet refusing to think of a thing when it seemed ever present was not going to do forever. Insensibly and subtly it might get a hold on her, never to be broken. Yet it was infinitely easier to dream than to think.

But the thought encroached upon her that it was not a dreamful habit of mind she had fallen into of late. When she dreamed or mused she lived vaguely and sweetly over past happy hours or dwelt in enchanted fancy upon a possible future. Carley had been told by a Columbia professor that she was a type of the present age—a modern young woman of materialistic mind. Be that as it might, she knew many things seemed loosening from the narrowness and tightness of her character, sloughing away like scales, exposing a new and strange and susceptible softness of fiber. And this blank habit of mind, when she did not think, and now realized that she was not dreaming, seemed to be the body of Carley Burch, and her heart and soul stripped of a shell. Nerve and emotion and spirit received something from her surroundings. She absorbed her environment. She felt. It was a delightful state. But when her own consciousness caused it to elude her, then she both resented and regretted. Anything that approached permanent attachment to this crude and untenanted West Carley would not tolerate for a moment. Reluctantly she admitted it had bettered her health, quickened her blood, and quite relegated Florida and the Adirondacks to little consideration.

"Well, as I told Glenn," soliloquized Carley, "every time I'm almost won over a little to Arizona she gives me a hard jolt. I'm getting near being mushy to-day. Now let's see what I'll get. I suppose that's my pessimism or materialism. Funny how Glenn keeps saying it's the jolts, the hard knocks, the fights that are best to remember afterward. I don't get that at all."

Five miles below West Fork a road branched off and climbed the left side of the canyon. It was a rather steep road, long and zigzaging, and full of rocks and ruts. Carley did not enjoy ascending it, but she preferred the going up to coming down. It took half an hour to climb.

Once up on the flat cedar-dotted desert she was met, full in the face, by a hot dusty wind coming from the south. Carley searched her pockets for her goggles, only to ascertain that she had forgotten them. Nothing, except a freezing sleety wind, annoyed and punished Carley so much as a hard puffy wind, full of sand and dust. Somewhere along the first few miles of this road she was to meet Glenn. If she turned back for any cause he would be worried, and, what concerned her more vitally, he would think she had not the courage to face a little dust. So Carley rode on.

The wind appeared to be gusty. It would blow hard awhile, then lull for a few moments. On the whole, however, it increased in volume and persistence until she was riding against a gale. She had now come to a bare, flat, gravelly region, scant of cedars and brush, and far ahead she could see a dull yellow pall rising high into the sky. It was a duststorm and it was sweeping down on the wings of that gale. Carley remembered that somewhere along this flat there was a log cabin which had before provided shelter for her and Flo when they were caught in a rainstorm. It seemed unlikely that she had passed by this cabin.

Resolutely she faced the gale and knew she had a task to find that refuge. If there had been a big rock or bushy cedar to offer shelter she would have welcomed it. But there was nothing. When the hard dusty gusts hit her, she found it absolutely necessary to shut her eyes. At intervals less windy she opened them, and rode on, peering through the yellow gloom for the cabin. Thus she got her eyes full of dust—an alkali dust that made them sting and smart. The fiercer puffs of wind carried pebbles large enough to hurt severely. Then the dust clogged her nose and sand got between her teeth. Added to these annoyances was a heat like a blast from a furnace. Carley perspired freely and that caked the dust on her face. She rode on, gradually growing more uncomfortable and miserable. Yet even then she did not utterly lose a sort of thrilling zest in being thrown upon her own responsibility. She could hate an obstacle, yet feel something of pride in holding her own against it.

Another mile of buffeting this increasing gale so exhausted Carley and wrought upon her nerves that she became nearly panic-stricken. It grew harder and harder not to turn back. At last she was about to give up when right at hand through the flying dust she espied the cabin. Riding behind it, she dismounted and tied the mustang to a post. Then she ran around to the door and entered.

What a welcome refuge! She was all right now, and when Glenn came along she would have added to her already considerable list another feat for which he would commend her. With aid of her handkerchief, and the tears that flowed so copiously, Carley presently freed her eyes of the blinding dust. But when she essayed to remove it from her face she discovered she would need a towel and soap and hot water.

The cabin appeared to be enveloped in a soft, swishing, hollow sound. It seeped and rustled. Then the sound lulled, only to rise again. Carley went to the door, relieved and glad to see that the duststorm was blowing by. The great sky-high pall of yellow had moved on to the north. Puffs of dust were whipping along the road, but no longer in one continuous cloud. In the west, low down the sun was sinking, a dull magenta in hue, quite weird and remarkable.

"I knew I'd get the jolt all right," soliloquized Carley, wearily, as she walked to a rude couch of poles and sat down upon it. She had begun to cool off. And there, feeling dirty and tired, and slowly wearing to the old depression, she composed herself to wait.

Suddenly she heard the clip-clop of hoofs. "There! that's Glenn," she cried, gladly, and rising, she ran to the door.

She saw a big bay horse bearing a burly rider. He discovered her at the same instant, and pulled his horse.

"Ho! Ho! if it ain't Pretty Eyes!" he called out, in gay, coarse voice.

Carley recognized the voice, and then the epithet, before her sight established the man as Haze Ruff. A singular stultifying shock passed over her.

"Wal, by all thet's lucky!" he said, dismounting. "I knowed we'd meet some day. I can't say I just laid fer you, but I kept my eyes open."

Manifestly he knew she was alone, for he did not glance into the cabin.

"I'm waiting for—Glenn," she said, with lips she tried to make stiff.

"Shore I reckoned thet," he replied, genially. "But he won't be along yet awhile."

He spoke with a cheerful inflection of tone, as if the fact

designated was one that would please her; and his swarthy, seamy face expanded into a good-humored, meaning smile. Then without any particular rudeness he pushed her back from the door, into the cabin, and stepped across the threshold.

"How dare—you!" cried Carley. A hot anger that stirred in her seemed to be beaten down and smothered by a cold shaking internal commotion, threatening collapse. This man loomed over her, huge, somehow monstrous in his brawny uncouth presence. And his knowing smile, and the hard, glinting twinkle of his light eyes, devilishly intelligent and keen, in no wise lessened the sheer brutal force of him physically. Sight of his bulk was enough to terrorize Carley.

"Me! Aw, I'm a darin' *hombre* an' a devil with the wimmin," he said, with a guffaw.

Carley could not collect her wits. The instant of his pushing her back into the cabin and following her had shocked her and almost paralyzed her will. If she saw him now any the less fearful she could not so quickly rally her reason to any advantage.

"Let me out of here," she demanded.

"Nope. I'm a-goin' to make a little love to you," he said, and he reached for her with great hairy hands.

Carley saw in them the strength that had so easily swung the sheep. She saw, too, that they were dirty, greasy hands. And they made her flesh creep.

"Glenn will kill—you," she panted.

"What fer?" he queried, in real or pretended surprise. "Aw, I know wimmin. You'll never tell him."

"Yes, I will."

"Wal, mebbe. I reckon you're lyin', Pretty Eyes," he replied, with a grin. "Anyhow, I'll take a chance."

"I tell you—he'll kill you," repeated Carley, backing away until her weak knees came against the couch.

"What fer, I ask you?" he demanded.

"For this—this insult."

"Huh! I'd like to know who's insulted you. Can't a man take an invitation to kiss an' hug a girl—without insultin' her?"

"Invitation! . . . Are you crazy?" queried Carley, bewildered.

"Nope, I'm not crazy, an' I shore said invitation. . . . I meant thet white shimmy dress you wore the night of Flo's party. Thet's my invitation to get a little fresh with you, Pretty Eyes!"

Carley could only stare at him. His words seemed to have some peculiar, unanswerable power.

"Wal, if it wasn't an invitation, what was it?" he asked, with another step that brought him within reach of her. He waited for her answer, which was not forthcoming.

"Wal, you're gettin' kinda pale around the gills," he went on, derisively. "I reckoned you was a real sport. . . . Come here."

He fastened one of his great hands in the front of her coat and gave her a pull. So powerful was it that Carley came hard against him, almost knocking her breathless. There he held her a moment and then put his other arm round her. It seemed to crush both breath and sense out of her. Suddenly limp, she sank strengthless. She seemed reeling in darkness. Then she felt herself thrust away from him with violence. She sank on the couch and her head and shoulders struck the wall.

"Say, if you're a-goin' to keel over like thet—I pass," declared Ruff, in disgust. "Can't you Eastern wimmin stand nothin'?"

Carley's eyes opened and beheld this man in an attitude of supremely derisive protest.

"You look like a sick kitten," he added. "When I get me a sweetheart or wife I want her to be a wild cat."

His scorn and repudiation of her gave Carley intense relief. She sat up and endeavored to collect her shattered nerves. Ruff gazed down at her with great disapproval and even disappointment.

"Say, did you have some fool idee I was a-goin' to kill you?" he queried, gruffly.

"I'm afraid—I did," faltered Carley. Her relief was a release; it was so strange that it was gratefulness.

"Wal, I reckon I wouldn't have hurt you. None of these flop-over Janes for me! . . . An' I'll give you a hunch, Pretty Eyes. You might have run acrost a fellar thet was no gentleman!"

Of all the amazing statements that had ever been made to Carley, this one seemed the most remarkable.

"What'd you wear thet onnatural white dress fer?" he demanded, as if he had a right to be her judge.

"Unnatural?" echoed Carley.

"Shore. Thet's what I said. Any woman's dress without top or bottom is onnatural. It's not right. Why, you looked like—like"—here he floundered for adequate expression— "like one of the devil's angels. An' I want to hear why you wore it."

"For the same reason I'd wear any dress," she felt forced to reply.

"Pretty Eyes, thet's a lie. An' you know it's a lie. You wore thet white dress to knock the daylights out of men. Only you ain't honest enough to say so. . . . Even me or my kind! Even us, who're dirt under your little feet. But all the same we're men, an' mebbe better men than you think. If you had to put that dress on, why didn't you stay in your room? Naw, you had to come down an' strut around an' show off your beauty. An' I ask you—if you're a nice girl like Flo Hutter—what'd you wear it fer?"

Carley not only was mute; she felt rise and burn in her a singular shame and surprise.

"I'm only a sheep dipper," went on Ruff, "but I ain't no fool. A fellar doesn't have to live East an' wear swell clothes to have sense. Mebbe you'll learn thet the West is bigger 'n you think. A man's a man East or West. But if your Eastern men stand for such dresses as thet white one they'd do well to come out West awhile, like your lover, Glenn Kilbourne. I've been rustlin' round here ten years, an' I never before seen a dress like yours—an' I never heerd of a girl bein' insulted, either. Mebbe you think I insulted you. Wal, I didn't. Fer I reckon *nothin'* could insult you in thet dress. . . . An' my last hunch is this, Pretty Eyes. You're not what a *hombre* like me calls either square or game. *Adios*."

His bulky figure darkened the doorway, passed out, and the light of the sky streamed into the cabin again. Carley sat staring. She heard Ruff's spurs tinkle, then the ring of steel on stirrup, a sodden leathery sound as he mounted, and after that a rapid pound of hoofs, quickly dying away.

He was gone. She had escaped something raw and violent. Dazedly she realized it, with unutterable relief. And she sat there slowly gathering the nervous force that had been shattered. Every word that he had uttered was stamped in startling characters upon her consciousness. But she was still under the deadening influence of shock. This raw experience was the worst the West had yet dealt her. It brought back former states of revulsion and formed them in one whole irrefutable and damning judgment that seemed to blot out the vaguely dawning and growing happy susceptibilities. It was, perhaps, just as well to have her mind reverted to realistic fact. The presence of Haze Ruff, the astounding truth of the contact with his huge sheep-defiled hands, had been profanation and degradation under which she sickened with fear and shame. Yet hovering back of her shame and rising anger seemed to be a pale, monstrous, and indefinable thought, insistent and accusing, with which she must sooner or later reckon. It might have been the voice of the new side of her nature, but at that moment of outraged womanhood, and of revolt against the West, she would not listen. It might, too, have been the still small voice of conscience. But decision of mind and energy coming to her then, she threw off the burden of emotion and perplexity, and forced herself into composure before the arrival of Glenn.

The dust had ceased to blow, although the wind had by no means died away. Sunset marked the west in old rose and gold, a vast flare. Carley espied a horseman far down the road, and presently recognized both rider and steed. He was coming fast. She went out and, mounting her mustang, she rode out to meet Glenn. It did not appeal to her to wait for him at the cabin; besides hoof tracks other than those made by her mustang might have been noticed by Glenn. Presently he came up to her and pulled his loping horse.

"Hello! I sure was worried," was his greeting, as his gloved hand went out to her. "Did you run into that sandstorm?"

"It ran into me, Glenn, and buried me," she laughed.

His fine eyes lingered on her face with glad and warm glance, and the keen, apprehensive penetration of a lover.

"Well, under all that dust you look scared," he said.

"Scared! I was worse than that. When I first ran into the flying dirt I was only afraid I'd lose my way—and my complexion. But when the worst of the storm hit me—then I feared I'd lose my breath."

"Did you face that sand and ride through it all?" he queried.

"No, not all. But enough. I went through the worst of it before I reached the cabin," she replied.

"Wasn't it great?"

"Yes—great bother and annoyance," she said, laconically.

Whereupon he reached with long arm and wrapped it round her as they rode side by side. Demonstrations of this nature were infrequent with Glenn. Despite losing one foot out of a stirrup and her seat in the saddle Carley rather encouraged it. He kissed her dusty face, and then set her back.

"By George! Carley, sometimes I think you've changed since you've been here," he said, with warmth. "To go through that sandstorm without one kick—one knock at my West!"

"Glenn, I always think of what Flo says—the worst is yet to come," replied Carley, trying to hide her unreasonable and tumultuous pleasure at words of praise from him.

"Carley Burch, you don't know yourself," he declared, enigmatically.

"What woman knows herself? But do you know me?"

"Not I. Yet sometimes I see depths in you—wonderful possibilities—submerged under your poise—under your fixed, complacent idle attitude toward life."

This seemed for Carley to be dangerously skating near thin ice, but she could not resist a retort: "Depths in me? Why I am a shallow, transparent stream like your West Fork! . . . And as for possibilities—may I ask what of them you imagine you see?"

"As a girl, before you were claimed by the world, you were earnest at heart. You had big hopes and dreams. And you had intellect, too. But you have wasted your talents, Carley. Having money, and spending it, living for pleasure, you have not realized your powers. . . . Now, don't look hurt. I'm not censuring you. It's just the way of modern life. And most of your friends have been more careless, thoughtless, useless than you. The aim of their existence is to be comfortable, free from work, worry, pain. They want pleasure, luxury. And what a pity it is! The best of you girls regard marriage as an escape, instead of responsibility.

You don't marry to get your shoulders, square against the old wheel of American progress—to help some man make good—to bring a troop of healthy American kids into the world. You bare your shoulders to the gaze of the multitude and like it best if you are strung with pearls."

"Glenn, you distress me when you talk like this," replied Carley, soberly. "You did not use to talk so. It seems to me you are bitter against women."

"Oh no, Carley! I am only sad," he said. "I only see where once I was blind. American women are the finest on earth, but as a race, if they don't change, they're doomed to extinction."

"How can you say such things?" demanded Carley, with spirit.

"I say them because they are true. Carley, on the level now, tell me how many of your immediate friends have children."

Put to a test, Carley rapidly went over in mind her circle of friends, with the result that she was somewhat shocked and amazed to realize how few of them were even married, and how the babies of her acquaintance were limited to three. It was not easy to admit this to Glenn.

"My dear," replied he, "if that does not show you the handwriting on the wall, nothing ever will."

"A girl has to find a husband, doesn't she?" asked Carley, roused to defense of her sex. "And if she's anybody she has to find one in her set. Well, husbands are not plentiful. Marriage certainly is not the end of existence these days. We have to get along somehow. The high cost of living is no inconsiderable factor to-day. Do you know that most of the better-class apartment houses in New York will not take children? Women are not all to blame. Take the speed mania. Men must have automobiles. I know one girl who wanted a baby, but her husband wanted a car. They couldn't afford both."

"Carley, I'm not blaming women more than men," returned Glenn. "I don't know that I blame them as a class. But in my own mind I have worked it all out. Every man or woman who is genuinely American should read the signs of the times, realize the crisis, and meet it in an American way. Otherwise we are done as a race. Money is God in the older countries. But it should never become God in America. If it does we will make the fall of Rome pale into insignificance."

"Glenn, let's put off the argument," appealed Carley. "I'm not—just up to fighting you to-day. Oh—you needn't smile. I'm not showing a yellow streak, as Flo puts it. I'll fight you some other time."

"You're right, Carley," he assented. "Here we are loafing six or seven miles from home. Let's rustle along."

Riding fast with Glenn was something Carley had only of late added to her achievements. She had greatest pride in it. So she urged her mustang to keep pace with Glenn's horse and gave herself up to the thrill of the motion and feel of wind and sense of flying along. At a good swinging lope Calico covered ground swiftly and did not tire. Carley rode the two miles to the rim of the canyon, keeping alongside of Glenn all the way. Indeed, for one long level stretch she and Glenn held hands. When they arrived at the descent, which necessitated slow and careful riding, she was hot and tingling and breathless, worked by the action into an exuberance of pleasure. Glenn complimented her riding as well as her rosy cheeks. There was indeed a sweetness in working at a task as she had worked to learn to ride in Western fashion. Every turn of her mind seemed to confront her with sobering antitheses of thought. Why had she come to love to ride down a lonely desert road, through ragged cedars where the wind whipped her face with fragrant wild breath, if at the same time she hated the West? Could she hate a country, however barren and rough, if it had saved the health and happiness of her future husband? Verily there were problems for Carley to solve.

Early twilight purple lay low in the hollows and clefts of the canyon. Over the western rim a pale ghost of the evening star seemed to smile at Carley, to bid her look and look. Like a strain of distant music, the dreamy hum of falling water, the murmur and melody of the stream, came again to Carley's sensitive ear.

"Do you love this?" asked Glenn, when they reached the green-forested canyon floor, with the yellow road winding away into the purple shadows.

"Yes, both the ride—and you," flashed Carley, contrarily. She knew he had meant the deep-walled canyon with its brooding solitude.

"But I want you to love Arizona," he said.

"Glenn, I'm a faithful creature. You should be glad of that. I love New York."

"Very well, then. Arizona to New York," he said, lightly brushing her cheek with his lips. And swerving back into his saddle, he spurred his horse and called back over his shoulder: "That mustang and Flo have beaten me many a time. Come on."

It was not so much his words as his tone and look that roused Carley. Had he resented her loyalty to the city of her nativity? Always there was a little rift in the lute. Had his tone and look meant that Flo might catch him if Carley could not? Absurd as the idea was, it spurred her to recklessness. Her mustang did not need any more than to know she wanted him to run. The road was of soft yellow earth flanked with green foliage and overspread by pines. In a moment she was racing at a speed she had never before half attained on a horse. Down the winding road Glenn's big steed sped, his head low, his stride tremendous, his action beautiful. But Carley saw the distance between them diminishing. Calico was overtaking the bay. She cried out in the thrilling excitement of the moment. Glenn saw her gaining and pressed his mount to greater speed. Still he could not draw away from Calico. Slowly the little mustang gained. It seemed to Carley that riding him required no effort at all. And at such fast pace, with the wind roaring in her ears, the walls of green vague and continuous in her sight, the sting of pine tips on cheek and neck, the yellow road streaming toward her, under her, there rose out of the depths of her, out of the tumult of her breast, a sense of glorious exultation. She closed in on Glenn. From the flying hoofs of his horse shot up showers of damp sand and gravel that covered Carley's riding habit and spattered in her face. She had to hold up a hand before her eyes. Perhaps this caused her to lose something of her confidence, or her swing in the saddle, for suddenly she realized she was not riding well. The pace was too fast for her inexperience. But nothing could have stopped her then. No fear or awkwardness of hers should be allowed to hamper that thoroughbred mustang. Carley felt that Calico understood the situation; or at least he knew he could catch and pass this big bay horse, and he intended to do it. Carley was hard put to it to hang on and keep the flying sand from blinding her.

When Calico drew alongside the bay horse and brought Carley breast to breast with Glenn, and then inch by inch forged ahead of him, Carley pealed out an exultant cry. Either it frightened Calico or inspired him, for he shot right ahead of Glenn's horse. Then he lost the smooth, wonderful action. He seemed hurtling through space at the expense of tremendous muscular action. Carley could feel it. She lost her equilibrium. She seemed rushing through a blurred green and black aisle of the forest with a gale in her face. Then, with a sharp jolt, a break, Calico plunged to the sand. Carley felt herself propelled forward out of the saddle into the air, and down to strike with a sliding, stunning force that ended in sudden dark oblivion.

Upon recovering consciousness she first felt a sensation of oppression in her chest and a dull numbness of her whole body. When she opened her eyes she saw Glenn bending over her, holding her head on his knee. A wet, cold, reviving sensation evidently came from the handkerchief with which he was mopping her face.

"Carley, you can't be hurt—really!" he was ejaculating, in eager hope. "It was some spill. But you lit on the sand and slid. You can't be hurt."

The look of his eyes, the tone of his voice, the feel of his hands were such that Carley chose for a moment to pretend to be very badly hurt indeed. It was worth taking a header to get so much from Glenn Kilbourne. But she believed she had suffered no more than a severe bruising and scraping.

"Glenn—dear," she whispered, very low and very eloquently. "I think—my back—is broken. . . . You'll be free—soon."

Glenn gave a terrible start and his face turned a deathly white. He burst out with quavering, inarticulate speech.

Carley gazed up at him and then closed her eyes. She could not look at him while carrying on such deceit. Yet the sight of him and the feel of him then were inexpressibly blissful to her. What she needed most was assurance of his love. She had it. Beyond doubt, beyond morbid fancy, the truth had proclaimed itself, filling her heart with joy.

Suddenly she flung her arms up around his neck. "Oh—Glenn! It was too good a chance to miss! . . . I'm not hurt a bit."

CHAPTER VII

The day came when Carley asked Mrs. Hutter: "Will you please put up a nice lunch for Glenn and me? I'm going to walk down to his farm where he's working, and surprise him."

"That's a downright fine idea," declared Mrs. Hutter, and forthwith bustled away to comply with Carley's request.

So presently Carley found herself carrying a bountiful basket on her arm, faring forth on an adventure that both thrilled and depressed her. Long before this hour something about Glenn's work had quickened her pulse and given rise to an inexplicable admiration. That he was big and strong enough to do such labor made her proud: that he might want to go on doing it made her ponder and brood.

The morning resembled one of the rare Eastern days in June, when the air appeared flooded by rich thick amber light. Only the sun here was hotter and the shade cooler.

Carley took to the trail below where West Fork emptied its golden-green waters into Oak Creek. The red walls seemed to dream and wait under the blaze of the sun; the heat lay like a blanket over the still foliage; the birds were quiet; only the murmuring stream broke the silence of the canyon. Never had Carley felt more the isolation and solitude of Oak Creek Canyon. Far indeed from the madding crowd! Only Carley's stubbornness kept her from acknowledging the sense of peace that enveloped her—that and the consciousness of her own discontent. What would it be like to come to this canyon—to give up to its enchantments? That, like many another disturbing thought, had to go unanswered, to be driven into the closed chambers of Carley's mind, there to germinate subconsciously, and stalk forth some day to overwhelm her.

The trail led along the creek, threading a maze of bowlders, passing into the shade of cotton-woods, and crossing sun-flecked patches of sand. Carley's every step seemed to become slower. Regrets were assailing her. Long indeed had she overstayed her visit to the West. She must not linger there indefinitely. And mingled with misgiving was a surprise that she had not tired of Oak Creek. In spite of all, and of the dislike she vaunted to herself, the truth stared at her—she was not tired.

The long-delayed visit to see Glenn working on his own farm must result in her talking to him about his work; and in a way not quite clear she regretted the necessity for it. To disapprove of Glenn! She received faint intimations of wavering, of uncertainty, of vague doubt. But these were cried down by the dominant and habitable voice of her personality.

Presently through the shaded and shadowed breadth of the belt of forest she saw gleams of a sunlit clearing. And crossing this space to the border of trees she peered forth, hoping to espy Glenn at his labors. She saw an old shack, and irregular lines of rude fence built of poles of all sizes and shapes, and several plots of bare yellow ground, leading up toward the west side of the canyon wall. Could this clearing be Glenn's farm? Surely she had missed it or had not gone far enough. This was not a farm, but a slash in the forested level of the canyon floor, bare and somehow hideous. Dead trees were standing in the lots. They had been ringed deeply at the base by an ax, to kill them, and so prevent their foliage from shading the soil. Carley saw a long pile of rocks that evidently had been carried from the plowed ground. There was no neatness, no regularity, although there was abundant evidence of toil. To clear that rugged space, to fence it, and plow it, appeared at once to Carley an extremely strenuous and useless task. Carley persuaded herself that this must be the plot of ground belonging to the herder Charley, and she was about to turn on down the creek when far up under the bluff she espied a man. He was stalking along and bending down, stalking along and bending down. She recognized Glenn. He was planting something in the yellow soil.

Curiously Carley watched him, and did not allow her mind to become concerned with a somewhat painful swell of her heart. What a stride he had! How vigorous he looked, and earnest! He was as intent upon this job as if he had been a rustic. He might have been failing to do it well, but he most certainly was doing it conscientiously. Once he had said to her that a man should never be judged by the result of his labors, but by the nature of his effort. A man might strive with all his heart and strength, yet fail. Carley watched him striding along and bending down, absorbed in his task, unmindful of the glaring hot sun, and somehow to her singularly detached from the life wherein he had once moved and to which she yearned to take him back. Suddenly an unaccountable flashing query assailed her conscience: How dare she want to take him back? She seemed as shocked as if some stranger had accosted her. What was this dimming of her eye, this inward tremulousness; this dammed tide beating at an unknown and riveted gate of her intelligence? She felt more then than she dared to face. She struggled against something in herself. The old habit of mind instinctively resisted the new, the strange. But she did not come off wholly victorious. The Carley Burch whom she recognized as of old, passionately hated this life and work of Glenn Kilbourne's, but the rebel self, an unaccountable and defiant Carley, loved him all the better for them.

Carley drew a long deep breath before she called Glenn. This meeting would be momentous and she felt no absolute surety of herself.

Manifestly he was surprised to hear her call, and, dropping his sack and implement, he hurried across the tilled ground, sending up puffs of dust. He vaulted the rude fence of poles, and upon sight of her called out lustily. How big and virile he looked! Yet he was gaunt and strained. It struck Carley that he had not looked so upon her arrival at Oak Creek. Had she worried him? The query gave her a pang.

"Sir Tiller of the Fields," said Carley, gayly, "see, your dinner! *I* brought it and *I* am going to share it."

"You old darling!" he replied, and gave her an embrace that left her cheek moist with the sweat of his. He smelled of dust and earth and his body was hot. "I wish to God it could be true for always!"

His loving, bearish onslaught and his words quite silenced Carley. How at critical moments he always said the thing that hurt her or inhibited her! She essayed a smile as she drew back from him.

"It's sure good of you," he said, taking the basket. "I was thinking I'd be through work sooner to-day, and was sorry I had not made a date with you. . . . Come, we'll find a place to sit."

Whereupon he led her back under the trees to a half-sunny, half-shady bench of rock overhanging the stream. Great pines overshadowed a still, eddying pool. A number of brown butterflies hovered over the water, and small trout floated like spotted feathers just under the surface. Drowsy summer enfolded the sylvan scene.

Glenn knelt at the edge of the brook, and, plunging his hands in, he splashed like a huge dog and bathed his hot face and head, and then turned to Carley with gay words and laughter, while he wiped himself dry with a large red scarf. Carley was not proof against the virility of him then, and at the moment, no matter what it was that had made him the man he looked, she loved it.

"I'll sit in the sun," he said, designating a place. "When you're hot you mustn't rest in the shade, unless you've coat or sweater. But you sit here in the shade."

"Glenn, that'll put us too far apart," complained Carley. "I'll sit in the sun with you."

The delightful simplicity and happiness of the ensuing hour was something Carley believed she would never forget.

"There! we've licked the platter clean," she said. "What starved bears we were! . . . I wonder if I shall enjoy eating—when I get home. I used to be so finnicky and picky."

"Carley, don't talk about home," said Glenn, appealingly.

"You dear old farmer, I'd love to stay here—and just dream—forever," replied Carley, earnestly. "But I came on purpose to talk seriously."

"Oh, you did! About what?" he returned, with some quick, indefinable change of tone and expression.

"Well, first about your work. I know I hurt your feelings when I wouldn't listen. But I wasn't ready. I wanted to—to just be gay with you for a while. Don't think I wasn't interested. I was. And now, I'm ready to hear all about it—and everything."

She smiled at him bravely, and she knew that unless

some unforeseen shock upset her composure, she would be able to conceal from him anything which might hurt his feelings.

"You do look serious," he said, with keen eyes on her.

"Just what are your business relations with Hutter?" she inquired.

"I'm simply working for him," replied Glenn. "My aim is to get an interest in his sheep, and I expect to, some day. We have some plans. And one of them is the development of that Deep Lake section. You remember—you were with us. The day Spillbeans spilled you?"

"Yes, I remember. It was a pretty place," she replied.

Carley did not tell him that for a month past she had owned the Deep Lake section of six hundred and forty acres. She had, in fact, instructed Hutter to purchase it, and to keep the transaction a secret for the present. Carley had never been able to understand the impulse that prompted her to do it. But as Hutter had assured her it was a remarkably good investment on very little capital, she had tried to persuade herself of its advantages. Back of it all had been an irresistible desire to be able some day to present to Glenn this ranch site he loved. She had concluded he would never wholly dissociate himself from this West; and as he would visit it now and then, she had already begun forming plans of her own. She could stand a month in Arizona at long intervals.

"Hutter and I will go into cattle raising some day," went on Glenn. "And that Deep Lake place is what I want for myself."

"What work are you doing for Hutter?" asked Carley.

"Anything from building fence to cutting timber," laughed Glenn. "I've not yet the experience to be a foreman like Lee Stanton. Besides, I have a little business all my own. I put all my money in that."

"You mean here—this—this farm?"

"Yes. And the stock I'm raising. You see I have to feed corn. And believe me, Carley, those cornfields represent some job."

"I can well believe that," replied Carley. "You—you looked it."

"Oh, the hard work is over. All I have to do now is to plant and keep the weeds out."

"Glenn, do sheep eat corn?"

"I plant corn to feed my hogs."

"Hogs?" she echoed, vaguely.

"Yes, hogs," he said, with quiet gravity. "The first day you visited my cabin I told you I raised hogs, and I fried my own ham for your dinner."

"Is that what you—put your money in?"

"Yes. And Hutter says I've done well."

"*Hogs!*" ejaculated Carley, aghast.

"My dear, are you growing dull of comprehension?" retorted Glenn. "H-o-g-s." He spelled the word out. "I'm in the hog-raising business, and pretty blamed well pleased over my success so far."

Carley caught herself in time to quell outwardly a shock of amaze and revulsion. She laughed, and exclaimed against her stupidity. The look of Glenn was no less astounding than the content of his words. He was actually proud of his work. Moreover, he showed not the least sign that he had any idea such information might be startlingly obnoxious to his fiancée.

"Glenn! It's so—so queer," she ejaculated. "That you—Glenn Kilbourne—should ever go in for—for hogs! . . . It's unbelievable. How'd you ever—ever happen to do it?"

"By Heaven! you're hard on me!" he burst out, in sudden dark, fierce passion. "How'd I ever happen to do it? . . . *What* was there left for me? I gave my soul and heart and body to the government—to fight for my country. I came home a wreck. *What* did my government do for me? *What* did my employers do for me? *What* did the people I fought for do for me? . . . Nothing—so help me God—*nothing!* . . . I got a ribbon and a bouquet—a little applause for an hour—and then the sight of me sickened my countrymen. I was broken and used. I was absolutely forgotten. . . . But my body, my life, my soul meant *all* to me. My future was ruined, but I wanted to live. I had killed men who never harmed me—I was not fit to die. . . . I *tried* to live. So I fought out my battle alone. Alone! . . . No one understood. No one cared. . . . I came West to keep from dying of consumption in sight of the indifferent mob for whom I had sacrificed myself. I chose to die on my feet away off alone somewhere. . . . But I got well. And what *made* me well—and *saved* my soul—was the first work that offered. *Raising and tending hogs!*"

The dead whiteness of Glenn's face, the lightning scorn of his eyes, the grim, stark strangeness of him then had for Carley a terrible harmony with this passionate denunciation of her, of her kind, of the America for whom he had lost all.

"Oh, Glenn!—forgive—me!" she faltered. "I was only— talking. What do I know? . . . Oh, I am blind—blind and little!"

She could not bear to face him for a moment, and she hung her head. Her intelligence seemed concentrating swift, wild thoughts round the shock to her consciousness. By that terrible expression of his face, by those thundering words of scorn, would she come to realize the mighty truth of his descent into the abyss and his rise to the heights. Vaguely she began to see. An awful sense of her deadness, of her soul-blighting selfishness, began to dawn upon her as something monstrous out of dim, gray obscurity. She trembled under the reality of thoughts that were not new. How she had babbled about Glenn and the crippled soldiers! How she had imagined she sympathized! But she had only been a vain, worldly, complacent, effusive little fool. She had here the shock of her life, and she sensed a greater one, impossible to grasp.

"Carley, that was coming to you," said Glenn, presently, with deep, heavy expulsion of breath.

"I only know I love you—more—more," she cried, wildly, looking up and wanting desperately to throw herself in his arms.

"I guess you do—a little," he replied. "Sometimes I feel you are a kid. Then again you represent the world—your world with its age-old custom—its unalterable . . . But, Carley, let's get back to my work."

"Yes—yes," exclaimed Carley, gladly. "I'm ready to—to go pet your hogs—anything."

"By George! I'll take you up," he declared. "I'll bet you won't go near one of my hogpens."

"Lead me to it!" she replied, with a hilarity that was only a nervous reversion of her state.

"Well, maybe I'd better hedge on the bet," he said, laughing again. "You have more in you than I suspect. You sure fooled me when you stood for the sheep-dip. But, come on, I'll take you anyway."

So that was how Carley found herself walking arm in arm with Glenn down the canyon trail. A few moments of action gave her at least an appearance of outward composure. And the state of her emotion was so strained and intense that her slightest show of interest must deceive Glenn into thinking her eager, responsive, enthusiastic. It certainly appeared to loosen his tongue. But Carley knew she was farther from normal than ever before in her life, and that the subtle, inscrutable woman's intuition of her presaged another shock. Just as she had seemed to change, so had the aspects of the canyon undergone some illusive transformation. The beauty of green foliage and amber stream and brown tree trunks and gray rocks and red walls was there; and the summer drowsiness and languor lay as deep; and the loneliness and solitude brooded with its same eternal significance. But some nameless enchantment, perhaps of hope, seemed no longer to encompass her. A blow had fallen upon her, the nature of which only time could divulge.

Glenn led her around the clearing and up to the base of the west wall, where against a shelving portion of the cliff had been constructed a rude fence of poles. It formed three sides of a pen, and the fourth side was solid rock. A bushy cedar tree stood in the center. Water flowed from under the cliff, which accounted for the boggy condition of the red earth. This pen was occupied by a huge sow and a litter of pigs.

Carley climbed on the fence and sat there while Glenn leaned over the top pole and began to wax eloquent on a subject evidently dear to his heart. To-day of all days Carley made an inspiring listener. Even the shiny, muddy, suspicious old sow in no wise daunted her fictitious courage. That filthy pen of mud a foot deep, and of odor rancid, had no terrors for her. With an arm round Glenn's shoulder she watched the rooting and squealing little pigs, and was amused and interested, as if they were far removed from the vital issue of the hour. But all the time as she looked and laughed, and encouraged Glenn to talk, there seemed to be a strange, solemn, oppressive knocking at her heart. Was it only the beat—beat—beat of blood?

"There were twelve pigs in that litter," Glenn was saying, "and now you see there are only nine. I've lost three. Mountain lions, bears, coyotes, wild cats are all likely to steal a pig. And at first I was sure one of these varmints had been robbing me. But as I could not find any tracks, I knew I had to lay the blame on something else. So I kept watch pretty closely in day-time, and at night I shut the pigs up in the corner there, where you see I've built a pen.

Yesterday I heard squealing—and, by George! I saw an eagle flying off with one of my pigs. Say, I was mad. A great old bald-headed eagle—the regal bird you see with America's stars and stripes—had degraded himself to the level of a coyote. I ran for my rifle, and I took some quick shots at him as he flew up. Tried to hit him, too, but I failed. And the old rascal hung on to my pig. I watched him carry it to that sharp crag way up there on the rim."

"Poor little piggy!" exclaimed Carley. "To think of our American emblem—our stately bird of noble warlike mien—our symbol of lonely grandeur and freedom of the heights—think of him being a robber of pigpens!—Glenn, I begin to appreciate the many-sidedness of things. Even my hide-bound narrowness is susceptible to change. It's never too late to learn. This should apply to the Society for the Preservation of the American Eagle."

Glenn led her along the base of the wall to three other pens, in each of which was a fat old sow with a litter. And at the last enclosure, that owing to dry soil was not so dirty, Glenn picked up a little pig and held it squealing out to Carley as she leaned over the fence. It was fairly white and clean, a little pink and fuzzy, and certainly cute with its curled tail.

"Carley Burch, take it in your hands," commanded Glenn.

The feat seemed monstrous and impossible of accomplishment for Carley. Yet such was her temper at the moment that she would have undertaken anything.

"Why, shore I will, as Flo says," replied Carley, extending her ungloved hands. "Come here, piggy. I christen you Pinky." And hiding an almost insupportable squeamishness from Glenn, she took the pig in her hands and fondled it.

"By George!" exclaimed Glenn, in huge delight. "I wouldn't have believed it. Carley, I hope you tell your fastidious and immaculate Morrison that you held one of my pigs in your beautiful hands."

"Wouldn't it please you more to tell him yourself?" asked Carley.

"Yes, it would," declared Glenn, grimly.

This incident inspired Glenn to a Homeric narration of his hog-raising experience. In spite of herself the content of his talk interested her. And as for the effect upon her of his singular enthusiasm, it was deep and compelling. The little-boned Berkshire razor-back hogs grew so large and fat and heavy that their bones broke under their weight. The Duroc Jerseys were the best breed in that latitude, owing to their larger and stronger bones, that enabled them to stand up under the greatest accumulation of fat.

Glenn told of his droves of pigs running wild in the canyon below. In summertime they fed upon vegetation, and at other seasons on acorns, roots, bugs, and grubs. Acorns, particularly, were good and fattening feed. They ate cedar and juniper berries, and piñon nuts. And therefore they lived off the land, at little or no expense to the owner. The only loss was from beasts and birds of prey. Glenn showed Carley how a profitable business could soon be established. He meant to fence off side canyons and to segregate droves of his hogs, and to raise abundance of corn for winter feed. At that time there was a splendid market for hogs, a condition Hutter claimed would continue indefinitely in a growing country. In conclusion Glenn eloquently told how in his necessity he had accepted gratefully the humblest of labors, to find in the hard pursuit of it a rejuvenation of body and mind, and a promise of independence and prosperity.

When he had finished, and excused himself to go repair a weak place in the corral fence, Carley sat silent, wrapped in strange meditation.

Whither had faded the vulgarity and ignominy she had attached to Glenn's raising of hogs? Gone—like other miasmas of her narrow mind! Partly she understood him now. She shirked consideration of his sacrifice to his country. That must wait. But she thought of his work, and the more she thought the less she wondered.

First he had labored with his hands. What infinite meaning lay unfolding to her vision! Somewhere out of it all came the conception that man was intended to earn his bread by the sweat of his brow. But there was more to it than that. By that toil and sweat, by the friction of horny palms, by the expansion and contraction of muscle, by the acceleration of blood, something great and enduring, something physical and spiritual, came to a man. She understood then why she would have wanted to surrender herself to a man made manly by toil; she understood how a woman instinctively leaned toward the protection of a man who had used his hands—who had strength and red blood and virility—who could fight like the progenitors of the race. Any toil was splendid that served this end for any man. It all went back to the survival of the fittest. And suddenly Carley thought of Morrison. He could dance and dangle attendance upon her, and amuse her—but how would he have acquitted himself in a moment of peril? She had her doubts. Most assuredly he could not have beaten down for her a ruffian like Haze Ruff. What then should be the significance of a man for a woman?

Carley's querying and answering mind reverted to Glenn. He had found a secret in this seeking for something through the labor of hands. All development of body must come through exercise of muscles. The virility of cell in tissue and bone depended upon that. Thus he had found in toil the pleasure and reward athletes had in their desultory training. But when a man learned this secret the need of work must become permanent. Did this explain the law of the Persians—that every man was required to sweat every day?

Carley tried to picture to herself Glenn's attitude of mind when he had first gone to work here in the West. Resolutely she now denied her shrinking, cowardly sensitiveness. She would go to the root of this matter, if she had intelligence enough. Crippled, ruined in health, wrecked and broken by an inexplicable war, soul-blighted by the heartless, callous neglect of government and public, on the verge of madness at the insupportable facts, he had yet been wonderful enough, true enough to himself and God, to fight for life with the instinct of a man, to fight for his mind with a noble and unquenchable faith. Alone—indeed he had been alone! And by some miracle beyond the power of understanding he had found day by day in his painful efforts some hope and strength to go on. He could not have had any illusions. For Glenn Kilbourne the health and happiness and success most men held so dear must have seemed impossible. His slow, daily, tragic, and terrible task must have been something he owed himself. Not for Carley Burch! She like all the others had failed him. How Carley shuddered in confession of that! Not for the country which had used him and cast him off! Carley divined now, as if by a flash of lightning, the meaning of Glenn's strange, cold, scornful, and aloof manner when he had encountered young men of his station, as capable and as strong as he, who had escaped the service of the army. For him these men did not exist. They were less than nothing. They had waxed fat on lucrative jobs; they had basked in the presence of girls whose brothers and lovers were in the trenches or on the turbulent sea, exposed to the ceaseless dread and almost ceaseless toil of war. If Glenn's spirit had lifted him to endurance of war for the sake of others, how then could it fail him in a precious duty of fidelity to himself? Carley could see him day by day toiling in his lonely canyon—plodding to his lonely cabin. He had been playing the game—fighting it out alone as surely he knew his brothers of like misfortune were fighting.

So Glenn Kilbourne loomed heroically in Carley's transfigured sight. He was one of Carlyle's battle-scarred warriors. Out of his travail he had climbed on stepping-stones of his dead self. *Resurgam!* That had been his unquenchable cry. Who had heard it? Only the solitude of his lonely canyon, only the waiting, dreaming, watching walls, only the silent midnight shadows, only the white, blinking, passionless stars, only the wild creatures of his haunts, only the moaning wind in the pines—only these had been with him in his agony. How near were these things to God?

Carley's heart seemed full to bursting. Not another single moment could her mounting love abide in a heart that held a double purpose. How bitter the assurance that she had not come West to help him! It was self, self, all self that had actuated her. Unworthy indeed was she of the love of this man. Only a lifetime of devotion to him could acquit her in the eyes of her better self. Sweetly and madly raced the thrill and tumult of her blood. There must be only one outcome to her romance. Yet the next instant there came a dull throbbing—an oppression which was pain—an impondering vague thought of catastrophe. Only the fearfulness of love perhaps!

She saw him complete his task and wipe his brown moist face and stride toward her, coming nearer, tall and erect with something added to his soldierly bearing, with a light in his eyes she could no longer bear.

The moment for which she had waited more than two months had come at last.

"Glenn—when will you go back East?" she asked, tensely and low.

The instant the words were spent upon her lips she realized that he had always been waiting and prepared for this question that had been so terrible for her to ask.

"Carley," he replied gently, though his voice rang, "I am never going back East."

An inward quivering hindered her articulation.

"Never?" she whispered.

"Never to live, or stay any while," he went on. "I might go some time for a little visit. . . . But never to live."

"Oh—Glenn!" she gasped, and her hands fluttered out to him. The shock was driving home. No amaze, no incredulity succeeded her reception of the fact. It was a slow stab. Carley felt the cold blanch of her skin. "Then—this is it—the something I felt strange between us?"

"Yes, I knew—and you never asked me," he replied.

"That was it? All the time you knew," she whispered, huskily. "You knew. . . . *I'd never—marry you—never live out here?"*

"Yes, Carley, I knew you'd never be woman enough— *American enough*—to help me reconstruct my broken life out here in the West," he replied, with a sad and bitter smile.

That flayed her. An insupportable shame and wounded vanity and clamoring love contended for dominance of her emotions. Love beat down all else.

"Dearest—I beg of you—don't break my heart," she implored.

"I love you, Carley," he answered, steadily, with piercing eyes on hers.

"Then come back—home—home with me."

"No. If you love me you will be my wife."

"Love you! Glenn, I worship you," she broke out, passionately. "But I could not live here—*I could not*."

"Carley, did you ever read of the woman who said, 'Whither thou goest, there will I go' . . . ?"

"Oh, don't be ruthless! Don't judge me. . . . I never dreamed of this. I came West to take you back."

"My dear, it was a mistake," he said, gently, softening to her distress. "I'm sorry I did not write you more plainly. But, Carley, I could not ask you to share this—this wilderness home with me. I don't ask it now. I always knew you couldn't do it. Yet you've changed so—that I hoped against hope. Love makes us blind even to what we see."

"Don't try to spare me. I'm slight and miserable. I stand abased in my own eyes. I thought I loved you. But I must love best the crowd—people—luxury—fashion—the damned round of things I was born to."

"Carley, you will realize their insufficiency too late," he replied, earnestly. "The things you were born to are love, work, children, happiness."

"Don't! don't! . . . they are hollow mockery for me," she cried, passionately. "Glenn, it is the end. It must come—quickly. . . . You are free."

"I do not ask to be free. Wait. Go home and look at it again with different eyes. Think things over. Remember what came to me out of the West. I will always love you—and I will be here—hoping—"

"I—I cannot listen," she returned, brokenly, and she clenched her hands tightly to keep from wringing them. "I—I cannot face you. . . . Here is—your ring. . . . You—are—free. . . . Don't stop me—don't come. . . . Oh, Glenn, good-by!"

With breaking heart she whirled away from him and hurried down the slope toward the trail. The shade of the forest enveloped her. Peering back through the trees, she saw Glenn standing where she had left him, as if already stricken by the loneliness that must be his lot. A sob broke from Carley's throat. She hated herself. She was in a terrible state of conflict. Decision had been wrenched from her, but she sensed unending strife. She dared not look back again. Stumbling and breathless, she hurried on. How changed the atmosphere and sunlight and shadow of the canyon! The looming walls had pitiless eyes for her flight. When she crossed the mouth of West Fork an almost irresistible force breathed to her from under the stately pines.

An hour later she had bidden farewell to the weeping Mrs. Hutter, and to the white-faced Flo, and Lolomi Lodge, and the murmuring waterfall, and the haunting loneliness of Oak Creek Canyon.

CHAPTER VIII

At Flagstaff, where Carley arrived a few minutes before train time, she was too busily engaged with tickets and baggage to think of herself or of the significance of leaving Arizona. But as she walked into the Pullman she overheard a passenger remark, "Regular old Arizona sunset," and that shook her heart. Suddenly she realized she had come to love the colorful sunsets, to watch and wait for them. And bitterly she thought how that was her way—to learn the value of something when it was gone.

The jerk and start of the train affected her with singular depressing shock. She had burned her last bridge behind her. Had she unconsciously hoped for some incredible reversion of Glenn's mind or of her own? A sense of irreparable loss flooded over her—the first check to shame and humiliation.

From her window she looked out to the southwest. Somewhere across the cedar and pine-greened uplands lay Oak Creek Canyon, going to sleep in its purple and gold shadows of sunset. Banks of broken clouds hung to the horizon, like continents and islands and reefs set in a turquoise sea. Shafts of sunlight streaked down through creamy-edged and purple-centered clouds. Vast flare of gold dominated the sunset background.

When the train rounded a curve Carley's strained vision became filled with the upheaved bulk of the San Francisco Mountains. Ragged gray grass slopes and green forests on end, and black fringed sky lines, all pointed to the sharp clear peaks spearing the sky. And as she watched, the peaks slowly flushed with sunset hues, and the sky flared golden, and the strength of the eternal mountains stood out in sculptured sublimity. Every day for two months and more Carley had watched these peaks, at all hours, in every mood; and they had unconsciously become a part of her thought. The train was relentlessly whirling her eastward. Soon they must become a memory. Tears blurred her sight. Poignant regret seemed added to the anguish she was suffering. Why had she not learned sooner to see the glory of the mountains, to appreciate the beauty and solitude? Why had she not understood herself?

The next day through New Mexico she followed magnificent ranges and valleys—so different from the country she had seen coming West—so supremely beautiful that she wondered if she had only acquired the harvest of a seeing eye.

But it was at sunset of the following day, when the train was speeding down the continental slope of prairie-land beyond the Rockies, that the West took its ruthless revenge.

Masses of strange cloud and singular light upon the green prairie, and a luminosity in the sky, drew Carley to the platform of her car, which was the last of the train. There she stood, gripping the iron gate, feeling the wind whip her hair and the iron-tracked ground speed from under her, spellbound and stricken at the sheer wonder and glory of the firmament, and the mountain range that it canopied so exquisitely.

A rich and mellow light, singularly clear, seemed to

flood out of some unknown source. For the sun was hidden. The clouds just above Carley hung low, and they were like thick, heavy smoke, mushrooming, coalescing, forming and massing, of strange yellow cast of mauve. It shaded westward into heliotrope and this into a purple so royal, so matchless and rare that Carley understood why the purple of the heavens could never be reproduced in paint. Here the cloud mass thinned and paled, and a tint of rose began to flush the billowy, flowery, creamy white. Then came the surpassing splendor of this cloud pageant—a vast canopy of shell pink, a sun-fired surface like an opal sea, rippled and webbed, with the exquisite texture of an Oriental fabric, pure, delicate, lovely as no work of human hands could be. It mirrored all the warm, pearly tints of the inside whorl of the tropic nautilus. And it ended abruptly, a rounded depth of bank, on a broad stream of clear sky, intensely blue, transparently blue, as if through the lambent depths shone the infinite firmament. The lower edge of this stream took the golden lightning of the sunset and was notched for all its horizon-long length by the wondrous white glistening-peaked range of the Rockies. Far to the north, standing aloof from the range, loomed up the grand black bulk and noble white dome of Pikes Peak.

Carley watched the sunset transfiguration of cloud and sky and mountain until all were cold and gray. And then she returned to her seat, thoughtful and sad, feeling that the West had mockingly flung at her one of its transient moments of loveliness.

Nor had the West wholly finished with her. Next day the mellow gold of the Kansas wheat fields, endless and boundless as a sunny sea, rich, waving in the wind, stretched away before her aching eyes for hours and hours. Here was the promise fulfilled, the bountiful harvest of the land, the strength of the West. The great middle state had a heart of gold.

East of Chicago Carley began to feel that the long days and nights of riding, the ceaseless turning of the wheels, the constant and wearing stress of emotion, had removed her an immeasurable distance of miles and time and feeling from the scene of her catastrophe. Many days seemed to have passed. Many had been the hours of her bitter regret and anguish.

Indiana and Ohio, with their green pastoral farms, and numberless villages, and thriving cities, denoted a country far removed and different from the West, and an approach to the populous East. Carley felt like a wanderer coming home. She was restlessly and impatiently glad. But her weariness of body and mind, and the close atmosphere of the car, rendered her extreme discomfort. Summer had laid its hot hand on the low country east of the Mississippi.

Carley had wired her aunt and two of her intimate friends to meet her at the Grand Central Station. This reunion soon to come affected Carley in recurrent emotions of relief, gladness, and shame. She did not sleep well, and arose early, and when the train reached Albany she felt that she could hardly endure the tedious hours. The majestic Hudson and the palatial mansions on the wooded bluffs proclaimed to Carley that she was back in the East. How long a time seemed to have passed! Either she was not the same or the aspect of everything had changed. But she believed that as soon as she got over the ordeal of meeting her friends, and was home again, she would soon see things rationally.

At last the train sheered away from the broad Hudson and entered the environs of New York. Carley sat perfectly still, to all outward appearances a calm, superbly-poised New York woman returning home, but inwardly raging with contending tides. In her own sight she was a disgraceful failure, a prodigal sneaking back to the ease and protection of loyal friends who did not know her truly. Every familiar landmark in the approach to the city gave her a thrill, yet a vague unsatisfied something lingered after each sensation.

Then the train with rush and roar crossed the Harlem River to enter New York City. As one waking from a dream Carley saw the blocks and squares of gray apartment houses and red buildings, the miles of roofs and chimneys, the long hot glaring streets full of playing children and cars. Then above the roar of the train sounded the high notes of a hurdy-gurdy. Indeed she was home. Next to startle her was the dark tunnel, and then the slowing of the train to a stop. As she walked behind a porter up the long incline toward the station gate her legs seemed to be dead.

In the circle of expectant faces beyond the gate she saw her aunt's, eager and agitated, then the handsome pale face of Eleanor Harmon, and beside her the sweet thin one of Beatrice Lovell. As they saw her how quick the change from expectancy to joy! It seemed they all rushed upon her, and embraced her, and exclaimed over her together. Carley never recalled what she said. But her heart was full.

"Oh, how perfectly stunning you look!" cried Eleanor, backing away from Carley and gazing with glad, surprised eyes.

"Carley!" gasped Beatrice. "You wonderful golden-skinned goddess! . . . You're *young* again, like you were in our school days."

It was before Aunt Mary's shrewd, penetrating, loving gaze that Carley quailed.

"Yes, Carley, you look well—better than I ever saw you, but—but—"

"But I don't look happy," interrupted Carley. "I am happy to get home—to see you all . . . But—my—my heart is broken!"

A little shocked silence ensued, then Carley found herself being led across the lower level and up the wide stairway. As she mounted to the vast-domed cathedral-like chamber of the station a strange sensation pierced her with a pang. Not the old thrill of leaving New York or returning! Nor was it welcome sight of the hurrying, well-dressed throng of travelers and commuters, nor the stately beauty of the station. Carley shut her eyes, and then she knew. The dim light of vast space above, the looming gray walls, shadowy with tracery of figures, the lofty dome like the blue sky, brought back to her the walls of Oak Creek Canyon and the great caverns under the ramparts. As suddenly as she had shut her eyes Carley opened them to face her friends.

"Let me get it over—quickly," she burst out, with hot blood surging to her face. "I—I hated the West. It was so raw—so violent—so big. I think I hate it more—now. . . . But it changed me—made me over physically—and did something to my soul—God knows what. . . . And it has saved Glenn. Oh! he is wonderful! You would never know him. . . . For long I had not the courage to tell him I came to bring him back East. I kept putting it off. And I rode, I climbed, I camped, I lived outdoors. At first it nearly killed me. Then it grew bearable, and easier, until I forgot. I wouldn't be honest if I didn't admit now that somehow I had a wonderful time, in spite of all. . . . Glenn's business is raising hogs. He has a hog ranch. Doesn't it sound sordid? But things are not always what they sound—or seem. Glenn is absorbed in his work. I hated it—I expected to ridicule it. But I ended by infinitely respecting him. I learned through his hog-raising the real nobility of work. . . . Well, at last I found courage to ask him when he was coming back to New York. He said—'never!' . . . I realized then my blindness, my selfishness. I could not be his wife and live there. I could not. I was too small, too miserable, too comfort-loving—too spoiled. And all the time he knew this—*knew* I'd never be big enough to marry him. . . . That broke my heart. . . . I left him free—and here I am. . . . I beg you—don't ask me any more—and never to mention it to me—so I can forget."

The tender unspoken sympathy of women who loved her proved comforting in that trying hour. With the confession ruthlessly made the hard compression in Carley's breast subsided, and her eyes cleared of a hateful dimness. When they reached the taxi stand outside the station Carley felt a rush of hot devitalized air from the street. She seemed not to be able to get air into her lungs.

"Isn't it dreadfully hot?" she asked.

"This is a cool spell to what we had last week," replied Eleanor.

"Cool!" exclaimed Carley, as she wiped her moist face. "I wonder if you Easterners know the real significance of words."

Then they entered a taxi, to be whisked away apparently through a labyrinthine maze of cars and streets, where pedestrians had to run and jump for their lives. A congestion of traffic at Fifth Avenue and Forty-second Street halted their taxi for a few moments, and here in the thick of it Carley had full assurance that she was back in the metropolis. Her sore heart eased somewhat at sight of the streams of people passing to and fro. How they rushed! Where were they going? What was their story? And all the while her aunt held her hand, and Beatrice and Eleanor talked as fast as their tongues could wag. Then the taxi clattered on up the Avenue, to turn down a side street and presently stop at Carley's home. It was a modest three-story brown-stone house. Carley had been so benumbed by sensations that she did not imagine she could experience a new one. But peering out of the taxi, she gazed dubiously at the brownish-red stone steps and front of her home.

"I'm going to have it painted," she muttered, as if to herself.

Her aunt and her friends laughed, glad and relieved to hear such a practical remark from Carley. How were they to divine that this brownish-red stone was the color of desert rocks and canyon walls?

In a few more moments Carley was inside the house, feeling a sense of protection in the familiar rooms that had been her home for seventeen years. Once in the sanctity of her room, which was exactly as she had left it, her first action was to look in the mirror at her weary, dusty, heated face. Neither the brownness of it nor the shadow appeared to harmonize with the image of her that haunted the mirror.

"Now!" she whispered low. "It's done. . . . I'm home. The old life—or a new life? How to meet either. Now!"

Thus she challenged her spirit. And her intelligence rang at her the imperative necessity for action, for excitement, for effort that left no time for rest or memory or wakefulness. She accepted the issue. She was glad of the stern fight ahead of her. She set her will and steeled her heart with all the pride and vanity and fury of a woman who had been defeated but who scorned defeat. She was what birth and breeding and circumstance had made her. She would seek what the old life held.

What with unpacking and chatting and telephoning and lunching, the day soon passed. Carley went to dinner with friends and later to a roof garden. The color and light, the gayety and music, the news of acquaintances, the humor of the actors—all, in fact, except the unaccustomed heat and noise, were most welcome and diverting. That night she slept the sleep of weariness.

Awakening early, she inaugurated a habit of getting up at once, instead of lolling in bed, and breakfasting there, and reading her mail, as had been her wont before going West. Then she went over business matters with her aunt, called on her lawyer and banker, took lunch with Rose Maynard, and spent the afternoon shopping. Strong as she was, the unaccustomed heat and the hard pavements and the jostle of shoppers and the continual rush of sensations wore her out so completely that she did not want any dinner. She talked to her aunt a while, then went to bed.

Next day Carley motored through Central Park, and out of town into Westchester County, finding some relief from the stifling heat. But she seemed to look at the dusty trees and the worn greens without really seeing them. In the afternoon she called on friends, and had dinner at home with her aunt, and then went to a theatre. The musical comedy was good, but the almost unbearable heat and the vitiated air spoiled her enjoyment. That night upon arriving home at midnight she stepped out of the taxi, and involuntarily, without thought, looked up to see the stars. But there were no stars. A murky yellow-tinged blackness hung low over the city. Carley recollected that stars, and sunrises and sunsets, and untainted air, and silence were not for city dwellers. She checked any continuation of the thought.

A few days sufficed to swing her into the old life. Many of Carley's friends had neither the leisure nor the means to go away from the city during the summer. Some there were who might have afforded that if they had seen fit to live in less showy apartments, or to dispense with cars. Other of her best friends were on their summer outings in the Adirondacks. Carley decided to go with her aunt to Lake Placid about the first of August. Meanwhile she would keep going and doing.

She had been a week in town before Morrison telephoned her and added his welcome. Despite the gay gladness of his voice, it irritated her. Really, she scarcely wanted to see him. But a meeting was inevitable, and besides, going out with him was in accordance with the plan she had adopted. So she made an engagement to meet him at the Plaza for dinner. When with slow and pondering action she hung up the receiver it occurred to her that she resented the idea of going to the Plaza. She did not dwell on the reason why.

When Carley went into the reception room of the Plaza that night Morrison was waiting for her—the same slim, fastidious, elegant, sallow-faced Morrison whose image she had in mind, yet somehow different. He had what Carley called the New York masculine face, blasé and lined, with eyes that gleamed, yet had no fire. But at sight of her his face lighted up.

"By Jove! but you've come back a peach!" he exclaimed, clasping her extended hand. "Eleanor told me you looked great. It's worth missing you to see you like this."

"Thanks, Larry," she replied. "I must look pretty well to win that compliment from you. And how are you feeling? You don't seem robust for a golfter and horseman. But then I'm used to husky Westerners."

"Oh, I'm fagged with the daily grind," he said. "I'll be glad to get up in the mountains next month. Let's go down to dinner."

They descended the spiral stairway to the grill-room, where an orchestra was playing jazz, and dancers gyrated on a polished floor, and diners in evening dress looked on over their cigarettes.

"Well, Carley, are you still finicky about the eats?" he queried, consulting the menu.

"No. But I prefer plain food," she replied.

"Have a cigarette," he said, holding out his silver monogrammed case.

"Thanks, Larry. I—I guess I'll not take up smoking again. You see, while I was West I got out of the habit."

"Yes, they told me you had changed," he returned. "How about drinking?"

"Why, I thought New York had gone dry!" she said, forcing a laugh.

THE CALL OF THE CANYON ★ 597

"Only on the surface. Underneath it's wetter than ever."

"Well, I'll obey the law."

He ordered a rather elaborate dinner, and then turning his attention to Carley, gave her closer scrutiny. Carley knew then that he had become acquainted with the fact of her broken engagement. It was a relief not to need to tell him.

"How's that big stiff, Kilbourne?" asked Morrison, suddenly. "Is it true he got well?"

"Oh—yes! He's fine," replied Carley with eyes cast down. A hot knot seemed to form deep within her and threatened to break and steal along her veins. "But if you please—I do not care to talk of him."

"Naturally. But I must tell you that one man's loss is another's gain."

Carley had rather expected renewed courtship from Morrison. She had not, however, been prepared for the beat of her pulse, the quiver of her nerves, the uprising of hot resentment at the mere mention of Kilbourne. It was only natural that Glenn's former rivals should speak of him, and perhaps disparagingly. But from this man Carley could not bear even a casual reference. Morrison had escaped the army service. He had been given a high-salaried post at the ship-yards—the duties of which, if there had been any, he performed wherever he happened to be. Morrison's father had made a fortune in leather during the war. And Carley remembered Glenn telling her he had seen two whole blocks in Paris piled twenty feet deep with leather army goods that were never used and probably had never been intended to be used. Morrison represented the not inconsiderable number of young men in New York who had gained at the expense of the valiant legion who had lost. But what had Morrison gained? Carley raised her eyes to gaze steadily at him. He looked well-fed, indolent, rich, effete, and supremely self-satisfied. She could not see that

he had gained anything. She would rather have been a crippled ruined soldier.

"Larry, I fear gain and loss are mere words," she said.
"The thing that counts with me is what you *are*."

He stared in well-bred surprise, and presently talked of
a new dance which had lately come into vogue. And from
that he passed on to gossip of the theatres. Once between
courses of the dinner he asked Carley to dance, and she
complied. The music would have stimulated an Egyptian
mummy, Carley thought, and the subdued rose lights, the
murmur of gay voices, the glide and grace and distortion
of the dancers, were exciting and pleasurable. Morrison
had the suppleness and skill of a dancing-master. But he
held Carley too tightly, and so she told him, and added,
"I imbibed some fresh pure air while I was out West—
something you haven't here—and I don't want it all
squeezed out of me."

The latter days of July Carley made busy—so busy that
she lost her tan and appetite, and something of her
splendid resistance to the dragging heat and late hours. Seldom was she without some of her friends. She accepted
almost any kind of an invitation, and went even to Coney
Island, to baseball games, to the motion pictures, which
were three forms of amusement not customary with her.
At Coney Island, which she visited with two of her younger
girl friends, she had the best time since her arrival home.
What had put her in accord with ordinary people? The
baseball games, likewise pleased her. The running of
the players and the screaming of the spectators amused
and excited her. But she hated the motion pictures with
their salacious and absurd misrepresentations of life, in
some cases capably acted by skillful actors, and in others
a silly series of scenes featuring some doll-faced girl.

But she refused to go horseback riding in Central Park.

She refused to go to the Plaza. And these refusals she made deliberately, without asking herself why.

On August 1st she accompanied her aunt and several friends to Lake Placid, where they established themselves at a hotel. How welcome to Carley's strained eyes were the green of mountains, the soft gleam of amber water! How sweet and refreshing a breath of cool pure air! The change from New York's glare and heat and dirt, and iron-red insulating walls, and thronging millions of people, and ceaseless roar and rush, was tremendously relieving to Carley. She had burned the candle at both ends. But the beauty of the hills and vales, the quiet of the forest, the sight of the stars, made it harder to forget. She had to rest. And when she rested she could not always converse, or read, or write.

For the most part her days held variety and pleasure. The place was beautiful, the weather pleasant, the people congenial. She motored over the forest roads, she canoed along the margin of the lake, she played golf and tennis. She wore exquisite gowns to dinner and danced during the evenings. But she seldom walked anywhere on the trails and, never alone, and she never climbed the mountains and never rode a horse.

Morrison arrived and added his attentions to those of other men. Carley neither accepted nor repelled them. She favored the association with married couples and older people, and rather shunned the pairing off peculiar to vacationists at summer hotels. She had always loved to play and romp with children, but here she found herself growing to avoid them, somehow hurt by sound of pattering feet and joyous laughter. She filled the days as best she could, and usually earned quick slumber at night. She staked all on present occupation and the truth of flying time.

CHAPTER IX

The latter part of September Carley returned to New York.

Soon after her arrival she received by letter a formal proposal of marriage from Elbert Harrington, who had been quietly attentive to her during her sojourn at Lake Placid. He was a lawyer of distinction, somewhat older than most of her friends, and a man of means and fine family. Carley was quite surprised. Harrington was really one of the few of her acquaintances whom she regarded as somewhat behind the times, and liked him the better for that. But she could not marry him, and replied to his letter in as kindly a manner as possible. Then he called personally.

"Carley, I've come to ask you to reconsider," he said, with a smile in his gray eyes. He was not a tall or handsome man, but he had what women called a nice strong face.

"Elbert, you embarrass me," she replied, trying to laugh it out. "Indeed I feel honored, and I thank you. But I can't marry you."

"Why not? he asked, quietly.

"Because I don't love you," she replied.

"I did not expect you to," he said. "I hoped in time you

might come to care. I've known you a good many years, Carley. Forgive me if I tell you I see you are breaking—wearing yourself down. Maybe it is not a husband you need so much now, but you do need a home and children. You are wasting your life."

"All you say may be true, my friend," replied Carley, with a helpless little upflinging of hands. "Yet it does not alter my feelings."

"But you will marry sooner or later?" he queried, persistently.

This straightforward question struck Carley as singularly as if it was one she might never have encountered. It forced her to think of things she had buried.

"I don't believe I ever will," she answered, thoughtfully.

"That is nonsense, Carley," he went on. "You'll have to marry. What else can you do? With all due respect to your feelings—that affair with Kilbourne is ended—and you're not the wishy-washy heartbreak kind of a girl."

"You can never tell what a woman will do," she said, somewhat coldly.

"Certainly not. That's why I refuse to take no. Carley, be reasonable. You like me—respect me, do you not?"

"Why, of course I do!"

"I'm only thirty-five, and I could give you all any sensible woman wants," he said. "Let's make a real American home. Have you thought at all about that, Carley? Something is wrong to-day. Men are not marrying. Wives are not having children. Of all the friends I have, not one has a real American home. Why, it is a terrible fact! But, Carley, you are not a sentimentalist, or a melancholiac. Nor are you a waster. You have fine qualities. You need something to do—some one to care for."

"Pray do not think me ungrateful, Elbert," she replied, "nor insensible to the truth of what you say. But my answer is no!"

When Harrington had gone Carley went to her room, and precisely as upon her return from Arizona she faced her mirror skeptically and relentlessly. "I am such a liar that I'll do well to look at myself," she meditated. "Here I am again. Now! The world expects me to marry. But *what* do I expect?"

There was a raw unhealed wound in Carley's heart. Seldom had she permitted herself to think about it, let alone to probe it with hard materialistic queries. But custom to her was as inexorable as life. If she chose to live in the world she must conform to its customs. For a woman marriage was the aim and the end and the all of existence. Nevertheless, for Carley it could not be without love. Before she had gone West she might have had many of the conventional modern ideas about women and marriage. But because out there in the wilds her love and perception had broadened, now her arraignment of herself and her sex was bigger, sterner, more exacting. The months she had been home seemed fuller than all the months of her life. She had tried to forget and enjoy; she had not succeeded; but she had looked with far-seeing eyes at her world. Glenn Kilbourne's tragic fate had opened her eyes. Either the world was all wrong or the people in it were. But if that were an extravagant and erroneous supposition, there certainly was proof positive that her own small individual world was wrong. The women did not do any real work; they did not bear children; they lived on excitement and luxury. They had no ideals. How greatly were men to blame? Carley doubted her judgment here. But as men could not live without the smiles and comradeship and love of women, it was only natural that they should give the women what they wanted. Indeed, they had no choice. It was give or go without. How much of real love entered into the marriages among her acquaintances? Before marriage Carley wanted a girl to be sweet, proud, aloof, with a heart of golden fire. Not attainable except through love! It would be better that no children be born at all unless born of such beautiful love. Perhaps that was why so few children were born. Nature's balance and revenge! In Arizona Carley had learned something of the ruthlessness and inevitableness of nature. She was finding out she had learned this with many other staggering facts.

"I love Glenn still," she whispered, passionately, with trembling lips, as she faced the tragic-eyed image of herself in the mirror. "I love him more—more. Oh, my God! if I were honest I'd cry out the truth! It is terrible. . . . I will always love him. How then could I marry any other man? I would be a lie, a cheat. If I could only forget him—only kill that love. Then I might love another man—and if I did love him—no matter what I had felt or done before, I would be worthy. I could feel worthy. I could give him just as much. But without such love I'd give only a husk—a body without soul."

Love, then, was the sacred and holy flame of life that sanctioned the begetting of children. Marriage might be a necessity of modern time, but it was not the vital issue. Carley's anguish revealed strange and hidden truths. In some inexplicable way Nature struck a terrible balance—revenged herself upon a people who had no children, or who brought into the world children not created by the divinity of love, unyearned for, and therefore somehow doomed to carry on the blunders and burdens of life.

Carley realized how right and true it might be for her to throw herself away upon an inferior man, even a fool or a knave, if she loved him with that great and natural love of woman; likewise it dawned upon her how false and wrong and sinful it would be to marry the greatest or the richest or the noblest man unless she had that supreme love to give him, and knew it was reciprocated.

"What am I going to do with my life?" she asked, bitterly

and aghast. "I have been—I am a waster. I've lived for nothing but pleasurable sensation. I'm utterly useless. I do absolutely no good on earth."

Thus she saw how Harrington's words rang true—how they had precipitated a crisis for which her unconscious brooding had long made preparation.

"Why not give up ideals and be like the rest of my kind?" she soliloquized.

That was one of the things which seemed wrong with modern life. She thrust the thought from her with passionate scorn. If poor, broken, ruined Glenn Kilbourne could cling to an ideal and fight for it, could not she, who had all the world esteemed worth while, be woman enough to do the same? The direction of her thought seemed to have changed. She had been ready for rebellion. Three months of the old life had shown her that for her it was empty, vain, farcical, without one redeeming feature. The naked truth was brutal, but it cut clean to wholesome consciousness. Such so-called social life as she had plunged into deliberately to forget her unhappiness had failed her utterly. If she had been shallow and frivolous it might have done otherwise. Stripped of all guise, her actions must have been construed by a penetrating and impartial judge as a mere parading of her decorated person before a number of males with the purpose of ultimate selection.

"I've got to find some work," she muttered, soberly.

At the moment she heard the postman's whistle outside; and a little later the servant brought up her mail. The first letter, large, soiled, thick, bore the postmark Flagstaff, and her address in Glenn Kilbourne's writing.

Carley stared at it. Her heart gave a great leap. Her hand shook. She sat down suddenly as if the strength of her legs was inadequate to uphold her.

"Glenn has—written me!" she whispered, in slow, halting realization. "For what? Oh, why?"

The other letters fell off her lap, to lie unnoticed. This big thick envelope fascinated her. It was one of the stamped envelopes she had seen in his cabin. It contained a letter that had been written on his rude table, before the open fire, in the light of the doorway, in that little log-cabin under the spreading pines of West Ford Canyon. Dared she read it? The shock to her heart passed; and with mounting swell, seemingly too full for her breast, it began to beat and throb a wild gladness through all her being. She tore the envelope apart and read:

DEAR CARLEY:

I'm surely glad for a good excuse to write you.

Once in a blue moon I get a letter, and to-day Hutter brought me one from a soldier pard of mine who was with me in the Argonne. His name is Virgil Rust—queer name, don't you think?—and he's from Wisconsin. Just a rough-diamond sort of chap, but fairly well educated. He and I were in some pretty hot places, and it was he who pulled me out of a shell crater. I'd "gone west" sure then if it hadn't been for Rust.

Well, he did all sorts of big things during the war. Was down several times with wounds. He liked to fight and he was a holy terror. We all thought he'd get medals and promotion. But he didn't get either. These much-desired things did not always go where they were best deserved.

Rust is now lying in a hospital in Bedford Park. His letter is pretty blue. All he says about why he's there is that he's knocked out. But he wrote a heap about his girl. It seems he was in love with a girl in his home town—a pretty, big-eyed lass whose picture I've seen—and while he was overseas she married one of the chaps who got out of fighting. Evidently Rust is deeply hurt. He wrote: "I'd not care so . . . if she'd thrown me down to marry an old man or a boy who couldn't have gone to war." You see, Carley, service men feel queer about that sort of thing. It's something we got over there, and none of us will ever outlive it. Now, the point of this is that I am asking you to go see Rust, and cheer him up, and do what you can for the poor devil. It's a good deal to ask of you, I know, especially as Rust saw *your* picture many a time and knows you were my girl. But you needn't tell him that you—we couldn't make a go of it.

And, as I am writing this to you, I see no reason why I shouldn't go on in behalf of myself.

The fact is, Carley, I miss writing to you more than I miss anything of my old life. I'll bet you have a trunkful of letters from me—unless you've destroyed them. I'm not going to say how I miss *your* letters. But I will say you wrote the most charming and fascinating letters of anyone I ever knew, quite aside from any sentiment. You knew, of course, that I had no other girl correspondent. Well, I got along fairly well before you came West, but I'd be an awful liar if I denied I didn't get lonely for you and your letters. It's different now that you've been to Oak Creek. I'm alone most of the time and I dream a lot, and I'm afraid I see you here in my cabin, and along the brook, and under the pines, and riding Calico—which you came to do well—and on my hogpen fence—and, oh, everywhere! I don't want you to think I'm down in the mouth, for I'm not. I'll take my medicine. But, Carley, you spoiled me, and I miss hearing from you, and I don't see why it wouldn't be all right for you to send me a friendly letter occasionally.

It is autumn now. I wish you could see Arizona canyons in their gorgeous colors. We have had frost right along and the mornings are great. There's a broad zigzag belt of gold halfway up the San Francisco peaks, and that is the aspen thickets taking on their fall coat. Here in the canyon you'd think there was blazing fire everywhere. The vines and the maples are red, scarlet, carmine, cerise, magenta, all the hues of flame. The oak leaves are turning russet gold, and the sycamores are yellow green. Up on the desert the other day I rode across a patch of asters, lilac and lavender, almost purple. I had to get off and pluck a handful. And then what do you think? I dug up the whole bunch, roots and all, and planted them on the sunny side of my cabin. I rather guess your love of flowers engendered this remarkable susceptibility in me.

I'm home early most every afternoon now, and I like the couple of hours loafing around. Guess it's bad for me, though. You know I seldom hunt, and the trout in the pool here are so tame now they'll almost eat out of my hand. I haven't the heart to fish for them. The squirrels, too, have grown tame and friendly. There's a red squirrel that climbs up on my table. And there's a chipmunk who lives in my cabin and runs over my bed. I've a new pet—the little pig you christened Pinky. After he had the wonderful good fortune to be caressed and named by you I couldn't think of letting him grow up in an ordinary pig-like manner. So I fetched him home. My dog, Moze, was jealous at first and did not like this intrusion, but now they are good friends and sleep together. Flo has a kitten she's going to give me, and then, as Hutter says, I'll be "Jake."

My occupation during these leisure hours perhaps would strike my old friends East as idle, silly, mawkish. But I believe you will understand me.

I have the pleasure of doing nothing, and of catching now and then a glimpse of supreme joy in the strange state of *thinking* nothing. Tennyson came close to this in his "Lotus Eaters." Only to see—only to feel is enough!

Sprawled on the warm sweet pine needles, I breathe through them the breath of the earth and am somehow no longer lonely. I cannot, of course, see the sunset, but I watch for its coming on the eastern wall of the canyon. I see the shadow slowly creep up, driving the gold before it, until at last the canyon rim and pines are turned to golden fire. I watch the sailing eagles as they streak across the gold, and swoop up into the blue, and pass out of sight. I watch the golden flush fade to gray, and then the canyon slowly fills with purple shadows. This hour of twilight is the silent and melancholy one. Seldom is there any sound save the soft rush of the water over the stones, and that seems to die away. For a moment, perhaps, I am Hiawatha alone in his forest home, or a more primitive savage, feeling the great, silent pulse of nature, happy in unconsciousness, like a beast of the wild. But only for an instant do I ever catch this fleeting state. Next I am Glenn Kilbourne of West Fork, doomed and haunted by memories of the past. The great looming walls then become no longer blank. They are vast pages of the history of my life, with its past and present, and, alas! its future. Everything time does is written on the stones. And my stream seems to murmur the sad and ceaseless flow of human life, with its music and its misery.

Then, descending from the sublime to the humdrum and necessary, I heave a sigh, and pull myself together, and go in to make biscuits and fry ham. But I should not forget to tell you that before I do go in, very often my looming, wonderful walls and crags weave in strange shadowy characters the beautiful and unforgettable face of Carley Burch!

I append what little news Oak Creek affords.

That blamed old bald eagle stole another of my pigs.

I am doing so well with my hog-raising that Hutter wants to come in with me, giving me an interest in his sheep.

It is rumored some one has bought the Deep Lake section I wanted for a ranch. I don't know who. Hutter was rather noncommittal.

Charley, the herder, had one of his queer spells the other day, and swore to me he had a letter from you. He told the blamed lie with a sincere and placid eye, and even a smile of pride. Queer guy, that Charley!

Flo and Lee Stanton had another quarrel—the worst yet, Lee tells me. Flo asked a girl friend out from Flag and threw her in Lee's way, so to speak, and when Lee retaliated by making love to the girl Flo got mad. Funny creatures, you girls! Flo rode with me from High Falls to West Fork, and never showed the slightest sign of trouble. In fact she was delightfully gay. She rode Calico, and beat me bad in a race.

Adios, Carley. Won't you write me?

GLENN.

No sooner had Carley read the letter through to the end than she began it all over again, and on this second perusal she lingered over passages—only to reread them. That suggestion of her face sculptured by shadows on the canyon walls seemed to thrill her very soul.

She leaped up from the reading to cry out something that was unutterable. All the intervening weeks of shame and anguish and fury and strife and pathos, and the endless striving to forget, were as if by the magic of a letter made nothing but vain oblations.

"He loves me still!" she whispered, and pressed her breast with clenching hands, and laughed in wild exultance, and paced her room like a caged lioness. It was as if she had just awakened to the assurance she was beloved.

That was the shibboleth—the cry by which she sounded the closed depths of her love and called to the stricken life of a woman's insatiate vanity.

Then she snatched up the letter, to scan it again, and, suddenly grasping the import of Glenn's request, she hurried to the telephone to find the number of the hospital in Bedford Park. A nurse informed her that visitors were received at certain hours and that any attention to disabled soldiers was most welcome.

Carley motored out there to find the hospital merely a long one-story frame structure, a barracks hastily thrown up for the care of invalided men of the service. The chauffeur informed her that it had been used for that purpose during the training period of the army, and later when injured soldiers began to arrive from France.

A nurse admitted Carley into a small bare anteroom. Carley made known her errand.

"I'm glad it's Rust you want to see," replied the nurse. "Some of these boys are going to die. And some will be worse off if they live. But Rust may get well if he'll only behave. You are a relative—or friend?"

"I don't know him," answered Carley. "But I have a friend who was with him in France."

The nurse led Carley into a long narrow room with a line of single beds down each side, a stove at each end, and a few chairs. Each bed appeared to have an occupant and those nearest Carley lay singularly quiet. At the far end of the room were soldiers on crutches, wearing bandages on their heads, carrying their arms in slings. Their merry voices contrasted discordantly with their sad appearance.

Presently Carley stood beside a bed and looked down upon a gaunt, haggard young man who lay propped up on pillows.

"Rust—a lady to see you," announced the nurse.

Carley had difficulty in introducing herself. Had Glenn ever looked like this? What a face! Its healed scar only emphasized the pallor and furrows of pain that assuredly came from present wounds. He had unnaturally bright dark eyes, and a flush of fever in his hollow cheeks.

"How do!" he said, with a wan smile. "Who're you?"

"I'm Glenn Kilbourne's fiancée," she replied, holding out her hand.

"Say, I ought to've known you," he said, eagerly, and a warmth of light changed the gray shade of his face. "You're the girl Carley! You're almost like my—my own girl. By golly! you're some looker! It was good of you to come. Tell me about Glenn."

Carley took the chair brought by the nurse, and pulling it close to the bed, she smiled down upon him and said: "I'll be glad to tell you all I know—presently. But first you tell me about yourself. Are you in pain? What is your trouble? You must let me do everything I can for you, and these other men."

Carley spent a poignant and depth-stirring hour at the bedside of Glenn's comrade. At last she learned from loyal lips the nature of Glenn Kilbourne's service to his country. How Carley clasped to her sore heart the praise of the man she loved—the simple proofs of his noble disregard of self! Rust said little about his own service to country or to comrade. But Carley saw enough in his face. He had been like Glenn. By these two Carley grasped the compelling truth of the spirit and sacrifice of the legion of boys who had upheld American traditions. Their children and their children's children, as the years rolled by into the future, would hold their heads higher and prouder. Some things could never die in the hearts and the blood of a race. These boys, and the girls who had the supreme glory of being loved by them, must be the ones to revive the Americanism of their forefathers. Nature and God would take care of the slackers, the cowards who cloaked their shame with bland excuses of home service, of disability, and of dependence.

Carley saw two forces in life—the destructive and constructive. On the one side greed, selfishness, materialism: on the other generosity, sacrifice, and idealism. Which of them builded for the future? She saw men as wolves, sharks, snakes, vermin, and opposed to them men as lions and eagles. She saw women who did not inspire men to fare forth to seek, to imagine, to dream, to hope, to work, to fight. She began to have a glimmering of what a woman might be.

That night she wrote swiftly and feverishly, page after page, to Glenn, only to destroy what she had written. She could not keep her heart out of her words, nor a hint of what was becoming a sleepless and eternal regret. She wrote until a late hour, and at last composed a letter she knew did not ring true, so stilted and restrained was it in all passages save those concerning news of Glenn's comrade and of her own friends. "I'll never—never write him again," she averred with stiff lips, and next moment could have laughed in mockery at the bitter truth. If she had ever had any courage, Glenn's letter had destroyed it. But had it not been a kind of selfish, false courage, roused to hide her hurt, to save her own future? Courage should have a thought of others. Yet shamed one moment at the consciousness she would write Glenn again and again, and exultant the next with the clamouring love, she seemed to have climbed beyond the self that had striven to forget. She would remember and think though she died of longing.

Carley, like a drowning woman, caught at straws. What a relief and joy to give up that endless nagging at her mind! For months she had kept ceaselessly active, by associations which were of no help to her and which did not make her happy, in her determination to forget. Suddenly then she gave up to remembrance. She would cease trying to get over her love for Glenn, and think of him and dream about him as much as memory dictated. This must constitute the only happiness she could have.

The change from strife to surrender was so novel and sweet that for days she felt renewed. It was augmented by her visits to the hospital in Bedford Park. Through her bountiful presence Virgil Rust and his comrades had many dull hours of pain and weariness alleviated and brightened. Interesting herself in the condition of the seriously disabled soldiers and possibility of their future took time and work Carley gave willingly and gladly. At first she endeavored to get acquaintances with means and leisure to help the boys, but these overtures met with such little success that she quit wasting valuable time she could herself devote to their interests.

Thus several weeks swiftly passed by. Several soldiers who had been more seriously injured than Rust improved to the extent that they were discharged. But Rust gained little or nothing. The nurse and doctor both informed Carley that Rust brightened for her, but when she was gone he lapsed into somber indifference. He did not care whether he ate or not, or whether he got well or died.

"If I do pull out, where'll I go and what'll I do?" he once asked the nurse.

Carley knew that Rust's hurt was more than loss of a leg, and she decided to talk earnestly to him and try to win him to hope and effort. He had come to have a sort of reverence for her. So, biding her time, she at length found opportunity to approach his bed while his comrades were asleep or out of hearing. He endeavored to laugh her off, and then tried subterfuge, and lastly he cast off his mask and let her see his naked soul.

"Carley, I don't want your money or that of your kind

friends—whoever they are—you say will help me to get into business," he said. "God knows I thank you and it warms me inside to find *some one* who appreciates what I've given. But I don't want charity. . . . And I guess I'm pretty sick of the game. I'm sorry the Boches didn't do the job right."

"Rust, that is morbid talk," replied Carley. "You're ill and you just can't see any hope. You must cheer up—fight *yourself;* and look at the brighter side. It's a horrible pity you must be a cripple, but Rust, indeed life can be worth living if you make it so."

"How could there be a brighter side when a man's only half a man?" he queried, bitterly.

"You can be just as much a man as ever," persisted Carley, trying to smile when she wanted to cry.

"Could you care for a man with only one leg?" he asked, deliberately.

"What a question! Why, of course I could!"

"Well, maybe you are different. Glenn always swore even if he was killed no slacker or no rich guy left at home could ever get you. Maybe you haven't any idea how much it means to us fellows to know there *are* true and faithful girls. But I'll tell you, Carley, we fellows who went across got to see things strange when we came home. The good old U. S. needs a lot of faithful girls just now, believe me."

"Indeed that's true," replied Carley. "It's a hard time for everybody, and particularly you boys who have lost so—so much."

"I lost *all,* except my life—and I wish to God I'd lost that," he replied, gloomily.

"Oh, don't talk so!" implored Carley in distress. "Forgive me, Rust, if I hurt you. But I must tell you—that—that Glenn wrote me—you'd lost your girl. Oh, I'm sorry! It is dreadful for you now. But if you got well—and went to work—and took up life where you left it—why soon your pain would grow easier. And you'd find some happiness yet."

"Never for me in this world."

"But why, Rust, *why?* You're no—no—Oh! I mean you have intelligence and courage. Why isn't there anything left for you?"

"Because something here's been killed," he replied, and put his hand to his heart.

"Your faith? Your love of—of everything? Did the war kill it?"

"I'd gotten over that, maybe," he said, drearily, with his somber eyes on space that seemed lettered for him. "But *she* half murdered it—and *they* did the rest."

"They? Whom do you mean, Rust?"

"Why, Carley, I mean the people I lost my leg for!" he replied, with terrible softness.

"The British? The French?" she queried, in bewilderment.

"No!" he cried, and turned his face to the wall.

Carley dared not ask him more. She was shocked. How helplessly impotent all her earnest sympathy! No longer could she feel an impersonal, however kindly, interest in this man. His last ringing word had linked her also to his misfortune and his suffering. Suddenly he turned away from the wall. She saw him swallow laboriously. How tragic that thin, shadowed face of agony! Carley saw it differently. But for the beautiful softness of light in his eyes, she would have been unable to endure gazing longer.

"Carley, I'm bitter," he said, "but I'm not rancorous and callous, like some of the boys. I know if you'd been my girl you'd have stuck to me."

"Yes," Carley whispered.

"That makes a difference," he went on, with a sad smile. "You see, we soldiers all had feelings. And in one thing we all felt alike. That was we were going to fight for our homes and our women. I should say women first. No matter what we read or heard about standing by our allies, fighting for liberty or civilization, the truth was we all felt the same, even if we never breathed it. . . . Glenn fought for you. I fought for Nell. . . . We were not going to let the Huns treat you as they treated French and Belgian girls. . . . And think! Nell was engaged to me—she *loved* me—and, by God! She married a slacker when I lay half dead on the battlefield!"

"She was not worth loving or fighting for," said Carley, with agitation.

"Ah! now you've said something," he declared. "If I can only hold to that truth! What does one girl amount to? *I* do not count. It is the sum that counts. We love America— our homes—our women! . . . Carley, I've had comfort and strength come to me through you. Glenn will have his reward in your love. Somehow I seem to share it, a little. Poor Glenn! He got his, too. Why, Carley, that guy wouldn't *let* you do what he could do *for you*. He was cut to pieces—"

"Please—Rust—don't say any more. I am unstrung," she pleaded.

"Why not? It's due you to know how splendid Glenn was. . . . I tell you, Carley, all the boys here love you for the way you've stuck to Glenn. Some of them knew him, and I've told the rest. We thought he'd never pull through. But he has, and we know how you helped. Going West to see him! He didn't write it to me, but I know. . . . I'm wise. I'm happy for him—the lucky dog. Next time you go West—"

"Hush!" cried Carley. She could endure no more. She could no longer be a lie.

"You're white—you're shaking," exclaimed Rust, in concern. "Oh, I—what did I say? Forgive me—"

"Rust, I am no more worth loving and fighting for than your Nell."

"What!" he ejaculated.

"I have not told you the truth," she said, swiftly. "I have let you believe a lie. . . . I shall never marry Glenn. I broke my engagement to him."

Slowly Rust sank back upon the pillow, his large luminous eyes piercingly fixed upon her, as if he would read her soul.

"I went West—yes—" continued Carley. "But it was selfishly. I wanted Glenn to come back here. . . . He had suffered as you have. He nearly died. But he fought—he fought—Oh! he went through hell! And after a long, slow, horrible struggle he began to mend. He worked. He went to raising hogs. He lived alone. He worked harder and harder. . . . The West and his work saved him, body and soul. . . . He had learned to love both the West and his work. I did not blame him. But I could not live out there. He needed me. But I was too little—too selfish. I could not marry him. I gave him up. . . . I left—him—alone!"

Carley shrank under the scorn in Rust's eyes.

"And there's another man," he said, "a clean, straight, unscarred fellow who wouldn't fight!"

"Oh, no—I—I swear there's not," whispered Carley.

"You, too," he replied, thickly. Then slowly he turned that worn dark face to the wall. His frail breast heaved. And his lean hand made her a slight gesture of dismissal, significant and imperious.

Carley fled. She could scarcely see to find the car. All her internal being seemed convulsed, and a deadly faintness made her sick and cold.

CHAPTER X

Carley's edifice of hopes, dreams, aspirations, and struggles fell in ruins about her. It had been built upon false sands. It had no ideal for foundation. It had to fall.

Something inevitable had forced her confession to Rust. Dissimulation had been a habit of her mind; it was more a habit of her class than sincerity. But she had reached a point in her mental strife where she could not stand before Rust and let him believe she was noble and faithful when she knew she was neither. Would not the next step in this painful metamorphosis of her character be a fierce and passionate repudiation of herself and all she represented?

She went home and locked herself in her room, deaf to telephone and servants. There she gave up to her shame. Scorned—despised—dismissed by that poor crippled flame-spirited Virgil Rust! He had reverenced her, and the truth had earned his hate. Would she ever forget his look—incredulous—shocked—bitter—and blazing with unutterable contempt? Carley Burch was only another Nell—a jilt—a mocker of the manhood of soldiers! Would she ever cease to shudder at memory of Rust's slight movement of hand? Go! Get out of my sight! Leave me to my agony as

you left Glenn Kilbourne alone to fight his! Men such as
I am do not want the smile of your face, the touch of your
hand! We gave for womanhood! Pass on to lesser men who
loved the fleshpots and who would buy your charms! So
Carley interpreted that slight gesture, and writhed in her
abasement.

Rust threw a white, illuminating light upon her desertion of Glenn. She had betrayed him. She had left him
alone. Dwarfed and stunted was her narrow soul! To a man
who had given all for her she had returned nothing. Stone
for bread! Betrayal for love! Cowardice for courage!

The hours of contending passions gave birth to vague,
slow-forming revolt.

She became haunted by memory pictures and sounds
and smells of Oak Creek Canyon. As from afar she saw
the great sculptured rent in the earth, green and red and
brown, with its shining, flashing ribbons of waterfalls
and streams. The mighty pines stood up magnificent
and stately. The walls loomed high, shadowed under the
shelves, gleaming in the sunlight, and they seemed dreaming, waiting, watching. For what? For her return to their
serene fastnesses—to the little gray log cabin. The thought
stormed Carley's soul.

Vivid and intense shone the images before her shut eyes.
She saw the winding forest floor, green with grass and
fern, colorful with flower and rock. A thousand aisles,
glades, nooks, and caverns called her to come. Nature was
every woman's mother. The populated city was a delusion.
Disease and death and corruption stalked in the shadows
of the streets. But her canyon promised hard work, play-
ful hours, dreaming idleness, beauty, health, fragrance,
loneliness, peace, wisdom, love, children, and long life. In
the hateful shut-in isolation of her room Carley stretched
forth her arms as if to embrace the vision. Pale close walls,
gleaming placid stretches of brook, churning amber and

white rapids, mossy banks and pine-matted ledges, the towers and turrets and ramparts where the eagles wheeled—she saw them all as beloved images lost to her save in anguished memory.

She heard the murmur of flowing water, soft, low, now loud, and again lulling, hollow and eager, tinkling over rocks, bellowing into the deep pools, washing with silky seep of wind-swept waves the hanging willows. Shrill and piercing and far-aloft pealed the scream of the eagle. And she seemed to listen to a mocking bird while he mocked her with his melody of many birds. The bees hummed, the wind moaned, the leaves rustled, the waterfall murmured. Then came the sharp rare note of a canyon swift, most mysterious of birds, significant of the heights.

A breath of fragrance seemed to blow with her shifting senses. The dry, sweet, tangy canyon smells returned to her—of fresh-cut timber, of wood smoke, of the cabin fire with its steaming pots, of flowers and earth, and of the wet stones, of the redolent pines and the pungent cedars.

And suddenly, clearly, amazingly, Carley beheld in her mind's sight the hard features, the bold eyes, the slight smile, the coarse face of Haze Ruff. She had forgotten him. But he now returned. And with memory of him flashed a revelation as to his meaning in her life. He had appeared merely a clout, a ruffian, an animal with man's shape and intelligence. But he was the embodiment of the raw, crude violence of the West. He was the eyes of the natural primitive man, believing what he saw. He had seen in Carley Burch the paraded charm, the unashamed and serene front, the woman seeking man. Haze Ruff had been neither vile nor base nor unnatural. It had been her subjection to the decadence of feminine dress that had been unnatural. But Ruff had found her a lie. She invited what she did not want. And his scorn had been commensurate with the falsehood of her. So might any man have been justified in his insult to her, in his rejection of her. Haze Ruff had found her unfit for his idea of dalliance. Virgil Rust had found her false to the ideals of womanhood for which he had sacrificed all but life itself. What then had Glenn Kilbourne found her? He possessed the greatness of noble love. He had loved her before the dark and changeful tide of war had come between them. How had he judged her? That last sight of him standing alone, leaning with head bowed, a solitary figure trenchant with suggestion of tragic resignation and strength, returned to flay Carley. He had loved, trusted, and hoped. She saw now what his hope had been— that she would have instilled into her blood the subtle, red, and revivifying essence of calling life in the open, the strength of the wives of earlier years, an emanation from canyon, desert, mountain, forest, of health, of spirit, of forward-gazing natural love, of the mysterious saving instinct he had gotten out of the West. And she had been too little—too steeped in the indulgence of luxurious life— too slight-natured and pale-blooded! And suddenly there pierced into the black storm of Carley's mind a blazing, white-streaked thought—she had left Glenn to the Western girl, Flo Hutter. Humiliated, and abased in her own sight, Carley fell prey to a fury of jealousy.

She went back to the old life. But it was in a bitter, restless, critical spirit, conscious of the fact that she could derive neither forgetfulness nor pleasure from it, nor see any release from the habit of years.

One afternoon, late in the fall, she motored out to a Long Island club where the last of the season's golf was being enjoyed by some of her most intimate friends. Carley did not play. Aimlessly she walked around the grounds, finding the autumn colors subdued and drab, like her mind. The air held a promise of early winter. She thought that she would go South before the cold came.

Always trying to escape anything rigorous, hard, painful, or disagreeable! Later she returned to the clubhouse to find her party assembled on an inclosed porch, chatting and partaking of refreshment. Morrison was there. He had not taken kindly to her late habit of denying herself to him.

During a lull in the idle conversation Morrison addressed Carley pointedly. "Well, Carley, how's your Arizona hog-raiser?" he queried, with a little gleam in his usually lusterless eyes.

"I have not heard lately," she replied, coldly.

The assembled company suddenly quieted with a portent inimical to their leisurely content of the moment. Carley felt them all looking at her, and underneath the exterior she preserved with extreme difficulty, there burned so fierce an anger that she seemed to have swelling veins of fire.

"Queer how Kilbourne went into raising hogs," observed Morrison. "Such a low-down sort of work, you know."

"He had no choice," replied Carley. "Glenn didn't have a father who made tainted millions out of the war. He had to work. And I must differ with you about its being low-down. No honest work is that. It is idleness that is low down."

"But so foolish of Glenn when he might have married money," rejoined Morrison, sarcastically.

"The honor of soldiers is beyond your ken, Mr. Morrison."

He flushed darkly and bit his lip.

"You women make a man sick with this rot about soldiers," he said, the gleam in his eye growing ugly. "A uniform goes to a woman's head no matter what's inside it. I don't see where your vaunted honor of soldiers comes in— considering how they accepted the let-down of women during and after the war."

"How could you see when you stayed comfortably at home?" retorted Carley.

"All I could see was women falling into soldiers' arms," he said, sullenly.

"Certainly. Could an American girl desire any greater happiness—or opportunity to prove her gratitude?" flashed Carley, with proud uplift of head.

"It didn't look like gratitude to me," returned Morrison.

"Well, it *was* gratitude," declared Carley, ringingly. "If women of America did throw themselves at soldiers it was not owing to the moral lapse of the day. It was woman's instinct to save the race! Always, in every war, women have sacrificed themselves to the future. Not vile, but noble! . . . You insult both soldiers and women, Mr. Morrison. I wonder—did any American girls throw themselves at *you?*"

Morrison turned a dead white, and his mouth twisted to a distorted checking of speech, disagreeable to see.

"No, you were a slacker," went on Carley, with scathing scorn. "You let the other men go fight for American girls. Do you imagine one of them will ever *marry* you? . . . All your life, Mr. Morrison, you will be a marked man— outside the pale of friendship with real American men and the respect of real American girls."

Morrison leaped up, almost knocking the table over, and he glared at Carley as he gathered up his hat and cane. She turned her back upon him. From that moment he ceased to exist for Carley. She never spoke to him again.

Next day Carley called upon her dearest friend, whom she had not seen for some time.

"Carley dear, you don't look so very well," said Eleanor, after greetings had been exchanged.

"Oh, what does it matter how I look?" queried Carley, impatiently.

"You were so wonderful when you got home from Arizona."

"If I was wonderful and am now commonplace you can thank your old New York for it."

"Carley, don't you care for New York any more?" asked Eleanor.

"Oh, New York is all right, I suppose. It's I who am wrong."

"My dear, you puzzle me these days. You've changed. I'm sorry. I'm afraid you're unhappy."

"Me? Oh, impossible! I'm in a seventh heaven," replied Carley, with a hard little laugh. "What're you doing this afternoon? Let's go out—riding—or somewhere."

"I'm expecting the dressmaker."

"Where are you going to-night?"

"Dinner and theater. It's a party, or I'd ask you."

"What did you do yesterday and the day before, and the days before that?"

Eleanor laughed indulgently, and acquainted Carley with a record of her social wanderings during the last few days.

"The same old things—over and over again! Eleanor don't you get sick of it?" queried Carley.

"Oh yes, to tell the truth," returned Eleanor, thoughtfully. "But there's nothing else to do."

"Eleanor, I'm no better than you," said Carley, with disdain. "I'm as useless and idle. But I'm beginning to see myself—and you—and all this rotten crowd of ours. We're no good. But you're married, Eleanor. You're settled in life. You ought to *do something*. I'm single and at loose ends. Oh, I'm in revolt! . . . Think, Eleanor, just think. Your husband works hard to keep you in this expensive apartment. You have a car. He dresses you in silks and satins. You wear diamonds. You eat your breakfast in bed. You loll around in a pink dressing gown all morning. You dress for lunch or tea. You ride or golf or worse than waste your time on some lounge lizard, dancing till time to come home to dress for dinner. You let other men make love to you. Oh, don't get sore. You do. . . . And so goes the round of your life. What good on earth are you, anyhow? You're just a—a gratification to the senses of your husband. And at that you don't see much of *him*."

"Carley, how you rave!" exclaimed her friend. "What has gotten into you lately? Why, everybody tells me you're—you're queer! The way you insulted Morrison—how unlike you, Carley!"

"I'm glad I found the nerve to do it. What do you think, Eleanor?"

"Oh, I despise him. But you can't say the things you feel."

"You'd be bigger and truer if you did. Some day I'll break out and flay you and your friends alive."

"But, Carley, you're my friend and you're just exactly like we are. Or you were, quite recently."

"Of course, I'm your friend. I've always loved you, Eleanor," went on Carley, earnestly. "I'm as deep in this—this damned stagnant muck as you, or anyone. But I'm no longer *blind*. There's something terribly wrong with us women, and it's not what Morrison hinted."

"Carley, the only thing wrong with you is that you jilted poor Glenn—and are breaking your heart over him still."

"Don't—don't!" cried Carley, shrinking. "God knows that is true. But there's more wrong with me than a blighted love affair."

"Yes, you mean the modern feminine unrest?"

"Eleanor, I positively hate that phrase 'modern feminine unrest!' It smacks of ultra—ultra—Oh! I don't know what. That phrase ought to be translated by a Western acquaintance of mine—one Haze Ruff. I'd not like to hurt your sensitive feelings with what he'd say. But this unrest means speed-mad, excitement-mad, fad-mad, dress-mad, or I should say *un*dress-mad, culture-mad, and Heaven only knows what else. The women of our set are idle, luxurious, selfish, pleasure-craving, lazy, useless, work-and-children shirking, absolutely no good."

"Well, if we are, who's to blame?" rejoined Eleanor, spiritedly. "Now, Carley Burch, you listen to me. I think the twentieth-century girl in America is the most wonderful female creation, of all the ages of the universe. I admit it. That is why we are a prey to the evils attending greatness. Listen. Here is a crying sin—an infernal paradox. Take this twentieth-century girl, this American girl who is the finest creation of the ages. A young and healthy girl, the most perfect type of culture possible to the freest and greatest city on earth—New York! She holds absolutely an unreal, untrue position in the scheme of existence. Surrounded by parents, relatives, friends, suitors, and instructive schools of every kind, colleges, institutions, is she really happy, is she really living?"

"Eleanor," interrupted Carley, earnestly, "she is *not*. . . . And I've been trying to tell you why."

"My dear, let me get a word in, will you," complained Eleanor. "You don't know it all. There are as many different points of view as there are people. . . . Well, if this girl happened to have a new frock, and a new beau to show it to, she'd say, 'I'm the happiest girl in the world.' But she is nothing of the kind. Only she doesn't know that. She approaches marriage, or, for that matter, a more matured life, having had too much, having been too well taken care of, *knowing too much*. Her masculine satellites—father, brothers, uncles, friends, lovers—all utterly spoil her. Mind you, I mean, girls like us, of the middle class—which is to say the largest and best class of Americans. We are spoiled. . . . This girl marries. And life goes on smoothly, as if its aim was to exclude friction and effort. Her husband makes it too easy for her. She is an ornament, or a toy, to be kept in a luxurious cage. To soil her pretty hands would be disgraceful! Even if she can't afford a maid, the modern devices of science make the care of her four-room apartment a farce. Electric dish-washer, clothes-washer, vacuum-cleaner, and the near-by delicatessen and the caterer simply rob a young wife of her housewifely heritage. If she has a baby—which happens occasionally, Carley, in spite of your assertion—it very soon goes to the kindergarten. Then what does she find to do with hours and hours? If she is not married, what on earth *can* she find to do?"

"She can work," replied Carley, bluntly.

"Oh yes, she can, but she doesn't," went on Eleanor. "*You* don't work. I never did. We both hated the idea. You're calling spades spades, Carley, but you seem to be riding a morbid, impractical thesis. Well, our young American girl or bride goes in for being rushed or she goes in for fads, the ultra stuff you mentioned. New York City gets all the great artists, lecturers, and surely the great fakirs. The New York women support them. The men laugh, but they furnish the money. They take the women to the theaters, but they cut out the reception to a Polish princess, a lecture by an Indian magician and mystic, or a benefit luncheon for a Home for Friendless Cats. The truth is most of our young girls or brides have a wonderful enthusiasm worthy of a better cause. What is to become of their surplus energy, the bottled-lightning spirit so characteristic of modern girls? Where is the outlet for intense feelings? What use can they make of education or of gifts? They just can't, that's all. I'm not taking into consideration the new-woman species, the faddist or the reformer. I mean normal girls like you and me. Just think, Carley. A girl's every wish, every need, is almost instantly satisfied without the slightest effort on her part to obtain it. No struggle, let alone work! If women crave to achieve something outside of the arts, you know, something universal and helpful which will make men acknowledge her worth, if not the equality, where is the opportunity?"

"Opportunities should be *made*," replied Carley.

"There are a million sides to this question of the modern young woman—the *fin-de-siècle* girl. I'm for her!"

"How about the extreme of style in dress for this remarkably-to-be-pitied American girl you champion so eloquently?" queried Carley, sarcastically.

"Immoral!" exclaimed Eleanor with frank disgust.

"You admit it?"

"To my shame, I do."

"Why do women wear extreme clothes? Why do you and I wear open-work silk stockings, skirts to our knees, gowns without sleeves or bodices?"

"We're slaves to fashion," replied Eleanor. "That's the popular excuse."

"Bah!" exclaimed Carley.

Eleanor laughed in spite of being half nettled. "Are you going to stop wearing what all the other women wear—and be looked at askance? Are you going to be dowdy and frumpy and old-fashioned?"

"No. But I'll never wear anything again that can be called immoral. I want to be able to say *why* I wear a dress. . . . You haven't answered my question yet. Why do you wear what you frankly admit is disgusting?"

"I don't know, Carley," replied Eleanor, helplessly. "How you harp on things! We must dress to make other women jealous and to attract men. To be a sensation! Perhaps the word 'immoral' is not what I mean. A woman will be shocking in her obsession to attract, but hardly more than that, if she knows it."

"Ah! So few women realize how they actually do look. Haze Ruff could tell them."

"Haze Ruff. Who in the world is he or she?" asked Eleanor.

"Haze Ruff is a he, all right," replied Carley, grimly.

"Well, who is he?"

"A sheep-dipper in Arizona," answered Carley, dreamily.

"Humph! And what can Mr. Ruff tell us?"

"He told *me* I looked like one of the devil's angels—and that I dressed to knock the daylights out of men."

"Well, Carley Burch, if that isn't rich!" exclaimed Eleanor, with a peal of laughter. "I dare say you appreciate that as an original compliment."

"No. . . . I wonder what Ruff would say about jazz—I just wonder," murmured Carley.

"Well, I wouldn't care what he said, and I don't care what *you* say," returned Eleanor. "The preachers and reformers and bishops and rabbis make me sick. They rave about jazz. Jazz—the discordant note of our decadence! Jazz—the harmonious expression of our musicless, mindless, soulless materialism!—The idiots! If they could be women for a while they would realize the error of their ways. But they will never, never abolish jazz—*never,* for it is the grandest, the most wonderful, the most absolutely necessary thing for women in this terrible age of smotheration."

"All right, Eleanor, we understand each other, even if we do not agree," said Carley. "You leave the future of women to chance, to life, to materialism, not to their own conscious efforts. I want to leave it to free will and idealism."

"Carley, you are getting a little beyond me," declared Eleanor, dubiously.

"What are you going to *do?* It all comes home to each individual woman. Her attitude toward life."

"I'll drift along with the current, Carley, and be a good sport," replied Eleanor, smiling.

"You don't care about the women and children of the

future? You'll not deny yourself now, and think and work, and suffer a little, in the interest of future humanity?"

"How you put things, Carley!" exclaimed Eleanor, wearily. "Of course I care—when you make me think of such things. But what have *I* to do with the lives of people in the years to come?"

"Everything. America for Americans! While you dawdle, the life blood is being sucked out of our great nation. It is a man's job to fight; it is a woman's to save. . . . I think you've made your choice, though you don't realize it. I'm praying to God that I'll rise to mine."

Carley had a visitor one morning earlier than the usual or conventional time for calls.

"He wouldn't give no name," said the maid. "He wears soldier clothes, ma'am, and he's pale, and walks with a cane."

"Tell him I'll be right down," replied Carley.

Her hands trembled while she hurriedly dressed. Could this caller be Virgil Rust? She hoped so, but she doubted.

As she entered the parlor a tall young man in worn khaki rose to meet her. At first glance she could not name him, though she recognized the pale face and light-blue eyes, direct and steady.

"Good morning, Miss Burch," he said. "I hope you'll excuse so early a call. You remember me, don't you? I'm George Burton, who had the bunk next to Rust's."

"Surely I remember you, Mr. Burton, and I'm glad to see you," replied Carley, shaking hands with him. "Please sit down. Your being here must mean you're discharged from the hospital."

"Yes, I was discharged, all right," he said.

"Which means you're well again. That is fine. I'm very glad."

"I was put out to make room for a fellow in bad shape.

I'm still shaky and weak," he replied. "But I'm glad to go. I've pulled through pretty good, and it'll not be long until I'm strong again. It was the 'flu' that kept me down."

"You must be careful. May I ask where you're going and what you expect to do?"

"Yes, that's what I came to tell you," he replied, frankly. "I want you to help me a little. I'm from Illinois and my people aren't so badly off. But I don't want to go back to my home town down and out, you know. Besides, the winters are cold there. The doctor advises me to go to a little milder climate. You see, I was gassed, and got the 'flu' afterward. But I know I'll be all right if I'm careful. . . . Well, I've always had a leaning toward agriculture, and I want to go to Kansas. Southern Kansas. I want to travel around till I find a place I like, and there I'll get a job. Not too hard a job at first—that's why I'll need a little money. I know what to do. I want to lose myself in the wheat country and forget the—the war. I'll not be afraid of work, presently. . . . Now, Miss Burch, you've been so kind—I'm going to ask you to lend me a little money. I'll pay it back. I can't promise just when. But some day. Will you?"

"Assuredly I will," she replied, heartily. "I'm happy to have the opportunity to help you. How much will you need for immediate use? Five hundred dollars?"

"Oh no, not so much as that," he replied. "Just railroad fare home, and then to Kansas, and to pay board while I get well, you know, and look around."

"We'll make it five hundred, anyway," she replied, and, rising, she went toward the library. "Excuse me a moment." She wrote the check and, returning, gave it to him.

"You're very good," he said, rather low.

"Not at all," replied Carley. "You have no idea how much it means to me to be permitted to help you. Before I forget, I must ask you, can you cash that check here in New York?"

"Not unless you identify me," he said, ruefully. "I don't know anyone I could ask."

"Well, when you leave here go at once to my bank—it's on Thirty-fourth Street—and I'll telephone the cashier. So you'll not have any difficulty. Will you leave New York at once?"

"I surely will. It's an awful place. Two years ago when I came here with my company I thought it was grand. But I guess I lost something over there. . . . I want to be where it's quiet. Where I won't see many people."

"I think I understand," returned Carley. "Then I suppose you're in a hurry to get home? Of course you have a girl you're just dying to see?"

"No, I'm sorry to say I haven't," he replied, simply. "I was glad I didn't have to leave a sweetheart behind, when I went to France. But it wouldn't be so bad to have one to go back to—now."

"Don't you worry!" exclaimed Carley. "You can take your choice presently. You have the open sesame to every real American girl's heart."

"And what is that?" he asked, with a blush.

"Your service to your country," she said, gravely.

"Well," he said, with a singular bluntness, "considering I didn't get any medals or bonuses, I'd like to draw a nice girl."

"You will," replied Carley, and made haste to change the subject. "By the way, did you meet Glenn Kilbourne in France?"

"Not that I remember," rejoined Burton, as he got up, rising rather stiffly by aid of his cane. "I must go, Miss Burch. Really I can't thank you enough. And I'll never forget it."

"Will you write me how you are getting along?" asked Carley, offering her hand.

"Yes."

Carley moved with him out into the hall and to the door. There was a question she wanted to ask, but found it strangely difficult of utterance. At the door Burton fixed a rather penetrating gaze upon her.

"You didn't ask me about Rust," he said.

"No, I—I didn't think of him—until now, in fact," Carley lied.

"Of course then you couldn't have heard about him. I was wondering."

"I have heard nothing."

"It was Rust who told me to come to you," said Burton. "We were talking one day, and he—well, he thought you were true blue. He said he knew you'd trust me and lend me money. I couldn't have asked you but for him."

"True blue! He believed that. I'm glad. . . . Has he spoken of me to you since I was last at the hospital?"

"Hardly," replied Burton, with the straight, strange glance on her again.

Carley met this glance and suddenly a coldness seemed to envelop her. It did not seem to come from within though her heart stopped beating. Burton had not changed—the warmth, the gratitude still lingered about him. But the light of his eyes! Carley had seen it in Glenn's, in Rust's—a strange, questioning, far-off light, infinitely aloof and unutterably sad. Then there came a lift of her heart that released a pang. She whispered with dread, with a tremor, with an instinct of calamity.

"How about—Rust?"

"He's dead."

The winter came, with its bleak sea winds and cold rains and blizzards of snow. Carley did not go South. She read and brooded, and gradually avoided all save those true friends who tolerated her.

She went to the theater a good deal, showing preference

for the drama of strife, and she did not go anywhere for amusement. Distraction and amusement seemed to be dead issues for her. But she could become absorbed in any argument on the good or evil of the present day. Socialism reached into her mind, to be rejected. She had never understood it clearly, but it seemed to her a state of mind where dissatisfied men and women wanted to share what harder working or more gifted people possessed. There were a few who had too much of the world's goods and many who had too little. A readjustment of such inequality and injustice must come, but Carley did not see the remedy in Socialism.

She devoured books on the war with a morbid curiosity and hope that she would find some illuminating truth as to the uselessness of sacrificing young men in the glory and prime of their lives. To her war appeared a matter of human nature rather than politics. Hate really was an effect of war. In her judgment future wars could be avoided only in two ways—by men becoming honest and just or by women refusing to have children to be sacrificed. As there seemed no indication whatever of the former, she wondered how soon all women of all races would meet on a common height, with the mounting spirit that consumed her own heart. Such time must come. She granted every argument for war and flung against it one ringing passionate truth—agony of mangled soldiers and agony of women and children. There was no justification for offensive war. It was monstrous and hideous. If nature and evolution proved the absolute need of strife, war, blood, and death in the progress of animal and man toward perfection, then it would be better to abandon this Christless code and let the race of man die out.

All through these weeks she longed for a letter from Glenn. But it did not come. Had he finally roused to the sweetness and worth and love of the western girl, Flo Hutter? Carley knew absolutely, through both intelligence and intuition, that Glenn Kilbourne would never love Flo. Yet such was her intensity and stress at times, especially in the darkness of waking hours, that jealousy overcame her and insidiously worked its havoc. Peace and a strange kind of joy came to her in dreams of her walks and rides and climbs in Arizona, of the lonely canyon where it always seemed afternoon, of the tremendous colored vastness of that Painted Desert. But she resisted these dreams now because when she awoke from them she suffered such a yearning that it became unbearable. Then she knew the feeling of the loneliness and solitude of the hills. Then she knew the sweetness of the murmur of falling water, the wind in the pines, the song of birds, the white radiance of the stars, the break of day and its gold-flushed close. But she had not yet divined their meaning. It was not all love for Glenn Kilbourne. Had city life palled upon her solely because of the absence of her lover? So Carley plodded on, like one groping in the night, fighting shadows.

One day she received a card from an old schoolmate, a girl who had married out of Carley's set, and had been ostracized. She was living down on Long Island, at a little country place named Wading River. Her husband was an electrician—something of an inventor. He worked hard. A baby boy had just come to them. Would not Carley run down on the train to see the youngster?

That was a strong and trenchant call. Carley went. She found indeed a country village, and on the outskirts of it a little cottage that must have been pretty in summer, when the green was on vines and trees. Her old schoolmate was rosy, plump, bright-eyed, and happy. She saw in Carley no change—a fact that somehow rebounded sweetly on Carley's consciousness. Elsie prattled of herself and her husband and how they had worked to earn this little home, and then the baby.

When Carley saw the adorable dark-eyed, pink-toed, curly-fisted baby she understood Elsie's happiness and reveled in it. When she felt the soft, warm, living little body in her arms, against her breast, then she absorbed some incalculable and mysterious strength. What were the trivial, sordid, and selfish feelings that kept her in tumult compared to this welling emotion? Had she the secret in her arms? Babies and Carley had never become closely acquainted in those infrequent meetings that were usually the result of chance. But Elsie's baby nestled to her breast and cooed to her and clung to her finger. When at length the youngster was laid in his crib it seemed to Carley that the fragrance and the soul of him remained with her.

"A real American boy!" she murmured.

"You can just bet he is," replied Elsie. "Carley you ought to see his dad."

"I'd like to meet him," said Carley, thoughtfully. "Elsie, was he in the service?"

"Yes. He was on one of the navy transports that took munitions to France. Think of me, carrying this baby, with my husband on a boat full of explosives and with German submarines roaming the ocean! Oh, it was horrible!"

"But he came back, and now all's well with you," said Carley, with a smile of earnestness. "I'm very glad, Elsie."

"Yes—but I shudder when I think of a possible war in the future. I'm going to raise boys, and girls, too, I hope—and the thought of war is torturing."

Carley found her return train somewhat late, and she took advantage of the delay to walk out to the wooded headlands above the Sound.

It was a raw March day, with a steely sun going down in a pale-gray sky. Patches of snow lingered in sheltered brushy places. This bit of woodland had a floor of soft sand that dragged at Carley's feet. There were sere and brown leaves still fluttering on the scrub-oaks. At length Carley came out on the edge of the bluff with the gray expanse of seat beneath her, and a long wandering shore line, ragged with wreckage or driftwood. The surge of water rolled in—a long, low, white, creeping line that softly roared on the beach and dragged the pebbles gratingly back. There was neither boat nor living creature in sight.

Carley felt the scene ease a clutching hand within her breast. Here was loneliness and solitude vastly different from that of Oak Creek Canyon, yet it held the same intangible power to soothe. The swish of the surf, the moan of the wind in the evergreens, were voices that called to her. How many more miles of lonely land than peopled cities! Then the sea—how vast! And over that the illimitable and infinite sky, and beyond, the endless realms of space. It helped her somehow to see and hear and feel the eternal presence of nature. In communion with nature the significance of life might be realized. She remembered Glenn quoting: "The world is too much with us. . . . Getting and spending, we lay waste our powers." What were our powers? What did God intend men to do with hands and bodies and gifts and souls? She gazed back over the bleak land and then out across the broad sea. Only a millionth part of the surface of the unsubmerged earth knew the populous abodes of man. And the lonely sea, inhospitable to stable homes of men, was thrice the area of the land. Were men intended, then, to congregate in few places, to squabble and to bicker and breed the discontents that led to injustice, hatred, and war? What a mystery it all was! But Nature was neither false nor little, however cruel she might be.

Once again Carley fell under the fury of her ordeal. Wavering now, restless and sleepless, given to violent starts and slow spells of apathy, she was wearing to defeat.

That spring day, one year from the day she had left New York for Arizona, she wished to spend alone. But her thoughts grew unbearable. She summed up the endless year. Could she live another like it? Something must break within her.

She went out. The air was warm and balmy, carrying that subtle current which caused the mild madness of spring fever. In the Park the greening of the grass, the opening of buds, the singing of birds, the gladness of children, the light on the water, the warm sun—all seemed to reproach her. Carley fled from the Park to the home of Beatrice Lovell; and there, unhappily, she encountered those of her acquaintance with whom she had least patience. They forced her to think too keenly of herself. They appeared care free while she was miserable.

Over teacups there were waging gossip and argument and criticism. When Carley entered with Beatrice there was a sudden hush and then a murmur.

"Hello, Carley! Now say it to our faces," called out Geralda Conners, a fair, handsome young woman of thirty, exquisitely gowned in the latest mode, and whose brilliantly tinted complexion was not the natural one of health.

"Say what, Geralda?" asked Carley. "I certainly would not say anything behind your backs that I wouldn't repeat here."

"Eleanor has been telling us how you simply burned us up."

"We did have an argument. And I'm not sure I said all I wanted to."

"Say the rest here," drawled a lazy, mellow voice. "For Heaven's sake, stir us up. If I could get a kick out of *anything* I'd bless it."

"Carley, go on the stage," advised another. "You've got

Elsie Ferguson tied to the mast for looks. And lately you're surely tragic enough."

"I wish you'd go somewhere far off," observed a third. "My husband is dippy about you."

"Girls, do you know that you actually have not one sensible idea in your heads?" retorted Carley.

"Sensible? I should hope not. Who wants to be sensible?"

Geralda battered her teacup on a saucer. "Listen," she called. "I wasn't kidding Carley. I am good and sore. She goes around knocking everybody and saying New York backs Sodom off the boards. I want her to come out with it right here."

"I dare say I've talked too much," returned Carley. "It's been a rather hard winter on me. Perhaps, indeed, I've tried the patience of my friends."

"See here, Carley," said Geralda, deliberately, "just because you've had life turn to bitter ashes in your mouth you've no right to poison it for us. We all find it pretty sweet. You're an *un*satisfied woman and if you don't marry somebody you'll end by being a reformer or fanatic."

"I'd rather end that way than rot in a shell," retorted Carley.

"I declare, you make me see red, Carley," flashed Geralda, angrily. "No wonder Morrison roasts you to everybody. He says Glenn Kilbourne threw you down for some Western girl. If that's true it's pretty small of you to vent your spleen on us."

Carley felt the gathering of a mighty resistless force. But Geralda Conners was nothing to her except the target for a thunderbolt.

"I have no spleen," she replied, with a dignity of passion. "I have only pity. I was as blind as you. If heartbreak tore the scales from my eyes, perhaps that is well for me.

For I see something terribly wrong in myself, in you, in all of us, in the life of to-day."

"You keep your pity to yourself. You need it," answered Geralda, with heat. "There's nothing wrong with me or my friends or life in good old New York."

"Nothing wrong!" cried Carley. "Listen. Nothing wrong in you or life to-day—nothing for you women to make right? You are blind as bats—as dead to living truth as if you were buried. Nothing wrong when thousands of crippled soldiers have no homes—no money—no friends—no work—in many cases no food or bed? . . . Splendid young men who went away in their prime to fight for *you* and came back ruined, suffering! Nothing wrong when sane women with the vote might rid politics of partisanship, greed, crookedness? Nothing wrong when prohibition is mocked by women—when the greatest boon ever granted this country is derided and beaten down and cheated? Nothing wrong when there are half a million defective children in this city? Nothing wrong when there are not enough schools and teachers to educate our boys and girls, when those teachers are shamefully underpaid? Nothing wrong when the mothers of this great country let their youngsters go to the dark motion-picture halls and night after night in thousands of towns over all this broad land see pictures that the juvenile court and the educators and keepers of reform schools say make burglars, crooks, and murderers of our boys and vampires of our girls? Nothing wrong when these young adolescent girls ape *you* and wear stockings rolled under their knees below their skirts and use a lip stick and paint their faces and darken their eyes and pluck their eyebrows and absolutely do not know what shame is? Nothing wrong when you may find in any city women standing at street corners distributing booklets on birth control? Nothing wrong when great magazines print no page or picture without its sex appeal?

Nothing wrong when the automobile, so convenient for the innocent little run out of town, presents the greatest evil that ever menaced American girls! Nothing wrong when money is god—when luxury, pleasure, excitement, speed are the striven for? Nothing wrong when some of your husbands spend more of their time with other women than with you? Nothing wrong with jazz—where the lights go out in the dance hall and the dancers jiggle and toddle and wiggle in a frenzy? Nothing wrong in a country where the greatest college cannot report birth of one child to each graduate in ten years? Nothing wrong with race suicide and the incoming horde of foreigners? . . . Nothing wrong with you women who cannot or will not stand childbirth? Nothing wrong with most of you, when if you *did* have a child, you could not nurse it? . . . Oh, my God, there's nothing wrong with America except that she staggers under a Titanic burden that only mothers of sons can remove! . . . You doll women, you parasites, you toys of men, you silken-wrapped geisha girls, you painted, idle, purring cats, you parody of the females of your species— find brains enough if you can to see the doom hanging over you and revolt before it is too late!"

CHAPTER XI

Carley burst in upon her aunt.

"Look at me, Aunt Mary!" she cried, radiant and exultant. "I'm going back out West to marry Glenn and live his life!"

The keen old eyes of her aunt softened and dimmed. "Dear Carley, I've known that for a long time. You've found yourself at last."

Then Carley breathlessly babbled her hastily formed plans, every word of which seemed to rush her onward.

"You're going to surprise Glenn again?" queried Aunt Mary.

"Oh, I must! I want to see his face when I tell him."

"Well, I hope he won't surprise *you*," declared the old lady. "When did you hear from him last?"

"In January. It seems ages—but—Aunt Mary, you don't imagine Glenn—"

"I imagine nothing," interposed her aunt. "It will turn out happily and I'll have some peace in my old age. But, Carley, what's to become of me?"

"Oh, I never thought!" replied Carley, blankly. "It will be lonely for you. Auntie, I'll come back in the fall for a few weeks. Glenn will let me."

"*Let* you? Ye gods! So you've come to that? Imperious Carley Burch! . . . Thank Heaven, you'll now be satisfied to be let do things."

"I'd—I'd crawl for him," breathed Carley.

"Well, child, as you can't be practical, I'll have to be," replied Aunt Mary, seriously. "Fortunately for you I am a woman of quick decision. Listen. I'll go West with you. I want to see the Grand Canyon. Then I'll go on to California, where I have old friends I've not seen for years. When you get your new home all fixed up I'll spend awhile with you. And if I want to come back to New York now and then I'll go to a hotel. It is settled. I think the change will benefit me."

"Auntie, you make me very happy. I could ask no more," said Carley.

Swiftly as endless tasks could make them the days passed. But those on the train dragged interminably.

Carley sent her aunt through to the Canyon while she stopped off at Flagstaff to store innumerable trunks and bags. The first news she heard of Glenn and the Hutters was that they had gone to the Tonto Basin to buy hogs and would be absent at least a month. This gave birth to a new plan in Carley's mind. She would doubly surprise Glenn. Wherefore she took council with some Flagstaff business men and engaged them to set a force of men at work on the Deep Lake property, making the improvements she desired, and hauling lumber, cement, bricks, machinery, supplies—all the necessaries for building construction. Also she instructed them to throw up a tent house for her to live in during the work, and to engage a reliable Mexican man with his wife for servants. When she left for the Canyon she was happier than ever before in her life.

* * *

I t was near the coming of sunset when Carley first looked down into the Grand Canyon. She had forgotten Glenn's tribute to this place. In her rapturous excitement of preparation and travel the Canyon had been merely a name. But now she saw it and she was stunned.

What a stupendous chasm, gorgeous in sunset color on the heights, purpling into mystic shadows in the depths! There was a wonderful brightness of all the millions of red and yellow and gray surfaces still exposed to the sun. Carley did not feel a thrill, because feeling seemed inhibited. She looked and looked, yet was reluctant to keep on looking. She possessed no image in mind with which to compare this grand and mystic spectacle. A transformation of color and shade appeared to be going on swiftly, as if gods were changing the scenes of a Titanic stage. As she gazed the dark fringed line of the north rim turned to burnished gold, and she watched that with fascinated eyes. It turned rose, it lost its fire, it faded to quiet cold gray. The sun had set.

Then the wind blew cool through the piñons on the rim. There was a sweet tang of cedar and sage on the air and that indefinable fragrance peculiar to the canyon country of Arizona. How it brought back to Carley remembrance of Oak Creek! In the west, across the purple notches of the abyss, a dull gold flare showed where the sun had gone down.

In the morning at eight o'clock there were great irregular black shadows under the domes and peaks and escarpments. Bright Angel Canyon was all dark, showing dimly its ragged lines. At noon there were no shadows and all the colossal gorge lay glaring under the sun. In the evening Carley watched the Canyon as again the sun was setting.

Deep dark-blue shadows, like purple sails of immense ships, in wonderful contrast with the bright sunlit slopes, grew and rose toward the east, down the canyons and up the walls that faced the west. For a long while there was no red color, and the first indication of it was a dull bronze. Carley looked down into the void, at the sailing birds, at the precipitous slopes, and the dwarf spruces and the weathered old yellow cliffs. When she looked up again the shadows out there were no longer dark. They were clear. The slopes and depths and ribs of rock could be seen through them. Then the tips of the highest peaks and domes turned bright red. Far to the east she discerned a strange shadow, slowly turning purple. One instant it grew vivid, then began to fade. Soon after that all the colors darkened and slowly the pale gray stole over all.

At night Carley gazed over and into the black void. But for the awful sense of depth she would not have known the Canyon to be there. A soundless movement of wind passed under her. The chasm seemed a grave of silence. It was as mysterious as the stars and as aloof and as inevitable. It had held her senses of beauty and proportion in abeyance.

At another sunrise the crown of the rim, a broad belt of bare rock, turned pale gold under its fringed dark line of pines. The tips of the peak gleamed opal. There was no sunrise red, no fire. The light in the east was a pale gold under a steely green-blue sky. All the abyss of the Canyon was soft, gray, transparent, and the belt of gold broadened downward, making shadows on the west slopes of the mesas and escarpments. Far down in the shadows she discerned the river, yellow, turgid, palely gleaming. By straining her ears Carley heard a low dull roar as of distant storm. She stood fearfully at the extreme edge of a stupendous cliff, where it sheered dark and forbidding, down and down, into what seemed red and boundless depths of Hades. She saw gold spots of sunlight on the dark shadows, proving that somewhere, impossible to discover, the sun was shining through wind-worn holes in the sharp ridges. Every instant Carley grasped a different effect. Her studied gaze absorbed an endless changing. And at last she realized that sun and light and stars and moon and night and shade, all working incessantly and mutably over shapes and lines and angles and surfaces too numerous and too great for the sight of man to hold, made an ever-changing spectacle of supreme beauty and colorful grandeur.

She talked very little while at the Canyon. It silenced her. She had come to see it at the critical time of her life and in the right mood. The superficialities of the world shrunk to their proper insignificance. Once she asked her aunt: "Why did not Glenn bring me here?" As if this Canyon proved the nature of all things!

But in the end Carley found that the rending strife of the transformation of her attitude toward life had insensibly ceased. It had ceased during the long watching of this cataclysm of nature, this canyon of gold-banded black-fringed ramparts, and red-walled mountains which sloped down to be lost in purple depths. That was final proof of the strength of nature to soothe, to clarify, to stabilize the tried and weary and upward-gazing soul. Stronger than the recorded deeds of saints, stronger than the eloquence of the gifted uplifters of men, stronger than any words ever written, was the grand, brooding, sculptured aspect of nature. And it must have been so because thousands of years before the age of saints or preachers—before the fret and symbol and figure were cut in stone—man must have watched with thought-developing sight the wonders of the earth, the monuments of time, the glooming of the dark-blue sea, the handiwork of God.

I n May, Carley returned to Flagstaff to take up with earnest inspiration the labors of home-building in a primitive land.

It required two trucks to transport her baggage and purchases out to Deep Lake. The road was good for eighteen miles of the distance, until it branched off to reach her land, and from there it was desert rock and sand. But eventually they made it; and Carley found herself and belongings dumped out into the windy and sunny open. The moment was singularly thrilling and full of transport. She was free. She had shaken off the shackles. She faced lonely, wild, barren desert that must be made habitable by the genius of her direction and the labor of her hands. Always a thought of Glenn hovered tenderly, dreamily in the back of her consciousness, but she welcomed the opportunity to have a few weeks of work and activity and solitude before taking up her life with him. She wanted to adapt herself to the metamorphosis that had been wrought in her.

To her amazement and delight, a very considerable progress had been made with her plans. Under a sheltered red cliff among the cedars had been erected the tents where she expected to live until the house was completed. These tents were large, with broad floors high off the ground, and there were four of them. Her living tent had a porch under a wide canvas awning. The bed was a boxlike affair, raised off the floor two feet, and it contained a great, fragrant mass of cedar boughs upon which the blankets were to be spread. At one end was a dresser with large mirror, and a chiffonier. There were table and lamp, a low rocking chair, a shelf for books, a row of hooks upon which to hang things, a washstand with its necessary accessories, a little stove and a neat stack of cedar chips and sticks. Navajo rugs on the floor lent brightness and comfort.

Carley heard the rustling of cedar branches over her head, and saw where they brushed against the tent roof. It appeared warm and fragrant inside, and protected from the wind, and a subdued white light filtered through the canvas. Almost she felt like reproving herself for the comfort surrounding her. For she had come West to welcome the hard knocks of primitive life.

It took less than an hour to have her trunks stored in one of the spare tents, and to unpack clothes and necessaries for immediate use. Carley donned the comfortable and somewhat shabby outdoor garb she had worn at Oak Creek the year before; and it seemed to be the last thing needed to make her fully realize the glorious truth of the present.

"I'm here," she said to her pale, yet happy face in the mirror. "The impossible has happened. I have accepted Glenn's life. I have answered that strange call out of the West."

She wanted to throw herself on the sunlit woolly blankets of her bed and hug them, to think and think of the bewildering present happiness, to dream of the future, but she could not lie or sit still, nor keep her mind from grasping at actualities and possibilities of this place, nor her hands from itching to do things.

It developed, presently, that she could not have idled away the time even if she had wanted to, for the Mexican woman came for her, with smiling gesticulation and jabber that manifestly meant dinner. Carley could not understand many Mexican words, and herein she saw another task. This swarthy woman and her sloe-eyed husband favorably impressed Carley.

Next to claim her was Hoyle, the superintendent. "Miss Burch," he said, "in the early days we could run up a log cabin in a jiffy. Axes, horses, strong arms, and a few pegs—that was all we needed. But this house you've planned is different. It's good you've come to take the responsibility."

Carley had chosen the site for her home on top of the knoll where Glenn had taken her to show her the magnificent view of mountains and desert. Carley climbed it now with beating heart and mingled emotions. A thousand times already that day, it seemed, she had turned to gaze up at the noble white-clad peaks. They were closer now, apparently looming over her, and she felt a great sense of peace and protection in the thought that they would always be there. But she had not yet seen the desert that had haunted her for a year. When she reached the summit of the knoll and gazed out across the open space it seemed that she must stand spellbound. How green the cedared foreground—how gray and barren the downward slope—how wonderful the painted steppes! The vision that had lived in her memory shrank to nothingness. The reality was immense, more than beautiful, appalling in its isolation, beyond comprehension with its lure and strength to uplift.

But the superintendent drew her attention to the business at hand.

Carley had planned an L-shaped house of one story. Some of her ideas appeared to be impractical, and these she abandoned. The framework was up and half a dozen carpenters were lustily at work with saw and hammer.

"We'd made better progress if this house was in an ordinary place," explained Hoyle. "But you see the wind blows here, so the framework had to be made as solid and strong as possible. In fact, it's bolted to the sills."

Both living room and sleeping room were arranged so that the Painted Desert could be seen from one window, and on the other side the whole of the San Francisco Mountains. Both rooms were to have open fireplaces. Carley's idea was for service and durability. She thought of comfort in the severe winters of that high latitude, but elegance and luxury had no more significance in her life.

Hoyle made his suggestions as to changes and adaptations, and, receiving her approval, he went on to show her what had been already accomplished. Back on higher ground a reservoir of concrete was being constructed near an ever-flowing spring of snow water from the peaks. This water was being piped by gravity to the house, and was a matter of greatest satisfaction to Hoyle, for he claimed that it would never freeze in winter, and would be cold and abundant during the hottest and driest of summers. This assurance solved the most difficult and serious problem of ranch life in the desert.

Next Hoyle led Carley down off the knoll to the wide cedar valley adjacent to the lake. He was enthusiastic over its possibilities. Two small corrals and a large one had been erected, the latter having a low flat barn connected with it. Ground was already being cleared along the lake where alfalfa and hay were to be raised. Carley saw the blue and yellow smoke from burning brush, and the fragrant odor thrilled her. Mexicans were chopping the cleared cedars into firewood for winter use.

The day was spent before she realized it. At sunset the carpenters and mechanics left in two old Ford cars for town. The Mexicans had a camp in the cedars, and the Hoyles had theirs at the spring under the knoll where Carley had camped with Glenn and the Hutters. Carley watched the golden rosy sunset, and as the day ended she breathed deeply as if in unutterable relief. Supper found her with appetite she had long since lost. Twilight brought cold wind, the staccato bark of coyotes, the flicker of camp fires through the cedars. She tried to embrace all her sensations, but they were so rapid and many that she failed.

The cold, clear, silent night brought back the charm of the desert. How flaming white the stars! The great spire-pointed peaks lifted cold pale-gray outlines up into the deep star-studded sky. Carley walked a little to and fro, loath to go to her tent, though tired. She wanted calm. But instead of achieving calmness she grew more and more towards a strange state of exultation.

Westward, only a matter of twenty or thirty miles, lay

the deep rent in the level desert—Oak Creek Canyon. If Glenn had been there this night would have been perfect, yet almost unendurable. She was again grateful for his absence. What a surprise she had in store for him! And she imagined his face in its change of expression when she met him. If only he never learned of her presence in Arizona until she made it known in person! That she most longed for. Chances were against it, but then her luck had changed. She looked to the eastward where a pale luminosity of afterglow shone in the heavens. Far distant seemed the home of her childhood, the friends she had scorned and forsaken, the city of complaining and striving millions. If only some miracle might illumine the minds of her friends, as she felt that hers was to be illumined here in the solitude. But she well realized that not all problems could be solved by a call out of the West. Any open and lonely land that might have saved Glenn Kilbourne would have sufficed for her. It was the spirit of the thing and not the letter. It was work of any kind and not only that of ranch life. Not only the raising of hogs!

Carley directed stumbling steps toward the light of her tent. Her eyes had not been used to such black shadow along the ground. She had, too, squeamish feminine fears of hydrophobia skunks, and nameless animals or reptiles that were imagined denizens of the darkness. She gained her tent and entered. The Mexican, Gino, as he called himself, had lighted her lamp and fire. Carley was chilled through, and the tent felt so warm and cozy that she could scarcely believe it. She fastened the screen door, laced the flaps across it, except at the top, and then gave herself up to the lulling and comforting heat.

There were plans to perfect; innumerable things to remember; a car and accessories, horses, saddles, outfits to buy. Carley knew she should sit down at her table and write and figure, but she could not do it then.

For a long time she sat over the little stove, toasting her knees and hands, adding some chips now and then to the red coals. And her mind seemed a kaleidoscope of changing visions, thoughts, feelings. At last she undressed and blew out the lamp and went to bed.

Instantly a thick blackness seemed to enfold her and silence as of a dead world settled down upon her. Drowsy as she was, she could not close her eyes nor refrain from listening. Darkness and silence were tangible things. She felt them. And they seemed suddenly potent with magic charm to still the tumult of her, to soothe and rest, to create thoughts she had never thought before. Rest was more than selfish indulgence. Loneliness was necessary to gain consciousness of the soul. Already far back in the past seemed Carley's other life.

By and by the dead stillness awoke to faint sounds not before perceptible to her—a low, mournful sough of the wind in the cedars, then the faint far-distant note of a coyote, sad as the night and infinitely wild.

Days passed. Carley worked in the mornings with her hands and her brains. In the afternoons she rode and walked and climbed with a double object, to work herself into fit physical condition and to explore every nook and corner of her six hundred and forty acres.

Then what she had expected and deliberately induced by her efforts quickly came to pass. Just as the year before she had suffered excruciating pain from aching muscles, and saddle blisters, and walking blisters, and a very rending of her bones, so now she fell victim to them again. In sunshine and rain she faced the desert. Sunburn and sting of sleet were equally to be endured. And that abomination, the hateful blinding sandstorm, did not daunt her. But the weary hours of abnegation to this physical torture at least held one consoling recompense as compared with her experience of last year, and it was that there was no one interested to watch for her weaknesses and failures and blunders. She could fight it out alone.

Three weeks of this self-imposed strenuous training wore by before Carley was free enough from weariness and pain to experience other sensations. Her general health, evidently, had not been so good as when she had first visited Arizona. She caught cold and suffered other ills attendant upon an abrupt change of climate and condition. But doggedly she kept at her task. She rode when she should have been in bed; she walked when she should have ridden; she climbed when she should have kept to level ground. And finally by degrees so gradual as not to be noticed except in the sum of them she began to mend.

Meanwhile the construction of her house went on with uninterrupted rapidity. When the low, slanting, wide-eaved roof was completed Carley lost further concern about rainstorms. Let them come. When the plumbing was all in and Carley saw verification of Hoyle's assurance that it would mean a gravity supply of water ample and continual, she lost her last concern as to the practicability of the work. That, and the earning of her endurance, seemed to bring closer a wonderful reward, still nameless and spiritual, that had been unattainable, but now breathed to her on the fragrant desert wind and in the brooding silence.

The time came when each afternoon's ride or climb called to Carley with increasing delight. But the fact that she must soon reveal to Glenn her presence and transformation did not seem to be all the cause. She could ride without pain, walk without losing her breath, work without blistering her hands; and in this there was compensation. The building of the house that was to become a home, the development of water resources and land that meant the making of a ranch—these did not altogether constitute the anticipation of content. To be active, to accomplish things, to recall to mind her knowledge of manual training, of domestic science, of designing and painting, to learn to cook—these were indeed measures full of reward, but they were not all. In her wondering, pondering meditation she arrived at the point where she tried to assign to her love the growing fullness of her life. This, too, splendid and all-pervading as it was, she had to reject. Some exceedingly illusive and vital significance of life had insidiously come to Carley.

One afternoon, with the sky full of white and black rolling clouds and a cold wind sweeping through the cedars, she halted to rest and escape the chilling gale for a while. In a sunny place, under the lee of a gravel bank, she sought refuge. It was warm here because of the reflected sunlight and the absence of wind. The sand at the bottom of the bank held a heat that felt good to her cold hands. All about her and over her swept the keen wind, rustling the sage, seeping the sand, swishing the cedars, but she was out of it, protected and insulated. The sky above showed blue between the threatening clouds. There were no birds or living creatures in sight. Certainly the place had little of color or beauty or grace, nor could she see beyond a few rods. Lying there, without any particular reason that she was conscious of, she suddenly felt shot through and through with exhilaration.

Another day, the warmest of the spring so far, she rode a Navajo mustang she had recently bought from a passing trader; and at the farthest end of her section, in rough wooded and ridged ground she had not explored, she found a canyon with red walls and pine trees and gleaming stream-let and glades of grass and jumbles of rock. It was a miniature canyon, to be sure, only a quarter of a mile long, and as deep as the height of a lofty pine, and so narrow that it seemed only the width of a lane, but it had all the features of Oak Creek Canyon, and so sufficed for the exultant joy of possession. She explored it. The willow brakes and oak thickets harbored rabbits and birds. She saw the white flags of deer running away down the open. Up at the head where the canyon boxed she flushed a flock of wild turkeys. They ran like ostriches and flew like great brown chickens. In a cavern Carley found the den of a bear, and in another place the bleached bones of a steer.

She lingered here in the shaded depths with a feeling as if she were indeed lost to the world. These big brown and seamy-barked pines with their spreading gnarled arms and webs of green needles belonged to her, as also the tiny brook, the blue bells smiling out of the ferns, the single stalk of mescal on a rocky ledge.

Never had sun and earth, tree and rock, seemed a part of her being until then. She would become a sun-worshiper and a lover of the earth. That canyon had opened there to sky and light for millions of years; and doubtless it had harbored sheep herders, Indians, cliff dwellers, barbarians. She was a woman with white skin and a cultivated mind, but the affinity for them existed in her. She felt it, and that an understanding of it would be good for body and soul.

Another day she found a little grove of jack pines growing on a flat mesalike bluff, the highest point on her land. The trees were small and close together, mingling their green needles over-head and their discarded brown ones on the ground. From here Carley could see afar to all points of the compass—the slow green descent to the south and the climb to the black-timbered distance; the ridged and canyoned country to the west, red vents choked with green and rimmed with gray; to the north the grand up-flung mountain kingdom crowned with snow; and to the east the vastness of illimitable space, the openness and wildness, the chased and beaten mosaic of colored sands and rocks.

Again and again she visited this lookout and came to love its isolation, its command of wondrous prospects, its power of suggestion to her thoughts. She became a creative being, in harmony with the live things around her. The great life-dispensing sun poured its rays down upon her, as if to ripen her; and the earth seemed warm, motherly, immense with its all-embracing arms. She no longer plucked the bluebells to press to her face, but leaned to them. Every blade of gramma grass, with its shining bronze-tufted seed head, had significance for her. The scents of the desert began to have meaning for her. She sensed within her the working of a great leveling process through which supreme happiness would come.

June! The rich, thick, amber light, like a transparent reflection from some intense golden medium, seemed to float in the warm air. The sky became an azure blue. In the still noontides, when the bees hummed drowsily and the flies buzzed, vast creamy-white columnar clouds rolled up from the horizon, like colossal ships with bulging sails. And summer with its rush of growing things was at hand.

Carley rode afar, seeking in strange places the secret that eluded her. Only a few days now until she would ride down to Oak Creek Canyon! There was a low, singing melody of wind in the cedars. The earth became too beautiful in her magnified sight. A great truth was dawning upon her—that the sacrifice of what she had held as necessary to the enjoyment of life—that the strain of conflict, the labor of hands, the forcing of weary body, the enduring of pain, the contact with the earth—had served somehow to rejuvenate her blood, quicken her pulse, intensify her sensorial faculties, thrill her very soul, lead her into the realm of enchantment.

One afternoon a dull, lead-black-colored cinder knoll tempted her to explore its bare heights. She rode up until her mustang sank to his knees and could climb no farther. From there she essayed the ascent on foot. It took labor. But at last she gained the summit, burning, sweating, panting.

The cinder hill was an extinct crater of a volcano. In the center of it lay a deep bowl, wondrously symmetrical, and of a dark lusterless hue. Not a blade of grass was there, nor a plant. Carley conceived a desire to go to the bottom of this pit. She tried the cinders of the edge of the slope. They had the same consistency as those of the ascent she had overcome. But here there was a steeper incline. A tingling rush of daring seemed to drive her over the rounded rim, and, once started down, it was as if she wore seven-league boots. Fear left her. Only an exhilarating emotion consumed her. If there were danger, it mattered not. She strode down with giant steps, she plunged, she started avalanches to ride them until they stopped, she leaped, and lastly she fell, to roll over the soft cinders to the pit.

There she lay. It seemed a comfortable resting place. The pit was scarcely six feet across. She gazed upward and was astounded. How steep was the rounded slope on all sides! There were no sides; it was a circle. She looked up at a round lake of deep translucent sky. Such depth of blue, such exquisite rare color! Carley imagined she could gaze through it to the infinite beyond.

She closed her eyes and rested. Soon the laboring of heart and breath calmed to normal, so that she could not hear them. Then she lay perfectly motionless. With eyes shut she seemed still to look, and what she saw was the sunlight through the blood and flesh of her eyelids. It was red, as rare a hue as the blue of sky. So piercing did it grow that she had to shade her eyes with her arm.

Again the strange, rapt glow suffused her body. Never in all her life had she been so absolutely alone. She might as well have been in her grave. She might have been dead to all earthy things and reveling in spirit in the glory of the physical that had escaped her in life. And she abandoned herself to this influence.

She loved these dry, dusty cinders; she loved the crater here hidden from all save birds; she loved the desert, the earth—above all, the sun. She was a product of the earth—a creation of the sun. She had been an infinitesimal atom of inert something that had quickened to life under the blazing magic of the sun. Soon her spirit would abandon her body and go on, while her flesh and bone returned to dust. This frame of hers, that carried the divine spark, belonged to the earth. She had only been ignorant, mindless, feelingless, absorbed in the seeking of gain, blind to the truth. She had to give. She had been created a woman; she belonged to nature; she was nothing save a mother of the future. She had loved neither Glenn Kilbourne nor life itself. False education, false standards, false environment had developed her into a woman who imagined she must feed her body on the milk and honey of indulgence.

She was abased now—woman as animal, though saved and uplifted by her power of immortality. Transcendental was her female power to link life with the future. The power of the plant seed, the power of the earth, the heat of the sun, the inscrutable creation—spirit of nature, almost the divinity of God—these were all hers because she was a woman. That was the great secret, aloof so long. That was what had been wrong with life—the woman blind to her meaning, her power, her mastery.

So she abandoned herself to the woman within her. She held out her arms to the blue abyss of heaven as if to embrace the universe. She was Nature. She kissed the dusty cinders and pressed her breast against the warm slope. Her heart swelled to bursting with a glorious and unutterable happiness.

* * *

That afternoon as the sun was setting under a gold-white scroll of cloud Carley got back to Deep Lake.

A familiar lounging figure crossed her sight. It approached to where she had dismounted. Charley, the sheep herder of Oak Creek!

"Howdy!" he drawled, with his queer smile. "So it was you-all who had this Deep Lake section?"

"Yes. And how are you, Charley?" she replied, shaking hands with him.

"Me? Aw, I'm tip-top. I'm shore glad you got this ranch. Reckon I'll hit you for a job."

"I'd give it to you. But aren't you working for the Hutters?"

"Nope. Not any more. Me an' Stanton had a row with them."

How droll and dry he was! His lean, olive-brown face, with its guileless clear eyes and his lanky figure in blue jeans vividly recalled Oak Creek to Carley.

"Oh, I'm—sorry," returned she haltingly, somehow checked in her warm rush of thought. "Stanton? . . . Did he quit too?"

"Yep. He sure did."

"What was the trouble?"

"Reckon because Flo made up to Kilbourne," replied Charley, with a grin.

"Ah! I—I see," murmured Carley. A blankness seemed to wave over her. It extended to the air without, to the sense of the golden sunset. It passed. What should she ask—what out of a thousand sudden flashing queries? "Are—are the Hutters back?"

"Sure. Been back several days. I reckoned Hoyle told you. Mebbe he didn't know, though. For nobody's been to town."

"How is—how are they all?" faltered Carley. There was a strange wall here between her thought and her utterance.

"Everybody satisfied, I reckon," replied Charley.

"Flo—how is she?" burst out Carley.

"Aw, Flo's loony over her husband," drawled Charley, his clear eyes on Carley's.

"Husband!" she gasped.

"Sure. Flo's gone an' went an' done what I swore on."

"*Who?*" whispered Carley, and the query was a terrible blade piercing her heart.

"Now who'd you reckon on?" asked Charley, with his slow grin.

Carley's lips were mute.

"Wal, it was your old beau thet you wouldn't have," returned Charley, as he gathered up his long frame, evidently to leave. "Kilbourne! He an' Flo came back from the Tonto all hitched up."

CHAPTER XII

Vague sense of movement, of darkness, and of cold attended Carley's consciousness for what seemed endless time.

A fall over rocks and a severe thrust from a sharp branch brought an acute appreciation of her position, if not of her mental state. Night had fallen. The stars were out. She had stumbled over a low ledge. Evidently she had wandered around, dazedly and aimlessly, until brought to her senses by pain. But for a gleam of camp fires through the cedars she would have been lost. It did not matter. She was lost, anyhow. What was it that had happened?

Charley, the sheep herder! Then the thunderbolt of his words burst upon her, and she collapsed to the cold stones. She lay quivering from head to toe. She dug her fingers into the moss and lichen. "Oh, God, to think— after all—it happened!" she moaned. There had been a rending within her breast, as of physical violence, from which she now suffered anguish. There were a thousand stinging nerves. There was a mortal sickness of horror, of insupportable heartbreaking loss. She could not endure it. She could not live under it.

She lay there until energy supplanted shock. Then she

rose to rush into the darkest shadows of the cedars, to grope here and there, hanging her head, wringing her hands, beating her breast. "It can't be true," she cried. "Not after my struggle—my victory—not *now!*" But there had been no victory. And now it was too late. She was betrayed, ruined, lost. That wonderful love had wrought transformation in her—and now havoc. Once she fell against the branches of a thick cedar that upheld her. The fragrance which had been sweet was now bitter. Life that had been bliss was now hateful! She could not keep still for a single moment.

Black night, cedars, brush, rocks, washes, seemed not to obstruct her. In a frenzy she rushed on, tearing her dress, her hands, her hair. Violence of some kind was imperative. All at once a pale gleaming open space, shimmering under the stars, lay before her. It was water. Deep Lake! And instantly a hideous terrible longing to destroy herself obsessed her. She had no fear. She could have welcomed the cold, slimy depths that meant oblivion. But could they really bring oblivion? A year ago she would have believed so, and would no longer have endured such agony. She had changed. A cursed strength had come to her, and it was this strength that now augmented her torture. She flung wide her arms to the pitiless white stars and looked up at them. "My hope, my faith, my love have failed me," she whispered. "They have been a lie. I went through hell for them. And now I've nothing to live for. . . . Oh, let me end it all!"

If she prayed to the stars for mercy, it was denied her. Passionlessly they blazed on. But she could not kill herself. In that hour death would have been the only relief and peace left to her. Stricken by the cruelty of her fate, she fell back against the stones and gave up to grief. Nothing was left but fierce pain. The youth and vitality and intensity of her then locked arms with anguish and torment and a cheated, unsatisfied love. Strength of mind and body involuntarily resisted the ravages of this catastrophe. Will power seemed nothing, but the flesh of her, that medium of exquisite sensation, so full of life, so prone to joy, refused to surrender. The part of her that felt fought terribly for its heritage.

All night long Carley lay there. The crescent moon went down, the stars moved on their course, the coyotes ceased to wail, the wind died away, the lapping of the waves along the lake shore wore to gentle splash, the whispering of the insects stopped as the cold of dawn approached. The darkest hour fell—hour of silence, solitude, and melancholy, when the desert lay tranced, cold, waiting, mournful without light of moon or stars or sun.

In the gray dawn Carley dragged her bruised and aching body back to her tent, and, fastening the door, she threw off wet clothes and boots and fell upon her bed. Slumber of exhaustion came to her.

When she awoke the tent was light and the moving shadows of cedar boughs on the white canvas told that the sun was straight above. Carley ached as never before. A deep pang seemed invested in every bone. Her heart felt swollen out of proportion to its space in her breast. Her breathing came slow and it hurt. Her blood was sluggish. Suddenly she shut her eyes. She loathed the light of day. What was it that had happened?

Then the brutal truth flashed over her again, in aspect new, with all the old bitterness. For an instant she experienced a suffocating sensation as if the canvas had sagged under the burden of heavy air and was crushing her breast and heart. Then wave after wave of emotion swept over her. The storm winds of grief and passion were loosened again. And she writhed in her misery.

Some one knocked on her door. The Mexican woman called anxiously. Carley awoke to the fact that her presence was not solitary on the physical earth, even if her soul seemed stricken to eternal loneliness. Even in the desert there was a world to consider. Vanity that had bled to death, pride that had been crushed, availed her not here. But something else came to her support. The lesson of the West had been to endure, not to shirk—to face an issue, not to hide. Carley got up, bathed, dressed, brushed and arranged her dishevelled hair. The face she saw in the mirror excited her amaze and pity. Then she went out in answer to the call for dinner. But she could not eat. The ordinary functions of life appeared to be deadened.

The day happened to be Sunday, and therefore the workmen were absent. Carley had the place to herself. How the half-completed house mocked her! She could not bear to look at it. What use could she make of it now? Flo Hutter had become the working comrade of Glenn Kilbourne, the mistress of his cabin. She was his wife and she would be the mother of his children.

That thought gave birth to the darkest hour of Carley Burch's life. She became possessed as by a thousand devils. She became merely a female robbed of her mate. Reason was not in her, nor charity, nor justice. All that was abnormal in human nature seemed coalesced in her, dominant, passionate, savage, terrible. She hated with an incredible and insane ferocity. In the seclusion of her tent, crouched on her bed, silent, locked, motionless, she yet was the embodiment of all terrible strife and storm in nature. Her heart was a maelstrom and would have whirled and sucked down to hell all the beings that were men. Her soul was a bottomless gulf, filled with the gales and the fires of jealousy, superhuman to destroy.

That fury consumed all her remaining strength, and from the relapse she sank to sleep.

Morning brought the inevitable reaction. However long her other struggles, this monumental and final one would be brief. She realized that, yet was unable to understand how it could be possible, unless shock or death or mental aberration ended the fight. An eternity of emotion lay back between this awakening of intelligence and the hour of her fall into the clutches of primitive passion.

That morning she faced herself in the mirror and asked, "Now—what do I owe *you?*" It was not her voice that answered. It was beyond her. But it said: "Go on! You are cut adrift. You are alone. You owe none but yourself! . . . Go on! Not backward—nor to the depths—but up—upward!"

She shuddered at such a decree. How impossible for her! All animal, all woman, all emotion, how could she live on the cold, pure heights? Yet she owed something intangible and inscrutable to herself. Was it the thing that woman lacked physically, yet contained hidden in her soul? An element of eternal spirit to rise! Because of heartbreak and ruin and irreparable loss must she fail? Was loss of love and husband and children only a test? The present hour would be swallowed in the sum of life's trials. She could not go back. She would not go down. There was wrenched from her tried and sore heart an unalterable and unquenchable decision—to make her own soul prove the evolution of woman. Vessel of blood and flesh she might be, doomed by nature to the reproduction of her kind, but she had in her the supreme spirit and power to carry on the progress of the ages—the climb of woman out of the darkness.

Carley went out to the workmen. The house should be completed and she would live in it. Always there was the stretching and illimitable desert to look at, and the grand heave upward of the mountains. Hoyle was full of zest for the practical details of the building. He saw nothing of the havoc wrought in her. Nor did the other workmen glance more than casually at her. In this Carley lost something of a shirking fear that her loss and grief were patent to all eyes.

That afternoon she mounted the most spirited of the mustangs she had purchased from the Indians. To govern him and stick on him required all her energy. And she rode him hard and far, out across the desert, across mile after mile of cedar forest, clear to the foothills. She rested there, absorbed in gazing desertward, and upon turning back again, she ran him over the level stretches. Wind and branch threshed her seemingly to ribbons. Violence seemed good for her. A fall had no fear for her now. She reached camp at dusk, hot as fire, breathless and strengthless. But she had earned something. Such action required constant use of muscle and mind. If need be she could drive both to the very furthermost limit. She could ride and ride—until the future, like the immensity of the desert there, might swallow her. She changed her clothes and rested a while. The call to supper found her hungry. In this fact she discovered mockery of her grief. Love was not the food of life. Exhausted nature's need of rest and sleep was no respecter of a woman's emotion.

Next day Carley rode northward, wildly and fearlessly, as if this conscious activity was the initiative of an endless number of rides that were to save her. As before the foothills called her, and she went on until she came to a very high one.

Carley dismounted from her panting horse, answering the familiar impulse to attain heights by her own effort.

"Am I only a weakling?" she asked herself. "Only a creature mined by the fever of the soul! . . . Thrown from one emotion to another? Never the same. Yearning, suffering, sacrificing, hoping, and changing—forever the same! What is it that drives *me*? A great city with all its attractions has failed to help me realize my life. So have friends failed. So has the world. What can solitude and grandeur do? . . . All this obsession of mine—all this strange feeling for simple elemental earthly things likewise will fail me. Yet I am driven. . . . They would call me a mad woman."

It took Carley a full hour of slow body-bending labor to climb to the summit of that hill. High, steep, and rugged, it resisted ascension. But at last she surmounted it and sat alone on the heights, with naked eyes, and an unconscious prayer on her lips.

What was it that had happened? Could there be here a different answer from that which always mocked her?

She had been a girl, not accountable for loss of mother, for choice of home and education. She had belonged to a class. She had grown to womanhood in it. She had loved, and in loving had escaped the evil of her day, if not its taint. She had lived only for herself. Conscience had awakened—but, alas! too late. She had overthrown the sordid, self-seeking habit of life; she had awakened to real womanhood; she had fought the insidious spell of modernity and she had defeated it; she had learned the thrill of taking root in new soil, the pain and joy of labor, the bliss of solitude, the promise of home and love and motherhood. But she had gathered all these marvelous things to her soul too late for happiness.

"*Now* it is answered," she declared aloud. "That is what has happened? . . . And all that is *past*. . . . Is there anything left? If so—*what?*"

She flung her query out to the winds of the desert. But the desert seemed too gray, too vast, too remote, too aloof, too measureless. It was not concerned with her little life. Then she turned to the mountain kingdom.

It seemed overpoweringly near at hand. It loomed above her to pierce the fleecy clouds. It was only a stupendous upheaval of earth-crust, grown over at the base by leagues and leagues of pine forest, belted along the middle by vast slanting zigzag slopes of aspen, rent and riven toward the heights into canyon and gorge, bared above to cliffs and corners of craggy rock, whitened at the sky-piercing peaks by snow. Its beauty and sublimity were lost upon Carley now; she was concerned with its travail, its age, its endurance, its strength. And she studied it with magnified sight.

What incomprehensible subterranean force had swelled those immense slopes and lifted the huge bulk aloft to the clouds? Cataclysm of nature—the expanding or shrinking of the earth—vast volcanic action under the surface! Whatever it had been, it had left its expression of the travail of the universe. This mountain mass had been hot gas when flung from the parent sun, and now it was solid granite. What had it endured in the making? What indeed had been its dimensions before the millions of years of its struggle?

Eruption, earthquake, avalanche, the attrition of glacier, the erosion of water, the cracking of frost, the weathering of rain and wind and snow—these it had eternally fought and resisted in vain, yet still it stood magnificent, frowning, battle-scarred and undefeated. Its sky-piercing peaks were as cries for mercy to the Infinite. This old mountain realized its doom. It had to go, perhaps to make room for a newer and better kingdom. But it endured because of the spirit of nature. The great notched circular line of rock below and between the peaks, in the body of the mountains, showed where in ages past the heart of living granite had blown out, to let loose on all the near surrounding desert the streams of black lava and the hills of black cinders. Despite its fringe of green it was hoary with age. Every looming gray-faced wall, massive and sublime, seemed a monument of its mastery over time. Every deep-cut canyon, showing the skeleton ribs, the caverns and caves, its avalanche-carved slides, its long, fan-shaped, spreading taluses, carried conviction to the spectator that it was but a frail bit of rock, that its life was little and brief, that upon it had been laid the merciless curse of nature. Change! Change must unknit the very knots of the center of the earth. So its strength lay in the sublimity of its defiance. It meant to endure to the last rolling grain of sand. It was a dead mountain of rock, without spirit, yet it taught a grand lesson to the seeing eye.

Life was only a part, perhaps an infinitely small part of nature's plan. Death and decay were just as important to her inscrutable design. The universe had not been created for life, ease, pleasure, and happiness of a man creature developed from lower organisms. If nature's secret was the developing of a spirit through all time, Carley divined that she had it within her. So the present meant little.

"I have no right to be unhappy," concluded Carley. "I had no right to Glenn Kilbourne. I failed him. In that I failed myself. Neither life nor nature failed me—nor love. It is no longer a mystery. Unhappiness is only a change. Happiness itself is only change. So what does it matter? The great thing is to see life—to understand—to feel—to work—to fight—to endure. It is not my fault I am here. But it is my fault if I leave this strange old earth the poorer for my failure. . . . I will no longer be little. I will find strength. I will endure. . . . I still have eyes, ears, nose, taste. I can feel the sun, the wind, the nip of frost. Must I slink like a craven because I've lost the love of *one* man? Must I hate Flo Hutter because she will make Glenn happy? Never! . . . All of this seems better so, because through it I am changed. I might have lived on, a selfish clod!"

Carley turned from the mountain kingdom and faced her future with the profound and sad and far-seeing look that had come with her lesson. She knew what to give. Sometime and somewhere there would be recompense. She would hide her wound in the faith that time would heal it. And the ordeal she set herself, to prove her sincerity and strength, was to ride down to Oak Creek Canyon.

Carley did not wait many days. Strange how the old vanity held her back until something of the havoc in her face should be gone!

One morning she set out early, riding her best horse, and she took a sheep trail across country. The distance by road was much farther. The June morning was cool, sparkling, fragrant. Mocking birds sang from the topmost twig of cedars; doves cooed in the pines; sparrow hawks sailed low over the open grassy patches. Desert primroses showed their rounded pink clusters in sunny places, and here and there burned the carmine of Indian paint-brush. Jack rabbits and cotton-tails bounded and scampered away through the sage. The desert had life and color and movement this June day. And as always there was the dry fragrance on the air.

Her mustang had been inured to long and consistent travel over the desert. Her weight was nothing to him and he kept to the swinging lope for miles. As she approached Oak Creek Canyon, however, she drew him to a trot, and then a walk. Sight of the deep red-walled and green-floored canyon was a shock to her.

The trail came out on the road that led to Ryan's sheep camp, at a point several miles west of the cabin where Carley had encountered Haze Ruff. She remembered the curves and stretches, and especially the steep jump-off where the road led down off the rim into the canyon. Here she dismounted and walked. From the foot of this descent she knew every rod of the way would be familiar to her, and, womanlike, she wanted to turn away and fly from them. But she kept on and mounted again at level ground.

The murmur of the creek suddenly assailed her ears—sweet, sad, memorable, strangely powerful to hurt. Yet the sound seemed of long ago. Down here summer had advanced. Rich thick foliage overspread the winding road of sand. Then out of the shade she passed into the sunnier regions of isolated pines. Along here she had raced Calico with Glenn's bay; and here she had caught him, and there was the place she had fallen. She halted a moment under the pine tree where Glenn had held her in his arms. Tears dimmed her eyes. If only she had known then the truth, the reality! But regrets were useless.

By and by a craggy red wall loomed above the trees, and its pipe-organ conformation was familiar to Carley. She left the road and turned to go down to the creek. Sycamores and maples and great bowlders, and mossy ledges overhanging the water, and a huge sentinel pine marked the spot where she and Glenn had eaten their lunch that last day. Her mustang splashed into the clear water and halted to drink. Beyond, through the trees, Carley saw the sunny red-earthed clearing that was Glenn's farm. She looked, and fought herself, and bit her quivering lip until she tasted blood. Then she rode out into the open.

The whole west side of the canyon had been cleared and cultivated and plowed. But she gazed no farther. She did not want to see the spot where she had given Glenn his ring and had parted from him. She rode on. If she could pass West Fork she believed her courage would rise to the completion of this ordeal. Places were what she feared. Places that she had loved while blindly believing she hated! There the narrow gap of green and blue split the looming red wall. She was looking into West Fork. Up there stood the cabin. How fierce a pang rent her breast! She faltered at the crossing of the branch stream, and almost surrendered. The water murmured, the leaves rustled, the bees hummed, the birds sang—all with some sad sweetness that seemed of the past.

Then the trail leading up West Fork was like a barrier. She saw horse tracks in it. Next she descried boot tracks the shape of which was so well-remembered that it shook her heart. There were fresh tracks in the sand, pointing in the direction of the Lodge. Ah! that was where Glenn lived now. Carley strained at her will to keep it fighting her memory. The glory and the dream were gone!

A touch of spur urged her mustang into a gallop. The splashing ford of the creek—the still, eddying pool beyond—the green orchards—the white lacy waterfall—and Lolomi Lodge!

Nothing had altered. But Carley seemed returning after many years. Slowly she dismounted—slowly she climbed the porch steps. Was there no one at home? Yet the vacant doorway, the silence—something attested to the knowledge of Carley's presence. Then suddenly Mrs. Hutter fluttered out with Flo behind her.

"You dear girl—I'm so glad!" cried Mrs. Hutter, her voice trembling.

"I'm glad to see you, too," said Carley, bending to receive Mrs. Hutter's embrace. Carley saw dim eyes—the stress of agitation, but no surprise.

"Oh, Carley!" burst out the Western girl, with voice rich and full, yet tremulous.

"Flo, I've come to wish you happiness," replied Carley, very low.

Was it the same Flo? This seemed more of a woman—strange now—white and strained—beautiful, eager, questioning. A cry of gladness burst from her. Carley felt herself enveloped in strong close clasp—and then a warm, quick kiss of joy. It shocked her, yet somehow thrilled. Sure was the welcome here. Sure was the strained situation, also, but the voice rang too glad a note for Carley. It touched her deeply, yet she could not understand. She had not measured the depth of Western, friendship.

"Have you—seen Glenn?" queried Flo, breathlessly.

"Oh no, indeed not," replied Carley, slowly gaining

composure. The nervous agitation of these women had stilled her own. "I just rode up the trail. Where is he?"

"He was here—a moment ago," panted Flo. "Oh, Carley, we sure are locoed. . . . Why, we only heard an hour ago—that *you* were at Deep Lake. . . . Charley rode in. He told us. . . . I thought my heart would break. Poor Glenn! When he heard it. . . . But never mind *me*. Jump your horse and run to West Fork!"

The spirit of her was like the strength of her arms as she hurried Carley across the porch and shoved her down the steps.

"Climb on and run, Carley," cried Flo. "If you only knew how glad he'll be that you came!"

Carley leaped into the saddle and wheeled the mustang. But she had no answer for the girl's singular, almost wild exultance. Then like a shot the spirited mustang was off down the lane. Carley wondered with swelling heart. Was her coming such a wondrous surprise—so unexpected and big in generosity—something that would make Kilbourne as glad as it had seemed to make, Flo? Carley thrilled to this assurance.

Down the lane she flew. The red walls blurred and the sweet wind whipped her face. At the trail she swerved the mustang, but did not check his gait. Under the great pines he sped and round the bulging wall. At the rocky incline leading to the creek she pulled the fiery animal to a trot. How low and clear the water! As Carley forded it fresh cool drops splashed into her face. Again she spurred her mount and again trees and walls rushed by. Up and down the yellow bits of trail—on over the brown mats of pine needles—until there in the sunlight shone the little gray log cabin with a tall form standing in the door. One instant the canyon tilted on end for Carley and she was riding into the blue sky. Then some magic of soul sustained her, so that she saw clearly. Reaching the cabin she reined in her mustang.

"Hello, Glenn! Look who's here!" she cried, not wholly failing of gayety.

He threw up his sombrero.

"Whoopee!" he yelled, in stentorian voice that rolled across the canyon and bellowed in hollow echo and then clapped from wall to wall. The unexpected Western yell, so strange from Glenn, disconcerted Carley. Had he only answered her spirit of greeting? Had hers rung false?

But he was coming to her. She had seen the bronze of his face turn to white. How gaunt and worn he looked. Older he appeared, with deeper lines and whiter hair. His jaw quivered.

"Carley Burch, so it was *you?*" he queried, hoarsely.

"Glenn, I reckon it was," she replied. "I bought your Deep Lake ranch site. I came back too late. . . . But it is never too late for some things. . . . I've come to wish you and Flo all the happiness in the world—and to say we must be friends."

The way he looked at her made her tremble. He strode up beside the mustang, and he was so tall that his shoulder came abreast of her. He placed a big warm hand on hers, as it rested, ungloved, on the pommel of the saddle.

"Have you seen Flo?" he asked.

"I just left her. It was funny—the way she rushed me off after you. As if there weren't two—"

Was it Glenn's eyes or the movement of his hand that checked her utterance? His gaze pierced her soul. His hand slid along her arm—to her waist—around it. Her heart seemed to burst.

"Kick your feet out of the stirrups," he ordered.

Instinctively she obeyed. Then with a strong pull he hauled her half out of the saddle, pellmell into his arms. Carley had no resistance. She sank limp, in an agony of amaze. Was this a dream? Swift and hard his lips met hers—and again—and again. . . .

"Oh, my God!—Glenn, are—you—mad?" she whispered, almost swooning.

"Sure—I reckon I am," he replied, huskily, and pulled her all the way out of the saddle.

Carley would have fallen but for his support. She could not think. She was all instinct. Only the amaze—the sudden horror—drifted—faded as before fires of her heart!

"Kiss me!" he commanded.

She would have kissed him if death were the penalty. How his face blurred in her dimmed sight! Was that a strange smile? Then he held her back from him.

"Carley—you came to wish Flo and me happiness?" he asked.

"Oh, yes—yes. . . . Pity me, Glenn—let me go. I meant well. . . . I should—never have come."

"Do you love me?" he went on, with passionate, shaking clasp.

"God help me—I do—I do! . . . And now it will kill me!"

"What did that damned fool Charley tell you?"

The strange content of his query, the trenchant force of it, brought her upright, with sight suddenly cleared. Was this giant the tragic Glenn who had strode to her from the cabin door?

"Charley told me—you and Flo—were married," she whispered.

"You didn't *believe* him!" returned Glenn.

She could no longer speak. She could only see her lover, as if transfigured, limned dark against the looming red wall.

"That was one of Charley's queer jokes. I told you to beware of him. Flo is married, yes—and very happy. . . . I'm unutterably happy, too—but I'm *not* married. Lee Stanton was the lucky bridegroom. . . . Carley, the moment I saw you I knew you had come back to me."

appear. Was this a dream? Swift and loud his hoofbeat
here—and then—ood again.

"Oh, my God!—Glenn, are you—mad?" she was
perspiration pouring.

"Sure—I reckon I am," he replied. Immediately, and pulled
her full the way out of the saddle.

Calley would have fallen but for his support. She could
not think. She was all instinct. Only the oncome—he self-
less horror—drifted—faded as before, fires of her heart.

"Kiss me!" he commanded.

She would have kissed him if death were the penalty.
Then, his face flounced in her agonized sight. Was that a
strange smile? Then he held her back from him.

Calley—you came to kiss Glenn and find happiness," he
asked.

Oh, yes—yes.... Pay me Glenn, let me go. I've gone
well.... I should... mean have to be.

"Do you love me?" he went on, with passionate, flashing cheer.

"God help me—I do—I do." And now it will kill me!"

"What did that darned fool Sharley tell me."

The sharp torment of his query, the incipient force of
it, brought her upright, with eight suddenly cleared. Yet
this gave the hope Glenn was held would to her from the
cabin door.

"Glenn, he told me—you and I—were married," she
whispered.

"You don't believe him," returned Glenn.

She could no longer speak. She could only see her lover.
She was figured, braced hard against the handguided wall.

"That was me on Carley's quicker jokes, I told you to
because of him. He wanted, yes... and very happy?
I'm mightily happy, too—but I'm not married.... de-
ception was the likely bridegroom.... Calley, the moment
I saw you I knew you had come back to me."